DEFENDING WALLS
Lee Wyndham

Published in 2009 by New Generation Publishing

Copyright © Lee Wyndham

First Edition

British Library C.I.P.
A CIP catalogue record for this title is available from the British Library

'Tis not the walls or purple that defends
A prince from foes, but 'tis his fort of friends.

The Languedoc, November 1645

May he dream treason, and believe that he
Meant to perform it, and confesses, and die,
And no record tell why.

Giraud de Chesnay had always loved autumn best, the time when he could leave his summer-green grief behind for the softer world of mists and fallen leaves, the faintly musty scent of fermenting grapes ready for their second decanting, the time of silent, spider-webbed orchards and of cool dew that looked like and presaged frost.

Summer, even with the rose-tinged light of the Languedoc dawns, had long since become too harshly reflecting a world for him, redolent of loss, resonating with guilt.

His father's blood in a pooled mockery of every sacrament, dark and accusing, shed not for many but for two boys who made it their secret communion and broke Church law as much as their dead sire. His brother's blood, threading onto the Carcassonne cobbles, broken out of the small, strong body by his own hand, and that for no-one at all, in the end.

Their sacraments of death and destruction, as binding as the transubstantiation, a black mass for their burdened souls.

With the autumn rains and burgeoning coolness, he could believe those stains gone, and every year he prayed it would be so.

But with every autumn, he waited, too, for a word of forgiveness that would never come, waited for news that he had no right to, and his sorrow seeped deeper and closer to his bones, so that he felt it course through him as the wine ran through the funnels in the cellars.

I do miss you. But I couldn't stay.

They had always been able to find kindness in the written word, and he could not stop his hope that they might again.

I'm all right. I promise.

Guyon, his brother, had known better at fourteen than he himself did at nearly thirty, had known that the only way to survive their inheritance was to discard it - something he could

1

not, would not do. Giraud pursued an adherence to Spain that he knew to be disaster, because he also, in his heart, believed it to be right. He allowed the Inquisition to praise his treatment of mysticism, all the time knowing that he tried to eliminate it, not through any belief, but through fear of what might befall his brother.

Of what might be waiting for his unborn child.

Every autumn, Giraud de Chesnay held a day of private prayer, tried to relinquish his guilt and his grief to God. He sat in the room that had been his father's sanctum and his little brother's first haven of learning, and read the old letters, every word in the handwriting that sharpened and matured along with the mind the words sprang from. Guyon's Athena-like missives, fully grown and armored from the first ink-blotched page.

He read his way through three years of regretful, gentle, undemanding love, and every time he read, he swallowed down the newest bottled vintage, coated his tongue in the sharpness of two years before, in measured mouthfuls, saying his annual farewell, trying to relinquish his brother to Paris, to academia, to a past in which he had no place any more.

He remembered the small boy with the blazing, brilliant, uncanny mind, who had fought him to a standstill to be allowed to go somewhere that would accept him - and who, when the standstill had been reached, and he had grown into an acceptance of it, a little taller and a little more widely-read, and no different, had simply walked out on the refusal. He had walked out and away and down the path they had seen flooded and sun-baked and snow-covered, walked half-way to Paris and ridden the rest of the way on a weapons-cart destined for the Guard, and sent him letters from every flea-ridden inn en route.

I'm all right, Giri. I promise. But I had to leave.

Guyon, his little besotted brother, studying at the Sorbonne, and still trying to tell him that he had found ease for the aching, tormented longing that his mind had become in the aftermath of their father's death.

I'm learning so much, and there's still so much more; I feel as though I'll never be filled, never be done. Is this what it's like to be in love?

2

He laughed every time he read that, thinking of Guyon's earnest, fifteen-year-old belief that love was some miracle, a thunderbolt from heaven, a possession and a consuming fire in one. He laughed, and then he wept, knowing that he had killed that belief with his own determination to fix Guyon's spirit to the world.

I love you, little brother.

He remembered the crack of thin leather on flesh, Guyon's agonized cry of refutation -

I cannot recant! I cannot recant! I am not this thing!

With every year, the letters grew more blurred, as every time he found new salt pain to weep over.

Do you ever think that perhaps the church was wrong?

What if Socrates was right, and not the priests?

Giri! Giri-mi!

He allowed himself to remember the last words his brother had ever spoken to him -

It's done. And so am I.

- remembered them, and put them aside, swallowing them down with the last pith-filled dregs of the final glass, residue gritty on his tongue and teeth.

He remembered, and he willed himself to forget.

Every autumn, he succeeded until the next dog-days of blazing rose light, and the memories of blood and hatred and arrant failure.

The Languedoc was his prison and his balm at once. He could not imagine leaving it, could not imagine tearing himself from the lands that sang to him. But sometimes, he wondered how he would survive if he did not.

*

Paris, February 1646.

Others near you shall whispering speak,
And wagers lay, at which side day will break,
And win by observing, then, whose hand it is
That opens first a curtain, hers or his :
This will be tried to-morrow after nine,
Till which hour, we thy day enlarge, O Valentine.

"A toast! A toast for the newlyweds!" The cry went out over the gathered crowd as Gottfried van Hesselink led his new bride to the front of the room. Ännchen was blushing a most becoming shade of pink as her father, Herr Kirschner, leaned in to kiss her cheek.

"A toast!" Peter heard Vincennes's voice take up the cry, echoed by *Ritter* Voorhees. "Yes, a toast!"

Guyon caught Peter's eye from the corner of the room, where he was doing his level best to blend in with the wall hangings of the Merchants' Guild, and made a small face. *Sentiment*, he mouthed, and rolled his eyes, but his clear, deep voice was at its best when it carried effortlessly across the room -

"God give you joy and a long life to share it."

He then leaned back, his eyes filled with sardonic amusement, as the couple tried to drain their glasses first, each trying to get to the small piece of bread before the other and claim mastery in the house. Somehow, it wasn't a surprise when they finished at the same time.

There was cheering and applause and much teasing of both Gottfried and Ännchen, most of it bawdy, as their friends gathered round to congratulate one and kiss the other. Peter wandered back across the room to Guyon, a smile on his face.

"Not going to kiss the bride, Gui?" Peter asked. "She'll be horribly disappointed if you do not."

"Later," Guyon said absently. He was turning his glass in his hand, apparently fascinated by the prisms of light caught in the delicate chasing. "It's Venetian," he added, catching Peter's eyes on the movement. "God knows how they got it. Gottfried," he added in the same tone of voice, "wants me to set up a subsidiary

4

school with him."

"Yes?" Peter blinked for a moment. In his opinion, this could only be a good thing. He had been worried about Guyon since his dismissal from the Sorbonne. It seemed that the only time he seemed challenged was when he was given a particularly difficult piece of code to work out, and that was not an acceptable pastime in either of their opinions. The decoding profited the spy master, Luc Corvay, and neither of them wished to forward that devil's plans even slightly. "Do you like the idea?"

"It would mean moving." Guyon's eyes searched out Herr Kirschner. "They're taking one of the big houses on the Rue des Esclangons - the *Herr's* eyesight is getting worse daily, you know, and Gottfried seems to like the idea of family. The idea is I take the top floor. There would be a couple of dormitories for the students, and teaching rooms, on the ground floor...but it means moving." He shrugged. "I've become...attached, I suppose. To two rooms and an old bed and a desk someone seems to have used for the relief of damaged feelings by returning the favor. Bah." He shifted off his odd mood, quicksilver laughter gleaming through. "*I* don't have to house twenty cadets and the *very* capable Lieutenant Wycombe."

"Indeed, not," And Peter gave a sigh at that. He needed to find quarters suitable for his motley bunch soon or he might just find himself, not only being the ex-Marshal, but also an ex-Captain. *I'll be demoted to scullion.* It's not that his lads were unruly, there were just...alright, they were unruly, and high spirited and not at all accustomed to dealing with the Court. "But I think you'll do well partnering with Gottfried."

"Mm. He can maintain order, I'll teach the fine art of chaos. We already have the next generation's de Barrion on a list of admittance - de Retz's secretary-lawyer, Andre Morel? Our noble Archbishop thinks I can do something with his mind." Guyon laughed. "So do I, but it involves poniards - oh, David, *must* you?"

"I must indeed, my dear one. For if Mohammed will not go to the mountain..." David Somers chuckled slightly, pushing an even pinker Ännchen toward the two men. "...then the mountain must go to Mohammed. Not that Ännchen is large enough to be a

5

mountain...More like a molehill, I'd 'spect."

"Will you not wish me joy?" the bride, who had obviously drunk more than one toast in the last few minutes, giggled at them.

"But of course, for I do," Guyon said quickly. He brushed his lips quickly across her cheek. "*May your hearth be always warm*," he said, and it was one of his more slurred utterances, the clear sign of a mental translation. An Occitan blessing, then, and Ännchen gave him the little private grin that Peter was only just learning not to feel jealousy over.

"And you, my chevalier? Will you do the same?" Bright eyes looked up at Peter, twinkling with happiness.

"And I." said Peter, bending down to give the woman he valued as much as his sister, a kiss on both cheeks. "I wish you joy, Ännchen. Many years of it."

"And what is this?" Gottfried's voice crackled joyfully over the end of Peter's words. "I leave you alone for two minutes and you're already consorting with soldiers?"

"Thus displaying her utter lack of sense, since she still hasn't run away with one," Guyon said amiably. "I'm not kissing you, you horror, you have birds nesting in that beard of yours."

"Then I'll have to kiss Peter instead," Gottfried suited action to words and planted a smacking kiss on the side of Peter's face.

David chuckled and offered Peter his handkerchief. "I don't think it will wipe off that blush though."

Yes, he was blushing. Peter sighed. All of Guyon's former students seemed to delight in causing him to blush. He would have thought he had become inured to it by now.

Guyon shot him a sympathetic look. "Vengeance *will* be Henri's, children, if you keep this up..."

"*Children* -!" Gottfried began to protest, and then laughed. "Oh, shut up, Guyon, damn you. Brat." Getting his license had freed Gottfried from any sense of restraint that had ever been doubtfully in his possession. He now treated his former tutor as the junior he was in years, rather than in any way his superior.

"Anyway, Henri won't, cause I'm a genius." David Somers, English herbalist and perennial student, collected more champagne from a passing servitor, smiling like a particularly cream-and-fish-fed blond cat. "*I* found Peter a home. Actually, I found him a hôtel. The Hôtel d'Orsay, to be exact."

"The Hôtel d'Orsay?" Peter stumbled a bit over the name. "Where is that, David? Do you think it's large enough?"

He had asked all of the scholars...*all of his friends*, he corrected...to watch for some place suitable for him. Part of him wondered if he were really desperate enough to take a recommendation from David, however. The Englishman was pleasant enough, and honestly did amuse Peter more often than not, but he so often went around with his head literally in the clouds that his judgment was often in question.

"*Large* enough?" Gottfried choked out. "David, you *are* a genius. Why didn't we think of that?"

"Because we are beautifully unworldly, above such matters, and thick as two short planks on a bargeman's head," said Guyon amusedly. "Good God, David, I'm impressed - Pèire, it's d'Orsay's old official residence, *of course* it's large enough, you could fit a standing army into it!"

"And unoccupied," David assured them. "Well, might be a few birds and some mice, I'd 'spect. But no people."

"Perhaps I should kiss David then," Peter said in relief. "God, it would be wonderful if it could be arranged. If I have to chase my lads out of the de Medici Courtyard again, her Majesty will have my head. I can not convince them that the fountain is not there for them to soak their feet after a march."

"It shouldn't be a problem - the Hôtel belongs to the Court," Guyon said with a shrug. "It's a mausoleum, no-one's used it for nearly a century - *but* it's within the provenance of gifts to the Lords Marshal. And you actually qualify..." He was grinning. "David, that was inspired."

"Coca leaves," David said cheerfully. "Everything goes numb except your brain."

"The only man in the world who finds this a desirable state of being," Henri de la Roche agreed, coming to join them. "I got the paper signed after Mass, Peter, you can move your men in - I think the exact phrase was *please and could that be sometime approaching now, thank you* - whenever you're ready." The organist and composer of the chapel Richelieu was, by his very position, close to the Court and able to pass on and deliver messages to and from it to those who were kept away by work, or, like Guyon, tried to avoid it as much as possible. He delighted in storing up his verbal messages to pass on at moments that were both unwanted and - whenever he could manage it - devastating.

Peter stood for a moment, silent and overwhelmed by the kindness of these men who had befriended him on blind faith and what had originally been a mere acquaintanceship with Guyon. He looked for the words to express his gratitude for their help, but in the end simply settled for a quiet, "Thank you."

There was a sort of communal shrug, and then -"Why can't you all find *me* a house?" said Gottfried plaintively, and everyone stared at him. Eventually, David ventured -

"I thought you had one?"

"I *do*. That's not the point. The point is - er." He snorted with laughter. "All right. No point."

"Pointless," Guyon agreed.

"You'd better remedy that before tonight," Henri said slyly, and Ännchen's pink deepened to red. "Oh, no, Anna, don't worry, I'm sure Gottfried will be - more than adequate. *I* meant Guyon."

"That's a problem we've never figured out how to remedy," Peter said softly, causing Guyon to cast him a sharp look before he continued. "Because it's a problem we've never encountered." He had long since learned how to deflect the scholars with his own slightly cruder humor, finding them easily distracted into bawdiness from wordplay.

"Oh *God*," said Guyon with feeling, as David hooted with glee. "I'm - going. Elsewhere. To talk to someone...er...else. Now." He made his way hurriedly across the room, rubbing at the back of his neck as though his shirt was chafing him.

"I think I'm in trouble," Peter chuckled, as he watched Guyon's swift departure.

The look Guyon sent him over one slightly hunched shoulder bore him out. It wasn't that Guyon hated having his private life made an open topic *in particular*. It was that Guyon hated being discussed *at all*, and he tended to have incredibly inventive ways of reinforcing his feelings on the matter.

Peter ducked his head over his glass to hide a grin. If Guyon ever found out he occasionally forced those moments, he had a feeling they would stop quite suddenly - and he had learned to turn them to his advantage too well to forfeit the pleasure he had learned to gain from them.

*

The Hôtel d'Orsay, Paris, late March 1646

Love, nature's plot, this great creation's soul,
The being and the harmony of things,
Doth still preserve and propagate the whole,
From whence man's happiness and safety springs:
The earliest, whitest, blessed'st times did draw
From her alone their universal law.
Friendship's an abstract of this noble flame,
'Tis love refined and purged from all its dross,
The next to angels' love, if not the same,
As strong in passion is, though not so gross:
It antedates a glad eternity,
And is an heaven in epitome.

Peter moved his troop into the Hôtel d'Orsay, lock, stock and tired feet. The place had been a shambles at first, pigeons in the rafters, doves in the attics, and whole families of mice and rats in every room, as well as a rather confused looking hedgehog who had taken up residence under the mahogany desk in the room Peter planned to make over into his office.

Fortunately for Peter, he had a whole troop of unruly cadets that needed something to keep them out of trouble. He set them to cleaning the place from top to bottom and evicting the unwelcome tenants. Punishment detail got to swill out the gutters and make sure the privies were clear. The place was livable in a record time, and once windows were replaced and grillwork repaired, they seemed to be not only free of stray creatures, but weather tight as well.

The place was still remarkably shabby, but Peter did have a budget for that, it was just a matter of having it done. All in all, David had done well.

Guyon, on the other hand, had either decided to demonstrate his complete lack of respect for all forms of life - which included the cadets, whom he viewed as being decidedly further down the chain of Peter's tenuous command than the hedgehog - or was proving that his sense of humor was indeed beyond repair. He had bequeathed his much hated and only remaining pupil, Andre

Morel, as a go-between lawyer between Peter and de Retz. Or rather, between the English Marshal and the Archbishop of Paris.

Peter did the best he could to disguise how he felt about Morel. He wondered at times if the young man was really as annoying as he seemed or if it was merely that he was *not* François Villon, which made him so intolerable. Two men could not be less alike, it was true. François had been fun loving and teasing, as quick to laugh at himself as he was at anyone else, and above all, well versed in the law and willing to help any of the students that needed it. Andre Morel, on the other hand, seemed to be self-centered and unbending. His humor was often at the expense of someone else and his sense of his own importance rather overly inflated for a mere student. Peter simply *could not* like him.

Perhaps he would have come to at least tolerate him, if not for the joyful, unequivocal, loving and dismissive presence of Guyon's former students in his Hôtel. They teased, adored, and laughed at his cadets in equal measure, patched up their self-inflicted wounds and gave cures for home-sickness that were the despair of the Watch and the boon of his Lieutenant. They brought in whisky gained from dicing illegally with the Scots Guards, taught them terrible songs that surpassed bawdy in favor of simply horrendous, and, under the charge of David Somers, proved that there were herbs that could be used to disinfect a wound and make a young man stay alert for three days, all at the same time.

But no-one ever taught or repeated the loving, lilting song that had belonged to François Villon, that had once mocked its way through the colonnades of the Louvre and the Sorbonne alike, and come to stand for a time that seemed now almost golden in its innocence, when a lawyer could work for the good of France and the best mind of the Sorbonne's scholars was not owned by a spymaster and bound by blackmail.

Auprès de ma blonde, ma blonde, ma blonde...

And yet sometimes, despite the unspoken embargo on the words and tune, Peter could hear that utterly insouciant voice echo down the halls - hear it when Guyon finally broke into unwilling laughter, see it when the strange green eyes that he had learned were *Languedocien* darkened to hazel out of their queer translucency. François in death was a more intrinsic part of Guyon de Chesnay that he had ever visibly or tangibly been in his short life.

Que donnerais vous, bèl...?

No, there was no way that Andre Morel would ever lessen the loss of François in any way. The only thing that made Morel's presence bearable was the amusing fact that the young man had, somehow, despite his most certain inclination towards and determined pursual of the female sex, developed a *tendre* of some peculiar kind for David Somers. He had to merely enter the room when Morel was there and the young lawyer became all calf eyes and obsequiousness.

And David - being David and so utterly oblivious to all that pertained to himself in any direct way - not only missed the point, but missed out on any possible deflection he might put up.

"A lawyer? And at such an age. You must be quite the clever one, my goodness, I'm impressed."

"Um...yes...I suppose I am rather young to be -" Andre stammered.

"And Peter, I see I'm interrupting." David grinned, his mind already drifting on to other things. "How very opportune of me. I've saved you again..."

"Indeed, David...I rely upon your rescue at all times. How ever else would I make it thorough my day?" Peter responded with dry sarcasm. "Now Monsieur Morel...if you'll wait a moment, I'll give you a message to take back with you."

David yawned, and stretched out like a welcome cat across Peter's desk, reaching out a hand to ruffle Peter's hair and then playing with the papers that he was half-lying on.

Andre, growing more uncomfortable by the moment, stared out of the window, at his feet, at the ceiling, and fidgeted. Finally, David took pity on him - or what, with David, might possibly pass for pity. With anyone else it would have been closer to a rather frightening non-sequitur, designed to alarm the recipient out of what remained of their coherency.

"Do you like herbs?"

"Um...herbs? I...I never gave them much thought, really."

Andre managed to stammer out. *Give him some credit, he managed a response,* Peter thought, before deciding to rescue him.

"Don't start, David...I do use this office for other things you know? That is, aside from a place for you to lounge." Peter tugged the papers from under David's hip, then leaned them against him like a book stand. David just smiled up, beatific and unmoving.

"Shame, really, because if you took out one of those windows and made the balcony into a greenhouse, I could use it for a wonderful poison garden."

Somewhere at the back of Peter's mind, Guyon's explosive, sudden laughter rang out, loving the ridiculous for him. *How nice!*

"You know about poisons too?" And Peter was, however unwillingly and embarrassedly, watching a young man gain stars in his eyes, blinding him to the obvious.

"Well, yes," David said, happily causing chaos amidst papers. "Peter doesn't like it when I kill people, so I sort of have to, really. Yes, we need a poison garden, Peter, I don't want your lovely guardsmen wandering around and sticking their fingers in foxgloves because they think it's funny how the flowers fit on their fingertips." He paused, sat up, and made a face at Peter. "Again."

Peter sighed, "Yes, Michael is an idiot. But he's young yet...he'll get better, hopefully without dying in the attempt."

"I'd still like it if he didn't have to be saved from himself five times a day before he gets there..."

"David...you have a home. You have a garden. You can keep your bloody killer weeds in your own place." Peter growled, then laughed behind his papers when he caught Morel scowling at him for doing so.

"It's full," David said cheerfully. "And Henri said he'd have a killer weed bonfire if I planted anything else in pots and put them on the harpsichord." He looked imploringly at Peter. "Oh, come on...just one more plot? I'll put a lock on it..."

"David, I am not funding your habits. Really. Go..." Peter waved his hand in a shooing manner. "I'm working. See if you can get Vincennes to let you use *his* balcony...He, at least, might have a use for the result."

"You're no fun at all, you know that?" David shook his head sadly. "And I *do* need that money by next week, or I'll let your infants all turn septic, and then where will you be? Goodbye, Monsieur Morel, and I hope you have better luck than I!" He raised his hand to them both, and left the room.

Morel, looking bereft, said to his absence, "Um...Goodbye...?" He stared at the closed door for a long moment before turning to Peter, "You are going to get him the money, aren't you? I mean...if he needs it?"

Peter gave him what he devoutly hoped was a quelling look. "I don't know why that would be your concern, but yes. Monsieur Somers keeps our medical supplies stocked for us...And is always paid promptly, in spite of his complaints."

"Oh. Is he here a lot, then?" Morel looked at the door again.

"Interminably..." Peter said, going back to his note and obviously dropping the subject.

"Does anyone around here know the differences between right and *left*?" howled a voice outside the door. "As in *my* right, *your* left, get your damn halberd *off my foot*!"

"Christ," Peter rolled his eyes, then raised his voice to be heard outside the door, "I'm working in here! Please confine your drill to the hall!"

Morel blinked. "What should I tell de Retz about the cadets?" he asked, perhaps unwisely.

"You must tell him nothing." Peter frowned. "All you need do is return my note." He sanded the ink, waved the paper to dry it a bit more then folded it in thirds and sealed it.

Morel took the paper with a sigh. "Couriers," he said sadly, "get paid more. I expect I shall see you within the week, my lord Marshal." He bowed, and made his way out of the room. There was a metallic clatter, the sound of someone half-falling into the gallery, and a chorus of "Sorry, sorry, sorry..." drifted up.

Peter looked up at the ceiling, "Young men do grow up. Young men do grow up. Young men do grow up."

"I refuse to," Guyon said cheerfully from the doorway. "It's the only alternative that isn't completely depressing. What

14

happened, did David feed them all laudanum with their breakfasts?"

"Gui, thank God," Peter rose to his feet. "Save me?"

"Well, I would, but are you sure you can leave the infants to their own devices?" Guyon waved a piece of paper at him. "Also we have a commission. And I do *not* think that counts for safety, do you?"

"The infants will do fine with Lt. Wycombe. Training them is his job." Peter moved to clear papers off of his deskside chair, waving Guyon into it.

"He's not very good at it," Guyon said critically. "Oh, well, what do I know." He handed Peter the piece of paper, and settled himself in the chair, drawing his legs up under him. His eyebrows raised mockingly. "Why, Peter, all these papers. You'll be employing a codemaster of your own, soon, when I would be advising a *secretary*. Are you trying to outdo our gracious Archbishop?"

Peter chuckled, "That is a decoy, I'm afraid. I keep that chair full of papers to help discourage people from lingering when I'm busy."

Guyon laughed. "I'm sure it works, knowing the inhabitants of this place. Anything that resembles work, they avoid with skill and grace, it's one of their few talents in this life..."

"Well, mostly it keeps them from sitting in the only other comfortable chair in the room." He waved at the bench pushed against the wall. "And that has broken springs that poke in very awkward places."

"An original thought here, *chérâme*. Buy some new furniture. And also will you *read* that damn thing, it took me five hours of interruptions to translate." Guyon, as always, was unimpressed by the entire setup of the Hôtel d'Orsay. He claimed it should have stayed as a piece of historical interest and saved everyone the effort of refurbishment.

"Yes, Guyon." Peter picked up the paper with a sigh and read through it, pausing to ask questions as he did.

*

15

Guyon sat in the window seat, looking out through the open casement at the familiar view, and feeling the faint chill of the early spring breeze drift past him into the room. He had learnt a little wisdom, since his last disastrous attempts to help Peter in the aftermath of Corvay's machinations. Learned wisdom, and understood both himself and Peter's stubborn, occasionally lunatic-seeming behavior a great deal better than he had a year since.

He might want more than anything, at times like this, when de Retz or Corvay showed them so incontrovertibly that their lives were not their own, or some demand came from the Court that seemed both irrelevant and ludicrous, to get Peter out of the Hôtel d'Orsay and back to his own rooms. But what he himself perceived as sanctuary, he understood enough now to know that to Peter, it was, rather, a living image of the trap that held him enclosed. All the elements of his life he most hated, the papers that were a constant reminder of Corvay, the shabbiness of Guyon's few possessions - enclosed in three rooms, it reinforced what had been done to them.

To stay in the Hôtel while the little missive from de Retz hung in the air, on the other hand, was impossible, would be disastrous, and would certainly end in an argument or a fight, with both of them still so often unsettled by their new lives. The *Shoe* had long since been taken over by other, newer students, the Pantheon library would be less than happy to hear them discussing something not pertaining to any course of study, and while they had started to become quite comfortable at the inn referred to by most as the *Quai*, they were almost guaranteed an infinite number of interruptions. Guyon scratched at his head irritably, and wondered how his world was so narrow and he so unconscious of it.

Peter, he knew, was irritable at the best of times, despite his surface levity. He had little to do that his mind found satisfying, even while he was often physically exhausted, and the combination was leading him to become a more autocratic personage than ever, the traits that made up the Marshal to the fore more often than not, and unsettling Guyon more than it ever did the cadets, who expected it. Guyon, who had come to know a man very far from even the Royalist Captain, saw the changes and hated them, and, himself made unhappy by de Retz's machinations, was in no mood to endure them.

Guyon could, of course, avoid all possibility of having to either evade or diffuse the half-irritation that was in the air, and insist on sending Peter off to his fencing master Marcelli, but he did not think that burning off any excess mental energy in pursuit of the *destreza's* perfection would do Peter any good - and he was not, himself, in the mood for observation of yet another world in which he had no part.

He was still feeling unnerved by the sudden wave of almost ferocious tenderness that had shaken him earlier, watching Peter pore over the little commission from de Retz that might just be the start of something that could help them, and had left him feeling, even now, as though he were finding his feet in the aftermath of a breaking fever.

"University meadows," he said abruptly, and got to his feet.

"What?" Peter looked up from where he was sitting, seemingly immersed in the information contained in de Retz's little missive - or rather the lack thereof.

"I haven't even *been* there this year," Guyon continued with a deliberate lack of concern, because he knew that if he started to show any, it would end up in a conversation he had promised himself he would never have, and quite possibly in a display of emotion, and he had really had quite enough of everything connected with his innermost thoughts and feelings for one day. He was fairly sure Peter had, as well. "The meadows behind the Sorbonne. It's probably where they got the snake, back last year in the spring...we need to go there. Now. While it's not raining. Or thinking about raining. Or having a pointless little localized hailstorm."

"Outside? Someplace that's not a garden, or a colonnade, but a real honest to goodness meadow?" Peter rose to his feet. "Yes...Please." He paused for a moment, as if wanting to make his next statement perfectly clear, "I'm not catching any snakes. Really not, Gui."

Guyon raised his eyebrows slowly. "No? What a shame. We could bring one back and he could eat that hedgehog you still haven't evicted." He started poking through the cupboards. "You know, whatever you may have been taught in the army, Pèire, it is in fact permissible to throw bread out when it goes gre - oh, my mistake, it is in fact cheese. Of course it is." He held up the dubious object with a frown. "And you were planning to do *what* with this?"

"Um...David...experiment...Um..." Peter laughed. "No, I've got no bluff for that, my dear, just forgot it was there, I suspect."

"Hm." Guyon fought down the urge to grin like a lunatic as he realized that he had somehow managed to hit on the happy combination of a good idea and the right tone of voice with which to approach it. "Do you actually have anything *edible* in here? Or am I going to be reduced to skewering your little prickly friend and stuffing him *a la zingaro*?"

"Now, Guyon, just because you didn't want a pet doesn't mean I don't," Peter chuckled. "Come, we'll stop and buy something along the way." He held his hand out for Guyon.

Usually, Guyon would have rolled his eyes and proved - perhaps with an acidic comment accompanying his gesture - that he could get to his feet by himself without difficulty, and the day he could not, a coffin needed to be bought. But not today. Today he had to walk the small, fragile line he had long ago laid out for his own feet, and not say any of the words he had vowed to keep his own.

Aşkin Cemal Olsun.

My heresy for my faith.

Bravura, bravado, stupidity, mocked the cold voice of his worst dreams, mimicking his longings.

Concealing a flinch away from his own store of carefully-preserved and self-created horrors, that would inevitably be misconstrued, he let Peter pull him to his feet.

*

The meadows were predictably beautiful, even this early in the year, frosted twigs and glazed dead leaves mingling with the first hints of cold-preserved green to create an almost magical atmosphere. They were also predictably scattered with people, and yet surprisingly easy to find relative solitude in. The scholars came there for peace and quiet, or for private conversation in the shade of trees, or for the solitude of their own thoughts and a long walk. It was the essence of the Sorbonne's self-created privacy, where all were free to look, and no-one ever saw.

Also predictably, Peter had woven through the grasses and people and found just the perfect spot - sheltered by a windbreak of trees, in the faint, weak sunlight, and possessed of rare, real solitude, for the 'perfect spot' was just behind a ridge that hid them from the casual view of passersby. Never let it be said that the military had not trained Peter in how to reconnoiter an area to his benefit.

Guyon watched him with the lazy eyes of afternoon and contentment, knew that this was as ingrained in Peter as it was for him to settle himself in a library with papers and books and ink to hand, gestures learned so thoroughly and so well that they were no longer even *learned*, but *part of*.

And when we are sent somewhere, it is always like this, and when it is night or winter, he will light a fire, and all without having to think. All just from knowing.

It somehow added to the faint warmth of the day.

Peter spread out the blanket he had grabbed as they went out the door, sat the basket of food and wine down upon it, and then wrapped himself in his cloak and collapsed onto the blanket as if it had all been far too exhausting. His eyes promptly closed and he waved a vague hand at Guyon. "You are more than three feet away, I can tell without looking. And you are thinking. No thinking is allowed when the air feels this good."

"It's outdoor space," Guyon said cheerfully, but he rolled over onto the blanket so that he was lying on his stomach and definitely within the prescribed area. He pulled the hood of his own cloak up over his head, the warmth of the fur stroking his ears with kind softness. "It's different." He started picking blades of damp, newly de-frosted grass, wondering whether to plait them or just poke them randomly at Peter's ears. In the end he set the longer ones aside for later consideration and when he felt like making the effort, and began the time-honored means of irritating someone foolish enough to close their eyes in a field.

At the first poke, Peter reached up and scratched at his ear. At the second poke, he opened one eye, peered at Guyon's innocent expression, and scratched at his ear. At the third poke, he peeked out again and growled, "Did no one ever warn you about teasing the bear?"

"Why, no," Guyon said innocently. "Is that like stirring up bees?" He had the offending piece of grass stuck between his teeth. It moved up and down and sideways, in an odd green blur, when he spoke.

"Poke me again and you may find out." Peter settled back down, closing his eyes once more and, just for good measure, scratching at his ear.

Guyon contemplated wisdom. It was unappealing.

He took one of the longer blades of grass and very, very gently, like a tentative spider finding a place to rest, brushed it over Peter's eyelashes.

And somehow, suddenly, he found himself weighted down, pressed into the blanket by the full weight of a madly grinning cavalier. "I knew you couldn't resist. I knew it."

"O Solomon, the depth of thy knowledge is incalculable," Guyon said in his best priestly tones, and knew he'd ruined it when his voice cracked with laughter at the end, the last syllable an indecipherable squawk more than a word ending. He grinned up unrepentantly.

"It is indeed," Peter agreed, his own attempt at being solemn defeated by a grin to match Guyon's. "And, O thou my Scholar of Unresisting, can you even guess what my vast knowledge is telling me at this very moment?"

"Um." Guyon could think of several, in fact, but since he doubted that either of them were up to breaking laws that would end *very definitely* at a Paris whipping post, and almost certainly in some unpleasant gaol before that, he was unwilling to hazard even a guess. "No?" he offered, widening his eyes.

"It tells me that you are ticklish...right there..." tormenting fingers went to work, running up and down ribs and in the bends of knees.

Guyon yelped, and his entire body tried to simultaneously curl up in a ball and get away from Peter, which resulted in his lying flat on his back and wheezing for breath between bouts of helpless laughter. He flailed rather wildly with his hands, and started to contemplate kicking.

Then, just as suddenly as he had begun his tortures, Peter stopped. "God, I want to kiss you right now. Have you any idea what you look like? All flushed and relaxed, smiling...Beautiful."

"It's - the not - breathing," Guyon managed. "'S...irresistible." He whooped in air rather painfully. He would rather Peter *had* kissed him - in the middle of a crowd - than commented on his looks. "The feeling's mutual," he said after a couple more breaths, and hoped the harsh bright light of the February sun was bleaching the blush that he could *feel* burning his neck and face, out into nothing noteworthy.

"You're irresistible..." Peter said softly, then shifted awkwardly, the cause of his discomfort all too obviously pressing against Guyon's hip. "But, since it's broad daylight and there are other people not twenty feet away, I suppose I will have to find some way of managing." He sighed and rolled back to his previous spot, although not flat on his back.

Guyon bit his lip unhappily, but said as lightly as he could, "Perhaps it should be *only* three feet between us, but for now no *less*, either?" Sometimes he hated the fact that he had to be the one who always thought, who could never lose himself even for a second of want or need or desire. Hated it - and in that moment of awareness as to just *how* much he hated it, forgot everything he had just reminded himself of and that Peter had said in one white-hot flash of resentful anger, because they *were* hidden, and some things were worth the risk.

Since I cannot prove the truth of my body other than with my body...

He leant over and kissed Peter - not seductive, or promising more than could be given, simply what it was, an affirmation of what *he* had said, of all the promises he had once vowed to his father he would never make. *The feeling's mutual. And I won't leave.*

There was silence when the kiss ended, with only Peter's soft and breathy, "*Beloved,*" breaking it. It hung in the air for several moments before Peter shifted and spoke again, somewhat more strongly this time, "We...we need a distraction. Yes. Yes. " He looked around, then announced, "Your English. This is a perfect time to practice."

"Jesus God, can't I have the cold water?" Guyon protested. "All right, I know, you're right, and I need to practice..." He made one of his worst and most horrific faces.

Peter switched to English, "It's not meant to be torture, Gui. Someday, I hope, you'll get to meet my sister. I want her to be able to understand you and she doesn't speak French. Not well, at least."

Guyon sighed. He could understand English perfectly, could read it fluently, could even *speak* it. He could also reduce Peter to helpless mirth with it, because what he could *not* do with any consistency or skill was pronounce it. "Per'aps you would be bett'r off payin' fo' a tuto' she could use?"

"God, no. Sarah is even more helpless at studying than I am." Peter chuckled. "I can only hope her offspring took after their father."

"I don'," Guyon said honestly. Whatever Peter might find to say to the good about Robert Macquarie, he felt no desire to soften his opinion of the man even a little. "An' you aren't." He gritted his teeth. "'Elpless. Or 'opeless." He damned all aspirants with a private venom.

"Well, whatever else I may or may not have been, I was never thought to be a scholar," Peter smiled. "You, however, are. Say the sound, Gui. Ha, ha, ha, ha."

Guyon just glared at him wordlessly - and soundlessly. *If I could say the sound, I damn well would have!*

"Don't glare at me." Peter chuckled. "You know you won't really be satisfied until you master this. And you won't master it if you don't keep trying."

"No, I would be quite content," Guyon said cheerfully, but sighed, and attempted it. He suspected he sounded more like a dying horse.

"A bit better," Peter allowed, "But it still needs work. And don't give me that look, Monsieur, I suffered through far worse when you helped me with my French."

"You didn' sound like somethin' asp'yixiatin'," Guyon pointed out.

"No, actually, the exact opposite. I sounded like a drunk with a three day head cold. Plus, you laughed." Peter somehow managed to keep a straight face.

Guyon rolled his eyes. "I wonde' *why*. You laugh. You laugh *inside*. I can tell."

"It's safer that way," Peter finally chuckled. "God, Gui, isn't this a perfect day? Can we just hold it like this? Bright and clear and somewhere we can breathe, and the two of us together?"

"I think that would be why God granted us a memory, hm?" Guyon did not feel like wishful thinking. He agreed with Peter too strongly for that to be possible, knew that if he discussed it further he would fall into lamentable sentimentality more laughable than his English.

"I suppose. And one could get tired even of peace and tranquility after awhile...eventually." Peter sighed. "And just think of all the clothiers and bootmakers and smiths we'd put out of business..."

"Ännchen would neve' fo'give us, you know this...nothin' mo' to mend, or to yell about..." Guyon sighed. "Te -" He frowned, concentrated. "*Terrible* 'ardship." He scowled in frustration. "I mean awful difficulty," he added in distinctly enunciated self-mockery.

"That really won't work, you know? You can't spend the rest of your days avoiding words that begin with 'H'."

"Yes I can." Guyon nodded vehemently. "A wonde'ful solution."

"Guyon, my family estates are called Hawthornden..." Peter pointed out.

"So, I will point, and say 'that ove' there,'" Guyon announced with no small amount of glee. "Or just...Scotland. A Rock in Scotland."

"Ah, yes...And if someone were to ask you for my title?"

"Lo'd of a Rock in Scotland," Guyon replied with spurious innocence. "With the sheep."

"Well, that's put me in my place then, hasn't it?" Peter chuckled. "And as Lord of a Rock in Scotland...With the sheep...I command you to get lunch."

Peter waved a hand vaguely in the direction of the basket then promptly stretched out in the sun, once again closing his eyes.

Guyon contemplated minor havoc for a moment, then grinned to himself, and rummaged in the basket for bread, cheese and wine, before making himself an impromptu edible plate, uncorking the bottle, and sitting there calmly eating and drinking. "I got lunch," he said after a moment. "It's reasonably good..."

Opening one eye, Peter peered out. "Bastard," he grumbled, then sat up and rummaged in the basket himself.

"Alas, no, for I am not," Guyon said amusedly. "Oh, *sorry*. You wanted me to get *you* lunch. The failin's of anothe' language..." He held his look of slow comprehension for all of five seconds, before snickering quietly. "Teach you to make me sound like an *horse*," he pointed out. He knew that he sounded more Spanish than anything, but reasoned that at least it would stop Peter's amused insistence.

"Hmmpf." Peter answered around his mouth full of food.

"Yes, *just* like that," Guyon agreed. *Everything is perfect. Everything is a lie, is tangible deceit. What price casuistry now?* All he had left in his mind these days was Corvay, de Retz, de Retz's commissions, Corvay's commissions, Corvay, Corvay, Corvay, like some sickening wheel of Fortune that took more than one revolution in a minute. He had once thought of Peter, in an odd moment of clarity, that his soul was wounded. He knew that those hurts had been added to, knew that he could do nothing to heal them. *His body is all I can reach*, he had thought then, in the June light of the evening.

And now, by virtue of where he had brought them, not even that was true.

Isn't this a perfect day? Can we just hold it like this?

If this is our perfection, then God help us both, Guyon thought, and covered his sudden despair by swallowing wine. *God help us both.*

"What's in Douai, do you think?" Peter asked suddenly, capturing the reason for Guyon's falling mood with a few well-chosen words. And that, of course, was the main reason for their practicing English. Not Guyon's dreadful accent, but the fact that no-one's attention would be particularly caught by their conversation as anything other than something vaguely amusing and to be politely ignored.

"A solution, de Retz thinks. A contact, I know. Info'mation - per'aps." Guyon sighed, and pulled his cloak more tightly around him. He understood Peter's need for escape, but it always left him suffering slightly. "Can y'excuse th' time away?"

"I have so far, even for Corvay," Peter pointed out, and Guyon sighed.

"Yes, but *Corvay* -"

"Keeps our secrets, as long as they're his?" This was a horribly accurate summation. Guyon sighed, and nodded ruefully.

"An' *this*, we must 'ide from him."

"You think we can?"

"No. But...I think we can conceal *what* we do, hm?"

"For long enough?"

Guyon shrugged. "Per'aps. We can try. An' your cadets an' the scholars will protect you, you know." Off Peter's blank look, he clarified, "You know that with all your successes, you just got promoted, *chevalier*. Straight through a marsh'ldom and right up to demi-god."

"Pffft!" Peter made a rude noise. "I'm just a nine days wonder. They'll be over it soon enough, and back to laughing at my scholarly pretensions."

"*Damn* it!" Guyon had tried. He had tried in every way he knew how, and somehow he never managed to make Peter hear him. *You hear but you don't listen.* He fell back into French. "They don't laugh at you. They have *never* laughed at you. Will you *for Christ's sake* get it into your head that they *admire* you!"

"For what?" Peter looked oddly amazed at the idea. "I mean I have been trying. And I've been reading, so I don't look like a complete idiot when they draw me into a conversation, but..."

I will not scream. I will not throw anything at him. I will keep my temper. "*No*, Pèire," Guyon said as calmly as he could. "Not what you do. *You*. Who you *are*. The rest just makes you...more approachable." He ran his hands through his hair in frustration. "You made them collectively break their rule," he said then. "They look at you and they *see* you - and they *like* you. Not

25

because of me. Not because of the English Queen and the Dieudonne's liking for you. Not because you went to the damned Pantheon. Because of *who you are.*"

"Oh." It was a simple monosyllable, but spoke volumes. It was obvious that Peter had never considered that possibility. Perhaps, it had been too much time spent with the backstabbing sycophants of Court, who only cared for those who could advance them, or perhaps it the betrayal he still felt at Robert Macquarie's actions, the fact that it was his own brother-in-law who had led to his exile here in France, but Guyon was certain that Peter was actually surprised at the thought.

"Oh," Guyon agreed wryly. "You turned me into a human being, and you avenged François. Even to that lunatic crew, it beats out defending a thesis by a league and more."

"Turned you -" Peter scowled. "You were always a human being, Gui. You stepped in when I didn't have a friend in the world and treated me like I was worth knowing. You and François both."

"No," Guyon said very quietly. "No, I wasn't." He looked down at his hands. "I was so...afraid. Afraid that if I was anything more than this...mind...I would lose the only home I had. I didn't even see it wasn't a home. Just - a hiding place. You accomplished in a few months what François had been trying to do for years, made me think about something that wasn't my set course of study, or teaching." He looked up, then, feeling the smile lie crookedly on his face. His honesty was his own coin of loving, but he knew that Peter, who expected no less from him, would not understand that. "You didn't do that for me by reading Montaigne."

"No," Peter said softly. "But don't think I had no ulterior motives. I...I was attracted to you from the start. From that first night at the *Shoe* when François tried to drive me away. It took all my courage to return."

Guyon took in a sharp, startled breath, trying to adjust his mind to that idea. *Even then?* He blinked, and found himself laughing. "Well, that sort of ulterior motive I can live with," he said lightly. He snorted. "It's a relief to find you aren't quite the selfless paragon I had taken you for..."

26

"Paragons are boring." Peter gave him a half-smile. "I hope to avoid that, at least."

"*Boring*?" Guyon choked. "Yes, that you most certainly avoid!" He shook his head. "You know," he said, "I keep saying this, but...I *am* going to change your view of yourself."

He did not repeat what he had said back at the Louvre, after Peter's duel with Lesueur. He never had, after that one night of half-confession, knew that he did not have to.

Because you gave me the time to do so.

He smiled. "So. When do we leave?"

*

They left for Douai three days later, on a morning when the sky was heavy, with graying clouds that spoke of rain to come. The ground, still wet with the previous day's rain, was not yet churned into a morass of mud, but Peter knew it was only a matter of time. Still, in spite of the poor weather and chilly wind, Peter felt as though springtime had arrived.

They were out of Paris. No inconvenient summonses from a Queen who seemed to know far more than she was willing to express. Peter's leave taking from her had been odd and full of perceptions that she 'officially' did not have and suggestions that she hadn't made, all disguised in a trivial but pointed discussion about artists.

There were also no bumbling cadets who, somehow, had achieved the age of seventeen without learning their left from their right. No uninspired students droning away in a tone guaranteed to turn Guyon into an infuriating mountain of snarkiness by the end of the day. Just fresh, if cold air, a good horse and Guyon's company as they set out on an adventure.

What more could he require of life?

"You know," Guyon said, sounding vaguely disturbed, "I never thought I would say this, but I feel *thankful* towards Corvay."

If Guyon had said the sky was turning a lovely shade of puce, he could not have surprised Peter more, "You what -?"

Guyon made a small face. "Well, if de Retz hadn't got the

27

information about him, and didn't want our help, then we wouldn't be going anywhere, and I would probably be looking at the Bastille for having murdered one or all of my students. Slowly, and with torture," he added.

"Ah," Peter nodded his understanding. "I would have insisted on adjoining cells. I am almost at the point of painting left and right on the toes of Cadet Mitchelson's boots, the tradesmen have flooded my office with samples of paint and fabric, and her Majesty has taken it into her head that I should have a portrait done. What *is* the penalty for locking one's monarch up in a cupboard?"

Guyon snorted out laughter. "I think it depends on how quickly the monarch is found," he said. "God knows, Peter, she'd probably give you another knighthood or something. Or more cadets."

"Why?" Peter looked at Guyon, a teasing smile twisting round his lips. "Do you suppose she'd like being shut in a cupboard and would reward me?"

"No," Guyon admitted, "but the *Dieudonne* would probably find it hysterical. So *she* would give you the cadets, and he would give you some honor that you could - hmmm, what was it you did with your official title again? Oh yes, stuff it in a drawer and ignore your lands completely."

"I wrote a letter to the estate manager," Peter defended himself. "What would you have me do? Just jaunt off there for a few months and leave you in town with Corvay? You know I'd never do that and I don't think you'd leave your students for something so trivial."

"Oh, trust me, I'd leave them behind in a heartbeat," Guyon said quickly. He didn't seem to have taken Peter's defensiveness badly, which was unusual - he had been expecting a scathing summary of *just what* he should and could be doing. "Unfortunately, I can't leave de Retz. Except when he asks me to." He waved a hand. "I love irony."

"And I love being away from Paris, if only for a few days." Peter's voice sounded utterly tired, even to himself. His new position as Marshal of the English troops, such as they were, was not that taxing, in spite of the frustrations of dealing with the cadets. The duties he still performed directly for her Majesty were not onerous, in spite of his joking and his dealings with the tradesman that was refurbishing the Hôtel was merely a minor annoyance. No, his tiredness was due to worry, he was sure. Worry for Guyon's safety and that of his family. Worry that somehow Corvay would find a way to bring the one person who meant more to Peter than his own life, more firmly under his thumb.

"Hm." Guyon shot him one of those uncomfortably sharp looks, where he seemed to see straight through Peter and into every thought process he possessed. Whatever he concluded, however, he seemed in no mood to pursue. "You just like the thought of going somewhere there's a chance of getting shot at, or hacked at, so you have an excuse to give me interminable lectures on vigilance and the importance of keeping up my sword practice.

"Of course," Peter agreed as the first damp splats of rain began to fall, "I live for those as you live for rain and mud."

Guyon's expression shifted from indecipherable into a snarl. "Oh hell," he said irritably, and hunched into his cloak. It was one of the few good items he possessed, and the cause of a jealousy Peter was hopefully never going to be stupid enough to express - the constant winter reminder of *why* Guyon did not love him, bequeathed by the dead François Villon. "I take it all back. I'm not grateful *at all*."

"Take heart, Gui, there's a village just ahead," Peter pointed at the faded marker at the side of the road. "If we hurry we might find ourselves settled snuggly in an Inn before it gets too bad."

He got a slit eyed glare in response. "Joy unbounded," Guyon said irritably, as the rain fell harder. "Yes, hurrying is certainly a thought. And besides, it's *your* fault I hate mud." And with that particularly incomprehensible remark, even for Guyon, he set his heels to his borrowed horse, and suited action to his words.

*

There was no-one in the Western hemisphere, Guyon sometimes thought, as unsuited to the business of intelligence-gathering as Peter. Not because he was mentally ill-equipped to do so - Guyon had long since noted that if he was the one with the ability to say *this is who, and this is how*, it was Peter who could always see the essential *why* of a man's actions - but because he was simply incapable of making himself invisible in any respect. The best that might have been hoped for his looks was that Guyon could explain him as Piedmontese - and he only had to open his mouth for that to be proved a falsehood - and his entire demeanor was simply *foreign*. It was of no comfort to Guyon that he strongly suspected that it was foreign to his home country, too, that it was Peter himself who tended to stand out, not his nationality or his voice.

It was a quite terrifying responsibility, and all Guyon could do on occasions such as this one was to thank God that de Retz gave official commissions to go with the truth of whatever they did, so that there was no need to disguise who and what they were. It might be seen as a decidedly *odd* move on the part of the Archbishop of Paris, to send the Queen of England's Marshal into the Spanish Netherlands, but it was his decision and his choice - and his authority, and no-one would question any of it.

For once, it was Guyon's presence that was in question. It would have been simpler had he been allowed to pretend a position of servant, but Peter's damnable honor would not permit that. The name *de Chesnay* was not always a wise one to use if they were to observe the alliance with the Dutch, and was a distinct drawback when they wanted to disassociate themselves from any Spanish dealings.

Guyon, who loved silence and books and the opportunity to create mild havoc with his ability to decipher coded documents, was therefore usually completely out of his league and simultaneously unable to take on any persona that would enable him to fit in. It drove him mildly insane.

He was currently praising some extremely indifferent cooking, so as to reassure the landlord of the innocuousness of his intentions, and pretending to cheerfulness in the fact that he was being forced to listen to a rhapsodic account of just how the flavor (which he himself thought to be downright peculiar) of the ale was got. He thought that if he heard nothing more about apple peelings for the next five days, it would be too soon.

The things I do for you, he thought venomously at an oblivious Peter, who had managed to strike up conversation with a group who quite definitely *wanted* the opportunity to say they had spoken to a Marshal, however doubtful his provenance. He was under no illusions as to why the landlord wanted his approval, and it most certainly was not because he had some peculiar fondness for damp Occitan travelers.

"And it wasn't a wolf after all?" Peter nodded slowly at the end of some tale that the foremost of the locals was just finishing up. "How clever you are to have figured it out."

The man beamed with pride that Peter was speaking to him as if to an equal, and nudged his friends to make them notice that as well.

Holy God, Guyon thought with a fair mixture of prayer and blasphemy, and stored that particular gem away for future occasions of tormenting Peter.

"My wife says I should put raisins in," the landlord said.

Guyon truly hoped he didn't mean the ale. "Well, perhaps you should try it once, and ask for opinions?" *Just not mine.*

Peter stood and stretched, "As lovely as it has been to spend time with you gentlemen, my friend and I have many things we need to discuss before we continue on our journey tomorrow." He leaned in as if telling a confidence, "Strategy you know..."

The other men nodded as if they knew exactly what Peter meant, and agreed with him completely.

"Landlord? Could I trouble you to have dinner brought up to our room later? We may not have time to come down for it?" Peter grinned when the man agreed. "Come, Guyon, if you're finished there?"

"Oh, I think so," Guyon said in his blandest tones, and watched with no small pleasure as Peter had to fight very hard not to laugh outright.

"It's good to talk to a man who understands these things," the landlord said with a sincerity that made Guyon feel guilty. "It may not be something that interests many, but people *notice*, and I like to create some pleasure where I can."

"And that is a truly worthy ambition," Guyon said with a bow, "and one in which you have most certainly succeeded in my case." He gave the somewhat random patrons one of his nicest and vaguest smiles, and hurried up the stairs.

Peter almost fell through the door to their room, covering his mouth with his hand to keep his chuckling from being heard back down the stairs, "Don't ever do that again. I don't want them to think we're actually laughing at them rather than each other."

Guyon opened his eyes wide. "Oh, we *were*?" he asked innocently, before succumbing to repressed laughter. "*Raisins*, Peter. *Wolves.* Oh *God.*"

"Ah, Gui, you know they were only telling us the things they feel important about. Not everyone in the world is caught up in politics and intrigue, thank God." He plunked himself down in chair and began struggling to remove his still damp boots. "Some invest a good deal of time and attention to lesser things...like raisins."

"I think he wanted to put them in his ale," Guyon said, caught in a sort of dreamy absurdity that not even Peter's reminder could dent, and then shook his head. "I mean, yes, Peter, you are of course right, and I should not mock." His mouth twitched.

His contrition, unfortunately, seemed to effect Peter completely inversely, causing him to lose his grip on his boot, tumble off the chair and onto the floor where he lay laughing like some kind of demented farm animal.

"Hm," said Guyon, peering down at him interestedly. "That's...no, I give up. What on *earth*?" He shook his head in amusement. "Very...decorative, Scudamore."

"Indeed," Peter agreed, in between gasped wheezes, until he finally managed to get his laughter under control. "Being decorative is what I am best known for after all. Just ask half the French Court." And that set him off again.

"Yes, do you mind awfully if I *don't*?" Guyon asked, and, giving up all pretences to the chance of sanity being restored, sat down on the floor with his legs crossed like a tailor, giving Peter his best look of demented and sideways-tilted interest.

Peter took a deep calming breath and then patted Guyon on the knee. "You'd think they'd have realized after all this time that, yes, I actually can speak French, and that I am not hard of hearing nor mentally diminished. But yet they so frequently speak about me as if I'm not there, it's rather amazing. I heard one of the ladies telling Lady Hepplewhyte that it was 'charming' that the Queen had chosen me for her Marshal, because I 'did look so lovely in my uniform'. "

"*Lovely*?" Guyon, caught between the ludicrity of such a statement and a fair amount of insult on Peter's behalf, heard the word escape him in a sort of horrified squeak. "*Charming*?" He choked.

"Yes, because, apparently that is my most outstanding feature...my looks." Peter sighed. "I suppose I should be grateful that they do not insinuate that I gained my position through peddling my charms in some way...or at least not within my hearing."

"*God*, I hate the court!" It wasn't that Guyon was unaware of insinuation and rumor - and downright unpleasantness - and it was not as though the Sorbonne did not have its fair share of all, though in slightly different ways, but it somehow seemed worse when it was Peter that was affected. He had no illusions as to why, and found himself ridiculous because of it, but even acknowledging his own foolish and ultimately useless sense of protectiveness did not diminish the sheer outrage he sometimes felt. "Maybe they *should* do so, and in your hearing, too, you could make them pay..."

"I would as well, if it were only my honor they were impinging, but usually such an accusation includes a second party." Peter shook his head. "I don't want anyone else having to suffer that."

Guyon's good mood had evaporated like autumn mist. "Shall we skip the part where I lecture you about the pointlessness of that sort of honor?" he asked wearily. "It's all right, I understand. I just -" He made a small, wholly involuntary face. "I hate that I can't help."

"You can," Peter gave a bit of a grimace. "Escort Ännchen when she comes to the Hôtel. My Lieutenant reported to me that one of the Cadets was commenting on her visits. The boy is an idiot, but I won't have careless words hurting her or Gottfried."

"Because having me at her services is so much more respectable?" Guyon asked blankly. "They'll think I'm either a procurator or worse!" He was about to go on, when he realized just what was being said. "No. They won't, will they. They'll see it as the local eunuch providing respectability on all sides." He sighed. "Well, that's an easy enough task. And hardly something for which I'll need to make up excuses. Of course I will."

"Don't be ridiculous." Peter gave a glancing swat to Guyon's shoulder, "I hadn't thought of that...they'll probably think we're sharing her instead. Just...make sure *someone* escorts her, hmm?"

"Yes," Guyon said absently. He chewed at his thumbnail, thinking. "She should take a maid with her anyway, I hadn't thought about that." He smiled wryly. "A lesson to us all to avoid entanglements with scholars, they never consider the obvious pitfalls of life."

"I hadn't considered it either, until it was pointed out to me, so perhaps that rule holds true of soldiers as well," Peter paused. "No, probably only of me. I was so used to looking at Ännchen as a sort of sister, or a part of Gottfried, that I never considered how others might see it. "

"No, well, why would you..." Guyon sighed. "Ännchen is so very beautiful. And it would not be inconceivable for the lord Marshal to have a mistress, you know that. The sight of you together – well. Conclusions are inevitable. What stuns me is how careless *she* has been." He waved a hand, wiping the conversation away. "I'll tell her to take one of the maids. I don't think I'll have to explain."

Peter reached up one long fingered hand and absently twisted one of Guyon's curls, "I have a master...no need for a mistress."

"You say the most ridiculous things, you know that?" Guyon asked dryly, but he could feel his bad mood starting to lift. "As though it were *possible* to command you!"

"Thou art my life, my love, my heart, The very eyes of me, And hast command of every part, To live and die for thee." Peter smiled, his finger now gently tracing along Guyon's jaw line.

"Oh, God, we're descending to Herrick?" Guyon turned his head, as though to bite Peter's finger, hoping that the gesture hid his sudden color. He hated that he craved these overt moments of sentimentality so much - and hated more that he could not respond to them without betraying the one secret he still kept.

34

"*Really*, Peter. *Sentiment.*" But he pressed his mouth into the palm of the long-fingered hand, after that, as much to silence himself as to take away the sting of his words.

"Yes, a descent into sentimentality," Peter agreed at once. "But I feel every bit of it, whether you do or not. I'm yours to command, in everything that is truly important."

Peter gave a small, crooked smile, then uncurled himself and stood up, "I still need to get these damned boots off, so they can dry out before morning."

Guyon, wishing there were some way he could ever get through these moments without either causing Peter pain or cursing himself, gestured to the bed. "If you sit there, you can only fall sideways instead of down, and I can get them off *for* you," he pointed out in oblique apology.

Obligingly, Peter settled down on the edge of the bed, then once again began to tug at his boots, "I'll get them. You're not my servant, Gui."

"No, but I object to being forced to laugh at you more than once a day," Guyon said, "and besides, you were busy instructing me not to, and how can I follow your instructions when you will *persist* in making me so tempted to defy all?" He tugged Peter's hands out of the way. "Also, this is quicker." He was proud of the fact that he had dragged the riding boots off and put them by the fire before Peter had either finished protesting or worked out just how easy it would be to kick him over.

"Thank you," Peter said simply, wiggling his stocking covered toes. "We should take yours off as well."

Guyon grinned at him. "Benefits of a complete lack of style or sense of taste," he said cheerfully, and simply toed them off as he stood by the hearth. He noticed with some irritation that he had a hole in his stocking. "My toes have a vendetta," he said thoughtfully, "but whether it's against me or staying dry, I'm not completely sure..."

Peter chuckled, "Poor thing. He looks so lonely poking out there all alone. Best have them off completely and give him company."

He rummaged through their pack and tossed clean, dry stockings towards Guyon.

Guyon made a face at him. "I'm not going to bother until tomorrow," he said. "I'll just wear through them again, or something, and then you'll be performing field surgery and amputating my toe just to shut me up..." He dropped the stockings on the chair, and came back over to the bed, prodding at it. "Think it has bedbugs?"

"If you're too worried, we can sleep on the floor, with whatever will appear once the lights are out." Peter raised an amused eyebrow.

"Oh God. Are you going to start telling Scottish ghost stories again?" Guyon glared at him, looking up from his pack-hunt for scissors, and settling in to perform a deeply uncomfortable task. "I *still* haven't forgiven you for the *sidhe*." Nor, he imagined, had the place they had been staying.

Peter just chuckled, returning to his seat near the fire, "Never again. I think my ribs still creak from the blows I received. You're rather nasty when awakened unexpectedly."

"Thank you," Guyon said, and beamed at him, collecting his clippings and throwing them into the fire, "It's a natural talent, honed by years of practice..." He padded over to where Peter was sitting, and sat by the hearth, feeding the fire twigs. "Are the cadets really that bad?" he asked the glowing depths, after a while. The fatigue in Peter's voice had worried him more than he cared to admit, as they traveled. Not that he thought there was anything he could do to help - he knew better - but it concerned him that Peter might already be so distanced by his new official work that there were things beginning to appear that he should know, and did not.

"No, they're not. Not really." Peter thought, then amended, "Well, not most of them. Young and brash and some of them hotheaded. The ones that bother me, actually, are the ones that are not. The ones that always have their eyes on you as if they're looking for a weak spot."

"Ah, then you're safe," Guyon said. "Any weak spots you have lead straight to Corvay, and only a fool would pursue further." He looked up, and seeing no responding amusement on Peter's face, sighed. "Always on your guard, then, *car-mi*?"

"I should be used to it. I've been on my guard since I arrived in France." Peter chuckled. "It's only when I'm with you that I can relax and know that someone's watching my back...and not because they want to stick a knife in it."

"I don't know whether to be flattered or terrified," Guyon said honestly. "You make me feel guilty at how carefree my existence is, these days."

"And boring?" Peter questioned. "But you can't miss this can you? Me dragging you away so that you can be embroiled in yet another demented imbroglio? No, I'm certain you're very much enjoying that bit of carefree existence, without all of my insanity."

"No," Guyon said, and would have left Peter to deduce whatever he wanted from that, save for the fact that he knew, no matter how he had stopped himself from seeing or acknowledging it, that he had hurt Peter earlier, another small cut to add to the myriad that he could not seem to stop inflicting. "You're the sanity."

"Guyon, you -" Whatever Peter had been going to say was interrupted by the sound of a knock on the door and a woman's voice announcing the arrival of their dinner.

Guyon got to his feet. "Come in," he called in his lightest voice. Had it been the landlord, he would have let Peter deal with it, but bar a very few - Ännchen included - Peter's awkwardness around women had a tendency to make the first impression of cold dislike, and he found that he did not have the energy to overcome that impression with charm. He took the tray from her with a smile. "Thank you."

She smiled back at him. "Will you be wanting anything else?" There was no mistaking the intent of her question. "Later?"

Guyon turned back from where he was setting the tray aside, and let regret enter his voice. "Alas, nothing but hot water in the morning," he said, and handed over a few coins to make his refusal the gentler.

"I saw her downstairs," Peter commented, when the girl had left the room. "She was watching you like you were the last bit of cheese in the pantry."

"The green bit that even the mice rejected?" Guyon asked lightly.

"Rather more like she'd like to get the first bite in," Peter snorted.

"Hm." Guyon laughed. He *knew* that. He had always known when someone was interested - except when it had been Peter, because he had actually wanted Peter in return, and it had blinded him with its suddenness, with the complete newness of desire coming to him for the first time, and the utterly unwanted and all-consuming emotions that had presaged it. "However, since I am *not* cheese, I can *choose* my consumer, and with care." He made sure to emphasize the singular, amidst his alliterative humor. He had still not forgotten that Peter could be inexplicably, bewilderingly and extremely painfully jealous at the oddest moments, and he was not sure that his current state of low-level exhaustion was one in which he could be laughed out of it.

"She would not have appreciated all of your nuances in any case," Peter moved to stand behind Guyon at the table, nuzzling his face down into his neck, "For you, it requires a gourmand."

"A -" Guyon choked on sudden, delighted laughter. *God, I love you*! In the surprise of that bubble of pure joy, he almost said it aloud, having to bite the inside of his lip hard before the words could escape him. "Thou very glutton," he said, and hoped that Peter would put the tremor in his voice down to either amusement or a response to his proximity.

"Glutton indeed," Peter whispered against his neck, "for something far more delectable than that." He waved a negligent hand towards the plates on the table.

"Which is hardly difficult," Guyon could not stop himself pointing out, but the shiver that ran through him this time *was* one of desire, his own body as ever a surprise to him, that the feel of breath on his skin, Peter's voice in his ear, could evoke a response in something he had thought of for years as nothing more than a shell to house his unreachable mind and spirit. But Peter reached all three, each and every time, and it still struck him like a bell, still reverberated within him almost physically. "Pèire -"

He had nothing to finish the sentence with in any case, simply needed to say something, anything, however meaningless, and turned around, stopping himself from some pointless tangle of words by kissing Peter, letting himself become uncaring of anything but the pleasure he knew he would never be able to wholly accept could be his.

*

Douai itself, of course, provided them with the usual selection of bafflement, unhelpfulness, and assorted attempts at assistance that were in fact more trouble than the deliberate stonewalling.

Guyon, whose gifts at questioning were never in the initial stages, but rather when they had found their target and were on established ground, had cheerfully left Peter to the tediousness of introductions and discretion, and set out to charm the owner of the inn they had chosen for their stay.

Peter, lost in a jointly-created fog of incomprehension and attempted assistance at the other tavern, while trying to avoid explaining why they were not staying with *this* particular landlord, could happily have kicked him.

"No. Monsieur *Renard*," he said again, repeating it slowly as if his pronunciation might be at fault. *How many people can there be by that name - or similar ones - in one town?*

"No, Monsieur, he has not been here for over a week now. Yes, Michel?" The landlord looked to his tapman for confirmation of his words.

At least he exists. It was sad that this was the most progress they had made to date, but equally sadly, the slowness and tedium of every tiny stage they managed to attain was by now almost an inevitable fact of life.

"Well, we are staying at *The Night In Jerusalem* if you see him. Please direct him there." Peter gave the man a few coins that, hopefully, would ensure the message delivered.

"Don't tell me," Guyon said as Peter came out. His voice carried through the rain from where he was sheltering beneath the eaves of one of the small houses. "No-one's seen him for days. Dear, dear, anyone would think he knew we were coming." He sneezed.

"Bless you." Peter joined him under the eaves and offered him his kerchief. "You should have stayed at the Inn, Gui. I could have done this alone."

"Yes, and then it would have been a trap and *I* would have been tearing Douai apart. Alone," Guyon said mockingly. "My presence ensures boredom, Peter, be grateful for it." He sneezed again, and blew his nose. "I think Douai is *made* out of moldy straw," he added grumpily.

"Ah. Is that what the translation is? And here I was thinking the name meant, *'Mudhole to irritate all visiting Scotsmen'*." Peter shook his head. "Either way there's nothing more to be done here at the moment. Let's get you back to the Inn."

"Like a parcel, inconspicuous and hidden, save for the sound of perpetual sneezing," Guyon said wryly. "Lord, I'm glad I didn't actually *come* to the University here!"

"So am I." Peter smiled softly as he fussed with Guyon's cloak, assuring it was pulled together in front before he lead the way out into the soggy landscape. "I would have had little occasion to come here."

"Yes," Guyon said dryly, "obviously that was my first consideration and not the *goddamned mould*!" He was curiously insistent that he was not suffering from a cold, but rather that the damp, musty-smelling air that did indeed seem to be coming from most of the roofs had got stuck in his nose. It was certainly making his temper worse than usual.

Peter filled him in on what he'd discovered at the tavern, or rather his lack of discovery, as they darted between sheltered spots. It really was infuriating how these things seemed to happen to him, but at least this time he did not have the imperative of save him or kill him to agonize over. If Monsieur was not there, it was simply a coincidence and of no concern, they had made two other contacts that morning and had a final one to speak with tomorrow. Between those three, they might have something.

"Mm." Guyon sounded skeptical, but not unhappy. He was obviously thinking again, and Peter knew from experience that he would be told none of it until every permutation of every vague idea that Guyon had was worked through. He stifled an amused grin as Guyon walked straight through a puddle while trying to avoid the drips from the eaves, looking down at his abused boots in consternation. "Ah," he said vaguely. He looked back at Peter, and his mouth twitched. "Let's get back to that inn of ours *fast*, shall we?"

"Yes, I think that might be wise." Some how, Peter managed to keep a straight face. "It's just down here."

"I do still have my sense of direction intact, yes, o he who got lost at Saint-Sulpice," Guyon said blandly. His eyes gleamed with the promise of havoc, in direct contrast to his smooth tones.

Peter refused to take insult, "Indeed. I still need to work on my written language skills, apparently."

Although his spoken skills had grown with leaps and bounds since he had arrived in France, Peter still had difficulty with the written language, often mistaking words each for the other. Much, he was often reminded, to Guyon's amusement.

"No, not *apparently,*" Guyon said on a breath of laughter. "*Definitely.*" He finished his peculiar dance between dripping eaves and slightly loose cobbles, and opened the door to the *Night in Jerusalem* with a flourish.

"Yes, well, we'll see how well you do when we visit Scotland and you have to ask for directions to 'a-torn-down'." Peter sniped back as he passed through the door, removing his cloak and shaking the water off of it.

"I'll just wave my hands a lot and smile optimistically," Guyon said cheerfully, closing the door and throwing his equally wet cloak onto a seat by the fire. "They will, of course, take pity on the poor idiot and send me *just* where I want to go."

Peter snorted, but chances were Guyon was correct. The scholar had the amazing ability to look helpless and innocent and slightly crazed when he wished, and would, he was certain, be able to charm even the most stubborn Scot into directing him straight to Hawthornden. "Luncheon? Or just something warm to drink?"

"Food and something *hot* to drink," Guyon said with emphasis. "It's cold, it's wet, I'm bored - does the landlord have a chess set?"

"It couldn't hurt to ask," Peter shrugged and moved to give their order and make the inquiry.

This was, in his opinion, the most difficult thing about having Guyon along with him. While they were actually doing something he was helpful, sharp and intense, but the moment that focus was removed his friend's razor sharp mind quickly craved something to occupy it.

He had managed to convince Guyon that they could not, in fact, take more than five books with them, but Guyon was still more likely to unpack his saddlebags to disclose far more than that and a complete lack of anything remotely useful. A passing interest in the mechanics of pistols had ensured for a while that he was at least armed, even if more in theory than in practice, but Peter was reasonably sure that now Guyon had worked out their construction to his satisfaction, the chances of his having anything more than an unloaded flintlock and some poor sad remnants of something mechanical that he had disemboweled several weeks previously and discarded were vanishingly small.

Thankfully though, the landlord did have a chess set and promised to bring it and their lunch into the small private room they had set aside. Peter picked up the two mugs of mulled wine he had been given and gestured for Guyon to follow him. "Grab the cloaks will you? We can spread them to dry in there."

"Mm." Guyon's expression was abstracted again as he draped the cloaks over his arm, following Peter into the little room. Rather than spreading them out, he hung them up by the fire, shaking out the folds as much as possible. The fur lining of his own was beginning to look a little sad. "Peter - I've been thinking."

Peter passed him the wine, then settled himself into a seat near the fire, "You are *always* thinking, Gui."

"Well, yes, so are you, it's the human condition, I meant I've been *specifically* thinking." Guyon rolled his eyes, and took a drink from his cup. "I don't think de Retz is going the right way about trapping Corvay."

"I can't say you're wrong," Peter told him with a sigh. "But I know no other way than gathering evidence and working toward proof. I just wish we were getting more."

Guyon bit his lip. He was staring down into his cup as though it held the secrets of the universe, and was silent for so long Peter thought he had fallen into a reverie, before he said very quietly. "I could *make* more."

"You what?" Peter frowned, convinced that he had misunderstood.

"I could make more," Guyon repeated clearly. "More proof." He was a little white around his mouth and eyes, usually a sign of temper, but he didn't seem angry.

Afraid, Peter thought, surprised, and then, with a small shock that struck him somewhere beneath his breastbone - *Afraid of* **me**.

"I know you could." Peter said quietly. "I could as well. But, damn, the man is corruption itself, surely we should not have to resort to any such thing."

He tried to keep his voice even, to show no trace of condemnation in his features. He knew what this meant to Guyon. Knew that he wanted to keep his family safe - even that damnable bastard that he called 'brother'. It were left to him, Giraud could go hang and Guyon would be better off. The idea of falsifying evidence went against his every belief, *but* he could understand Guyon's suggesting it.

"No," Guyon said quietly. "We should not. But I think -" He stopped, and sighed, running a hand over his face. "You're right," he said quietly. "It does no good to try and stop corruption if the only means of doing so is to become as tainted oneself. I'm sorry. I should never have said anything."

"God no, don't apologize for that. I understand. Don't you think that if I truly felt we could not do this some other way that I would not be considering your suggestion right now?" That was surely the truth, although Peter hoped it would never come to that. For Guyon he would lie. He would perjure himself and do whatever it took to get his friend, his beloved, free from Corvay's clutches.

"Honestly?" Guyon smiled at him a little wryly. "No. I do not. I think you will *always* believe there is another way, *chérâme.*" He walked across the room, taking the seat opposite Peter and leaning forward to brush his fingers, fleetingly, over the back of Peter's hand. "Don't change."

"Hmmpf." Peter snorted indignantly, but could not contain the smile that twinkled in his eyes. "I love you, you know?"

He said it oh-so-casually, as if he were discussing the rain or the mud. There were times when he simply could not hold back the words, no matter what Guyon's feelings in the matter.

"God love the Scots," was Guyon's only response, "for someone needs to save them from their sentimentality." But he was smiling, for once free of any sort of wry twist, and for the thousandth pointless time, Peter let himself hope that one day those words would be returned.

*

It was evening by the time the message came for them. Guyon was playing chess with himself under a series of complicated rules that he had tried, briefly, to explain, before seeing the glazed look in Peter's eyes and giving up. He had pretended not to notice the sheer relief on Peter's face as he started the solitaire game, and simply raised a hand in acknowledgement when Peter announced his intention of going to the taproom and finding company that wasn't obsessed with keeping its own thoughts hidden from itself.

So enthralled was he, in fact, with this mental exercise that it took him a moment to realize that Peter had returned some time later. Returned and had apparently been standing over him saying his name. Several times, it would be assumed, from the slightly frustrated and yet amused look on Peter's face when he finally looked up.

"Yes?" he asked politely, as though it were the first time Peter had said his name, and not, which was all too possible, the tenth. "Can I help you, my Lord Marshal?"

Peter reached down and slid a rook across the board, "Checkmate. Now you're done and we are expected back at the *'Eagle Eye'*. Renard is there and, by his message, has some kind of...*package* for us."

Guyon, who had spent the best part of twenty minutes trying to get *out* from under that move, closed his eyes in frustration. "Thank you," he said with what he thought was remarkable calm. "What *would* I have done without your help?" He sighed, and got to his feet, retrieving his now-dry cloak from the hook by the fire. "I hope it's a *pretty* package," he added dryly. "Lots of letters and numbers, all tied up with a bow..."

44

"Oh, God, so do I." Peter grinned, "If only to give you something to do."

Picking up his own cloak and settling it over his shoulders, Peter led the way out.

"I *was* doing something," Guyon began to protest, and stopped mid-complaint as they stepped outside. "My God, it's *still* raining."

"Yes," Peter replied dryly as he negotiated the large puddle that just in front of the door. "Either that or the angels are weeping in commiseration for your boredom."

"No, that's just you, and it doesn't count as commiseration when it's based in pure desperation," Guyon shot back. It was moments like this when he was closest to deciding that his self-imposed rule could go and choke itself by its own knotted morality. What most people took for contempt, Peter took and returned quickly, fitting into his world of words and creation as no-one else had ever managed.

"I am never that desperate, Gui, but most of the ways I know to distract you involve things that can't easily be done in public," Peter peeked back at Guyon around the edge of his cloak, his eyes twinkling brightly.

"In this case, they'd have to be mad enough to be in public," Guyon retorted. "And no, Peter, the taproom doesn't count, since I don't think anyone's *ever* noticed what's done in a taproom."

There was a snort of amused laughter from Peter as he led them the last few yards to the 'Eagle Eye'. "*This* I think they might notice."

"Really?" Guyon asked innocently, blowing drops of water off his nose. "And why would that be, please?" He managed to time his query and his look of completely spurious ignorance to coincide with Peter's opening the door and turning to look at him. He stepped backwards, laughing in disbelief, and missed the small step behind him, so that his arrival in the room was more of a heavy jump than any sort of dignified entrance. Guyon smirked, and stepped in neatly behind him.

"Bastard," Peter muttered under his breath, as he moved to question the tapman about Renard's location.

"Critic," Guyon murmured back sweetly, taking up his usual

position in the shadows by the side of the fireplace, watching the room.

Peter carried on a quick conversation with the tapman and then an even quicker conversation with the man, Renard apparently, at the other end of the bar. A bare twenty words were exchanged before other man exited through the rear of the tavern and Peter walked over to where Guyon stood.

"Other than potential syphilis," Guyon said quietly, having noted the rather strange appearance of the man's nose, "what does he have?"

"I'm not sure," Peter frowned. "But whatever it is, we need to meet him out back in the stables. He says he can't bring it in here."

"Oh, damn, it's not papers," Guyon said, thoroughly disappointed. "Unless it's a chest of them, which is very unlikely. It's probably an anvil, or...oh, God, who cares. It's really not going to be useful, is it?" He sighed, and went towards the rear of the tavern himself, going out of the smaller door and into the wet courtyard, before making a dash across to the small light he could see in one of the tiny stable windows. He lifted the latch on the door, and went into the warmth of horses and straw and fermenting grass.

Peter hurried after him, muttering to himself, "Oh, no Gottfried, I'm so terribly sorry, but your partner got himself skewered by dashing into a stable to get out of the rain. What? No, of course he didn't let me go first to see if it was a trap...just dashed right in...*Christ, Guyon!*"

Guyon, who had heard most of the muttering via the oddly magnifying effect of wet cobbles and the close stone walls of the courtyard, rolled his eyes. "*Are* you going to skewer me?" he asked Renard with interest, ignoring Peter.

"Ah, not today, I think," Renard answered him with amusement as Peter stomped through the door. "That assignment is usually left in the hands of my 'package'."

He stepped aside to reveal a man, bound and gagged, laying in one of the stalls.

"Good God."

Peter's gasp was not for the state of the 'package', but rather because he recognized the man far too well.

"How nice," Guyon said, wondering what on earth was going on. "A tied up and rather smelly individual who seems to mean something to everyone but me. Anyone care to enlighten the ignorant among you?" The man in the stall made a few muffled noises, and he sighed. "No, you can talk later, my fragrant friend. Anyone who is *not* currently tied up and smelling like the Seine in midsummer want to try?"

"'s Martelle," Peter choked out, his face going stiff and stark.

"And that was extremely unhelpful, but at least I know what to call him when I'm torturing information from him lat - *ah*." Guyon went very still, as his mind connected Peter's odd reaction to the man with the almost communal twitch everyone had given when he mentioned torture. "Well, well. Now this *is* someone I've been wanting to meet. Thank you, Renard. I can't see what use he'll be in the abstract, but at least he'll give me a few hours amusement. How kind of you."

Martelle had been one of the leaders of the insurgents at the time Peter had been sent to Poitou, by Corvay. He was also the man who had run Peter through when he tried to effect the escape of Michel Duvane, another operative. That wound had nearly killed Peter as he made his way back to Paris, dodging those who were searching for him. His recovery had taken months.

And now here he was, bound, gagged and at their mercy.

"So much for your gift - which I'll show due gratitude for in time," Guyon continued, wishing that Peter would contribute more than to stand there looking at Martelle as though his eyes alone could induce the pain of the damned. "But you wrote to de Retz saying that you had proof against Corvay." As Renard looked at him blankly, he turned away, kicking the stall door in frustration. "Oh *Christ*. Tell me, someone tell me, that this smelly object isn't your *proof*!"

"Well...yes," Renard looked bemused. "Well, that and this..."

He reached inside his tunic and withdrew a small sheaf of papers. The writing was familiar, very much so - Corvay's.

"*Ah*." Guyon took the papers gratefully. "Now *these* I may be able to use. *Him* -" he prodded at Martelle with the toe of his boot - "I think unfortunately *not*. Unless for target practice. Or the

47

Place de la Greve. Or possibly the fine art of fingernail removal, but proof, alas, no. Peter? Any suggestions? He is *your* acquaintance, after all, it should be on your word that his fate is decided, I believe."

"We'll turn him over to de Retz," Peter's voice was still strained. "Perhaps he can be convinced to give witness against Corvay."

"The bird will sing," Renard assured them. "Especially once word is put out that he was a double agent."

"Oh for the love of -" Guyon bit the inside of his lip, hard. Peter looked as though he were looking at a ghost, which in many ways Guyon supposed he was, and coming up with something that did not involve personalized and intricate revenge had obviously been the limit of his adherence to any sort of structured thought or behavior. Renard he was beginning to think possessed all the lack of sense of a stunned trout. Martelle, obviously, was no use at all, but unfortunately for him, he was no use at all in any respect. "Listen," he said in a more measured voice. "I'm sure that word getting out to the insurgents that he was a double agent will make his life nasty, brutish and short should he attempt to go back to them. I am equally sure that the thought of having to do so under those circumstances will turn him into a veritable waterfall of words. But *unfortunately*, none of those words will do us any good at all, because he's *already condemned* and his testimony will be deemed irrelevant and inadmissible!"

"Bloody Hell..." Peter suddenly burst out of his frozen state, babbling in English, "it doesn't matter. We have to take him back for his own trial whether he's of use or not. But I..." Peter ran one hand through his long hair, "I don't want responsibility for him. We'll find someone else to do it."

"All right," Guyon said calmly, "Renard can do it. He seems to think he can convince everyone of others being double agents, let's see if he can pull off a conversion to the One True Faith." He smiled at Renard nastily. "The head of which, my fiendishly stupid friend, is de Retz. Start thinking of a *very* good story. Because believe me, I am *not* the man you want to have to ask to save you from the fate which is, quite inevitably, going to be Martelle's." It was irrational of him, it was probably foolish to

48

expose his interests in this way, but he found it very difficult to care. His determination to destroy Corvay had begun with a small, simple statement that the bound man in front of him had been responsible for.

And then it was raining and all the footprints had gone.

He had no more forgotten than Peter had the details he knew of the events in Toulouse. And he would never, as long as he lived, forgive the authors of that moment of pure, singing hate that had been his first step on the road from academia and into Corvay's clutches. He was damned, and doomed to remain so. But the causes of it - those he could ensure met the same fate.

"I want," he said grimly, "a priest with at least a vague knowledge of a bishop's name, a lawyer, and a magistrate."

Renard blinked at him. "Now?"

"*Right* now," Guyon confirmed, before turning to Peter. "And you, I'm afraid, need to go back to our lodgings." He sighed. "Some things, I think, are outside the provenance of the English Marshal."

Thank God, he thought involuntarily, hoping his expression did not give away his rather savage joy at the knowledge that here, at last, was where the scant powers de Retz was able to give him came into their own. At Court and in the army, Peter was infinitely, effortlessly his superior. Within the Church, however, Guyon was the Archbishop of Paris's mouthpiece abroad, and his suggestion to an ecclesiastical court that Martelle should be condemned would be taken as a decree.

That it would be an ecclesiastical court in the first place who tried Martelle was not in question. Peter might have been working for the State, but without Duvane's testimony and an admission from Corvay as to what he did, there would be nothing but an unwilling acquittal. The Church, however, would be Martelle's first attempted point of refuge, if they did not move to stop that avenue of escape before it was attempted. A man condemned by the State might be saved by the Church in acknowledgement of his soul's innocence. But should the Church condemn him - and Guyon intended to make sure that in Martelle's case, it did - the State had no choice but to follow.

And even though a local priest, a magistrate, and a lawyer

were really no more than paying face value to the idea of justice, Guyon knew that it was appearance alone that would count here. Martelle had damned himself from the moment he tried to run, and Guyon, bearer of de Retz's written approval to his orders, was more than happy to be the author of that damnation.

*

The dream, when it came, was as unpleasant as it was expected. The sight of Martelle had stirred up fevered memories of Peter's trek from Toulouse. Waves of mud and pain and a feeling of loss, all tangled together with the unending drive and belief that if he could just get home, somehow, all would be made right.

He had just reached the point in the confusion where he had to fight...someone...Corvay, Martelle...even his brother-in-law, Robert, in a few of his more confused moments...when the dream changed. Peter was still immersed in ever rising water and mud, but now Guyon stood on the bank his hand extended toward him... reaching. In the dream, Peter fought, struggled, battled the mud, but just as he reached the shore, his fingers mere inches from Guyon's... the reaching hand disappeared and all he could see was the distant curly-haired figure, walking away, never pausing or taking even a moment to look back, deserting him.

Peter woke in a cold sweat and eased out of bed, going to sit by the fire, while he willed his breathing back to normal.

"I have in no way questioned Martelle," Guyon said quietly as he came into the room, "there was in no way an ecclesiastical court held, and your honor is in no way compromised by the fact you undoubtedly woke making love to feathers and hard linen . In other words -" The insouciant, soft voice stopped abruptly, moving into quick understanding. "*Jesu*, Pèire!" The blunt, cold, fingers were sudden and hard on his face, strong and demanding in their pressure. "You dreamt. *Damn it.*"

"Is that not allowed?" Peter returned, his sarcasm lessened by his muted voice and shaking hands.

"In fact of fact and point of point, no, I forbid it," Guyon said gently. "At least not when I am from the room to be *able* to forbid

50

it." He took Peter's hands in his own, smaller ones, and kissed them. "*Tolon, bèl-mi?*"

"Of course Toulouse," Peter shrugged.   "Not as bad as it might have been, you were there to save me."

But you didn't...you didn't. Still, the words were not a lie, Guyon's presence in the dream had made it less stressful up until the end.

"Was I, so? Evidently I am kinder in sleep than in waking," Guyon said, as though hearing his thoughts. "Martelle is damned for attempted murder, Pèire, I summoned the ecclesiastical court tonight."

"Here?" Peter blinked.   "No..no..no...of course, here. Sorry. I'm still about half asleep, I think."

Half asleep and scared out of my mind that my dream will come true. That you'll leave me drowning and alone.

Peter scrubbed one hand over his face. "Do we need to stay and give evidence...or something?"

"No, *car-mi.* We do not." Guyon shrugged it away. "Now tell me, what did I do?" He had not let go of Peter's hands.

"Do?" Peter looked at him blankly. "You summoned the court...didn't you?'

No...no...no... Keep your ridiculous insecurities to yourself for once, Scudamore. It was a dream.

"Mm. Except you didn't know that and you look like hell - Pèire. Don't try to hide. I know each and every variation of that journey, what did I do in this variation of your nightmare's ride through it? Did my hand wield the knife or did I simply walk away as you bled to death from Martelle's wound?"

"It's ridiculous, Gui. It was a *dream*, for Christ's sake." Peter dropped his head down on his chest and closed his eyes. "Just one more in a line of many I've had about that damn trip. It just makes me angry, because I thought I was past them."

"Oh, you're angry?" Guyon's eyes were bright in the firelight. "So, you want to spar, not to be told - *it doesn't matter. That wasn't me. I will always find you.*" The last of it was breathed into Peter's ear as he was drawn forward into the faint chill of the outside that still clung to Guyon's clothes, and the faint scents of bergamot and woodsmoke. "Don't spar, Pèire-mi. Don't spar, my soldier. I am too easy to defeat."

Peter gave a rough bark of a laugh and reached out his hands. *Guyon is here...here...here...Thank God.* He wrapped his arms around Guyon's waist and drew him closer, burying his face against his stomach.

"Please don't - leave me alone." The words were choked out of him, leaving Peter feeling somewhat embarrassed that he had allowed a dream to affect him so strongly.

"Never," Guyon said strongly. "While I am wi-*without him*, I am dead until I be *with him*." The English words were strongly accented, but accurate and sure. "You are the one sure thing in my life, you sentimental dreaming foolish Scot."

Peter rubbed his face against Guyon's tunic, feeling the hard muscle underneath the soft cloth, "As you are mine, you sarcastic, infuriating brat of an Occitan.. Just...remember that, alright?"

"I am terrib'y, dreadfu'y, 'orribly aware," Guyon said, wry and confident. "I pray God to deliver me and in the same breath pray 'im not to every day." He kissed the top of Peter's head. "Ah, your nightmares 'ave come out through the top of your 'ead, you are damp!" He was still speaking in English. "My God, thou always so dear and very idiot!"

Against all Peter's half-voiced protestations, he was out of his nightshirt and into a clean, dry piece of linen that was far too short in every way, and being pressed to drink something that was sweet, and herbal, and kindly took all the skin out of the back of his throat when he swallowed it. It burned through him, dispelling the last of the clinging chill, and not for the first time, he wondered how Guyon found things that walked the line between drugs and folk remedies so easily.

"Bed," Guyon said then, firmly.

"Yes, sir..." Peter had learned that when Guyon got like this, his instant and complete obedience was easiest...also rather nice. He spent so much damn time being in charge of everything - the Cadets, the Hôtel, her Majesty's security, himself - that letting go of it was almost cathartic.

Guyon laughed, soft and kind and deep. "Mm. My tired Marshal. Ah, the English are so desolate, for you leave them to the depths of slumber, to the Isles of the Hesperides..." As he spoke, he pulled Peter into bed with him, so that it was not so much as surrender, as a glad and very forgettable relinquishment of something he had no words for. "We shall sail to find those golden apples, the source of immortality. We shall meet those maidens and seduce them with your song and my words, we shall put them aside and bite into the fruit of the blessed isles, and be with Achilles..." He cupped Peter's head in the hollow of his shoulder, creating beautiful, shimmering nonsense for a web of peace, and Peter slept, slowly falling between a tale and the reality of a warm shoulder, between deft blunt fingers and softly repeating words.

*

As Peter fell into sleep, Guyon's voice changed, following words that were soothing only to him, resonating within his soul and mind, allowing himself a rare expression of love.

"In true friendship, it is a general and universal heat, and equally tempered, a constant and settled heat, all pleasure and smoothness, that hath no pricking or stinging in it, which the more it is in lustful love, the more is it but a raging and mad desire in following that which flies us."

Have you finished Montaigne yet? He kept asking that, hoping that Peter would read there the words he was incapable of saying for himself, that it would be made clear how deeply and strongly his emotions ran, no matter how he refuted them when asked.

Sentiment! It was his perennial mockery of himself, not of Peter, though there was no way Scudamore could ever be expected to know that. Sentiment, yes, but it was his own that he mocked, not Peter's, no matter how it sounded to those who heard him.

"I am quite certain that I love you, you know," he said quietly in Occitan, slurring his soft way into Peter's sleep. "I don't know how I'm supposed to do it right, and it's for sure not how I do feel it that can of all possibility be right, I know that much, but...you are so much a part of me now that not to love you would be to lose all that remains to me of myself. I have a heart and soul as well as an intellect, and they are so often at war, *chérâme*, so very often. Don't spar with me, Peter, not in this, not in the world of love or dreams. I meant it - I'm so easy to defeat. So very easy."

He sighed.

"And truly, if without that, such a genuine and voluntary acquaintance might be contracted, where not only minds had this entire joy, but also bodies, a share of the alliance, and where a man might wholly be engaged: then it is certain, that friendship would thereby be more complete and full. It is said, though, that our sex could never yet by any example attain unto it, and is therefore by ancient schools rejected thence. It's not, you know. They see what we have as perfection. They see what I cannot say as folly, as a laughable mistake, for how can you deny love? And yet I do, my very dear, I do, and I must. Our genuine and voluntary acquaintance will be curtailed until the day I die, because my love is - my love is too absolute. Too final, too all in all. You could, and should, have others, and I cannot, and that is - is unfair, is wrong for you and leaves you blameless of my errors. I am - warped in the making, no matter how strong and enduring my love for you may otherwise be."

Peter stirred, and Guyon pressed his lips to the fine, feather-like golden hairs above the pale temple, breathing out the only warmth he knew himself to possess.

"This is my luxury. This is my peace, why I never teach you Occitan as I promised, so that I can use my words and soothe my tongue. I love you, in breath and shadow and in sleep and sunlight, in thought and unconsciousness, in the very essence of what I cannot be, I *am you.* I would tear apart the world to save you, I would die and count myself happy, I would kill, I would defy God and still know myself whole. You double me and take me away from myself, you possess me and enhance me, you are the very heart of my heart and the blood in my veins. I will love you until the sea runs dry and turns to pure salt, until my limbs atrophy and turn to dust. I can live knowing that I am not what you need, as long as I can hold my silence and yet have moments such as this."

He stared blindly into the faint firelight, and wished damnation on Martelle, a greater one than would ever meet him in the Bastille, a greater one than any man could bring to bear.

"When you dream," he whispered, "dream this. I will always find you. In the worst and the darkest of times, I am the one sure thing, for I too am the darkest and the worst, and in those places, those unspoken of horrors, I am at home. I will never promise, *car-mi*. But I can say that...that I am. I am, I exist. I *will be*. I will move through shadows and light and set the whole world ablaze, I will do the forbidden and the most dreadful of all, to hold you safe for one moment in which you will reject me.

"Wholly, completely, and utterly," he vowed, as Peter shifted against his shoulder, turning his face so that lips and eyelashes moved alike against Guyon's neck. "Wholly. Completely. Utterly. *Thine.*"

He looked across the room at the fire, and let his mind sink into the light.

All that I am...

All that I will be...

Clear and cold came the voice of his madness, the voice of Peter's night outside Toulouse, the words new if not the tone of them -

"You will lose all you hold dear for this."

Guyon smiled into the flames, and saw his ruin.

"So be it," he whispered in English, and fell into sleep.

His lips moved in dreams, his mind moving upon silences and truths and understandings that he would never have dared admit to awake, knowing and discarding costs even while he slept.

Illam mea si partem animæ tulit,
Maturior vis, quid moror altera,
Nec charus æque nec superestes,
Integer? Ille dies utramque
Duxit ruinam.

"Since now from that part of my soul fate has torn me,
Why stay I here and mourn the other part he left me?
Not so dear, nor entire, while here I rest:
That day hath in one ruin both oppressed."

His eyes opened, unseeing.

"His hands will be in the shackles. And they will watch. And I cannot be his monk to pray for a soul still bleeding. *It will happen*," he said clearly into the night. "*And I shall be the author of it.*"

*

Paris, April 1646

But yet the wheel in turning round,
At last may lift us from the ground;
And when our fortune's most severe,
The less we have, the less we fear.

Guyon tried more often than even Peter gave him credit for to control his temper around Corvay - something which was not always feasible, given that he held him responsible for the two great griefs of his life; Giraud's permanent endangerment and François Villon's death. But a summons from him when he was dealing with a disappointed de Retz, the aftermath of an ecclesiastical court that he probably should not have summoned, and his own worry over Peter, was the one thing guaranteed to remove all traces of his ever-tenuous control and send him straight into a state of spitting, far-too-coherent fury that even he hoped would have worn off by the time he and Peter reached Corvay's house on the Rue Ferou.

Oddly, it seemed the more furious he became, the quieter Peter was. He seemed to withdraw into himself, his face giving little clue as to his thoughts. Guyon was unsure if this was just Peter controlling his temper in some new way, or if the retrospect of meeting the man who almost killed him and Corvay's possible connection to it was still weighing on him.

It went further than anything towards slowly killing his anger, subsuming it beneath the worry that was ever more familiar these days. "It's all right," he said at last. "I won't say anything but the minimum in there, I promise. No embarrassing rants that lead to more holds on your time."

"Nothing you do embarrasses me, Gui." Peter spoke softly as they walked. "I - I just hate coming here. I hate Corvay, and I hate that he can call us like trained dogs, and that we have to do his bidding. And most of all...I hate myself for ever getting you mixed up in this."

"You didn't," Guyon said, as he always did, and wondered when Peter would realize that he was telling the truth, that Corvay had always wanted him, and that if it had not been Peter who had provided the means to that end, the spy master would have found another way. It was the doomed legacy of the Languedoc, the tainted, warped beliefs that had led Giraud to defy the kingdom and himself to try and hide in the ivory sanctum of academia, that had first attracted Luc Corvay, and it was not Peter's fault that he had found Guyon such a surprisingly willing tool. "And you shouldn't. Hate Corvay by all means, to your last breath if you have to, but not yourself, not for this. We're all responsible for our own actions." He grinned. "Even I am, you know."

Peter gave a small smile, "Even you?" And it seemed as if that small jest lightened something in him. He took a long, deep breath and then put his hand on Guyon's shoulder, "Thank you for that. I still can't help but think that if I hadn't suggested you - Well never mind, it's done, isn't it? Now we just look for how to move forward and get out."

"And that has made me annoyed all over again," Guyon said, making a face, "and mostly at de Retz and his ideas as to what constitutes preparation. I know he wants to help, but Christ, for a man whose true Bible is Machiavelli, he's worse than I am at intrigue." He frowned, his temper dissolving into one of his sudden, quicksilver grins even as he did so. "Which is hard, isn't it, and mildly disturbing as a thought..."

"You're actually good at it," Peter said as they paused in the street in front of Corvay's house. "You're good at holding your true thoughts, and - well, you're much better than I am. Not so obvious."

"Right up until the point where I open my mouth and explain in graphic detail what I'm thinking and why," Guyon agreed, still amused. "You know, it's a source of continual amazement to me that Corvay actually thought we'd be useful for anything but starting fights - oh, I know, between him and de Retz, we're getting better, but while we're not so bad at the intelligence bit, spies we truly are not to any competent degree."

"As you say," Peter chuckled a bit and then looked at the house. "Busy today. I wonder what's happening." Several people had entered and exited the house while they stood there. Some Guyon recognized from previous visits, but most were odd types, sailors, merchants, recognizable villains.

Guyon sighed. "Nothing we really want to know about, I'd lay down good money - oh, come on, let's get this over with." His irritability was back in full force.

"Everything we can find out about what Corvay is doing could be useful." Peter shrugged. "But yes...sooner begun, sooner done."

Guyon, briefly and pleasurably, contemplated a world where people could be mesmerized into forgetting annoying rhyming aphorisms, felt instantly guilty for wanting to change Peter in the slightest, and greeted Corvay's secretary with a look that set him stepping back and announcing their arrival without any delaying formalities at all.

"See," Peter leaned in and whispered, "you're intimidating enough to be a good spy."

"Then don't make me laugh," Guyon hissed back, feeling his mood lighten instantly, and it was truly ludicrous, how Peter could be worried and tense and in an abysmally self-deprecating mood, and still manage to make life seem bearable.

"Gentlemen, how was Douai?" asked Corvay in his most nastily avuncular voice, and the feeling of bearability vanished instantly.

"Wet," Guyon replied with honesty. "And moldy." Beside him, Peter made a noise like a stifled sneeze.

"As always then," Corvay nodded. "Which brings me to wonder exactly why the two of you decided you must go there."

"There's a monastery," Guyon replied. "For some reason, I can't be trusted to go to them alone."

Corvay gave a snort of disbelief, "I'd be more afraid of setting the lascivious wolf among the sheep than you." He nodded in Peter's direction, making his reference to Peter's preference for men even more pronounced.

"No, no, *no*," Guyon said with limpidly innocent amusement, "not the *monks*, the *books*. Really, Corvay, you need to spend a little money of an evening, if you turn your mind so wistfully towards the unwashed and hair-shirt wearing among us."

"No word games today, my little Occitan, I haven't the time nor the inclination to play with you," Corvay growled out the words and then looked at Peter. "Why did you go to Douai?"

"I'd never been there before," Peter shrugged. Well, that was certainly no lie.

"You went to Douai because *he* wanted to look at a book -"

"*Books*," Guyon interjected, with the air of one insistent upon accuracy.

"- and *you* had never been there before?"

"Never," Peter asserted again. "Might be a nice place if it dried out. I find that mud disagrees with me."

Briefly, Guyon looked down at the toes of his boots, knowing that however good his control, Corvay would see the quick flicker of rage in his eyes at that small comment. "And with my boots," he agreed, hoping that the second's pause would not have been enough to betray him. "I shall have to get them re-soled."

He looked up to see Corvay looking at them both with undisguised irritation. "And the ecclesiastical court in Douai?" he demanded.

"Is hell's own idea of boring?" Guyon suggested helpfully. "We didn't attend, did you want us to?"

"Please, don't think you can toy with me, de Chesnay. You want me to believe that you two being in town and the fact that an ecclesiastical court was called is mere coincidence?"

"Since we weren't the subjects of investigation, and you didn't summon it - *yes*," Guyon said pointedly. "You may have forced me to make my head a grave, and refute Browne in the doing of it, Corvay, but you have not yet succeeded in dulling my wits to the point where I am not *sure* there is nothing that occurs in France without your express involvement." *Now tell me the truth, and admit this once de Retz held the upper hand, and I shall die of shock.*

Corvay snorted, "It doesn't matter. I will find out at any rate. It couldn't have been anything of import or you'd both be all too willing to wave it in my face."

He looked from Guyon to Peter and then back to Guyon, a smirk on his face. "All too willing...yes."

"Yes, willing to the point of absurdity, that's us," Guyon agreed, beginning to feel tired of Corvay and the conversation, and forcing himself to concentrate and focus, refusing to let things slip from simple ennui. "Did you *want* anything?"

Corvay was now prowling around them, his expression one of speculation, his eyes on Peter. "There are many things I want. But the timing isn't yet right." He gave a chuckle there.

"Lord, let us not upset your sense of timing, by any means." Guyon had reached the point he always did, where one more minute of watching Corvay contemplate just how he was going to destroy Peter's life next, and he would put a knife straight into the spy-master's eye. "Are you *quite* sure you wouldn't like me to send to the brothels for someone willing to dress as a monk? It might improve your temper."

"You do so amuse me, de Chesnay." Corvay said it in a way that meant the exact opposite. "I think I'm done with you...for now. I'll have the information I want, never fear."

"I never do fear," Guyon agreed blandly, and resisted the urge to make the English bowman's salute that his students loved, right in Corvay's face. "Pleasant though this has been, and *so* to the point, I'll bid you farewell, in that case."

"I will want you here again soon," Corvay continued as if Guyon had not spoken. "There is a tempest brewing and, somehow, I do believe you'll want to be in the middle of that as well."

He waved a hand as if in dismissal, then turned to walk away.

Guyon looked at Peter, his eyebrows raised. "Hopefully not in a fishing boat," he muttered. "*Christ.* Let's get out of here."

"Less mud in a fishing boat," Peter muttered nonsensically as they left. "God, hate this place."

"Really? I thought it was ideally situated for a holiday," Guyon sniped, then grimaced. "Sorry. I'm *not* in a bad temper with *you*."

Peter gave an exasperated sigh, "I know that, Gui. Facing Corvay always puts me in a foul mood, let alone you."

"I can never *shut up* when he starts," Guyon said furiously. "I have to - to push, and poke, and *damn*, he turns the *week* sour!"

"Ah, yes, that would explain his resemblance to a dried up lemon," Peter snorted out an unamused laugh. "And now, I have the added joy of greeting six new recruits and hoping that *they* at least know their left from their right." He paused for a moment, now that they had reached the street. "Are you free later?"

"Always, for the Lord Marshal," Guyon said teasingly. "I'll let Ännchen tuck the students in and read them a story. Unless they've managed to make Gottfried eat chalk again, in which case *I'll* read them a bedtime story and let Philippe deal with the resulting nightmares." It amused him to act as though his group of one-year students, desperately cramming all the information they could find into their minds before they attempted entry to the Sorbonne, were in fact infants still in need of wet-nursing.

Peter chuckled over the image, but then raised an eyebrow as they continued their fast paced walk, both of them unconsciously putting space between themselves and Corvay, "For the Lord Marshal? What about some time for plain Peter Scudamore?"

"Ah, well, *he* doesn't even have to ask," Guyon said with a smile. "The Hôtel, then? Or do you need to escape?"

"Meet me there and we'll decide?" Peter slowed his pace. "I don't know - Whenever Corvay summons me, I feel the need to prove to myself that there are still good things in my life. And that's you, you know?"

"*Car-mi*, you have the worst priorities of any man I have ever met." *And God help me, but I love you for them.* He wished, as he so often did, that he could be as unself-conscious when he cared as when he felt only mild affection. He could casually walk about the streets with his arm through that of Vincennes or Gottfried, but with Peter, he was convinced that he broadcast his every emotion to the world as soon as he touched him. "But I admit to an element of returned truth in that. Mostly, of course, because you give me an ideal reason to avoid supper."

"I knew there was another reason you agreed so quickly." Peter grinned. "Is Ännchen trying out another new recipe? Or simply destroying an old one?"

"I'm...not sure," Guyon admitted. "It's involved eggs." It was inadequate, as far as describing the horror of things that were half-raw and slimy and peppered with what he had optimistically taken to be spices, and had turned out to be the scraped out remnants of a burned pan, but it was nonetheless true.

"Oh, God." Peter shook his head in sympathy. "Then by all means, the Lord Marshal *commands* your presence, for your own well-being."

Guyon laughed. "Well, tell him when you see him that I thank him profusely and profoundly. And with that - I leave you to engage in an afternoon of torture. Theirs, rather than mine, I hope."

*

Peter was stretched out on a padded bench in his room when Guyon arrived later that day. He had greeted the new recruits, finished up several reports and sent de Retz's new secretary/lawyer/errand boy on his way. He was now enjoying a few moments peace, reading an essay by Montaigne. *"Of diverting and diversion"*...it seemed appropriate somehow, considering what they had been doing earlier that day.

"Good God, haven't you finished that yet?" Guyon asked amusedly. "What are you doing, committing each line to memory before you continue?"

"Indeed," Peter said softly, setting the book aside and going to greet Guyon. He did not like to admit that his spoken French still far exceeded his grasp of the written word. "I see you managed to escape the terrible infants unscathed."

"Oh, yes." Guyon half-laughed. "Ännchen made them soup for lunch, so I took pity on them and sent them out to observe the architecture of the Pont Neuf."

"And if they really get bored, perhaps one of them will jump in the Seine," Peter chuckled. "You know, we've upset the balance of interaction between the Guard and the Scholars?"

"However did we manage that?" Guyon sounded genuinely curious. "The only time they talk to each other is to become even more confused than they were to start with..."

"Yes, but at least they are not taunting each other into fistfights," Peter pointed out. "Definitely an improvement."

"And *that* is the balance? Honestly, Pèire, you worry me!" Guyon laughed. "So, do any of yours know their left from their right - in order to help their fists connect correctly?"

"Now that is a pertinent question," Peter chuckled. Really though, with the students running in and out, threading themselves through the often diabolical mish mash of drilling, they did seem to be gaining some kind of tolerance for one another.

"I'm always pertinent - oh wait, that's *im*pertinent." Guyon's eyes were gleaming with amusement. "So is this the philosophy Montaigne leads you to? Increased tolerance for the morbidly foolish?"

"No, that's my own slant on life, I fear." Peter closed his book and sat it aside. "I suppose I just want them to get along. I don't want -" *I don't want to have to bandage up any more Watch-baiters, the way I did you.* Peter began again. "I don't want to have to deal with any more diatribes from the Magister."

Guyon, as always, seemed to have heard what Peter was carefully *not* saying, as well as what he had. "No, well, who does? But Peter - you know that you cannot stop the Sorbonne feuding with the city Watch. It's a worthy concept, but not even you can erase the tradition of centuries with a few tolerant cadets."

"Perhaps not," Peter agreed, "but I can hope...and maybe get them to confine it to the Watch and keep my Cadets from being an extension of it."

"Y-eees..." Guyon said slowly and doubtfully, and then laughed and shook his head. "Yes, why not! You will lead by example and change Paris, I can see it now..."

"Yes, laugh at me," Peter said, standing and tugging Guyon into his arms. "But it has been done before, you know?"

He gave a nod back towards his book.

"Ah, yes, but they were unique. Montaigne himself says so." Oddly, Guyon looked suddenly hopeful, his eyes clear and alight, the look fading as Peter frowned in slight bewilderment. "Never mind. You'll know when you read it. I *hate* people who give the plot away before I've finished, so I won't spoil it for you."

"You may have to wait sometime then. I'm not -" Peter cut back the words. He still did not like giving voice to the inadequacies he felt about his imperfect understanding of anything he considered 'learned'. "I don't have as much time to read as I might wish."

"I don't *think* he's going anywhere," Guyon said teasingly. "And we all know my patience is unlimited, I can wait." He brushed a hand over Peter's face. "Really. I always can, for the things I consider worth it."

"I know about your patience," Peter chuckled. "I say prayers for its continuance on a daily basis." He leaned in and brushed a light kiss over Guyon's lips, "Hungry?"

Guyon's eyebrows raised. "What a very leading question. Yes, in fact and in metaphor both, and Herr Kirschner, convinced that all you and your cadets drink is bad ale, has sent you some wine and your men some barrels of a good German *weissbier*. He also said something about lemons, but I conveniently went deaf at that point." He grinned. "Just...not eggs, please."

"No, no...I actually seem to have a couple of cadets from large families that do know how to cook decently. They should have something ready for us pretty soon." Peter smiled down at Guyon. "I do love having you here, you know? It's more like a home than when I was at the Louvre."

"Peter, I firmly believe that a small hovel on the banks of the Seine's worst overflow would be more a home than the Louvre, but I thank you for the sentiment." Guyon's eyes softened into the rare, private kindness that only Peter, and very occasionally his old students, got to see. "I may think the money being spent on this place is an absurdity, but I *am* fond of it and its chipped marble and horrible old tapestries with that terrible metallic thread, and even that glowering old portrait they all worship so."

"Yes, they really have become attached to that monstrosity." Peter chuckled. He didn't see the resemblance between himself and the old portrait that hung in his office, aside from the blond hair, but his cadets did and they made it seem lucky to them. "I have to credit Ännchen with my own rooms. She's done more to make it comfortable than anyone."

She had indeed, sewing curtains and making pillows, helping him choose furniture that was sturdy but still comfortable. He didn't know what he would have done without her.

Guyon chuckled. "She's found an outlet. I won't let her near mine, and she knows it - and patching endless socks simply isn't as fulfilling." It had turned out that Herr Kirschner had encouraged Ännchen's work as a seamstress in order to *dis*courage suitors who might have had hopes of his not inconsiderable wealth. Now that she was married to Gottfried, who would have actively encouraged her to continue in her work, he had insisted she stop. Ännchen's skills were confined to favors for friends and darning three-times turned cloaks for Gottfried and Guyon's scholars, and she was frustrated almost beyond measure. It probably explained the cooking, though not how bad she was at it.

"Well, I am more than happy to be the recipient of what she excels at as opposed to the victim of those skills she lacks." Peter chuckled, nuzzling his nose into the bend of Guyon's neck. It was one of his favorite places, he had to admit. Warm and safe, smelling oddly of ink and chalk and...hmmm...apples?

"And if you were a cat, I would be coming to the conclusion that I was in desperate need of a bath." Guyon, the human fire-damper to any sentimental or romantic considerations, though his reaction belied his flat tone as he kissed the side of Peter's head. "You are a strange, strange man, *bèl-mi*."

"So I have been told...many, many times." Peter chuckled and nipped the spot he had been nuzzling, as a knock sounded at the door.

He straightened and stepped away before answering. "Come in."

Guyon made a face at him from the other side of the room, indicative of his displeasure at being interrupted. It was astonishing how the arrogant, often mask-like features could suddenly convey such a range of almost conversational emotions, when he was in private.

One of the cadets peered in. "Are you ready for your dinner, sir?"

Peter glanced at Guyon, his lip twitching, "Oh, yes, quite ready."

The door opened further and two other cadets entered, complete with trays and cloths and food, setting up his table and arranging everything, then disappearing without another word.

"*Very* efficient," Guyon said mockingly. "And so *quiet*. If not precisely...well-timed." He grinned.

"And so very difficult to teach *that* to them, if discretion is to be maintained," Peter grinned moving back to Guyon's side. "Now, may I continue? Or would you care to relieve other hungers first?"

"Oh, continue, continue!" Guyon laughed. "Far be it from me to interrupt your *thought patterns*. It seems so desperately unkind..."

"Yes," Peter agreed, sliding his arms around Guyon once more. "And I am so desperately in need of some...kindness."

Guyon gave a little, delighted choke of laughter, and kissed him, but with none of the kindness he had been told was needed, rather with the half-startled thoroughness that showed more clearly than anything how angry and unsettled he still was after their meeting with Corvay. Even after his summoning of the needfully closed ecclesiastical court, and his ensuing irritation, he had been more inclined to gentleness than he ever was for days after a single encounter with the spy-master.

"Guyon..." Peter led him over to the table and sat him down. "Here. Food. Eat. And tell me all of it. We will neither have any peace until we get that over with."

Guyon sighed. "There isn't anything to tell. The court was summoned, de Retz presided in absentia - which I'm sure was a blessing he thanked God for - Martelle was convicted and your name kept out of it. Aiding and fraternizing with the enemy and a little treason garnish, all evidence provided by myself and the very helpful M. Renard." He poured himself some wine. "One down, a hundred more to go, and all to no use, for Corvay remains untouched, if a little annoyed."

"It won't always be so, Gui." Peter assured him. "He'll make that one mistake, or someone will, and we will have him."

It had to be true, Peter would accept no other solution.

"And in the meantime, I must watch you endure his looks and his insinuations and his *damned* hold on you *that I gave him*." Guyon, oddly tolerant of mistakes in others, left no room for even the slightest error in his own life. "I should kill him. If I were not such a coward, I *would*."

And that was it, the heart of Guyon's always quickly reawoken fury, his perception of his own lack.

"No." Peter insisted. "No. This way is better. Beating him at his own game will hurt him worse than simply killing him would. And we don't know what orders he has in place...what would happen if he were to be killed."

That the man could hurt them, hurt Guyon, even after he was dead was an all too real fear.

"But would it be worth it, would the cost be worth it?" Guyon rubbed his hands over his face. "I keep wondering. If the cost is to me, then perhaps...I *hate* that I am afraid." He laughed sharply. "You're the only one I'd admit that I *am* afraid to."

"And only then because you know I don't believe it's true," Peter smiled softly. "I wish this were all different. I'd kill him myself if I thought it would be simpler, better, but I don't really believe that. It's better that we bring him down than we kill him. So do you, really."

Guyon's eyebrows raised sharply. "Do I? Hm. You have a faith in me I find quite frightening all on its own. But whatever else you believe...believe this. I want Corvay *dead.* Not disgraced, not in prison, not tortured, *dead.* Everything else I do is simply a means to that end." He shrugged. "I don't have your morality, Peter. I sometimes think I don't have *any* morality. And scruples are...alien. I'm sorry. I know you want to think better of me, but the court..." His voice dropped. "If I had to, I would have lied to the court. With no compunction."

"Never lie for me, Gui. You know I would never want you to do that." Peter hated that thought. It was bad enough that Guyon had compromised so much for him, had lost so much for him, really - his peace, his position. He would never ask for his integrity as well.

"Yes," Guyon agreed. He looked suddenly very tired, and a thousand miles away. "I know. But I would have lied *for me.*" He sighed, and stretched out his hand across the table. "It doesn't matter. I think I'm glad you don't understand, I prefer you to retain some illusions about me." He quirked a small smile.

"Here then, enough talk about Corvay," Peter said, "before you completely lose your appetite. And that would be a shame as this actually smells like it will be fairly good."

Guyon's mouth twitched. "Do I want to know how they managed to get venison?" he asked dryly. "Or is that an arcanity of the English Army in France that I am better off not knowing *anything* about?"

"I never do," Peter admitted. "I just enjoy."

He uncovered the plates and bowls and took a deep breath, drinking in the aromas. "Of course, if you have qualms, I'm sure that Ännchen will have leftovers..."

"And how would the English Marshal like to *wear* his venison today?" Guyon retorted. "No, I thank you!"

Peter just chuckled and began to fill their plates, "Wycombe is talking about assigning one of the cadets to be my valet."

"How very nice *that* will be," Guyon said, looking mildly confused. "Interruptions without end, all in the name of assistance..."

"Not if I train him properly," Peter said. "I want someone bilingual too. Gad, personal servants. I'll be spoiled in no time."

"You?" Guyon did laugh, then, genuinely amused. "Never. He will be, having nothing to do, but you? Never."

"You do know me well." Peter chuckled, "Would you pour me some wine?"

"I would make a terrible valet, I have to be asked," Guyon said amusedly, pouring the wine as he spoke. "*Not* a second career, I think." He handed Peter the cup.

"Well, if you're volunteering, I'm sure I could find some...position for you," Peter took a drink of the wine, his eyes twinkling.

"And since you've obviously given it some thought, I'll leave that to you," Guyon agreed with an almost-concealed smirk.

"We could discuss it later, perhaps?" Peter suggested, taking a bite of the venison. God, he loved Guyon this way - playful and teasing in spite of how their day had begun. He could never get enough of this, if he lived a thousand years - Guyon's mocking intransigence softened in its rare outward-turning.

"No, no, I think this is still at the hypothesis stage, empirical experimentation is required before you can discuss your thesis." Guyon's mouth was twitching uncontrollably now, his hand poised in mid air as he tried to control his breathing enough to risk eating.

"Hmmm..." Peter said, slowly chewing and then swallowing his food. "Who would you suggest for a test subject?"

"Well, I *was* about to volunteer, in the noble pursuit of

science, but of course if you had someone else in mind..." Guyon looked innocently enquiring, finally taking a bite of food.

"I could want no one but you," Peter's own voice almost surprised him, so strong and so serious, the teasing suddenly gone.

"Because I make such a good test case?" But Guyon's expression was no longer teasing, rather it had softened into the private, focused clarity that so often belied his tone and words.

"Because you are you." Peter answered him simply. "Because I am me. Because it is us."

Guyon stared at him. "Yes," he said in an odd tone. "Because it is me, because it is you." His hand shook a little as he lifted his wine cup. "A proven synthesis," he said obscurely, and drank.

*

"No! No! Je...je voux trouver Monsieur Scudamore, damn you!" Robert Macquarie, newly arrived in Paris and already beginning to loathe it to the depths of his being, vented his frustration with trying to speak French. "Does no one here speak any bloody English? Well?"

The men he was speaking with smiled amiably at him, looking at him as they would any poor madman.

Robert took a deep breath and tried again, "Il est le capitaine ...Comprenez-vous capitaine? Le capitaine de la reine anglaise. Christ! There's only one English Queen in the whole bloody country, this shouldn't be that hard!"

There was a snort of laughter from behind him, and he turned to see a man with hair so blond as to be almost white, dressed in the most richly embroidered clothes he had ever seen, openly amused by his discomfiture. "'El-*lo*," he said, still grinning, and bowed.

Eyeing this vision, Robert bowed tiredly and replied, "Hello, yerself. Don't suppose you speak English do you?"

"Small," said the man cheerfully. Robert was beginning to feel annoyed at the way he kept smiling. "Am Boronskaya," he added, which actually beat everybody else he had encountered for pure, incomprehensible unhelpfulness. "Russe."

"Russe..." Robert felt as blank as he was sure his face must look. "Oh. You're Russian? God, I hope your 'small' English is better than my 'small' French, because I don't know word one of Russian."

Almost invisible eyebrows raised over dark, soft eyes that looked as though they had a bloom of pollen dusted over their surface. "No," Boronskaya agreed politely, but the damn amused smile was still there. "You look for the capitan Anglais? Is no possib'. They make fun. Is Maréchal now."

"Maréchal...Maréchal..." Robert tossed that around for a moment. "Marshal? You're talking about Peter Scudamore? He's been promoted?"

That would be Peter, all right, if he'd understood correctly. Peter always was one for impressing people, all without ever trying. Not that Peter wasn't good at things, but people always seemed to see that he was, whereas he, himself, had to really work for recognition.

"Yes?" The smile turned blank, a veneer of politeness. It was as though the Russian had seen straight through his questions and into the faint resentment that he tried so hard to keep hidden - seen through to it and disapproved. Then he nodded, as though confirming something he had been asking himself, rather than Robert's questions. "Yes."

"Yes," Robert hedged. "I'm Robert Macquarie. I'm...um...Je suis... Je suis son frère? God, I hope that's right. I'm trying to find him. J'essaye de le trouver. But I don't know exactly where.... Um... Sauvez-vous où il est?"

Robert was hoping that between French and English, the Russian would be able to piece together enough for him to be understood. *Or he'll be even more confused.*

"Son frère?" The man laughed again, deep and rolling and infinitely amused. "Come. I will make map pour trouver vot-re frère."

Well, that would certainly be easier than trying to understand directions, but it also meant Peter was no longer residing at the Louvre. Robert sighed, and resigned himself to a far longer day than he had ever thought possible.

"Thank you...Merci." Robert picked up his bag and followed

after Boronskaya, which he assumed was the man's name. "I hope it's not too difficult to get to where he is. Je n'ai ici avant jamais été. I don't want to get lost."

"No." Again that strangely neutral, half-amused acquiescence. It really was vaguely disturbing, but the room he was led into was a clean and well-appointed study, and the servant who appeared as soon as they entered showed that the embroidery on his clothing was not just an ostentatious sign of wealth, but of consequence. However unnerving he might be, then, this man was obviously someone who could help, and not just another court member who thought the highlight of an afternoon was to further confuse an already bewildered stranger.

Boronskaya scratched out a few lines on a piece of trimmed paper, labeled it in neat and slightly childish handwriting, sanded it down, and handed it over to Robert with a smile. "You go to there. You find."

"Rue d'Esclangon?" Robert's pronunciation and accent rendered it almost unrecognizable. "That's where he lives? Eh... C'est sa maison?"

It wasn't very far away, if he was reading the map properly.

"Is how you find him." It wasn't really an answer. It was that odd sort-of agreement again, but that was probably the language barrier, which was fairly impressive, between them both. "Say I send."

"Yes." Robert nodded, looking at the little map again. "Merci, monsieur...Monsieur Boronskaya."

He bowed to the other man, honestly grateful for his help. Not enough people helped strangers these days. Robert's lip twitched. Not enough people were like Peter.

"De rien," Boronskaya replied gravely, and seemed to mean it - it really had been nothing to him, this little formality. He inclined his head to Robert, the odd little smile back on his mouth, and then quite simply walked out of the room, leaving the door open.

"Guess that means we're done," Robert quirked his head and walked out the door.

And now, on to the greater task and more humiliating of eating crow. He'd come to set things right with Peter, or at least

72

to try. He wouldn't blame his brother-in-law if he sent him packing without hearing a word that he had to say.

But Peter wouldn't do that. That was what Robert was counting on, the inherent fairness in Peter's nature. *At least he'll hear me out before he tells me to go hang.*

*

The house, strangely for a high-ranking soldier, was on a street that even Robert recognized as being mostly owned by members of the Merchants' Guild. The insignias above doors and on gates were similar to the ones he had seen in Edinburgh, and he wondered what on earth Peter was doing in an area where bales of cloth were a more commonplace sight than steel.

"P'rhaps he's staying with friends..." Robert muttered as he located the proper house and knocked on the door.

It was opened a moment later by a young blonde woman, obviously the mistress of the house, rather than a servant. Her hair was neatly pinned up and she smiled at him from beneath a cap. "Bonjour, monsieur."

A very lovely friend. Robert blinked at her for a moment. *My, my, Peter, have you changed that much?*

"Um," he said, feeling utterly wrong-footed and hopeless. "Je suis -" Oh, Lord, no, that was wrong. "Uh, je cherche? Je suis cherche?"

Her mouth twitched. "Vraiment," she agreed, and Robert sighed.

"Le mare - the Marshal - oh, damn it all. Peter Scudamore?" he finished up desperately.

"Oh, *Peter*..." The girl grinned at him. Her accent wasn't true, Robert realized. She was German, he guessed, or possibly Dutch. Leave it to him to keep running into people that he couldn't communicate with even in his limited French. "Il n'est pas ici aujourd'hui, mais - venez avec moi, monsieur."

She gestured to him, inviting him inside, "Um...yes? Merci."

He hadn't quite gotten all of that, but hoped it meant she was taking him to Peter.

She led him through a cool hallway that smelled of beeswax

and lavender, and, oddly, of chalk, and into a large, airy room that seemed to be in the middle of being decorated, or possibly gutted - whatever it was had been drastically and enthusiastically undertaken and abandoned halfway through.

"Attendez-vous," she said, with a smile that left Robert wondering all over again whether Peter had finally developed some taste, gestured to a chair, and left him. It seemed to be the day's theme.

He sat for a moment and studied the room. Aside from the destruction and odd bits of renovation, there were some more personal effects. A globe, a desk, and a small crate that held books. He frowned. Peter, in spite of his disagreements with his tutors, had always been one for reading. It was the one thing that his guardian, his Uncle William, had instilled in him. It was never something that Robert, himself, set much store by. Books never tilled a field or cut peat or helped with a lambing, so for him, they were rather useless.

There was the sound of rapid-fire French from the hallway, two voices overlapping and sounding thoroughly fed up with each other, and then a young man, still talking over his shoulder, came into the room. Robert could only discern a few words in what he thought might have been every twenty of the rapid speech. "...mais certainme - non, parce-qu'il... les cadets... non, Gottfried ...oc, pour le prochain -" he cut himself off, and turned to Robert with an exasperated expression. "Can I 'elp?"

"Oh. Thank goodness you speak some English. My French, I'm afraid, is not very good." Robert sighed in relief. "Mon Français est très mauvais," he added, just in case.

"Yes, it is," said the young man amusedly. "I think the wo'd is atrocious." It was said completely without malice. He had obviously been called in from doing something that had required his full concentration - perhaps dealing with another room, Robert thought, since his shirtsleeves were rolled up and his arms and hands smudged with something white. "I am Guyon de Chesnay - Gottfried's English is wo'se than mine, I regret to say, and Anna's does not exist, so -" he shrugged. "Fo'give me. We may 'ave not understood quite clea'ly. You came here for Peter?"

"Yes. Peter Scudamore. A man...A Russian...His name was

Bor...Hmmm...Boronsky? Somethin' similar leastways. He said I could find Peter here." Robert tried to get the words out quickly. If Peter wasn't here, then he wanted to move on and find him. Sooner started, sooner done, as Sarah always said.

"Boronskaya," said the young man resignedly, and shook his head, running his hands over his untidy hair. "'E suffers from - hm...a sense of 'umor." He made an apologetic little face. "Peter lives at the 'Otel d'Orsay, but comes 'ere often. I can - send word? If you give you' name..." He waved a hand encouragingly, and Robert was struck by the strange eyes that looked up at him, like washed glass.

"I'd be very much obliged to ya." Robert said gratefully. "I'm Robert Macquarie. Peter's my wife's brother."

The odd eyes darkened to a grey-green. "*I know,*" Guyon de Chesnay said in a voice that made the hair stand up on the back of Robert's neck, and while he was wondering what the hell difference his name could make to the previously cheerful and exasperated man in front of him, who was now looking as though he had met a speaking viper, pain exploded in his jaw, and he went reeling back towards the seat the pretty girl had gestured him towards earlier, flailing a hand out to try and regain his balance, and finding that everything was beyond his grasp as he fell over the crate of books and landed hard on the floor.

"Bloody cryin' Saints!" Robert cursed from his place on the floor. Were all the people in this damnable place insane?

Of course, if this was a friend of Peter's, a good friend, then he probably knew about...

He looked up at the small but strong man standing over him, obviously ready to knock him down again if he made a wrong move. "Aye. I suppose I deserve that...and worse. Will Peter knock me down too, do you suppose?"

"I *hope* so," came the furious response, "I do not care to find out without 'e is at least warned. Cagar! You should never 'ave come!"

"Ya might be right, but still in all, here I am." Robert felt his jaw, waggling it back and forth. Sore, but not broken, it would probably be purple by morning. "And determined ta see Peter, just the same."

*

Far from ameliorating his sudden fury, Guyon found that having knocked Robert down had exacerbated it instead, leaving him almost shaking with the need to convey his feelings in some language that the man in front of him could understand. "No," he said firmly. "Not without 'e knows first. To choose if 'e sees you."

"He will." Robert's answer was decidedly strong, without any doubt shading it. "He will because he's Peter, and fair, no matter what kind of idiot I've been. 'Course he may toss me out on me arse right after, but he'll see me."

Guyon contemplated hitting the man in front of him again, wondering if anything was able to get through that impermeable conviction. *You have no idea what you've done, do you?* he thought wearily. *Oh, you know the concept. But you have no understanding of what you caused...*"Yes. But I am not fair. Not to anyone but Peter. It does not concern me to be so, you see?"

"Didn't ask you ta be, did I?" Robert shrugged off the words, but watched Guyon warily. "It's not you I have ta convince, it's Peter. Nay, let me reword that. I'm not here to convince him of anything, really. I'm just ta have my say and leave the rest ta him."

"No, you leave it all to 'im." Guyon sighed. "*Him.* You made your decision. You forfeited all right to 'ave your say. Now 'e decides. What you want..." he waved a hand in the air, fumbling for the right word, and found it. "Irrelevant. What you want is irrelevant." He took a deep breath. "I will tell 'im. Say you are 'ere."

"Do you want me to wait here?" Robert asked uncertainly, and Guyon's irritation flared up all over again.

"No I do *not*," he said with some force. "Go back to the Louvre. Go back to your lodgings. Go and *wait*, pretend at least to common courtesy even if you are wholly devoid of decency." He pushed Robert ahead of him through the small garden, and through the little gate into the back street. Once outside, he shoved Macquarie's mistreated hat into his arms, and inclined his head. "Go *home*, Scotsman," he said irritably, and hurried off towards the Rue St. Antoine.

Damn him, damn him, damn him! Damn him for coming here, damn him for all he has done, damn him for his very existence! The familiar streets passed by Guyon in a blur of fury. He did not stop to think that a great deal of his anger was in fact aimed at the absent Giraud, and not at all at the unfortunate Robert, who had after all expressed his desire to make amends.

His concern, however, was real, and untainted by personal motives save for the overriding one, that Peter *was* one of his few concerns, and that Macquarie's appearance could cause nothing but pain.

"He was seduced alright and tried to drag me in for a ménage a trois. Almost got locked up when I refused and I had to leave. Leave my home, Guyon, like I was cast out."

Guyon had promised himself that night that if he ever met the man who had wounded Peter that deeply, caused the terrible damage to his soul that had allowed Corvay his handholds, he would kill him. Knocking him down had been a poor substitute, but he was very much afraid that Peter would not forgive him if he actually followed through on this particular self-made promise.

Like a singularly righteous thunderstorm Guyon, at last, entered the Hôtel d'Orsay, the usual crowd of Guardsmen and Cadets falling to the side to make a path for him. They had learned, apparently, that when de Chesnay was in a mood, it was best to give him rein. Better to make oneself scarce, because if the Marshal was the cause of his temper, it would mean extra drills and inspections and damn hard work until the disruption of their personal peace could be repaired.

Usually, Guyon would have felt some faint sense of satisfaction at the idea that the most peculiar collective in Paris had apparently begun to learn wisdom - at least where he was concerned - but for once, he could not bring himself to care, other than to hope it extended to not eavesdropping, a factor they had considered their absolute right until the fourth time he flung the door open quite literally in their faces.

He was under no illusions that bruises were a true deterrent - another reason he was anxious to talk to Peter. He was convinced that Robert would do nothing so sensible as follow his instructions, and equally sure that Peter would receive a visit from him within the hour.

As he took the last three steps up toward Peter's office, he heard Peter's voice raised on a frustrated tone. At any other time, he might have felt amusement at the topic. "No. No brocade. No velveteen. And no damn satin." The last was said almost with a growl. "This is a place for soldiers, not a Court salon, and I want something that will hold up to leather and spurs and roughhousing. Strong cloth that will hide stains and good solid wood. Is that so difficult for you to understand? If it is, say so and I will take my trade elsewhere."

Guyon shook his head in a sort of confused irritation at the constant trivialities that seemed to beset them these days, and pushed open the door. "But you can put gilt anywhere you want," he said kindly to the cloth-festooned merchant in the center of the room. "Especially in random corners. Peter, I need to talk to you. Now."

Peter looked toward Guyon for a moment, his eyes narrowing, a frown forming on his face. He turned back to the merchant for just a moment, "No gilt. None." He pointed toward the door. "Go. Now." There was flutter of cloth as the man and his assistant quickly scurried out, leaving Peter and Guyon in the now silent office. "What is it? What's wrong?"

Guyon winced. "Perhaps it isn't *wrong*," he said tentatively. *I think so, but there are so many things we perceive differently.* There was no way he could be oblique about this, no way of letting Peter think he had come to this conclusion himself - unless he *did* already know, and was avoiding the fact, which was something Guyon did not want to consider, being as he was ill-equipped to deal with this in the first place. "Robert Macquarie is in Paris. He came to see me earlier, looking for you."

"Christ...." The word was barely a whisper.

*

Robert Macquarie is in Paris. Is in Paris. Right now, at this moment.

78

"Christ..."

Peter had often thought about what he would do when he saw Robert again, and no, tempting though it might be, homicide had not been the predominant feature of those thoughts. He valued his sister's love far too much to actually kill the man and, truth be told, he valued the friendship they had shared in younger days too much to do more than contemplate it as more than a rage empowered fantasy. *Robert Macquarie is in Paris.* And now that he was, what did it mean?

"He wants to make amends." Guyon's voice was utterly flat and expressionless, which meant, in Peter's experience, that he was thinking and feeling forty thousand things at once and did not want to express any of them. He moved across the room, and his hand came up to grip the back of Peter's neck in the old, old gesture of forced attention. "Give the order to bar him entry to the Hôtel, Pèire, and I promise, I'll see it done."

Peter let his eyes slide shut for only a moment, melting into that touch, that utterly trusting and protected feeling it engendered. But a moment was all he could allow himself, "I can't, Guyon. As much as I'd like for you to deal with this, and never see the man again, I owe it to the love I bear for my sister to at least listen to him."

Guyon sighed sharply. "*Oc.* How did I know you would say that? You and your sentiment, Peter, I swear..."

"Don't." Peter interrupted him. "This will be the first direct word I've had from home since I left, Gui. How can I turn that down? Even from him?"

Guyon nodded, and dropped his hand. "I would have thought - *with ease*," he said lightly, "but then as we all know, I have no care for such things. Nor affection for rocks, which is why no-one will ever grant me lordship over one. Well." He shrugged. "You had best send him word, then." His neutral expression flashed into pure, gleeful wickedness. "And do sign it with *all* your titles, *chérâme.*"

"You are an evil man, beloved," Peter laughed. "And being just as evil myself, I have a mind to let him sit and stew for a day or so, before I see him, hmmm?"

"Oh, I think at least that," Guyon agreed, "but the question is, will he be so obliging as to wait? I did - *reinforce* - my opinion that he should wait on your say-so, but I doubt he will hold that in mind."

"True. I'm not exactly difficult to find," Peter agreed, "which begs the question of why someone directed him to you, rather than straight here."

Guyon chuckled. "Because your brother-in-Christ was unfortunate enough to meet Boronskaya at the Louvre," he said with distinct amusement. "And our dearest of Socratian liars thought someone else should suffer from Court obliquities."

"Ah...well..." Peter shook his head at that, then chuckled suddenly, his mind filled with images of that conversation, both of them stumbling away in their broken French, the only language that Robert and Alexei would have in common, to the best of his knowledge. "That would have been an interesting conversation." Peter ran one hand through his hair, "This isn't an easy thing for me to do, Gui, you know? I just...Would you mind staying here for awhile?" Guyon would keep him on track. Keep him from doing something utterly idiotic.

"Of course," Guyon said easily, and then, on a sudden splutter of laughter, "Oh, Christ, poor Gottfried!"

"Poor Gottfried?" Peter asked, then frowned, "Robert wasn't bothering him as well, was he?"

"No, no!" Guyon waved a hand dismissively. "But I left him with our worst group after giving them something quite certainly not their subjects to discuss, and they are so very...*talkative*!"

"And I repeat, *you* are evil," Peter chuckled. "Look, I need to go out and watch the Cadets drill for a while. It shows interest on my part and it keeps them on their toes. I know it will probably bore you to death but...come?"

"By all means," Guyon said. "And your cadets are *never* boring. They are a source of perpetual entertainment even to the wholly unskilled." He grinned. "It's rather like watching puppies deal with a basket of snakes."

"They will improve, Gui...it's inevitable." Peter prayed that it was, at least. Too many of those innocent young faces would find their way to the gravedigger if not.

"Ah, in that case, lead the way to the inevitable," Guyon said with a faint grimace. "Or save your lieutenant from it, whichever is more applicable..."

With that, Peter swept open the door, and made his most courtly bow, "After you, chér."

Guyon made a face at him, and walked out into the gallery. "*Cagar,*" he said with feeling, stopping dead.

"Oh, *Christ,* what are they doing n - Robert." That was him, alright. Same dark hair, same reddish beard, same look of growing aggravation as he attempted to wend his way through the milling guards and cadets.

Guyon was very still. "Damn it," he said softly. "He followed me. I should have *thought* -" He bit off whatever he was going to say next, his hand clenching and unclenching on the rail, obviously waiting for whatever Peter decided before making his next move. The expression on his face suggested it would not be one that Robert would find pleasant.

"No.. it's alright. This is my territory now - territory that he has no claim on." Peter turned toward the stairs. "A fact I intend to make very, very clear."

"Oh, this *is* going to be interesting," Guyon murmured, following him. There was no humor at all in his voice.

As Peter came down the stairs there was a call to attention. Suddenly the milling mass of cadets was formed up in lines, positions correct, eyes straight ahead. This at least, was something they got right. Protocol and procedure and respect to their commanders, not always the easiest thing to drum into a bunch of young men, but this group, somehow had taken to that easily.

Now if they could just get their swordplay and weapon firing as accurate, I'd be a very happy man. Peter continued to the front of the group, Guyon still one pace behind him.

"Peter. Thank God, I -" Robert's voice rang out in the sudden silence, cut off as he saw Peter's face, cold and commanding.

"Lieutenant, you may begin."

Guyon fixed utterly translucent, colorless eyes on Robert, jerking his head to the side in a gesture to follow him as he went to the far side of the room, leaning against the wall, his arms folded.

"I -" Macquarie began, and Guyon cut him off without even

favoring him with a look.

"*Don't. Bother,*" he said icily. He might have had no other interest in the world but the cadets.

The Lieutenant began putting the cadets through their paces as Peter prowled the room, speaking a word here, correcting a position there. His commands were obeyed instantly, but with no obvious signs of resentment from any of the cadets. As they neared the end of a particularly difficult musket formation, Peter moved back to the front of the group. "Well done, gentlemen. Well done indeed." Peter smiled. "I am more than happy with your improvement. Mitchelson, we may yet get you to tell your left from your right." There was a general chuckling from the group and a blush from the young man in question, but it was obvious that the comment was praise rather than a punishment.

"I'd forgotten..." Robert murmured, and Guyon *did* turn then.

"Had you?" he asked in his clearest voice. "So it's only Royalist Captains in *general* that you betray to Cromwell. How reassuring."

Peter's voice continued, raising to cover the other conversation in the room, "I will expect to see a corresponding improvement in your sword work by the end of the week. Practice not only makes perfect, Gentlemen, it can save your life." He nodded to the Lieutenant, who then dismissed the cadets. "Good job, Lieutenant." Peter walked over and clapped the man on the shoulder. "Come to my office later with your report."

"Sir." The lieutenant came to attention, looking pleased, before turning and ordering the cadets into the courtyard, accompanying their departure with a scathing summary that was in no way as contented in its assessment as Peter's had been. In his case, however, there were more than a few retorts in the same tone.

The hall was left empty, save for Guyon, still leaning against the wall with an expression of cold disinterest, and Robert, looking utterly wrong-footed.

Peter really did not feel up to this confrontation, but he knew he never would, so best just to get on with it, "Macquarie."

"Peter. Can't we...isn't there somewhere more private?" Robert looked as though he were regretting to his toenails having made the decision to follow Guyon to the Hôtel d'Orsay.

"Private?" Peter raised an eyebrow. "If you wish. My office is upstairs." He turned sharply after a quick glance at Guyon, then moved toward the stairs.

"After you," Guyon said to Robert, a mixture of amusement and dislike shivering through his voice. Being as unless he was in a real temper, he never showed anything he did not want to when he spoke in front of anyone but Peter, it was a moment of calculated insult that Peter could not help but appreciate even under the horrifically awkward circumstances.

When they entered the office, Peter moved immediately to sit behind his desk, leaving Robert to stand in front of him like a misbehaving school boy. He knew Guyon would approve of the maneuver, it being similar to some of the things he'd used himself. "You may have fifteen minutes. Macquarie." Peter sounded as if whether the man stayed or left was a matter of complete indifference.

Robert rubbed at his jaw, and Guyon's faint smirk turned into an outright grin, though he said nothing, staying by the door. "I came to say you were right," he said suddenly and abruptly. "Cromwell doesn't want to lessen absolute power. He wants it for himself. And since that is the thing I couldn't stand in the first place, I thought my change in support was something you deserved to hear before anyone. Along with a heartfelt apology - because I *am* sorry. I know that saying I truly believed I was behaving for the best isn't an excuse, but I did. I believed as strongly in Cromwell's cause as you did in the King's. And in all conscience - I can't. Not now. Not any more."

Peter's eyes sought out Guyon, knowing that in spite of his limits in speaking English, his understanding was almost perfect, "So what is it you want from me? You say this and I'm to - what? Say 'Oh that's too bad, Robert.' and all is forgiven? I protect my Queen daily, from men with more plausible stories."

"I was expecting more emphasis than 'that's too bad'," Robert admitted. "Possibly along with some pointed comments about my idiocy." He sighed. "I'm not trying to be plausible. I just came to tell you."

"I'm quite 'appy t'make the pointed comments," Guyon said

quietly from the doorway, and Robert swung on him.

"And I suppose you would know!"

Guyon tilted his head. "Mm." He smiled unpleasantly. "Then again, I 'ave stronge' wo'ds fo' betraye's than *idiot*. But you are right, Peter would be kind enough to call you that. And I do *hate* presumption." The word *hate* came out with a distinctly Spanish snarl to it.

"Either way, " Peter's voice snapped out, drawing Robert's attention back to him, "plausible or implausible, what is it you want from me, Macquarie? You didn't come all this way for that alone, I'm certain sure."

"No. I came to apologize. To say that...if you still thought of Hawthornden as home, if you are prepared to consider us family even with my presence, with all I have done, you are welcome. *More* than welcome. Wanted." He smiled ruefully. "You always were, of course, I'm not fool enough to think I rule my household in any way save in name."

Guyon took a sudden, audible breath, and caught it as quickly, his lips pressed together. "You are right," he said in quick French. "This is private. Your lieutenant must be in need of entertainment by now..." He opened the door without turning, and stepped out through it backwards, closing it behind him with a dull thump.

Peter looked at the door, somehow managing to keep his shock internal, not a sign showing on his face. Guyon had left him to this? Left him alone with Robert, after saying he would stay? He was very confused. "That's very easy to claim, Robert," Peter raised his chin defiantly, "considering the fact that you know that I can't take you up on it, even if I wished too." He was silent for several long moments before he continued, "And you've left Sarah there, alone. Did it never occur to you that she might well be in danger if Cromwell hears of your change of heart?"

"Scotland's safe." Robert's mouth twitched. "Internal politics and perpetual backbiting, better than a whole cavalry. I wouldn't have left if I'd even considered it an issue, no matter how many times I was threatened with a poker."

That caused a small answering twitch in Peter's lips. He could see Sarah doing just that, threatening Robert with a poker...or a broom handle...Christ knows she used to threaten him enough when she didn't get her way. "I'm sorry, Robert. This is just too damn easy." Peter shook his head. "You'll have to do more than give me words to prove you've returned your loyalty to where it should be."

Robert made an oddly helpless gesture. "What else do I have?" he demanded. It was evident that he thought the question rhetorical. "I can't stay here under your command, I'm no soldier and never was."

"No, I know that but -" Peter paused as the tiny glimmer of a thought skimmed across his brain. "Would you be willing to do something for me? Me personally?"

"If I can," Robert agreed. "I'll hope it's feasible."

"I'm not selfish enough to ask the impossible, Robert," Peter frowned. "I just- Look, go back to your...to where ever you're staying. Be back here in two days time and I'll give you the conditions of what I want...spelled out."

"I'll just hope it's not a roc's egg," Robert said. He made a movement as though to hold his hand out, then shook his head, bowed, and left the room

Peter watched him go, his face bland and impassionate as he lost himself in thought. Could this be what he was waiting for? Could this surprise visit, as unwanted as it was, actually lead to something good? This was something Peter would have to consider very long and hard, for if Robert Macquarie were to complete the mission that Peter had in mind...he just might *have* to forgive him.

*

While he was a tutor at the Sorbonne, Guyon had been forced to exercise control over his outward reactions almost constantly, always bearing in mind the myriad of things that could get him dismissed. It was a skill he had needed to employ less and less in the intervening six months, however, and so he could no longer rely on that ability - something that had been forcibly brought home to him as he was unable to disguise the shock Robert's admission and offer had dealt to him.

He had not, as he had said, gone down into the courtyard to observe the cadets' training, but had waited in the gallery, caught between the knowledge that whether he had used the notion of privacy as an excuse or not, it was *true*, and the fact that Peter had asked him to stay, and he had been unable to fulfill even so simple a request.

As so many times in his life, therefore, he was left kicking his heels, unable to return to the room he had just exited, and reluctant to go further away. He told himself that it was because he *might* be needed, because he did not trust Robert, because it was one way of at least keeping vaguely to his given word, but in truth it was because while he did not want to hear that Peter *was* leaving for Scotland, he did not want to be left in ignorance, either.

Guyon was all too aware that it was Corvay's hold over *him* that kept Peter working for the spymaster, his ridiculous concepts of protection and honor binding him in service to a man he hated more than he ever had been when he considered himself to be doing the right thing and helping the English Crown by completing Corvay's missions. He had no doubt that if - *when* - Peter left for Scotland, he would ask for his company, and knew quite as well that he could not leave. Could not, because it would mean his brother's death, and could not because he had promised Corvay that the day Giraud died, the spymaster himself would breathe his last. Could not, as well, because the Archbishop, the still-scheming de Retz, had given him sanction to bring Corvay down, and Guyon, more than anything, wanted that revenge for François Villon. The death of Lesueur, Villon's actual murderer, at Peter's hand had not satisfied his need for personal satisfaction, for some action of his own that would, if not nullify his grief, make it comprehensible.

So, there he stood, halfway between obedience and abandonment, when Robert Macquarie came out of the room, looking almost as torn as he himself.

"Oh...I -" Robert looked at Guyon, as if he weren't certain if he should greet him or knock him down the stairs. "You're here."

"It's an occupational 'azard," Guyon said non-committally. "I take it you will be staying in Paris fo' a while?"

Robert looked back at the door, making a half-step in that direction as if he were considering going back in, then stopped, sighed and focused his attention fully on Guyon, "It would appear so." He shook his head, "Look, my French is not the best, but, considering the way you greeted me, I'm assuming you're a good friend of my brother-in-law?"

Guyon snorted with sudden and completely unexpected amusement. "Why, do good friends of 'is always greet you in that way? Yes. I am." It was the one thing he never even thought to query in his usually questionable life.

"No," Robert shook his head. "But unless you normally greet visitors in such a violent fashion, I have to assume that you knew a little bit about the trouble between Peter and I. That you knew enough to be angered on his behalf. And Peter, what ever else I can say about him, is not normally a person that would tell his troubles to just anyone."

"No," Guyon said blandly. He knew that it could have been taken as refutation or agreement. "What do you want, Macquarie? Even if I 'ad any influence over Peter, I would not use it, if that was what you 'ad in mind to ask me."

Robert looked Guyon over slowly, just once, then turned his eyes toward the room below before continuing, "No, I do not expect that you would, nor would I ask it. Peter always did have an easy way about him. It was always so easy for him to make friends." Robert stopped for a moment, as if considering, "No, that's not quite right. He had very few true friends, but there were many who were loyal to him, in spite of not being close. It was as if, even without the closeness that true friendship would have given them, they knew, just knew, that they could trust him. That's probably what makes him such a good leader."

Lord, God, tell me something new and interesting or leave me be! Guyon sighed. "Yes. 'E can be trusted. A shame you did not, a shame you 'ave forfeited that trust, I 'ope you feel this shame, *why* are you telling me this?"

"I'm telling you this because, I think, Peter has gifted you with that true friendship." Robert turned his head now, looking at Guyon obliquely. "I miss it. Truly. But I'm glad he found someone here that he could share that with."

"I'll be sure and convey your inexpressible joy," said Guyon dryly. Robert may have been feeling the need to divulge his thoughts and feelings, perhaps in the strange sense of confidence that talking to a stranger could sometimes induce, perhaps because he thought he was telling Guyon something of which he had somehow remained unaware, but Guyon, who guarded his own emotions like the inner sanctum of the Vatican itself, had no intention of following suit.

Robert gave a wry chuckle, "God, the two of you must make a pair. Both of you prickly as hedgehogs. No.. no.. you needn't poke me any further, I'm leaving."

"Let me convey *my* inexpressible joy," said Guyon in the same tone, and then, thinking that if he could not offer any sort of confidence or encouragement, he could at least issue a warning that he knew Peter would not have considered - "Macquarie. If you receive a summons or a letter from a man named Corvay - then no matter what 'e 'ints at, no matter what 'e seems to be offering - even if 'e 'olds Peter's life or reputation up to bargain or threaten with - *do not answer it.* Do not attend 'im. If it is written, bring it to my 'ouse, if 'e sends it by word of mouth, inform Alexei Boronskaya."

"Boronsk - Ah, the snickering Russian that directed me to you." Robert gave a nod. "This...Corvay? He's trying to hurt Peter in some way? No, you don't have to explain. If he were not, you would not feel the need to warn me. Thank you."

He turned to leave then, trotting down the stairs without another look.

Guyon, left feeling as though whatever he had done had been somehow inadequate, that he had misunderstood or misinterpreted whatever it was that Macquarie had been trying to tell him, sighed in complete exasperation and tapped his foot thoughtfully against the gallery rails as he watched Peter's brother-in-law leave the Hôtel. "Damn it," he said softly, "don't tell me there's another good man arrived in Paris. The city will fall in ruins around my head."

He ran his hands over his face, trying to compose himself, and went back to Peter's office, pitching his voice to its lightest as he pushed the door open.

"Did you know that our Alexei was a 'snickering Russian'?" he asked conversationally.

"Hmmm?" Peter turned away from the map of France he had hanging on the wall of his office, "Oh. No, although I could see him in that role. He does seem to have a sense of the absurd, though, and for him to send Robert to you rather than here would probably have amused him, whether he knew who Robert was or not."

"Hm. I'm not sure he does things out of amusement, whatever he may claim," Guyon felt bound to point out. Then he laughed. "Hypocritical though it may be of me, I feel I should remind you that he *is* a spy." Innate fairness made him add, "among other things." When Peter made no response, he winced slightly, and, tentative as always when it came to any form of demonstrativeness, crossed the room and touched Peter's arm briefly. "Is...are you all right?"

"I will be." Peter answered with a small nod, then raised his eyes to Guyon's own, "Why did you leave? I thought - No, never mind, it's not important. Robert was here. We spoke. The world did not end and I did not kill my sister's husband. Everything will be alright."

"I was about to lose my temper," Guyon said. *A partial truth, and oh, my sins of omission grow by the day!* "I thought it might be *one* experience of this Hôtel that Macquarie might not deserve, and you *certainly* could do without." He quirked a smile. "Wasn't it noble of me?"

"Indeed," Peter smiled then, placing both his hands on Guyon's shoulders. "Thank you for coming to warn me. It would have been quite a shock otherwise. And, I suppose, I should thank Alexei as well, when I see him." He leaned forward, brushing a quick kiss over Guyon's lips. "Although, my thanks to him will remain verbal only."

"Alas, poor unkissed Alexei," said Guyon wryly. Since Boronskaya had the habit of saluting those he considered his friends almost precisely like that, he did not think it was a statement that would hold true for very long, but he saw no reason to remind Peter of the fact. "So, all's forgiven, then?"

"All's for - No, it's not." Peter frowned. "I don't know if it ever will be. I just don't trust him and that's hard. I see him and, right there, that's my childhood friend. The one that taught me to swim. The one who was there the first time I got drunk. *Christ*, the one who gave me the liquor that got me drunk." Peter laughed and smoothed his hand through his hair, taking an uneasy step away. "And the man who betrayed that friendship. It's all twisted in knots and confused and...I'm not making much sense, am I?"

Guyon shrugged. "It makes sense to me," he offered. It did. He had no idea what his feelings would be should Giraud suddenly walk into his home as Robert had, but he suspected that part of him would forever see the older brother whom he had admired and emulated, the man he had always considered to be a bastion of integrity. "He *is* both. Neither fact negates the other, that's not possible with truths."

"He supported Cromwell against the King. He tried to get me to join him and when I wouldn't, he forced me from my own home." Peter gave a deep sigh, "I don't trust him, I doubt I ever will again. But I have to give him a chance to prove himself to me - if only for Sarah's sake."

"That's a good reason," Guyon said, quelling his desire to say *Don't give him a chance! It works both ways, you leave the door open for renewed betrayal!* But his own view of things was not, and never would be, Peter's. He was not a good man, had no honor or integrity of his own, but he could still recognize it in others, and as strongly as he knew Peter was possessed of it, so he also suspected that even in its every misguided demonstration, so was Robert Macquarie. "And remember, I have never thought that supporting Cromwell's originally stated ethics was so bad an ideology. Perhaps he was simply in need of enlightenment. If he found it, it cannot have been a pleasant experience."

"No, I'm sure of that." Peter nodded his agreement. "Doubly hard for Robert, because he's as stubborn as the day is long. It would have to have been something major for him to recant his support."

"Mm." Guyon made a face. "I find myself lacking in sympathy, though, I confess. I had promised myself I would kill him, you know." He kept his voice light, inconsequential. "He will never know the restraint I exercised in merely greeting him with a blow from my fist, and not from a dagger."

Peter stepped closer to Guyon then, taking his hand and lifting it, "You bruised your knuckles. Amazing the damage that inflicting pain can cause." He ran his thumb gently over the injured spots.

"I once advised you to hit those who angered you, and not innocent masonry," Guyon said in the same light voice, "and as you know, I have ever taken my own advice." He shook his head, unable as ever to maintain the full strength of his defenses under Peter's touch. "I think I hate him *for* you. I'm sorry." He meant his apology with all his heart. If Peter *was* intending to forgive Macquarie, under whatever conditions or pretexts, then he would have to learn grace.

But at that moment, he was very far from feeling it, and he was forcibly reminded of just *why* he guarded his defenses so jealously, that they worked as well to protect others from the worse side of his nature as they did to keep himself safe from the world.

"Don't be," Peter whispered, placing a kiss on Guyon's knuckles before he released them. "I can't do it myself, I'm afraid. Distrust, yes. More than I can even explain. But hate? No. Even with all that is between us."

"Ah, but that is because you are a good man," Guyon said, and then, changing the subject before he said something else that he would regret, and felt forced to negate it by saying something they would *both* regret, "which is why you agreed to eat dinner with the van Hesselink household tonight."

"Oh, God...I'd forgotten." Peter gave a heart-felt groan. "Please tell me that Ännchen is not trying something new?"

"I have no idea," Guyon said innocently. "Perhaps all of today's luck will be overturned, and she will have burnt it too badly to be eaten."

*

What did one bring as a gift for a wine merchant's daughter? Peter wondered as he trudged through the streets towards Guyon's new residence. He had finally settled on a set of combs for

Ännchen and a copy of Hobbes's *Elementorum Philosophiae*, a relatively new treatise that was currently making the rounds, for Gottfried. Nothing extravagant, but they'd be appreciated, he'd no doubt.

Far more appreciated than the stomachache he expected to get out of the evenings festivities. Ännchen, lovely girl that she was, simply could not cook. She was working at it though and, well, improvement could always be hoped for. Besides, the company would more than make up for any deficiencies in the meal - or at least that was what he told himself, as he approached the building that held the newlyweds' home.

He knocked sharply on the side door and waited for an answer, looking around him and noting the neatly kept appearance of the building. Ännchen's doing, he had no doubt, as neither Gottfried nor Guyon would normally have raised their noses up from their books long enough to notice flaking paint or a loose stair, unless it tripped them up.

In a singular fit of optimism, Ännchen had bullied them a few weeks ago into at least giving the ceiling of the teaching room a new coat of paint. Two days later she had conceded defeat and a desire not to see any more white footprints clearly marking their passage through the house and particularly up and down the cellar stairs, and hired workmen to do the complete interior - the same ones that Peter had been speaking to before Robert's arrival. They had done a plain and competent job, and seemed like the ideal solution – when viewed in the abstract.

Unfortunately, confronted with a place of the Hôtel d'Orsay's magnitude and assuming Peter had pockets to match, the design and prices had escalated to impossible and unwanted standards, and Peter was left wondering if just letting his cadets kick the paneling to pieces and tear down every curtain for makeshift muffle-cloaks was a better idea. Then, at least, they could move.

One of the van Hesselinks' three servants came to open the door, and Peter was left wondering why, given that they could obviously afford that number, who had so very little to do, Ännchen did not simply employ a cook.

He was led inside and to the small parlor that sat at the front of the building. Gottfried and Guyon were already there, as well as Ännchen's father, Herr Kirschner. "Good evening," Peter smiled and walked over to where the vintner sat.

Ännchen's father looked up at him through his small, heavy glasses, and smiled in welcome. "Ah, good," he said cheerfully. "Now I shall have conversation I can understand with my indigestion."

Peter bit back his amusement, "I'm sure your understanding is always superior, Herr Claus, indigestion or not."

"Hmf. If it were, I should be dining out." Herr Kirschner loved his daughter, but he was very far from idolizing her - unlike Gottfried, who Guyon claimed was a walking example of just what love could do to destroy a man. Not only had Gottfried's every sense become inflamed, he had once said acidly, but infected, gangrenous, and amputated, all without his noticing. Guyon himself, who claimed not to care what he ate, tended nevertheless to feign deafness and absorption at mealtimes, and subsisted on bread and cheese eaten hurriedly in his rooms as often as he could get away with it.

That idolization was a far cry from what Peter felt for Guyon, not better or worse, just different. He loved Guyon, but he was awake to his faults and loved him all the more for them. That this love did not appear to be returned, at least not in words, never altered his feelings.

"Hello, Gottfried, Guyon," Peter greeted the two other men. "Oh...here, Gottfried." He handed van Hesselink the treatise and the smaller package. "That's for Ännchen."

"Hobbes." Gottfried stuck the smaller package on the mantelpiece and opened the octavo volume. "Guyon, didn't you say we needed this?

"I said *you* needed it," Guyon murmured, "but yes." His eyes gleamed with amusement. "Will you exercise the theories on the inhabitants of your Hôtel, Pèire?"

"I believe I already have," Peter chuckled. "No brawling in the Hôtel is a primary rule of the establishment. So far it's been upheld. A microcosm of the belief, no doubt, but I call it home."

"And we all wait on tenterhooks for that equilibrium to finally collapse," Guyon said wryly. "Probably on the day when some infant genius works out the difference between right and left and someone else's foot."

"You are not to corrupt the good Marshal, Guyon," said Herr Kirschner, not moving from his seat. "I like him better unphilosophized."

One of Guyon's rare, genuine smiles flickered over his face. "Yes, sir, but then you hate pepper in your food as well."

"You needn't fear anything on that score, sir," Peter said, chuckling over Guyon's retort. "My tutor never managed to make me 'philosophized', and he used his cane."

"Oh, excellent man," Gottfried said wistfully. "Why can't we have students young enough for similar threats, Guyon?"

"Because I would kill them," Guyon said simply. "Untutored minds are bad enough, but add extreme youth to that burden, and I would be at the Place de la Greve before the week was out."

"Instead you merely send out a cannonade of ink encrusted paper wads," Peter pointed out. "I suppose they should count themselves lucky that you've no shoes handy."

"No, no, I *save* my shoes for important visitors," Guyon retorted. He looked down at his battered and endlessly-resoled boots. "And my boots I waste on no-one."

"A fact for which the students thank God, daily," Gottfried chuckled.

Peter spared a fond look at those old and disreputable bits of footwear, as much a part of Guyon as his paper, ink and books. He often worried about what would happen when they finally wore through and were more patches than solid leather.

Guyon made a face at them both. "Very amusing," he said, waving a hand at them, "don't cut yourselves on this lethally sharp wit, will you?"

"Be useful instead," Herr Kirschner admonished them. "If we wait for your servants to realize we might want our cups filling, Gottfried, my wine will have dust in it and be ruined."

Gottfried just chuckled at his father-in-law, and went to see about more wine. Herr Kirschner picked up the treatise from where Gottfried had laid it down and turned it toward the light. Peter watched as he moved it closer and closer to his face, trying to make out the words, then stopping to rub his eyes and peer at it again. The man's eyesight seemed to be worsening daily, and

Peter knew his pride did not allow him to admit it, in spite of how obvious it was becoming.

The skin tightened over Guyon's jaw as he noticed the same thing, but he said nothing either. Another man might have pretended that the copy was bad, but Herr Kirschner, while he was indisputably proud, was not a man to inflict unnecessary criticism on a gift to protect his image. He simply laid the book back down with a faint huff of exasperation. "Well," he said, "it seems I will need *someone* to philosophize, after all."

"Oh, choose Peter or Gottfried," said Guyon lightly. "I've had enough of war's philosophies for a lifetime."

Peter smiled and picked up the book, "*Etsi studiis docendi occupati, parum spatii ad scribendum habeamus, quoniam tamen multos vestes philosophiae abscindentes, et cum panniculis arreptis, totam sibi eam cessisse credentes...*" The Latin syllables spilled out so much more easily than they had when he had first learned them. That, he supposed, was a matter of growing older and more inclined to study, whereas when he was younger, sitting still for the amount of time his lessons required was always a trial.

Guyon snorted quietly, but refrained from comment, going to the door to relieve Gottfried of some of his clinking burden. As usual, they remained completely unconcerned as to whether something was being read aloud and might require concentration, but Peter suspected it might be a greater distraction to Herr Kirschner than to him, being as they were talking in German.

Peter read a bit more, "*Aer igitur est luna usque ad terram, qui quanto est terrae propinquior, tanto humidior et spissior: quanto remotior, siccior, et splendidior. Hic cum sit suppositus soli, ex eo calorem et lucem accipit.* Christ, Gottfried, I don't think I've done you any favors. Hobbes might have some interesting ideas but his manner of expressing them is just...horrid."

"That'll teach you to succumb to those already seduced by Euclid over Aristotle," Guyon said slyly, and Gottfried swiped at his head. Guyon dodged him, laughing. "Oh, the chill wind of science...don't insult Hobbes, Pèire, he's Gottfried's role-model." The little evil chuckle that followed the last word would have made it a lie even if Gottfried had not succumbed to teasing rather than Euclid and begun to protest.

Peter sat the book down with a grin, and moved to block Guyon, "Such insults, Gottfried. Should we stand for them, do you think? Or shall I subdue the brat while you berate him?" He slid his arms around Guyon, pinning him in place.

"*Brat*?" Guyon demanded, and Peter did not have to see his expression to know that the black eyebrows would be arched to their highest point. "Oh, you one to comment!" His foot slid over Peter's, clear warning that, if he felt the need, he would extricate himself and cause as much pain as possible in the process.

"Three very overgrown brats, from what I can see," Ännchen's laughing voice drifted from the doorway. "Really, Father, can you not make them behave?"

Herr Kirschner choked on laughter. "I never even succeeded with one daughter, how should I with three young men who have no filial ties to make them listen to me?"

"Because we're *terribly* polite, deep down," Guyon said, kicking Peter's ankle.

"*Yipe!*" Peter literally squeaked and let go of Guyon, wondering if he really needed to rethink his sentimentality about those damn hard boots. He looked at Ännchen pleadingly, "I'm polite...and wounded. Have pity."

"Or kick him again," Guyon said sweetly, moving smoothly and not altogether as nonchalantly as he would probably have liked to the other side of the room.

Anna Kirschner, all five feet six inches of her, threw up her hands and turned to her father, "I suppose I shall just have to thank you then."

"Thank me?" Herr Kirschner looked puzzled, "For what?"

"Because you did not give me any brothers."

"Ah, I'm glad to hear you recognize my perfections, sweeting..."

"Speaking of brothers," Gottfried said thoughtfully, "did yours find you, Peter?"

Peter's eyes flashed up at the other man, suddenly narrowing. "I don't have any brothers, Gottfried. You must have met Robert, my sister's husband." God, had the man just wandered through town accosting random strangers and asking for his whereabouts?

"Oh, I didn't *meet* him." Gottfried chuckled. "No-one thought to introduce us, but even I can distinguish *fraire* out of Guyon's Occitan babble - especially when it's at top volume."

"Jesus," said Guyon on a groan. "Shut up, van Hesselink."

Peter smiled at that, "Yes, Gottfried. Surely you will not claim that Guyon might have been, oh, defending me in some way?"

Ännchen's blue eyes widened, then narrowed and fixed on Guyon.

"Heaven forbid," he murmured obligingly, even as Gottfried, conceding defeat, raised his hands in acknowledgment of his need to drop the subject and shook his head.

"As if I would say something so outrageous!"

*

It was difficult, Peter thought, to explain the devil to someone who has never met him, someone who has never experienced true evil. That was the way Peter felt when he tried to explain Corvay's machinations to Robert.

"He has no loyalty. Not to crown, nor family, nor friend, only to himself. And no conscience, Robert. He will do whatever it takes to achieve a goal, no matter who dies or is broken." Peter sat behind his desk, his fingers toying with the small knife he used to open letters. "He has power and somehow has protected himself and done enough outwardly loyal acts to put him in the position he now holds."

"And that's all very disturbing, and now I'm clear on why yon frustrating little academic of yours gave me a warning, but what the hell's he got to do with you?" Robert wasn't looking any more enlightened as to why Peter had finally sent for him, pleasure and relief rapidly giving way to equally visible frustration.

"I'm rather like you in this, Robert. I first agreed to work with Corvay as a way to help her majesty and, I'll admit, to relieve my own boredom. The ways of court were never mine, you know, I have to be doing *something*." Peter looked down at the knife again. *I'm fidgeting. Even thoughts of Corvay disturb me, let alone his presence.* "I grew to dislike him rather quickly, but still

I was, I thought, doing needful work."

Robert nodded. "Aye, I've no problems seeing that. But why d'ye not just tell the man you'll not work for him any more? He can't force ya to, not now you've the Marshaldom an' more titles and lands to your name than the great Argyle!"

"I wish it was that simple." Peter shook his head. "He blackmails people to ensure their loyalty. Sometimes with information of deeds they have done...sometimes through their families."

"Well, there's nothing you or I have done that's not known to the world," Robert said, scratching at his head. "The dear Lord knows the world must see me as a precious idiot, but that shouldn't hold you, and we all know Sarah's been past reproach since she could breathe!" He grinned ruefully. "There's no more family to speak of, is there? Or have we some hidden mad aunt you're feeling terrible protective of?"

"No." Peter said softly, his English slurring back into its more normal patterns, "But I have a friend, one as close ta me as you've ever been, and he has family. And, Saints forgive me, it's my fault he's caught in this."

Robert snorted, and rubbed at his jaw in painful reminiscence. There was still a greenish-blue mark there, fading slowly to yellow around the edges. "I'm thinking *that* one can take care of himself and half Paris. *And* might have a wee bit of a dispute with this point of view as to fault that ye're holding."

"He might at that." Peter gave a short terse laugh, "But don't ya see? This is my job, Robert, my choice - to be a soldier, to risk my neck for her Majesty - not his. He was a scholar, a student at the Sorbonne. And me, I knew how smart he was, so I brought his name up. 'Ask for de Chesnay to help' I said, plain and bright, never thinking what it might mean. And for friendship's sake Guyon agreed to do just that. He had no interest in the court or intrigue, it was merely another puzzle set before him."

Robert's hand moved up to rub thoughtfully over his mouth. "And it's his family Corvay's got the hold on," he said, musingly. As Peter looked at him, slightly startled that he had made the connection had been made so quickly, Robert snorted, and waved a hand. "Ye're planning to ask me for help, and ye'd never think

of it for you or for him his own self. So, then, it'll be his family."
He chuckled. "Ye've put too high a rating on these academics of
yours, Peter, if y'forget we can all think as well as them!"

"No..." Peter began. "I mean yes, it's his family, but not for
their own sake. As far as I'm concerned his brother can go ta the
devil...but still an' all, it's Guyon's family and it would break him
if something happened ta hurt them."

"And ye're quite sure of that, are ye?" There was no malice in
Robert's tone, just a faint curiosity about a group of men he did
not know.

"It's why he's still working for Corvay." Peter let those words
speak for themselves. Those were the reasons - Guyon loved his
family, in spite of how they'd treated him, and Peter loved Guyon.

"*Is* it, now?" Robert nodded slowly. "Well then, what're
y'wanting me to do? Seems to me killing Corvay would be the
most sensible, but ye'd hardly be asking me for that."

"No, I hope ta have the pleasure of doing that myself one
day," Peter nodded solemnly. "I want ya ta go to Carcassonne...to
his home...convince his brother ta take the rest o' his family and
leave. To give up his idiocies against th' crown and get out. He's
no good ta anyone since he's been found out anyway."

"His brother's against the -" Robert suddenly hooted with
laughter. "Christ's breeks, Perry! What did you two do, meet for a
lament as to your boneheaded relations?"

Peter's voice went cold again, "I'm afraid that I don't find the
same amusement in the situation that you do, Robert. But then
again, I'm the one who was driven from his home, and Guyon is
the one whose brother is in danger, whether by his own stupidity
or not."

"Well now, didn't *that* put me in my place, huh?" Robert
sighed. "No, y'wouldn't see the joke in this. I tell ye what, though,
Marshal. Ye'd better bloody hope this Carcassonne brother of
your little academic's can see the funny side. A man's got to laugh
at himself before he'll change his mind."

"Well, that's your job then isn't it?" Peter spoke blandly. "To
make him laugh and get the hell out. I've arranged for a safe
place...for his transportation...all of that."

"The price of my forgiveness. Another man's brother." Robert sighed. "Aye, makes sense. And tells me where I stand now." His mouth closed, and firmed. "I'm hoping to God you're going to give me a map," he said in a lighter tone, "for I'll be damned if I go back to that bloody Russian for directions."

"I do and I'll send one of the cadets with you," Peter said, trying to relax. God, he wanted to trust Robert, wanted back his friend, his brother, Robbie. But he couldn't just trust him. Trust could kill you if offered unthinkingly.

"That's good of you," Robert said, retreating inch by inch back into formality. "Oh, aye, one other thing. What do I call this stupid brother of yer friend's?"

"Giraud de Chesnay, the Marqués de Carcassonne," Peter said the name with no small amount of venom. "I don't know what other of his family is there, but get out as many as will go, the close ones at least, and any Giraud think might also be found out."

Robert nodded. "I hate to be asking ye this, what with all the transportation sorted and the safe place found," he said quietly, "but if I canna persuade him?"

That was the crux of the whole, wasn't it? Peter wished he could tell Robert to just put the man on the bloody ship and get him out no matter what...but he couldn't.

"We'll think on that if you fail." Peter said, maintaining, at least outwardly, his cool expression.. And if he did fail, what then? Would he still refuse to believe Robert's apology? Would he send him back home and still harbor his resentment for the past? Peter wasn't sure if he had the strength to do that, even if he should.

Robert nodded, a kind of grim humor in his eyes. "I suppose that we will," he agreed. "Send your cadet to my lodgings when he's ready, then, Peter. I'll be fit to travel within the hour." This time, he didn't even hesitate over whether to shake hands or not. He gave a small, clipped, awkward bow. "And I'll bid ye good day."

Peter didn't watch him go. Couldn't watch him go, if the truth be told, it took all his strength not to call him back and tell him simply to try his best, to do it because there was no one he trusted more to do this. Because that was the truth, not the story he had given to Robbie. If anyone could persuade someone out of pigheadedness, it was the most pigheaded of them all, the man who had, once and disastrously, put his beliefs above private affection, and held to that way of behaving even when disaster struck.

The man who was probably closer to understanding what drove Giraud de Chesnay than any other man now in France.

"God keep you safe, Robbie. God keep you safe."

*

The Languedoc, late April 1646

Essential honor must be in a friend,
Not such as every breath fans to and fro;
But born within, is its own judge and end,
And dares not sin though sure that none should know.
Where friendship's spoke, honesty's understood;
For none can be a friend that is not good.

The kindest thing Robert Macquarie had found to say about his brother in law in the last few days was that perhaps - *perhaps* - Peter hadn't known just how bad his French was. If he had, there was absolutely no excuse for sending him to an area of France where even their supposedly native tongue was incomprehensible half the time, and an entirely different language the other half.

And Giraud de Chesnay might speak English - in fact, he had bloody well better speak English, or Robert was completely doomed - but he had left Robert waiting in one of the coldest halls it had ever been his misfortune to enter, with an old man whose preferred form of entertainment seemed to be to spit at the too-small fire.

And miss.

"Bit cold in here," he ventured. "Which is surprising as the night's fairly mild."

The old man looked at him with a sneer. *Or perhaps that's just his usual expression.* It wouldn't have been the least bit surprising, all things considered.

Robert was beginning to wonder if the cadet was not the one better off, being as he had yet to return from the stables where it was warm, dry, and, last he saw, had people ready to offer assistance and mulled ale. What he had was an uncommunicative elder who looked at him as though he was something to be scraped off the bottom of a shoe, and an absent host. Not that the host had known he was going to be a host, but since Robert had come a bloody long way to talk to him, an appearance would have been more than appreciated.

He peered into the shadows of the room, trying to see what the place was like, but it was nearly impossible. The room was ill

102

lit and the windows, though uncovered to allow in the late afternoon sun, high and narrow. The place was more like a fortress than a home, and a sharp contrast to Hawthornden. His home was warm and bright, like the people who owned it, open and welcoming. His Sarah would have wilted in a place like this. *Or had me knocking the walls out to give more light, more like.*

"Sorr' t've kep' you." What was merely a small, slurring elide in Guyon's voice was an almost complete lack of word endings in Giraud's. "I'ad t'ge' dress'. Ah, no, I mean, I 'ad to *re*dress. For th'comp'ny."

He was both taller and somehow wirier than Guyon, the build of a man who either had been, or should have been, a soldier, brisk and assessing. But it was the same strange eyes which had glared at Robert as he lay on the floor that peered through the dusk of the room now. "I am *le Marqués*. Is...*honor*, Seigneur Macquarie."

"Ye might not be thinking' it as much once we have our talk, Marqués de Chesnay." But Robert held out his hand in greeting. "Can we go somewheres else to talk? What I've got ta say is fer yer ears alone, I'm afraid." He didn't want to insult either Giraud or the old man near the fire, but even as straightforward as he was, he didn't want to just blurt this out in company.

"*Oc, ta ben.*" Giraud strode across the room and took his hand, grasping it firmly, and looking intently at Robert. "You'e f'om Paris. You *come* from Paris. Is. My *fraire*, Guyon, 'e - is *well*?" Even in the darkened room, he was very white. "No, is of no - come. You tell me. Come." He released Robert's hand abruptly, turning away before he could answer, and leading the way out of the room.

"First off, yer brother's well, or leastways was when I left town," Robert said as he took the seat that Giraud offered him. "Fine and feisty as a lone cock in the yard."

Giraud blinked at him, and then laughed, sudden and deep. "In *Anglais*, this is good?" he asked at last, but the color had come back to his face with the laughter.

"Aye, verra good...unless yer on the bad side of his temper," Robert rubbed one hand along his still slightly discolored jaw. "But that's not why I've come. At least, not directly."

Giraud sighed. "'E did no' sen' you. Ah well. I 'oped..." He shrugged. "Please, continue."

"No, he didn't send me," Robert frowned hoping he was deciphering all the word bits that the other man was using. *Be like me ta get it wrong and get the other brother ta knock me down.* "As a matter of fact, I doubt he knows I've come at all."

"Ver' sorr', I don'...un'erstan'." Giraud was very obviously trying to be polite, but he was beginning to frown. "Please t'explain?"

"Sorry, myself. I'll get to my point, then you can toss me out or listen to the rest," Robert was prepared for either eventuality, not knowing if Giraud was as stubborn as his brother or not. "A friend of yer brother has sent me here. I'll say it right out. It's known that yer making deals with the Spaniards, and it's going ta be getting a bit dangerous fer you verra soon."

There was a long, uncomfortable silence. Giraud stared at him, the strange eyes seeming to be making an attempt at seeing through his skull straight into his thoughts, before he dropped his head into his hands and said something quick and slurred and incomprehensible. When he straightened, he looked both embarrassed and angry, a combination that Robert knew from experience never led to anything good. "An' so...it woul' be...*easier*...fo' my *fraire*. If I we'e to...*vanish*?"

"Don't know that," Robert shrugged. He didn't know Guyon well enough to guess at his motivations. "But the one who sent me? He said that yer brother worried for yer safety. He's being blackmailed for it, matter of fact. This man...Corvay...knows what yer doing and is using yer continued safety ta hold yer brother in his control."

"*Corvay?*" What *was* this man, that his very name held such power to evoke dread? "Guyon is - *sciecco mi* ! 'E was nev' s'pose'...*neve'*. *Fotu!*" The tray on the neatly laid out table went flying across the room with one sweep of Giraud's arm as he got to his feet. "You. You tell Villon he is a *dead* man. For to no' protec'. 'E *swore!*"

Robert was up out of his chair before the tray hit the floor, "Who? Don't know anyone named Villon. He a cadet or something'?"

"*Non.* A friend, a lawye'...ah *Cristi.*" Giraud's temper was gone as suddenly as it had exploded into the neat room. "'E is dead, then." He closed his eyes. "The'e a'e too many cand'es, Robe't Macquarie. Too many."

"I light a few myself, come Sundays. Just as soon not ta have more." Robert agreed. "Spare Guyon a few and give up this...well, what ever ya think yer doing."

"You 'ave never done what you though' right fo' the sake of you' lan's?" Giraud half-laughed. "Fortuna'e man." He ran his hands over his head, smoothing over hair that was heavy and straight where his brother's was wild. "*Oc.* I do it. But I...I mus' tell my wife, you un'erstan'?"

"That's ta be the hard part, eh?" Robert gave an understanding nod. "And, about yer other question, I have done. Still am...but it's my wife's land really, and her brother's. Still and all, I love it and do my best fer it.."

"Hah." It wasn't any sort of mockery, rather a choking laugh of comprehension. "*Oc,* is the 'ard part. Who...sended you?"

"I told you. A friend of yer brother's," Robert repeated, his lip twitching. "Who just happens ta be my wife's brother."

"*Ah.*" There was a sudden corresponding amusement in Giraud's eyes. "Oh fortuna'e son of *l'Ecosse.*" He gestured at the room. "You mus'...be at 'ome. I will sen' someone, you say to 'im what you need. Now I 'ave...*the 'ard part.*" He smiled wryly.

"Aye, and good luck with that." Robert nodded, settling back into his chair. Well, that had gone fairly well. He only hoped that Giraud had less trouble convincing his wife of what was to be, than he knew he'd have trying to convince Sarah.

*

It was several hours later that Robert found himself seated at a table in the somewhat dim dining room. Candles and lamps had been lit but, somehow, did little to dispel the darkness of the place. Still and all, the light was soft and flattering and showed off his hostess, Maria Catalina Margareta Elena García-Carrión de Chesnay y Martínez, if he had managed to catch all the names that Giraud had tumbled out with, to her best advantage. Not that she needed it, because she was a lovely little thing, not as outspoken as his Sarah of course, but not backward in giving her opinions either, although they might have been watered down since Giraud was translating between them.

And she had told him, in her somewhat limited English, to call her 'Lina' because, "The res'? It is too much."

He had to agree with her there.

But it was she who leaned across the table and put her hand on her husband's wrist as he yet again attempted polite conversation. "Párese, querido," she said gently, and turned her large eyes on Robert. "Now. You tell why we leave. I know...what he do. An' I know why. Which...is more than you, eh? So now tell. Is for the *hermanito*? Is for Guyon?"

"Yes...is...I mean, yes, for Guyon indeed." Robbie stumbled just a bit. "He's got himself in a mess, I take it. No, that's not quite right either. He was dragged in and can't get out because they're holding him hostage for yer safety. It's hard fer me to explain since I was just given the bare bones. Seems this man, Corvay, has a verra watchful eye and Peter wanted me on the way before he had any clue as ta what was planned."

She frowned, and when Giraud tried to translate, held up a small, jewelled hand. "No. Is *mine*. Wait." She smiled at Giraud, then, quiet and private and somehow making Robert want to leave, or perhaps just dive under the table, but it was Robert she spoke to when she said calmly and confidently, "Verr' well. Is his penance. We go to where?"

Robert blinked for a moment. Obviously Lina was a bit more like his Sarah than he'd given her credit for, making the decisions that were needed without complaint. "Portugal, it seems. Peter has arranged it all - a ship, a place for you ta stay, all done. He said he'd contact you later, when it was safer, and arrange something more permanent if yer not happy there."

"I have state." Lina shrugged, her pale shoulders outlined by the warm light, and reached out for another serving of fish and almond cream. At Robert's slightly stunned look, she grinned, and added, "I eat for two. Most nice."

"She means," Giraud said to the table, his dark face a deeper color even in the soft light, "that she 'as *estates*. She'as estates

106

ev'where. Also I think you un'erstan' the rest. Also, I think you can *see.*"

Lina laughed quietly, and stuffed a forkful of fish in his mouth. "Quiet," she said, her voice shaking with laughter. "No polite."

"You have lands in Portugal." Robert nodded. That would make things easier on all concerned, he was sure. This woman that Guyon's brother had married was a gem, and apparently about to make him an uncle. "Shouldn't be too hard ta get ya to them once ye land, then. Peter has someone meeting ya and they'll help with the rest."

Lina said something quick and angry-sounding to Giraud in the odd, slurred language that wasn't French or Spanish, and Giraud, if possible, went a deeper red. "My husband is sometimes most appalling stupid," she said then, and got to her feet. "And now I am for to pack things. Or make for others to pack things. Is same." She almost stamped out of the room, her skirts muffling the effect, and Giraud groaned.

"Do the Scottish drink *aguardente*?" he asked wearily. "Because *per Dio*! I will!"

"Not sure as I know what that is, but I'm willing ta try," Robbie grimaced. "I know I find a good bottle of whiskey helps set me ta right when my Sarah's set the rough edge of her tongue at me."

Or flung her shoes at my head...Or taken a broom after me.

"You' - *ah*. You' wife." Giraud smiled a little. "An' you' wife, she take the rough of 'er tongue to you abou' you' brothe'?" He picked up the small bell by the side of his plate, shook it once, and even Robert could tell that it was a series of quiet requests, and not demands, that he gave to the man who entered.

"Aye," Robert nodded as the man left the room. "Quite a bit lately. Peter and I had a bit of a fallin' out. My fault, really, but neither one of us was quick ta make it up. So he was here and I was home and Sarah wasn't verra happy about any of it. But, now I'm here and I'm trying ta patch us back tagether."

"A bit of a -" Giraud snorted, choked, and waved off the servant who came in with a tray laden with glasses, a bottle of clear liquid, nuts, cheese and fruit, as he set it down and came over to pat Giraud on the back. "*Na.* Go." He took a deep breath, sat upright, and filled the two heavy glasses with the clear drink. "*Aguardente.* Good 'ealth."

"And ta yers and yer good wife's as well," Robert added and took a drink of the Aguardente. It was sharp and strong going in, but for one used to whiskey it had little flavor. Still, the taste was not the point of the drink if he knew anything about it.

"Tell me...abou' you' brothe'." Giraud added something in his own language that must have been *love*, and not *lover*, because otherwise Robert's scant smattering of French was worse than he thought it.

"Peter? Ah, he's tall and strong, has blond hair and blue eyes and..." Robert took another drink of the liquor before he continued. "He has a smile that can warm ya like the sun and a scowl that can make ya wonder just what the hell ya did. But he smiles more'n scowls so ya know when you see that it must have been something' verra bad." Robert paused to chuckle. "And he's almost as stubborn as me."

Giraud looked as though he were about to cry, his mouth twisting. "An'...'e makes for Guyon to smile back?"

"Well, that I can't really say," Robert began, then shrugged, "but I 'spect he does. And that Guyon makes him smile just as often."

Giraud looked straight at him, the strange eyes hard and somehow clean-cut, like washed glass, and said distinctly, "God damn them both." He poured himself another glass of *aguardente*, drained it, and got to his feet. "Fo' Po'tugal, then. *Bonne nuit,* Robert." And with that, he was gone from the room.

Well, that was an odd reaction. Robert suddenly wondered if Giraud had, indeed, understood what he'd said. How could the man not be pleased that his brother had found as good a friend as Robert knew Peter could be? That he found some measure of happiness in their companionship? There was more going on here than he knew, obviously, and he hoped that none of it would keep him from accomplishing what Peter wished.

*

As Robert trudged back towards the Hôtel d'Orsay more than a fortnight later, all he had in his mind was reporting to Peter and hearing, please God, the sound of some plain English. The cadet that Peter had sent as his guide was a pleasant young man who, at least, spoke English rather commendably, but with such an accent that Robert had to train his ears to understand him.

Still the young man had been excellent help in getting Giraud and Catalina packed up and then loaded on board their Portugal bound ship. Helpful in spite of, so the cadet had explained, their own language differences.

And here Robert had thought they were both speaking French - he had a lot to learn, apparently, for the cadet, Jean, was speaking French, the de Chesnays Occitan. Robert wasn't quite sure what the difference was, apart from what his ears told him, but still, he was quite glad to have Jean to deal with it.

"Nearly home," Jean said cheerfully as they went past a tavern in which Robert was convinced he recognized half of Peter's cadets. "And then supper and beer and a proper sleep." He was absolutely undentable, Robert thought enviously, having as much energy now as when they had set off. He, on the other hand, felt as though he had aged ten years overnight, and all of them weighed actual pounds that were hanging from his shoulders.

"Yes, and I'm sure I can find my way from here," Robert looked down the street, catching a glimpse of the Hôtel's roof. "Go. Off with ya then, join yer friends and have a beer for me."

"I'll have six," Jean agreed with a grin, and almost bounced into the tavern. The yells of delight proved that Robert had not been mistaken, and he wondered suddenly if he had ever, in his entire life, been that young. Shaking his head, he carried on to the hôtel, which was, as it had been on both previous occasions he had been there, a hive of seemingly pointless activity that nevertheless seemed to involve everyone's complete concentration, and above it all, a voice that was now oddly familiar after days spent with its almost precise echo - "My God, Philippe, do you need lessons on breathing, now?"

If Jean had energy to spare then, Robert thought, Guyon de Chesnay actually *was* energy, tightly bound and controlled by the strength of his mind. Energy that, at the moment was directing a hapless young man to do...what? Whatever it was, the young man, Philippe, seemed rather unhappy about the whole thing.

"You take a breath, you hold it with your diaphragm, you use it as a cushion for your voice. So. You breathe in, you store it, you start to speak."

"Most people can talk without help, sir!"

"Are you *arguing* with me?" Guyon demanded, and then stopped dead, as something large and metallic-sounding was knocked over and came down the staircase, turning out to be an incredibly elderly suit of armor that had apparently been made for a giant, and was now in several pieces. There was the familiar chorus of 'Sorry, sorry, sorry!' from the gallery, and then an equally familiar shout of "For Christ's sake!" following.

Just like home. The sudden thought amused Robert completely. He and Peter had always been in some kind of mischief, aided and abetted by both their friend Brian MacInerney and Sarah. He was sure they'd been a great trial to Peter's Uncle William, as well as his own parents, and now his own sons and even his daughter had taken over from where they had left off, distracting and chaos-creating and secure beyond belief in their parents' love.

"And now you have woken the Marshal from his - ah - paperwork," Guyon sounded deeply amused. "Yes, go on, Philippe, help them clear up, at least something can be done right here...*Robert*." He had no idea what emotion Guyon was feeling at his reappearance, but it was strong enough to make his voice change completely, sharpening into an even louder tone than was usual for the Hôtel.

"Yes," Robert gave him a nod. "I'm back."

Like that's not completely obvious, Robert. He could hear Sarah's voice in his head. She hated his habit of pointing things out.

"Peter's here then, I take it?" Obviousness again.

"In 'is office," Guyon agreed. After Giraud's heavy accent, he sounded almost English by comparison. "You should go up, I think?"

"Most probably should," Robert agreed, and started up the

stairs, wending his way around the bits of armor scattered over its length. He was halfway up when he realized that Guyon was following him. *Probably wants to knock me down again if I say one wrong word ta Peter.*

But then again, if Peter was going to forgive him, which he devoutly hoped, Guyon was going to owe him, and that surely meant no more blows to the face.

No, said the exasperated voice of Sarah in his mind, *he'll go for something more painful, with his foot.*

The door to Peter's office was open, and Robert found himself, unexpectedly nervous, hovering on the gallery steps and trying to convince himself that everything was going to be fine.

"Jus' barge in," Guyon advised, his voice carefully even. "Eve'y one else seems to."

Yes, Robert was sure they did, but somehow that didn't feel right at the moment. He raised his hand and knocked sharply.

"Ye gods and little fishes," Guyon muttered exasperatedly, and moved past him into the office. "Peter, Robert's back. Again." He gestured rather extravagantly in Robert's direction. "See?"

Damn insufferable brat. But Robert was still grateful that Peter had found such a friend during his exile. Peter was never meant for solitude, and the thought that he'd been suffering from it so far from home had often invaded Robert's thoughts during their disaffection with each other.

"Robert?" Peter's voice was oddly cold, Robert thought as he entered. *But maybe he's expecting me to have failed.*

Feeling a little like a magician unveiling his final trick, Robert grinned with a triumph he could no longer hide, and said, "One brother safely delivered to Portugal, wife and household goods included."

Peter stood and walked around the end of the desk, stopping just in front of him. "Thank God," he whispered out, then pulled Robert into a fierce hug.

Relief almost singing through him, Robert returned the embrace with equal strength, wondering as he did how Peter had changed so much that he could go from the icily distant demeanor of seconds before to this infinitely more wanted familiarity.

"You do realize," said Guyon's clear voice from behind him, "that I really need some kind of explanation?"

Peter whirled around then, and somehow, Robert was sure that if he had not been present he'd have grabbed up the shorter man and swung him around in circles. *And probably gotten his ears boxed for daring it.* Robert chuckled softly.

"Robert's done it, Gui." Peter's voice was shaking with some kind of emotion. "He's got your brother away and safe."

Guyon went very, very still, somehow seeming to absorb all the light and energy in the room into himself. "*My God,*" he whispered at last, and Robert, looking at him, caught sight of something so unbelievable as to be impossible - a stark, soul-deep terror that made him catch his breath. He was on the verge of saying something, but in the next instant, Guyon blinked, and the look was gone, leaving Robert half-convinced he had imagined it. "I don't have the words," he added in a constricted voice.

Peter moved forward, placing his hand on Guyon's shoulder. He'd felt that touch often enough himself to recognize it. Comfort, reassurance...all the things that Peter was so apt at giving.

"It means you're free. Finally, totally free." But there was something odd in Peter's voice, as if he expected, somehow, for that freedom to change their friendship. "No more Corvay. No more blackmail. Free."

"You did this? *You* did this." All Guyon's attention was on Peter, and Robert might as well not have existed - or gone to see his rotten brother at all, he thought, repressing a laugh. "And if I am, then so are you." He twitched a smile. "And so, I believe, is Giraud, hm?" His voice shook a little on the name.

"We've drawn the wolf's fangs, Gui. Next we lead him to the slaughter," Peter nodded, his face taking on a determined expression.

Robert frowned slightly. He wasn't sure what Peter was referring to, but it sounded dangerous. He didn't want to lose his brother as quick as he'd gained him back.

He was about to say something when he felt poke and a rustle of paper from within his tunic. "Oh, Guyon, yer brother asked me to give you this." He pulled the letter out and passed it to Guyon.

112

"Thank you," Guyon said quietly. "I -" he made an odd little gesture with the hand not holding the letter, towards the balcony. "I'll just -" He walked to the glass-paned doors, and opened one, going out onto the balcony and closing the door behind him. Robert shifted uneasily.

"Is he all right? He's not looking as though ecstasy's taken him over."

"No," Peter sighed. "He and his brother have had...problems. But he still cares for him, I know. Plus, it's probably going to take awhile for it all to hit him."

*If he doesn't perk up and thank Peter properly I'll see about hitting **him**,* Robert thought, uncharitably. He'd done this for him as much as for Peter. Well, yes, it had been for himself as well, but helping Peter was his main goal. And if helping Guyon helped Peter, then he'd help Guyon.

"Aye, well he seemed nice enough," Robert ventured. "Or he was t'me. And his wife's a right gem."

He forced himself not to think about Giraud's outburst, the night of his arrival. *God damn them both.* It had never been repeated, the feelings that had provoked it never as much as hinted at again, and there was no reason to spoil the moment by mentioning it now, and besides, Peter wasn't really paying attention to him, all his focus on the man on the other side of the balcony doors.

Outside on the balcony, Guyon, head back, was staring at the sky, the hand with the open letter in it fallen to his side. Then he straightened, and came back in, folding the letter away into his doublet as he did so.

"I can never repay you," was the first thing he said when he re-entered. "Thank you, Robert. From the bottom of my heart."

"You're welcome." Robert knew what those words must have cost the other man. One thing that Robert had learned about Guyon de Chesnay during their short association was how independent he was. For him to thank another for doing something that he could not accomplish must have been terribly hard.

"And thank you, Robert, from myself as well," Peter's voice interrupted his thoughts. "There's no one else I would have trusted ta try this, ya know?"

"Ach, I know that," Robert said with a grin. "Doesn't mean I'll not be asking you to repeat it a few dozen times, but." He was surprised at the fact it was Guyon who laughed at that, warmth entering the strange eyes as they regarded him for the first time.

"Start now," Guyon advised, and dodged a swat from Peter quite automatically. "And Peter? We are going, I think, on a wolf-hunt." His smile was appropriately feral.

"Tomorrow, I think, will be soon enough?" Peter said, and it startled Robert to see that his smile matched Guyon's to an alarming degree. *Peter, you have changed some, haven't you?*

Robert shook himself out of that thought, "Tomorrow?"

"Because tonight? We celebrate." And that grin, at least, was more natural.

"Whiskey?'

"Whiskey." Peter gave a nod, then laughed at the disgusted look on Guyon's face.

"Oh *God*," was all Guyon said, with an odd fervency. "Wine? Please?" He widened his eyes to an almost impossible degree, exaggeratedly pleading. "*Please*?"

*

Guyon knew that he should be ecstatic. Corvay's one real hold over them was gone - had left for Portugal five days before, in fact, leaving him with a long letter of remorseful intent that had somehow managed to be too much and far too little, and instructions about the Languedoc estates that could have been summarized by 'keep paying the estate manager and he'll take care of the rest'. But that was all he had seen of his brother, all he would ever have in terms of resolution until Corvay was dealt with in some permanent way.

He wanted to ask Robert 'Has he changed? Does he still talk in the same way, does he still throw his head back when he laughs, is he still my brother, still?' but Robert would not know, had no answers to those questions that crowded at the back of his throat and choked him before he could speak.

Guyon could not even admit his conflicting feelings to Peter, who was taking one of his more absolutist viewpoint stances on Giraud. Peter was delighted that Corvay could no longer use the renegade Marqués against them, and truly relieved and pleased that it *had* been Robert who had accomplished this - because now his brother-in-law could be forgiven, had shown he could be trusted, had proved his worth. Guyon, whose brother was a traitor now twice over, and who had done nothing but cause immeasurable pain and grief to others, knew that he had no room to comment, no right to whisper even a hint of his wish to have spoken to Giraud, no allowance for regret or resentment.

"Wasn't such a bad sort, really." Robert growled out, his hands wrapped around a large cup full of whisky. "Saw sense much quicker than I would have thought he would have. Can credit his wife with that, I'm certain." Robert snorted a laugh. "Not that I'd know anything about being managed by a woman."

Guyon winced. *I didn't even know. Even Corvay assumed I knew, or he would have taken delight in telling me. But I had no idea. My brother and his Spanish wife - no wonder he was supporting them, he was a genuine ally.* "Of course you wouldn't," he agreed dryly, hoping that nothing of his unhappy, whirling thoughts showed on his face.

Peter snorted, refilling his cup, "Sarah's been managing him since he was fourteen. But he didn't admit it until he turned twenty."

"And she managed you up until then," Robert claimed. "But I was much more satisfying."

"Gad, Robert. That's my sister and I do *not* want to hear that." Peter covered his ears.

"And yet the rest of the world can breathe a sigh of relief," Guyon said in his blandest voice, wondering if they were even capable of grasping the implications.

"Too true," Robert agreed, with a fond smile. "If there were more women like my Sarah, the world would not be safe for men."

Guyon hastily covered his laugh with a cough. "Hm. Yes, I had not considered that. I should thank God."

"On bended knees," Peter emphasized and was promptly swatted on the back of the head by his brother-in-law.

Guyon, by now, was completely wrongfooted as to whether they were all discussing true devotion or a rather more private kind, and bitterly regretting his decision to stay sober. He would have drained his cup, but reminded himself of aquavit, of François's funeral and his long-ago destruction of Henri, and contented himself with raising his eyebrows. "I did not realize you were so against prayer, Robert," he said with not altogether feigned amusement.

Now Robert snorted. It appeared to be a family trait. "You'd have ta meet my Sarah to completely understand. She can be stubborn and bossy one minute, then the softest rose that ever grew in the churchyard the next. Keeps ya on yer toes, let me just say."

"I can imagine," Guyon said in a voice that he hoped would convey his utter displeasure at being made to do so.

"Eh?" Peter looked over at him as he drained his cup. "Oh...come on, Robbie, it's kind of rude for us ta be going on so, when Guyon doesn't know Sarah...and is sober besides." His accent was getting stronger the more he drank, Robert's heavy, lilting tones seemingly contagious.

Robert eyed Peter, "You haven't told him much about home then have you? About me and Sarah, or Brian either, I'd suspect."

Peter's ears suddenly turned an exceptional shade of pink.

Guyon stared at them both. "Well, I'm a quizzity, the very embodiment of an incurious cat," he said lightly. "I never asked, either." *Though I would like to now, if only to discover the source of your embarrassment...*"I have the terrible tendency to assume people will tell me what I need to know."

If anything, Peter's blush just deepened, "He's just a friend from home, Guyon. We - We used to get up to a lot of mischief together, the three of us."

"Aye," Robert agreed with a smirk, "Mischief is what they called it."

Guyon rather thought that mischief was the least of what 'they' had probably called it, but kept that thought to himself. "Well, your rock still stands," he said lightly, "so it can't have been much worse than that."

"His rock stood a'right." Robert chuckled into his cup.

"Robert!" Peter covered his head with his arms, his forehead now resting on the table as if he wanted to, somehow, bury himself in the surface.

Guyon, by now thoroughly lost, stared from one to the other. "I do not," he said rather grimly, "speak Scottish. A fact which I have long since added to my numerous debts of gratitude to the Almighty, but which in this case is distinctly annoying, particularly as you seem to have found a way of mutilating perfectly good French in order to do so. *What*?"

Peter peeked up from where he was attempting to hide, "My dear 'brother' is referring to the fact that it was he and Brian who shoved me into the arms of my first woman. I was sixteen. I was terrified."

Guyon, the man who had managed to avoid even a Twelfth Night kiss until he was almost twenty-two, felt nothing but purest sympathy. "Knowing your temper when afraid or uncertain, Pèire, I rather think it is *Robert* who should thank God daily. That he *survived*." He let his mouth curl into a faint smile, and shook his head slightly at Peter. *It's not important.*

"God, yes!" Robert refilled his glass, "The man was an absolute wretch ta Brian and I for over a month. Brian brought him 'round though. Peter never could stay mad at him for long."

The faintest stirrings of unease prickled at the base of Guyon's spine. Robert's too-overt amusement was at odds with Peter's undiminished embarrassment, and while he was quite prepared to believe that both reactions were exacerbated by the whiskey, he was also fairly sure that for once, Robert was trying *not* to demonstrate how much more he knew about Peter than Guyon did, which was a new and disturbing development. "I knew someone rather similar," he said, while his mind raced. "Although I generally wanted to avoid the spaniel imitation."

The look of relief on Peter's face would almost have been comical under other circumstances, but considering the conversation, Guyon wasn't quite sure what it meant.

"You would have loved François, Robbie. Or maybe you would have tried to kill him. He was that sort, ya know? Smart he was and quick with a joke, but could infuriate you just as quick." Peter smiled softly at Guyon then, his eyes full of reminiscence.

"He was a good friend ta have. The best."

"Yes, when he wasn't irritating you and half of Paris to a state of homicide," Guyon agreed lightly. It was rare for him even to show his true feelings to Peter - with Robert there he was more guarded than ever, not only for the sake of his inner privacy, but because while it did not matter if the whole of the Sorbonne suspected the real nature of this friendship with Peter, he felt that for Robert to guess at his inclinations would be disastrous.

"Well, you'll have ta introduce Guyon ta Brian sometime," Robert continued, seemingly unaware of any undercurrents floating around him. "I'm sure they'd get on."

"Aye." Peter agreed, his eyes twinkling, "There are few that don't get on with Brian." He looked at Robert and they both started laughing.

For a second, Guyon was silenced by complete and irrational anger. He understood that Robert had achieved something incredible. He understood that Peter wanted to celebrate it - he understood that it was in all respects *worth celebrating* - but he wished that they could see it was not that simple for him, that for him it was mixed with grief, with the past, with the knowledge that he really *had* lost his brother now, in ways he had not before. And he could not cope with all the things he had no right to ask about, had no part of, had no knowledge of, being forced on him in one evening.

He could not manage to try and understand all the layers of amusement, could not untangle from all the hidden meanings whether it was himself or Brian who was being laughed at.

Stupidly and childishly, he wished suddenly that he could just go back to his rooms on the merchants' street, lock his door, and hide until all these conflicting emotions had passed. Instead, he said cheerfully - "Oh, I'm quite sure I could manage. I can get anyone to dislike me with enormous rapidity, you know..."

"The only people who dislike you, are ones who do not deserve to have you like them." Peter's manic laughter had suddenly faded at Guyon's words, "I always wondered how I managed it."

You have no idea, Guyon thought passionately, *and please God, you never will.* "You threw shoes onto my desk," he said, feeling the bright dazzle of his feigned happiness soften into something real, and honest, and ultimately private. He hoped Robert was too whiskey-blurred to notice. "How could I not like you after that?"

"Far too easily," Peter looked up with whisky-bright eyes. "I was there to tell ya off. I was that sure that you had purposely played a trick on me." He reached over and put one hand on the side of Guyon's face, softly rubbing his cheek with the pad of his thumb. "I'm so glad that wasn't. That it was just a misunderstanding."

Guyon could, so easily, have turned his head and pressed his lips to the inside of Peter's wrist, to the heel of his palm, and for one moment, the instinct - the *desire* - to do so was so great that he thought he had. For an instant, he met Robert's dark, surprised gaze, and was tempted to laugh, to brush off Peter's gesture as mere drunken affection and let it go - and was as instantly ashamed of himself. Peter *trusted* Robert, had done so for years before their estrangement, was not so drunk that he did not know precisely what he was implying by his actions.

Guyon might not be capable of allowing himself to be demonstrative in company, but he was also not willing to let anyone think for a second that he was ashamed or an unwilling partner.

"But misunderstandings are our specialty, *bèl*," he said, and touched the back of Peter's hand where it lay against his face. "You can't deny natural talent..."

"Christ, no," Peter said fervently, tugging Guyon closer. "Though it's the one talent I wish we'd never honed."

Guyon huffed out a little breath of laughter, and nodded, letting himself be pulled closer, wholly unresisting.

"I think I might *need* to hone it," Robert said in an odd combination of understanding and irritation. "Good lord. Give me some room for doubt, would you?"

Peter turned his head to look at Robert, "This is one time ya need ta have no doubt, Robbie. This is me. This is what I want. Who I want. The one that makes me happy the way Sarah does you. It's not the drink talking, and I'll not deny it when I'm sober."

Guyon drew in sharp, startled air, and almost choked on it as he did so. "*Père* -" He wondered whether he would have to kill Robert after all. If the man said something to hurt Peter, after that, it was going to be a *pleasure*, not a commitment. He was overwhelmed with the strange, furious protectiveness that no-one and nothing else but Peter could evoke in him, the sudden blaze of pride that someone like this could be so unashamed of him, the dazzled wonder that Peter could support his claims to love with the same strength of self that he brought to his own honor - and wanting at the same time to plead *don't, don't leave yourself open, not like this, not for me, don't...*

There was silence, Robert's eyes darting between Guyon and Peter for several long moments, as if judging something. When he spoke he seemed to have come to a decision. "You'll have ta explain it ta Sarah, though. I'm not getting in the middle of that argument."

Peter laughed, burying his face against Guyon's neck, "Sarah will get used to it. She'll have no choice."

"Oh, and you said she'd *like* me," Guyon snorted. "You love to self-defeat your own prophecies, don't you?" He ran a hand over Peter's head, letting it rest on the nape of his neck, not quite the familiar, attention-demanding grip, but an assurance of his presence, confirmation that he had heard, and understood, and was holding to his months-ago given word and staying.

Peter suddenly looked up, his face as serious as Guyon had ever seen it, "Doesn't matter if she does or not. You understand that? I love my sister but...she has no say in this."

Guyon wished Peter would stop saying things that seemed calculated to steal every particle of air from his lungs, and wished even more that he had the ability to respond in any way to his declarations. "Yes," he managed at last. He had no idea what expression was on his face, but it seemed to be enough to compensate for his lack of vocabulary. He suspected that if it hadn't been, Robert might have tried to kill *him*, and he would have been completely deserving of the attempt. "Yes, I understand."

The words seemed to satisfy Peter, for he nuzzled his face back into Guyon's neck, after placing a soft kiss on his jaw line. "Good."

"Come on now, enough of yer mush," Robert broke the serious mood. "Are ya drinking with me or not?"

"No," Guyon said amusedly. "I *like* being able to talk. That stuff removes throat linings from the inside out." *And has the potential to turn me into a raving lunatic of the sort that deserves to die, if it's as similar to aquavit as I suspect.* "And *mush*? You must have spent time with the Scots Guards, Macquarie, you're obviously thinking of porridge again..."

Peter snorted from his spot at Guyon's neck, "Nay, that was our deal. I'd uphold the honor of the family and Robbie would keep the Hall from decaying and falling down around our ears."

"It was a fair trade, Peter." Robert sputtered. "You hate being the **Laird.**" The word was pronounced with every bit of accent that Robert owned.

Guyon chuckled. "Except when he's demonstrating its innate power over the cadets..." He tilted his head to slant a grin at Peter, who showed no signs of moving. "And *are* you upholding your end of the bargain?" he asked Robert mockingly.

Robert chuckled, "The Hall wasn't ever in any danger of caving in, really. Peter's exaggerating because he hates keeping books and dealing with tenants."

"And you *like* it?" It sounded like a form of hell. "Isn't that why bailiffs were invented?"

"Bailiffs will keep the estate running...but they don't improve it, generally," Robert took another drink of his whisky.

"And Robbie has done that," Peter's voice came out muffled against Guyon's chest. "Turned a nice piece of that rock I called home into good farmland that will take a plow without breaking it."

"Poor old sheep," said Guyon. "Peter, I am not a bolster, and if you begin trying to make me into a more comfortable shape you will find I prove that point with some force. What do you *grow*, for God's sake? I thought it was windy and rained all the time and had gravel for earth..."

"Well, we still mostly have sheep," Robert admitted. "But we have a good cash crop. Rye."

Peter chuckled and muttered a snip of a song against Guyon's stomach.

"I have no idea what 'bonny at morn' means," Guyon said wryly, "but I suspect it will not be you tomorrow. Rye...? Ah. For your horrible drink." He gestured at the cup in Robert's hand, and grinned.

Robert grinned back then, "Sin and drink always pay well. But Sarah'd have our hide if we tried ta make a living from the first."

Somehow Peter, who had managed to stretch out full length on the bench and was now laying on his back with his head in Guyon's lap, thought that was terribly funny, "No...that's Brian's job."

Guyon stared down at him. "You might want to explain that...or at least clarify it," he suggested, raising his eyebrows. At Peter's blank look back at him, he sighed, and said, "What are you talking about?"

"Half the bastards in the village claim Brian as father." Robert spoke up before Peter could answer. "He's our friend, but we know his faults after all these years."

"Hm. That sounds more as if it would be expensive than a way of making a living," Guyon pointed out. "Still, as long as he acknowledges them..." The faint feeling of unease that he had about Brian still remained with him, though, and he put it down to his generally unsettled state. *Don't take it out on someone you don't even know, de Chesnay.*

"Oh, aye, he does. And probably some that aren't his as well." Robert shrugged. "The man never did understand the idea of faithfulness." Robert paused for a long moment, "But that's all water under the bridge."

"How nice for Brian," Guyon murmured. A bubble of not-quite laughter seemed to have stuck in his throat, because sometimes, *just sometimes*, being both intelligent and the only sober person in the room was a terrible, terrible thing.

This is one time ya need ta have no doubt, Robbie.

It's not the drink talking, and I'll not deny it when I'm sober.

The man never did understand the idea of faithfulness.

He looked steadily at Robert. "But somewhat empty, for an existence's creed," he said in the same neutral tones.

"Aye, that it is," Robert agreed softly, looking down into his cup. There was another silence then, broken only by the soft sounds of Peter's gentle snoring.

"He *really* can't drink," Guyon said to Robert amusedly, and the moment that had just passed between them might never have been. "At least he just goes to sleep. Well." Honesty overtook him, along with his inappropriate sense of humor. "*Eventually*."

"There's sense in that," Robert nodded, climbing shakily to his feet. "I'm for my bed too."

"Will you be all right to get back?" Guyon enquired with genuine concern, though it was more born from a desire to *not* get Robert out of the Watch House first thing in the morning than any selfless motives.

"He's got me a bed in the officer's quarters," Robert nodded. "He knew we'd be late."

"Hm." Guyon was slightly relieved to find that he wasn't the only one being managed. "You'll forgive me if I don't get up." He looked down at the still-sleeping Peter, shaking his head. "It was a most enlightening evening, Robert. Thank you. And thank you for everything you have done."

"Don't." Robert held up a hand. "I needed to do it. Had to prove myself to him and to you. And...some things are just wrong. This man. This Corvay. He's just wrong." Robert turned then and staggered towards the door.

Guyon tilted his head back, resting it against the wall, and closed his eyes. "You have no idea," he whispered, and had no idea whether he was talking to the departed Robert, to Peter, or to himself. "You have no idea..."

*

There was a spike in his head. Or a nail at the very least. It ran from just behind his right eyeball, through his brain and out through the top of his head. He wasn't sure how he was still able to think, or live really, with such a large bit of metal skewering something so important as his brain, but somehow he appeared to be managing it.

"Guyo - ohhhhh..." Peter cringed, putting one hand on either side of his head. "Help...."

It was a pitiful and weak plea, but heartfelt in its perfect misery.

"How, reverse time and stop you drinking a bottle of alcoholic peat-water?" came the snippy reply. "Sorry, beyond my capabilities." Guyon peered at him interestedly, and apparently from an upside down position. "Good heavens."

"Oh, God. I think something is wrong with my eyes." Peter closed them, quickly. "Or someone has played a horrid trick on me and has nailed me to the ceiling."

That would certainly go a long way towards explaining the spike through his head.

Guyon snorted, but quietly, which was one good thing. "No, you have a hangover," he said with a mixture of patience and amusement. "And *I* have some of Vincennes's tea-cure."

"I don't know if that means you care about me...or hate me...but at this point I'm even willing to try something Vincennes has brewed." Peter groaned, but managed to pry his eyes open about half way, "If it kills me, you can salvage the metal and use it to pay for the funeral."

"The metal?" Guyon asked in rare, genuine bewilderment. "What metal?" He shook his head in a sort of blur of too-bright light and unfocused movement. "Never mind, spare me." He was holding out a mug.

Peter reached for it, a bit unsteadily, but managed to get it to his lips and slowly drink it down with a shudder, "Vincennes has not gotten any better since becoming a real physician."

"I could have given you David's cure instead," Guyon pointed out amicably. He sat on the end of the bed, curling his legs under him and leaning against the post.

"God no," Peter whimpered. "I'd probably not know who I was for a week."

Guyon stifled a laugh with the back of his hand. "Are you sure that isn't something you *want*?" he asked. "You could treat it as a holiday. Your cadets would treat it as a *public* holiday."

"Would you care for me in my addled condition?" Peter sighed softly, then made a face. "I don't know which is worse- the taste of Vincennes concoction, or the small badger that apparently has died in my mouth."

Guyon's expression was faintly horrified. "I'm certainly not caring for you if it *has*," he said with less tact than honesty. "What a revolting thought." He rubbed his hand over the back of his head. "Um. Water? I'd offer to make tea, but I do terrible things to it..."

"I'll make it..." Peter tried to stand, but the mere motion drove the spike just that much further into his brain. "That's it then. The cadets won't have to worry because I may never be able to stand again."

Guyon rubbed a thumb down by the side of his mouth, but not in time to stop the revealing twitch at its corner. "Your lieutenant has them studying the mathematics of trajectory. And when they have finished, they have the basic theories of Euclid's geometry. And when they have finished *that*, he is taking them out to watch the drills at the Champ de Mars. So it's you who don't have to worry, they are well in hand." He nudged Peter with a companionable foot. "Let the drugs work, then you can make enough tea to drown yourself."

Peter sighed with relief, closing his eyes. He'd obviously chosen the right man to leave in charge of his cadets, long ago before his now-skewered brain had lost all sense. "Drowning might help." He peeked one eye open and looked at Guyon, "I'm sorry. I sound rather pathetic, don't I?"

"You sound hung-over," Guyon said patiently. "I've heard worse." Considering the Sorbonne students, that was almost certainly true, and possibly an understatement. His mouth twitched again. "You *look* pathetic, though."

"Christ, then I look like dead gone three days." Peter shuddered. "Possibly with rot...and maggots."

And no, he should not have mentioned maggots because the thought of them rather made his stomach lurch.

"*No*," said Guyon with an odd emphasis, and since when was he squeamish? "No maggots. No weevils." He sighed, his half-amused, relaxed mood completely gone. "I'll get you some water."

"Gui?" Peter slowly straightened, opening his eyes completely now, although squinted a bit against the morning light coming in through the windows. "I.. I didn't do or say anything really stupid last night...did I?"

He knew how he got when he drank, but with only Robert for company and Guyon not drinking, he had felt safe to indulge. But what if he had done something indiscreet?

"Hm?" Guyon was seemingly focused on pouring the water, and his eyes were slightly anxious when he turned. "No. No, I - I don't think so." He handed Peter the water. "I don't know. You might think so. I don't know."

Peter took the water, but caught at Guyon's hand before he could move away. "Tell me. Please?"

Guyon sighed, shifting his shoulders in something that was not quite a shrug. "You told Robert," he said, his voice stiff with awkwardness. "About - about us." It obviously cost him an enormous effort even to say that much.

"Christ, I didn't bloody well give details, did I?" Peter was horrified. That was something private between the two of them, and not even his 'brother' needed to know any of that.

"*No*," Guyon said with an equally horrified expression. Then he choked on an almost laugh. "Well, not the sort I'm thinking of, or the sort I think Robbie might actually cross another ocean to avoid hearing. You were...you were very eloquent as to my importance in your life, but...not detailed."

"Oh...that's fine then." Peter's relief was immense. "I would have told him sooner or later anyway."

Although he would have chosen a time when they were both sober, and more settled back into their old camaraderie. Robbie was family, more or less, and had been a good friend to him since they were children. This was something he had never considered keeping a secret from him. He loved Guyon, and wanted his family to understand his happiness.

But Guyon - How did he feel about Peter's announcement? What if he had never planned on anyone knowing outright? He had taken things into his own hands again and blundered on without discussing it first. He had just *managed* it, like Guyon accused him of doing so often.

"Oh, God. I'm sorry..." Peter looked up with wary bloodshot eyes.

Guyon's face closed up like a trap, but not before Peter had seen hurt flash, quickly and inexplicably, across the changeable eyes. "Yes, I thought you might be, when you sobered up," he said in a softly neutral voice. "I wouldn't worry, I doubt that Robert remembers much more than you."

"I'm an idiot." Peter looked down at the glass that was still in his hand. "You might not have wanted anyone to know. I never considered that. It was wrong of me to give away a confidence that you share without talking to you about it first."

It wasn't like most of Guyon's little group of scholars didn't suspect or know outright without being told, but this was not one of Guyon's friends. He barely knew Robert and would probably not have chosen to share something so...intimate with a stranger.

"Oh." Guyon's shrug was real, this time. "No, Robert's your brother in law, you had every right..." He trailed off, and blew out a small, irritated puff of air. "You had every right," he repeated. He sounded sincere.

"No." Peter shook his head. It wasn't right. "Everything you say of me is true, Guyon. I run roughshod over what you want and I do things without thinking. Or maybe I just think I know what's best. I don't know...I just know it's wrong and -" *I don't know how much longer you'll put up with it - put up with me.* "I'm sorry."

"Oh, for -" There were white lines of temper around Guyon's mouth and eyes, all too familiar. "Peter, you choose the *absolute worst* times to apologize, and subjects where - when - of all the - how do you manage to -" He stopped again, his mouth snapping shut. "I have students," he said in a clipped voice. "And no excuse to abandon them for the day." He took a deep breath, his expression smoothing over and closing at the same time. "I'll see you when your head is less painful," he said politely, inclined his head, and left the room.

Peter stared at the door for a long moment. He'd done it again. He'd stupidly missed some point that Guyon was expecting him to see. It was not, apparently, about his drunken disclosure to Robert, but something else. Something that was like and yet very far from his apology, and had been close enough to his confession to have touched a very real nerve, not one of irritation, but of anger. Something that Guyon felt was far more important than what Robert knew of his emotions or his private life. And Peter was utterly lost as to what that could be, and distressed at the results of whatever he had done.

This was supposed to be a time for elation. Guyon's brother was safe and Corvay could no longer have any hold over him. Guyon should have been happy, or at the very least, relieved. But he wasn't. And there was some *stupidity* in Peter that was keeping him from seeing the real reason.

It was another failure.

Peter wondered if this would be his final one.

*

Paris, May 1646

Men's weakness makes Love so severe,
They give him power by their fear,
And make the shackles which they wear.
Who to another does his heart submit,
Makes his own Idol, and then worships it.

It was, all of it, beginning to be ridiculous. No one man, even Guyon, could be so busy all the time. He'd gone by the school in the morning, only to be told that Guyon was with a student and could not be interrupted. The same in the afternoon. Peter had thought to invite him to dinner, only to be told that Guyon wasn't home at all. Four days. Four days he had not been able to meet up with Guyon.

It wasn't that they never got busy, caught up in their own duties and responsibilities, but it usually was not for so long, and never before had Peter been denied admittance to Guyon's rooms, students or no students. The thought that Guyon might be avoiding him had hit about mid-way through day three, but after digging through his brain he dismissed the idea. Hadn't they just taken care of their biggest problem, when Robbie had helped Guyon's family to flee to Portugal? Corvay no longer had that hold over them and Guyon should have been relieved. Not that he would have expected gratitude, but neither had he expected this...whatever it was. No, there must be some explanation for it. Possibly just bad timing and luck. Peter stepped up to the door of the school, and raised his hand to knock.

"Well he's not -" The door was pulled open before he could hit the wood, and Ännchen blinked down at him from the top step. "Oh. Peter. Hullo."

"Good morning, Anna." Peter peered past her, trying not to look too hopeful. "Is Guyon at home?"

"Do you want the nice answer or the honest answer?" Ännchen asked tiredly, pushing her hair back into the escaping plaits.

"The honest answer, always." Peter told her then reached his hand out to her, encouraging her to take a seat on the steps. "Is he on a rant about something?" Unspoken were the words *Is he on a rant about me?*

"No," Ännchen said bluntly. "He's not talking at all. Except four days ago, to say that he's at home. To *everyone* but you. Peter..." she went a little pink, "what did you *do*? He's not *talking*. He's not sleeping, or eating, or - *anything*. And he is really, *really* angry at you."

Guyon had been avoiding him. Peter's worst fears were confirmed. And the worst part was that he had no real idea why. "I don't know, Ännchen. And I can't even try to fix it if he won't see me." Peter scowled up toward the second story window. "Do you think if I just went up anyway...I could get him to talk?"

"Um. *No.*" Ännchen went, if possible, a deeper shade of rose-pink. "He - really, Peter, *no.*"

"But how can I -?" Peter started pacing, trying to think. "He won't see me and won't tell anyone what I did. I could write him a note?" He looked hopefully over at Ännchen, but sighed when she shook her head. "Damn it! What do I do then? I can't -" He suddenly froze. "He's changed his mind, hasn't he? The big stupid Scot isn't amusing anymore...he's...God, Anna, he's what? What do I do?"

"He what?" Ännchen blinked at him. "I don't think he *ever* thought you were funny, Peter. But right now, he's so angry at you he *can't talk.* And I don't know what you did, so I don't know what you should do!"

"But..." Peter looked at her, his face puzzled and woebegone. "There must be something - I can't just leave this. Or maybe I should. Maybe he'll talk to me after he calms down some more?" Yes. After Guyon calmed down he'd see Peter. He'd tell Peter just why he was angry. And Peter would wait...wait like a patient dog. "No...it's been four days...damn him, how much time does he need?" Peter was angry now. "Don't I at least deserve to know what I did?"

"Yes," Ännchen agreed, her blue eyes unchanging in their kindness. "Of course, you do, and if I knew, I would tell you. Truly I would. But Peter...I don't know what I have to say to make you understand. *He isn't talking.* Not to me, not *about* you, not *to* Gottfried, he's not -" She sighed. "He's here, of course, but

130

he's not *here.* And all he asked is that I send you away."

Peter's shoulders slumped in defeat, "I'm sorry, Ännchen. I know you'd help if you could. But - Guyon is all there is for me. He doesn't understand that yet. But he is." Peter sighed. "And I'm afraid." *Because he doesn't feel the same and I keep waiting for him to decide I'm not worth it.*

"I know," Ännchen said, and her voice was utterly without comfort. "I'm sorry."

*

Peter made his way back to the Hôtel in record time, never knowing how quickly people had been scurrying out of his path. His hair was loose and flying behind him, his face a dark and brooding mask. But it was his eyes that had caused the most fear - fire and holocaust lurked in their depths, making even the redoubtable and normally unflappable Lt. Wycombe think twice before approaching him.

He was angry and hurt. What had he done to deserve this? Had he even done anything at all? Or was Guyon simply bored with his company now that he had been won free of Corvay's machinations?

Peter could answer none of those questions and that made him even angrier. He finally entered his office to find the decorators waiting for him.

"If Monsieur le Maréchal would just look at these samples, the -"

"Bloody hell!!" Peter bellowed. "Out! Just out! I don't care if you bloody well paint the place pink with green polka dots. Write out your suggestions, along with prices and give the lot to Lt. Wycombe. Out!"

The men scurried out and Peter slammed the door behind them.

It opened again, slowly, and Robert poked his head around the widening gap. "Polka dots?" he said curiously. "You sure that was a good thing t'say? Because they might, y'know..." he trailed off, blinking at Peter. "Are you all right?" he asked hesitantly.

"M'fine." Peter jerked his chair out from behind his desk and slouched into it. "And I've got a lot to do, Robert, so if you don't mind." He pointedly picked up a piece of parchment and began reading it.

"Ah, well, *yes*, I do mind, an' that'd be the list *you* made this morning of what everyone *else'll* be doing." Robert had perfected the tone of voice that made actually seeing him roll his eyes completely unnecessary. "I thought y'were going ta show me Paris." He sounded suddenly petulant. "Ye said ye'd cleared yer schedule."

"Things change, Robert." Peter put the paper down. "Things change."

People leave, refuse to talk to you, and the worst pain is not knowing why. *God, Guyon...*

"Charming," Robert grumbled. "What crawled into yer brain and died?" He snorted suddenly, a startled sound a bit like a frustrated horse. "Oh, I see. He's still not talking to you." He chuckled. "Has anyone ever told that man he's a rare brat?"

"*He's not!*" Peter snapped, then took a deep calming breath. "Yes, I suppose he can be but...bloody hell, Robbie. I must have done something to make him do this. I just can't figure out what." Peter's voice settled down to a pained crack. "I don't know what to do."

Robert shrugged. "Ignore him right back? Certain sure, he'll get bored if he's makin' a point, and if he's not and he really doesn't want to see you ever again, there's nothing that'll have changed." He came around the desk and put his hands on Peter's shoulder's, shaking him slightly. "It's not the end of the world, y'know. And ye don't really need someone in a permanent sulk clouding yer days."

"You don't know him well enough to talk that way about him." Peter snapped again. "Do not begin to judge what you don't know. "

Robert's eye roll was back in his voice. "Well, make up yer mind," he said. "Either ye're acceptin' that he's having some sort o' childish fit, or ye're going to keep haunting his street like some lovestruck hound. And man alive, go with the first, for it's a hell of a lot more appealing to live with!"

"I feel like a lovestruck hound." Peter ground out. "And I feel angry and hurt and - I damn well feel *everything*!"

"Um," Robert said. He was not very good with emotions that weren't either his or simplistic. Love and hate, loyalty and anger, that was Robbie, and only one of each at any given time. "At least ye're feelin'?"

Peter twisted round and stared at him incredulously. Robert shrugged. "Well, what *should* I say? Telling y'not ta worry doesn't bloody work, does it?"

"No. It doesn't." Peter said simply. "I wish it did." He gave a small tight chuckle, "You know, I never thought I'd wish that I were more like Brian, but right now, it would be damn bloody convenient."

"Ye don't think he's angry about *that*, do ya?" Robert asked suddenly. "And Christ, no y'don't, one Brian is all I can stand without committing murder as the least of it."

"No." Peter sighed. "Guyon doesn't understand about jealousy. I wish that *was* it. I could fix that."

"Eh?" Robert blinked. "How do ye mean - oh, never mind. He's quite mad, y'know." It appeared to be an attempt at consolation. "Ye'll just have to get him to talk to ya." He put up his hands defensively. "Aye, I know, what do I think ye've been trying to do and so on and so on, but you'll just have ta - try harder?"

"I have to." Peter said slowly. "Otherwise? I'll be the one who's mad."

"Right," said Robert cheerfully. "So, were ye wantin' me to sit on him or just tie him to a chair? Or I could put him in irons..." He looked thoughtful. Peter wondered how he had managed to forget that it was *Robert* who had instigated half the havoc of their years growing up.

*

Guyon was not a man who went in for self-justification. He always knew why he had chosen his courses of action, knew whether they were right or wrong in the eyes of the world and his contemporaries, knew every detail of the rationale behind them. If it was hard, or unkind, or against his principles, it was still a conscious choice, and he held to it until he was shown clearly why he should not. *Could* not had not been something that had ever entered his way of thought or system of belief.

Until now.

Guyon had known when he left Peter's rooms that morning, abandoning him to a hangover and the dubious mercies of Robert, that Peter had no idea of what he had done, no concept of the depths to which Guyon felt betrayed. And Guyon knew no other way to deal with how he felt than to leave and to stay away until Peter *did* realize, until he saw that he had taken that step back into protecting Guyon from his own life that was wholly unforgivable to someone who already had to fight Corvay's intrusion into all aspects of it, had little or no control over his soul and body in any case, and had now had the last of all events that should have been his to manage wrested from his grip.

But he was suffering, and suffering badly, decision made or not. He longed for Peter, physically and mentally, found himself reaching out as he had done when Peter was about to fight Lesueur, and kept having to stop himself. He caught himself again and again, staring at the candle or at a fire, his mind trying to escape him, his own thoughts betraying him as his yearning proved stronger than his will. He hardly dared speak, except to teach, following set patterns in familiar methods where he could be sure he would not betray himself. He deprived his body of other things it needed, of sleep and food and mental rest, hoping that the other, more immediate necessities would take precedence, and kept hoping, even when they did not.

He avoided Peter successfully, always managing to be where the English Marshal was not, setting Ännchen to tell him not to try and see him. His eyes felt strained, and wide, always looking for that flicker of movement at the end of the street, in a doorway of an inn, in the Richelieu Chapel. Because Peter, damn him, had obviously decided that thinking for himself was not an option, and was utterly determined to force a meeting. And he had Robert Macquarie's unquestioning help.

In despair at himself and at Peter, Guyon enlisted the aid of his former students at the Sorbonne, and found Voorhees, at least, willing to keep an eye out while he tried to force his brain into

134

patterns of study. Which meant leaving his rooms and going to the Pantheon - a respite he was fairly sure his pupils and Gottfried were almost pathetically grateful for.

"Hmmpf." If Voorhees had been unfailingly helpful, Charles de Barrion was, as usual showing his unmitigated disapproval of the whole matter. "It's ridiculous. Do you intend to spend the rest of your days avoiding the man? Because that's how long it will take for that idiot Scot to have even a clue of what you want from him. Whatever it is, since you have neglected to tell even us, will be as much a mystery to him as everything else." He slumped into his chair, scowling at both Guyon and Voorhees, "I won't be a party to any of this insanity, and neither should you, Rudolf. Look at him. He looks horrible and you're just encouraging him."

"I am not encooragink him to look horrible," Voorhees replied in his usual mild tones. "He does not vant to see Pieter. So I am makink sure he does not see Pieter. It is de moost interestink thing I have done in *veeks*. And it makes you study." The serene grey eyes twinkled in his bland, rather heavy face. "Iss all to the gut."

"Then your idea of good is rather skewed." And with that, de Barrion opened his book and went back to reading. Or at least he was pretending to read, Guyon had his doubts since he had been reading before his little tirade but still seemed to be aware of everything he and Rudolf had discussed.

Voorhees rolled his eyes at Guyon. "You know, in a year he vill have students."

"The academic world trembles," Guyon agreed.

De Barrion made a very Anglo-Saxon gesture at them without taking his eyes from his book.

Guyon pulled his own text toward him, pen and parchment under his hand. Yes, this would work. The calm soothing of the written word, the scratch of his pen and all would return to normal. No thoughts but those related to philosophy. No urges except for those of the mental variety - the quest for knowledge. These were the things he understood, the things that kept him sane.

Will and intellect are one and the same thing, said Spinoza.

135

Only if you're in hell, he scrawled beside the point, continuing in his own unique shorthand. *Uncnqrb. will of Stn? Spn. chll gods - Grk? Athens?*

He tapped the quill against his nose, and scowled as it itched. *Philsp as anti-rel?*

"Uh. Guyon." Voorhees tapped his arm, and he jerked, nearly oversetting his inkpot.

"Hm?"

Voorhees jerked his head at the far end of the stacks. Guyon hissed out irritated breath. "*Cagar*!"

There was Peter, talking to Lt. Wycombe, but with his eyes locked on Guyon like a starving man at a banquet. There was a faint crease of worry on his forehead and a haunted look around his eyes that said he had, most probably, not gotten much more sleep in recent days than Guyon had himself.

He finished whatever he was saying to the good Lieutenant, then directed him to another section of the library. When he had gone off, Peter hesitated for a moment, as if gathering his thoughts, or possibly his courage, then moved toward where Guyon was sitting.

"Oh God," said Guyon in panic, and bolted, abandoning notes and pen and ink and books on the table. Behind him, he heard Voorhees and de Barrion starting an argument that would delay Peter for at least two minutes -

"I *warned* you, you're a nursemaid!"

"Ant you vill never know!"

"Did you just -"

"I *did* joost -"

"Will you two *move*?"

"Oh, hallo, Pieter."

Guyon stifled a grin, and climbed out of the window. He edged along until he came to the guttering, then swung his legs enough to gain his balance, and jumped into the gardens

His landing was soft and he did avoid smashing any of the plants, but he had only managed to gain a few yards when he heard Peter's voice behind him, from the window.

"Damn you, Guyon." The words weren't loud, but they carried to him over the sound of his own footsteps on the grassy ground. "I don't know what you want from me."

"Pieter, he does not vant to see you joost yet."

"Yes, so it would appear." And then the window was shut with a very firm and final sounding click.

I want you to stop doing this to me, he thought, and then the pain caught him, sudden and unexpected and *savage*, enough that he could almost believe it were real and not some phantom product of his tormented imagination. It took his breath out of his lungs, and closed over his throat. For a moment of blank terror, he thought perhaps his heart had stopped, before it beat again, hard and foundering.

But he did not stop, and he did not turn around, or go back to the Pantheon to retrieve his notes, even though Peter would have long gone by the evening. He retreated to his rooms, bolting the doors, and staring at the strange and rather ugly vase-like thing that Peter had presented to him when he moved into the van Hesselinks' new house.

Indian rubies and the gold of Samarkand...

"I won't," he said, and was unsure of what he was denying, only that he had to. "I won't." His head throbbed, and he rubbed his hands over the strong bones of his forehead and jaw, trying to ease the tension. "I won't."

He ignored the other, frightened voice inside his mind, the one that beat like trapped birds, fluttering, frantic wings against his consciousness.

I can't, I can't, I can't...

He spent the night not thinking of the look on Peter's face, or the tone in his voice. And he went down to face his morning pupils with a savagery that even took Gottfried by surprise, while all the time the voice beat against the glass of his surface thoughts. *I can't. I can't. I can't.*

*

It had been ten days since Peter had last seen Guyon. Ten days since he had awoken with a hangover and said something that caused Guyon to leave. It had been six days since an apologetic Ännchen had finally told Peter that, yes, Guyon was in

137

fact avoiding him and would not see him. It had been four days since he finally believed it to be true - when Guyon had actually climbed out of the window of the Pantheon rather than speak to him.

If Peter's cadets had once been tolerant of his occasional fits of ill temper, they were now avoiding his presence whenever possible. The main courtyard, normally a bustling gathering spot for those on or off duty, was almost deserted. The only souls who had consigned themselves to the possible vagaries of Peter's temper were those who were already on punishment details or being given remedial drill practice. The large foyer below Peter's rooms were also surprisingly empty of activity, Lt. Wycombe having deigned that, discretion being the better part of valor, the cadets needed the experience of being on bivouac *now, right now, lads, move your stumps.*

This, having removed one of Peter's main means of working out his bad temper, left him rather at odd ends, growling internally and frustrated. He was eating only when Robert bullied him into it, and drove himself, physically, to the point of exhaustion each day, falling into his bed for only an hour or two of fitful sleep, only to arise and start the cycle all over again.

He was no longer attempting to see Guyon, no longer making trips to the Shoe or the Pantheon, nor appearing on the street near Gottfried's school. Instead he rode out every morning on his great brown horse, tearing through the Sorbonne meadow as if demons were on his trail then returning to stalk off to the fencing school to lose himself in the mindless forms of the Destreza for hour after hour.

It was only there that he appeared to find any comfort, blanking his mind to fall into the patterns and movements of that much vaunted discipline. Improving and honing his skills, and allowing his troubled spirit to gain some rest.

He was finding that invisible line between skill and simply existing in the moment - becoming the weapon instead of using it. It was getting easier for him all the time, and he was finding he craved that blank feeling as surcease from the pain that otherwise haunted him. It wasn't a numbness, as much at it was an ascendancy, giving him a power over something that he could not find otherwise.

He understood, now, the point of Marcelli's constant *again*. It wasn't - or at least, wasn't any more - because it hadn't been right the first time. It was because it had to go beyond *getting it right*, beyond thought, become as involuntary a response as breathing, not only natural but integral.

The line that is the centre.

The paradox of the circle's philosophy.

"Again," said Marcelli, coming up under Peter's guard. Peter wondered, briefly, *how* Marcelli was always this self-possessed. But then - sometimes it was him under *Marcelli's* guard, and still the same instructions.

Hours of it. And more hours of it, until Peter wondered that their blades were not worn to paper thinness, from the clash and scrape. But it didn't matter, in the short term at least. It was again, and again, and again, until all thoughts were driven away. No pain except the ache of overworked muscles, and nothing to think of except *now* and *this* and *again.*

"Aren't you bored?" he asked Robert, who seemed to have appointed himself an unofficial shadow to Peter's every move. They were walking to the school, Robert still eating breakfast as they went, and Peter tried very hard not to think about the way Guyon always forgot food was necessary, and still always stole apples if you gave him a second's chance, as though, never truly having been a schoolboy, there was a small part of him that would never lose its delight in being one.

"No," Robert, oblivious to the sorrowful track his thoughts had taken once again, said with his mouth full. It came out more as a negatory splutter, rather akin to *Nsshf*. He swallowed. "Ver' inshruc'ive."

"Really, Robert, this isn't at all necessary." Peter stopped just outside the doors to the school. "I'm going to survive this. I always knew...I mean I was always aware that this could happen. Because he...never felt the way that I did. Not the way he felt for François. And now - I'll be fine. Really. You should go back home."

Robert snorted. It came out in a spray of crumbs. When he had finished coughing, he said, "Because I really want to use all this new knowledge on my *wife*? Jesu, Peter!" Rolling his eyes, he went in through the doors, letting them swing back in Peter's face as he made his way to the viewing gallery.

God save me from family. Peter shook his head then turned to walk out onto the exercise floor and began limbering up muscles that still seemed to be tight from the previous day's lessons.

Marcelli was talking to someone Peter could not see, in the corridor that led from the far side of the room to the private areas. Whoever it was had obviously merited time and courtesy, if not complete attention, for Marcelli caught Peter's eye, mid-sentence, and nodded at him. He turned back to his invisible visitor and said something quickly, then, in his own dialect of Italian, the words too quiet for Peter to pick up anything but the tone of wry amusement, and shrugged at whatever the response was, shaking his head with a half-laugh. Then he inclined his head in farewell, and came back across to Peter.

"You might like to sleep," he said, and the look of almost-exasperated humor was still in his eyes. "It is astounding to me how much easier the body feels after *rest*."

"Yes, I would imagine that's true." Peter did not bother to say that sleep seemed to have deserted him when Guyon had. He simply continued stretching out his tense muscles.

It seemed to be everyone's day for rolling their eyes at him. "Of course it is," Marcelli said, and chuckled. "I never lie."

Peter gave a final stretch, causing several of his vertebrae to pop, then moved to retrieve his sword. "Where do we begin today?"

Marcelli's eyes crinkled in his rare, silent laughter. "Where we always begin," he said, and Peter groaned, saying with him, "*Again.*"

*

Robert sat and watched Peter from the viewing gallery as he began his daily torment. There were times when *he* would have gladly smacked Master Marcelli with the remains of his breakfast if he heard *again* one more time. He, quite frankly, did not understand how Peter bore it.

Of course, Robert was no soldier and never claimed to be, but he saw little difference between the first time Peter performed a form and the thirtieth time. It was almost maddening. However, he had to admit that Peter now seemed to be the one with more *points* by the end of each session, so he must be improving.

He yawned, and stretched, turning his head from side to side as he tried to get the cramps out of his shoulders. The bed in the room at the hôtel was stuffed with horsehair, which made him sneeze and compressed his head down into his back with unfailing regularity. Along with Peter's foul mood, which, while he might be kind enough to make allowances for due to its very real source of unhappiness, was nonetheless a strain to live with, it was proving to be a severe deterrent to his usual accepting outlook on life.

He leaned forward on the rail, resting his head on his hands, and tried again to get the kink out of the right side of his neck, twisting his head round as far as he could, and craning backwards toward the shadows of the doorway.

The strange eyes that met his as he did so, wide and startled, could only belong to one man.

Guyon. Robert gave a small quiet bark of a laugh. So, the odd little Occitan had not left Peter as completely as he wanted it to be believed. *Unless he was here for some other reason.* Robert frowned and considered that but could not come up with one other reason for the man's presence. He was here to see Peter, but did not want Peter to know it.

Well, to Hell with that. Robert got up slowly and made his way to where Guyon was, yes, lurking was the only word for it.

"*Spy,*" he said quietly. The other man did not move for a moment. Then he sighed, and turned to look fully at Robert.

"Yes," he agreed in English, and there was a terrible bleakness in his voice. "I 'aunt shadows. Like an assassin." The black eyebrows raised. "You probably think I am comparable, hm?"

Robert took a good long look at Guyon. He had lost weight in the days since their drunken night, and looked like he had slept even less than Peter. His hair, which had always been clean and shiny if not always tidy, was now lackluster and dirty looking. He also seemed to have lost that energy that he'd had on their first meeting, looking somehow diminished as a whole. For once, it was evident that he was a small, spare man, with little physical presence to him. *I never knew an always-working mind could do so much for someone,* Robert thought, unwanted understanding, as so often these days, assailing him.

"No." Robert responded, hoping none of those thoughts had shown on his face, and shook his head. "I thought so at first, but now, I think yer hurtin' yerself as much as Peter. I don't know why ya'd want to do either. Seems pretty stupid for someone as intelligent as Peter claims you are."

"No." Guyon smiled wryly. "You don't know an' *he* don't know. Per'aps it *is* stupid." He sighed. "We cannot talk 'ere. *Here.*" The correction made him smile painfully, and the next words left him more smoothly. "He will know I am watching if I keep speaking."

"He doesn't seem to notice much of anything once they begin," Robert glanced back at where Peter and Master Marcelli were clashing on the exercise floor. "No, perhaps yer right. Where do we go?"

Guyon shrugged. "Faubourg Gardens," he said, and Robert wondered how two people who looked so unalike could look so very similar, as Guyon's eyes went almost black with a pain that seemed, impossibly, physical. It was the same look that kept crossing Peter's face. *Can't mention anything, I swear. Faubourg Gardens, apples, books, wish someone a good bloody morning, put a log on the fire and Peter snaps your head off and none of us the wiser as to why...*"Perhaps they will have a dancing bear."

I do not *want to know.* "Fine by me," Robert said out loud, retaining his deliberate cheerfulness with some effort.

They walked out of the fencing school, enough people calling out greetings to Guyon that it became clear his presence here was as frequent as Peter's. Robert grinned.

"Now what," Guyon said exasperatedly, "could *possibly* be funny?"

"Both of you." Robert gave a sharp bark of a laugh. "No, don't scowl at me, I'll not laugh again. How far do we go?"

"Oh, it's...quarter of an hour. At most." Guyon pointed.

"Left." They walked in silence for a few minutes and then he said, "I will not go back on this, you know."

"Oh, of course not, " Robert said amiably. "Yer just as bloody stubborn as he is."

"Yes." A faint, flickering smile was his reward for that. "*Worse*," Guyon said then, and the amusement was gone from his face, leaving it hard and angry. For the first time, Robert understood what everyone had been trying to tell Peter.

He's really, really angry with you.

Yes, he was. And the amount of pain he was *also* in didn't change that for a second.

Robert, wisely, kept his own counsel after that realization until they got to the Faubourg.

"So...no dancing bears and no chance o' Peter overhearing us." Robert said by way of an opening remark. It wasn't very witty, he knew, but wit was not his strongest point.

"No," Guyon said. He looked desperately uncertain, and Robert was very conscious of the thing everyone seemed to be aware of but Peter himself, that Guyon did not like or trust almost anyone *but* Peter, which made conversation with him at the best of times like ice-skating, and was more like taking a walk by a crevasse, right then. "Robert...my brother. Was he - was he well?"

"He seemed ta be." Robert nodded. "A bit frustrated with that damned uncle of yours, but very happy with his new wife. She's a pretty little thing, all dark curls and big eyes. Seems to be fair bright as well."

"Spanish." Guyon chewed on his lip for a moment. "I didn't know. That he had got married. I think - I think I would have *liked* to know."

So that was it. Robert caught his breath in surprise. Not only, it appeared, was he an idiot - which he had long ago accepted with a fair amount of cheerful resignation - but so was Peter. All this effort to patch up a brotherhood, and they had managed to completely ignore the fact that they were dealing with *someone else's* in order to do so.

"Brothers can be a good thing ta have," Robert ventured. "Mistakes can be made, all 'round. You argue. Sometimes even raise yer fists to one another, but none 'o that matters really, does it?"

He wanted to make a point here, really, but wasn't sure how to get it across. "Peter 's a year younger than me, you know? But no matter what I've done, he's always been there when I've needed him. That's why this...mess with Cromwell, hit us both sa hard. Was my fault and I didn't listen ta him. For the first time ever, I didn't listen. I broke it and didn't know how ta fix it ya see? Because Peter's always been there ta fix things for me...and now he wasn't."

"*Yes,*" Guyon said fervently. "But Robert - *he is not my brother.* I *have* a brother. Who breaks things. I break things. But he is always my brother. I do not *need* Peter to fix things. Not like that. I need -" He stopped, shaking his head.

"I can understand that," Robert nodded slowly. "But just the same, you've got ta understand Peter. Taking care of people is what he does. Me, Sarah, all the people at Hawthornden and the village and now her Majesty.....and you. And *we've* all let him, because, well, he's that good at it. It's probably not been fair ta Peter a lot of times, but he's never complained about it, because he loves us."

"You will forgive me," Guyon said in a small tight voice, "if that piece of information does not surprise me in the slightest. Well, Peter is about to get a dose of being fair. Because I *will not let him.* He is always saying we are equals." He looked grimly out across the gardens. "He needs to remember that. He needs to *learn* that. The day I need taking care of by virtue of Peter Scudamore's love -" He shook his head. "That sort of obligation - Robert, I know very little of such things, but I do know that without understanding, without even the *attempt* to understand the one you try and fulfill this self-imposed obligation to - it is not love. And it would be - it would be better that I never spoke to him again - better that I should lose my right hand, better I cut it from my wrist *myself* - than that I bore the sin of allowing him to keep thinking it is."

Robert sighed. Obviously he'd cocked this up, hadn't explained it properly. "It's not an obligation ta Peter. I don't think he's ever thought of it that way. It's just...a part of him." He sighed, trying to order his thoughts into a pattern this intensely

144

intelligent and oddly foolish man could understand. "Look, de Chesnay, Peter only thinks he's good at one thing in life, and that's being a soldier. And soldiers, more or less, take care of people. So, ya need ta see that it's going ta take more than you having a temper tantrum for Peter to drop years of training. He'll try, for you, but it's going to be a long hard road. If ya care about him at all, you'll work with him and not set him ta founder on his own."

"Ah," said Guyon, and just like that, he was utterly unreachable once again, a being so alien to all Robert knew he might as well have come from the backside of the moon. "But perhaps you did not hear. Only a monster would do that. And *that*, Macquarie, is precisely what I am." He bowed. "Thank you for your company."

Robert made no attempt to stop him from leaving. He watched the small figure cross the Faubourg Gardens, and sighed. *Perry, next time? Just adopt a viper.*

But he had learned something. Guyon de Chesnay was a long, long way from invulnerable. And if he was reduced to trying to horrify Robert...

Robert grinned. "Ya know," he said cheerfully to a passing man with his head in a book, "why they call the Scots bloody-minded?"

The man looked like he had several damn good ideas, all of which he would very much like to share with Robert, but he shook his head.

"We know that giving up is *really stupid*," Robert said, and went on his way, back to the fencing school. *And what sort of brother would I be if I let mine start ta do so now?*

*

In spite of the sure knowledge that he was a good doctor, and his driving confidence that bore him along with that fact, there were still only a few things in the world that Pierre Vincennes was positive about. One, that although he would never touch Ibn Ibrahim's skill as a surgeon, he was probably far better than him as a doctor of general medicine, if only for his much better bedside manner. Two, that if it had not been for the help of Guyon de Chesnay he would never have managed to present his dissertation and get his degree. And three, that Peter Scudamore, in spite of their frequent disagreements and the one time that he had been accused, unjustly it should be said, of coming between he and his beloved, actually did like him.

Therefore he had been a bit surprised, when walking calmly across the Sorbonne meadow that morning, to be knocked off his feet by a huge brown stallion ridden by that same Peter Scudamore. Even more surprised when other than a quick backwards glace to ascertain that he lived, Peter had ridden off without a word. It was enough to make him wonder if Peter's eyesight were going or if he, somehow, had acquired a twin and an evil twin at that.

It was with no small sense of righteous indignation then, that he turned into the Rue des Esclangons and approached the school operated by Gottfried van Hesselink and that very same Guyon de Chesnay. Sensibly, he wondered if somehow Peter had allowed that former unjust accusation to resurface and had actually been attempting to injure him on purpose. He mulled that over in his brain, as he knocked on the door and then was led up to the third floor study which was Guyon's private tutoring room.

"I have a terrible sense of deja vu," Guyon said without turning round from where he was bent over his desk, his back to the door. "Vincennes, I can recognize your peculiar form of hovering at twenty paces, and I am completely at a loss as to what on *earth* you want."

"Well, whatever it is, I refuse to stand here and address it to your backside." Vincennes muttered. "Good day to you, Guyon. And isn't it a nice one?"

Really, he hadn't had much time to see any of his friends from the Sorbonne lately, but that was no reason to treat him badly, was it?

"No," Guyon said briefly. It sounded like general negation of the sort that would have had Vincennes fleeing, had he still been Guyon's student, but since he also turned around as he spoke, Vincennes held his ground. "There," he said. "I'm facing you. What?"

Vincennes froze. *Good God*, what was going on around here. First Peter racing over the meadow as if the Devil were keeping him hard pressed and now Guyon who looked...looked..."You look like Death. Death on toast. When is the last time you slept?"

He stepped forward and raised one hand to Guyon's cheek, peering into his eyes. "Or ate for that matter?"

The familiar, blunt-fingered hand grasped his arm, and forced his hand back down to his side with a bruising pressure that made him give a little cry of pain. "Vincennes, you were an extremely good student, I am reasonably fond of you, and if you ever touch me again without my permission I will break your arms," Guyon said in an utterly inflectionless voice. His eyes were almost completely translucent in the afternoon light. "And the answers to your questions are I have no idea and I do not care."

"Damn it, Guyon," Vincennes shook his arm, which he was certain, would be sporting a lovely multi-hued bruise the next day. "I haven't seen you look like this since right after -" *François died*. "- after the last time you went Watch baiting. You haven't begun that again, have you? Really, no wonder Peter looked so angry."

"No, I haven't," Guyon said acidly. "And Peter's angry? *Peter's* angry?" There was a hint of real disbelieving astonishment in his voice. "*Good*." The last word was spat out with some venom. "Perhaps it will make him *think*." He stepped back. "Now, what are you here for?"

"This, apparently," Vincennes felt somewhat confused. Guyon was glad that Peter was angry? That was, *damn*, unthinkable. "The man practically ran me down in the University meadow. He was riding like a maniac and you need to get him to stop before he actually does hurt some innocent person or that beast throws him off and breaks his neck."

Guyon snorted. "Both of which are as likely as you suddenly sprouting wings," he said disbelievingly. "Wait, you came to tell me you don't approve of Peter's riding patterns? What exactly do you expect I can do about *that*?" He turned back to his desk dismissively, but not quickly enough to hide the sudden flash of fear in his eyes.

"Oh, well, excuse me for thinking that you might have some

stock in keeping alive the person that you almost single-handedly brought back from death's door," Vincennes shrugged. This was so very, very wrong. Guyon should have been more overtly worried over Peter, he always was. No, most people would not have seen it, but those who knew the Occitan knew that his acerbic demeanor hid the fact that he cared and cared for Peter most of all.

"Vincennes," Guyon said sweetly, "I have an idea. It's a marvelous idea, so don't interrupt. *Get out!*" He swung around, his eyes blazing with rage that even Vincennes knew was unfeigned. "And don't *ever* presume to think about what I should be feeling again! It's none of your damned business and it never was - even if I were forty fathoms deep in love with Peter, even if I was breaking my heart for it, *even if I were going to my death for it*, it is nothing, *nothing* to do with you! Now *get out of my rooms!*"

"Fine, yes, none of my business," Vincennes held up his hands, as if to ward off Guyon's anger. "If even simple friendship could mean so little to you, there is nothing more for me to say...*to you.*"

Vincennes turned, taking his discretion and his valor and making a hasty retreat to the lower floor, to see if Ännchen could tell him *what the hell* was going on.

Behind him, something smashed against the door, and he picked up his pace.

"You know," Gottfried said from the door to the teaching room, as Vincennes arrived somewhat breathlessly at the foot of the stairs, "most people with any sense listen to him the first time."

"Never claimed to have any sense," Vincennes shrugged. "Especially when it comes to friends acting like idiots."

"*Hah!*" Gottfried's choked-off laugh was the most welcomingly familiar sound Vincennes had heard in what felt like weeks. "That's true enough, you don't. So what brought you to beard the lion in his den, my friend?"

"A very intimate encounter with Peter," Vincennes related what had happened in the meadow. "If you think Guyon looks demon-ridden, you should see him."

"I think Guyon looks like a spoilt brat who's refusing to go to bed," Gottfried said wryly, "but I'm in a minority in this house. Me, I'd like to string him up for how he treats Peter."

"But what happened?" Vincennes was truly at a loss. "The last time I saw them they were very much...well...together and happy. Or at least it looked like it."

"You think I'm suicidal?" Gottfried demanded. "I haven't *asked*! Besides, you're wrong. How can they have been happy when only one of them is capable of any sort of real affection? If you ask me, Guyon's just finally doing the right thing."

"Hmmpf." Vincennes shook his head. "Somehow, I doubt Peter is feeling the same way."

*

When Peter received his summons from Corvay, his first thought was, *Now we can tell him to go hang.* It was followed with his second thought and a stabbing pain, *There is no longer a 'we'.* He should not have been surprised that this happened, hadn't he been half-way expecting it? Always? But the pain was still there, awake or asleep, although mostly awake because he appeared to have given up sleep for the present.

This is no good, Scudamore. You need sleep and your wits if you must deal with Corvay.

So he had tried for some sleep. Had dismissed his secretary and gone to his rooms for two hours and actually had managed to finally fall into a rough and restless sleep. It had left him grumpy feeling and groggy, and the coffee he had demanded now sat in his stomach like acid.

All in all, as he made his final turn into the Rue Ferou, he did not feel at all improved.

Guyon was already waiting in the shade of the house farther along from Corvay's, glaring up at the shuttered windows as though mere force of will could set it ablaze, his narrowed eyes focused on something that probably was not even there for other people to see. He looked very close to how Peter felt, the shadows beneath his slitted eyes suggesting that even two hours broken and unhappy sleep were a damn sight more than he had been getting. As Peter approached, he became, if possible, even more tightly-wound in his stance.

"Peter." The usually smooth voice was rasping and hard.

Even rough, the sound of it wrapped around Peter's heart, making it beat more strongly than it had in weeks. It took all the strength that he had not to break the distance they were carefully keeping between them and simply lay his head on Guyon's shoulder begging him, somehow, for forgiveness. Forgiveness for this...whatever it was...that was keeping them apart.

"Guyon," Peter nodded, briefly turning toward the house and staring at it - anything to avoid those pale eyes.

Ironic really, that it was Corvay that had brought them together at last, when nothing Peter could do had made any difference.

"You're ready for this?" Guyon asked in his deep, soft voice, utterly familiar and yet completely alien in its impersonal smoothness. Peter could feel that attention turned on him, now, hotter and stronger than the reflecting sun, making his skin prickle with its intensity.

"I had better be," Peter said tersely. What choice did they have really? They'd go in, tell Corvay that they were having nothing more to do with him and that there was nothing more he held over them, then walk away...from Corvay and each other. "We...we need to be united here, Guyon." Somehow, one last time, if that was what was to be.

"I know." Guyon shrugged one shoulder up, a restless, protective movement that half-hid his face. He sighed. "This should have been a pleasure. Instead -" He shook his head. "Just one more task. Maybe that's better."

Peter drew in a slow ragged breath, "It probably is. Then you can...go back to being a tutor. You're so very good at it, you know?" Peter stumbled over his words. "And.. And I'll continue to try to find more evidence against him. I won't leave you out, though. I'll keep you informed."

He owed him that much. He owed François that much.

"If you think," Guyon said quickly and furiously, "that I have so far forgotten *myself* as to even consider leaving you to *ever* deal with this snake alone, you truly don't know a single thing about me. Christ, Peter! I wouldn't do that to my worst enemy, if I had another one than Corvay!"

"I -" Peter stopped, not sure what to say. "I assumed you'd think yourself well out of the whole thing. Done with him...done with me...and -"

Peter could not stop the next words from pouring out, "I don't know what I did. I probably never will...but I'm sorry for whatever it was. I know that doesn't mean much and I don't expect it to change your mind but - I just wanted you to know...before..." He waved his hand vaguely at Corvay's house.

"I know," Guyon said quietly. When Peter glanced over at him, wondering if this meant some slight thaw in Guyon's unyielding attitude, he was greeted with a small, sad smile. "Unfortunately, that's the problem." As Peter stared at him, thinking *Well, that made even less sense than I was expecting*, and wondering what he was missing all the time, Guyon drew a deep breath, and closed his eyes briefly, before straightening with a shake of his head. "Come on," he said. "Time to make a wolfskin rug."

"Indeed," Peter agreed, giving the first real smile he'd actually had in weeks. Behind it though, there was some small worry. Even if they put up a united front, Corvay had to know that it wasn't true. Peter had every faith that the Spy Master knew of their disaffection and would, somehow, use it against them.

"He can't," Guyon said, almost absently, his uncanny ability to answer what Peter was thinking rather than what surface words he chose to put to it, coming to the fore. "Whatever new leverage he may have, it isn't about *us*. He's completely lacking in personal perception, had you noticed? Information and manipulation, yes, but understanding? No."

"He's going to take one look at us and know something's not right, Gui." Peter had to point out. "We both look a bit...trampled on." It wouldn't take much perception at all to figure that out.

"And there was I, thinking my appearance was perfection itself," Guyon said with a flicker of amusement. "Bah. There are a thousand explanations, and all of them good. You'll see, he may make some comment, but he won't *care* why."

Peter gave a nod of agreement as they approached the door

and knocked. No, Corvay would not care why. Guyon was right, as usual. He spared a moment to wonder what he was going to do without that steady sense to ground him. He wanted so much to say something, anything, that would make this all right between them, but he had no idea what it would be, and luckily, the door opening kept him from saying something completely stupid.

"And you opened the door *yourself*," Guyon said to Corvay as soon as he realized who was there. "My heavens, the honor..."

"No honor intended, of course," Corvay said dryly. "Well, none except to the servant that now does not have to gaze upon such a sight. What have you two been up to? Some kind of contest to see who can look most like Death?"

"I'm touched," Peter smirked, "you noticed. Aren't you touched, Guyon?"

"Deeply," Guyon said, and the corner of his mouth quirked downwards in an involuntary little inverted smile. "To the core. Or the quick. Or the heart. Possibly the stomach, all this worry for our well-being is almost nauseating."

"And here I was thinking it was merely the stench of Corvay that was turning my stomach," Peter continued lightly. Baiting the wolf was probably not a very smart idea, but somehow he could not resist.

Corvay merely frowned and turned back toward the inside of the house without another word, apparently expecting them to follow.

Guyon slanted a delighted little look of pure glee at Peter, and murmured, "You know, if we stayed here, we could probably make him start chewing the carpet with frustration..." He raised an eyebrow, looking hopeful, and then sighed. "No, I suppose not. Ah well." He went after Corvay, humming under his breath.

Peter trailed after him, not bothering to close the front door behind him. He, after all, was no longer Corvay's servant. The act might have been petty but it was no less satisfying for all of that

They were led into Corvay's office. Led in and left to stand like recalcitrant school boys, while Corvay took a seat behind his desk. Peter knew that this was meant to be a disconcerting position, but, long used to standing just so before her Majesty it no longer had the power it once might have.

152

Guyon, who had obviously decided that today was the day to take out his horrific mood on someone other than Peter, sat himself on the desk corner, swinging one leg backwards and forwards so that his battered boot hit the polished, ornate leg of the desk rhythmically, steadily, and with a nerve-jangling precision. "You wanted to see us?" The rest of the sentence was as clear as if he had spoken it. *You must be out of your mind.*

"You think you're free of me, don't you?" Corvay cut right to the heart of the matter. "Yes, I know you think you're clever, getting that idiotic Scot to scurry your brother away."

His voice wasn't even slightly annoyed, a fact that immediately sent alarums screaming into Peter's head. Why wasn't he annoyed? Had he, somehow, stopped Giraud's escape? Did he have Robert now? *No,* he had seen Robert when he left the Hôtel - had grumbled a greeting to him even. It had to be something though."

"Now that's not very flattering," Guyon said amusedly. "Giraud *never* scurries. He stomps, he stamps, he occasionally, much though I hate to say this of my own brother, *flounces*, but scurry?" He paused, apparently considering. "No. No, I've never known him scurry." To anyone else, and hopefully to Corvay, he would have seemed as unconcerned as when he entered, but there was a fine, almost undetectable tension in the light voice now, a faint wariness in his eyes.

"It doesn't matter really," Corvay picked up his letter opener, gesturing with the sharp, rather deadly looking implement as he continued. "It is of no great concern where your brother or his little heiress have gone. Spain, Greece...or Portugal..."

"Norway, I should think," Guyon said absently. "They link so well with the Scots, you know, all those years of alliances...oh, wait, was that Denmark? I can never remember." He yawned. "What did you *want*, Corvay? We're busy. My students are busy. Peter's cadets are busy. We *do* have things to accomplish other than waiting for some pearl of wisdom to escape you, you know..."

"As I was saying..." Corvay shot both Peter and Guyon a silencing look, "...it is the Languedoc that concerns me, not your brother's whereabouts. There are obviously other's there that share his sympathies and must be rooted out. A few troops, I think...some *pointed* questioning of the locals...."

"That's nice," Guyon said sweetly. "Who were you planning on having do that?"

"Come, now," said Corvay. He smiled, the old, sharp, unpleasant expression that Guyon had once confessed always made him want to carve off the man's face slowly. "Who else but the brother of the Marqués?"

Peter blinked. He wanted Guyon to go back home? Back to that place where -? "I'll go, Corvay. You'll need someone more official to vouch for the information, especially if you want troops to be deployed there."

"But they won't trust you, Marshal," Corvay pointed out. "Are you so eager to repeat your experience in Toulouse?"

Peter, somehow, managed not to flinch at the words, "They don't have to trust me, Corvay. The only ones that have to trust me are my contacts. I do have a few of those too, you know? Since I *am* the Marshal."

He didn't really have any in the Languedoc, but Corvay did not necessarily know that, and it should not be too difficult for him to redirect a few to that area in any case.

"You'd let him go alone?" Corvay turned back to Guyon. "You disappoint me. I had such hopes that your friendship, at least, was real."

"And absolutely none of your business," Guyon said. "No. If someone is to destroy the Languedoc, then -" his mouth twisted. "Ah, why not. I owe God a death, why not my country's?"

Peter looked sharply at Guyon but did not comment. He fully intended to convince Guyon that his presence was unnecessary, but he'd not do it here, not in front of Corvay. "There. All taken care of, then? You have your 'brother of the Marqués' and someone official, and you'll have your answers no matter that this is probably all something you've made up in your mind as some kind of odd revenge. You waste time, Corvay...I'd thought better of your intellect."

And that speech proves I can lie with a straight face.

He gave a nod to Guyon and began to turn toward the door.

"Dear, dear," he heard Guyon say lightly. "You can't even

impress soldiers these days. Poor Corvay. How sad to feel your powers wane. How sad to begin your decrepitude so early." There was a faint thump as Guyon's feet hit the ground, and then - "I'll bid you good day, *spy master.*" Somehow, it sounded like the worst obscenity imaginable.

"And good day to you, *little scholar.*"

Peter froze there. Hearing the endearment that François had so often used, on Corvay's lips almost driving him to a reaction he knew he would regret.

It's not time, Scudamore. Not yet.

Guyon was moving past him almost before Corvay had finished speaking, his jaw clenched so tightly that Peter could see the small muscles standing out in sharp relief as he walked by at speed.

Peter followed quickly, through the house and out the front door, which he pointedly left open behind them. He caught up with Guyon as he reached the street.

"I'm sorry, Gui. I'd keep him from you if I could." Peter's voice was soft and hesitant. "He has no right to those words." *I have no right to them either.*

"He has no right to the Languedoc, and no right to threaten you, either," Guyon said wearily. "However, somehow he manages all these things despite his total lack of rights, proving yet again that Virgil and Horace talked complete rubbish about fortune." He sighed. "I'm going back to the school. Life does, alas, go on..."

"It does," Peter agreed with a small sad smile. *It goes on and on and on, broken heart or not.* "I'll see you then...soon." He hated how his voice sounded, needy and small. "To plan for the trip, of course." That was a bit better, stronger. "And...in spite of what Corvay says, if you don't wish to go, I'm sure I can manage alone." *I don't want to, but I will.* He owed it to Guyon to spare him that pain, at least. He wouldn't make him return to those memories.

Guyon gave him a long look, and shook his head. "No," he said quietly. "Some things even I -" He broke off, biting his lip. "I'll see you soon," he agreed quietly, sketched an odd little salute, touching the tips of his fingers to his forehead, bowed, and turned to make his way back to the house on the Rue des Esclangons.

Peter watched him go, holding him with his eyes until the last moment when he turned the corner. Then he snapped his eyes shut, not wanting the possible bad luck of watching someone out of sight. He'd had enough of that kind of luck to last him a lifetime, even without tempting fate.

He turned then, going back toward the hôtel, wending his way past a group of street musicians and the inevitable vegetable carts.

At least Guyon had spoken to him, briefly but not unkindly. He tried to keep down the spark of hope it gave him, but it threatened to flare into flame with even the slightest bit of fuel. There had to be something he could do...some little something to show that he still cared, no matter what their misunderstandings were.

*

Corvay's plans for the Languedoc, and his fury at Giraud's removal from his manipulations, should have been the topmost concern in Guyon's mind, but instead they were pushed into the background by the simple factor of his having been put in the position of working with Peter again - and the simple ease with which he had done so. It had been easy for him to forget, in his determined holding on to what he knew was justified resentment and even more justified anger at Peter's continuing failure to understand it, that they worked well together - had *always* worked well together, from the first time Peter had brought him a code snatched from an English spy, and expected him to be unable to translate it.

As soon as Corvay had started speaking, all other considerations had been set aside. Whatever Peter had been enduring - and forcing others to endure - in order to try and deal with Guyon's continuing refusal to see or speak to him had become irrelevant, their ability to merge their differing abilities *to the same purpose* seemingly stronger than anything else. In one quick look, everything pertaining to Corvay's new bargain had been exchanged, leaving them free to listen and pretend agreement.

I won't betray the Languedoc for him.
I'll help you stop him.

Guyon sat at his paper-covered desk, and sighed, putting his head in his hands. He could no more withstand Peter in person than the Rock of Gibraltar could avoid being in the sea, and he was, for the first time, feeling a fair amount of guilt added to his continuing painful decision.

Peter had looked *appalling*, as bad as he had been feeling for the last two weeks, and he knew that the stories people had gone to great lengths to ensure he had heard - of the bullied cadets, Peter's unusual behavior with Robert, the brawls and the insane rides, stemmed from his own anger, his own refusal to give way until Peter *saw* what he had done.

"Aşkin Cemal Olsun," he whispered to his hands, and felt ludicrously close to tears of pure despair. "I *can't tell you,* Pèire."

This miserable contemplation was brought up short by a hesitant knock on his door, *thank God and all his angels*, and the sound of Ännchen's voice, "Guyon?"

He ran his shirt sleeve over his face, and looked up, "Come in."

Ännchen's face was all dimples as she peeped round the door. "You have *got*," she said, ignoring both his obviously unhappy state, as she always did, praise her sense, and the fact that his room was getting perfectly uninhabitable, "to come and see this. Or listen." She giggled.

Guyon stared at her. "Huh?" he managed coherently.

"There's a viol," Ännchen said, and spluttered on laughter. "Among other things. In the garden."

A viol in the garden. Guyon knew his face must reflect his puzzlement. Either that was what Ännchen had just said, or his hearing was going. Or quite possibly he was hallucinating due to lack of sleep and food. But in any case he allowed her to draw him behind her to go and look.

There was, indeed, a viol in the garden. It was accompanied by a viol *player*, a lutenist, an oboe player, and an instrument-free individual who waved up at Guyon and Ännchen when they leant out of the window.

He then turned back to the assemblage and, raising a hand,

directed them to begin playing. They began softly, with some kind of hushed introductive piece.

"Who do you think sent them?" Ännchen asked. "It must have been someone unless random musicians are now taking it into their heads to gather here, as well as the students."

Guyon shrugged. "Perhaps you have a follower who wishes to praise your blue eyes, your golden hair, and your kindly nature," he said dryly.

But the song that started was in the *langue d'oc*, and Guyon dropped his head onto the windowsill. "Oh my *God*," he said with feeling.

"What is it?" Ännchen asked, listening intently to the song. "Oh..."

She stepped closer then, placing one small hand lightly on Guyon's shoulder, "Peter."

Yes, Peter. Who else would do something so silly, so sweet and so full of what he felt, and at the same time so utterly not what Guyon wanted to hear?

"Love then bids me stir
such a song as to be neither second nor third,
but first in sweetening a sour heart..."

Guyon winced. "Ah," he said through a constricted and painful throat, "You know me too well..."

"...and don't think I turn my heart elsewhere,
since neither prayer nor game nor viol
can part us the length of a reed...
what did I say? God, help my merits
or may the bitter ocean have me."

Guyon went utterly, perfectly still. "No," he whispered. *Arnaut Daniel himself would be envious. Oh God, what have I done?* "No."

"With shame along with distress
I shall sing, since I can't do otherwise
for he must indeed be ashamed
who has a great privilege
and then, through right or wrong
loses it, regardless of how well he loves."

"So sweet and sad," was Ännchen's only comment, but her

hand remained, unmoving on Guyon's shoulder, a reminder that she was there, whether he wished to keep himself under control or wished to break down to her comfort. Utterly accepting.

"It's a goddamned troubadour song, Ännchen, it's supposed to be," Guyon forced out through his teeth.

It was as though he were caught in some hell, forced to listen to the plaintive little song to its end. His hands clenched on the wood of the window frame

"But I do not seem as wretched
as I am, wherefore a great ill comes to me;
but God can't harm me more by death;
and of that too I shall be glad...
Therefore, he is at fault
who believes all he hears from such people;
and you, if you at any moment loved me,
how could you even suspect
that I could fail you so awfully?"
Don't send me away.
Lo jure. I won't.

Guyon closed his eyes in agony. *Stop. For the love of God, stop.*

The bell swung wildly within him.

"And therefore, presently, without hesitation,
for mercy's sake, return me to your favor,
if you don't agree to my death or its equivalent!"

Something shattered inside Guyon's mind. "*No!*" He slammed the casement shut, narrowly missing Ännchen's fingers. "No! *No!*" He turned, and the world spun with him dizzily, his feet somehow finding a floor that tilted and swayed more than any ship could endure the strain of, and fled for his room, dimly aware of Ännchen following him, and helpless to prevent her.

She entered his rooms barely a pace behind him, then stopped, watching him closely with affection and sadness in her eyes, "Oh, Guyon, could you not just -"

Her words were cut off and she took a deep breath, shaking her head as if she'd thought better of what she'd been about to say.

"No." It seemed to be all he was capable of saying. The air was thin, and too hot, and he could not force down his grief with its weight. He backed away from Ännchen, pressing his back to the wall. *You don't know, you don't know, no-one knows, my last refuge...*"No, I -" *It would be the last betrayal. Better if I did kill him, far better, than letting him know what I am, what I am capable of...*"Oh, God. *What have I done?*" He slid down the wall, burying his face in his hands. "God forgive me, God forgive me..."

"What have you done," Ännchen whispered, "to need His forgiveness? You have merely stuck to what you believe is right. Can there be true harm in that?"

"*Right?*" Guyon said incredulously. "Is that what you all -" But wasn't it? Wasn't that what he had been trying to do? "No," he said, and shook his head, painful and rapid. "And *yes*. There is more harm - I have caused more harm -" *I have hurt the only person in the world I have ever loved with both parts of my divided soul.* "You don't know what I am," he whispered at last. *No-one does.* "You don't know..." *He doesn't know.* "I love him, you see," he said simply. "And he must never, ever know."

Never.

Guyon put his head down on his knees, and wept.

*

This really had been the very last thing he could think of, if Guyon still wouldn't speak to him, he'd just have to...Peter's thoughts froze there. None of the choices he could think of were the least bit acceptable to him. He missed Guyon with a misery that he could barely explain to himself, let alone express to anyone else. He ached with it, morning and night. Went to bed miserable and woke the same way. His cadets, who had been tolerant of his occasional flare of temper, now cringed whenever he entered the room. He'd taken so much of his mood out on them that they were now actively avoiding him whenever possible.

Even Robert, who had been so happy at their return to accord, was barely managing a smile when he saw Peter. And damn it, he didn't blame any of them. Not Robbie or the cadets, or David whose head he had almost chewed off for bringing him coffee instead of tea. Something had to be done.

160

Perhaps, well, perhaps it would be just as well if he went to Carcassonne without Guyon. God and Peter both knew that he didn't wish to return there, this side of death, so maybe if Peter went alone, it would have a two fold benefit - No horrible trial for Guyon and himself out of the other man's presence long enough that...That what? He'd forget why he was angry?

Well, perhaps not that, but be better relaxed by distance that they could, perhaps, become friends again. Peter could ask for little more.

It wasn't much consolation that Guyon had looked little better than he felt, that morning in Corvay's rooms - as though, rather than burning itself out, his anger were burning *him* out, instead, Corvay's new demand of them evoking little response bar a tired laugh, even the infamous temper subsumed into his extraordinary withdrawal.

He had not, though, seemed averse to Peter's company - just tired, and unwilling to discuss anything, and Peter hadn't been able to find a reason to keep him, not while knowing that Guyon was having to face the thought of going back to the Languedoc, that he would have to consider betraying what was, surely, what he thought of as his home.

He could only hope that the musicians had at least woken Guyon's somewhat unpredictable sense of humor - even if it was turned on him.

By the time Peter arrived at the building where Gottfried and Guyon lived, he had changed his mind half a dozen times about just how he should approach the other man. Now he was standing in the lane, just a short distance from the front steps, staring up at the third floor window that opened into the side of Guyon's study room. The window was closed, and from where he stood all he could see was the globe, a bit of ceiling and the end of a bookcase - none of which told him anything about the mood of the inhabitant. He took four steps towards the front door, then stopped and retreated three.

God help me. I was once thought to be brave.

But he felt no such courage now, just worry and anxiety and an overwhelming sense of loss and loneliness.

"If I want a guide, I have my named one upstairs!" came the

161

frustrated voice of Herr Kirschner. Despite the success of Ibn Ibrahim's operation, Gottfried and Ännchen still had a tendency to fuss over him if he showed too many signs of independence, and it never failed to infuriate the German merchant. The door shut with a bang, and the grey-haired man came down the steps, shaking his head.

"Ah, Marshal, is good to see you." He beamed at his own joke, and shook his head, rolling his eyes upwards exaggeratedly. "Ach, this house. Gottfried sulks and stomps like a bear, and my daughter is like a boiling pot. Your scholar is a wise man, he hides away in his room!"

His scholar. Simple words to hurt so much.

"He always has been wise, Herr Kirschner. I wish more of it had rubbed off on me." Peter gave the older man a small smile.

"Ja, well, for that you would need to be here, but your brother must take much of your time. Families." He snorted. "I am going for a very long walk, and I think also I shall go to an inn and drink far too much beer." He chuckled. "Perhaps I shall sing when I come home." He patted Peter on the arm. "You can find me at the *Oise Grise*. Bring Guyon, hmm? We should make *him* sing, he is too silent." He nodded genially, and continued on his way.

Yes, brothers could take a lot of time, but unfortunately that wasn't what had been keeping him away. Nor had duties. Nor had a million and one other things that might be considered important. The only thing that had been keeping him away, was Guyon's refusal to see him.

He stared at the door as if doing so would will it to knock itself.

Coward.

It was sad, really, that he almost wished that Vincennes would appear, dithering on about some problem with his dissertation, sweeping Peter with him up to the top of the stairs. At his point, he would almost have been grateful for de Barrion.

"Are you coming in?" Gottfried's voice demanded, and Peter looked up to see him leaning out from a second-floor window, "or have you taken root? And I need to have a -" The casement suddenly slammed down, cutting off his sentence.

That was rather odd, but Peter had seen stranger interplay

between the van Hesselink pair. They seemed to tease as much as breathe, neither one offering the other the upper hand on a regular basis.

But yes, he should go in. He lifted the latch and opened the door, stepping into the entryway and starting slowly up the stairs.

"I really do need to talk to you -" Gottfried said, meeting him on the landing, and Ännchen snapped -

"No you *don't*!" from beyond him. "Just - no more musicians, please, Peter. They trampled the flowerbeds."

She looked flushed and annoyed, but her ire seemed, rather inexplicably, to be bent on her husband.

"I'm sorry, Ännchen." Peter grimaced. "I expected them to be more - Well, no...no more musicians, don't worry. Probably didn't help anyway, so...."

He had to stop this. Had to begin speaking in whole sentences before he got to the top of the stairs. Guyon always hated it when he didn't complete his thoughts.

"No, they damn well didn't," Gottfried said irascibly. "I *know*, Anna, I'm to shut up and go downstairs. But it's not right. It's not fair on you, Peter."

"Darling mine, believe me when I say I'm five seconds away from dismissing the cook you so kindly employed to spare me time," Ännchen said with poisonous sweetness. "Go away. *Now*."

Gottfried growled, and stomped down the stairs, in a way that bore out Herr Kirschner's complaint.

The door to the schoolroom shut with a decided click, before Peter turned back to Ännchen, "I really am sorry if they caused a problem, Anna. I thought they might amuse Guyon, but...well...I've not been very good at guessing his moods lately. I probably got it completely wrong and he still won't speak to me."

Peter wondered if his face looked as hangdog as he felt - miserable and out of sorts and just pained.

Ännchen sighed. "Well, it wasn't the cleverest idea you've had," she said, pushing back her hair, "but ignore Gottfried. I think it might have been exactly what was needed. Just - don't start a fight with him this time, would you? As a favor. I'm not sure whether he's got a headache, but I really do." She smiled. "Now I have to go and apologize for being a shrew, so - just have a little courage." She went down the stairs, and after Gottfried into the schoolroom, the door shutting a second time rather more quietly.

A headache? Wonderful. Peter suddenly wondered if he should just call it a day, go have a beer with Herr Kirschner and try this another time.

No, he'd put this off long enough. Either Guyon would speak with him or he wouldn't and that was that. They need to plan, or at least make some decision about going to Carcassonne and quickly. Peter turned and walked quietly up the last set of stairs, knocking softly on the door when he reached the top.

"It's open," Guyon's voice called from somewhere inside. "Just come in, I'll be through in a minute..."

Peter stepped in, but went no further, hovering uncertainly near the door, "Gui - Guyon, it's me, Peter. I...I can come back later if you're busy. But, I thought - Well, never mind what I thought. We need to talk soon, about this trip."

There, that was mostly complete sentences.

There was the sound of something quite comprehensively breaking from the next room, and a yelp of pain, followed by a string of curses, before Guyon emerged, toweling his head and face, and limping. "Sorry, that was my basin, I was -" he gestured at his damp hair. "Headache," he added.

He looked it.

"Sorry," Peter spoke quietly. "Do you want me to come back later?"

Then, "Did you hurt yourself?"

Peter almost bit his tongue, willing those last words back into his mouth. But he *was* concerned. No matter what was between them, he would *always* be concerned.

"Not really," Guyon said vaguely. "Well, other than yes, I've just had a damn great bowl full of water drop on my foot, I didn't." He smiled ruefully. "Sorry. If you want sense from me, it's not a good time. I'm as shattered as the blasted basin."

"You're tired," Peter nodded, "and I showed up on your doorstep like the unwanted cat. Just send me a message about a better time. All right?"

"*No!*" Guyon looked as startled as Peter felt at his sudden reaction. He blinked, and laughed a little. "I mean - stay. You're not unwanted. Or a cat," he added.

Peter gave a very small chuckle, "You *are* tired. Here, would you like me to -"

It was a very small gesture, and he made it as tentatively as that cat would have done, but he placed his hand on the nape of Guyon's neck, rubbing gently to soothe the tension that sat there all too obviously. But, even as he did it, he prepared himself to be pushed away, having even this small touch rejected.

He was surprised when Guyon only dropped his head, pressing a thumb to the point between his eyebrows and swallowing. "Got a week?" he asked a little raggedly. "Sorry. Yes." He was shaking a little, not visibly, but easily discernable to the touch, the fine, constant tremors of complete exhaustion, as though he had completed some act of immense physical exertion and was paying for it.

"I have as much time as it takes at the moment. Here. Sit down. That will help." Not stopping his ministrations, Peter indicated the nearby chair.

He did have time. He'd already arranged the time he'd need for the journey to Carcassonne, had spoken to her Majesty, had given commands to his lieutenants that would take effect upon his departure. Talking to Guyon, really, was the final step.

"Sitting down will help?" Guyon offered him a small smile. "I wonder why I never thought of that. *Jesus,* Pèire, your *damned* musicians!" He sat in the chair and dropped his head into his hands.

"I meant it would help me do this better," Peter brought up his other hand, massaging all along the tension spots, neck, temples, scalp. "I'm sorry about the musicians. Were they really that horrid? No, I suppose they must have been or you'd not complain."

"What?" Guyon looked up at him. "Oh - no, I think they were quite competent. They just hit me with the force of a consignment of bricks, that's all."

"Oh...too loud?" Peter grimaced sympathetically. "Well, I am sorry. I just wanted to amuse you, really. Sorry it didn't work."

He could do this, keep up his end of small talk, and sink into the feeling of being able to touch Guyon for the first time in weeks. He just had to keep the feeling tightly reined in or he'd probably do something stupid and wind up out on the doorstep.

Guyon snorted. It didn't even sound remotely like laughter. "That's one way of putting it," he said into his hands. "I take it you weren't actually *trying* to tell me that my behavior has been appalling, unbearable, and ridiculous?"

Peter froze, "What? No. I - Your behavior hasn't been any of that...well, no worse than mine, I'm sure."

What had those bloody musicians played for Christ's sake?

"*Love then bids me stir such a song as to be neither second nor third, but first in sweetening a sour heart,*" Guyon said with appropriate sourness. "Somehow I don't think that was you."

Peter cringed mentally. "No. Most definitely not."

He was actually surprised that Guyon hadn't flung the basin at his head rather than dropping it on his own foot.

"Again...sorry." He moved his hands down to Guyon's shoulders, working out knots there.

"*Oc.*" Guyon moved a hand from his face, and his cold fingers grasped Peter's. "So am I. I was angry because you saved my brother." He shook his head. "Christ, it sounds even more ridiculous out loud..."

Now Peter was confused. That was it? But why would that have upset Guyon? His brother was safe and free and he hadn't had to do anything...

Oh...

"I'm incredibly stupid sometimes, Gui. I admit it freely and without reservation. I did this for you. Truly. That was my motivation in all this. I wanted your family safe so that you no longer needed to worry...no longer needed to feel threatened by Corvay." Peter paused and took a deep breath. "It honestly never occurred to me that I was...once again...by-passing you when I did it."

"I know." Guyon sighed. "I know, I know, I know...I'm not *rational* about it, I can't be, I'm sorry..." His voice was shaking. "I'm never going to see him again. You know that, *I* know that. And *Robert* -" He choked, and stopped. His free hand rubbed over his face roughly. "I resent that. I'm sorry."

"No...I understand." Peter felt horrible that he had unthinkingly robbed his friend of this chance. Even with the pure hatred that somehow sparked up when he thought of how Guyon's brother had treated him, he could still understand how it was with family. "But Gui, never say never. I thought that I'd never be reconciled with my family...and now...."

"It's just *slightly* different," Guyon said wryly, but he didn't elaborate. "And now Corvay wants me to damn the Languedoc." He looked up at Peter with red-rimmed eyes. "Well I won't."

"No...we'll figure out something. We'll prove him wrong." If the determination in his voice alone could have made it so, they wouldn't even have had to leave Paris.

*

The Rue des Esclangons, late May, 1646.

Our hearts are mutual victims laid,
While they, such power in friendship lies,
Are altars, priests, and off'rings made ;
And each heart which thus kindly dies
Grows deathless by the sacrifice.

Usually, Guyon was capable of offering a reasonable degree of hospitality - wine, at least, if nothing more, and usually coffee, which suited his tastes if no-one else's. Now, of course, when it would have been a perfect time to use it to smooth over the remaining and rather painful awkwardnesses, he had nothing, not even the offer of badly-made tea, to help him. He still *had* tea, in the odd little caddy he'd bought at a stall back before Christmas, but he didn't want Peter to think that he'd been taking his return for granted by keeping it, and he certainly didn't want to admit the real reason he still had it, which was that he quite simply couldn't bear to get rid of it, even knowing he might never renew their friendship.

Going down to the cellar to find some wine that hadn't been set aside for some specific date, therefore, he was slightly startled to run into Gottfried.

"Um, sorry," he said, about to edge past him. "Wine." It struck him as rather sad that the only things he had said to his co-tutor recently tended to be apologies, which reminded him - "Gottfried, I'm taking a leave of absence."

Gottfried started at him for a moment, then broke into a blinding grin, and caught him up in a bearhug. "Hah! Ännchen was right, you *are* capable of seeing sense!"

"Oof," Guyon managed in mild protest. "Thank you?" *What?*

"Stay away as long as you need," Gottfried said cheerfully. "I won't let the school go under." He released Guyon at last, and continued to beam at him. "I should apologize, my friend, I underestimated you," he said, and patted him on the shoulder.

"Er, don't worry about it," said Guyon, thoroughly bewildered, and watched as Gottfried went back upstairs, whistling. *I don't want to know.* He shook his head, and went to get the wine.

When he returned upstairs it was to find Peter still standing in almost exactly the spot he had left him, as if he were taking care not do disturb anything by even so much as moving a chair. It made him feel even more awkward somehow, all this leftover tension.

"Have you taken a vow of deprivation of the senses?" he asked, taking care to keep his voice light. "Have a seat. Go through into comfort. Whatever you want, for goodness' sake!" He managed a smile. "I really have *done* with being angry."

"What?" Peter blinked as if his thoughts were far away, then moved to sit down in the chair. "I was just thinking. Or woolgathering would probably be more accurate."

"Oh?" The smile felt better, this time, his skin hurting less in what had become an unfamiliar movement of the small muscles around his mouth. "I'll give you a glass of good wine for a bag of it..."

"It's rather an inferior grade, I'm afraid." Peter smiled back, almost shyly. "Full of burrs."

Guyon laughed, almost unwillingly. It took him a little by surprise that he still could, but he hadn't sounded mocking, or unpleasant, or any of the things he had been taking such care to portray over the last couple of weeks, so he thought it might be all right. "So I'll pick them out," he said, and handed Peter one of his good glasses, pouring the wine. He hoped that the fact he had taken a beaker for himself would pass unnoticed, but he didn't think he could actually hold anything delicate for very long at the moment without either his grip breaking it, or simply dropping it.

Given what had happened to a whole basin earlier, he suspected he was going to be lucky if it didn't happen to the wine bottle, either. He sat on the faded piece of carpet by the hearth, drawing his knees up. "There, payment." He tilted his head, inviting. "Tell me?"

Peter took a drink of the wine, as if fortifying himself for the conversation. "If I do, will you at least hear me through before you get angry or...anything? I'm not making a demand or telling you what to do. I simply want to offer a suggestion."

"Consider me the equivalent of Niobe, turned to stone with

calm," Guyon agreed. Niobe had turned to a statue from grief, the stone still weeping, but he didn't think Peter was likely to pick up on that particular slip. "I'm listening."

"I know that going back to Carcassonne is one of the last things you want to do." Peter began. "I wanted to suggest that I go alone. And no, this is not coming from some misguided thought that you aren't up to the trip. It just might be easier."

Oh, God. Guyon was too tired for anger, or he suspected he might have felt some. Not because of Peter's suggestion - or at least, not because of the daft, honorable, misguided motives that had *led* to that suggestion - but because of his own ridiculous, irrational behavior that had made Peter think he had to make it. "No," he said slowly. "No, it wouldn't be." It was his turn to drink wine, choosing his words with care. "Peter...you're right. I don't want to go back. I would be insane if I did, and while we both know my grasp on the sane may be occasionally tenuous, it isn't quite that bad. But I wouldn't let *anyone* go alone there - well, perhaps to the area, but not when having to deal with my family. It's one of the reasons I was so annoyed about Robert. And you - you are the *last* person -" Everything was too close to the surface for him to continue with that particular sentence. "I couldn't live with myself," he finished, honest and deceptive at once.

"I wanted to spare you the upset and, well, I thought, perhaps you would not wish to spend quite so much time in my company just at the moment." Peter looked down into his glass, swirling the contents absently. "I wouldn't go alone, if that is what you're concerned about. I'd take one of the Guard with me. But," he continued quickly before Guyon could say anything more, "if I'm being honest, I would much rather I have *you* with me, for so many reasons."

"I do hope not all of them are practical," Guyon said. His voice shook. "I'm *sorry*. I just wanted you to *see*, I suppose." Make Peter see what he had nearly done to Robert, the idiocy of not involving Guyon - make him see that *without* telling him what Carcassonne had really been about, and Guyon was sometimes amazed, considering all this, that he was supposed to be the one with a working intelligence. God help him. "I hate being out of control. Having it - taken away. I know you did the right thing, but Pèire - you have no idea how it makes me feel. As though -" it struck him suddenly that drinking wine on an extremely empty stomach after two weeks of complete abstinence wasn't the most sensible thing he could have done, but he did, in fact, want to explain this - "as though I'm on a rock in the middle of some flooded river, and everything I value is rushing by me, and I'm not quick enough to hold on to any of it." He sighed. "I told you once. I would trust a thousand strangers - risk my life, my soul for them, if you asked, if I knew that I was allowed to be your friend at the end of it. Carcassonne...it's unpleasantness. It's nothing. My pride." He shrugged. "I can't stand the thought of you having to endure all the things Maurice can - and *will* - come up with, without me there."

"I'm beginning to see that this has all been a part of my infernal idiocy. All of this. Our estrangement...or whatever this has been." Peter finally raised his head, but still did not look directly at Guyon. "I want so very much to do things *for you*, but it always winds up that I'm doing them *to you* and I can't seem to see the difference. It appears that I will have to learn to simply ask. That's a difficult lesson for me to learn." He cleared his throat. "Please come with me, Guyon. I'm asking."

Guyon was extremely glad that he was not standing up, because the relief that rushed through him felt as though it were turning every muscle and tendon into water, leaving him completely unstrung and pithless. "I'll come," he said, and humor returned to give him a little strength, the ability to joke, however badly and awkwardly. "But I don't *want* to." He grinned at Peter, knowing it was completely crooked and odd-looking, but having no other way at all of expressing how he felt. "Thank you."

Peter let out a long slow exhalation of air, as if he had been holding his breath. And perhaps he had, for he only now, finally, looked at Guyon. "How long will you need to get everything arranged?"

"It's done," Guyon said with a thankful return to stable ground. "I told Gottfried I was leaving for a while, and he said to take as long as I need - and he *hugged* me." He shook his head. "He's completely insane."

"Probably more relieved that I won't be haunting his doorstep anymore with a face like the very devil." Peter guessed. "It will take me a day or two to get the cadets settled and make some preparations."

"You can't settle them," Guyon said automatically. "They're unsettleable. Or something." He refilled his beaker. It was quite nice to have the edges of things starting to be less painfully sharp. "Peter - when we get to the Languedoc...the man Maurice de Chesnay. The one Robert was telling you about - the one he didn't like." He could not repress a faint smile at that. "He's very, *very* dangerous. So please - whatever he says, whatever he suggests, whatever he asks - don't listen to a word. Promise me."

"I will use the utmost caution in all my dealings there," Peter nodded. "Just the few things Robert had to say and the way you have been treated are more than enough to warn me of the folly of complacency."

"Oh - *that*." Guyon could not help his smile. That Peter, even not knowing the *why* of what had been done to him at the pelourinho, so completely assumed his innocence, was a source of unutterable relief to him - if of a somewhat guilty sort. "Christ. You realize, whatever happens, whether we succeed in saving the idiot denizens of that area from their own folly or not, we're free of Corvay after this?"

"Of course, I realize it." Peter nodded. "My only question is as to the next step. How do we remove him?"

"I'll leave that to de Retz. I'm *happy* to leave that to de Retz." Guyon meant it. He had personal preferences as to what he would *like* to happen to Corvay, but he was wise enough to know that was one thing that really was outside his influence. "Unless...we use this. Use the Languedoc. He wants to - why shouldn't we?"

"No reason," Peter agreed, "but how?"

"Corvay wants us to prove the Languedoc is what everyone thinks it." Guyon made a face. "Heretics, traitors - and Spanish allies." He chuckled. "It probably is, but I must tell you, I don't care. But Corvay has been *using* the Spanish - we know this. We can prove this. It's not quite enough to convict him of anything, but we have a start, so - what if all the proof that should lead to the Languedociens led to him instead?"

"Since it's true, it should not be that difficult to find the proof." Peter nodded. "One more piece of his downfall in place."

Guyon nodded. "And keeps my idiot countrymen's necks safe - for now," he added a little grimly. "God, I'll be glad to get out of this. I know you all think I'm good at intelligence work, but I really am *not* equipped for spying."

Peter's expression grew a bit grim at that, "I know. I'm sorry you ever had to become involved."

"I involved myself, Peter." Guyon never cared how many times he had to say that. "I would have whether you asked or not, eventually. You know that." He had his own quixotism, of a different nature to Peter's incomprehensible code of honor, but of a strong enough sort that he could see its windmill-tilting elements for what they were. "Besides, I'm glad I did, or you would have long ago killed Corvay and be in the Bastille, or worse."

"Hmmphf." Peter snorted, then gave Guyon that same shy smile. "You're probably right."

Guyon hated, with a sort of detached viciousness, that he had created that new awkwardness in Peter. It was devastating to him, as bad as the musicians, to know that all the efforts he had tried to make to get Peter to see his own worth, to give him some sort of confidence in the things that were *not* solely the province of the Queen's Marshal, he had single-handedly destroyed for the sake of his own pride. "Of course I am," he said lightly, and tried not to think of what Ännchen had said to him, after his appalling bout of shameful grief had passed.

*There's always the lover and the beloved in any relationship, Guyon. You're the beloved. I know, because so am I. And everyone thinks that we have all the power, but it's not true, because we won't know - we'll **never** know - why we're loved. And we'll never know if this is the one time we've pushed too far, too hard, and managed to put an end to it. I'm not surprised you're scared. I never have been surprised. Honestly.* "Peter...I need to tell you..." He stopped, unable to finish.

*If one day I were to tell you...*He had stopped himself then, too, that time in the courtyard, the moment between worlds and the strokes of midnight lost to him. *You don't know what I am.*

But Peter's eyes, seemingly ever alert for any need that

Guyon felt, centered on him with unerring accuracy, "What, Gui? Tell me."

"Nothing." He shook his head. "I think I'm a little drunk. I was going to ask you if you believed in demons, of all things!" He forced a laugh.

"But why would -?" Peter looked confused for a moment, then seemed to consider Guyon's words. "If you mean events and actions that can haunt you with regrets for the rest of your life...yes. If you mean Biblical demons, actual, physical ones?" Peter shook his head, "I've seen too many odd things out on the heath late at night to doubt that they could exist. And I've felt..." Peter shook his head again. "You'll be thinking that I'm daft now.

"No." Guyon shook his head. *Considering I have a tendency to hear and see things that really do **not** exist, no.* "What?" Then he narrowed his eyes. "Are you setting me up to be frightened by a sheet again...?"

"Never again," Peter ran one hand over his ribs in remembrance. "But I can say that there's truth in all those old stories, Guyon, somewhere. I'm not sure what it is, but I'm sure it's there."

"So am I," Guyon said, and then shook his head. "I'm sorry. You'll now think I've lost the remainder of my wits." He half-laughed, and waved a hand, dismissing the subject. "Would the Lord Marshal's absence be noted tonight?"

Peter shrugged, "I make it a point to not be too predictable, and considering my mood of late, there will probably be a party in honor of my absence."

"Then stay here," Guyon said. He didn't mean it to sound quite as pleading as it did, but that might, he recognized, be for the best, all things considered. "Please," he added, with a wry twist to the word.

The look Peter gave him was odd and hesitant, but his answer came quickly enough, "Yes. Yes, of course."

"Thank you," Guyon said, in very real gratitude. He had no idea if he was going to be able to sleep or not, but at least, however selfishly asked for, he would have some rest. He offered up one of his best smiles, and tried to make it real. "I told you I'm idiotic when I'm tired, but I find myself needing to know you're not, in fact, some product of my imagination." And *that* was a good deal more than he had meant to let slip past his defenses, and he had no idea how he was going to answer any questions Peter followed it up with.

"I'm here. I'm real." Peter tried to reassure him. "And I've missed you so much. I - I haven't been sleeping very well. And, Christ knows, I'm lucky that anyone is still speaking to me the way I've been snapping at them."

Guyon snorted in genuine, if painful amusement. "Well, you're up several on me for luck, then," he said. "Other than Ännchen, *no-one's* speaking to me. *Very well* is something only applicable to those who *do* sleep. And my students are ready to leave Paris, let alone the school! And *while I remember* -" He got up onto his knees, leaning forward so that he was only inches from Peter - "Bad temper and riding. You are never to do that again. Vincennes is still shaking, and he's convinced you were going to kill *yourself.* Now while I have a *little* more faith in your abilities than that, terrifying the physicians of Paris is *not* a good plan."

"Christ. Was that Vincennes?" Peter suddenly chuckled. "Yes, well...I certainly didn't mean to frighten him."

"*Peter...*" It was very close to a growl, which was a long way from the effect he had been intending to create, but it was too late to alter his tone. He gripped Peter's arms. "Never again." He gritted his teeth, and admitted, "You frightened *me*, damn it."

"I have never been thrown. But yes, I promise, never again." Peter assured him solemnly. "Never again."

Guyon closed his eyes in relief. He suspected he was being humored, and could not even find the necessary energy to care or protest. "Thank you," he said fervently. "And now I am going to bed, before I make an even greater spectacle of myself than begging you for ridiculous promises on my knees. You are *more* than welcome, incidentally, to join me, though I don't think I shall provide any more guaranteed pleasure than some very faint snoring. And possibly the occasional twitch."

Peter's lip twitched in amusement, "I live for those snores. They are sweet music that give my heart ease."

"Have you been letting David at the water again?" Guyon

demanded, and got to his feet. "*Honestly.* You're deaf and demented."

"And in love." The words were so soft that Guyon barely heard them.

But he *had* heard them, and he was starting to quite thoroughly believe them, and if he couldn't admit to returning it, he could at least accept the emotion with grace. "No excuse," he said sternly, and smiled. "But a damn good explanation."

*

When Peter awoke, groggily, during the night it was with the disconcerting feeling of a warm weight on his chest. A part of him wondered if one of the cadets had snuck a cat into his room and it had taken up residence on top of him while he slept. The weight was, indeed, rather on the furry side, but as he reached torn between petting it and moving it off of him, he heard a soft sound. It wasn't purring, that much was certain, although it was a relaxed and rather rumbling sound.

Peter batted his eyes, fighting his way to complete wakefulness as he realized that the sound was a snore and it was coming from Guyon, who at some point had apparently decided that he was more comfortable than a pillow. He smiled, gently smoothing back the mass of unruly dark curls, until he could easily see Guyon's face in the dim light of the room.

"Mrr?" Slitted eyes stared in an unfocused manner somewhere around his chin, and that, too, was like a cat, albeit a cranky and disturbed one who had been napping on a nice warm person, *thank you and kindly leave me be*, and was about to demonstrate just what claws were for. Then Guyon opened his eyes properly, blinking a great deal but aware. "Ah. Sorry. Sh'd move?" He yawned, and made a face. His eyelids started to slide shut again.

"Not on my account," Peter said softly. This...this was what he had missed. The closeness and the sounds of holding the person he loved in his arms...or on his chest. He'd almost given up hope that he'd ever feel this again.

Guyon did not so much frown, as his face made a peculiar

effort to concentrate for him. "Mm. It's. It's night." He looked briefly disconcerted, and apparently that had not been quite what he meant to say. Then a rusty-sounding laugh rasped out of him. "Nice? It is night..." The laughter sounded more like a soft sneezing fit, now, shaking them both. He dropped his forehead onto Peter's chest, his breath coming in warm little snorts of air, in contrast to his cool skin. "Heh."

"It is, indeed." Peter chuckled and nodded as if speaking to a child. "And then when the sun begins to rise, it shall be morning and the whole day to follow until night falls again."

He felt the eyebrows rise sharply against his skin before the change in Guyon's voice and posture told him that the last of sleep had left him. "Good God, and I never knew that." All the cat-like languor had left him, replaced by the familiar mockery that still, somehow, managed to be uncertain.

But Peter continued to stroke his fingers through Guyon's hair, and spoke gently, "Stay with me, and a few good things will be learned. Though who the tutor and who the student, shall be a mystery to us both."

Guyon muttered something that might have been agreement or negation. It was certainly warm, and slightly damp, in the way that breath trapped between skin tended to be. One of his hands moved, tracing over the old Newbury scar on Peter's hip. He never understood why that was the one that fascinated Guyon so much, but he had certainly discovered it was still more sensitive than the surrounding area.

The feeling was delicious, sending tiny shivers of sensation running through him, as those maddening fingers stroked over him. It wasn't *quite* arousing, but it wasn't quite relaxing either.

"Checking," Guyon said in his soft slurred voice, the one that belonged utterly to night and privacy and *them.* "You sounded all...philosophical. But when I dream, I never get this right."

"You can't control a dream." And he should know, he'd dreamt this repeatedly over the last few weeks. Dreamt it and longed for it, and cursed the daylight that took him away from what little pretense he could manage.

Guyon lifted his head, eyes glittering. "Ten to four, odds on." He didn't look happy. His hand stopped moving, fell to the mattress with a faint sound of skin on cotton. "Sorry. I just -" The muscles in his back tensed and bunched up, preparatory to movement, the familiar presage to his leaving the bed.

"Please don't." Peter spoke quickly, his voice rough and tender. "Please don't go. I...I've missed you so much, Gui. Please stay."

"I *think*," Guyon said, staying still but his breathing a little too fast, "I *have* to get up. If you want sleep."

"I want *you*." Peter knew he sounded desperate, but was in the grip of...whatever this was - reconciliation or mere tolerance. He ached for Guyon. He could admit it to himself, if no one else.

Guyon's shoulders unknotted slightly, the glitter in his eyes changing to one of amusement as his lips quirked faintly. "*Want* me?" He shifted against Peter, rendering the question completely unambiguous, despite the teasing note in his voice.

"God, yes." That was all it had taken, that shift of weight and Peter could feel himself harden. It always took him by surprise, the way he responded so quickly to Guyon. His touch, his voice, even his look at times.

Guyon kissed him, tentative and sudden. It was as though the last months had never been, leaving him awkward and uncertain once again - though still with that startled, banked ferocity, the fine veneer of simple desire over something Peter was always unsure he wanted to fully understand - and certainly did not want to now, needing instead a confirmation of this renewal of the once-familiar.

"Guyon..." Peter whispered the name, then leaned in to claim his lips in an insistent kiss. If his dreams had been full of Guyon's presence, then the ones where he was free to touch and taste had been the most vivid, often waking him to heat and sweat and the raging pain of arousal. Those dream had kept his nights short, even self-release giving no comfort.

It was awkward and harsh, all of it. They both seemed to have new angles, corners. Guyon hit his elbow on the bedpost, and what would usually have provoked laughter that led to some heightened wave of sweetness, brought only a sharp curse, bitten and jagged. They were uncomfortable, and desperate, and too hot, even Guyon. Where they managed to find some sort of fit was too slick with the heat, with sweat. Guyon's hands were damp, and still cold, and his bitten thumbnails were rasping little catches of pain. One of the old bolsters lost its tenuous grasp on cohesion, and what felt like every single pointed base of each individual feather jammed sideways into Peter's neck.

And when they were finished, both of them coming with half-pained shouts of release, and collapsing onto the bed in a panting wheezing mess, they wrapped their arms around each other, still tense and a bit strained. Peter wondered if they would, eventually, manage to relax together again, or if this was to be their fate - this fevered passion that contained none of the humor or companionship that they had felt before.

He had forgotten about Guyon's persistent, mocking honesty. "You were right," he said with surprising cheerfulness. "About the *learning*, anyhow, not about the *good*."

Peter looked at him for a long moment, his expression flashing from confusion to horror to regret and finally settling on amusement. He started laughing, pulling Guyon into a real embrace at last and covering his neck with chuckling kisses.

"Hm," Guyon contributed amusedly, picking feathers out of Peter's hair and rubbing a somehow far more soothing thumb over the prickling scratches. "Go to sleep, *car-mi*. Apparently Morpheus now has wings..."

He was still carefully piling feathers somewhere to his left when Peter *did* manage to fall asleep, his quiet voice still constructing some theory about sleep and wings and different kinds of bars on feathers that all blurred into something incomprehensible and soft and oddly welcoming.

He dreamed, comfortably, of goosedown.

*

The grain of wood on Peter's desk was exceptional, smooth and even to the eye and to the touch, with just enough whorls and knots to keep it interesting. It had been stained a rich dark shade, and the polish on it was thick and satiny, kept that way by the hands of the cadets, whose chores often included such trivial tasks. It was also, Peter hoped, a good strong wood, because if he had to explain his decorating preferences to the two merchants standing in front of him one more time, he was probably going to attempt to punch his fist through it...or his head.

"No. I don't care what you heard. No gilt. No brocade. No velvet. This is a military establishment, not a bloody brothel! I want simple serviceable paint and wood. If you -"

"'Scuse me, sir." One of the cadets stuck his head in the door. "Will you be wanting your tea in here? Or your private quarters?"

"Here's fine." The cadet saluted and scurried out. "As I was saying...If you do not feel up to providing what I am asking for, I'm certain that I can find -" There was a knock on the door. "Yes! What!"

"Just checking," said David with one of his best imbecilic grins. "In case everyone was hallucinating." He came in and perched on the desk. "H'llo, Guyon."

Guyon flapped a hand at him irritably, and carried on explaining to the new secretary that Lt. Wycombe had found just why the alphabet was necessary, a task that should have been unneeded seeing that the new secretary was Philippe, one of Guyon's students.

"David...is this really essential right now?" Peter asked, with a sigh and went back to his other conversation without waiting for an answer. "Gentlemen, either you will provide what I have asked for or I will find someone who will. You may leave now." He dismissed them, as if they had been two of his Cadets, and he hoped his stance and demeanor would finally put paid to their ridiculous notions. "Oh! Whatever other changes you might make to this place...that portrait must stay exactly where it is."

"But it's hideous, sir!" protested one of the merchants, and then took a step backwards as David turned to look at him with an identical expression to that of the portrait's subject, mocking all concerns and similarities at once. "Oh. I - a relative?"

Guyon's explanation of filing was choked off in a sudden abrupt snort. His shoulders shook.

"Out!" Peter bellowed. "Now!" The two tradesmen left in a flurry of drapery samples and measuring tape. Peter walked around the desk, taking up a position in front of the portrait. He knew his men had become rather superstitious about the ugly old thing. The frame was mis-set, its gilt edges mostly worn off, and the painting itself was obviously not the work of a highly skilled painter. Yet...there was a bit of resemblance between the subject and Peter, if only for the blonde hair, long aristocratic nose and full lips. His men had certainly noticed it from the moment they had set up occupancy, and had taken the hideous thing on as kind of a good luck charm.

"Can I go, too?" asked the secretary plaintively.

"Don't ask me," said Guyon. "I just explain alphabets, I don't employ you...you know, that thing really is disturbing, Peter."

"Yes. This is what I envision every time her Majesty brings up the subject of having my portrait done." Peter gave a small shiver of distaste. "What do you think? Will I look like this in fifteen years?"

"Hopefully a bit less peeling," David said cheerfully, lying across the desk and cushioning his head and arms on a pile of papers. "And less...well, ugly. Of course, if you had your portrait painted and then waited a hundred years, then the *painting* might look like that."

"No," said Guyon rather more succinctly. "Not in fifteen, not in thirty."

Peter chuckled, brushing his hand over the scrollwork of the frame, then turning around, "Well, in either - Yes, yes, Philippe...for goodness sake, go." He scowled at his new secretary, then looked at David. "You know...I have a perfectly serviceable bed down the hall if you're that exhausted." He tugged his stack of papers out from under David's arms.

"But have you changed the sheets?" David asked with a limpid innocence that made Peter's fingers itch to clamp around his throat. "Oh, sorry, it doesn't matter. Since you weren't *here* last night."

Guyon gave Peter a hard look. "And that was no-one noticing your absence, was it?" He snorted.

"No one of importance," Peter tried to laugh it off, but could feel the tips of his ears going red. "Although, I didn't clarify that, did I?"

Guyon shook his head. It was impossible to tell whether he was annoyed or amused, and who either emotion might have been directed at.

There was another knock at the door, "Come in," Peter called for what felt like the thousandth time that day, and added, "Why not? Everyone else has."

A young cadet, laden with tea things, peered in cautiously. "Sir...you said you wanted this here."

"No. No, Thomas. It's fine. Just put that down over -" Peter scowled. "David, do get off my desk, would you?"

"I like your desk. It's a nice desk." David rolled onto his back, his gilt curls falling out across the polished wood like a profane version of a saint's icon. He beamed up at the cadet. "Hello. That's tea."

"Y-yes?" The cadet looked wildly at Peter for help.

"Off," Guyon said firmly, and pushed David to the floor. He landed with a graceless thump.

"There now, Thomas. Just put it there." Peter pointed at the desk. The cadet sat down the tray and left as quickly as he could.

"Tea." Guyon's mouth twitched. "Very civilized. Is it my imagination, by the way, or is that man absolutely terrified of you?"

Peter sighed. "I'm afraid that Thomas and I didn't...begin very well. Entirely my fault, I'm sure." Yes, he was sure. Thomas had just been assigned as his valet about the time he actually realized that Guyon was avoiding him. The boy's kind and solicitous nature had prompted him to make some offers of warm milk and brandy or reading aloud to help Peter sleep. Peter had told him, in no uncertain terms, exactly what he could do with his warm milk. "Oh, that reminds me..." Peter changed the subject. "Do you know anyone who might be willing to do some tutoring for the cadets?

Guyon's eyebrows raised. "I take it you aren't asking me, since they seem quite petrified enough of life as it is? Gottfried would do it, I am sure. And de Barrion has his license, you might ask him." He lifted the lid of the teapot, and sniffed suspiciously. "It still smells like - *David*!" It was a growl of real anger.

David didn't even pretend he didn't know what Guyon was angry about, which made him at least one step ahead of Peter, for once. "I didn't know you'd be here!"

"That's an *excuse*?"

"Someone had to -"

"Not like that -"

"What?" Peter just looked confused, then leaned in to sniff at the tea. "Alright, what did you put in there, David?"

"Mandrake," David muttered. "Look, you need to *sleep*!"

Peter moved back from the teapot as if it were about to jump up and pour itself down his throat. "No. No drugs, damnit. I don't. I can't." Poitiers and drugs and fevered dreams flashed through Peter's head, and he grabbed David by the wrist, holding it at a painful angle. "Never ever try to give me anything that I don't know about. Never."

"Right, because you take it when you know about it!" David was, as always, impervious to threats.

"If I do or I don't, it's not your bloody business." Peter flung David's hand away.

"And please excuse me for breathing," David snapped, "but it's my job."

"Drugging the Lord Marshal?" Guyon's voice was a dangerous little purr. "Who employs you, then, Somers? *Corvay*?"

"*Damn* you, Guyon, at least I *cared*!"

"*Hey*!" Henri's voice cracked out from the door. "They can hear you all over the Hôtel!"

"And how did you convince Thomas to let you put that in my tea?" Peter growled, ignoring Henri for the moment. "Or was he in this with you? Hot milk and brandy, my arse..."

"Hot *milk*?" It was a sort of incredulous squawk from a temporarily distracted Guyon.

David rolled his eyes. "Obviously *not*," he said disgustedly. "He's far too scared of you for anything so useful."

"That's. Not. The point." Peter threw his hands up in the air. "Look, David, thank you so much for worrying about me, but I am an adult and.... Just don't, alright? Don't try this again."

"Hot milk?" Guyon asked the room helplessly.

"Bah," said David sulkily. "Fool."

"Just promise him," Henri said on a sort of groan, and David made a face.

"Oh, all *right*!"

Peter let out a puff of air, "Thank you, David. And thank you, Henri. And yes, hot milk." There was a silence as Peter moved to prowl towards Guyon. "I vaguely remember someone offering me something similar...Of course, I think I almost passed out at your feet before I got more than a sip in me."

There was an explosion of laughter from Henri. "*Guyon!*"

"Oh, be quiet," Guyon said sulkily.

"No, really, is that why you asked?" It was a gleeful howl. "You spent all that money - and you didn't even know - and all because some book said about that stupid Scottish drink - and you hate milk - and *hee*!"

"Henri, *shut up*," Guyon pleaded. He blinked at Peter. "Um. Yes?"

"It's alright, Gui. I've been known to drink it on quiet winter evenings...It's not bad, really." Peter stepped a bit closer, lowering his voice. "But, you see, I didn't want it from him...not after you'd given it to me. It just...It wasn't right, somehow."

"Oh - *sentiment*!" Guyon said on a gasped laugh, and looked away. "*Really*, Pèire, am I never to provide you with any sort of refreshment again?"

"Only this," Peter smiled, gently placed his hands on either side of Guyon's face, and kissed him.

He realized his mistake as soon as he felt Guyon respond, knowing that Guyon was not ready - perhaps never *would* be ready - to allow that kind of exposure in front of anyone, even in front of Henri or David. He was surprised, then, when Guyon only drew back a little, putting his hands down gently, and said with a small, wry twist to his mouth,

"Oh, is that all?"

It was a small reminder, driven home with kindness at least, that in spite of the fact that they had, ostensibly, *made up*, Guyon still did not feel for him what he felt. Affection perhaps, but not love. *Never love.* Peter tried to turn it into a joke, "Well, there is also your coffee. No one quite seems to make it the same."

"I thought that was a *good* thing?" At least Guyon was quick with the balm of humor, if nothing more. Then he glared past Peter. "I'm sorry, did you two want something?"

"I want," David considered his answer, "some wine. And then

perhaps, some of these rolls." He snagged one off of the tea tray and began to liberally spread butter on it.

Guyon rubbed a thumb between his eyebrows. "I asked," he said dryly. There was a knock at the door. "Lord, *God*! It's not always like this, I'd remember!"

"Only recently." Peter sighed and then raised his voice, "Come in."

Robert poked his head around the door. "Only if no-one's going to throw anything," he said cheerfully. "Hello, Guy!"

"Yer quite safe ta join the asylum, Robbie," Peter told him in English.

"Not if he calls me Guy he isn't," Guyon growled irritably.

"Ah then, excuse me, Gee-ohne," Robert exaggerated the pronunciation of his name, "Just in time for tea, am I?" He moved to pour himself a cup.

Guyon stared at him. The skin around his mouth tightened, and his eyes went a little wider, anger starting to glitter in them, and Peter braced himself for an explosion. But instead of the usual quick-flashing temper, Guyon just sighed, and dropped his shoulders, forcing relaxation on himself like a well-worn cloak. He looked suddenly tired. "So it would seem," he agreed quietly.

"Robert," Peter growled out a warning. "Just don't start this. Alright?"

"Me?" Robert grinned at him, putting cream and sugar into his tea. "Wouldn't dream of it. Really. Oooh, lemon tarts." He plucked one off the tray, "Amazing what your lot of Cadets manages with as little French as they know."

He garnered a round of very blank looks for that. "I never knew that was a hindrance to training," Henri ventured at last. "Not with - well. Them being English and Peter being English and -"

"It *is* the English Marshal's Hôtel," David agreed.

Robert picked up his tea cup, "Not fer that. But they're living in France, ya know. They need ta be able ta buy food, arrange for it ta be cooked. I'd say only two or three in the whole company knows enough French to arrange fer this." He gestured with the cup. "Hell, I'd be willin' ta bet that only one in five of them can read or write even in English." He took a sip of the tea and frowned, "I think your cream's gone wrong."

Guyon snorted. It was a suspiciously happy sound. "Perhaps they ordered the wrong cream," he said smoothly.

"Like from goat's milk?" Robert took another sip.

"Mandrake," Peter bumped against Guyon with a wry grin.

"Mandrake's milk?" Robert frowned, "Never heard of that."

"Very rare," David agreed in a sort of blissful croak.

"Hmmm..." Robert took another sip. "Can't say I care for the flavor." He sat the cup down and took a bite of the tart instead.

"It's an acquired taste," Peter's lip twitched, "but very relaxing."

It was like watching the cogs of a watch fall into place. Robert stared at Peter, his cup, the ecstatic expression on Guyon's face, and groaned. "*Thanks*," he said, putting his head in his hands, and then, "*Mandrake*. Right idiot that makes me."

"Did I say a word?" Guyon asked the ceiling sweetly.

David started giggling his contagious giggle, leaning against Henri, whose deeper laughter joined in counterpoint. "It's alright, Robbie, it won't hurt ya and isn't it you that's been telling' me fer days that sleep is good for you?" Peter smirked.

"Raveled sleeve of care," David agreed a little incoherently. "'S all right, half a cup won't be - you'll just be a bit -"

"Sleepy?" Guyon suggested, and lost control of his twitching mouth completely.

*

There was a time for everything, or so Robert Macquarie had been taught. A time to greet friends, a time for adventures, and a time to bloody well go home. And this? This was definitely the latter, before one of his brother-in-law's demented friends did more to him than knock him out with mandrake.

Really, he wasn't sure how Peter dealt with all the lunacy that seemed to surround him from day to day. Cadets tumbling off balconies. Students tying cadets up, naked...on statues...painted blue. Doctors and pharmacists discussing the best undetectable ways to kill people. It was all a bit too much for staid, intractable Robert. Chaos was simply too...chaotic.

186

And through it all wove the unspoken-of, frightening influence of Corvay, of the Church, of the French Court that no-one dealt with and yet no-one seemed able to be free of, and while Robert admired Peter's ability to deal with it all face-on, and was beginning to develop a faint sense of awe as to Guyon's ability to remain imperviously acerbic in his attitude to the whole thing, he wanted out. Mostly because he was starting to understand all too well the temptation to join in, and was quite aware that his wife's tolerance, never a bedrock of his existence in the best of times, would certainly be like fine-ground sand in the face of a heavy fine from the authorities. He didn't, being a reasonably kindly man, say any of this when he announced that he had booked his passage, however, restricting himself to the bare fact of his departure.

Peter had given him a sad, but understanding expression, "So soon? Aye, but you're probably missing Sarah and the children. I can understand that. I miss her too, you know?"

Of course his homesickness had been growing, but it really did rank very low on the scale of his reasoning, "She misses you as well, Perry. Ya should come back soon, at least for a bit."

Which proved he was able to evade and ignore with the best of them, because while he knew he had to say it, he knew just as well what Peter's answer would be, and wondered which part of the decision would be influenced by the horrible sense of responsibility he still seemed bound by this time. Even if de Chesnay had proved that he was no ward, to be looked after and protected from the unpleasantnesses of life, the cadets *were*, and Peter could scarcely ship them all over with him for a few weeks' visit.

"I'll come when I can, Robbie. You know that." Peter gave a definite nod. "And I'll give you a letter to take to her."

It wasn't as much as Sarah would be happy with, but sometimes Sarah had expectations that had nothing to do with how the world actually worked. Bless her.

"And that'll keep her quiet for all of ten seconds." Robbie sighed. "Ah well, you know what ye're about." *I hope. Most of the time, anyway.*

The author of the times Robbie privately suspected Peter

187

didn't have a damn clue came hurriedly into the room, frowning. "Robert, you are leaving?" Guyon looked worried and a little flushed, as though he had run from wherever he had been to get to the Hôtel. "Is everything well?"

"Aye." Robbie nodded. "It's just time. As much as its Laird avoids running the place, Hawthornden does require a bit of work."

Odd that. Guyon's eyes kept shifting back and forth from himself to Peter and back. It was almost as if -

He thinks Peter will leave.

That startling thought butted right up against another. *Surely he knows how strong Peter's sense of honor and duty is?*

But, of course, none of that mattered where hearts were concerned, did it? All those fears of disappointment and disappointing, could be almost crippling. He remembered that much, at least, from his early days with Sarah.

"Poor rock," Guyon said, and his eyes were still, as though he had realized where Robbie's thoughts had gone. "Neglected geological points of interest are a sad thing." The frown flickered over his face again, and Robert knew that he was searching for an inoffensive way of putting what he really wanted to say. It was almost amusing, watching the usually silver-tongued little man struggle, until he said - "I had thought perhaps - you would stay until Peter returned."

Not *we*. Peter. Until *Peter* returned. Guyon didn't think Peter *would* leave, he thought he *should*. In all the misery of the preceding weeks and his frustration with Guyon's behavior, Robert had forgotten his own moment of understanding, out in the spring warmth of the Faubourg Gardens, seeing that no matter what Peter might say or believe, his love was returned, and in full.

And I thought Brian and his selfishness were bad enough. This one's got a streak of self-sacrifice as bad as Peter's, and it's worse to deal with. Who'd have thought it?

"Whenever that might be." Peter snorted. "As much as I love Robbie, I can't imagine my sister would be any happier with him being gone indefinitely either."

"He's right." Robbie nodded. "And even as strong willed as she is, it's only so long that most of the tenants will take her word as mine. Plus, I'll not be waiting around until the sea gets rough with winter. I'm not *that* good a sailor."

Guyon made a little face. "I am no sailor at all, you 'ave my sympathy," he said in one of the small rare moments of candor that had been the first thing Robbie had ever liked about him. "Travel safely, my...hmm. My regards to your family, and - thank you. For all you 'ave done for me. I know it was for Peter, but - I thank you all the same. Whatever I can do for you in the future - you 'ave only to ask." He didn't extend his hand, or make a court bow, but simply inclined his head a little, before turning to Peter. "*I'll call on you this evening,*" he said in quick French, and was gone.

"He's an odd fellow," The words slipped out of Robbie's mouth before he could catch them. He stumbled to correct them because, really, he liked Guyon. He liked how Peter seemed to relax when the other man was in the room. His brother needed more of that, desperately. "I mean...he must be if he puts up with you."

He watched Peter recognize his fumbling for exactly what it was, looking at him with a faint grin on his face. The look in his eyes was utterly false encouragement, the sort that Robbie had fallen for one too many times in their childhood. "Oh no," he said quickly, "No, I'll go no further down that road!"

Peter snorted out another laugh, "You're getting smarter in your old age, Robbie mine. Much smarter."

They looked at each other for a long amused moment before Peter continued, "So, tomorrow is it? Or today?"

"At four, with the tide," Robbie said, surprised to feel a faint twinge of regret. "I sent my baggage on ahead, *and* all the silks and laces that dressmaking friend o' yours seems to think Sarah will want." He couldn't help the laugh that escaped him. "Aye well, better that than her recipe book, I'm thinking!"

"God, yes." Peter's protestation was vehement. "As much as I adore Ännchen, Sarah does not need any help from her in that regard."

Peter stood up from his desk then, stepping around it to where Robbie stood, "I just wish...No, I'll not start that or I'll be blubberin' and caterwaulin' and making a sight of myself. We can't come with you...not yet...so there's no use in me even wishin' it."

"And I'll have my fill of salt water, so I'll thank you for stoppin' there," Robbie agreed, unsure as to whether he was pleased or unhappy as to how far they had come since his unwanted arrival. "I'll be finding life dull very soon, I've no doubts." He restrained himself from adding how much he was looking forward to the moment that feeling of dullness assailed him, and settled for the more familiar expression of farewell, with silence and an embrace.

Peter gave him a couple of firm slaps on the back before releasing him, "I'll miss ya, Robbie. I can't tell ya how happy I am that we've made this up."

That was really the first time either of them had actually mentioned their reconciliation to each other, oddly enough. It almost made Robert feel a bit weepy himself.

"Aye, well. You or a poker, a broom, and a cold bed. Wasn't much of a choice." He grinned quite genuinely, then, thinking not only of Sarah, but his varied, frustrating, demanding brood, who would all want to know why he hadn't brought Peter back with him, preferably tied in a ribbon for effect. The image made him laugh. "No, just thinking." He sobered. "I'm only sorry it took me so long."

"Stone headed, like all yer kin." Peter smiled, rapping his knuckles gently against Robbie's forehead. "Let me get a letter written for Sarah, then we'll have a bit of lunch and I'll go to the dock with ya."

Robbie, who hated goodbyes of any sort, thought that Peter was out of his mind, and discovered that he, too, shared in the trait of self-sacrifice that seemed to be so contagious, because instead of refusing point-blank, he found himself agreeing meekly and behaving as though nothing would suit him better.

*

In the end, it appeared, that neither of them were quite as brave or as self-sacrificing as they had intended to be. Their conversation dwindled off after lunch at the Quai, both of them

190

lost in thoughts of home and their imminent separation. Robbie finally sent Peter off, back to the Hôtel with a rough hug and an adamant order to, "be off before we're both cryin' like babes, ya great idiot."

And Peter left, leaving Robbie to nurse what passed for ale and await the tide.

"And I *still* don't understand why you're suddenly interested in ships," he heard a half-familiar voice say in perplexity.

"Because my deep and burning desire is to find out whether one coils rope to the left or the right," said Guyon's soft voice. The wry smile was audible. "Or do they call it something else when it's on board?

"It all depends on what it's attached to, as far as I can tell. Lines, I think..." Vincennes shrugged, apparently and completely disinterested in anything to do with ships, other than the possibility of them carrying in rats and disease.

"It's attached to - or it is - oh, never mind." Guyon sighed, then, catching sight of Robbie, visibly brightened. "Robert. Your ship, you will be pleased to hear, is plague-free. Vincennes was removed minutes since."

Said plague sputtered something incoherent into his ale, and excused himself with remarkable alacrity, even compared to his usual rather scatterbrained behavior, seating himself at a vocal and incomprehensible table who were surrounded by discarded books, bags and gowns, and immediately losing himself in some argument Robbie didn't even want to try and decipher.

"So...this is what ya do when yer not teachin'? Haunt the *Quai* and torment yer other friends?" There was teasing in Robbie's voice, he'd come to appreciate Guyon's wit and scathingly mocking manner in the peaceful days since Guyon and Peter had 'made up'. Somehow it made him think, more than a little, of his Sarah - a comparison he was certain that Guyon would not appreciate.

"I *am* teaching. Tolerance." Guyon said solemnly, and then ruined the effect by grinning. "Of my company, that is. No, usually I am to be found gazing very mournfully at a skull and contemplating the infinite - that is, sleeping with my eyes open. But torment others - oh yes, that I do most excellently well. And do not tell Vincennes this, but I miss 'is company at times, and 'ave learned to call an excuse to see 'im good."

"You've got a mixed bag here, don't ya?" Robbie nodded. "It's int'restin'. Now I'll go home and it'll be just me and Sarah and the children, and the same faces that I've seen since I was a old enough ta see."

Robbie leaned back and gazed out over the rumbling playful mix of students and cadets that flowed in and out of the Quai during the day. There were a few snaps and shoves every now and then, but it was all puppy fights; noise and growls and no teeth. "I'll miss this...but home is...Home. And there's nothing and nowhere I want more."

"Mm. I think the same is true of Peter. But he will not leave." Guyon shrugged, though indifference was evidently the last thing he felt. "Will all be well for you, at 'ome? Not your family, but...I think it may be difficult for you to keep your new beliefs, per'aps?"

He had never heard a suggestion of renewed betrayal phrased quite so delicately.

"You're afraid I'll hurt Peter again," Robbie nodded. "Fair enough and I deserve that, I do. But no, Guy, ya'd have ta know Hawthornden. We're a bit off the beaten track and not apt ta call down troops on us. As long as we're quiet we'll be left ta ourselves, I'm thinkin'."

"That is not what concerns me." Guyon looked down at the battered table, his blunt index finger tracing out some pattern Robbie could not follow. "I am more...hm. As far as I can, I will protect 'im in Paris. But I am not the one who must pass through Edinburgh or can be accessed by some English version of Corvay. I fear for *you,* my Scot of convictions, as much as for Pèire. I am the most..." He paused, searching for words. "I am the most intransigent man alive, or so they say, and even I can be...bent to a purpose."

"There's not a man as can't be, Guy." Robbie agreed. "But I'll be home where I have friends, even in Edinburgh. Keep yer worries fer Peter. I'm...I'm countin' on ya there, ya know?"

Because if he was leaving, and he was, then there was no one else he trusted more to watch Peter's back than this short Occitan scholar, *God help them both.* "Nay, don't look daggers at me. I know I can and I know ya will, for the love you bear him. Just need ta have it be said."

"I live by words," Guyon said very dryly, "and yet - 'ow they are overrated! I think there are three people in the world who would dare say that to me and know I would accept it. *Oc.* You know I will." His strange eyes came up from their perusal of the table, and looked straight into Robbie's. "You know I *'ave.*"

Robbie looked down at his drink and then out over the wash of people around them, "I know. I know. But I'm not sure Peter does. And he needs ta, badly. He'd walk through fire for you Guy. Walk through fire and dance barefoot on the coals if he thought it would prove his love. Don't make him do that, would ya?"

"What do you think I try so 'ard to prevent?" Guyon asked sadly. "I tell 'im again and again not to prove it. Not to -" He took a deep breath, visibly regaining control. "As far as any man can stop another from such actions, yes. I promise."

"No...no you don't." Robbie almost snapped it back. "Oh, not that you don't want to, but that's not here nor there. Does ya no good ta want or don't want, Peter loves you. You just need ta decide if that's more important than what you think you're protecting him from...or protecting yourself from."

"Protecting *myself?*" Guyon's face went stark white, and his laugh sounded as though it had been pulled over jagged glass. "Oh, I stopped trying *that* months since. But nothing - *nothing* - is more important to me than protecting 'im. Not 'is love, not mine, not any kingdom. Christ. You are all blind. You - you think Peter is the only one who would dance barefoot on coals? You are wrong, Robbie. So would I. Because I *do not 'ave those words.*"

Robbie looked suddenly into eyes gone from clear to the flare of green fire. What must it be, he wondered, to have all that you might want and be unable to say so?

Suddenly, he felt very sad for Guyon, and for Peter as well. Peter he knew, needed the words and it appeared he might never receive them. And Guyon? He was trapped in his silence, more trapped than anyone he'd ever seen.

"If I were...what I let you all think me, I would 'ave walked away," Guyon said more gently. "I would 'ave found some way to save my brother. I would 'ave told Peter I did not love 'im, and sent 'im away for good. But with all I 'ave done, I 'ave never lied." His smile was a crooked little travesty. "I do promise, Robbie."

"Those words are important ta you, aren't they? Not just because ya want me ta believe ya?" Robbie could tell, from the strained sound of Guyon's voice that they were not ones he spoke often or lightly. "I do though, somehow. Just...."

Robbie looked off in the direction that Peter had traveled when he left the Quai, his eyes bright with farewell. "Bring him home ta us eventually will ya, Guy? He needs Hawthornden and we need him."

"You provide the damn coals *for* me," Guyon said wearily. "Yes, I will. When I can. As soon as I can." He made an odd little gesture. "I can't fight 'im, you know. I never could."

"Not many can," Robbie agreed. "And those as can...aren't worth their salt for much more than amusement's sake." He stood, "There now. It's time for me to go. Tide will have turned and I sit here blatherin'."

"I shall pray for...what is it? Fair winds and a following sea, I think," Guyon said, and got to his feet as well, all his intensity dimmed once his eyes were no longer on the same level as Robbie's. "Good fortune, Robert Macquarie. Be safe."

He had never seen Guyon make any demonstrative gesture towards any man but Peter, and even those had always been brief and half-embarrassed, but there was nothing but a strange kind steadiness in the farewell embrace that was offered him, nothing hurried or awkward about the formal brush of lips to his cheeks and forehead.

Robbie chuckled softly, and reverently returned the farewell, "Best you remember that I said for ya ta *bring* him home, right? Take care, Guyon, keep safe."

And with no other word or glance, he turned and moved off down the docks, leaving behind a friend.

*

To say that things were settling down in Peter's world, would perhaps be a misstatement. Robbie was gone back to Scotland and, yes, he and Guyon were once again speaking, were once again 'together' and working towards their old amicability, if not ease, and he was sleeping again, with no resort to any of David's vile concoctions. But, it seemed that chaos had sensed a vacuum and was attempting to fill it up at the Hôtel d'Orsay

The cadets, sensing or knowing that Peter's mood had greatly improved, returned to their usual activities with much enthusiasm, and apparently, felt the freedom to traipse in and out of his office on the slightest excuse. It made him feel rather like some kind of oddity presented for view, but he allowed it in an effort to reestablish an even keel. He trusted Philippe and Thomas Granger, his young valet, to make sure that nothing truly important was interrupted and so far that seemed to be working

The only real annoyance in his life at the moment was embodied in the personage of one Kees van Rijn, the young Dutch painter that Peter had finally agreed to allow her Majesty to commission to paint his portrait - agreed being a slight blurring of the truth. It was more that she refused to accept any more of his excuses about time or activities and told him when his first sitting was. It appeared however that for the moment, Kees was happy with spending a few hours a day, following Peter around and sketching him in odd moments. It wasn't as disruptive as Peter had envisioned and he hoped that it would remain the case.

At the moment, he had a whole office full of empty and quiet. Kees had gone, rubbing charcoal smudges off his fingers. Most of the cadets had been taken off by Wycombe for a brisk march, to be followed by a half day leave and Peter...well, to say he suddenly found himself at a loss in the quiet might be an overstatement, but he found himself, increasingly simply staring out the window.

"Well, if you will drop a pike on your foot pointy-side down..." Vincennes's unsympathetic tones drifted up the stairs. "Oh, God, someone translate for me? Pointy. Pointy end. Don't put it through your *foot*."

There was a soft consultation, and then the voice of Thomas, whose French was probably the best of any of the cadets', due to his French mother, explaining to Vincennes that, "Deighton says he didn't do it on purpose...that's why they call it an accident." It was a close enough translation, leaving out only Roger Deighton's calling Vincennes a *prat*.

"Um, yes. That's...in fact, I have no words," Vincennes said. He sounded tired. "Right, you need to keep your weight off this for at least a week, or it won't heal. Accident or not. And why is that man *sketching* me? No, really, why *are* you sketching me? Go away."

"I haf to work. I am paid."

"You're paid to drive Peter mad, not me."

"Thought that was de Chesnay's cause of living," said Philippe's voice slyly, and the too-familiar sound of Andre Morel's little hooting laugh followed it. Peter hoped, with sudden fervor, that the student lawyer was *not* there to see him.

"As amusing and as truthful as that might be," Vincennes said, with a voice that sounded neither amused nor particularly willing to be amused at that moment, "I would suggest that you do not repeat that in either de Chesnay's or Scudamore's hearing...if you value your position."

"They are a rather...volatile pair of friends," Thomas, *bless him*, even with a French mother his manners were completely English.

"Says the man who doesn't have to study with a deranged Occitan who challenges world order," said Philippe gloomily. "And makes *you* challenge world order."

"And rewrite things when they're *fine*." Andre sounded extremely sulky.

"You haf ve law wronk." Peter might have been imagining things, but there was a note in van Rijn's voice that suggested he had rather enjoyed whatever Guyon had done to Morel. "Ant he iss no matter zan ve *Maréchal*." There was an obviously uncomprehending silence, and he sighed into it in explanation, "No more *deranged*."

"Makes you wonder, don't it?" Roger Deighton's thick tones there, translated swiftly by Thomas once again.

"Wonder what?" Vincennes's voice was rather abrupt, as if he were growing impatient with this picking apart of men who were his friends.

"Not saying he's not brilliant or something, de Chesnay, but he's no soldier, and got no talent for it."

"Yes, that's not exactly *news*," Vincennes said irritably. "Really, we'll be sending you to the school next, if you keep being all observant like that." He did something that made Deighton yelp with pain, but the cadet carried on, undeterred if a little shaken-sounding -

"No, but why'd's he come here?"

"Oh, you *baby*," said Morel scathingly.

"*Mouth*, Morel." Vincennes's voice was a sharp warning. "Watch it."

"They obviously care for each other," Thomas again. "You know the Marshal was beside himself when they had their falling out. I'm sure that Monsieur de Chesnay was just as bad, from the little I saw of him then."

"Exactly." Vincennes sounded as if his agreement should be all that it took.

"Care for each other or not, there's got to be more than that." Andre Morel again. Peter had never heard a smirk quite so audible in a voice before. "Guyon de Chesnay was the darling of the Sorbonne from the moment he arrived, from all I've heard, and for him to spend so much time with, *excuse me but it's true*, a soldier...well, it can't be very challenging for him."

"Mm." Peter wondered, even as he contemplated the havoc Guyon would wreak in Morel's life if he found out about this conversation, whether Vincennes was deliberately imitating his former tutor's ability to convey an infinite amount of things with one small syllable. In this case it was disagreement and contempt at once. "But you *heard* that about Guyon, Morel, you weren't there to *know*. And in fact it would seem that for all your hearing, you don't know anything for certain." He chuckled, the sound soft and genuinely amused. "*Darling's* not the word anyone sane would use."

Deflection in debate. Peter recognized it with surprise, even as he also saw how deep Guyon's teaching ran in the young physician.

"Well at least he's *un vrai chevalier*!" Roger Deighton was apparently undeflectable. *Thank you so much*, Peter thought with

197

a total lack of gratitude for his cadet's defense.

"Well, semantics aside," Morel continued, seemingly not a bit put off by Vincennes's comments, "how long do you think it will go on before de Chesnay realizes that your Maréchal can not keep up with him intellectually? I'm sure that his own interest in swords and muskets and famous battles is less than minimal."

"Oh, put your *shoe* in your mouth, you idiot," muttered Vincennes.

"I'd say the Lord Marshal will tire of his prosy company far sooner," said Thomas with sudden and unwanted clarity. "In fact? I'd *lay odds*."

"Oh, my *God. No*," said Vincennes with feeling. "They'll find out and they'll *kill* you."

"Twenty to one. On de Chesnay." Morel's voice overlapped his.

"Done," Thomas said quickly. "And the rest of you?"

"I think you need to set the terms of this little wager," That was Philippe again. "Perhaps it is not who will leave who...but exactly when?"

Yes, Peter sighed softly. He did, after all, have no ties on Guyon - not of love, at least, and how long did he really think that Guyon would remain with him otherwise? He had already walked away from Peter on three different occasions, when would the final time come? Was it truly just a matter of time? Was he simply deluding himself?

"Oh, I'll give de Chesnay a month," Morel said confidently. "Probably won't notice he's bored until then."

Peter couldn't listen to anymore. He stood and stepped out onto the balcony, shutting the glassed doors behind him. He hadn't thought the things he feared most were so transparently obvious to anyone but himself. He'd obviously been wrong. Even that pack of youngsters downstairs had seen the obvious defects in his relationship with Guyon. Disparities in education and intelligence that no amount of study on his part would ever bridge.

And yet, as long as he had any hope of Guyon wanting him, how could he not still try to keep up? Try to do whatever it took to keep Guyon with him even a few hours longer? He had to, because admitting defeat before the battle was done was something he had never learned to do. And, if he were forced to endure a life without Guyon in it, he wanted to store up every moment he could...good or bad.

*

Guyon had suffered through an intensely unprofitable afternoon with Gottfried, the account books, and the legal documents of their school. The conversation had got stuck on the point of 'What do you mean, in case you don't come back?' and had not moved on for three hours. Guyon was absurdly touched by his colleague's concern and desperately irritated by it in slightly greater measure, helped on by the lack of any breeze whatsoever that day, which had rendered the usually airy main room stifling and heavy with the usually faint smells of chalk and slate and ink and very young men who had not quite gathered the necessity of actually *bathing*, as opposed to simply washing their faces and aiming in the vague direction of respectability.

Guyon had escaped with considerable relief, therefore, only to find that to an already protesting and insulted nose, Paris in late May smelled worse than the teaching-room. Hoping that David had recognized the need for strategically placed herbs in the Hôtel d'Orsay, he had reached it with vague optimism, which had immediately been dispelled when he found three of his students, only one of whom, the painter van Rijn, *should* have been there, Vincennes, and two red-faced young cadets, all in the main foyer and looking surprisingly guilty.

"Whatever you killed, I'm blaming Morel," he said with completely feigned cheerfulness. "What are you still doing here, Philippe? I *know* you have a debate tomorrow, Peter won't thank you if you miss the morning sleeping because you burned night's candles out trying to prepare for it."

"As you say, Monsieur," Philippe looked almost relieved that someone was suggesting he leave. He, oddly enough, gave van Rijn a pat on the back that looked almost sympathetic before hurrying out of the Hôtel.

Guyon took in Vincennes's annoyance, van Rijn's unease, and

finally turned his attention to a far-too smug looking Morel. *Ah. Well, de Barrion grew out of it, for the main part - there may be hope for this one yet...*

"And my dear apprentice of a lawyer, what are you doing here *at all*? If de Retz sent you, you should be with the Marshal, not wasting the time of his cadets, surely? My apologies, gentlemen, I can teach my students to debate, but manners are still beyond them."

"You would have me restricted in my friendships then, Monsieur?" Andre smirked. "As often as I am here, do you not think I could possibly have private business as well as that of the Archbishop?"

"If you do, it is not with anyone in this foyer," Guyon said curtly, and was pleased to see the look of discomfiture, however fleeting, that passed over Morel's face. "And *if* you do, as I said, you should not until after the Archbishop's formal hours are ended, since you do not have permission to be anywhere but with him, working for him, or in my glorious and esteemed company until then. *Do you.*" It was not a question. "Out, Andre. Go home. Now."

The young man's face grew stony and slightly red around the edges, but whether it was embarrassment or anger that tinted his cheeks, was a moot point. He bowed to Guyon and turned to go, tossing a final comment over his shoulder as he departed, "We'll speak more of this later, Thomas. You can be sure of it."

"I'll look forward to it, Monsieur!" Thomas called back. He was still pink-faced with annoyance

"Mm," said Guyon. "Then you're in an unique and enviable position here in Paris, because no-one else does. Vincennes, is Peter upstairs?"

Vincennes gave a start, and looked up from where he had been putting his supplies back in his bag. "Oh, yes, possibly. I haven't seen him since I arrived. I was a bit occupied with convincing this young....man...that his foot was not a good stand for his pike." He seemed far more annoyed than the cadet's clumsiness would warrant.

"Well, that must hurt," Guyon said to the still seated cadet with a cheerful almost-sympathy that he usually found worked wonders on unsettled students. "Still, you're in good hands." He took a narrow look at the four young men, and sighed. "Look. Whatever this was, don't tell me. Please. When I say I don't want to know about something, believe me, I mean it. But Morel is pushing his boundaries, and you should ignore him." He raised his eyebrows a little. "Vincennes, you usually do better than this."

"Yes, I do." He gave a tired little exhalation of air. "Maybe I'm just getting old and have less patience than you do. Or less than I used to." Vincennes chuckled then, shaking his head, "Or maybe I need to ignore them all and go have a drink. Maybe you can drag Peter away from all this, and meet me later?"

"Oh, I'll certainly try hard," Guyon said amusedly. "Down by the *Quai*, then? You and Peter can insult the merchants unloading."

"More like check for plague," said Vincennes, making a face. "Ibn Ibrahim's already got the 'comes in summer months, comes with cargoes' thing going night and day."

"Ugh. *Not* the *Quai*, in that case. The *Oise Grise* all right as an alternative?"

"That's fine. I'll meet you there after sundown," Vincennes picked up his bag, then glanced up the stairs. "Don't let him refuse, eh? He needs to get out more."

Guyon made a face. "The boat of my powers of persuasion sailed long since, I'm afraid. I will *try*." He shrugged a little helplessly, and Vincennes sighed.

"Well, if you can't, the rest of us are doomed."

"I'll try," Guyon repeated.

Vincennes nodded, gave the Cadets and van Rijn a farewell scowl, then went out the door.

"Monsieur de Chesnay, have you a moment? I promise to be brief." Kees interrupted before Guyon could move toward the stairs.

"I have *a* moment," Guyon said to the young painter who attended his classes and heard about a fifth of them, being more absorbed in sketching his fellow students than in any of the topics at hand. "And be *very* brief, please."

"I vant to know.. My sketches. Which you t'ink is mos' like de Maréchal?" Kees opened his sketch book. "De English

201

Queen...she says to paint and I paint soon, but the...Monsieur Scudamore.. He is diff'cult. He changes."

"Yes, he does," Guyon agreed absently, taking the sketchbook from him. "Kees, these are -" *Busily seeking in continual change. And one look here that you will never see, and I may have killed in him, complete absorption, and utter joy.* "- they're very good," he finished, lamely, turning the pages over, and then caught his breath on a little choke of recognition, seeing the faint quirk of a half-exasperated smile, the way two faint creases lay below one eye, and only one beneath the other, the small bracket of amusement curving down towards the faint shadow of Peter's stubborn jaw. "This," he said, his fingers resting on that familiar determined line, half-unconsciously. "This one."

Kees nodded agreement, "I tot so, but it is good to be sure. Thank you." He closed the book back up, gave them all a small bow and then followed in Vincennes' wake.

"*What?*" Guyon snapped at Thomas and the unfortunate bandaged-foot cadet. Getting no response, he shook his head, at the end of all patience with the world, and went up the stairs to find Peter, whom he found out on his balcony, looking out at Paris with a distinctly jaundiced expression.

"Perhaps Kees should paint you like that," Guyon said lightly, "and then it could act like Perseus's shield, turning the unwary to stone. Bad day, *chérâme?*"

"Just long and tiring and rather pointless, actually." Peter shrugged and continued his perusal of the skyline. "Can I hope yours was a bit better?"

"About the same," Guyon admitted. "With added accounts. And Gottfried *fretting*, for which I don't know whether to bless or curse him." He stifled a sigh. Before his unequivocal decision to force understanding on Peter, he would have gone out to the balcony to join him without thinking, but now he could only stand awkwardly by the glass doors, and wait to be invited, or for Peter to come to him. *Somewhere, the God of Chaos and Irony is laughing at me.*

"I think he's caught that from Ännchen," Peter smiled crookedly for a moment before turning his face towards Guyon. "Could you...? Would you like to share the sunset with me? It might be wishful thinking, but I think I felt a wisp of a breeze."

"Oh, definitely you imagining things," Guyon said, having paused for a moment to make sure he had the right note ready to transfuse into his voice. "It'll be a *relief* to get out of Paris, even this early." He leant on the stone balustrade, letting his arm and the back of his hand lie along Peter's, mirror images. Undemanding, uncomplicated, easy to move from without offence.

"Yes...about that..." Peter didn't move, but his voice sounded as far away as Scotland in that moment. "You know, you still have the choice to stay here. I know you said you'd go. And I know I would rather have no one else with me...but...No...Never mind. I keep rethinking everything. I feel like I'm on eggshells and nothing's quite right and I want so badly to make it better...but then that would be me, taking over again. I'm trying, Gui, really. But then, I was trying before and I mucked it all up so...."

"Trying, but not *thinking*," Guyon said with a lot more gentleness than he felt. He was starting to see, belatedly, just what Robert had meant by Peter using his taking responsibility as a means of showing love. Guyon had taken that form of expression away from him, and silenced him as effectively as when he had forbidden any mention of that emotion. "And I was doing the opposite. Normally we complement each other...this time we didn't. It's not the end of the world, *car-mi*. Just a small hurt. And the eggshells," he added mockingly, "are hurting my feet. I think we should get rid of them."

Peter's chuckle was a bit broken sounding, but still a laugh, bright and sincere, "I'd like to try. I'm certainly not enjoying them either. Just...just talk to me, please? Tell me if I'm heading the wrong direction. And I'll try to remember to ask first."

"What do I need to do?" Guyon could have bitten his tongue out the moment he said the words, because God help him, *he knew*. It would be easy, so easy, to give in, to let the bell-swing take his mouth, say *I love you*, and stop his lies of omission once and for all, say *I feel my soul within me, but it's you*, and lose it all. And they were going to the Languedoc, back to where everyone knew what he was, back to where Peter would find out

203

what he was, and he would not give Peter the impossible burden of his love to carry away with him from that. *These fragments have I shored against my ruins. My broken shards of dulled honor.*

"I don't know," Peter's head dropped forward, his eyes scanning the street below. "Kick me in the arse, maybe. Or the head. Whichever will do the most good." Peter looked back up at Guyon, "I can learn this. Really. Just give me time?"

"Oh *Jesus*, Pèire -" *You're breaking my heart.* From somewhere, he found the strength to silence himself, and even smile, a little. "All the time you want or need," he said.

"Thank you," Peter straightened up, and put one arm around Guyon's shoulders. He didn't pull him close though, as he once might have done, but left space between them, open and vacant.

Guyon, who knew that the justice in what had been said worked both ways - *thinking, and not trying* - leant into the seemingly endless space, wondering if that small gesture, all he had in him, would ever add up to enough, if repeated, to bridge the chasm that right now seemed so terrifyingly vast.

Peter's arm tightened almost at once and the sigh that escaped him seemed to have equal parts of relief, fatigue and contentment. "Thank you," Peter whispered again, but Guyon wasn't sure if the words were to him - they sounded almost prayerful.

But Guyon, seeing his doom approaching in the shape of his home country, could not find it within himself to pray or feel gratitude. He could only wait, and take the brief comfort of this moment for what it was.

*

The Languedoc, June 1646

All Love is sacred, and the marriage-tie
Hath much of honor and divinity.
But Lust, Design, or some unworthy ends
May mingle there, which are despis'd by Friends.
Passion hath violent extremes, and thus
All oppositions are contiguous.
So when the end is serv'd their Love will bate,
If Friendship make it not more fortunate:
Friendship, that Love's elixir, that pure fire
Which burns the clearer 'cause it burns the higher.

It was odd, Peter thought, how often they took comfort in avoidance. Here they were, on their way to Guyon's home but were they discussing what they would find there? What they could expect? No. Completely the opposite.

Somehow, that they held so true to form *was* comforting to Peter - if this remained the same, then perhaps, he could have faith in other things, in *equilibrium* and in *gravity*.

"So will Scotland kill me, or I it?" Guyon asked, amused and obviously willing to run with their latest branch into possible and might-be for as long as he could.

"More like the voyage will do you in."

"A most excellent point," Guyon said sourly, his precise, weary diction indicating quite clearly that Peter had thoroughly missed some point he was striving to make.

Peter caught the odd tone, more usual to the teaching rooms and evening, rather than their private conversations, and looked over at Guyon, "But you won't...You mean you would? I mean..." He stopped for a moment, as his brain churned over what had been said. "You'd go there?"

Guyon shrugged. "Your King is making - admittedly by force, but he *is* making - an alliance with the Scots, who, for some reason known only to the Almighty, will, I think, decide to support him. You have reallied with Macquarie. You want to leave Corvay. Unless you had plans on associating with the Dutch Army, I assumed that was where we were headed - or at least, where we *should* head."

Peter looked down at Guyon. *We*. That had a better sound than anything he had hoped for. "So...you'll go? With me, I mean?" Peter's voice was hesitant, something he'd thought he was long past.

"No," Guyon said acidly, "I thought I'd stay behind and keep Paris warm for you - preferably by burning it down and starting with the Louvre."

"Well, if that's your preference," Peter said, dryly. "But I think you'd prefer Scotland."

"Now, you see, that was my thinking," Guyon said with equal asperity. "But of course, you could always stay here, and help with the conflagration."

"The smell of burning paint and lacquer could never compete with a turf fire, Guyon. Trust me on that one." A smile flittered over Peter's face. "And much nicer for sitting beside after a long day."

"In terms of durability, at least," Guyon agreed, obviously letting Peter take that one however he wanted. He looked completely, blandly innocent, though, which never boded well for his actual intentions.

"There is a lot to be said for durability." Peter agreed, a smile twitching around his lips. "And flexibility...and endurance."

"Mm." The odd, non-committal noise. "Well, you are the one whose house is built upon a rock, after all. And God knows I'm intransigent enough to pass for one."

"God knows." Peter agreed and then began to chuckle. "I can't wait to get you and Sarah together. I'll just stand back and watch the fur fly."

"We might even like each other," Guyon suggested. "Then you would have to hide."

"Oh, I'm certain you will like each other." Yes, Peter was certain. But he and Sarah liked each other too, and it had never kept the two of them from going at it, toe to toe. Or maybe that was the result of familial love and always wanting the best for each other, and then disagreeing as to just what that best was.

Guyon looked rather as though he wanted to hit something. "That will be nice," he said in his smoothest tones.

"It will." Peter leaned closer and lowered his voice. "But it doesn't matter either way. If...If you're with me, it'll be alright."

*

Night had come upon them rather unexpectedly, and they found themselves too far from a sizable town to make their way to an inn. But, thanks to Peter's cachet and Guyon's persuasive charm they had convinced a farmwife to allow them to bed down in her barn for the night. It was rough, but she offered them a warm meal and clean blankets, so bedding down in the hay was not too onerous.

"Tell me again why we are set on the Languedoc, hm?" Guyon asked. It was unclear whether he wanted reassurance or an argument.

"Have you a better idea? Collect the information, direct from the source, and then out. For good." Peter gave a definitive nod. If Guyon wanted to start this debate up again, he was going to make it hard work - not because he didn't want to provide the reassurance or the distraction of an argument, but because it wouldn't be distraction any more, all the paths of possibility too well worn for anything but the weary familiarity of contempt.

"I merely warn you that your much-vaunted Scottish turf fires had better be warm, for nothing more will compensate for the chill of our reception." It seemed that Guyon felt the same way, for it was less a complaint than a somewhat dispassionate statement.

"I will always keep you warm, Guyon, no matter where we are or our reception." Peter assured him, as he spread their bedding out over the fresh smelling hay. "And do not make a joke of that, for I am quite serious."

"Do you remember I told you once, the more serious it is, the more you must be sure to make it into a jest?" Guyon shrugged. "Ta ben. I do not wish to go to the Languedoc, and nor should you. But - I have faith." His mouth twisted into something midway between a smile and a grimace. "I have faith in you, at any rate. So, we will get our information, and we will give it to Corvay, and we will go - home."

"Yes, God, we shall." Peter nodded solemnly, but then, in answer to Guyon's first comment, he continued. "It's going to be very difficult to explain you to the sheep."

"Oh, well, just say I overwhelmed you with the dazzling intellect they are sadly not even collectively in possession of," Guyon said quickly.

"You did, indeed." Peter agreed, then tugged Guyon closer and wrapped his arms around him. "I shall also say that you're much more fun to sleep with...although as long as we have been on the road, the smell is not that different."

Guyon choked on laughter. "Oh, you rose garden, you one-to-comment! I tell you, that will be the first thing I do. Order a bath and stay in it for an hour. No, two."

"Let me share it?" Peter nuzzled his face into Guyon's neck. "I'll scrub your back for you."

"Oh, if you want to fold yourself into a wooden tub -!" Guyon put his hands up at the back of Peter's neck. "Give me a reason, *chérâme*. One more reason. Add it to the list."

"Because I'll also scrub your front? Because it will be warmer and cozier?" Peter nibbled gently on Guyon's neck. "Because I love you?"

"I'll take the first and the last, I thank your kind -" Guyon broke off. "I don't know love, Peter, though I know you believe you feel it for me. I can't give more, but - I'll still act as your blade, though, in the Languedoc. That much I know."

"I'll take whatever you think you can give me, Guyon. I don't demand that my love be returned - it doesn't work like that." Peter whispered softly against Guyon's neck. "And I will just thank you for the rest, I think."

"You ask too little, and I think I hate that," Guyon murmured, but he still leant his head back, one quick second of evident indulgence. "Bah. Protect me from the sheep in three months, and we'll call it evens." He dropped his hands. "I am bored with my own sentiments. How many miles do you dictate for the day, magister?"

Peter gave a heartfelt sigh, "You really are a bucket of cold water on my plans for a lusty seduction, you know?"

"Oh - I -" Guyon laughed. "Very cold. Poor impoverished

Scot, did no-one tumble you in a hayloft, then?"

"Not recently, no." Peter attempted to look forlorn and pitiable.

Guyon shouted with laughter, and spun around. "Spare me the details, m'ecosse. Let me explain, instead, for you see, there is all this hay for a purpose..." He pushed Peter backwards, laughing still, and then brought his hands up to cup Peter's face, kissing him. "Aux tous les matin' du mond', t'ete l'gloir'..." he murmured indistinctly, and then pushed backwards, tumbling them both over into the hay.

Peter landed with a laughing 'oof', Guyon sprawling over the top of him, "And the purpose is to keep you from breaking me during the fall?"

"For sure, better than you breaking me, long length of nothing," Guyon agreed cheerfully.

"Ah, yes. I am as nothing..." Peter lay his head back, eyes closed and threw his arms out in surrender. "I am yours. Have your way with me."

"But that's too easy," Guyon said, mockingly, and flicked straw at his nose.

"Would it be easier for you simply to confess your love and let it be, then?" Peter asked, and regretted it almost instantly, as Guyon's teasing was replaced by the old, familiar, shuttered look.

"No," Guyon said shortly, and rolled off him. "It would not." He got to his feet. "I'll give everything a last check before we sleep, I think."

He was out of the barn before Peter could either protest or apologise, leaving his cloak behind.

It came as no surprise when he did not return until Peter was at least feigning sleep, lying down with a faint sigh, his head pillowed in the crook of his arm with no care for finding comfort. His eyes could have been open or closed in the deep shadows, and Peter did not have the courage, as he viewed the blanched face in the dim light, to find out which it was.

Why can't you love me? he wanted to ask, and did not dare voice the question, afraid in some essential part of himself that if he pushed his need for that knowledge too far, he might, God help him, receive it.

He was not sure he would survive whatever it was.

*

They awoke the next morning, a subdued pair. Peter, silent with having missed the answer to his question. Almost sorry not to have asked it, and still relieved he had not, for fear of what Guyon's reply might have been. Almost sorry, then, but not entirely, for it was impossible to regret what silence he had managed when compared to the reaction his words had evoked.

He disentangled himself from his cloak, standing with a slight wince and a stretch, brushing hay off of his sleep-damp body. He stretched again, then froze, feeling eyes on his back. Turning he spoke softly, "Will you wake? Or sleep longer?"

There was a considering silence. "I'm admitting I'm awake by answering that, aren't I?" Guyon said at last. "It's not right, the way your mind actually works first thing in the morning. It should be illegal." He yawned. "Illegalized. Something. Urgh, I have hay everywhere."

"Yes, that happens." Peter lowered himself back down to the ground, chuckling and picking bits of hay out of Guyon's curly hair. "You look rather debauched, actually. I like it."

"It's the village idiot look," Guyon agreed, "I'm returning to my roots." He rubbed a knuckle under his mouth, looking awkward. "You're - all right, then?" He sounded as though the words were being extracted from him with pliers. "Lord, why do I ask, all soldiers think hay is but a luxury and a bare floor heaven."

All right? That hadn't exactly been what Peter had been hoping to hear. Guyon rarely avoided the unpleasant so absolutely, preferring blunt confrontation to evasion whenever he could manage it. But, he supposed, it was Guyon, through and through - avoid the emotional by focusing on the practical. He looked up, studying Guyon's face, afraid as always that he would see regret there. "Yes. I'm fine. A bit stiff but fine."

Relief showed briefly on Guyon's face, followed by an equally fleeting look of embarrassment at having been caught worrying. "Good," he mumbled, focusing on some bits of hay that had somehow woven themselves into his shirt. Then he smiled tightly, all evidence of any sort of affection wiped away. "So we should make good time today, then."

"Yes. I suppose we will." Peter watched Guyon's hands, absently. He'd much rather remain here in their little island of quiet, trying to regain the mood he had so thoroughly destroyed the night before. He sighed, recognizing it as an impossibility, and retreated to the walls of fact and practicality that Guyon so embraced.

"Breakfast?" he suggested.

It was a non sequitur, but what he had been dwelling on would only have led to more of the same imaginings, and of how he could manage to convince Guyon to follow his mind's path.

Guyon gave him a look that suggested he knew damn well he was being unduly optimistic for listening to Peter, but was going to indulge himself anyway. "We have breakfast?"

"Well...not as such...but..." Peter rummaged around in his pack and pulled out a couple of rather dry looking apples, tossing one to Guyon.

Guyon gave him a disbelieving grin. "Apples and hay," he said amusedly. "What a lucky horse I am." He looked speculatively at the small handful of hay he had collected, then at the apple. "Decisions, decisions..."

"Oh...well, if you'll eat hay, I'll take the apple back and save it for later," Peter held out his hand.

Guyon bit hastily into the rather desiccated looking fruit. "No, no, luxury first," he said in a rather muffled voice. He swallowed. "Though on second thoughts, the hay might be less dry..."

Peter sniffed out a laugh, then stretched back out, using Guyon's leg for a pillow. "There must be a village or two ahead of us. I promise to feed you there. Real food...that must be prepared and cooked."

Guyon snorted. "Promise? More like a threat. Unless you're going to find someone who is not you to cook this real food while you're at it..." He threw the apple core in the vague direction of the barn door, and started getting the last of the hay out of Peter's hair. "Same damn color," he said. "Give you a few hours and you'd have blended in completely."

"Mmmmm..." A contented expression covered Peter's face and his eyes drifted shut. "And then you'd have to come look for me."

Peter wondered just how long he'd get away with this before Guyon realized he was stalling and call him back to the business at hand, continuing their journey.

"I wouldn't look," Guyon corrected him with utter, breathtaking arrogance. "I'd *find*." His fingers tugged a little, sharply, in Peter's hair. "Up, Scudamore. I will not be lulled into sentimentality without coffee."

Not very long, obviously.

"Ow! I'm up. I'm up." Peter clambered to his feet holding his hand out to Guyon.

Guyon's slanting smile was pure devilry. "Any response," he said with mocking over-dignity, "would be beneath me." He took Peter's hand and scrambled to his feet. "Come on. I want to find this village."

"After you," Peter gather up their packs and bowed Guyon toward the door, swinging a wild playful kick at his backside as he passed.

The look Guyon gave him, as he made a futile attempt to get the dusty footprint off his already-abused clothes, suggested that revenge was going to be later, rather than sooner, and extremely unpleasant.

*

Guyon would have known blindfold the moment his horse set foot in the Languedoc, known from the sound of water and the shifts in air, even from the sound of leaves. But even after nearly a day of its poignant, familiar movement around him, he was unprepared for the very real lurch of his heart, the pain that seemed to catch him beneath his ribs, at the first sight of Carcassonne's turrets, the red roofs and high stone walls, the green surrounding it beyond which the moat lay.

He was also unprepared for the sight of Peter, his eyes sharp and interested, taking in everything they passed as if he were mapping it for some future conflict. No, perhaps conflict was a poor choice of words. As if he were weighing it against something he knew and finding the measure a good match.

"I didn't know you had an interest in city architecture," he said, and tried not to wince at the sharply nasty little edge to his voice. *It's beautiful. You know it. Let him alone.* But, like a tongue at a sore tooth, he felt driven to poke and prod at the ache. "Dazzled or merely speculative?"

Peter's lips gave a small twitch of a smile, "Just imagining what you were like as a boy. The mischief you could have gotten into. Or Hell, the mischief *I* would have gotten into in such a place."

"I was hardly ever here," Guyon said, amused despite himself. He *had* spent some time on the roofs, it was how he had been so good at evading the Watch in Paris, but it had been strictly forbidden for him to do so once his predilection for all things high and dangerous had been discovered. "The house is - it's not like this."

"Now you're going to tell me you were raised in a hovel?" Peter looked at him with amusement. "I don't think I'll believe you."

"N-o..." Guyon said slowly, "but...it's very different." How to explain to Peter the closed walls, the small high windows that were mere slits on all but the south-facing side, the quiet darkness and the old wood? He had loved it, once thought it a palace beyond imagining, but to a man who had gone straight from the Louvre to the airy, grand dilapidation of the Hôtel d'Orsay? It would be unthinkable.

Peter looked at him, then shook his head, "Last night we slept in a barn. It was one of the most peaceful nights I've spent in ages. As long as you're with me, nothing else will matter. I hope that someday you'll believe that."

"If I were you," Guyon said, starting to feel less pained and more depressed, "I'd restrain myself from judgment until you see the place. You may think the barn *preferable.*" Because the barn, dear God, had not had *Paire* Maurice in it. And the house, Christ preserve them both, most certainly would.

I hope that someday you'll believe that.

So do I, he thought wearily, wondering if he would always be incapable of doing so, as he was of saying the words that were starting to haunt his every waking moment, with fear of saying them, with fear of not. "Do you...do you want to go into the town?" *Please, no.*

Peter looked up at the sky, judging the time, "No. There'll be time for that later once we decide who we need to talk to. And besides, it's probably best we arrive before it gets much later, yes?"

"Yes," Guyon said in enormous relief. "We really don't want to arrive in the dark..."

They really didn't. The servants, other than the stablemen, had always lived in the village, going home after supper had been prepared, and he couldn't imagine that had changed. And he had no intention of introducing Peter to Maurice in anything other than broad daylight. The man had always used the shadows as his weapons, and Guyon, who tended towards the same behavior when at his unhappiest, was determined that this first encounter, however grim it would be, would not be something to haunt Peter's dreams. He had enough of those for his own.

"Right enough," Peter nodded. "Which way?" He paused for a moment though, before they could proceed, peering out over a meadow with a distracted look on his face, "You insufferable brat!"

"I *what*?" Guyon asked blankly. He couldn't think of what he might possibly have done to the rather innocuous looking meadow. "*What* did you call me?"

"All these months...teasing me...acting like you barely knew that wool *came* from sheep and look at them." Peter waved a hand toward the meadow, a vast wave of rolling green interrupted only by the fluffy whiteness of a flock of sheep.

"Oh, those are sheep?" Guyon said innocently. "Dear dear, and I thought they were small perambulating clouds. Alas, all these years, and I've been so horribly wrong..." He snorted. "It's more vineyards round here, you must have noticed. I simply...had my mind on higher things - oh hell!" The last, he was a little ashamed to note, was more a yelp, as Peter started to come towards him with evident mayhem on his mind. He set his heels to the sides of his horse and headed off down the path as fast as he could make the rather surprised and recalcitrant animal move.

"You'll pay, de Chesnay...just you wait!" With a wild laugh, Peter charged after his friend, forward toward their destination.

*

Guyon was not a fool. He knew exactly what Peter was doing, and was grateful for it. Any sharpness he evinced was ignored, coaxed away from him, made into some quirked little jest that he could not ignore, puncturing the air bubbles of misery that seemed to be surrounding his mind each and every time they began to swamp him. And that was horribly often, coming over him in small waves of sorrow and regret with every landmark they passed. The large stones by the side of the path, that he had once thought a broken giant's pavement, the soft yellow of gorse and the blue haze of the wild lavender that grew in the scrub beyond. All the soft scents and quiet, blurred colors of his childhood.

All the memories of what had driven him away.

You're a monster, warped from the time you drew breath. Don't you know what you are? Can't you see?

Your back reflects your soul, Guyon. Every time someone draws their breath in horror - and they will - it will be because they know you for what you are.

I cannot recant!

He drew in a sharp breath, trying to quell the voices, and looked down into the dip below them. "There," he said, pointing at the house.

Unchanged, unyielding, unlit, the outbuildings showing no movement. Grey and impenetrable, the small windows mere dark lines from their vantage point, narrowed eyes in a closed stone face.

"Oh, dear." Peter's voice was quiet, pitched only for Guyon's ears. "It is a bit forbidding, isn't it? Rather like having *Magister* Benichou questioning you. That man always makes me feel as if I were six years old and dirty-faced."

"Does he?" Guyon asked absently. "He always makes me wonder if I've got holes in my shoes again." He wondered what

Peter would say, if he turned to him and said - *My home is here. Here, not a room with fifteen books and mice in the wainscoting. Here, in my blood and my marrow. And I want it cut out, drained, I want it gone. It's poison.* "Sorry," he offered. "I did try and warn you..."

"So you did," Peter nodded. "But still, I've seen worse. Did I tell you about the place we bivouacked in with all the spiders? Big as your hand some of them were, I swear it." Peter urged his horse forward, leading the way toward the house, his tale growing more and more outlandish as they approached.

"...And when I got up the next morning one of my boots was missing. I'm sure they carried it off."

Guyon resurfaced from an odd fog of pure loathing for Corvay, de Retz, his past, Giraud, Maurice, and the entire Languedoc to blink at him. "The *spiders* carried your boot off?" he repeated incredulously. "More like one of your men *ate* it. The boot, that is, not the -" They were at the outer wall. "Do you know, I'm really not all that sure I'm capable of doing this," he said, vaguely surprised at himself, though whether it was for the admission or the emotion itself, he was not quite sure.

"It's up to you, Gui," Peter's voice was soft, soothing. "We can find an inn someplace. We don't need to stay here."

"Yes, I think there'll be quite enough talk without that," Guyon said, shaking himself slightly. He felt slightly muzzy, as though everything was not quite real, or the lavender had fogged his sight. "No, it's - I'm indulging in a moment's cowardice, that's all."

Peter nodded his understanding, "So, ahead then?"

Guyon gave him his best sardonic look. "Yes, that *is* the normal way of proceeding, unless there's some miraculous soldierly method you haven't told me about..."

"Well, it is...unless you're going for the element of surprise." Peter said it matter-of-factly, as if Guyon were seriously asking him a question. "Then you could circle in from the side...or use a zigzag pattern... Or, and I've used this myself a time or two, although it wouldn't work here, jump down from above..."

All the time he spoke he rode forward, into the courtyard.

Guyon suffered from a sudden and rather peculiar mental

image of Peter doing all three of those things, still on his horse and causing chaos. He shook his head again, rather more rapidly. "Er, right," he managed. "The. Um. Stables. Are to the left."

At least he was managing coherency, if not precisely sentences. He looked down, and saw that the courtyard had not been repaved in all the years since he had left. Moss grew between the stones, dry in the summer heat and tinged with a faint, sickly yellow. It was not that anyone ever meant to leave them untended, it never had been, but they simply never had enough servants...

They, he reiterated mentally, forcing himself to lead the way, instead of giving in to the desire to let Peter make every first move. *They. Not* we. *Not* us. *They.*

Dismounting at the stable door, Peter looked around, "Will we be expected? I hadn't thought to ask if you'd written...or anything."

"I wrote," Guyon said briefly. *If only because anything Maurice could have prepared to say will be better than an involuntary reaction.* "I don't think it will have made a difference." He wondered when Peter was going to understand just how unwelcome he was.

"Ah.. So they're being purposely unwelcoming as opposed to accidentally?" Peter smirked. "It doesn't bother me, Guyon, truly. I've been to many places where I was unwelcome, including, as I am sure you will recall, the Court."

"Yes," Guyon agreed, feeling rather tired, "but even on my worst and most self-pitying and aggrandizing days, I have never held myself to blame for the *Court.*" His legs were atrociously stiff, and he blamed the fact he needed to lean briefly against the horse on dismounting on that fact. "*This,* on the other hand, is an instance where I cannot convince myself of the opposite." He sighed, looking round without much hope for one of the stablemen.

"Pfft..." Peter gave a snort, then led the horses into the stables and began unsaddling them. "Somehow, even with all your vast skills, I don't see how you could force someone to comply with your wishes for hospitality, all the way from Paris."

"Are you doubting the power of my written rhetoric?" Guyon

asked. Even to his own ears, it didn't have the snap he was aiming for. "No, don't answer that..." He looked around the stables, and found that he was actually relieved at the lack of change here, at the same rafters where he and Giraud had carved their initials still lying above his head, the same cool, dark air, whirling with dust motes and the musty smells of straw and horse. "Well, you were the one extolling the virtues of hay." He managed a smile. "If things are too bad, we can simply sleep here..."

"Mmmm...If I can have the same greeting as I got this morning, it's a deal, " Peter winked at Guyon, then moved to make sure the horses had plenty of food and water.

Guyon found himself breathing out a laugh. "Alas, Peter, the mysteriously vanished help *will* be back by tomorrow, and I doubt they would react well to such a - er - *display*. I'm afraid we are doomed either to damp and frowned-upon accommodation or hay-smothered celibacy."

"That's it then...we're not staying in the barn," Peter chuckled as he finished his work.

"Damn," Guyon muttered, past caring if that made any sense in relation to his earlier remarks. From the vaguely offended and very confused look Peter gave him, he gathered that it had been taken entirely the wrong way. "I just meant - oh *Christ,* let's get this over with before I drive you insane to match me!"

Peter moved closer then, looping one hand loosely around Guyon's wrist, and placing the other on his shoulder, "Guyon, please listen to me for one moment. We're in this together, both the investigation and anything else that comes up against us. Together - do you understand?"

Guyon blinked, hard, and nodded, not trusting himself to say anything. *Until Maurice tells you what I am. Until you know the why of the pelourinho. Until the inevitable.* "I understand," he said quietly at last, and even managed something approximating a smile. "I'm sorry -" He stopped himself, quickly. The rest of that sentence was *I love you, please don't leave me, even when you're told, please* - and there were some forms of humiliation he wasn't prepared to live with.

"It's alright." Peter lifted the wrist his hand encircled and placed a gentle kiss against the pulse point. "It *will* be all right. I promise."

"I know," Guyon said, and the sadness he felt was not for himself, but for Peter, who would be forced to break his word. He leant his head, briefly, into Peter's shoulder, taking what comfort he could while it was possible, hiding his expression. "Thank you."

"You don't need to do that, Gui, but you're welcome."

"Nice to know I am with someone," Guyon said, straightening. "Well. Since I doubt anything's changed in terms of unopenable doors, we'd better go around to the back..."

"That's always been *my* preferred entrance," Peter said lightly. "No pomp and no formality...plus you can usually flatter the cook into parting with something good."

Guyon gave him a deliberately blank look. "*Cook?*" he enquired. "My God, the optimism is palpable!" He led the way out into the small yard, closing the stable door behind them, and started to walk past the outbuildings to the back of the house. Wisteria, the blossoms long since gone in the summer sun, grew low on one wall that ran along beside the pathway, overgrown with convolvulus in a tangle of green and white. It had been there for as long as Guyon could remember, the images from his mind so clear that he could almost catch the perfume from the flowers on his tongue, believe the heavy, pale purple hung like strange grapes amidst the green.

But it was too late in the year, too late altogether. Giraud might have seen it, before he left. *My brother and his Spanish wife. I don't even know her name...*

Guyon sighed, and put out his hand to touch the corner of the house as he passed it, the sharp stone edge worn smooth by the thousands of passing fingers that had made that same gesture as they turned towards the back door.

The door, too, was overgrown, but by ivy, the sheared leaves near the hinges and handle showing that it was the more usual entrance, clipping the growth every time the heavy wood was moved. He put out his hand to the slightly rusted doorknob, knowing that it would not turn, as it never had, and quirked a smile at Peter. "I'd better give you what welcome you'll have now," he said dryly, and pushed the door open.

"Not going to carry me in?" Peter quipped as he peered into the dark interior. "I thought it was customary."

"No, that's washing your back, I think," Guyon said. "At least, it is if I want to observe the laws of hospitality and save *my* back." He sighed. "There should be a tinderbox and candle on the shelf to your left, by the way."

"Or is it washing feet?" Peter pondered as he fumbled for and found both tinderbox and candle and got a meager light glowing.

"It may very well be," Guyon said with a grin, "but I'm afraid of sudden death." Now that his eyes were adjusting, he could see that there were the remnants of a fire in the kitchen grate, still glowing. "Look for more candles, I'll get the fire started properly. Oh. This? This is the kitchen." He made a face. "Good luck with flattering that cook of yours..."

"Gone the way of the grooms, I take it?" Peter walked carefully through the room, peering into cupboards until he found more candles. "Ah, well, we're more than capable of making do, I'm sure."

"More than," Guyon agreed. He was starting to relax. Fending for himself was something he knew he was perfectly able to do - fending for himself with Peter's running commentary on just why anyone would want to put walnuts in oil, and oh God, was it really necessary to cut eggs in half before pickling them, because they were *looking* at him, was even more familiar and was going a long way towards steadying him, as was finding the usual curses to lay on the head of whoever had failed dismally to light the fire properly.

"How very ill-mannered of you, Guyon," said an amused, equally familiar voice from the door to the main house, and a great deal more light suddenly came into the room, along with a grey-haired, stocky man. Guyon looked up sharply, standing upright, and Maurice smiled at him, enjoying his discomfiture openly. "Not back in our bosom five minutes, and already you're criticizing. Parisian manners, I suppose?"

"Oh, about as Parisian as allowing guests to arrive ungreeted and unwelcomed," Peter said, his smile matched that of Maurice, but there was obviously steel behind it, "even less so when it's family."

"And you brought another of your useless scholar friends with you," Maurice said, dropping into Occitan. "How thoughtful."

Guyon gritted his teeth. He was not seventeen, he was not afraid of himself or of Maurice, and he was suddenly very angry indeed at Maurice's deliberate rudeness. *Couldn't we at least have pretended to civility for half an hour?*

"Why no, *Paire*," he said smoothly in French. "May I introduce the English Marshal, Lord of Brocéliande and Hawthornden, to you? Peter, forgive my great-uncle his manners. It's a family trait. This is Maurice de Chesnay." He made the flat lack of even a courtesy title a pointed contrast.

Peter's curt nod was his only movement, "Monsieur de Chesnay."

It was quite obvious that Maurice had completely set his foot wrong with Peter. Gone was the easy going man who had been teasing him mere moments before and in his place stood all that Peter truly was - every title and honor sitting on his shoulders for all to see. It was in the way he stood, his expression and bearing.

It was a moment of illumination for Guyon so bright that, like the aftermath of a lightning flash, he seemed to see its imprint in dark, repeating dazzle before his eyes. *It is not only Peter I love. I love the Maréchal, too, I love the Seigneur. All facets, all guises. I love him entire.*

"Was there anything you wanted, *Paire*?" he asked lightly, none of his sudden self-understanding showing in his voice. "Or was this your idea of a host's greeting?"

The green-glass eyes turned to Peter, completely ignoring Guyon other than to jerk a thumb in his direction. "Watch out for this one. He'll make your life a hell and expect gratitude."

With that, Maurice turned and stumped out of the room.

"*Jesus,*" said Guyon, involuntarily leaning back against the bricks of the fireplace. "And the horrifying thing is - *that went well.*"

*

Peter remained where he was, his entire body tensed as if for battle. He was furious. No, more than furious, he was appalled. The man could have spit in his face and Peter would have merely wiped it away, but for him to treat Guyon like that...was too much. Even at their worst he and Robert had, at least, always been polite.

"Guyon..." Peter's jaw worked tightly, "your uncle is an ass."

"No," Guyon said, and then his mouth quirked. "Well, *yes*. But he is also the most dangerous man you will ever meet." His throat worked. "Like looking in a mirror," he said, almost to himself, and turned back to the fire.

Up to that moment, Peter would have dismissed the man with barely another thought. Would have written him off as a petty, mean-minded tyrant with an overly inflated sense of his own importance. But he had to rethink that with Guyon's words. He would have thought that the description his friend had just given would have more closely pertained to Corvay, but if not, he was certainly not turning his back on Maurice.

"Forewarned is forearmed," Peter nodded. "I'll assume everything he says is a lie or some kind of manipulation."

Guyon nodded, the movement of his head a shadowy blur against the growing fire. "Good," he said, and then turned to face Peter again. "So, did you find anything that wasn't staring eggs?" It was an obvious effort, but it was an *effort*, and Peter had known through all the days of Guyon's darkening mood, as they approached the Languedoc, that he would have to take such small things and make the best of them.

"Mutton and cabbage," Peter teased. "No, really there's quite a bit of food here. We won't starve at least. I saw a ham hanging in the corner...and everything seems to be packed quite safe. Whoever your uncle has in to keep the kitchen has done a good job, at least."

"So he hasn't actually let the servants *go*, then," Guyon said in evident relief. "Thank God for that, I had visions of spending the first two weeks dealing with outraged evictees..." He brightened. "Don't get your hopes up, but there may even be clean linen, if not a prepared room..."

Once again Peter's anger flared, even stronger because Guyon seemed to accept that his uncle treated him this way. He stamped it back down, immediately, know that nothing he could say would help and it would probably just distress Guyon even more that he had noticed it. "There is still the barn."

"Yes, the horses will be infinitely better company than Maurice, for sure," Guyon said with a smile. "But no, *someone* has to play the host if Maurice won't, and if nothing else, I can provide you with a bed. There's a reasonably good cellar, too, though it won't match up to Herr Kirschner's."

"But then, few do." Peter tried for and managed a fairly natural smile. "On then. We'll reconnoiter, find a place to sleep, then come back a put together our dinner. And along the way, you can show me the nooks and crannies of *your* great pile of rocks."

"I - right. Yes." Guyon obviously thought better of whatever he was going to say, and nodded. "It's - mostly - I mean, Giraud married, it may have changed, his wife may have - I don't know." He looked tired and slightly disorientated, as though he had been hit very hard on the head a few hours before, and was trying to clear his thoughts through a haze of pain. Then he shook his head, sharp and rapid, and took one of the candles from the dresser. "It seems to be lit better out there, but - I don't know about the upstairs." He led the way out of the kitchen, and into the hall outside.

This was going to be rough. Even in the short time they'd been there, Peter had seen how Guyon's mood had dropped. He'd get them through this though. Keep Guyon going with jokes and an easy going attitude, find the information they needed and then get them the hell out.

And somehow, somewhere, in this place - not the great stone edifice they were standing in now, assuredly, but in this town, there had to be someone, somewhere, who remembered his love with kindness. Someone who actually had missed him and would be glad that he had returned.

Peter swore he'd find that person, if he had to scour every home in the damn place.

*

223

"Gallery," Guyon said rather obviously, holding up the makeshift lamp. "And paintings hung up extremely randomly along the wall of said gallery." His ancestors didn't seem to have ever been able to afford a decent portrait painter in their lives, and no-one had bothered since his grandfather, so it was probably an obvious *and* a useless remark, since it was fairly unusual to find one that looked like a replica of a human being, let alone find a family resemblance.

"Hmm...I think we're going to let Kees do yours. These are.... Well, um..." Peter looked at him sheepishly. "Sorry...they're not very good, Gui. ...But...um...Not that I know anything about art, really."

"No, they're really not," Guyon agreed, feeling a bit more cheerful. "Actually, they're awful. And my great-grandfather appears to have been descended from a crow and an owl, frightening thought. And Kees? Pèire, you just don't want to suffer alone! I have *no* desire to have my port...r...ait..." he trailed off and sighed, as Peter gave him his best imploring expression, and he found himself, as always, wanting to promise whatever might be wanted. "Yes, Peter," he said meekly and with obvious insincerity.

"We'll sit together. Two fast friends in shared suffering." Peter offered with a chuckle, his arm going around Guyon's shoulders for a quick hug.

"If we survive this," Guyon said grimly, "I'll sit for whatever you ask. Peter. Listen. Maurice...there are things..." He couldn't find the words. He couldn't *admit* to the words, and he stood there, the lantern beginning to shake in his hand as cold assailed him.

Peter's eyes never left Guyon's face, "I trust that if it's important for me to know, you'll tell me in your own time. I trust you, Guyon."

Guyon wanted to put his fist through something. He wanted to get back to Paris and have the Watch put their boots into him. Anything would have been preferable to the way he felt when Peter said things like that, as though he could trust him, tell him anything, everything.

"Jesus," he whispered. "Sorry. I should never have come

back here. I should have had you kidnapped and taken to Portugal yourself before I let you come here."

Peter reached out, taking Guyon's wrist in a loose grip, fingers soothing gently over the thrum of his pulse, "We won't be here long. I promise. We'll ferret out something and be gone right after."

Guyon nodded. "Did I mention a few hundred times yet how much I don't want to be here at all?" he asked with a feeble attempt at his usual levity.

"At least," Peter nodded. "Now, a dry spot for sleep and in the morning we begin. Sarah used to wake me in the morning with some such thing...something about the sooner you begin the sooner you'll be done."

Peter huffed, trying to lighten the mood, "Luckily you can't commit homicide with a thrown pillow, or I would have been short a sister."

Guyon felt his mouth twitch with real humor. "But you like mornings," he said, too-innocently. "Or at least that's what you keep telling me..."

"I do like mornings. It was Sarah I didn't like," Peter asserted. "She was a horrid child. Fortunately, she got better as I got older."

"Oh, what a good thing she had such an example of perfection before her, to show her how to behave..." Guyon pushed open a door, and sniffed the air inside suspiciously. "Damp," he said, returning to his former gloom.

"Light the fire and open the window...we've a bit of time before dark for it to dry out." Peter shrugged. "Or on to the next?"

"Do you think it will be more depressing, or reassuring to find out everywhere is the same?" Guyon enquired, genuinely interested.

"I think I will simply be happy if we do not choose a dry room, only to discover that it belongs to Uncle Maurice." Peter gave an expansive shrug, his face holding amusement. "I, for one, would not relish sharing with him. He looks like a snorer."

Guyon felt his eyes go wide with delight. "He is," he agreed, but that wasn't the source of his pleasure. "Peter...you must always call him Uncle Maurice." He felt the smile curl at his mouth, and let it. "He'll hate it."

"Then by your command, Uncle Maurice he shall be." Peter chuckled. "See, there's humor in everything if you look hard enough. I think Sarah told me that once as well."

"I think if she did, you told her first," Guyon pointed out, but decided not to share his next thought, which was that he wanted to know why Peter always attributed to Sarah things that were obviously his own thoughts to start with. *Do I dismiss him that quickly?* he wondered, and was forced, in all honesty, to answer himself *yes*. "Careful, Peter, I may begin to find hell bearable."

Peter lifted the wrist that he still held and placed a soft, warm kiss over the pulse point, "No, you'd better be careful, or I might begin to spout romantic platitudes that will put you completely out of humor with me again."

"It's the platitudes that I hate, not the romance," Guyon admitted, then made a face. "Bah. Half an hour here and my brain has softened past oatmeal."

"You're tired." Peter nodded, thumb back to stroking gently over Guyon's wrist. "I am too. So...do we try to dry this out? Or look further?"

"Oh, let's just dry it out, I'll give you the Grand Tour later." Guyon knew how childish he sounded, and didn't much care. He wanted to go back to Paris, wanted the safety of his shabby bed and the only promise he had ever made. He wanted to curl up like a cat into Peter's touch, to indulge his own need for contact. He wanted to say all the words he kept thinking.

He suspected he needed a keeper, or fifteen hours sleep, and he wasn't going to get either. "I'll open the window," he said, and pulled away gently.

*

Peter snuggled closer to the warm body next to him, nuzzling his nose into tangled dark curls. In spite of his usual morning alertness, he seldom managed to wake before Guyon. Seldom had the luxury of simply holding the other man while he slept. On the few occasions he had been able to share a bed with him,

Guyon had always moved away before Peter had awakened, leaving him feeling a bit bereft and lonely.

But this? This was heaven and contentment and a half dozen other comfortable feelings that he wanted to share, but knew he never could, not while Guyon still kept him at a distance.

Guyon slept on undisturbed, curling closer to the other warm body in blind, instinctive rest. He was still an intriguing mystery to Peter, after many months of friendship and more than a few nights of shared pleasure. It wasn't just that he was intelligent, Christ, half the court was *intelligent*, had to be to survive, and bloody Corvay excelled at it; occasionally Peter dared suspect he wasn't too stupid himself. Guyon, though, was different, more complicated. He always kept a certain cool distance between himself and the world, never stopped analyzing, as he saw every problem from several angles.

Peter couldn't imagine what it would feel like, having that frightening, brilliant mind. He could rarely guess what Guyon was thinking - simple surface things, yes, but not the two and three cross-currents of other thoughts underneath.

It was what kept him endlessly fascinated with Guyon, but it was also, unfortunately, what was still keeping them apart. There were times when Peter wanted to grab him by the shoulders and shake him until he couldn't think. To make him only feel - only want and love and ache the way that he himself did.

But no, that wouldn't be Guyon, so it would all be pointless.

A subtle change in the skin and muscle he touched warned him that Guyon was awake, or close to it. He shifted, but didn't move away. "What time is it?"

"Early...I didn't mean to wake you. Go back to sleep." Peter spoke softly, hardly daring to move, for fear Guyon would instantly pull away.

"You didn't." Guyon yawned, buried himself deeper. He wrapped thankfully-warm hands over Peter's arms. "Good. Avoidance. Let's avoid breakfast. Let's avoid Uncle Maurice. Oh God, let's avoid everyone else." He was sounding more and more alert.

Peter chuckled softly, placing a kiss on Guyon's temple, "That would rather make this whole long trip a bit pointless, wouldn't it?"

Guyon laughed into the sheets. Sleep seemed to have restored him to his usual half-acerbic, half-amused self. "Mm-hm," he agreed with enthusiasm. "And annoy everyone." He yawned again, stretched. Peter could feel the cold feet point downwards, before determinedly pushing between his ankles. "You're always warm..." It wasn't a complaint, as such, despite the tone.

"Yes, because my heart is pure." Peter snickered. "No...always have been. A survival tactic, I'd say, from long nights on wolf watch. "

Guyon twisted round, eyes dark and narrowed. "Wolf watch," he said skeptically.

Peter shrugged, "I took my turn like everyone else. It gets very cold and windy out on the rock I call home, and a fire tends to only warm one side of you at a time. Compared to that, your icy feet are barely a cool draft."

"Hm." Guyon looked thoughtful. "We have wolf hunts here. I could arrange one. It would be a wonderful way of putting you at risk and making everyone else happy."

"Me being at risk would make everyone happy?" Peter had to think about that a moment. "Because I'm Scottish? Or something else?"

"Oh, because they'd expect you to be bad at it," Guyon shrugged, his body thrumming with tension and at odds with his light voice. "Then they could watch you fail." He laughed, the tone a little unpleasant. "Only you wouldn't."

"Ah...so the idea is for me to give the optimum amount of annoyance I'm capable of while I'm here?" Peter looked down at Guyon, one eyebrow raised. "Then I suppose I could begin by annoying you?" He lowered his head to Guyon's shoulder, giving it rough biting kiss just this side of painful, "Let me know if I succeed."

Guyon pulled away. "You succeed," he said flatly, and swung his legs over the edge of the bed. "I'll go and see if anyone else is around."

"No." Peter tugged him back. "Don't." An explosion of temper was imminent, of that Peter was sure, unless he could find a way of diffusing it. "Let me go with you. *Please.* I'm completely prepared to pout like a four year old if you deny me, Guyon."

"Oh -!" There was a world of frustration in that small sound, and then Guyon seemed to physically shake himself into his everyday detachment, sitting up and pulling it on with his worn shirt. "Yes, by all means, let us avoid that."

Peter sighed and climbed out of bed, shrugging on his own clothes and muttering under his breath the whole time, "Of course, avoid...avoid...all we ever do. Could win an award for that by now. Champions at the whole thing."

Guyon made an odd noise, and threw Peter's jerkin at him. "I did say that was my plan for the day," he pointed out.

"Yes, you did. And yet, here we go, to actually seek out people." Peter put on his jerkin and looked around for his boots. "I liked my idea much better."

"Of course you did," Guyon said indulgently, and then - "Wait, you didn't *have* an idea, did you?"

"Well, two actually..." Peter shrugged. "And how did one of my boots wind up under the bed and the other across the room under the chair?"

Guyon looked improbably innocent. "You're a very untidy man," he said, in the face of all evidence. "Why ask me? And what were these great plans, then, O Master of Planning?"

"Well, the first one involved the avoidance that you said you wished to have, mostly by sleeping a lot longer than we have and allowing them to come to us." Peter tugged on the first boot. "Obviously, you already hate that idea."

"Thank you, but I've been woken enough times in my life by *Paire* shouting about my soul's defilement," Guyon said politely. "And the other?"

"So I suppose I should definitely mark defilement off my list?" Peter's lips quirked. "And I was so looking forward to that bit."

Guyon snorted. "My *soul's* defilement, you Scottish infidel barbarian! And we'll get that with breakfast in any case. Other plan."

"Pretty much similar but without the extra sleep," Peter

quipped. "There must be some one here that will be happier to see you than Uncle Maurice was. We just...wander...until they find us."

"You're insane," Guyon said blankly. "Believe me, no-one is going to be happy to see me. At all. And we are not simply going to 'wander', thank you. With our luck, someone practicing assassination will find us."

Holding his tongue at that moment was one of the hardest things that Peter had ever done. He wanted to tell Guyon that of course there had to be someone in this place that had missed him, that would be glad to see him back. How could they not miss that wonderful snippy sense of humor and sarcastic wit? Or the warmth that could shine out of those strange eyes when given half a chance? He knew, however, that no matter what he said, Guyon would deny the facts, determined that he was as unwanted here as the wolves they had spoken of earlier.

"Well, then, your plan it is." Peter shrugged and pulled his last boot up over his foot.

*

The state of Guyon's home was obvious at once as they had tried to settle in that night. The whole place held an air of general neglect, as if its current resident and, quite possibly those before Maurice, had not been sure how to keep up with it, or what was most important. Or perhaps they simply did not care. Windows stuck. Rooms needed airing. The wooden stairs creaked and the stone ones had dust in their corners. And Guyon apologized to Peter, frequently and awkwardly, with an air of responsibility quite out of keeping with his usual casual eye on housework.

Peter just ignored it for the most part, helped to find a room that was more habitable that the one they spent their first night in and set it to rights, then worked the next day or two with tools and what few servants that Maurice deemed necessary, to get the place in some sort of order, while Guyon roamed the lands. It was a good division of labor, Peter thought, and as a bonus it got his friend out of the house for long hours, which seemed to be just what he needed. He wasn't sure what it was yet about his ancestral home that made Guyon as jumpy as a hare, but he was not going to begrudge him any absence until they could settle in.

"I'm surprised," Maurice said acerbically from his seat near the fire in the hall, as Peter stopped his futile explanation to the servant who was more usually - and hopefully more usefully - employed as a general cleaner-of-all in the kitchen, of the necessary difference between warm water and *hot* water, while simultaneously realizing for the tenth time that day alone that Guyon really hadn't been joking when he said that Occitan was not a dialect, but a completely different language, and that it was also about as far from his Anglicized French as it was possible to get - "that Guyon didn't re-establish himself in his old room. Or his brother's room, now that he's ousted him. Or indeed his father's rooms, but then those boys were always completely *ridiculous* about that wing, I never understood it." His large eyes gleamed with the firelight and with what Peter recognized as straight malice. He just had no idea *why*.

"And I am surprised that rooms were not made ready for visitors when you received Guyon's letter," Peter again searched through his scant knowledge of Occitan and with some pantomime and emphasis, sent the servant off back to the kitchen, hopefully with an understanding of what he wanted. "You really are not fooling anyone, you know?"

"But I'm not trying to," Maurice said, sounding surprised. "I'm merely stating facts."

"You're overstepping your boundaries, *Paire*, is what you're doing," Guyon's dry voice called down from the gallery - and how the hell had he got to there without passing Peter in the hall? "Peter, let him molder by the fire if that's where he feels safest - *holy unblemished corpse of Christ!*" The servant had come back with what was undoubtedly, judging from Guyon's expression, very cold water indeed, and doused him with it liberally. Guyon gaped at him. "What on *earth?*"

"Bloody Hell." Peter lapsed into English. "Get your idiotic self back to the kitchen and figure out if there is any way on *God's Earth* that what I told you could in any way be translated into dousing your Master with cold water. Then if your brain is still functioning after that undoubtedly difficult task, get the grease scrubbed off of the damned windows!"

He gave the man a shove in the right direction and turned back to Guyon with a grim expression, "Yes...yes...I'm going to learn Occitan...tomorrow in fact. Sorry..."

Guyon mopped at his face with an equally drenched sleeve. "Um. Yes...that might -" He rubbed at his mouth, obviously trying not to laugh. "That might be a good idea," he agreed eventually, his voice shaking with badly controlled amusement. "Do I want to know what you *thought* you said?"

"Pretty much what I just told him in English, which means he's probably even more confused." Peter handed Guyon his kerchief and shook his head. "Do we have someone who can translate for me for a week or two until I can get a better handle on the language?"

Guyon gave him a rather confused look. "Er, me?" he suggested. "Or Maurice..." he made a face. "Wait, de Tourvel may have a Parisian servant. In fact, I'm sure he does. He *used* to have several, they can't all have died in five years." He looked at the kerchief, and raised his eyebrows. "Thank you, but I think this may prove a little inadequate. Er, did you find anything that could be used to dry people without tearing in half or simply disintegrating?"

"Yes, amazingly, you do have actual linens that appear to be fairly new. If I were to hazard a guess I'd say they were dower goods," Peter shrugged. "Who's de Tourvel?"

"He owns the estates on the other side," Guyon explained. "They were a gift after the war, when he served with my father. He doesn't have a title, so -" He broke off and grinned. "That wouldn't matter to you, but it made for some damn uncomfortable silences when my father insisted on everyone treating him as his equal. Being *Captain* around here doesn't really mean very much."

"Then I should thank God that I have a title and a bit of rock to go with it, eh?" Peter chuckled then paused with a sheepish grin. "Well, a bit more than that now I'm Marshal. I keep forgetting."

"Just a bit," Guyon agreed, rolling his eyes. "Hm. We should go and see him, I suppose. Just as soon as I'm..." he gestured rather uselessly. "Dry? Presentable? Both?"

"Aye." Peter laughed again. "Captain or Lord, I doubt he'll take kindly to a sodden mess dripping its way into his sitting room."

"No, I wouldn't have thought so," Guyon agreed, and headed off for the room Peter had been so assiduously making habitable.

Peter looked down at the puddle on the floor, sighed, and went down the stairs to the kitchen to try to convince someone to mop it up. By the time he was finished and out in the stables getting their horses saddled, Guyon came out of the house, much drier.

"Your friend from the kitchens," he said, looking rather perplexed, "is trying to mop the entire gallery floor using the rather small puddle of water that was left by his earlier assistance with my ablutions. I think we should go, *now*, before he gets any more wonderful ideas."

"Indeed," Peter just shook his head. Yes, learning Occitan was definitely going to be high on his list.

"Guyon - tell me a bit more about de Tourvel." He always liked to be prepared before meeting someone he was asking a favor of.

"What sort of thing?" Guyon asked, his frown deepening. While his tendency to take people for themselves alone was one of his few endearing characteristics, it also meant that he never had any idea what someone else would want to know. He was as likely to think Peter would understand de Tourvel perfectly if he said 'he once read a poem by Catullus out loud' as if he said 'oh, didn't I mention? Actually he comes from China.'

"Oh, you know, does he have any family? Children? Is he as intimidating as Magister Benichou or more like Herr Kirschner?" Peter let the stableman give him a leg-up and settled on his horse.

"He has a daughter," Guyon said, rather less formally getting onto his horse by way of the mounting-block. "A little girl, Jehanne. His wife died soon after, I don't really remember her at all. He's -" He shrugged. "I like him," he added, making a face that showed he knew just how inadequate that was as a description. "He's very - blunt."

"Ah," Peter nodded. "He was a soldier. They often tend to

be."

"I've noticed," Guyon agreed blandly, but his mouth twitched a little, giving his amusement away. "On occasion. Actually, on *several* occasions." He grinned across at Peter.

Guyon was more relaxed than he had seen him since their arrival and Peter wondered how much this visit to de Tourvel had to do with it, and how much him spending most of his time away from the house. It didn't matter, really, but somehow it made him feel much more inclined to like de Tourvel, sight unseen. "I'll have you know that I am considered the height of social blandness. Or would be if the court were not so busy discussing all my other defects."

"Was that *blandness* or *bluntness*?" Guyon enquired sweetly. "Because either way, I can quite see your point." He chuckled. "You don't have any defects, Pèire, you're the perfect knight."

"Hmmpf." Peter snorted out in disgust. He always hated to be called a perfect anything, being all too well aware of all of his shortcomings. "I think your standards are remarkably low. My hair is too long, too blond. I'm too tall. My accent is horrible, my manners barbaric and, the unforgivable, I do not court their daughters...or possibly their wives...I've not quite got that bit straight."

"I suppose it depends on the courtier," Guyon said, looking horribly fascinated. "And whatever you do, you'll displease the *wives*." He scowled thoughtfully. "I wonder how tall you're *supposed* to be?"

"Yes, that is the question," Peter looked around. This would be where de Tourvel's lands began and Guyon's ended, demarked by a small stream. It was good land, but Peter thought the de Chesnay lands were better. *Yes, Peter and you'd think the de Chesnay middens better as well.*

"No, just *a* question among the many that confuse me," Guyon said matter-of-factly. His horse walked down the small bank and into the stream, where it stopped and had a very noisy drink. Guyon rolled his eyes. "Yes, obedient thing, you are, aren't you?" he asked the space between its ears.

"Just as obedient as its owner," Peter teased and gave his own mount enough lead to drink. "So, how old would de Tourvel's daughter be?"

Guyon scratched at his chin. "Er. Fourteen? Something like that." He shrugged. "Maybe younger."

"Oh...lovely." Peter shook his head and chuckled. "I'll hope for younger."

It was fortunate, he thought, that Mademoiselle de Tourvel had no mother, fathers were usually much less apt to push their daughters at him. Even those women at court who did not care for his company had attempted to bring their daughters to his attention, the Marshal of her English Majesty's troops in France, being too great an opportunity to let pass by.

Guyon had helpfully pointed out that it was, in fact, a *bonus* rather than a drawback that there were not, as yet, any actual troops, and said that if he really wanted to discourage any and all matchmaking, all he needed to do was introduce a few of the cadets at court. While the idea had merit, Peter suspected it stemmed more from Guyon's desire to cause mayhem than any real urge to help, and had so far resisted.

Guyon gave him a look that suggested he had not understood Peter at all, and shrugged. "Well, she seemed fairly rational when I was here last, and I can't see that older would necessarily be preferable, so as you wish, Peter..." He moved his horse up onto the other bank.

Peter snorted, "Why is it I always worry when you are being agreeable?"

"I don't know," Guyon said innocently. "I thought I always was."

And what was there to be said to that?

"Is de Tourvel's home as old as the one on your land?" Peter changed the subject. Guyon's home was...defensible, but not what you would think of as homelike. The inside could easily be made more so but the exterior would always look like what it was, an outpost of past troubled times.

Guyon laughed. "God, no. Lucky old bastard, he took his war chest and built himself a decent place. He based it on the hunting lodges he'd seen in Germany, but like everything else around here, it keeps shape shifting into a farmhouse. In bits." He grinned, his eyes reminiscent. "It was a good place to visit - if you were nine, of course." The crinkles around his eyes suggested it had been no worse in the following or preceding years, either.

"Nothing wrong with a good farmhouse, Gui," Peter chuckled and looked up just in time for his first glimpse of the place. "And...That is one *big* farmhouse."

"Mm," Guyon agreed in amusement. "Did I mention that he decided to build this hunting lodge of his on a slightly...*larger* scale than usually advised?"

"All that just for himself and his daughter." Peter shook his head. It was sad, really, when you thought about it. Undoubtedly de Tourvel had built it before the death of his wife, planning a larger family than one daughter. He wondered that the man had never remarried, but -

He looked at Guyon and knew, easily, how that could be.

"I don't think -" Guyon started, and then looked back at him, and smiled ruefully. "Ah. I don't have to explain, do I? I suppose he could have moved, but...he was settled by then, I think. And he's well-liked here."

They entered the stable yard and had just dismounted when a groom came out to take their horses. Yes, this is the way it should have been when they arrived at Margarittes, attentive servants who actually did their jobs. And without prompting, Peter had to add.

"This is nice. Very nice." The place was obviously well-tended and well loved besides.

"Yes," Guyon agreed quietly. "You know, it didn't use to be so bad, our house, not back when -" He stopped, and shrugged. "It didn't use to be so bad," he repeated, and smiled at the groom. "Thank you."

"I know, Gui. A house is only as good as the man who is its master...and Maurice..." Peter let his voice drift. He had only contempt for the old man so far, mostly for his continued baiting of Guyon.

Guyon made a small sound of agreement. "We'll talk about it later," he said unexpectedly - unexpected because any information about the place usually had to be dragged out of him by a handler with no sensitivity and hide gloves on. "For now, I'll introduce you to someone *worth* knowing." He led the way around to the front of the house, but knocked on a smaller door to the side, rather than the great oak double doors that were more suited to a cathedral than a home.

They were let in by a servant and stood in the foyer while they were announced to de Tourvel. It was no hardship to stand there and Peter snooped shamelessly, looking at what he could see of the rest of the interior.

"Gervaise? Who was at -" A young girl came into the hall. She had long, reddish hair, and a rounded face common to girls of her age, the whole overlaid with a promise of beauty that might or might not vanish as she grew older, but more familiar to Peter was the intelligence that sparkled behind the large greenish-brown eyes, grown suddenly wider when she saw them. "Oh! Oh! *Guyon?*"

It was amazing, Peter thought, how quickly any hint of maidenly modesty left the girl as she flung herself at his friend, wrapping her arms around him.

Well, he had said he would find someone in this dismal town who would be glad to see Guyon, this just wasn't exactly what he had in mind.

"Christ! Off! Get off!" Guyon, unlike some character from a fairytale, did not melt instantly into some avatar of affection and sentimentality. He looked thoroughly disconcerted as he prised the girl's arms from around his neck, and held her at arm's length. "Jeannine," he said wryly. "Well, you grew *stronger*, I'll grant you that."

"They told me you were back, but I didn't believe it." Jeannine did not seem at all put off by Guyon's reaction. "You've been gone so very, very long, you grouchy bear. And I am quite angry that you never wrote."

Peter choked out a laugh at 'grouchy bear', then covered his grin with his hand when Guyon scowled at him.

"You're hardly illiterate, you spoilt brat, so that works both ways," Guyon said, completely unperturbed by the concept of someone being annoyed at him. It was, Peter had to admit, not exactly a novelty. "Behave. I brought you an English Marshal, which I hope may get me into a great deal less trouble than the organ-grinder's monkey you wanted, and who is *infinitely* better company. Peter, this undisciplined hoyden, as you've probably gathered, is Jehanne de Tourvel. Jeannine, meet Peter Scudamore, lord of Brocéliande and Hawthornden - and a very dear friend."

And, Peter thought, it was just as amazing how quickly the maidenly modesty returned when she heard his titles.

"Oh...forgive me, my Lord," Jeannine curtsied, extending her hand for him to take. He kindly obliged her, even brushing his lips just above her knuckles as if they were at Court.

"Mademoiselle de Tourvel, it is indeed an honor to meet any friend of Guyon's." He smiled at her and helped her to rise from her curtsy.

"Jesus," said Guyon. He didn't sound at all prayerful, unless he'd taken up invoking Beelzebub in his spare time. It wasn't altogether an impossibility...but it *was* unlikely that he would have chosen that word and someone else's house to start demonstrating. "Where's your father, Jeannine?"

"What? Oh, probably in the study. He usually does his accounts this time of day." She had been staring at Peter with a speculative look on her face, one that made him feel suddenly uncomfortable. He shouldn't have treated her like an adult. That was his first mistake. Even as adorably unpracticed as her curtsey had been he should have laughed rather than taking it seriously. When would he learn?

The look on Guyon's face, as he turned on his heel and gestured towards the far end of the house, seemed to be asking him exactly the same question.

He fell in step immediately, not giving Jeannine another glance.

"Sorry," he whispered as they moved away. "I'm an idiot."

"Mm. And blindsided." Guyon's mouth twitched. "Don't worry. Even though you *are*," he agreed, the faint residue of his good humor, at least, returning. "The study's just down here..." he turned at the end of the hallway and knocked at a baize-covered door. "Cap?"

"*Giraud*?" said an amazed voice from inside, and the door opened with a jerk. "You're supposed to be - *my God, boy, did you forget how to write?*"

Peter couldn't help noticing that even though *this* embrace made Guyon huff out a surprised breath of compressed air, he didn't protest or try to draw away at all. "Pretty much, Cap," he said in a rather constricted voice. "Sorry about that."

It was obvious this was Jeannine's father, the man had the same intelligent hazel eyes, the same smile, and the same searching look as those sharp eyes scanned Guyon from head to toes. "You look well, boy. Taller, stronger...and...much better than when I last saw you, thank God."

And just like that, Guyon's face went hard and closed and still, the mask of the Sorbonne scholar falling over it like a glass shutter, transparent and somehow impermeable. "Well, it wasn't hard," he said lightly, and Peter wondered if de Tourvel was as little fooled by the soft tones as he was. "Cap, this is Peter Scudamore. The English Marshal in Paris." Oddly, he didn't give any of Peter's titles, as he had been so careful to up until now. "Peter - this is Captain de Tourvel. My father's friend."

"I'm honored, sir." Peter extended his hand, and honestly meant his greeting. Although, *his father's friend*, rather than his own? He wasn't sure what could be read into that.

"The honor is mine," de Tourvel said with a grin, and gripped Peter's hand quickly and firmly, the assessing look he received oddly familiar from day after day of commanding officers, but not unkind. "You're staying for dinner, of course?"

Guyon chuckled. "Only if you still keep country hours, or we'll have to go back to try and salvage whatever has been done to the chicken *today*."

"Oh, has Maurice annoyed Esmée again? He should know better by now. He annoys her and she stomps off, sometimes for weeks until he decides that even apologizing is better than doing without her cooking skills." There was a snort of laughter from de Tourvel. "Some day he's going to annoy her so badly that she won't return, and he'll starve to death."

Guyon simply raised his eyebrows. De Tourvel snorted again. "Well, yes. But that's beside the point."

"Mm." It wasn't really agreement. "On the other hand, Cap, everyone's all too happy to do whatever Peter wants...*but* - there's a small linguistic difficulty. They can't understand a word he says to them, and the ones they do they misinterpret. Think you could lend us someone for a couple of weeks to translate?"

"I'm sure I do but..." he shook his head and gave an amused snort, "you and I both know that now you're home Jeannine will be haunting your doorstep with this book and that question and unwanted and unasked for insights on poetry to give you, so it would seem to be a redundant idea. I'm sure she'd be more than happy to help."

Peter hoped that either de Tourvel had forgotten what Guyon looked like when trying very, very hard not to wince, or that it was a new expression that had developed since the two had seen each other.

"Yes," Guyon said, and Peter had to admit that his unfaltering cheerfulness was deserving of some sort of award. "Although - *please* make sure she brings someone with her, would you? I know you think I'm beyond reproach, but the town won't."

"Ah, of course," the man nodded, "I forget my daughter is now of an age for that to be a concern. It is so easy to think of her as always being about six, you know, in spite of the evidence before my eyes."

Peter nodded, and wished that Jeannine had been about six, it would surely make all of their lives easier.

Guyon's eyes gleamed sudden laughter over at him, and Peter could read what he was thinking as clearly as if he had spoken aloud. *Trust me. It really wasn't even when she was.*

He started to smile back, and then de Tourvel was ushering them along to a more comfortable room, talking about something he wanted to do with cloisonné and tables that was making Guyon choke on little shouts of laughter, and Peter knew that whatever had just happened, it would have to wait.

*

"You have been blessed with a most excellent chef, Captain de Tourvel, " Peter could say it most honestly, as they finished their meal. The chicken, the fish, all the vegetables, everything had been perfectly done in spite of their unexpected arrival.

They were sitting in the study now, just the three of them, a fact for which Peter was most grateful. Jeannine, dressed in silk

240

too rich for her age, and her hair bound up, had spent the better part of the meal staring at him like a butterfly on a pin, a fact which made Peter even more glad of the perfection of the meal, because otherwise he would have worried himself into a case of indigestion.

"I was not *blessed* with him, I *employed* him," de Tourvel said amusedly. "I thought Guyon told you - I bring my servants from Paris, when I can."

"I thought you might have stopped doing that, so no, I didn't," Guyon pointed out quietly. He was standing at the window, drinking wine without any seeming desire to change to the more settling spirits that de Tourvel and Peter had already been given, and smoking a pipe rather awkwardly, holding it like a pen between his blunt fingers.

"And why would I have done that?" the Captain asked. "They tend to be more loyal and are much less likely to desert me for a sick father, or in a fit of pique, which can be a problem with servants who are native to the area."

Peter looked at de Tourvel for a long moment. This was someone that Guyon trusted, a man who had served the Crown honorably, so surely he could trust him as well. "That is part of what I...we...wanted to discuss with you, sir. The loyalties of this whole area have lately come into question."

"Or rather more so than usual," Guyon said to the wisteria that was making a determined bid for entry. "Giraud appears to have...created a conundrum."

Yes, that was one way of putting it. Peter would probably have said 'God's own mess' if it had been left to him.

"A conundrum?" The question was asked lightly, "Of what type?"

"That the Languedoc is, in name at least, allied to the Spanish, and there is just cause for warring with it as great as there is with Spain," Guyon said calmly. "Also, your wisteria needs a great deal of water. Though I do not think that was Giraud's doing."

De Tourvel barked out a laugh, although for a moment Peter was unsure if it was to refute Guyon's claims, or because of his remark about the wisteria, "That is ridiculous. Oh, I'm not saying that there may not be some sympathizers here, but most of my tenants, at least, are exceedingly loyal to the Crown."

Guyon turned, and his face was perfectly still, utterly white. "Really?" he asked, and the small word fell like a stone into the centre of the room, the shimmer of belief beneath it sending out ripples that even Peter could feel. "*Loyal*?" His clear eyes widened. "What a deal of trust for such a small thing that will never touch you - *if* I do nothing while I stay here."

"Your people are loyal because you are." Peter nodded his head. "But Giraud...he married a Spaniard...that can cause loyalties to shift. Are you certain, Captain, that such was not the case?"

"Positive," de Tourvel assured them. "I might have questioned it at one time, but once he married, all Giraud wanted was peace. Catalina was a beautiful but very sensible girl and, well, to put it bluntly, there is no money to be made in rebellion."

"All Giraud wanted was peace," Guyon repeated mockingly, and said something, fast and angry, in Occitan, gesturing at Peter, before - "*Fraire d'Carcassonne, piense d'm'en a oblis?*"

Carcassonne's brother. You think I would ever forget that?

Tolon.

We'll take the long road.

Oh, Christ, Guyon knew.

Peter had not understood the reference when he'd first heard it. Hadn't known of Carcassonne, nor of Guyon's connections to it. Then later, when he knew of Giraud, he had kept it to himself, and when Corvay revealed Giraud's perfidy he thought it pointless to tell something that Guyon surely knew. But now he did know...

And now Peter did as well, "That's it...That's it. That's why Martelle was questioning Duvane about Carcassonne's brother. You...you...it was you they were talking about. Because Giraud had switched on them. Betrayed them. And...Christ. So much worry and trouble." Peter gave a desperate laugh.

"No, *bèl-mi*," Guyon said, and distantly, Peter registered de Tourvel's quick, startled look at them, and then forgot it as quickly, as Guyon knelt in front of him, gripping his hands. "Not because of Giraud. Or *you*, chérâme. Corvay had already given them my name. *Not you*," he repeated, and there were no shadows in his eyes when they met Peter's.

I have never lied to you.

De Tourvel regained their attention with a clearing of his throat, "Is that why that confused Scot landed on Giraud's doorstep insisting he needed to leave for Portugal immediately? Someone had learned of his past indiscretions?"

"*Oh, Robbie,*" Guyon said on a gasped breath of laughter, an affection that Peter had never really suspected existed, clear in his voice, and then, recovering himself, "Mm. Something like that."

"My sister's husband," Peter explained. "We...we feared for Giraud's safety."

The words almost stuck in Peter's mouth, but he had truly, even if it was only for Guyon's sake.

And it was worth it, almost, for the sheer gratitude in Guyon's eyes before he got to his feet and faced de Tourvel. "Please, Cap," he said softly, the little coaxing flute of a voice that only de Retz and Benichou - and once, Peter - had heard directed on them. "Please understand I want to *save* us."

And, slowly, his eyes far away and assessing and somehow not seeing them at all, de Tourvel nodded. "All right, my lads," he said at last. "I'll trust the English Marshal, Guyon, even if you have your own agenda. Fair?"

Guyon blew out a breath of pure relief. "Lord. More than," he said, and then - "*Thank you.*"

"Thank you, sir." Peter said formally. "And please know that I have nothing but the best in mind for Guyon's family and friends."

De Tourvel laughed, short and sharp, and ran a hand over his face. "Thank *you*, *Maréchal*," he said rather dryly, and then grinned at them both. "Enough. Come to my study. We'll have the *ratafia de Coings* and be damned to my vintner." He wrapped an arm around Guyon, and pulled Peter to his feet. "Come." He laughed again, and added - "As the Hawk would say - *for tomorrow we die.*"

And Peter knew that if de Tourvel could sense the stiffness that had entered Guyon's body at that simple repetition of the Epicureans' motto, he was the only one ever who would know how much of a blow that little statement had struck.

The Hawk, he thought, and then remembered Guyon saying - *We'll talk later.*

Yes, he agreed silently. *We damn well will.*

*

Dusk was falling by the time they finally made their farewells to de Tourvel. Jeannine came out, trying her best to look demure, and failing miserably as her delight at the idea of acting as Peter's translator - which meant unlimited time at the de Chesnay estate - showed through quite transparently. Guyon wondered why on earth she would want it, but supposed it had something to do with her attempts at freedom, that had been a source of annoyance to everyone practically from the time she could walk. He himself would have happily stayed where he was - *anything,* in fact, rather than be forced to take part in the conversation he had no doubt Peter was itching to begin.

They had made it all the way back to the creek dividing the two properties, however, before Peter brought his horse up short, dismounted and sat down on a nearby hummock, leaving his horse to graze. He didn't say a word, just looked up at Guyon expectantly.

Damn.

Well, at least they were away from the house and away from Maurice. If they had to have this conversation those were two things that he would have insisted upon.

He sighed, and slid off his horse. "It's becoming a theme," he murmured to it, patting its neck. "You hold me up and I pretend I like you." He took a deep breath, resting his head briefly against the long face, and then stood straight, walking over to the patch of grass with a distinct feeling of dread. "Ask," he said shortly.

"Who's the *Hawk*?" Peter asked, simply. Somehow, out of all that de Tourvel had said that evening, that was what he wanted to know first, as if that was the key to everything else that they would discuss. And maybe it was.

Guyon tried not to wince. "My father," he said with equal simplicity. "He was de Tourvel's commanding officer, they retired from the army at the same time. They called him the Hawk because - he was a predator. Fierce." He shrugged. "So we were told, anyway."

"I can see that." Peter nodded slowly. "There is some of that in you. As I have some of my father in me. But...'you were told'? You do not remember?"

"Well I wasn't quite old enough to be in the army," Guyon said rather dryly, "so obviously I have no idea. And it wasn't an aspect of his character I ever saw turned on me, so -" he shrugged. "How would I know? By the time I was nine our lives were -" *unbearable, intolerable, why do you think I would forgive Giraud anything* - "changed, and I had run away from here and thought never to come back before I had quite reached fourteen. I'm not the best person to ask all this, Peter. You know I never wanted to come back, that I love - I love this country, but I hate who I am in it."

"I know that," Peter's sincerity shone out brilliantly even in the dim light. "But there is no-one else I can ask it of. There is de Tourvel...and there is you. I'm sure you don't mean for me to ask that idiot that you claim is your uncle." There was a short silence before Peter continued, "I just want to understand, Gui...to understand you, at least a little better."

That, Guyon thought with grim amusement, *is the stupidest thing you have ever said. Because believe me, you **don't**.* Aloud, he said only - "I know. But I'm not sure what to say...how I can help. Though you're right, asking Maurice isn't something I really want you to do. All I can do is try -" *to evade* - "to answer."

"Come and sit down, please." Peter gestured at a spot next to him. "You said things changed. How did they change?"

"Hm. My mother died. And my father...oh, he loved us, we never doubted that, but - all his life, all his...all of what he was - it was hers. *He* was hers." How to explain this to Peter, who loved so easily and pleasantly - even loved *him*, Guyon knew that now and believed it, but loved with none of that obsessive, single-minded turning of the self, none of the absorption that had led to accusations of heresy and his father's lonely death. "And...he tried. He tried so hard, but - in the end, he simply did not want to live without her. There was nothing for him here - nothing and no-one. All he wanted - was elsewhere."

All he wanted or needed was dead and gone. Love isn't a blessing from some kindly god, it's a curse and it's damnation, and you don't want mine. But thank you for reminding me why I keep my word and don't betray you by mentioning it. And I won't betray my father by telling you of his death. Giri and I kept that secret; and as long as I have the choice, I always will. "He followed her." It was as good a description as any.

"I see," Peter said, although Guyon could see that he didn't, not really. "I understand that a bit...maybe. I know when my parents died it was all a shock to Sarah and me. Uncle William tried hard but he wasn't a parent...not really. I was still pretty ill when they told me, but I can remember thinking that it was good that they had gone together. They would have hated being separated after so long."

"Something very like, then, yes," Guyon agreed, with a small sigh of relief. *Thank God. Thank God he will never have any idea of this, or what it means. Thank God for that small mercy.* "I don't think your Uncle William did such a bad job," he added with a small smile. "What happened? Plague?" He knew he sounded unsympathetic, knew too that Peter would have no idea that it was one more symptom of the damnably twisted emotion he felt, that all he could focus on and care for was the knowledge gained from those few small sentences, that Peter *could* have died, and had survived instead. *I wish I could make other things matter. I must. I must pretend, if nothing else.*

"Sweating sickness," Peter said quietly. "I brought it home with me from one of the crofters. They sent Sarah away so she wouldn't get it but mother and father stayed to take care of me. That's how they contracted it."

"Mm...I think more they contracted it because it was in the area, my friend, but I'm not in the habit of assuaging guilt for God's mistakes." Guyon raised his eyebrows. "I know of the sweating sickness, Pèire, it came to France, too. And I know that it can decimate an area and leave one man alive at the heart of it, or take one member of a family and leave the rest untouched. So I think perhaps your facts are a little...inaccurate. Hm?" *He doesn't know anything except taking responsibility for people. Jesus,*

246

Robert, you call that a warning? He felt the absurd urge to find Robert Macquarie out and thump him again for the sheer pleasure of relieved feelings.

"Yes, but I was the most likely source." Peter shrugged. "It's alright, Gui. I got over that guilt a long time ago. That's one thing my uncle did do for me. He explained to me how illnesses can travel even in air we breathe. He...he was a very smart man. He wasn't schooled but he, well, he knew a little about most everything." Peter paused for a moment, "This wasn't really what I wanted to talk about."

Guyon scratched absently at a small bite on his wrist and hoped to God it was something small and airborne that had bitten *him*, and not something in his bed. "No. Of course, I didn't - I'm sorry. I didn't mean to behave like a member of the Inquisition. What *did* you want to talk about?" *And I think I owe your uncle's soul a novena.*

"Why did you come back?" The words were small and quiet, almost as if Peter had feared to ask them. "Not this time...but when you were fourteen."

"Ah." Guyon sighed. *Damn it. François, you should never have died, and then I would not be answering this.* "No, I *left* at fourteen - well, just before. I came back when I was seventeen. I thought...things would be better. That they had changed. I had taken my degrees, was on the point of being granted my license, and I thought - I thought after all that time away that I was independent enough, strong enough, to deal with whatever was left, thought I could salvage my brother's love, at least. But Maurice was here." *Maurice and his pet priest and my brother was so afraid for me...*"You know the result of that somewhat...arrogant error of mine." He rubbed his hands over his face. "The only thing that saved me was the fact I had a friend with enough sense to insist on accompanying me."

"Thank God for François," Peter muttered shakily. "I - just thank God."

"I very much didn't, at the time," Guyon admitted, giving a small personal fact in a kind of apology for how much he was withholding. "I cursed him to the far ends of the earth." He touched Peter's wrist, briefly. "It was a long time ago, you know.

And I healed." *Mostly.*

"We all heal, Guyon, on the outside. But those scars run deeper than skin." Peter ran his hand over the spot that Guyon had touched, as if he were rubbing the feeling deeper into his skin. "And they reopen far too easily."

Guyon resisted the urge to snap *Then stop taking a knife and running it along their edges to see what happens, damn you!* and swallowed down words and sudden bile together. "I know," he said quietly. "I'm sorry. I am *trying.*" *Harder than you know, and it's costing more and more the closer I let you. You're under my skin, Pèire, you're creeping into my soul, and I don't know how to shut you out any more except with distance. And here - here where I am most myself, my most quiet and most hidden self, I have to keep that distance or destroy you.*

"I understand," Peter said, looking up at the night sky, "Or...or I'm trying to. I'm trying not to push or ask for too much. But I know I do. Just...just tell me when it's too much. I don't always recognize when I'm pressing you."

"I know," Guyon said, feeling tired, and sorrowful, and somehow beaten, as though he had lost a battle or some match of wits he had not even realized he was participating in. "It's not too much, *chérâme,* but please. For now. Enough. I can't - I don't think about any of this, all that often. And I'm no good at finding the words. So...give me a while, hm? In time...I'll answer more. I promise." *I may even tell you that you're the only person in this life I have ever said that to willingly.* He leant back on his hands, and followed Peter's gaze to the emerging stars.

*

Guyon didn't particularly want to go back to the Hall. It wasn't an unpleasant night, and if he had brought a cloak, he would have been quite content to remain out until it was dawn. As it was, he only had his riding jacket, and while serviceable enough, it was entirely unsuited to a night out of doors. Besides, even if he had been better prepared, he could scarcely ask it of Peter. Soldier or not, there had to be limits to what he asked the man to endure simply on a whim.

"It's nice out here," Peter said suddenly. "Relaxing and...alright, I'm stalling, I know. But you're right about the Hall, somehow it's just...depressing at times. I think it's the lack of proper light."

"The south side's all right," Guyon said dully, and then shook himself. "I'm sorry. It's - have you ever felt like this? That you can hate somewhere, but the instant anyone else criticizes it -" He sighed. "Ridiculous. I'm ridiculous. The place is horrendous, it should have been knocked down years ago."

"Yes...I have a little place like that near Hawthornden," Peter chuckled in understanding. "And no, I don't think your Hall should be knocked down, Guyon, just...I don't know. It just needs light. Or less Uncle Maurice. Or something."

"The *world*," Guyon said with feeling, "could do with less Uncle Maurice. A lot less Uncle Maurice. A complete absence of Uncle Maurice, in fact." He breathed out a laugh. "Have I happened to mention, *chérâme*, that you are in fact the entirety of my equilibrium? Like the quartz in the *Grotte de Limousis*. Without it, they would be...empty, mere rock and sand."

"Well, certainly there have been many that compared me to a rock, Gui," Peter's eyes twinkled in the darkness. "But never...quartz, was it? What is the Grotte de Limousis?"

"Mm." Guyon had never actually had to explain what the *Grotte* was before, and he found himself fumbling for words. "I - caves? Caverns? They're underground - well, no, almost underground, in the hillside. There are streams, and pools, and great rooms like cathedrals - and quartz," he added with a grin. "We were always told they were haunted, but...I think if they were, it was by very warm and alive bandits."

"That would not be surprising," Peter agreed. "Uncle William told us that the attics of Hawthorndon were haunted. That a bloody warrior with a sword as long as we were tall, walked there, waiting for mortal souls to steal. That when he'd gotten enough, he would be released from his imprisonment there and be allowed to return to life. It wasn't until we snuck up there one night to try to catch a glimpse of the ghost that he realized that his tale had just made the place more enticing and he finally explained that he simply did not want us playing up there until repairs could be made to the flooring. It was very disillusioning."

Guyon laughed. "Well, bandits are *not* disillusioning," he said dryly. "Dispossessing, perhaps, dispossessing you of your property, but not disillusioning." He felt, suddenly, a lot less amused. Peter had obviously not changed in his ability to do the most astoundingly idiotic things when either curious or bored, and the Languedoc seemed to be bringing both those emotions to the fore on a horrifically regular basis. "So if you feel the sudden desire to go exploring, *bèl-mi*, do it in the daylight where no-one can mistake you for anything but who you are, hm?"

"How sad, no midnight exploring..."

"It's going to be a damn sight sadder trying to explain to some very cross smugglers just why we felt the need to use those caves..." Guyon said with a snort. "And I thought you wanted *more* light, not less." He laughed, and relaxed. "But Peter...the *Grotte* might not actually contain ghouls and ogres and a troll with diamond teeth, but...it is dangerous. People have vanished there. We warn children because..." He gave up. If Peter wanted to go into the Grotte at two in the morning, nothing was going to stop him anyway. "I went," he admitted then, and laughed up at Peter's startled expression. "What, you think you're the only one who wanted to see a ghost?" He brought his hand up, and gripped the back of Peter's neck. "Alas, you were an ordinary child."

"And still all too ordinary," Peter admitted, leaning into Guyon's grip. "But I've outgrown taking risks out of mere curiosity, I should hope."

Guyon quirked an eyebrow at him. "Hm," he said disbelievingly, letting a silence fall in which he hoped Peter was remembering each and every time that had been decidedly not the case. After a few uncomfortable seconds, he leaned in and quickly, fleetingly, brushed his lips across Peter's. "Good," he said then, and let Peter feel his smile as the night grew steadily darker.

*

There were so many parts of Margarittes Hall that had been let go. Let go to the point of disuse. Peter could not understand it.

It was not as though they were things that took more than a bit of sweat and labor, either. The bushes needed to be trimmed, the beds in the kitchen garden weeded, all the hinges were in desperate need of oil and the windows, what few there were, needed to be cleaned and caulked.

And the drive was the worst. It was a wonder that the carters still agreed to make deliveries, so broken up was the paving, and so unevenly set at the places where it was whole. So *that*, Peter had declared and Guyon, slightly less enthusiastically, agreed, was to be their task of the day. It was hard and hot work, leaving and replacing stones, scrubbing away moss, and it had Peter, at least, stripped down to his breeches after an hour. But still, it felt good to be working outside rather than trapped in the dim interior of the Hall.

It would have been perfect, in fact, if not for the constantly moving storm cloud of drear that was Guyon's Uncle Maurice. Peter wondered if this was why Giraud had not taken care of so many of the smaller problems. Maurice's insistent nagging and overseeing would be enough to put anyone off.

"Feel free," Guyon said to Maurice eventually, gesturing with his hard brush and a piece of lye soap, "to join in at any moment. Really. There is an almost infinite amount of moss, and a corresponding degree of cold water in the well."

"I'd not waste my time as you've seen fit to. First rain and they'll be right back to this." Maurice folded his arms with a huff, taking a shaded seat on the rock wall that lined the drive. "But I don't need to be listened to. I don't know anything after living here my whole life."

"Well, yes, we *know* that," Guyon said with mock-kindness. He looked contemplatively at the stone he had balanced on its edge further along the wall, as though wondering just how much effort it would take to throw it at Maurice. Catching Peter's eye on him, he ducked his head with a small, embarrassed grin, and began using the graveled sand to lay a bed down for the cleaned slab instead.

Peter shook his head, and picked up his pry bar to prize the next uneven and cracked stone out of spot. If it came out whole he'd clean it and refit it. If it broke, well, he had plenty of previously broken stones to fill in the gaps.

He pressed down on the lever and, not surprisingly, nothing happened. Several years' worth of redistributed mud and roots and moss held the stone in place.

"Gui, can you give me a hand here, please?" It would probably take both their weights to get enough leverage.

"And do what, jump up and down on that metal bar of yours?" Sometimes, Peter could see just why Guyon said he was like Maurice. The same ever-present, sharp-tongued mockery was in both of them, but in Maurice's case it never turned inwards, never created the strange feeling of a glowing sphere of amusement being thrown out for his entertainment. Not, that was, unless it glowed out black unpleasantness. "Archimedes never had to deal with paving stones," Guyon added, wrapping his hands around the bar below Peter's, and leaning forward like one of the disparaged fulcrums.

Peter gave a wheezing choke as his soldier's brain took Guyon's comment in a direction that he certainly was *not* going to be sharing with Uncle Maurice, now or ever. "On three then. One...two..."

The pry bar simply stayed lodged exactly where it was under the paving - and bent in a very Archimedean curve. Guyon, in one of his more unnerving moments of working out just what Peter was thinking, looked wide-eyed at it and doubled up with laughter.

"Guyon..." Peter tried his hardest to keep a straight face, "...you bent my bar."

But that was as much as he could manage, his shoulders shaking with restrained laughter until it all burst out of him with an explosive cackle.

Guyon, still shaking with completely silent laughter, didn't even have to look up in order to connect the flat of his hand with the back of Peter's head. "Damn it," he said rather croakily. "Unfair, Scudamore, unfair..."

It was rare, Peter knew, for the sound of laughter to ring anywhere within the environs of Margarittes Hall, and it only took a moment more for him to be made clear as to the real cause.

"Do the two of you have no discretion at all?" Uncle Maurice huffed out from beneath his shady tree.

Guyon straightened quickly, all humor gone from his face, and his rare, annihilating temper carving lines on either side of his mouth. "*Paire*," he said, in soft warning, and if Peter had been in any doubt as to just how little the people at his home now knew Guyon, it was removed by the fact that Maurice, rather than either apologizing or removing his unwanted presence, simply stayed where he was, shaking his head a little and smiling faintly.

It was an expression that Peter was beginning to dislike intensely, attached to a man that he was coming to loathe altogether. But he held back both feelings, instead moving to extract the bent pry bar from beneath the stone and setting it aside.

"Water, do you think?" He asked Guyon as he looked back down at the stone. As distractions went it wasn't brilliant, he knew, but it was all he had.

Guyon ignored him, still staring at Maurice as though they were having an entire conversation merely by looking at each other with those odd, translucent eyes that were both similar and entirely different at once.

"I see your heresy has taken a more traditional form," Maurice said at last, "but we still failed. It grieves me that no effort of those who love you could drive it from your flesh."

Peter spun around at that and would have moved forward if not for Guyon's restraining hand.

Guyon is competent to fight his own battles, he told himself. *He doesn't need or want me to do it.*

But those words were a challenge to himself as well, to the love he held for Guyon, and coming from Maurice they were almost more bitter than Peter could stand.

"No," Guyon said, and his voice was as cold and soft as snow, his hand like a manacle of ice around Peter's wrist. "It could not."

"And you still think yourself innocent." Maurice looked at him with utter disbelief, and Guyon snorted.

"I disabused myself of that folly long since," he replied, his voice still oddly quiet. "It has been a long time since I did anything other than glory in the appellation of heretic, and longer still since I regretted the decisions it led me to."

Heretic? Heretic? Peter was sick of the repetition of that damnable word. Sick too of not knowing *exactly* what anyone meant by it. He knew that his love for Guyon could be called that, although this was one place where he and the Church parted company, but he also knew that what they shared had nothing to do with Maurice's claims.

"You're a fool, Guyon," Maurice said, and got to his feet. "You should have followed the path your father set out for you to its end."

"I expect I should," Guyon said wearily. "So should you, but then we're hardly a family known for our services to existence, are we?"

And oddly, it was Maurice who stepped back at that, as though Guyon had dealt some blow that he had not been thought capable of. Guyon remained unmoving, the faint pulse in his throat the only thing proving he still lived. Then Maurice nodded, and turned away, walking up the grassy side of the drive towards the house.

"Guyon?" Peter wanted to ask a million questions, but still he hesitated. Would Guyon tell him even if he did ask?

And, more importantly, did he really want to know the answers?

The answer there was "of course" and "yes", because this mystery, this not knowing seemed to be making everything worse. It was like going into battle completely blind, not knowing how many troops your enemy had, nor even how many *you* had.

"Mm." Guyon's hand slackened around his wrist, and the cold fingers released him. "Sorry about that."

Peter rubbed absently at his wrist. There would probably be a bruise there by morning but he hadn't even noticed the grip at the time, he had been so caught up in the latest of Maurice's dramas. He wondered, really, what the man's reason was for constantly stirring the pot.

"He's trying to keep us agitated, isn't he? He thinks that if we are we won't do what we came here to do." Peter huffed out a breath then looked at Guyon. "It...it would be far easier for me to deflect him, if I knew just exactly what he was talking about, rather than having to dig through sly innuendo and insult."

He felt like he were balancing, precarious and tottering. If Guyon did not trust him - No, that did not bear thinking about. The idea was all the more painful for having the ring of truth.

"Pèire -" Guyon looked at him, and for one strange moment Peter was back in a long-ago dream, not the one born of Toulouse and repeated by fear, but the one he had vowed not to forget, all brightness and ringing steel.

Shall I tell you the moment I knew that you lived?

"- he's just a foul old man who knows exactly how to put me at my worst," Guyon finished with a sigh, and his eyelids lowered like shutters, closing Peter out. "Don't worry about it."

He did indeed, but there was no heresy in that, only annoyance. But yet -

Shall I tell you the moment I knew that you lived?

What if -? Peter mind suddenly swirled with that and a million more. *What if? What if? What if?*

What if there was some...reality to their accusations? What if...he had actually heard Guyon as he tried through his fever and pain to stitch himself up in that lamentable and tiny barn? What if - Guyon were not what he appeared to be?

No. It didn't matter. If he was, or if he was not, he was Guyon.

"The wonderful thing about summer," said the object of his thoughts, "is how very long the days are. Come on. More stones."

The discussion, such as it had been, was apparently over. Peter sighed, and went to rescue his pry bar. Somehow its state didn't seem even vaguely amusing, any more.

*

Guyon had never learned, as most people did in the painfully awkward years between discovering love and becoming an accepted lover, how to dissemble - either in feigning interest or in concealing desire. His only way of dealing with the fact that he had no option but to show how he felt - *precisely* how he felt - was to withdraw his presence completely. Unfortunately, as he was discovering, while it might be an easy task to do so when his lover's rooms were a good mile away and so put a large portion of Paris between them, it was a damn sight harder even to start evading Peter's company when they shared a bed as well as a room.

It was made even more difficult when the object of his affections was actively nuzzling his slightly chilly nose into the hollow of his collar and pulling his icy hands against his own chest to warm them.

Guyon, with some difficulty, restrained himself from explaining with the help of some extremely explicit Occitan phrases just what he would like Peter to do with his affection, his caring, and his inevitable physical effect on Guyon, and managed to say something which he hoped was reasonably civil about paperwork. The fact that there wasn't any paperwork other than in his sadly uninventive hoard of excuses not to come to bed did nothing to improve his irrationally unstable temper - mostly because this meant another night trying to keep warm before coming to bed and hoping to God Peter was actually asleep.

Peter's morose expression did little to alleviate his upset, nor did the faint offer, "I can help, if you like?" that accompanied it.

"No, it's..." *non-existent, so I really have to do it alone, and isn't that an interesting conundrum?* - "It's all right. I'll probably be quicker on my own," he said unthinkingly, and could have bitten his tongue out in the next second, because while he didn't want to admit his need for Peter, while he was damned if he would ever expose a single emotion or even the beginnings of the depths of his desire to the ever-spying Maurice, he had also been trying very hard not to use any means of doing so that would wound the very person he was trying to protect. Unfortunately, the only way to keep Peter at arm's length was to *push* him there, and it never seemed possible to do so with any degree of pleasantness.

"Oh...sorry." Peter's face, if anything, became even more sad looking. "You're right. I know my Occitan is still pretty horrid. I'll...I'll just leave you to it then."

"No, it's - I left it downstairs in any case, so -" Guyon trailed off. *One day, one of us will finish a sentence with grace and accuracy, and the world will cease to revolve*, he thought bitterly, and gathered enough coherency to say - "I'll try not to wake you when I come up."

"When have I ever cared if you woke me?" Peter had turned now, and was looking out of the small window that graced one side of their room. "But, I may still be awake. I wanted to read a bit."

There was, Guyon thought despairingly, indeed no God. At least not at Margarittes - or at least not one that cared a single whit for his sanity. That his body betrayed him when he was awake to the point where he had to keep this enforced distance was bad enough - but that he should be tormented so continually, without even the respite of sleep for one of them - without even a few hours of peace so that at least he could hide the fraying threads of his resolution to some extent, seemed if anything a cruelty that was born of hell.

"I'm not sure I could sleep anyway," Peter continued, then shifted his position a bit, giving a small grunt as he moved his shoulders. "Some of those paving stones were...heavier than they looked."

Peter, Guyon thought, was either being wilfully obtuse or knew precisely what he was doing - and either answer was one which made him think longingly of violence. Unfortunately, barring a swift death for one or the other of them, the violence would end up exactly where Peter wanted and where he was trying to avoid, and the hell with aching shoulders. If he had found more courage before they left, had either been capable of telling the truth or of outright lying, of admitting his love or denying it absolutely, then none of this would be happening.

It was not God, then, or His absence, that was the cause of this, but Guyon's own inadequacies, his own failings, his own appalling lacks, made visible even when he tried with all that was in him to do something right, to be for Peter what he had promised - his sword in the Languedoc. If he was steel, then he was flawed in the making, and would shatter the first time he was tried.

I should have said I loved him or said I did not. I could have saved us both, and now it is too late, and we must both endure.

"I'll...send someone with hot water and a bath," he said desperately, and fled.

It was exactly like being back in Paris, before any of this had been thought of, before the furious confrontation that had followed Peter's journey to Argenteuil, before his one moment of unfettered decision.

But now - now he knew what he was refusing, knew all too well just what he so continually longed for, what he was costing Peter as well as himself - and now, just as then, he could not admit that it was fear which was forcing him to behave like this. Before, it had been fear of the unknown. Now, though, after Maurice's unveiled threats outside the house, it was fear of the only thing he *had* known before Peter, the constant, hovering knowledge of where any display of love or affection would lead, of what it could cause.

Your back reflects your soul, Guyon. Every time someone draws their breath in horror - and they will - it will be because they know you for what you are.

And every time he slept, his body betrayed him, turning his back towards Peter not in rejection, as he knew his friend saw it, but in unconscious search of the only protection he had ever known, and the only trust he had ever truly felt.

He had never wished before to so great an extent that he had not lied when he said he could not feel love.

*

The garden of Margarittes Hall, Peter was finding out, was much more pleasant than remaining indoors. Especially since, for some reason, every time he turned around he seemed to run into Uncle Maurice. If there really were ghosts in that Hall, he was beginning to think that Maurice was the chief phantom.

The garden though, was lovely, and he suspected that it was the one place that Catalina de Chesnay had defied her husband's uncle and had actually improved. The high walls were covered with flowering vines; roses, clematis, and passion flower all had their own place. The walks were nicely graveled, and although apparently no one had seen to them recently, relatively free of weeds and grasses. There was a fountain at its center, with a statue of a young girl bearing a pitcher. It wasn't running at present though, its basin filled with wet leaves from the last wind. But still it was calm and quiet, lots of sunshine and peace. For some reason it made Peter think of the Fountain Courtyard at the Sorbonne, although really there were nothing alike. Perhaps, it was just that he would ever link fountains with that night, the Twelfth Night Celebration, the first that they truly felt in accord.

Guyon, who claimed he could kill plants without difficulty from behind closed doors, was proving impossible to bring into it without lengthy coercion, and, that morning, had proved himself lacking in amenability even to that, for once, taking himself off somewhere before breakfast and still not back. Gone for most of the night and now out early. How one man could disappear so effectively had always been a mystery to Peter, and the Hall seemed only to enhance that ability. He assumed Guyon was with Jeannine, as so often in recent days, but when she called his name, sounding utterly frustrated, he was forced to revise his assumption.

"Have you seen him *at all* today?" she demanded without preamble.

"Guyon? Not since before breakfast." Peter admitted. "Was...was he expecting you?"

Not that it seemed to matter, since every day Jeannine showed up and they went off together, chattering about books and legends and poetry that Peter had little or no knowledge of. If he had felt inferior to Guyon's students at the Sorbonne, at least they joked with him and gave him great lists of books to read that he'd have taken two lifetimes to get through. But with Jeannine, he couldn't interrupt because then she turned into some kind of flirting kitten that irritated Guyon and put him out of sorts for the remainder of the day.

"Yes," she said crossly, and then, with equal irritation, "Well, no, but yes. He knew I'd *be* here, anyway." She looked around the garden, and laughed, not the little practiced sound that had been driving him insane, but a real giggle. "Lina would be thrilled, it's gone all overgrown," she said, and then - "Giraud's wife, the Marquesa, I mean."

"She'd prefer it that way?" Peter looked puzzled. "I would have thought the opposite to be true. Someone has obviously put a lot of care into this garden. I assumed it was she."

"Well...yes." Jeannine frowned at him. "She doesn't like things neat. You can take care of things without them being all in lines and rows and trimmed up till it's silly, you know, and this way - loads more flowers, I think it must have been what she was aiming for all spring. She wanted a wildflower garden when she first came, but -" Jeannine snorted, "it got a mole. It wasn't a garden for very long, after that."

"No, I can imagine not," Peter nodded, then looked around the garden again, judging it with this new vision. The colors she had chosen and how they were grouped were lush and brazen, flowing together and fighting for dominance. The scents were heady as the morning breeze shifted and brought them closer. But still, Peter had to admit, he preferred neat paths, although they did not have to be straight, it made it much easier to enjoy the garden. "This is beautiful though."

"Nice that you think something is around here," Jeannine said a bit grumpily, and sat down on the edge of the fountain with a fine disregard for her skirts. "And *how* does Guyon still do that disappearing thing?"

"If I knew that I would be far ahead of the game," Peter answered with a snort. "I'm not even certain *why* most of the time, let alone *where* or *how*."

"Don't know, don't know, don't know, always has," Jeannine answered, ticking the points off on her fingers. "I bet he's *fun* in Paris." She sounded utterly sincere.

"He can be." *When I've not annoyed him past all bearing. When I don't tell him things that he doesn't wish to hear...like 'I love you'. Or is it just that even without saying it, he knows? Could it be -?* No, Guyon often seemed to know what he was thinking, but that could more easily be put down to his transparency, than any foresight on Guyon's part. "But I'm not a little prejudiced, you know. He is, above all else, my very best friend." *Very best, heretic or devil.*

"So why weren't you here? Back then?" Jeannine's eyes were utterly guileless, her tone unaccusing. She simply wanted to know. "He stopped writing, after that. Stopped everything. He *really* disappeared." She looked suddenly sad. "I wasn't *his* best friend, but he was probably mine. And I missed him. Giraud did, too. He used to read the letters, to remind himself." She sighed. "I did, too, but mine were letters for a little girl, and -" she shrugged. "I grew up, so they're not important any more."

"We hadn't met then," Peter explained quietly, "but he had...François, for which I am very grateful." He *was* grateful. He *was*. As jealous as he felt of the other man at times, even now that he was gone, he still felt that gratitude that François had been there for Guyon when he could not.

And what, he wondered, had François thought about the charges against Guyon? Had he believed them? *He's not exactly...like other people.* No, it was probably simpler than that. If François had believed the charges, he had accepted them, too.

Peter drew a deep breath, "Never think that something is not important just because you were younger. I'm sure that Guyon's letters were special, as he is himself."

"Now *you're* treating me like a little girl," Jeannine said, and rolled her eyes. "No matter how pleased I am that a Sorbonne scholar remembered to ask after my doll's well-being, I *really* don't need to be reminded of that fact by a letter. *Or* that the writer must have been pretty much unique. But *Giraud*..." she made a small face. "Lina's nice," she added more quietly. Peter was quite sure that was supposed to mean something to him, but Jeannine's methods of conversation left him feeling as though he were at sea. In the fog. In a very small boat that leaked.

"You...you don't care for Giraud?" That much had been fairly plain. "I've never met him but - " Peter wasn't sure he was willing to tell this girl-child how he truly felt about the man who had flayed the skin off his own brother's back, no matter what the reason.

Jeannine shrugged. "I suppose he's all right. But all he cares about is the Languedoc, on and on and on, and the legacy of his father, and family name, and -" She kicked at the fountain base. "Guyon ran away, you know," she said, a bit irrelevantly. "I would have, too, but the Sorbonne doesn't take girls."

"No...no it doesn't." Peter didn't know what to think about

that, and it caused him to frown. "But you'd have missed your father, soon enough, I'm sure. And Giraud is the Marqués, I suppose that's enough of a reason for some, to have such concerns." He never thought about it himself, but then again, he was only the Lord of a Rock, in Scotland, with sheep. That thought, delivered to his brain in all of Guyon's slurred tones, made him smile.

Jeannine looked at him, and suddenly started to laugh. "Peter Scudamore, no university in the *world* will admit women! I mean, they did. I think. In Ancient Greece. But not now. And it's started to be quite clear I can't disguise myself as a boy. *Apart* from the fact Guyon would have recognized me and killed me dead. Anyway, Giraud's not concerned, he's obsessed," she finished up calmly, and sat back with an air of satisfaction. *Probably at the fact she's completely confused me.*

"Obsessed?" Peter started with one of the clearer concepts.

"Oh, their father," Jeannine explained. "God and duty and responsibility, and Giraud tries to do it all better and harder. *Guyon*," she repeated with pleasure, "ran away."

"Yes, I can see that he would have," Giraud was obviously more of an idiot than Peter had already given him credit for. "Maybe Giraud thought he had to, somehow, redeem himself?"

He didn't know if Jeannine knew any more than he did, but felt certain that if she did, she would not be quite so closed mouthed about it.

"Well, *yes*," Jeannine said in bewilderment. "You know...most people here? They think someone like Guyon's amazing. You shouldn't believe all the stuff Maurice talks about. Honestly, it's mostly this stupid family." She got to her feet. "I suppose I'd better go home." Her eyes danced with sudden mischief, and she leant in closer to Peter. "You know...I bet Giraud left those letters right where they were," she said quietly. "In his father's rooms." She grinned, stepped back, and dropped a far more graceful curtsey than the one she had first greeted him with. "Good luck." She straightened, and made her way back out through the garden with a small wave over her shoulder.

"Um.. Yes...thank you..." Peter watched her leave with a puzzled expression. Granted most women or girls left him in a state of confusion at the best of times, but Jeannine seemed even more cryptic than most. Could she really be hinting that he take advantage of her suggestion? He stood up and looked around the planned wildness of the gardens.

You can take care of things without them being all in lines and rows and trimmed up till it's silly, you know...

They think someone like Guyon's amazing.

Someone like Guyon? Did she mean his intelligence? Or was she hinting at something else? Damn! Why couldn't he just ask the question and expect a straight answer?

He used to read the letters, to remind himself.

I bet Giraud left those letters right where they were.

Jeannine did confuse him, but she liked Guyon. Liked him a lot. She obviously wanted to help him in whatever way she could and wanted to Peter to do the same. She had almost come straight out and told him to invade Guyon's privacy.

Peter straightened, well aware that he was now contemplating doing something that he normally would have disapproved of in the strictest of terms...but he was beginning to feel desperate to do something, anything. He knew deep down that lack of knowledge could only be his downfall.

*

Margarittes Hall, the Languedoc, June 1646

But yet the most discreet believe,
The Schools this jewel do receive,
And thus far's true without dispute,
Knowledge is still the sweetest fruit.
But whilst men seek for Truth they lose their peace;
And who heaps knowledge, sorrow doth increase.

Peter wasn't sure if he should feel guilty about this or not. Here he stood, contemplating a horrible breach of privacy, Guyon's privacy. Well, more than contemplating, because he had already slipped away and into a room where he really had no business being. But he needed answers, craved them like he craved Guyon's love, and had no one who would answer them. So here he was in the turret rooms that had belonged to Guyon's father and mother, holding a packet of letters in his hand. Letters, that he was sure would hold answers to so many of his questions. Private letters from Guyon to Giraud - and from Guyon's father.

He had, of course, read through other people's mail before, both on assignments from Corvay and his Queen. He had snuck into private chambers while their owners were away, gathered evidence that either exonerated or condemned, and felt little guilt over doing it. But this was different. This was Guyon.

Guyon, who it seemed had always written as he thought, on whatever scraps of paper came to hand, the handwriting dating the letters as definitely as the scrawled numbers at the top, the sprawling letters firming and tightening into the familiar upright, cramped strokes that could cover a page in what seemed like seconds. Phrases leapt out at Peter -

Please don't worry. I have a room at the University, and they have been kind.

I'm learning something every day, something new.

It is as though some vast abyss inside me exists, as though I read, and read, and argue, and define, and still there's room.

This was the Guyon that set his mind burning as well as his body. The Guyon that could get lost in the simple phrases of a text or the complexities of a code. The one who drew him out, tried to tangle his simple soldier's brain around issues that he often felt inadequate to comment on, and then, when he did, made him feel as if he had said something wonderful and worth listening to. This was one of the pieces of Guyon that first drew his admiration, this never-ceasing need to understand everything.

François Villon said today that the laws of heresy should be revised, that he intends to work with the archbishop to do this.

Do you ever think our father was wrong? Do you ever wonder if Socrates was right and not the Church?

I miss you, sometimes. It seems strange not to have someone to follow. I do think of you. But I couldn't stay.

And these were the seeds, this was what must first have poked at Giraud de Chesnay to think his brother's soul in danger. Damn him. It was pure idiocy to fear that questioning and curiosity were signs of heresy. Did not the Disciples question Our Lord daily? How else were they to learn God's will if not like that?

Peter shook his head. He should, he knew, probably pray to God that he could forgive Giraud, but somehow he did not have the goodness in his own soul to do that yet.

If we are part of the universe, children of the infinite, do our decisions matter in the end? Or are they part of this Great Design, the Potter's Wheel they talk of in Persia? Are we cups thrown from clay, made to be filled, and if so, why not by the three strands of the ancients? Why not by knowledge and love and truth? Why not?

"What the *hell* do you think you're doing?" demanded Guyon from the door.

To Peter's credit, he managed not to drop the letters and scatter them on the floor like a schoolboy caught cheating. Instead, he calmly refolded the last sheet, and placed the whole packet back where he had found it.

"I'm learning you," he answered. He bit his lip to keep from apologizing. He couldn't be sorry, not really, but he feared what he would read in Guyon's face when he looked up.

"I thought it was called an unforgivable intrusion of privacy," Guyon said tightly. "How nice to know there's a more pleasant term. I did *not* write those for *you*."

"No. You did not." Peter answered softly. What was he to say? *You never give me anything of yourself. You've never written anything for me to keep.* The thoughts would be wasted at this moment.

"Why did you come up here?" Guyon didn't sound particularly angry, really, as much as he sounded tired and unhappy and somehow disappointed. "There's nothing of value to you."

That gave Peter pause for a moment - surely Guyon did not think him a thief? But no, it was a more personal type of value that he was speaking of - sentiment and privacy, perhaps.

"Everything that is you, is of value to me." The words were true, but still not an apology nor an explanation.

"Not this." Guyon took the packet from where Peter had replaced it. "The maunderings of a selfish, uncomprehending child who thought love mattered." He smiled sourly. "I assume Giraud kept them to remind himself he was right, and I was wrong. They are of no interest to anyone living, and these - these are my father's rooms. They're - private."

Private. Not for Peter. Not to be shared, like so many things in Guyon's life. No matter how much love he felt, Peter was going to be left on the outside, time and again, because Guyon did not feel the same way. The thought was like a stone sitting in his stomach.

"Love does matter," but even as Peter said the words, he knew they would not be given credence.

"Yes, Peter." Guyon's eyes were sad, and kind, and his voice was very soft. "But why? In the end? Because it's the greatest betrayal man is capable of." He turned on his heel, and left the room, carrying the packet of papers with him.

Because it's the greatest betrayal man is capable of.

The words told Peter all. They told Peter nothing. He understood the betrayal of love, had fallen victim to it himself long ago. He understood how Giraud had betrayed Guyon's love for his brother. But he also knew that he would never, could never, betray Guyon in that way.

The idea that Guyon thought otherwise settled over him like a pall, one more weight to hold him down, utterly at odds with the vehemently underscored words that had been on the last page, the sound of the flight of eagles that had rung through the Sorbonne at Guyon's thesis presentation:

Are we cups thrown from clay, made to be filled, and if so, why not by the three strands of the ancients? Why not by knowledge and love and truth? Why not?

*

For all his attempts at light heartedness, Peter was beginning to feel the weight of Guyon's home dragging down on him. It was as if the heavy stones of the foundations, the fortifications and the turrets themselves were resting on his shoulders, oppressing his spirits and making him more glum as days passed. Of course, his altercation with Guyon over his father's letters had not helped; he was never at his best when the two of them were on the outs and Guyon showed no sign of wanting even to discuss their disagreement.

Instead, he was in the library with Jeannine, studying. What they were studying Peter had not yet discerned but it seemed to involve quite a bit of close conversation and occasional laughter. Laughter that Peter ached to join, but did not wish to intrude upon. Jeannine and her father seemed the only people in this hellacious place that were truly glad to see Guyon return, and Peter could not bring himself to disrupt even a moment of any pleasure he could take out of it.

The laughter was more Jeannine's than Guyon's, though, even in the times when they were not arguing, fast and quiet and not meant to be overheard, deliberately curtailing and slurring their words one into another so that even if Peter *did* hear them clearly, he would not be able to discern more than the tone. Jeannine might amuse Guyon, in the strange, half-bitter way that his students did from time to time, but she did not lighten his spirits. Whatever part of himself Guyon had withdrawn, he had done so from everyone, and not even the pleasant difference in mood that Jeannine brought with her could change that.

So, no talking with Peter, little laughter with or without him, and no news on what they had come for in the first place. Peter felt more than useless, to Guyon and to himself. He watched the two, listened to their tones since he could not *quite* make out the words, then took himself out into the barn. There at least he had something to do, even if it was only *talking* to the horses, all their care having been done by the day help from the village.

It was unreasonable of him to resent the sound of voices when the two finally left the library - *at Jeannine's prompting*, he thought with a faint tinge of resentment, *Guyon leaving even that dreadful collection of books would never be his own idea* - and came across the yard, but he did, the clear voices disturbing the stillness of the air and the sense of detachment he was trying to cultivate.

"You're not too old or too dignified for me to drop you in the water-trough," Guyon was pointing out brightly, as they came towards the stables.

Unreasonable of him to resent it, but he did. Now he'd have to pretend there was nothing wrong, that he was fine, and oh, yes, he'd had an actual reason for leaving the house which was to....Oh! Curry his horse. He grabbed a brush and stepped into the stall, smoothing hand and brush over the sleek hide.

"And I still know how to use a pitchfork."

"Of course you do, don't all the devils in hell?" Guyon asked amicably, and then, catching sight of Peter, sobered. "Père, we should invite the Captain to a dinner here, I think. His idea of conversation with his daughter does *not* include anything helpful." He ignored Jeannine's spluttered beginning of a protest, shrugging one shoulder up irritably. "It *doesn't*, brat, no matter how many pretty words you put around it."

"Hmmm..." Peter murmured noncommittally. "What would you consider to actually be helpful? Darning socks? Cooking bacon on a kettle lid?"

He smiled softly to himself, leaning down to run the brush down to the horse's belly. He had memories of Guyon doing both those things, one clumsily and the other...well, he'd interrupted so he could not vouch for Guyon's skills there.

Guyon looked at him rather blankly, "Well, personally I was hoping he'd found out a bit more about Spanish...er...inanities, but if you need your socks darned, I'm sure he's more than competent..." He snorted suddenly. "Surprised at the request, but more than competent. No, Jeannine, you may *not* have the privilege of darning Peter's socks, but you *can* go home and extend an invitation to your father for tomorrow night."

"But I am rather good at it," Jeannine gave Guyon a twisted grin. "I can also play a harpsichord, sing, play several dozen card games, organize a household and sew up a wound. There are no ends to my skills." She paused and looked hopefully over at Peter, "I even know how to curry a horse."

"And yet the one thing we are curiously not short of is stable boys, so I think not," Guyon said with surprising briskness, given Jeannine's wistful tone. "As to organizing a household, you've so far succeeded in organizing our poor kitchen-lad out of what were remaining to him of his wits, so forgive me if I fail to be entirely overawed by your skills. Card games, however, might be useful. I shall send you to play with Maurice while we talk to your father." He smiled at Jeannine's open-mouthed outrage, and added encouragingly, "Or you could go home, and find that by the time tomorrow comes, I've forgotten my good idea."

"Yes, very well, my grumpy bear," She leaned in and planted a kiss on Guyon's cheek, dancing back before he could retaliate in anyway. "I'll send word in the morning about the time and I'll see you then."

Peter thought for a moment that she was going to attempt the same move on him, but Guyon's scowl apparently deterred her enough that she merely waved at him before she left.

Guyon groaned, and leant against one of the doors. "Lord, God, have you any idea how much I crave *silence*, these days?" He ran his hands over his unruly hair. "It's...I missed her, to an extent, but..." He made a wry little face at Peter. "The trials I endure with the undereducated..."

"Yes...yes, I'm sure you do." Peter had often wondered why Guyon had any patience with him at all. Perhaps it was merely because he knew that Peter tried so hard to keep up.

"There's a very fine line between my sanity and this place," Guyon said, apparently at random, and with a calmness that was completely at odds with what he was saying, "and I should probably point out that you're currently the one thing stopping me from crossing it. Maurice, on the other hand," he continued in exactly the same tones, "is almost guaranteed to ensure that I *do* cross it, so would you mind accompanying me while I try and find out what he's done with the keys to all the cabinets *this* time?"

Well, it appeared then that there were one or two things that he was still useful for, but whether it was being a buffer between Maurice and Guyon, or a strong arm to force the other man into doing what he should, was unclear. Still, this was one of the things he was there for, to help Guyon, so help he would.

"Certainly," Peter put the curry brush away and gave the horse a final friendly pat before leaving the stall. "Am I to glower and look formidable?"

For a moment, Guyon looked sadder than Peter had ever seen him - not grief-stricken, not hurt or angry or distressed, simply *sad* - before he moved into the sunlight that was coming in through one of the open windows, and the clear rich light wiped all expression from his face and all color from his eyes. *Illusion of shadows, like so much in this damn place. And I'm starting to be affected too.* "No, just stop me from shaking them out of him," he said distantly.

"Just pretend he's Vincennes on the eighth draft of his thesis," Peter moved to stand beside Guyon, putting a hand on his shoulder. "That should remind you of your patience."

"I don't remember ever in fact *employing* patience with Vincennes," Guyon said with a faint grin, "so perhaps we need another example..."

"You're patient with me," Peter ventured. He tried to keep the words light as he continued, "And everyone knows what a trial I can be. You should ask Robbie. I'm sure I drove him quite mad at times."

Guyon's blank look returned. "You? But I don't -" He stopped, and brought his hand up to touch Peter's where it still lay on his shoulder. "I *will* ask Robbie," he said, his mouth quirking into a real smile. "And I have no doubt you'll regret it..."

"No, Robbie will tell you true...it's you talking to Sarah that I worry over," Peter chuckled now, his mood lightening a bit. "She'll have you believing I tormented her and locked her in a cupboard when she disagreed with me." Peter's lip twitched, "Really...it was only the once..."

"But of course you *did*, didn't you?" Guyon seemed to be coming back a little from behind the protective barriers of steel that had slammed up after he found Peter reading the letters - and the difference was so small and yet so acute that it was next to painful, *would* have been painful if it had not been such a relief.

"Well, of course," Peter chuckled again. "She thought she was grown and she was going to marry Robbie...and.. I was being rather an idiot about it. I wasn't ready to lose her and I thought...well, I knew Robbie, ya see. I love him like a brother but I didn't see how he could possibly be serious about my bit of a girl. But he was...and they did...and now I have two nephews and a niece."

"Robert Macquarie," said Guyon in one of his moments of strange illumination, "is only serious about one thing, but it's not just Sarah. It's your family. But of course you know that." He laughed then, half-awkward and mostly embarrassed. "Yes, yes, next I shall go and find a nice old lady to call Grandmother, and instruct her in the art of egg-sucking."

"I know it now, Gui, but I didn't always," Peter lifted the hand from Guyon's shoulder and teased a finger over his jaw line. "You don't know Robbie that well, but you saw it."

Guyon saw so many things about people, it made him wonder at times what was different about him. How Guyon could see that Robbie loved his family, but not how he, Peter, loved Guyon.

"Robbie," Guyon said, "has a way of getting through to the most obtuse of men. And of...poking vipers, all ready and willing to be bitten, if he thinks their venom might be efficacious to his brother-in-Christ." He leant into the touch a little, another small sign of thaw.

"He does that," Peter nodded. "Always has. He's a bit single-minded about things though. That's why I was so surprised that he finally changed his mind about Cromwell. It's not - He doesn't often change his mind once it's set."

"Mmmm." It was a softer, more considering sound than the usual non-committal hum. "Peter...ah, never mind. I'm in danger of sentiment." He made a face. "Come on. Maurice, death to every softer emotion, awaits."

"Ah, yes, indeed. Lead on." Peter waved Guyon ahead, falling into step as they went back to the house.

Just once he hoped, sometime, Guyon would let that sentiment out. Let him know where he really stood. He loved Guyon so much that he ached with it, but he didn't want him to have him around merely because he liked him, or found him useful, or even because he desired him. Desire was a wonderful thing, but as Peter had found out at a rather young age, desire often lied. Peter wanted love and if that was not what Guyon was prepared to offer him, he would-- he would stay for as long as Guyon needed him, and then let him go on to find what love he could., if that was what he wanted.

Peter shook his head. Even a meeting with Maurice was better than dwelling on those thoughts.

*

Peter had helped retrieve the wayward keys from Maurice and then found himself at loose ends. He and Guyon were still at odds and edgy in each others company. Neither of them mentioned the letters or Peter's ill mannered reading of them, or even Guyon's anger. They just hemmed and hawed and skirted the issue. The tension was almost intolerable at times.

And, even as much as he had learned of Guyon from the letters, they weren't as useful as they might have been if he'd had the replies to hand as well. He felt a deep seated need to know more, to ferret out exactly what had happened to Guyon and why. But Gui was, obviously, not going to tell him voluntarily, and his other sources, *de Tourvel and Jeannine,* either did not feel it was their place or, *Maurice,* were not trustworthy enough for him to bother with.

So he was approaching his final option - the church. True, Guyon said that de Retz had arranged for the records to be purged, but Peter still hoped that something might have been missed or that the Priest would deign to explain something to him.

He was used to parish priests with their own houses, often

shared with a curate or perhaps a younger priest, or, in the case of the Protestant church leaders, a wife and often children. He had somehow come to assume that priests took responsibility at a certain age and were always under instruction before that - but the man who answered the door of the slightly ramshackle cottage could not have been much over twenty, and yet obviously lived there alone, since there wasn't even room for half another priest, let alone a supervising one. The thought of this man being the senior church leader was a rather terrifying thought, so it was almost reassuring to think that if he had no room for a supervisor, he had no room to be one, either.

This also made him quite aware that this young man was probably not the priest that had officiated at Guyon's trial or punishment.

"Good afternoon, Father," Peter nodded and held out his hand in greeting. "I'm Peter Scudamore, Lord Hawthornden. I'm visiting at Margarittes Hall."

The priest gave him a decidedly odd look, before shaking his hand. "I hear confessions...Saturday," he said in very slow and heavily accented French, which was infinitely worse than Peter's and depended rather heavily on Latin.

Oh, wonderful. Peter would have, somehow, to scrape by on his slowly gained Occitan and the dreaded Latin. "You don't speak French? I...I have little Occitan, but I will try."

"I speak French," the priest said rather inflectionlessly. It was impossible to tell whether he meant precisely the opposite, was trying to be helpful, or was simply mimicking Peter and had missed out a word. Then he scratched at his head, and smiled a bit, the bland look dissolving instantly. "Would be better than trying your Occitan, I am thinking."

It was the first time Peter had heard someone really struggling with the divide between Occitan and French. He had got used to not being understood and not understanding, he had even begun to hear the divisions in the eliding, slurred phrases, but it was a shock to hear the careful, slightly odd phrasing that Guyon used when tired or trying hard to be precise emphasized and exaggerated. It was like having Guyon's often-repeated avowal - *I'm not French, not really* - brought to life and proved.

273

"You're probably quite right." Peter smiled at the other man, and did reply in somewhat broken Occitan, "We'll both do what we can manage, yes?"

He hoped against hope that they'd manage something, because this was important *damn it* and he needed to know.

"I am sure we will," the priest agreed. He still looked a little confused. "But confessions. Still for Saturday. Unless for weighty and pressing sins, and I would have heard those already, most probable." The expression on his face spoke of Maurice without need for further explanation. It seemed to be a look that more than five minutes in the man's company evoked in most people. "So I am not sure as to how I can help you."

"I'm not here for confession," Peter replied. "Not that I'm unaware that I probably need to confess my many and varied sins on a regular basis, but.... I'm more in need of information today, really."

"Information," the priest repeated, nodding slowly and obviously completely lost now, if he hadn't been to begin with. "On what? Or is it of what?" He blinked a little, shook his head, and then said abruptly, "You should come in." As invitations went, it was probably sad that this was neither the most ungracious nor the most awkwardly phrased Peter had ever heard, but it was, quite evidently, meant for one.

Peter stepped in through the door, and stood, "Thank you, Father. I need to take a look at your registers for a particular time span. Is...is that allowed?"

God, he was fidgeting. He was reduced to 6 years old and standing before Father Augustus, waiting to be told how many errors he had just made in conjugating the verb *live*.

"Of course, yes, they are kept so you can. Er." The priest scratched at his head again. Peter was beginning to wonder if he had fleas. "Not just you. Anyone. So anyone can. Yes. Follow me."

Peter followed obediently, taking in what he could see of the small, very tidy residence. "I'm sorry, Father, I wasn't told your name."

"Michael," said the priest a bit absently, going through the keys that hung from his belt and muttering under his breath. Peter couldn't make out all the words, but the tone of irritation and the repeated checking of five keys in particular would have been familiar in some language from the other side of the world. Apparently being convinced that something had been *right there,* and should *still* be there, even when it quite evidently was not, was not a phenomenon confined to Guyon's students or his own cadets.

Peter waited patiently, wondering how poorly it would go over if he volunteered to pick the lock? It was not a skill he bragged about, but one he had learned during his various errands for Corvay and was some times extremely useful.

Father Michael solved the problem by kicking with surprising force at the small wooden door set into the wall. The ease with which it swung open and the rather thorough splintering sound accompanying its movement showed that this was the more usual way employed of getting it to unlock. Peter wondered if it ever actually *got* locked, or just jammed shut.

"I'm specifically looking for the autumn of 1640, Father Michael. If you can point me in the proper direction, I shouldn't have to bother you anymore until I'm done." *Or until I scream in frustration that I've still found nothing.*

They both looked at the cupboard stuffed full of scrolls and badly-bound documents. "Ah," said Father Michael.

Peter sighed, resigned to a long afternoon and some very unhelpful help.

"Is there some type of...organization to this?" Peter said wearily. "Any at all?"

"Oh yes. We have all been very organized." Father Michael winced. "I am the sixth priest since then. And no-one made any record of *how* they organized. I think perhaps they invented just as I did...but perhaps it is like soil."

"Like   soil?"   Peter   frowned,   puzzled. "Because...um...confusion grows?"

"No, because it stays still and more somehow is on top," said Father Michael, looking in some despair at the overstuffed shelves. "So...maybe if we start halfway?" He tugged experimentally at one of the fat registers, and successfully withdrew it. The papers followed nature's law regarding vacuums, and cascaded downwards to fill the space. "Oh."

"Indeed," Peter agreed, and revised his estimate - a long afternoon *and* early evening.

Father Michael, though, was more helpful than his rather disordered behavior would have suggested, if only because he could tell from the first glance at a document or register book when and where it belonged, saving them both the need for thorough perusal of the not-always legible records. He finally put a weighty-looking tome in front of Peter where he sat on one side of the battered desk, and nodded encouragingly. "Here. This will have all we wrote down," he said. "I will get some more light."

Peter hoped he meant candles.

He began flipping through pages, squinting and looking at dates which were at least *usually* legible. He suddenly had a horrible sense of déjà vu and saw himself asking Guyon to help him find the autokey to decode the rest.

Father Michael brought in a very badly trimmed oil lamp, a jug, and a cup, all jostling rather uncomfortably for balance and position on top of a plate of cheese. "The mice had the bread," he said, more in explanation than apology.

"Oh...well, um...all God's creatures have to eat?" Peter really had little to say on the subject of mice, other than they made unusual pets if you were terribly bored. "Margarittes seems to have the same problem. Thank you though...for this..."

He hadn't expected this much in the way of hospitality after his dealings with Uncle Maurice. It made him forget that there were still people who still held to the laws of propriety.

"Yes," said Father Michael, though whether he was referring to the mice, Peter's thanks, or was agreeing with his own thoughts was rather hard to tell. "You must excuse. Mass." He gestured at the clock.

"Yes," Peter agreed. "Thank you again."

He watched the priest leave and wondered if he were as confused as Peter felt. Father Michael probably didn't understand a third of what he had said, but still was more gracious than Maurice had been to him during his whole stay.

Pulling the lamp closer, he began to slowly work his way through the register.

It didn't take him long to find what he was looking for. If the excised pages of August had not been enough, the closely-written, beautiful hand of a well-educated man, strangely at odds with the careful block printing of the then-incumbent priest, would have been out of place enough to alert him. The elaborate signature, embellished to the point where it filled all the paper left blank on the final page, was final proof. Maurice de Chesnay, who had maliciously incriminated and damned his great-nephew, his testimony still there as proof of his hatred, if not of what it had brought about. For a moment, Peter was overcome by the desire to seal the paper away again, and look no further.

But no, this is what he had come from, and although it was from Maurice, surely he would be able to judge what was truth and what was more of Maurice's venom? At least, he hoped he would.

He skipped over the opening paragraph, it being merely the details of who Guyon was and how he was related to Maurice and the family in general and what crime he was accusing his nephew of. Peter had known all this. The following paragraphs related to the actual "crime".

> *"Guyon feels himself closer to God than other mortals, evidenced in copies of letters (attached) that he has sent to his brother over the years of his absence from home. He repeatedly gives argument to the beliefs of the church, questions their correctness and their very understanding."*

The letters of course, were gone, expunged by de Retz. But Peter was well aware of what they said. They could, of course, been interpreted in the way he stated, but anyone who knew Guyon, as he had, would know they were more of a request, a prayer nearly, for more complete understanding.

> *"We should grant leniency though rather than the usual sentence of death, as we must always be aware of Astor's teachings, which his sons have so diligently sought to avoid. That Guyon went to the Sorbonne's halls of learning in order to defeat his leanings must be seen as proof positive of his desire for absolution, and not as further evidence of his heretical tendencies."*

Since no-one *but* Maurice had considered Guyon's traveling to the Sorbonne as anything but a desire for learning, before that, Peter had to admire, even while he loathed, the sheer manipulative gall of the man.

"Mention it in the same context as your accusation, and they'll never see beyond the connection. You didn't give anyone a chance, did you, you old bastard?"

Peter shook his head and reached for the cup that Father Michael had left. It was filled with a rather nice smelling yellowish concoction that tasted of herbs. The cheese was rather dry but complimented the drink and Peter, again, thanked the absent priest for his kind hospitality.

He shook his head again and returned to Maurice's testimony.

"We must also remember that Guyon has returned here, willingly, to face these accusations. That is, in fact, heartening..."

"Heartening? Did you give him even a clue before hand what he was being called home for? Or did you just spring it on him like some...demented birthday surprise?" Peter frowned, sure he knew the truth and again, thanked all the saints and angels that François had chosen to accompany Guyon.

But no matter what he felt, no matter how much he wanted to inflict the same agonies on Maurice, no matter how incomprehensible it all seemed, he could not ignore the memory of Guyon's soft, resigned voice the night he had pleaded with Peter to hear de Retz out.

I don't want to tell you why. Suffice it to say - it was deserved.

Peter hadn't believed that then any more than he did now, even knowing far less. But what he *did* have to believe was that some part of Guyon, at least, whether he knew what he came back to face or no, had acquiesced to what had been done.

Guyon had *agreed* to his judgment, to his punishment. Of all the things de Retz had excised from the records, even the slightest hint of Guyon attempting to defend himself would not have been among them.

Not only had he not tried, but he must have been compelling in his arguments to let this demented mockery of a trial proceed, for he had also stopped François, somehow, from coming to his defense - François who would have changed every law in France if he thought it would benefit his friend.

Did Guyon, then, *believe* what Maurice had written?

He must have done, Peter assumed, or he would not have claimed it was deserved. But still-

> *"My nephew understands the severity of these accusations and has said he will not refute them. He is willing to undergo the scourging of the self, in order to remind him of his humility, of his ties to earth and man, rather than any thoughts of commerce with the dead or spirits of any kind."*

It seemed all so fantastical. All of it. That they could believe Guyon guilty of such things as speaking to the dead, seeing angels, thinking himself above other men in his connection to God. Fantastical, exaggerated and patently ridiculous.

More than that, after Lesueur's death, when Peter had lived through his own time of fantastical impossibility in the form of a dream that seemed to both compress and span years of his life - *Shall I tell you the moment I knew that you lived?* - Guyon had dreamed of something that had truly happened - had *admitted* that was what he had done, in a rare moment of confidence.

And Peter, trying to fix each and every second of his own strange dream in his mind, could still remember what Guyon had said, half-asleep and locked in despair.

I have never seen an angel...

It had made no sense at all at the time, was almost frighteningly comprehensible now. Divine visitation or belief that he experienced them was hardly Guyon's style - denial of it, whether despairing or amused, was far more likely. So why had he agreed to something he, too, knew to be untrue?

Peter took another drink of the yellowish liquor and leaned back in the chair, Maurice momentarily forgotten as he puzzled everything out.

Alright, yes, the Guyon he now knew was, he assumed, different than the one that had agreed to be punished for these crimes. That Guyon, he assumed, was more willing to take on the punishment to appease his family. He could understand that, knowing how many things he had done to protect Sarah, and even

Robbie.

And Guyon might not be willing now to give in to what was wanted or demanded of him, but he would still endure Corvay to buy Giraud's safety, would no more consider evicting Maurice than he would have set down traps and poison for the mice in his old rooms. In a moment of lightning-dazzled understanding, Peter found one more piece to the puzzle, the reason Guyon feared and hated the word love. What Maurice had called an abomination, what Giraud had tried to whip from him, what the church had condemned and de Retz felt constrained to hide - all the little damning attempts to save Guyon from himself - from this inexplicable and ludicrous *heresy* - Guyon had called it love, and probably still did.

You're the best man I know.

You don't love me, Peter. You can't.

Of course he did not. Peter dropped his head into his hands, a bitter laugh escaping him. It was Guyon's prerogative, after all, to be damned. He was the perfect knight, so how could he be some twisted thing to be feared and destroyed?

You're the best man I know.

He had never realized until now that it was a curse.

A curse to be what he was. A curse to love what Guyon, *somehow*, thought he was. And *Love* the greatest curse of all...because so much had been done to him in the name of it.

"Oh, Gui." Peter wanted to take all of it way - the memories and the doubts - and keep Guyon from ever having to experience such pain again.

But the truth was he couldn't. Couldn't remove the past and couldn't mend the future, because Guyon would not allow it.

No wonder Guyon had dreaded their coming here. He would have known before they even set out that Peter would finally understand the full extent of how hopeless the task he had set himself was - to convince Guyon love was not something to be endured, but gloried in. He probably assumed that, understanding at last just how futile his attempts had always been, Peter would withdraw even his friendship - and Guyon had never left him in any doubt of how much that meant to him, even if he had shrunk away from all else. Guyon would not allow understanding, would

280

not allow any attempts at loving him *despite* knowing his past - Peter stood no chance of convincing him that it was not despite, and never had been, but rather *because.*

If Guyon's heresy was love, then Giraud and Maurice had succeeded in their attempt. All traces of it had indeed been beaten from Guyon at the Carcassonne whipping-post.

And now, it appeared, that Guyon was prepared to withdraw himself from Peter, rather than the obverse. Well, at least as far as anything beyond mere friendship went. He spent more time with Jeannine than with Peter. More time away from him than with him. And even when they were together, they weren't - Guyon having fended off or completely refused any kind of intimate contact since their arrival.

Was it, indeed time? Time for Peter to accept that he would not only never have Guyon's love in return, but that Guyon might be better off without his presence reminding him of what Peter wanted? Of what Peter was?

Of Peter at all?

The jug of herbal whatever-it-was had long since been emptied, and the oil lamp was more than needed by the time Peter clawed himself out of his shroud-like thoughts and into a more immediate awareness of the day - or rather rapidly-descending evening - and his surroundings. He put the book back into the overcrowded cupboard, and closed the door, jamming it shut by setting it off its hinges slightly, as was obviously the usual means of ensuring it stayed closed. Not wanting to intrude too much on Father Michael's living space, he left the used plate, jug and cup in a neat stack on the desk, and blew out the oil lamp, before leaving the room and going to find out if his horse was still where he had left it. As he did so, he realized that the herbal drink had been very far from innocuous, and that he was quite definitely drunk.

"Lovely." Peter shook his head and blinked. Big mistake, apparently, as the ground suddenly did some odd sort of jump and bounce along with him and almost dumped him on his arse.

He carefully made his way around to the side of the parish house and found his horse calmly cropping the grass and making some inroads into Father Michael's hedge. He managed to get hold of the reins and climb, somewhat inelegantly, into the saddle.

Well, if he could find his way back to Paris while almost unconscious with pain and fever, he could certainly find his way the few miles to Margarittes while drunk, especially on a horse that knew it's way home.

His reception, however, was surprisingly similar, if a little less relieved and a great deal more acerbic.

"Good God," Guyon said as he came into the main hall, looking up from what seemed to be the world's largest and most badly-drawn map, which was spread out on the floor in front of the hearth. He was standing in the middle of it, holding a pair of compasses and looking rather confused. "You smell like an entire monastery broke their rules of abstinence at once. What on earth?"

"It was yellow...and tasted of herbs...and..." Peter leaned toward the door frame and almost missed.

He knew he would regret his condition come morning, but somehow he couldn't, currently, make himself care. He'd sleep and, at least for one more night, not worry about how his attentions would be rebuked or refused, distasteful as they seemed to have become.

"Ah," Guyon said a little more sympathetically. "I probably don't want to know how you got it or who you drank it with, but I would definitely suggest you drink a lot of water before the inevitable desire to sleep wins you over - because if I remember correctly, the nice herbal flavor in your mouth will be far more like decaying socks when you wake up."

"Yes. Right..." Peter said quietly. No, Guyon wouldn't want to know. He no longer held much interest for him, apparently. He turned toward the stairs and the daunting prospect of climbing them.

He turned round carefully, to see Guyon once more crouched down over black and red lines, trying to measure them out with the decidedly inadequate compasses. He looked up, and offered Peter a wry little grin. "I never claimed to be a geographer," he pointed out, and bent back to his task. Feeling rather as though he were a dismissed schoolboy, Peter set off up the stairs.

*

Guyon had no idea as to how to order or arrange a dinner party, but he was, at least, capable of telling Esmée to provide a supper suitable for the Captain. What he was not capable of, unfortunately, was arranging for Maurice to eat separately and still keep an eye on him, so it was a decidedly awkward group that were attempting to hold what felt like six different conversations over some extremely indifferently prepared fish.

And Peter was looking a bit hard pressed at times, fielding snide comment from Maurice, seriously answering the Captain's questions, and fending off Jeannine's attempts at practicing her flirtations, while not being completely rude. It would have been amusing under other circumstances, in some other place, but not here, *God,* not here.

De Tourvel made a rather filthy joke about the quality of the fish that went straight over Jeannine's head - Guyon hoped, at least - made Maurice crack out a laugh, and inspired Peter, whom Guyon had first truly seen displaying a sense of humor in a Parisian steam bath with regards to the comparative freshness of chicken and women, to quote a foully-pronounced Spanish proverb that set de Tourvel to howling with glee. Jeannine frowned over at Guyon.

"That really meant what I think?" she mouthed. Guyon shrugged and nodded, and wished for a dog or one of Ännchen's damnable kittens, to feed his supper to. He was starting to feel as though his entire skin was going to crawl off his body with loathing of the whole situation.

But at least Peter looked a bit more relaxed after the joke. This was, after all, another military man he was chatting with, not one of the pretenders at Court. For that, at least, Guyon could be grateful, if only marginally.

"Is it the supper or the conversation that's not to your taste?" Maurice asked Guyon with abrupt, false, solicitude, and all faint traces of gratitude Guyon had been feeling instantly evaporated. De Tourvel looked faintly interested, Peter simply murderous, and he sighed.

"I have no taste," he said blandly, "so I think the question is moot." Under the table, he felt Jeannine's small hand grip his with sudden sympathy, and felt her willing him to keep his composure.

He returned the pressure, gratefully, using the warm little touch to ground him as Maurice continued -

"No, indeed, but then how could you have, after your...*exposure* to Parisian life. And so young, as well, no wonder that friend of yours - Villon, was it? - hasn't returned with you. Or did you simply discard him?"

"François is dead." Peter's voice snapped out with sudden cold clarity. "And I would thank you, Monsieur, to keep your thinly veiled accusations to yourself. François Villon happened to be a very good friend of mine as well."

"Well." Maurice smiled. "Let the dead bury the dead, I suppose." He looked across the table at Guyon, and his eyes were triumphant, for some reason Guyon could not fathom.

"What an *excellent* idea," Guyon retorted, before he could remember to guard his tongue. "But *Paire*, how were you planning to put it to the test?" He held Maurice's gaze, daring him to take this further.

"Me?" Maurice turned a face that was all sanctified innocence toward Peter, then back to Guyon. "How should I put anything to the test? I'm just here upon your sufferance after all. I keep the place running, it's true, but I have no true claim on it, do I?"

"I wouldn't know," Guyon said calmly. "Did you expect one? Or would you like one? I'm never sure of these things. And please. Let us not call it my sufferance." He gave Maurice his nastiest little grin. "I don't have any." He turned to Jeannine. "I'm sorry, we're being very rude. Private jokes are unforgivable when it is not only family present."

"It's alright," Jeannine tried to give him a reassuring grin, then shared it around the table indiscriminately. "Father and I often shock even the servants at times, I'd imagine."

"How very risqué of you, Cap," Guyon said lightly. De Tourvel was looking a little worried, and he toned down his expression to something less terrifying and more appropriate to the evening they were ostensibly having. "Tell us more, do!" He couldn't look at Peter, terrified that if he did he would show all

284

the real misery and shock he was feeling. Maurice was pushing, deliberately pushing, not for Guyon to be forced to say just what the accusation had been that had led to the pelourinho, but for de Tourvel, who would assume Peter knew, to say something - or, God help them all, Jeannine.

"Well, I dare say that it was the person I was discussing it with, rather than the subject matter," de Tourvel gave a shrug. "I tend to tell my girl things that most fathers would never discuss with their daughters. She has a good mind though, you know, and I value her opinion."

Yes, that was better. Trust Cap to try to put things back on a more reasonable level. He knew Maurice too and what he was capable of.

"Only to argue with it," Jeannine said with a pout.

"But that is what all good opinions are for." Guyon did look at Peter then, slanting a small, genuine smile in his direction, and caught his breath at the look of blank misery he surprised him in. He swallowed down the desire to demand what had happened, and continued, "Without debate, life is worthless."

"You would say that," Jeannine gave a short laugh. "But mostly because you love to argue above all things."

"It is my life," Guyon agreed quietly, risking another quick glance at Peter, who for some reason, now seemed quite enamored of his food, looking down at his plate and eating, somewhat mechanically. "Debate, though, it's more than argument. It's expansion, it's taking things further than ever, your mind, your ideas. There are no horizons, the sky is limitless and thoughts stretch on forever. And when you meet someone who is your equal...who forces you to look beyond the limits you didn't realize you had...it *is* life. It is the world, and greater than it." They were all looking at him now, and he shrugged. "That's how it *should* be," he amended with a small laugh. *That's how it is.*

"Yes...yes..." Jeannine jumped in with an agreement. "It's finding just the right words to express yourself. Just the right turn of phrase to allow someone to know just exactly what you mean. It happens so rarely though, doesn't it?" She paused for a moment's consideration. "Or perhaps I just need to learn more words."

"Or find the right person to give them to you," Guyon agreed. An irritable little devil, snickering at his discomfort at the back of his mind, prompted him to say, "Read what Montaigne has to say about it."

Her eyes met his, startled, and he let his mouth curl into the faintest of smiles. *Yes.*

"I shall," She answered quietly, reaching out one hand to pat his where it lay on the table, then moving it to pick up her fork.

"Here, we've grow so serious," de Tourvel suddenly spoke out, his more jovial tones overpowering their quieter tones. "So serious that our chevalier has had to actually turn his attention to his food to lighten his mood."

"The worst possible fate," Guyon said, trying not to frown. These people weren't Robbie, and he would never have trusted Maurice for long enough to let the man draw breath, let alone put the suspicions he must have by now into more than nebulous thoughts, but surely, Peter *must* have understood what he had just said?

"You know how it is," Peter said, his voice neither loud nor soft, but decidedly neutral. "A soldier learns to take what he is given, when he is given it. You never know when the chance might be taken away from you."

Somehow, strangely, Guyon had the feeling that Peter was not only talking about food.

"And alas, some of us are given cadets and a hedgehog, as proof of the unkindness of the adage," he said, trying to diffuse the strange sadness that was somehow pervading the air. De Tourvel seemed unaware of it, Jeannine, more perceptive, only confused. And Maurice, whom Guyon had never wanted to hit more, was *reveling* in the whole damn thing.

Suddenly and clearly and not even with surprise, Guyon was convinced that it was Maurice who had caused this, though he was unsure how his great-uncle could possibly have brought it about. He was equally convinced that it was he himself who had made it stone, and yet he had no idea how.

*

There were times when Peter detested his jealous nature. After dinner he sat with Monsieur de Tourvel, asking his advice about some estate papers, and covertly watching Guyon and Jeannine at the other end of the room. He could not hear them well enough to catch the words but the occasional giggle from Jeannine or the low pitched chuckle from Guyon lead him to believe they were much enjoying their conversation. *Damn it.* He thought - no, he *believed* - that nothing was going on between the two but honest friendship, but still those laughs felt like knife blades, every one.

"These look right in order," de Tourvel said, rolling up the papers and passing them back to Peter. "But I would have been surprised if they had not. Guyon was always more in tune with the estate than his brother, even as a child."

"Hmmm? Oh, yes, quite." Peter tore his eyes away and turned back to de Tourvel.

"Hm." It was the same little sound that Guyon made, acknowledgment and preface to something more. For the first time, Peter thought that rather than a personal quirk of Guyon's, it might be part of the slurring accent, as tied to home as Robbie's grunted 'Ach!' or his own swallowed vowels. "Come walk with me, Scudamore. I feel the need for some night air."

"Oh, yes...Of course, sir." Peter stood, giving one long glance back at Guyon and Jeannine before following.

"He never talks about Astor, does he?" de Tourvel asked as he made his way out into the courtyard.

"I'm sorry, sir, but who?" Peter was trying to enjoy the warm evening, but his thoughts were still a jealous jumble.

"Apparently not," de Tourvel said, in amused agreement with himself. "His father. Astor the Hawk. This house - it's his shrine, didn't you realize?"

"Guyon seldom talks about any of his family." Peter looked down and poked at a rock with the toe of his boot. Anything to distract him from this, yet another part of his life that Guyon would not trust to Peter. *He didn't even tell me his father's real name - I had to read it for myself. Is it that he won't talk about his family, or is that an excuse I'm making to soothe myself? Isn't it really that he can't trust me with even that much?*

"No, he wouldn't," de Tourvel said, and there was a significant amount of *something* not being said there. "Astor was my friend. A long time ago, before - he died." He laid his hand on Peter's arm. "You must understand, Scudamore, *he died.*"

"I see," Peter frowned for a moment. True, Astor de Chesnay would have been rather young but still..."People do. My own parents did when I was fourteen."

De Tourvel sighed. "Yes. Yes, they do. But they do not - *choose* their death, nor are they condemned first." He seemed to be trying to tell Peter something more with his eyes alone. "We say he died. The truth is that he was condemned to death and would have met his end in any case. He made - his own way."

"He killed himself?" Peter's shocked face turned back towards the house, as if he could see Guyon through the walls. In fact, he wished he could. It was said that the touch of melancholy that would cause a man to take his own life could be inherited and Peter had a sudden urge to see Guyon, to search his face for any hint that he might, somehow, follow his father.

"He made his own way," de Tourvel repeated. "He wished - to save his sons from the taint of heresy." His mouth twisted with an old, old regret. "He did them no favors."

"Heresy?" Peter scowled, suddenly angered. "Is this place fixated on that? Guyon's father and then Guyon? Christ! What crime was his father accused of?"

"Necromancy. He claimed to be able to speak to the dead. So, yes, Giraud was fixated on heresy. He thought he would lose his brother to the same madness, and a solution was offered. Guyon agreed. In full faith, he agreed. Had it been left to them - perhaps..." He sighed, and shook his head. "No, there is no perhaps. It was wrong. I should have stepped in, but - I watched Astor fall into despair, I had heard him claim he could speak to the dead, and like Giraud, I saw the same traits in his son, and I was afraid for him."

"So he almost killed his brother...to save him?" Peter wanted to rage. God, he wanted to go to Portugal and beat Giraud to within an inch of *his* life...or more fitting, *whip* him. Even after reading Maurice's testimony it was a shock to have it confirmed by someone face-to-face.

"It was not supposed to be - as it was." De Tourvel's voice was still gentle, but his eyes were haunted - haunted and looking back over the distance of nearly six years, to mistakes that could have been stopped then and there. "It was designed to be a reminder - something done in name only. But Maurice - Maurice manipulated them both, and I did not know. I did not know until it was happening in front of me, and then it was too late."

He sighed. "I thought those boys believed the story. That their father had died, and God save the Hawk, but he had willed his death, and so it was, God rest our Seigneur. *But they knew.* They had always known, and kept it hidden. Damn Astor for his madness, he *wrote* his decision."

"He what?" Peter tore his eyes once again away from the house, away from where Guyon was. He wanted to go to him. To tell him that he would fix everything. That he would right all the wrongs that had ever been done him.

But he couldn't do that. Guyon would not have allowed it – would, in fact, have been angered even at the suggestion.

"He wrote letters," de Tourvel said patiently. "One to each, explaining in terms that both would understand. So yes, Guyon always knew what his father did for them. When he ran away to Paris at fourteen, we thought it was from arrogance, when he brought that lawyer back with him, three years later, we could not understand. But he knew. He knows. That madness is hereditary, *all of it.* The Hawk's desire to reach the unknown, his love of death, his search for the infinite through prayer and faith - it is part of your friend. François Villon knew that and protected him from himself, but - I saw no acceptance in that boy's eyes, even when he stood up from the post. Now, though -" He, too, looked towards the house. "The boy I knew, with all his secrets - he is a man, he is close as can be to his father, and his father was a soldier of God. If Guyon's overcome his horror of cold steel for your sake, you must have influence beyond imagining."

"He never told me." Christ! Peter cursed himself. He hadn't found any of Astor's letters before Guyon interrupted his search - assuming they were even there to be found. "He let me bully him into it and never said a word." *No wonder he accuses me of so often running over his wishes, his concerns - I do.*

"No." De Tourvel's smile was a formality. "But I have. I could not protect that boy. But I can stop the man following his father's path. I see that despair in his eyes, Scudamore, and it is not the past which puts it there. It is the present. Villon would have given his life to protect him. You are giving yours up to ensure damnation."

"I would protect Guyon to my last breath." Peter shook his head. *He knows...he knows.* *He knows and thinks it's wrong.* Peter glanced back to the house. Would he keep Guyon from seeing Jeannine? From seeing the one person in this whole damn place that seemed happy to see him with no reservations? How could he allow that? "If you've any doubt of that, then you are the one who is mad."

"Cautious, perhaps, not mad." De Tourvel's voice remained even and calm. "I have reason, do I not?"

"No, you do not." Peter raised a stubborn chin. He refused, *refused,* to bow his head meekly to the idea that his love for Guyon was forbidden, blasphemous. It was what it was...Love. It could never be wrong.

De Tourvel drew a breath, then shrugged. "Hm. Then I give way to your knowledge. But look at him, Scudamore. Look at him and then tell yourself that he is not on that path. Look at him and continue to tell yourself he shares your sanguinity. Look at him and say he does not feel despair." He made a small gesture with his hands held upwards, his palms exposed in a gesture of good intent. "If you can say all that to me in good faith, then I shall ask forgiveness. But I do not think I will have to." He inclined his head, and went back towards the house.

Peter dropped his head. If de Tourvel had asked him that before François' death, he would have given a flat no. If he had asked him that as little as three months ago, he might have laughed in the man's face. But from the day the Languedoc had begun to have a part in their lives things had changed. Guyon had longer and longer moments of brooding and sadness.

But that was because of this place and its memories, wasn't it? It had nothing to do with him.

Did it?

*

Peter, having made his excuses and feigned tiredness in order to be able to retire before their guests left, stood at the rail of the darkened gallery, looking down at the pleasant scene below. Guyon and Jeannine, both of them sprawled out on the floor near the fireplace, books and papers scattered untidily around them. Guyon's dark curly mop, recently and ruthlessly cut by Jeannine's maid to a more local style, was mere inches away from Jeannine's untidily pinned chestnut coif, as he explained some point, citing a passage in the book spread between them. There was a deep blurred laugh and a lighter giggle, wrapping around each other and drifting up to him, where he stood. They looked so relaxed together, those two, brilliant minds and sharp tongues matching in a way that Peter envied.

It was the first time in days that he had seen Guyon smile with any real feeling behind it.

"They make a fine pair, don't they?" a voice whispered from the shadows just behind him. Peter turned sharply to see Uncle Maurice standing there.

As Peter remained silent, he continued, "Perhaps it was for the best, his being away so long. Growing up in proximity might have made their feelings more suited to siblings than is ideal in an affianced pair."

Affianced? No.. that couldn't be true. They had all but killed Guyon, the three of them, Maurice, Giraud and that damn priest. How could they then have also made marriage plans for him?

But still, the two of them did look very content down there, he had to admit again. And not at all like siblings.

"Oh?" Peter said, his voice low enough that it wouldn't be heard by the pair below. "How long has this been decided?"

"Since Jeannine was born. Her father's lands would have been an asset at the time - of course, he long since sold them to us and bought other property, but it seemed like a sensible solution. Guyon's mother was the most in favor of it, of course, his father was...well, I'm sure Guyon has told you of his other preoccupations. It could still be a good match." Maurice nodded approvingly, bestowing benediction. "It would be good for all of us."

As if Guyon would do anything that Maurice so heartily approved of, Peter thought, giving a tiny mental snort then looking once again at the scene below. Guyon reached out a hand, smoothing back a piece of hair that had managed to work its way out of Jeannine's pins, then tapped her on the end of the nose with a smile and pointed back toward the book in her hand.

Good for all of them. Good for Jeannine and, Peter felt a niggling of worry, *good for Guyon*. He'd be away from Paris, away from all his memories of what he had lost at the Sorbonne and what had been taken away from him when he lost François.

But Guyon would not want to be here, would he? There were horrible memories here too. Memories of his father's death and other things...

He brought François here. It was one of the first things Maurice had said - *What did you do with the other one?* - still expecting François and not him. It should not have mattered. Guyon was not a man who wrote home, Robert would surely have retained enough sense not to mention him. But still, it had been a sharp reminder of all he would never be, and now Maurice was delivering a further pointed blow, this one driven by all things he *could not* be. Peter looked up at the almost-familiar features, lined with bitterness as well as age, the deceptively clear eyes.

"Don't you think?" asked the rich, dark voice.

"Perhaps so," Peter said softly, his own words cutting into his chest like a surgeon's blade.

And suddenly everything felt wrong. He was tying Guyon to him, when he knew that he was just a poor substitute for what had been lost. He was keeping Guyon from moving forward into a future that would be far easier and better for him than anything Peter could offer. A future with someone whose interests and intelligence matched Guyon's own far better than Peter ever could or would, no matter how hard he studied. A future with Jeannine and a family of his own, here in Carcassonne, where all the painful memories of François would not intrude. And maybe, with all that around him, all that love...he could forget the bad memories and create new ones.

"Excuse me, would you?" Peter did not wait for a reply, but

walked quickly down the gallery and back toward his room.

*

Jeannine de Tourvel might only be fourteen years old, but she knew what she wanted in life, both at the moment and in the near future. She wanted out. Out of the environs of Carcassonne and out of the Languedoc, and as soon as humanly possible. As she saw it, Peter Scudamore, Lord Hawthornden and Brocéliande, Marshal of the troops of the English Court in Exile, was her best bet for achieving her goal.

She'd marry him if that was what it took, although that was not her first choice. Better, she thought, to slip under his defenses and cajole him into taking her to Paris, where her choice of matches would be far broader than an exiled Scottish Lord, no matter what titles he'd been granted since his arrival.

She had not bargained on the fact that Guyon de Chesnay knew her as well at fourteen as he had done at eight, and while his knowledge was tempered these days with understanding and sympathy, neither of those factors changed his straightforward outlook. If she wanted to go to Paris, he would help her. His condition, unfortunately, was that she relinquish the one aspect she knew she could have relied on - Peter Scudamore's help and sense of honorable behavior.

"He has reasons enough to think badly of us all," Guyon said softly. "Please, my dear, don't add to them."

"But Guyon," Jeannine spoke just as softly, leaning toward him just slightly, "Peter could do so much for me, if he only would. I don't intend to arrive in Paris as a bumpkin, with no cachet to back me up. Peter could introduce me to the Court...to both Courts."

"I do not think so," Guyon said, and there was real ice in his voice now, taking him further still from the affectionate irritability she had grown used to. "You will *not* use him. There are other ways, more practical ways and more honorable ways, and I am *disturbed* that they were not what first occurred to you."

Jeannine dropped her head at that, a faint blush tinting her cheeks. Yes, certainly there were other ways, but Peter was there and had all the correct contacts, so of course that would be the most simple and direct path to what she wanted. But she could see Guyon's point of view in this, and after all, Peter was his friend. He'd not want him taken advantage of. "I'm sorry. You're right, of course."

"Does that mean 'yes, Guyon, you're right, and I'm going to carry on with my plans as soon as your back is turned anyway'?" he asked, and he didn't sound cold any more, just deeply, terribly tired. "Or does it mean 'you're right and I'm going to leave Peter alone from now on'? Because quite honestly, I would like it if one area of my life didn't have to be guarded at all times from those I should be able to trust."

"It means, 'yes, Guyon, you're right and I'm going to leave Peter alone from now on," Jeannine assured him, but then continued, "But Guyon...if he *offers* to help me...I refuse to turn him down."

"Christ." Guyon rubbed his hands over his head. "No wonder they say we're all demon spawn in this area."

Jeannine just grinned brightly at him, then began to question about *just how exactly* he would convince her father to allow her to return to Paris with them.

*

Peter entered his room, and resisted the urge to simply collapse on the bed. The horrible feelings stirred up by seeing Guyon and Jeannine so happy in each other's company, felt like a physical blow, taking all the strength from him.

And yet, with all this pain, he still felt deep inside that he had to do this. That it would all be for the best where Guyon was concerned. He could get on with his life. Have children. Be happy. Have all the things that he should have had here in his home, and would have had if his brother had been a better man. He could give him that. A last loving gift.

Slowly, Peter began to put his things into his bag to prepare for the ride back to Paris. He'd just have to deal with Corvay. Explain to him that in spite of rumors there was nothing to fear from the denizens of Carcassonne, or the Languedoc.

Then Peter would -

Christ, what would he do? He couldn't, somehow, see himself remaining in Paris, duty or no duty. He'd have to renounce his marshaldom and return to England, hopefully to redeem himself in direct service to the king. If things went well, he'd go back to Scotland to live out his days.

Suddenly the years ahead stretched out before him in a long and endless wave of dark loneliness. Years without Guyon. And yet, how could he let that sway him? This was his choice - to ensure that Guyon's life, at least, would be a better one.

But with all his determination, all the clarity of vision that Maurice had so unkindly granted him in the gallery, it was difficult not to think that his leaving was also a betrayal of some kind, that he might *know* it was the right thing to do, but that Guyon would not. His offer to come to Scotland might have been dry and emotionless, and had probably been born of the need for convenience, but it had nonetheless been made, and, this being Guyon, had therefore been *meant*. Peter would have to give him a reason for his change of mind - for his apparent change of *heart* - and did not think that it was an interview which would go well or easily.

If he had some reason to give - some answer to the problems they had found waiting them in the Languedoc, or some new means of defeating Corvay that required Guyon to remain here and *demanded* he leave France alone - then, perhaps, his departure would be accepted. But not like this, without added information, with no change in their circumstances.

Peter moved towards the desk to pick up the few scattered objects that were his - the long-ago Twelfth Night gift of inkwell and pens, the papers that he would need to regain entry to Paris, the bits and pieces of proof that Guyon had managed to piece together for the safety of the Languedoc's inhabitants - and stopped as he came to a folded and sealed note, lying on the very edge of the desk, and addressed to him in an unfamiliar handwriting.

He picked it up, examining the plain paper before breaking the seal.

Your information is more correct than you know, Chevalier.

Go to the Grotte de Limousis tonight, by 10 of the clock, if you want the final pieces.

There was no signature, and no clue as to who he was supposed to meet. Both bits of neglect sent alarm bells ringing in Peter's head, however, since this could be a way of getting answers even if it was a trap of some kind, he was determined to go.

He sat his bag down on the foot of the bed and looked up at the clock. If he left now he'd have just enough time to check out the area before the appointed hour. That would, at least, give him a bit of an advantage.

He was to realize, later, that the writer of the note must have known him, had known, too, that he would not involve Guyon, and that considering everything Guyon had said about the area - *I may not own these rocks, but I know each and every one of them. The caves were my palaces, and I believed in Merlin and his crystal prison* - it was extremely short-sighted of him not to have at least wondered why the note was not addressed to the man who was utterly familiar with every inch of the surrounding area. But all he could think of, at that moment in time, was that this might be the solution to the problems he would face by leaving, and a chance at an irrefutable answer to give Guyon's inevitable protests.

It did not occur to him that no-one in their right mind would attempt to navigate the caves by night. Having never entered them, he had a mental image of something like the coastal caves, smoothed out and narrow and often mere scrapes of shelter in the cliff sides. But the caves of the Languedoc were labyrinthine caverns, and Guyon had not referred to Merlin's legend for nothing.

No-one had thought to warn him, being as he was no child to go exploring and be lost, and so when he left the high-windowed house to scope out the territory before his assignation, he was utterly unaware of the fact that two people within it would have knocked him unconscious before permitting him to leave, and a third had planned this moment for days in the full knowledge - and indeed hope - of what would ensue.

*

Guyon might pretend to indifference as to the court and its ways, but it did not mean that he was devoid of knowledge as to how it operated or how to survive it. He explained to Jeannine exactly what interest and offers she could hope to command with her dowry, and what additional consideration might be brought to mind by the knowledge that she would inherit her father's lands and properties. Not being someone who disparaged the art and subtleties of the great courtesans and acknowledged mistresses of the time, he also explained what options would be open to her there, as well, and why a far better education would be needed in that instance than if she wished only for marriage.

Amoral as he was, he was slightly taken aback at her cold assessment of the facts, her acknowledgement that she would be better off taking a husband first, and choosing one who would fit her needs, before taking a superior lover after her tastes and interests were better educated. As a plan, it was flawless. As something coming from the lips, however pretty, of a girl he still thought of as a child, it was mildly horrifying. Reminded for the hundredth time that day alone why he preferred to avoid women whenever he could and had chosen a life of academia long before his own interests had been made apparent to him, he said his somewhat relieved farewells to her and her curiously quiet father, and escaped from the hall and up to Peter's room. He did not think for a moment that the man would be sleeping, and was already talking as he pushed open the door.

"Lord, I am not as open-minded as I thought -" he began, and stopped, puzzled, glancing around the room. "What -"

The room had been cleared of all of Peter's effects. No brushes on the chest. No scissors or knife. No neatly folded articles of clothing. Nothing to say that Peter had been in the room at all, aside from a vaguely wrinkled blanket on the bed and, yes, Peter's pack stuffed full and sitting at the foot of the bed.

Guyon approached it cautiously, as if it were a poisonous snake warily watching his approach.

He undid the leather flap, and peered inside. He would never dare disturb Peter's methodical, and to him wholly arcane, style of packing, but he had no idea whether this was some strange freak of neatness that Peter had taken into his head, or a genuine preparation to leave. "What's going *on*?" he muttered irritably, seeing the inkwell he had given so long ago lying neatly padded by a rolled shirt on the top of the pack. Even if Peter had felt a sudden need to be completely free of clutter, he *needed* the inkwell, and certainly needed it filled with ink, rather than empty and clean and packed away.

Guyon chewed on his lip, wandering over to the desk in the hope that there would be some clue there as to what was going on. The next moment, he was running down the gallery to Maurice's room, in the kind of temper that he had not felt since the night Peter had come back from Corvay and told him that he knew of the hold the spymaster had on Guyon. He did not stop to request admittance, simply kicked the door open.

"*Wake up*!" he roared at the sleeping figure in the great bed. "Wake up, you unconscionable bastard, *wake up*!"

"Guyon? What are you doing? Get out of my room!" Maurice's voice was sharp and angry, with no sounds of recent awakening apparent in its tone.

"*Your* room? You are here on sufferance, *Paire - my* sufferance. *Nothing* is yours. *How dare you presume*!" Guyon was furious beyond all reason or sense, having seen the handwriting on the note and recognized it all too well.

"Will you cast me out then? I doubt it. You haven't the stomach for such things, never did." But Maurice did climb out of the bed, wrapping himself in his dressing gown so he could add the benefit of being dressed and standing taller than Guyon to his attempt at intimidation. "Why have you come barging in here?"

"I got your note," Guyon said, feeling his skin crawl and tighten with rage. "I want you to swear on the *saint-Segùr* that you have not knowingly sent Peter Scudamore to his death. I want you to stand here, and look in my eyes, and have the *effrontery* to lie to my face and to God and to all we hold sacred to save your sorry skin." As Maurice paused, he caught up the front lapels of his dressing gown in his hands and flung him against the wall, holding him pinned there. "*Go on! Tell* me! *Swear* to me,

298

Maurice, *go on!*"

There was a loud oof as Maurice hit the wall, but his voice was still steady when he replied, "What? Why would I do such a thing, Guyon? If your *friend* wants information that is where he will find it. I merely pointed the way."

"To the Grotte? What information have you conjured out of air? You know as well as I no-one would go there at night knowingly - what have you been telling him?" Anger was slowly being replaced by fear in Guyon's mind. *Leaving. He was leaving anyway. My God, what have we done?* The bell was silent within him, silent and still, not even a faint reverberation to reassure him. *Would you believe I know every moment that you live?* "Christ, Maurice, what have you *done*?"

"I have done only what needed to be done. Your Chevalier should have left long since with as little information as he had when he arrived." Maurice looked at Guyon, his eyes cold and calculating. "That he did not, you may blame on yourself and your interference."

"*My* blame I take to myself. *Yours* I call betrayal." Guyon knew that his voice could conceal any emotion, and he was making sure it did so now. "You fool, Maurice. You blind, bloody fool. Do you want the whole area in flames again?" He shook his head. "Don't answer. Just tell me who you have waiting for Peter at the Grotte, and we'll call our follies even."

"Who knows who will be there? And who cares?" Maurice snorted. "But *someone* shall discourage your *friend* from asking any further questions."

"You had better hope," Guyon said calmly, "that you are wrong. Because *I* care, Maurice. And so will de Tourvel." His lips twitched into something that was not a smile. "And the penalty for minor treason is still the same here, is it not?" He dropped his hands, letting Maurice slide onto his feet, and added, "*I* will not use the whip with love on my lips. Bear in mind, *Paire,* I know full well that it was *you* who caused Giraud to take the word of love from me, it is *you* whom I credit with making me the monster that I am." He turned towards the door. "Pray for Scudamore's survival, *Paire*, and pray hard. For I swear to God, if he dies, there will be nothing and no one to stop me from showing you what monsters do."

Peter Scudamore was a soldier and good at it. He knew how to lead men, how to gain their loyalty, and how, as much as it pained him, to send them into battle knowing that a goodly portion of them might never return. Why then did it feel like what he was getting ready to do was one of the bravest things that he would ever accomplish?

No, not going to the *Grotte de Limousis* in the dark of night, although that of itself was enough to make the hair on the back of his neck stand up, but walking away from Guyon. It would be so much simpler if he could be selfish. If he could ignore what his eyes and mind told him and follow only his heart. But he couldn't. Guyon still could not say he loved him and that was that. He needed to step aside and allow the other man a way to move on with his life with no guilt or feelings of responsibility toward himself. That would never happen if Peter remained, mooning around Guyon like a love-struck pup, craving his belly rubbed. He had to make a clean break. He would get the information that Corvay wanted and then turn in his resignation.

Pray God that the Queen would accept it, for since Peter had been declared Marshal, the small band of guards he had commanded had nearly doubled. It would certainly be within her Majesty's purview to refuse him, in light of his fine job. What he would do in that instance he was not sure. Not that it mattered. He would still be leaving and only a command that he should be detained in the Bastille would deter him.

Peter looked once again at the dark shadow that marked the opening of the Grotte. He'd been watching that entrance since he'd settled into this hiding spot, over twenty minutes earlier, and so far he had seen several shadowy figures slip in and out of it. Or at least he assumed it was several. It could possibly have been the same men several times. They all wore heavy concealing cloaks and their lanterns were shuttered, allowing light to shine out and down with almost none leaking back to illuminate who carried them.

He waited patiently until the movement ceased and the last person, he hoped, exited the caverns. Several long moments passed before Peter slipped out of hiding to creep into the Grotte. It was dark as pitch after the first few feet, but Peter was afraid to light his lantern until he was a bit further from the door, so he walked slowly with one hand just brushing the wall.

His next footstep ended in a small splash, and brought him up short. There was water ahead of him and he couldn't tell how much or how deep. He'd have to chance his lantern or wind up going for an unexpected swim. He slowly opened the shutter, sweeping the area around him in a gentle arc, being careful to keep the light directed away from the opening he had just come through. That might not keep anyone from seeing the lantern's beam but at least they might not be able to get a quick fix on where *he* was.

There were noises now, some faint, some sharp, but all of them impossible to place in the echoing cavern. They could have been twenty feet away, or twenty inches and he'd have known no difference. There was a short sharp splash, and he swung his lantern back towards the pool just in front of him. He saw that the surface had been disturbed, but had it been a fish? A frog? Or a rock disturbed by the passing of a foot?

This is insane. Guyon had told him tales of the Grotte and now he was imagining ghosts and specters where there were none. The mysterious figures that he had seen *were all gone* and what he needed to do was discover why they had been in the caves in the first place.

Peter moved forward, skirting the pool to move deeper into the cavern, keeping the exit always to his right and behind. Getting lost was not something he even wanted to contemplate. He shouldn't have to go in far, he hoped. None of the figures seemed to remain inside for very long, meaning they hadn't penetrated very deeply into this labyrinthine darkness. A side cavern perhaps? Not easily seen from the entrance but not far. He move his lantern again, side to side, looking for any openings, his light reflecting back to him from the many pools and glittering minerals that had formed stalactites and stalagmites all through the area he was traversing.

How much time had passed? How far had he come from the opening of the cavern? Without the stars and light to give even the slightest guide, he had no idea. He was rounding the end of a sickly white calcified spill of limestone when he saw it. An opening into another cavern - a pale stream of flickering light giving the tell that a candle or torch burned some where beyond that. Peter gave an almost relieved sigh of breath and then reshuttered his lantern before moving closer.

Were those voices ahead? A sudden chill broke over him as he realized just how foolhardy he might have been to have come here alone. Wandering through dark and unfamiliar territory to find or meet who knows what? But he hadn't thought of that before he had left and now? Now was not the time for retreat, in spite of his greater misgivings. He had to find out what lay ahead.

He drew his musket from his belt and slipped quietly closer, into the mouth of the opening.

"How long are we supposed to stay here?"

"Another half hour. Just like we were told."

"Wouldn't mind if it wasn't so cold in this damn place."

Peter couldn't see who was attached to the voices, and moving forward was not an option. The torch light would have illuminated his dark figure against the pale sparkle of the limestone and give him away in an instant.

"The things I do for a few sous. I could be home in my warm bed, if I didn't need old Maurice's coins."

Maurice? What would he have to do with this? And what was he paying these men to do besides stand around in a cold cavern in the middle of the night?

Peter moved to the other side of the opening, hoping a different angle and point of view might allow him to see the two men.

Yes, he could see more from this position, but it still did not help. A dark cloak covering a slim figure with dark hair, his back towards the opening and a leg encased in dirty but serviceable broadcloth and heavy boots. It wouldn't be enough to identify them now or later.

Something disturbed the air behind Peter, and he turned, just in time to see a flash of light, and the deeper more painful flash of stars behind his eyelids as a heavy shuttered lantern came crashing down on his head.

*

Guyon knew that if he had one besetting sin, it was his uncertain and too-easily piqued temper, and, though most people who knew him would not have believed it, he made efforts to control it accordingly. By the time he reached the *Grotte*, however, he was close to the angriest he had ever been in his life, and in no way minded to contain or conceal the emotion. Strangely, despite his recognition of the complete lunacy with which Peter had behaved, very little of his annoyance was directed at him - it was all saved for Maurice, for Corvay, and most of all for himself, for his own intransigent behavior, his own determination to prevent disaster that had *never worked in the past* and had assuredly been doomed to failure in the one place that had always rendered him subservient to fate.

He tied his horse up to one of the stubby trees near the *Grotte*'s entrance, and slipped in to the dark shadows.

Guyon hadn't, however, managed more than a few yards before a beam of light had him dodging into a dark cleft.

"I don't like this. Not at all."

"Not yours to like or not. Just yours to do as you were paid to do and then get yourself out."

Not Peter, obviously. The voices sounded vaguely familiar, but not enough that Guyon could place them without seeing the faces hidden by the muffling cloaks and the caves' darkness.

He knew, without having to hear more, certainly without having to be told more explicitly, that these were the men Maurice had hired. He would have thought one enough, given the time and Peter's lack of experience with the caves, but then he had never been the one who thought of ways and means by which to dispose of - *unwanted problems*. Rather sickly, he wondered just how often the beauty of the *Grotte* had been used for these purposes, concealing horror with an overlay of glittering, embellished fantasy.

The footsteps separated, and a figure passed by his hiding place. Guyon stepped out, his thin-soled feet silent on the fine, powdery sand, and caught the man from behind, with one hand gripping his chin and forcing it up, his other arm locking the man in place by his chest. He tightened his grip, clear warning - *I can break your neck* - and felt the struggling stop, the man going still against him.

"Wise," he breathed against the man's ear. "Is he dead yet?"

"No...I don't know." The words were a bare grunt. "He wasn't, but...." He gasped for breath as Guyon's grip tightened further, "I didn't know this is what they'd planned. He's in the second room, past the large limestone spill."

If I had any sense, I would kill you now and stop you following me or running straight to Maurice, Guyon thought, but even practicality could not take him that final step. He nodded meaninglessly, before moving back quickly and slamming the man's head into the wall, feeling him go instantly limp. Guyon checked cursorily for breath and pulse, and finding both, shrugged and moved through towards the second room.

It would have been a slow journey even with Guyon's knowledge of the caverns, but the third member of this little ambush had obviously decided that stealth was no longer required and had completely unshuttered his lantern, leaving it perched on a nearby ledge. The scene, as Guyon approached was something from a bad dream, shadows and reflections wavering in the flickering light. Peter, blood running over his face, sprawled out on the floor as a large hulking figure pawed over him, going through his pockets for anything that might be of value.

"*Aplantar!*" The Occitan command cracked out of him without conscious thought, and he was already moving past the pillar as the word echoed into the shadows, stepping into the shifting patterns of light.

The man stopped only briefly, though, his attention caught by the noise, and looked over at Guyon with incurious recognition. "De Chesnay. *Daissez-nos.*"

"*Leave?*" Guyon took an incredulous breath. "*What -*" and realized in the same second that he was being played for a fool, distracted into his own rage - too well-known or too well-

304

described, and either fatal to Peter.

Light caught the steel in the other man's hand, and Guyon moved fast, unthinking, his clasp-knife out of his belt and open before his mind had registered his fingers' actions.

He struck upwards with the full force of his move across the cavern floor, driving the knife in under the breastbone as he propelled them both into one of the twisted limestone pillars, pinning the would-be assassin against it with his forearm wedged into the joint between shoulder and arm.

There was a horrid gasp, air and blood bubbling from the larger man's lips as he struggled vainly, a look of utter surprise in his eyes. Eyes which soon grew blank and glassy as his heart and lungs caught up with his brain in knowing he was done. It was only moments before Guyon found himself pinning nothing but dead weight up against the pillar.

He stepped back, letting Maurice's paid assassin fall amidst powdered quartz and shale and limestone, leaving his knife where it was. He was fairly certain he was never going to want to use it again under any circumstance. Then he took a deep breath, and all his courage, and turned around.

"Pèire?" he asked hesitantly, and knew that his voice would not have even awakened a sleeping cat. He crossed the few steps across the floor to where Peter lay, and knelt down, extending one tentative hand to touch his shoulder. "*Pèire.*" Both voice and hand shook, that time.

There was a slight stirring, a bare breath of a sound, both lasting not much more than a heartbeat, but it gave Guyon hope.

"Pèire?" His voice was a bit stronger this time. He swallowed, tasting limestone and sand, and summoned the last of his control and his lightest voice. "I don't suppose you'd consider opening your eyes, would you?"

There was more of a response this time. A groan and fluttering of lashes, hands moving feebly as if to ward off another blow.

Guyon thought that it was probably the most damning indictment he had ever received, to realize that no attempts at reassurance would work with anything close to the efficacy of a renewal of his usual scathing commentary. "Or you could just keep having a nice sleep on a cave floor," he said, trying not to let his throat close over. He lifted a hand to rub at his face, and hastily dropped it back to his side, scrubbing it in the sand as he saw that it was covered in blood.

"Gui -" The voice was pitifully weak and pained sounding, but the fact that he recognized Guyon's voice was a starting point. "I - Where?"

"For some reason known only to your peculiar sense of what to do after dinner in the Languedoc, in the *Grotte de Limousis*." Guyon sighed. "You know, when I said not to listen to anything Maurice said, it was *not* a suggestion."

"Hurts," Peter shifted, trying to raise up, and promptly lost what dinner still remained in his stomach.

"And I thought the entry to Avernus was in Italy," Guyon said wearily to the shadowy alcoves of the cave ceiling, and decided that moving Peter as best he could nearer to a wall - and preferably far away from the corpse of his would-be assassin - was the only vague plan he'd had so far that was feasible. Ignoring the semi-coherent protests, he put his idea into practice, and sat back on his heels exhaustedly, trying to summon up a coherent glare, if nothing else. "I'm quite sure it does hurt, yes." He sighed. While he did not have much experience of looking after unconscious people who had been hit on the head, his time Watch-baiting had left him more than familiar with the *conscious* variety. "You know, I really, *really* want to know what you thought you were doing," he said grimly.

"No." That seemed to be all Peter could manage at the moment, eyes rolling in his head like he'd been on a 5 day drunk. His face, under the blood, looked pale and grayish.

"Hm. Well, about two hours ago would actually have been a superb time to master the negative," Guyon said, trying to hold on to acerbity. He just sounded plaintive, the effects magnified by the pillars and high ceiling. "Of course, it would also have been a damn good time for me to think of bringing some water. Or some - *ah*." He rose to his feet, before adding, with horrible memories of Peter's tendency towards fixated determination when hurt - "Don't move."

He went over to the man he had just killed, faintly horrified by the remaining warmth in the body, and by the fact that he was now doing what he had in fact killed for, only minutes before - thievery. *He's dead,* he reminded himself sternly, *and Peter wasn't. Focus, de Chesnay, you coward*!

He didn't find water, but he did, as he had suspected, find a flask. He unstoppered it, and sniffed suspiciously, finding it to be local brandy, which at least would not kill anyone - something which was more than he was sure of as to the water in the pools, despite stories he had heard about people surviving by drinking it.

And, surprisingly, Peter was still where he had left him, although Guyon was crediting this fact more to continued dizziness and pain than any true thought of him having obeyed his earlier injunction.

He slid one arm around Peter to steady him and raised the flask to the injured man's lips. "Drink this. No arguments."

He flinched at his own words even as he heard himself speaking them. They were too close to far too many things that he tried, in his blacker moments, not to think about - but this was no waking dream, this was a hard reality, this was where he walked the thin, high wire of rejection once again, and did so this time in the knowledge that there would be no-one to catch him when he fell.

Even if Peter was obeying him now, Guyon suspected it would not be long before the odd revulsion of the time after Toulouse and Poitiers came back to the fore - and this time, without François to steady him, he did not think he would survive the experience.

"Loving you," he said softly, "is worse than any sentence of torture the Inquisition could devise."

Peter sputtered and coughed as the brandy hit his stomach, then raised one hand up to brace his head, "Don't, Gui...Just...." He clutched his stomach with the other hand, and for a moment Guyon wondered if the brandy was going to follow the way of his dinner.

"You with me yet?" he asked, trying - and, he knew, failing miserably - to manage a smile. He put his clean hand up to touch the undamaged side of Peter's face - *God, we're the Grotte's own phantoms* - and scanned his eyes anxiously in the dim light.

"'M here." Peter answered, but his voice sounded almost as bleak as his expression. "Need to go. You'll be cold."

"Yes, and whichever country that made sense in, please let us never go there," Guyon said, shaking his head. *What is going on here?* he wondered confusedly, and then, still not sure of what had happened in the first place, settled on one conviction he knew to be true. *Maurice.* "I really *am* going to kill him," he said under his breath. "God knows, it's easy enough!"

Peter just looked at him blankly. "Should go," he repeated.

Guyon thought of just how interesting the journey back to the house was going to be, and winced. "Mm. Yes. Take a minute. Take several. Remember where your legs are, that sort of thing..." He *did* manage to smile, that time, his hand still on Peter's face. "It always helps..."

"Got 'em." Peter waved a hand vaguely downward. "It's alright."

"It really isn't," Guyon corrected him, "but it's going to be. It will be." Since Peter probably wasn't going to remember a damn thing about any of this conversation - *ever* - Guyon felt perfectly safe in trying out the words he had strangled in his throat for so long, the ones he had thought himself so strong for not saying, and had come to realize that his vow to keep silent was his greatest act of cowardice, the reason that his father had warned him against giving false promises. "I love you. Not -" He snorted with disbelieving laughter at how he always seemed to get things wrong, even when he was trying to overcome *himself,* for God's sake - "not that that would make anything automatically all right, but - I do."

"Don't, Gui." Peter struggled to push away from the pillar and stand alone. "I just can't -" His stance was wavery, but he didn't look as if he were going to fall. "My horse. You'll be fine."

"I'm not worried about me!" Guyon yelled, before clamping his mouth shut as the sound echoed. He imagined that had to have hurt. "Sorry. Sorry. Um. I've got a horse. It's fine. There are two horses." He snorted. "I can count, too."

"You don't." Peter started slowly toward the entrance, his path not exactly straight, but generally true. "Should go. I'm fine."

"You're *deranged,* is what you are," Guyon snarled, heading

308

after him. "Look, just, just - *stop*. All right. You're fine. We're going. Just...slow down, would you? We don't have to do this at top speed. Really." He put his hand, very gently, on Peter's arm. *He's not even thinking, so don't shout, and don't push, and just get him home.* "There's time." *And then you can tie him up and make him listen.*

"No." Peter stopped, his head lowering until his chin was almost on his chest. "There's not. Never will be."

Why does having a conversation with someone who's been hit on the head always sound like a demented form of philosophical debate? Guyon wondered with the faintest beginnings of hysterical laughter creeping into the edges of his thoughts. "Yes," he said with a firmness he was a very long way from feeling. "Yes, there is. Right now, there is. Honestly. So take it slow, have a bit of care, and we'll get out of here."

"It's past time." Peter told him, but didn't struggle as Guyon lead him toward the horses.

"And if you actually *had* a stone head, we wouldn't be having this conversation," Guyon said with a faint grin. "Fairy tales. Good God." He knew that Peter hadn't meant the old story at all, but hearing his own voice was at least reminding *him* to cling on to sanity.

He managed to get Peter to his horse, and with a fair amount of struggling, up and onto it. For a moment it seemed as if Peter was going to pass out and slide off the other side, but a firm grip and another dose of brandy kept him awake and steady until Guyon could climb up behind him.

He noted that the other horse was quite content where it was, had a reasonable amount of grazing surrounding it, and would definitely be more than all right until someone arrived to bring it back in a couple of hours - more to avoid getting shouted at for negligence when Peter was more awake than for any particular care over what happened to it. Experience had taught him that horses were more than capable of looking after themselves when the need arose.

He was never more thankful for that fact than when he realized he was going to have to navigate the paths mostly blind.

*

Guyon had grown up on these paths. He knew them by day and night, had once traversed them blindfolded and bareback on an insane bet with his brother that he could do more than table accounts for the estate and in fact knew the lands themselves, as well as he knew his own mind. This was infinitely harder, for he now lacked the bravado of a thirteen-year-old, and had to worry about more than his own foolhardy neck.

"Not that I ever cared much for that," he muttered, more to hear the sound of something that wasn't hoofbeats than because he thought any sort of remark would be responded to.

He was veering between panic and relief and a sort of unstrung, melancholic fatalism, accepting that he needed help and knowing he had no way of getting it with the immediacy that would have been his if he had not been so utterly, *damnably* self-reliant and taken someone with him to the caves.

"Or if *you* had," he said unkindly to Peter, his voice sharp in the warm, clear air.

When he saw the other rider, he almost stopped breathing with a combination of hope and ridiculous fear, both replaced by the sudden thought -

If you're another of Maurice's, this time I won't bother with a knife. I'll use my bare hands, I swear to Christ.

"*Holy Mary!* What happened?" A concerned cry came from the other rider, definitely female, and definitely Jeannine. "Is Peter alright?"

Peter shifted to one side, throwing a hand up in defense against the sharp tones, and almost toppling himself and Guyon off the horse.

"*No,*" Guyon said acidly. "Peter, I'm close to shooting *you* right at this moment, just to stop one concern, so *stay put.* Jeannine -" He dropped into Occitan, not wanting what he had to say to get through into Peter's decidedly blurry and distorted sense of awareness. "Get your father, and tell him to come to the house. I want Maurice arrested and in Carcassonne before midnight, and if he makes one murmur about *can't,* tell him I'm calling in the debt he owes me from over five years ago."

"But Peter - How are you going to -? " Jeannine stopped short when she suddenly saw true fire in Guyon's eyes. "Yes. I'll hurry."

She turned her horse and put spur to it, tearing off into the dark, before Guyon could think to question just why she was out riding over his lands, at night, all alone.

"Jesus," he said wearily. "Never thought I'd be grateful for the fact she can't do a damn thing she's supposed to. And *you*, what were you trying to do? Concuss *me,* as well?"

"Sorry...sorry. Won't be a trouble much longer...'promise." Peter's groggy voice came drifting back to him. "Be gone soon."

"Yes, you keep saying that, and it never makes sense," Guyon said, the frustrated, febrile half-anger leaving him all at once as he realized he was back in whatever twilight, nonsensical world Peter was inhabiting. He felt more tired than ever. "Do you think you could *stop*? I realize the words are so very-coherent to you, but from here, they truly are *not.*" He nudged the horse back into reluctant movement.

"Cause I'll be in Scotlan'...And you'll be..." Peter spoke in English, waving a rather vague, limp hand at their surroundings, "...here...I s'pose."

I want a drink. Guyon, who hated being drunk, had never wanted to be so more in his life. "Why," he enquired in what he knew was extremely close to a whine, "*why,* in every one of Dante's hells, *all* of which I think I am inhabiting, am I going to be *here*?" Even if Peter had no recollection at all of his somewhat peculiar declaration in the cave, he *had* to remember their conversation en route to the Languedoc.

I thought I was going with you. It seemed that the habitual irony of his mental voice had been replaced by that of an unhappy and uncomprehending child.

Be gone soon.

He swallowed. *He's been hit on the head, his brains are rattled, for God's sake, stop expecting sense.* "Why am I going to be here?" he asked in a rather more brisk tone.

"Ye've got someone ya care about." Peter's voice was soft and slurred. "Don't want ta be in your way." Peter drifted for a moment, his voice reduced to a mere mutter, "Can't stay...hurts..."

"Um," Guyon managed. It seemed to be the limit of his coherency. "How can you be in your own way?" was the next word order that his mouth managed to drag from his brain. *Wonderful, it seems I was hit on the head too.* Irritation with his own inadequacy, as always, came to his rescue. "I'm sorry it hurts, I wish I could do something, and - Peter, I'm utterly lost. I hate being lost. You *know* I hate being lost, it makes me snakeish. And I want to know what state of concussion exists to make you think that you would either be in my way, or how it would, in fact, help *anyone* to have the person they care about leave. I'm used to illogic, but I'm missing the entire thesis here!"

Peter tried to turn about and look at Guyon, "Jeannine's leavin'? No...I'll fix it. She can't."

It was, apparently, Guyon's turn to make the horse want to throw them onto the path, as he pulled it to an abrupt stop. This time, they both nearly went off the back. "What the *hell* has Jeannine got to do with it?" he managed in a sort of strangled gasp, once the world had stabilized a bit. He reached around Peter, and smacked the horse hard between the ears as it twisted its head and tried very hard to bite Peter's leg - again. "Stop that."

"Can't stop..." Peter said sadly. "Want ya ta be happy...when you and Jeannie get...married."

"*What*?" Guyon had no idea what he sounded like. He wasn't even sure if the question had made it past his lips, let alone been a coherent syllable. "I'm not marrying Jeannine, you Scottish lunatic! You're insane!" He had definitely said that. The syllables rang off the path.

"Probably am...or will be. Hurts.." Peter's voice cracked, but he tried to pull himself up to sit straighter. "Don't think de Tourvel will let ya have her another way."

"Good God." Guyon had heard people say that their mind had gone blank, but he had never actually experienced it before. He could almost see it, black and infinite and utterly devoid of anything that made sense. "Peter..." The sudden pain shot across the emptiness of his mind like a shooting star. "*Why in God's name must you accuse me of infidelity when it has never been among my sins?*"

Which had not, in any way, been what he meant to say. He

had meant to aim for calm rationality, somehow, had mean to dismiss whatever idiocy had entered Peter's head with the blow from the lantern, had meant, somehow, to reassure. And all of his intentions had been obliterated by the sudden knowledge that he had, in all ignorance, managed to make Peter lose all faith in him, and he had not even noticed.

"Didn't..." Peter answered back, weaving a bit unsteadily in his seat. "I...I'll miss ya so." And with those words, Peter went limp, once again succumbing to unconsciousness.

"I think," Guyon said to the middle of the Languedoc, "that I have done something absolutely irreparable."

It would have been nice if I had noticed myself doing it.

He set his jaw. *Get to the house. Get him to bed. Deal with Maurice. And then somehow, God help me, fix this.*

It felt decidedly overwhelming. He took a deep breath. *Very well. Step by step.* "House," he said aloud.

For some reason, it didn't feel any more manageable as an idea. Guyon closed his eyes, and fought back the very real urge to give into despair. "House," he repeated grimly.

At least his voice sounded certain.

Still, the trip did not take as long as he had worried it would, what with having to peer around the taller form in front of him, and holding Peter in place as he drifted in and out of alertness. But it was still a relief to see the sprawling shape of the hall as they approached it. *Which is something I never thought I'd feel.*

"That wasn't too appalling," he said as cheerfully as he could. "Well, all right, it wasn't too appalling for *me*, but that's the enormous bonus of pure selfishness..." His *own* head was beginning to thump at the concept of how the hell they were going to get inside, let alone up the stairs and to a room. "I don't suppose you'd like to aim for consciousness for a bit once I get into the grounds, would you?"

For a moment he feared his only answer was going to be small grunt and a lift of shoulders, but then Peter spoke. "I'll try."

Guyon took a deep, shaking breath of relief, and hung on to what was left of his composure with what felt like the fingernails of his willpower. "Thank you," he said fervently.

Getting into the house was every bit as difficult as he had

feared - even though Peter was doing his damnedest to stay reasonably alert and be of some assistance. Dreading the stairs with all his spare emotional energy, Guyon found that in fact he had more than spare, at the sight of Maurice standing - and presumably waiting for them, or possibly, and less forgivably, waiting for *just him* - at the rail of the gallery.

"Hmmpf." A huff of breath and a disdainful look was all the greeting they received as they began their rough and tiring climb up the stairs. Maurice was obviously not going to raise one hand to help. With most of Peter's weight resting on him, Guyon was uncertain whether he was grateful for that or not.

"Your man's dead," he managed in his flattest tones as they reached the gallery. "*Isn't* killing people easy, *Paire?*" He waited until full understanding reached Maurice's eyes, and smiled sharply. "Stay out of my way, Maurice. I'm in no mood for leniency."

*

Margarittes Hall, June - July 1646

I opened to my beloved; but my beloved had withdrawn himself, and was gone: my soul failed when he spake: I sought him, but I could not find him; I called him, but he gave me no answer.

Guyon had never been more grateful for the peculiar efficiency bequeathed to him by years of taking care of the Sorbonne scholars. Admittedly, they were less frequently severely damaged, and rather more usually drunk and completely incapable, but the fervent wish that the object of his attention would simply pass out and stop trying to have what passed in his addled mind for a conversation was quite perfectly familiar.

Toulouse was worse, he reminded himself, and instantly regretted it, because the memories of opening up a badly-stitched wound, cleaning it, and re-stitching the thing only to find that Peter had been awake through the whole process were not ones he ever willingly recalled.

This is different. This is different.

But he could almost see the teeth in the shadows, almost hear the whispering, and he had never been more afraid of his demons than in that moment, knowing that with all that was to happen when de Tourvel arrived, he would need coherency and calm above all.

He suspected he was in danger of losing both.

"He was big," Peter muttered. "Dark and....how did you? You always do...save me. Save me from me even and.... I have to give you this..."

But even with the weakness of his voice, Peter seemed somehow, horribly heartbroken.

"And if you really wanted to help, you stubborn, thickheaded - although right now I'm thanking God and all his angels for that - Scot, you'd give me unconsciousness." Guyon kept his voice conversational. "How's this for a plan? You go to sleep, we talk when you're capable of making sense, and I'll save you from the cringing embarrassment of ever repeating the gibberish you're currently spouting. Also, you have *wax* in your hair. How the *hell* - oh, never mind, why am I asking, you probably think I'm talking about flying albino monkeys." He wished that getting any sort of injury clean wasn't both so essential and so painful for the sufferer. "Hm. Me with hot water and torn linen. How familiar this is becoming. How very much I wish it were not..."

"Sorry...sorry...Should go...won't make any trouble," Peter looked as if he meant it, freezing as much in place as his dizziness would allow.

"You're not," Guyon said automatically. *You're troubling my heart, but that will have to wait, I think.* "Sorry. Try and remind yourself that the bed is actually still, even if it does feel like a ship in a gale. Probably doesn't to you, but - hm. How a ship in a gale would feel to me?" He was deciding that he hated head wounds with an equal intensity to old knife wounds across the ribs. "I'm not actually expecting responses, *bèl-mi*. I'm just a bit averse to silence. When I run out of completely unstrung words, I'll move on to quoting, and then you'll at least be assured I haven't got any better at this."

He flinched as he encountered the worst of what had been done. "Um. You have splinters," he said at last. "Well, more...bits. Really." He sighed. "At the risk of being a terrible cliché, my friend, this is going to hurt...and yes, I know." He was unable to resist a small snort of laughter. "It already does..."

"'S alright." Peter said solemnly, "...can't hurt worse...You'll get it.."

Do not, Guyon thought, furiously swallowing down a sudden grief he didn't quite understand, *do not choose now to have blind faith in me. Do not.* "Obviously," he said aloud. "I'm simply brilliant, I know, so naturally I'll get it." *Get what? I haven't got a blasted thing, and it seems I haven't for days.* He started removing splinters and sand and small bits of quartz that had somehow got stuck in the debris of the lantern, and wished he were someone else, a long way away. It seemed to take forever, and was worse than darning socks. By the time he had finished, he was quite prepared to go back to the *Grotte* and practice necromancy for the pure satisfaction of causing death for a second and slower time.

"Done?" It was a tiny pained question, but still Peter had not moved. He had also not complained or groaned or made any other of the sounds that Guyon was sure he must have felt like making.

"You bloody-minded, pig-headed -" Guyon started, and then closed his eyes and his mouth, and counted backwards from ten in Arabic, very slowly. "Yes," he said in more controlled tones, and sat, carefully, on the edge of the bed. *I should be able to offer comfort, this time. Why can't I?* "Yes, it's done."

"Thank you," The words were careful and controlled. "I'll try not to bother you any more."

"*Pèire* -" He couldn't take that careful withdrawal. Not now, not with his own painful decisions made and with all that was to come not even begun yet. He took Peter's hand in his, and lifted it to his mouth, whispering into the palm, "Don't. Don't."

The knock on the door was a kind of terrifying relief.

"Guyon, are you there?" The voice came through the door strong and confident. De Tourvel, of course.

Guyon closed his eyes, letting Peter's hand go and pressing his fingertips into the sockets until red and bright green exploded in his vision. He took a deep breath, and got to his feet. "Don't...go anywhere," he said with manufactured dryness, and crossed the room to open the door. "I'm here," he said softly. He let the cold, betrayed anger flood through him again, out of the small, terrible hidden place that was usually his alone, and a thing to conquer and overrule. "I'm here."

"Jeannine said you needed me to come. She said that Scudamore had been hurt and -" There was a pause as de Tourvel apparently took in the sight of Peter, his bloody shirt laying on the floor and the bandage on his head. "*Mon Dieu!* She wasn't exaggerating this time, was she? What happened?"

"Maurice set Peter up in the *Grotte*," Guyon said in an expressionless voice. "I want him arrested for treason against the Crown. Since that's who keep being told we all work for and serve. I want him out of this house and in the Carcassonne jail. And I'm *not* asking you. I'm *telling* you. I have a note in his handwriting as proof. And you have my word." He clenched his teeth together, and swallowed bile and fear together. "I want it done *now*."

"Maurice?" Brown eyes flashed from Guyon to Peter and then

back towards the door. "Surely he didn't - No, you said set up. Who actually did this?"

"I have no idea - can we talk about this *out* of here?" Guyon, feeling mildly exasperated now, rather than afraid, tugged de Tourvel into the hallway. "I killed one. I think the other's only stunned. Maurice had paid them to kill Peter, but who they were?" He ran a hand over his head. "I didn't feel it was the right time for introductions."

"Damn." There was frustration in de Tourvel's voice as he continued his questions, "You said you have proof beyond your own word? And you'll swear out a complaint? Tomorrow of course, I'm sure you don't want to leave Peter in this state." The Captain shook his head, "Where is Maurice?"

"Down in the main hall, in his bedroom, or skulking in the gallery," Guyon said. He snorted. "What else? And yes, whatever it takes. I'll sign his death warrant in de Retz's name if I have to."

"This wasn't always him, you know? Maurice was once - No, you don't want to hear that now, I'm sure." De Tourvel turned back toward the hallway. "You take care of Peter, and I'll see you in the morning. Oh...Jeannine is going to stay here, if you don't mind. She insisted on riding back with me and I don't want to drag her all over."

"I don't mind." Guyon shrugged. As long as Jeannine didn't get too much in his way, he didn't care what she did. "And - you're right, I don't want to hear." He thought he had succeeded in keeping his voice mild and calm, but he had obviously not quite concealed what he felt, because de Tourvel winced a little and nodded. "Cap? Lock Maurice in *carefully*."

"I know my responsibilities, Guyon, even with someone I've known for years," de Tourvel gave him a tight smile and left, heading first towards Maurice's room.

"Not enough to save me when I needed you to," Guyon said quietly to himself, and drew in a short, startled breath, putting his hand out to the wall to steady himself. That had been François's accusation, never his, that someone should have stepped in, someone who dealt with the laws - *someone who had known the truth*. "I don't trust you," he whispered. "Good Christ, I still don't trust you. How strange..." He realized that he was shaking slightly, cold sweat on the back of his neck, and swallowed. "Oh God."

There was a sudden movement and a shaking hand pressed lightly on his shoulder, "Gui...It's alright...." Peter, even in his dulled and muddled state, was offering him what comfort he was able, still swaying unsteadily.

Guyon, for one brief, appalled moment, thought that he did not have the strength to withstand that compassion, to hold himself intact for one more second, and even as he thought it, was swept with sick horror that he could even contemplate such selfishness. His wounds were old, long since healed, the damage they had done a fact of his life, not some fresh bruise and pain that needed another's help. "It is," he agreed, "and it's going to be even more so when you break the habit of a lifetime, do what I tell you, and get back to bed and *stay* there, hm?" He managed to keep the shake in his voice contained, his deep, steadying breath quiet. "Come on," he said, and even managed a small smile.

*

Guyon was uncertain whether Peter was asleep on his feet or simply unconscious by the time they got back across the room, and he was past caring either way. Shaken by his sudden understanding of himself, by Peter's unhappiness, by his own conviction that he was about to cause Maurice's death, he could not have stood one more second of support from someone in no fit state to give it. He felt that one more emotion added to the conflicting ocean inside him might actually stop his heart and breath entirely.

What he wanted to do was lock the door, curl up on the bed beside Peter, and pretend that none of this was happening or had happened. But he could not, even for a few minutes of sanity and peace, fall into that trap. He had to stay in one piece, had to at least put on a facade of competence that would reassure Peter when he woke and convince the world.

He was drenched in icy sweat, and shivering convulsively, unable to control even that much, and he dropped gracelessly into a chair by the fire, automatically feeding it with small branches that had been laid out.

It was there that Jeannine found him, sometime later, laying a hand on his sweat-damp back, and feeling the heat of his skin through the fine cambric. "Guyon -" she began, and stopped, her fingers involuntarily flinching back, the raised slick ridges of scars imprinting themselves on her palm and fingerpads.
"*Guyon -*"

"Did you think it was a night-time frightener?" he asked bleakly. "Ask your father. Ask your father what happened in Carcassonne. And while you're doing that, my little innocent, ask him *why*. And never laud and praise what I am again, because it is *that*."

Jeannine shook her head, a blur of half-glimpsed copper in the firelight from the corner of his eye. "No. It doesn't matter. It's – Guyon, listen. I know why they do that here, and I know that it's – I know...but punishing you for that is like punishing you for having brown hair or blue eyes. It's how you were born, not something you looked for."

Guyon didn't turn his head, staring at the flames. "And since I have neither brown hair nor blue eyes, what is there to discuss? That I was born what I am and warped in the refinement?"

"If anything could warp a good person into a bad one...it would have been this." A small warm hand traced the scar that came up over Guyon's shoulder. "I remember you. I told you I did. You were such...fun. I was sad for days when they told me you left. I was so young but...I remember it."

"It was better that I left." Guyon shrugged himself away, restlessly, and got to his feet, walking across the room and back to the bed. "They remember what my father was - a good man, a *kind* man. They would have expected the same from me, and I have none to give. *None*." His hand reached out, automatic and thoughtless, touching the blanket over Peter's shoulder. "Save to him." He looked into her young, clear eyes, and sighed. "They say that it is our intellects which divide us from becoming blind brutes. Perhaps it is so. For most of us. But not for me, Jeannine, not for me. For me - it is only the fact that here, here and only here, I can love. *I do love*. That is the core of my argument, my living truth. *He* is my living truth. Without him - I am wholly an

320

empty mind, reaching for some symbol I will never grasp, feeling my soul within me and yet unable to fulfill it. I can never be what I was. But for him...I think sometimes I could be something more." The last was a whisper, the things that lay in the dark of his mind, illuminated only by the sometimes-flicker that could be hope, if he let himself dare. He turned, slowly, trying to smile. "For him I would, perhaps, *want* to be more." He waited for incomprehension, and found only the understanding of youth, the longing for that something *more* that had driven Jeannine ever since he had known her, the firm belief of a child hardening slowly into the bedrock knowledge that inspired an adult.

"Then I'll thank God for Monsieur Scudamore and include him in my prayers along with you," Jeannine gave a definitive nod, her still-soft face tightening over the fine bones into something stronger. *In another life,* Guyon thought, *I would have known you and seen you now as I saw Peter in the colonnades of the Louvre. But it is not I who will see you and it is someone better who will.* He gasped with the suddenness of knowing what he saw for truth, and Jeannine put out her hand, misunderstanding. "For you deserve to be that 'something more'. And Peter deserves to have what he wants."

"*Oc.*" Guyon laughed, and ran a hand over his face, dispelling knowledge and his shadows at once. "Yes, that he does. I am not sure, though, lovedy, that he wants what he has." He looked at her perplexed expression, and shook his head. "Never mind. Just...do something for me?"

"Of course," she said at once, then paused and clarified. "If I can."

"You can." Guyon gave her his best smile. "Get me some string, *pica,* and lend me your scissors."

Jeannine's eyes narrowed suddenly, "Going to tie him to the bed so he can't leave? I think you'd be better with strong rope for that."

"If that were what I was going to do, yes it would." Guyon grinned at her. "But I'm going to tie him to *me*. And I refuse to make it inextricable."

"I think he already is, and it is, string or no string." Jeannine leaned in and kissed Guyon's cheek. "You know what I said about convincing him to marry me? I just want you to know, I would have always shared him with you." And with that disturbing revelation, she was gone.

"You know," Guyon said to the still-unconscious Peter, as dryly as if the man were awake, "I accused Maurice of creating a monster. I am not quite sure that I have not followed in his footsteps."

And it is someone better who will. The voice was the one that had spoken in his dreams, lit by the fire in the hearth at Douai, but, intent upon Peter, he neither heard it nor recognized it. He never knew that he had said his farewell to the other world he had so briefly glimpsed.

*

The world was a gray aching cloud of fuzziness when Peter cautiously opened his eyes. Grey...and fuzzy and it smelled rather of soap for some odd reason. Soap and cave dirt. The cave dirt at least made some kind of strange sense, because it definitely formed part of some of the last of his clear memories.

"Oh, God..." He gave a little moan, reaching his hand up towards his head. The hand did not cooperate as easily as he had expected it to, and his head was throbbing so badly Peter wasn't sure quite where the dressing on it stopped and the bed linens began. "Am I going to die? Or just feel as though I wish to?"

"I don't think I can do anything about your wanting to, but no, you aren't going to." Guyon's voice came from the other side of the room, "I'd take it as a personal favor if you stopped trying, of course, but we can have that particular discussion another time."

"Yes." Peter's voice went suddenly dry as memories began flashing into his brain. Guyon and Jeannine. That was as it should be. Uncle Maurice's words had not convinced Peter, but rather had simply brought together everything he already knew. Guyon did not love him. And although he might not yet love Jeannine, there was affection there and shared memories and...

Perhaps the cave ceiling had actually collapsed on him and he was, even now laying dazed under that suffocating weight. That would certainly explain his aching head, and the horrible pain in his chest and stomach. Guyon's voice was just a hallucination brought on by lack of oxygen and sorrow.

"Think you can risk water?" The tone in Guyon's voice was familiar, and somehow made the weight worse. He had thought it his alone, until he walked in to hear Guyon giving his then-student Vincennes that same softly acerbic reassurance.

Do you want me to stop caring?

Yes, was the bitter answer. *Yes, I do, because it doesn't mean anything except that you hate people to be unhappy or unwell.* It seemed typical that even an hallucination gave him exactly what he didn't want.

"I suppose." But it didn't really matter...nothing did. Nothing except getting past this painful ache and on to numbness. He could live with that. He would not be sad, particularly, nor happy, particularly. He would simply exist, a frozen simulacrum of life.

"Er." The small syllable managed to contain an incredible amount of dubious protestation. Then Guyon blew out a small, sharp breath that sounded almost, impossibly, amused. "Right, water." A battered pewter beaker appeared in Peter's vision, and the mattress dipped as his weight slid onto the side where Peter's head hurt least. "Um, this is *not* going to..." The beaker disappeared, and there was a small metallic clunk that reverberated painfully, as it was set down on something. "Sorry about this." He was shifted, slowly and painfully, onto a linen-covered shoulder that also smelled of soap, and a little of horse, and mostly of the odd burned-out roughness that was Guyon's skin when he was at his most exhausted. "Tell me when you've had enough." The beaker was cool and smooth against his mouth.

I've had enough now, he wanted to say. Enough pain, enough of being unwanted, enough of feeling so much that was not and never would be returned. But he couldn't say that, Guyon had put up with enough of that from him. And hadn't he promised himself that he'd let the other man go? Let him have a more normal life, free from Peter's demands?

He patted Guyon's arm to signal that he'd had enough water. "Thank you."

Guyon took the cup away, but he didn't move, the fingers of

323

his other hand tracing small patterns on the parts of Peter's temple that weren't covered in bandaging. "Hm. Poor hero of mine, lanterns are unkind objects, aren't they?"

"Is that what it was?" It was indeed, unkind, because it hadn't struck harder, taking him away. *God, where was that wondrous numbness?* Please let it be there soon.

"Apparently. There was a lot of wood." Guyon didn't elaborate. His fingers still moved, cool and deliberate and gentle. "I'm sorry, *car-mi*. You were...rather insistent on my not giving you drugs. And even if the pain's as bad as I suspect, I don't think I can give you anything for a while."

"It's alright. I'll be fine." The pain would at least give him something else to think about.

"Oh, you're impossible," Guyon said affectionately. "Yes, of course you will be, but I'm more concerned with now. And alas, the only things that would help you are as impossible for me to give as a phoenix. Well, I don't believe in phoenixes, but the principle's the same - if you try and lift up a bit, I can reach the back of your neck."

"I said I was fine, Guyon." His voice was just this side of snappish, but he couldn't control it. "Go on...Go back to who - whatever you were doing before this...whole thing happened."

The shoulder beneath his head shifted suddenly, and Guyon's very green and very angry eyes glared into his. "*That*," he said, with a distinct lack of affection or reassurance, "would be *you*. So where, precisely, would you like me to go? Because *this whole thing* started more than a year since. What did you have in mind, Peter? The Sorbonne?"

He didn't look as though he were trying to make one of his terrible jokes. He looked both furious and hurt, as though Peter were pulling him over thorns, and he was wholly unappreciative of the entire experience.

"You've had enough of nursemaiding me then, surely," The words were bleak, dark. *God, how could he do this?* For the first time in his life, Peter wasn't sure if he was strong enough to do 'what was right'.

Guyon's eyes narrowed into a perplexed squint. "I what? I - no, I'm sorry, I'm sorry, I don't - *what*? I appreciate you've been hit on the head, really I do, I have been trying to appreciate it for an interminable length of time, but *what are you talking about?*" He didn't look angry any more, but rather confused.

"I'm tired. I'm probably not making sense." *I'm a coward.* He tried to hedge for time. If he could get Guyon out of the room, he could find his damn clothes and leave...again. "I'll just rest...it will be better."

"Mm." Guyon's expression softened, something small and aching in his strange eyes. "I don't think I'm allowed to let you sleep, but yes, rest. Pèire -" He took a breath, and sighed. "It's never going to be the right time, and I am never going to find the right words, but I love you. You must know that. So I don't - it doesn't - it's all unimportant, you see."

Peter's eyes flashed up at Guyon much too quickly and for a moment the room spun in an irritatingly fuzzy circle. "You don't need to say that. I'm not dying, surely, so don't say words that you'll only regret when you're past this...worry."

"I have never," Guyon said with irritating calm, "said anything I regret. Although I have occasionally felt apology for the tone in which I said it. And I am not worried. I *was* worried. Now I am not. I regret not having said I loved you sooner, true, but that is omission and not deliberation. I do not believe my emotions are contingent upon concern, neither. Therefore - I love you, I regret *not* saying I love you, and I love you. Thesis, antithesis, synthesis."

"As you say," Peter's tired voice denied it all. He didn't know what had brought on this sudden spate of words, words that he could not bring himself to believe after all this time, but he wished that Guyon would stop. It would only hurt that much more when they were reversed and Guyon told him that he had been mistaken. It was really only worry...or worse, pity.

"You know what the worst thing is?" Guyon said very quietly. "I've earned each and every second of this - well, not the idiocy, that's just...extra, but you not listening? I've earned it. In spades." He brushed his hand down over Peter's forehead, smoothing his thumb gently over bruised-feeling eyelids. "Rest," he said quietly, and then - "I'm going to prove I mean it. I'm your friend. And I love you. And that's not going to change. I'm going to *prove* it."

Peter just sighed softly and lay back against the pillows. He deserved this mockery. He had put Guyon through worse, with his unwanted affections. He'd just have to take it...then leave when he could. He hoped Jeannine would be what Guyon really wanted and needed, since it seemed, he never would be.

*

Carrying a tray upstairs while trying to keep the lid on a teapot, not fall over loops of string, not pull on the string, and not fall up the stairs due to the sheer perversity of gravity was something Guyon was finding surprisingly hard. It was a relief to reach the comparatively level floor of the creaking gallery, and balance the tray on the newel post for a moment while he caught his breath. He refused to think about all the reasons his usually steady hands were shaking, focusing instead on controlling his breathing and trying to stop the teapot lid from bubbling up and down with the water pressure from inside it. When the small tremors had subsided enough that he felt he could pick the tray up again without causing chaos, he started again.

Getting to the door was one thing. Pushing it open with his hands full and not dislodging the recalcitrant lid was going to be quite another. Balancing the tray on one knee while he tried to untangle some of the string from around his feet with his teeth, Guyon became aware that he could hear Peter talking to himself inside the room.

His first reaction of amusement was swiftly dispelled as he realized that Peter was using the solitude in order to reinforce to himself what he must have already decided before going up to the caves. Guyon, who had left rationalizations behind him before his insane dash out of the Hall the same evening, found himself listening to all-too familiar reasoning.

That Guyon would be better off in a life of his own. That he would be better off in the Languedoc. And, finally, that Peter should leave.

"Consider this string an iron chain, Scudamore," Guyon muttered through his teeth, and finally got the door to swing open.

"It's really the - " Peter's words were cut short as Guyon entered the room. He was pretty much, in exactly the same position Guyon had left him, although, there was a suspicious looking red mark on his forearm. Peter had, Guyon suspected, resorted to pinching himself into wakefulness, on top of the running commentary about his plans. "You made tea. Thank you."

"You're right, it's better in pottery," Guyon said with equal blandness, and then the lid *did* fall off the teapot, and very audibly broke its spout. "Oh, blind plague-ridden *rats*," he said uselessly. "I swear, this thing has a vendetta against me."

"It's alright." Peter's voice was as bland and distant as his expression. "I didn't mean to put you to any trouble."

"No, that much I *do* know," Guyon said wryly, and set the tray of badly-made and now possibly lethal tea down on the chest by the side of the bed. "I have...something to tell you." He picked up the string, and showed off its coils, wrapped around his fist.

Peter looked at the string, a slightly puzzled expression on his face. *That was better*, Guyon thought. Well, better than the cold, calm, dead eyes of moments before. "What?"

"It's...a quizzity." Somehow, Guyon managed to smile. As he did so, he slipped the first coil over his clenched fist, and pulled on the other end. The triple knot obligingly tightened. Before Peter could react, he looped the other end just under the strength of the wide-boned rawness that was somehow so much Peter, and so much not, and tied the free string tightly. "There."

There was a small sigh, as Peter looked down at his anchored wrist, then over at Guyon. "I'm really not sure I'm up for a game, Gui. Can we do this some other time? I'm sure that any skills I might have for it have been driven away by this headache."

"It's not a game." Guyon had never used his tutor's voice on Peter before, never employed the deep softness of *trust me* on someone he cared for. But François had always known when he meant it, and no-one else had ever cared whether it was genuine or not, only if he used it at all; and Guyon was tired, tired to his soul, of omission and pretence. "It's how it is." He tugged on the string, unfolding it to its fullest length, and then, deliberately, measured out that length in steps, to press Jeannine's pair of small

327

golden scissors into Peter's free hand. "I can't undo either knot," he said. "One's too tight, and the other I can't reach. But - you can cut it. Cut the string. If you truly do not believe I love you."

Peter looked from the scissors to Guyon's face to the string and back, his expression becoming more and more panicked. "No. Don't ask me to do that...I.... Damn it, Guyon, how can you ask me? Can't you even leave me one small shred - *something* to cling to?"

"No," Guyon said bluntly. "Since you do not, in fact, believe I have given you any shreds at all. What, Peter! You do not *think* I shall marry Jeannine, and stay, you *accuse* me! Accuse me and make all my unspoken love a mockery! So *make* it nothing! Nullify me! Tell me I do not love you - *go on, cut that string*! And when you do, you are the only one it will have made a difference to, in admitting you do not believe me, for I shall still love you, and I shall be silent once more."

And that was the heart of it really. Could Peter condemn him to the limbo he had been placed in himself? To love and never speak of it? Guyon hoped he understood Peter as well as he thought. Understood him well enough to know that he at least had to give the idea some thought.

"I can't." Peter's voice came to him then, soft and pained. "It would be like cutting off my arm, to take that last hope away."

"Is it hope?" Guyon was at the last remnants of his own string, frayed and limp with use. "Is it? Or is it dullness, to have said you loved me all this time and received no response, and now it is too late..."

"You know it's not. It's just -" Peter looked up wildly, as if trapped. "I'm trying to do what's right. And if...if you say this now...and it's not...*God,* how will I live?"

"As I do," Guyon said gently. "Knowing that all you have ever said or done was wrong." He did not dare touch Peter, in case it was the last coercion. "I love you. Whether or not you wish me to - that is your choice."

"I -" Peter slumped then, his hands going up to rub over his temples at the edge of the bandage. "I have to think, Guyon. Can you let me do that, at least?"

"No, in fact," Guyon said quickly. This much, at least, he was sure of. "Because then you will talk yourself back into leaving, and Pèire, perhaps you might cut that string and do so, *but I will cross the Pyrenees to find you again.* So *no.* No. No!"

The sudden silence that came next was almost as loud as Guyon's words, ringing and echoing between them, just as much a physical tie as the string. And into that silence Peter's voice rasped, as if forced from him.

"You know I can not."

"No, I don't," Guyon said gently, letting his voice lilt into the little, coaxing flute of persuasion. "I *don't* know, my dear. You love me, but you might wish to be away from me. If you do not believe that I love you, with the whole of my divided soul, then perhaps you would be better off to do so."

"How *can* you?" The words were sharp and bitten off, as bitter as a winter wind. "I would have died to hear those words a month ago, even a week ago...but they never came. And now...you...do? What made you decide this, now, and not then?"

"I didn't *decide*!" Guyon had never before had words taken from him, and if he had, only ever away from his lips and into silence, but now they were wrenched, raw and bleeding, into open and cold and rasping air. "I always felt it. *Pèire!*" He felt the last of his assumptions leave him with a breath of disbelief. "I told you. I *always* told you! I have loved you for so long that I even forgot the words!"

With a sudden swift movement, Peter threw the scissors across the room where they hit the hearth with a bright, sharp, clatter of sound. "I love you, Gui...Please...tell me."

"That I love you?" Guyon was still dazed from his own realization, that for every declaration of Peter's, he had given an annulment to that blunt understanding. "Peter, I *have* told you. Again and again, *I tell you.* I love you. I love you, *chérâme,* my best beloved, *bèl-mi,* my most beautiful, my more beautiful than all others, *car-mi,* the heart of my heart, the essence of my breath and existence, I tell you when I speak, when I breathe, whatever I have done, be it good or bad, I have been telling you - *I love you.*"

Peter spread his arms wide, his eyes never leaving Guyon. "Show me."

Guyon felt his eyes go wide. "But - you're hurt -" he started, and then laughed, and pulled Peter up off the heaped pillows, kissing him with all the force and passion he had tried to warn Peter against evoking. Half-laughing and half-despairing, all his barriers down and the ferocity François had tried to put him on his guard against to the fore. The kiss was all teeth and roughness and desire and the only way he knew love could feel, annihilation and pain and longing.

It was all he, at least, needed to know.

*

When Guyon had finally let him sleep - Peter had other ideas about what he'd rather be doing, but Guyon had denied those as well - Peter had gone under deep. Exhaustion, mental and physical, combined with pain, made for a heady cocktail. It had to have been hours, he was sure, because as he recalled the room was bright with midday sun when he had been allowed to drift off and now it was barely pink with dawn's light. The bed was soft and warm and smelt of -

"Guyon?" Peter sat up quickly, almost panicked when he discovered he was alone. Had that all been a dream? Was he now to leave? To go on alone?

He groaned miserably, his confusion mixing with his headache to double his pain.

There was a thump from the other side of the room, and then Guyon's voice said from somewhere surprisingly near floor level -

"You know, I keep meaning to ask you *why* you so loathe the concept of me and chairs. Or is it just chairs?" He yawned, mumbled something, and then said, still from the floor, "Sorry. I was asleep." He snorted. "Obviously. But sorry."

"But why were you sleeping over -" Peter, still groggy, reached down to wrap his hand around his wrist, sighing with relief when he discovered the string there...*still there, not a dream...*" - over there instead of here with me?"

"Cause I went to - oh *God* -" Guyon yawned again, and his voice swooped into sudden coherence as he got to his feet and became visible - "feed the fire, and I sat down, and I was warm, and I went to sleep. In the chair." He brushed dust off his knees,

330

looking a little embarrassed. "Sorry. I meant to read, I think, I thought I was awake..." He was quite evidently not completely so, even now. "Sorry. I - water? I can make tea. I brought the -" another yawn - "tea. Upstairs."

"Come back to bed." Peter hated that he sounded so weak, so needy. *But you do need him, Scudamore, admit it. Love you or hate you, there's no denying it.* "Please."

Guyon squinted at him, his eyes little cat-slits of narrow green in the pale, bright light. "Is that with tea or without?" he asked with all the earnestness of the truly confused.

"Without, thank you." Peter said softly, pulling back the blankets to welcome Guyon in. "You're still half asleep and I'm not much better."

Guyon snorted. "Oh. I was wondering. Mostly why either of us were awake at all, but definitely wondering..."

"We are both awake...because I am here...and you are way over there." It sounded like nonsense, but Peter always slept better with Guyon next to him, icy hands and all.

"Should I be worried that you make more sense with a broken head than at any other time?" Guyon asked, half-laughing and half-yawning, and crawling under the covers to press icy feet and hands and *dear God knees, how the hell are his* knees *cold?* - against Peter.

"No. I only make more sense when you are half asleep," Peter shivered, shifting to allow those frozen appendages better access to his warmth and give Guyon the place where his sleeping body had warmed the bed. "Otherwise I'd sound just as ridiculous as always."

"Mm. No. *I* make sense when half asleep, you always make sense." It was one of Guyon's rare moments of sheer, transparent veracity. He yawned again, his breath warm against Peter's skin. "You didn't dream it, by the way," he said, as though the sudden intake of air had given him the clarity of a man on a high mountain-top. "I *do* love you."

Peter's arms tightened around Guyon involuntarily at the words, and he had to force himself to relax, "I did wonder. Slept too deep, I suppose, for clarity."

How long would it be, he wondered, before those words

ceased to catch him unaware? How long before his heart stopped leaping at the sound of them and beating as if to burst from his chest? And how long, before he stopped waiting for the last line of the joke - where Guyon told it and then laughed at him for believing?

"Also, some unfeeling and decidedly dead individual hit you over the head, so any confusion is understandable." Guyon's laugh was oddly shaken. "I'm sorry. I'm sorry it took me so long to - it wasn't *you* I didn't trust, you do know that, correct? It was myself. A new thing to add to the collection of new understandings. I can be a coward, and not know it. I thought - I was being brave. Noble." He shrugged, his whole body restless and taut. "Wrong, is actually the word."

"Guyon..." Peter sighed his name, half in negation, half in amusement. "We've both made mistakes. If - If we're going to do this, we need to leave that behind and just move forward."

Peter knew there were mistakes of his own that he would rather not have brought up. Leaving had been one. He'd said he wouldn't leave unless sent...and he had tried to do just that. No matter what his motivations, that was something he was not proud of - no matter that his heart told him he wouldn't have made it past the third mile marker before he'd have turned around.

"Ah, Pèire, you're a fool. I told you, I would have crossed the Pyrenees if I had to, to bring you back. You made no mistakes except to think I had changed when I am incapable of doing so." How was it, that he had never noticed before how Guyon's real smiles warmed his whole body through, tangibly and unmistakably?

Peter placed a warm kiss on Guyon's forehead where it rested against his chest, "Then I love you as I am a fool - once, today and forever. Poor Gui, are you certain you wish to be tied to a lunatic?"

"Oh, *that!*" It was a suddenly familiar tone, and it was like cold water on Peter's face, bringing him to full awareness as he realized that Guyon had not been exaggerating, that with that much simplicity and for that long, he had been saying the words Peter wanted to hear so badly.

I tell you when I speak, when I breathe, whatever I have done,

be it good or bad, I have been telling you -
"But of course."
He was, indeed, a fool.

*

Peter woke the second time with a far less painful head, a feeling of contentment that warmed through him into an involuntary, sleepy smile, and suddenly discovered that he couldn't move. It was not only because of the warm body that was partially draped over him, but somehow Guyon's amazing amount of string had conspired to twist around and pin his free arm to the headboard. "Gui?" He shifted, trying to wake the other man without tightening the string any further than it already was. "Guyon? I need your help. Please wake up."

"I'm awake." Guyon sputtered into laughter and coherency at once. "I'm *trapped*!"

"Indeed," Peter chuckled. "The web has ensnared the spider as well as the fly. Or is it more like fish and the fisherman? I'm not sure which is less flattering."

"Webs and nets - oh, *cagar*..." Guyon gasped out a breath of pure amusement. "Either seems appropriate. And deserved!" He tried to untangle the mesh of string, and yelped quietly. "Oh damn, I don't think...well, I can't exactly jump through *this*!"

Peter gave a small sigh, "Well, we knew we'd have to cut it sooner or later. The scissors are still on the table...can you just? Or maybe if I shifted like -" They both moved and the thought struck Peter that they were now in one of those oddly athletic sexual poses that he'd seen drawings of once. It had been in some book that a foreign visitor had given to Rupert. The thought made him laugh and move his arm, which tightened the string.

Guyon shook with laughter. "Well, you did once promise me Scheherazade," he said, his voice shivering with amusement. "But I'd rather not re-enact the Arabian Nights. Thank you, however, for the offer...oh God, just grab the damn scissors!"

With the shifting of Guyon's weight, Peter was now able to twist enough to reach back over his shoulder and, with careful fingertips, pick up the scissors. He handed them to Guyon with an

333

amused smile. "Where will you first choose to cut us free?"

"I was rather thinking of the middle - *ah!*" Guyon snipped through several loops at once, and shook his arm free, string trailing from his wrist. "You should be able to move now."

A devilish glint twinkled in Peter's eyes and he made a not very subtle shift of his hips, "Yes, movement is, indeed, possible."

"Yes, and should I actually *hit* your head to prove why it is not actually *desirable*?" Guyon asked snappishly.

"Already, been done." Peter replied, now subdued. "Sorry."

"Oh, it's not my headache." Guyon sounded crosser than ever. "By all means, continue. Knock out what remains of your brain, feel free, go on, after all, why in God's name should *I* care?" His voice spiraled upwards, the words almost spitting out in a complete contrast to his usual amused drawl.

"Guyon?" Peter raised his hand up to rest on his friend's cheek. "I was just joking. I'm sorry if I upset you. Truly."

"I think I left my entire sense of humor about anything to do with your safety in the *Grotte de Limousis*," Guyon said flatly. "And I think it may be staying there for the foreseeable future."

"You can't lock me up in a padded box, Gui," Peter spoke softly, his thumb smoothing over the beard roughened cheek, "no more than I can you. But, if it will help, I promise to do my best to avoid anything dangerous as much as possible, as long as we're here."

"I'll settle for no more notes on a table and bags that don't disappear," Guyon said in the same expressionless voice. "I'll settle for letting the Languedoc go to Corvay's dubious mercy. I'll settle for crossing the whole of Europe to find you. It would appear, in fact, that I'll settle for just about anything." His mouth twisted. "I always did, you know."

"I don't want you to 'settle' for anything you don't want," Peter muttered. "My trying to leave was wrong, I can see that now. But then? I just wanted you to be happy and thought that I was keeping you from it, somehow." Peter drew in a deep breath before he continued, "Besides, you didn't always have to 'settle' for me, in a good way or a bad."

"No," Guyon agreed. "I didn't. I wasn't, that's not what I

meant. I just..." He sighed, sharply. "I meant what I said, back in Paris, but I said it wrong. I should have said - I should have said that it doesn't matter. None of it matters. As long as I'm *allowed* to love you. Not know you. *Love* you. As long as I'm allowed that, then - none of it's important."

"It's not a matter of allow. I want you to. I encourage you to." Peter chuckled softly, "I've dreamed of it for so long that I should be ashamed."

"I couldn't *say* it," Guyon said painfully, and the effort it cost him to admit that was visible, color flooding across his face in red patches. "I thought it was the last thing you needed to hear, to be honest, and I -" He laughed, sudden and sharp and rueful. "God, I hate it when *you're* noble, I don't know why I thought it would be a good idea for me to try and emulate that sort of behavior."

"It's alright, Guyon." Peter told him, "As much as it hurt me, I always knew part of why you couldn't or wouldn't. I was willing to wait, always, until I felt that I was more in the way than waiting."

"Hm." A little spark of amusement re-entered Guyon's voice. "Should have hit *me* with a piece of wood."

"Or a lantern," Peter grimaced. "That's what got me."

Guyon blinked. "It - a - *oh.* I know." He put tentative fingers over the bandage, and said hopefully, "I suppose you can say you weren't singed..."

"Only by love," Peter smiled softly, leaning carefully into the touch. "Singed, consumed and reborn."

"I told you," Guyon said with consummate dryness, "I don't *believe* in the phoenix." He made a face. "Just you."

Laughing, Peter pulled Guyon closer, burying his face in his neck, "I'm sorry. I have reduced you to sentimentality, which I know you hate."

"Well, I hate anything I'm bad at," Guyon said with somewhat disarming honesty, and rubbed a very gentle hand over the back of Peter's neck. "So please, get your head to heal soon, and then I won't have to be bad at not holding on to you like a form of woodsman's vice."

"I like when you hold on to me," Peter told him. "However, this whole tied up thing could get a bit old." He looked pointedly up to where his arm was still rather tangled with the headboard.

"Ah." Guyon, perhaps not so surprisingly, grinned with delight. "But you have to stay *still*..." He chuckled, and began to detach the string with quick fingers. "There. You should trim it, though, or it will do something equally entertaining to a bedpost."

"Could you?" Peter held up his wrist, "Just cut it loose, but...leave this bit." He indicated the first loop, tied in a loose circle around his wrist. "I want to keep that."

Guyon's eyes were suddenly very wide in the dim light, and a little bright. "'S easy enough," he said roughly, and clipped off the string with less than an inch to spare by the knot. "There." He slid his index finger between the string and Peter's wrist. "It'll probably slip off anyway..."

"If it does, you'll just need to replace it," Peter told him. "I want to be tied to you. This will be a symbol of it."

"And it'll wear through..."

"And as often as it does, I'll have you put on more." It was a gentle explanation and utterly sincere. "Renewing it for as long as you wish it to be."

"You do realize I'm going to start hiding scissors..." It would have sounded nonsensical save for the fact that Guyon was the one who had devised the whole idea whereby Peter was the one who had to choose to use the blades, not him. Like its user, Guyon's affection was an odd and prickly thing.

"You don't need to," Peter wanted to reassure him, to tell him that the only way he would ever cut the string was if Guyon asked him to. But it was all too new for both of them and such confidence would only come with time. In time they would not need string or scissors or anything so concrete. They might still retain them, but it would be for sentiment rather than proof.

"Hm." Guyon hadn't moved his finger. "Maybe not," he conceded at last, and turned his head to kiss Peter. "Maybe not."

When the kiss broke, Peter looked around with a small grin, "Am I allowed to leave the bed today? Or am I your prisoner? Because if I am your prisoner, I'm going to be rather demanding that you feed me soon."

The seriousness with which Guyon considered the question was slightly frightening. "You're allowed," he said eventually, and then he laughed, ruining the contemplative effect. "But only because the kitchen terrifies me and I think the cupboards have a vendetta..."

*

Guyon, much to his embarrassment, was discovering that ten years since he had last been in the kitchen to any purpose was more than enough time for most things to have been changed around and for him to have forgotten the rest. He had managed to discover where the bread was kept, and inspected the pantry to find that it was no longer a pantry but a vegetable store of some sort, with flower bulbs on the top shelf. He found a bottle of wine on a shelf that didn't seem to have any particular purpose, and was trying to work out where on earth the actual pantry now was, with a startling lack of success in anything other than to make Peter laugh at him.

"Pantry...pantry...pantry," Peter chuckled, methodically starting at the back door and working his way around the room opening and shutting doors. So far he had almost had a repeat of his head cracking experience with a broom, a sack of turnips and, oddly enough, a wad of knitting, half-finished with the needles poked through it. "Esmée didn't strike me as the knitting type."

"If she is," Guyon said from inside a cupboard, "I never want to know what she knits. Nooses?" He snickered, the sound echoing slightly and reverberating just enough to send him backing out of the cupboard, shaking his head at the faint buzz it had set up in his jaw and teeth. "Aha!" He yanked on a particularly recalcitrant door that looked as though it should lead to cellar steps, and staggered backwards as it came off one hinge. "Er. Well, I found it..." He wondered how he was going to re set the damn thing without the decidedly terrifying Esmée finding out. He could think of other ways she would be happy to use her needles, if she thought he'd damaged her arena of expertise.

"Indeed," Peter nodded, peering around Guyon and helping him set the now-broken door to one side. "Hmmm...Smells like food, at least. How many rats do you think?"

"The ones I am intending to roast for the Lord Marshal's

dinner? Oh, several, I do hope," said Guyon acidly. Mice he could stand. Mice he was used to. Rats, on the other hand, he thoroughly and sincerely loathed - or at least, that was the emotion he would admit to feeling about them. Privately, they horrified him.

"Oh, don't go to any extra trouble on my account," Peter said softly as he picked up a candle and the broom. "I'll just take a look, alright?"

On the other hand, nothing was actually private any more, and he *could* still feel shame at his own inadequacies. "No, no. My cellar - er, well, pantry, apparently, I really would like to know *why* -" He groaned, realizing that he was talking too much, and giving himself away. "I'll go...er...hunting. You're supposed to have a headache, anyway, shouldn't you be sitting down and being stoical?"

"I told you I was hungry. If there are rats in here...I'm fighting for my share." He leaned in, carefully holding the candle away, and kissed Guyon. "For luck."

"Yes, you didn't set me on fire," Guyon agreed. *I am always telling you. Do you see that, now?* "Oh, for heaven's sake, I doubt eggs are going to bite..."

They didn't. The shelf that fell off the wall and hit his foot, the nail doubling as a peg on one of the walls, and the broken milk-jug waiting to be mended, however, all did. Peter, who had avoided each and every trap, and was trying not to laugh at him any more - *probably in case I kill him* - Guyon admitted, had managed to find a decent amount of food that didn't require two hours' cooking before being palatable. Guyon, who strongly suspected he had a broken toe, and who *did* have a ripped shirt and a cut thumb, envied him.

Peter set about slicing ham and some cheese and bread and setting a kettle on the hearth, then looked over to where Guyon was now putting his cut thumb in a pan of cold water. "You know when I promised to try to go for the foreseeable future without injuring myself, I had no idea that you intended to take my place."

"I told you the cupboards had a vendetta," Guyon said with a small grin. "But would you believe me? Why no, no, you thought I was exaggerating." He took his thumb out of the pan, sighed irritably, and tore the ragged cuff off his sleeve to tie around it, before going over to open the wine. "*Not* tea," he said firmly. "Well, not in my cup. I drank far too much already."

"It's good for you," Peter asserted, carrying a tray laden with food over to the table. "Keeps you alert....and...besides I like to see the faces you make when you drink it."

"Yes, because you are completely insane," Guyon said, taking Peter at his word and bestowing one of his more gargoyle-like expressions on him. "Swamp-water, I tell you. Completely evil." He smirked.

Peter laughed again and sat down, popping a bit of cheese into his mouth. "Your taste buds have just been killed from too many years drinking that acid they served at the Shoe."

"It's not acid," Guyon said patiently, "it's cat's piss, I keep telling you that, but do you listen? No, you insist upon a chemical impossibility." He picked up a piece of bread and stared at it for a moment of complete blankness, wondering what the hell he was supposed to do with it, before snorting. "Er, remind me which one of us got hit on the head again?" he asked, half-sincerely. "Unbelievable though it may sound, I think I'm still *tired*!"

"Me too," Peter nodded. He picked up a slice of ham, rolled it up in a piece of bread then dunked it in a bowl of honey he had sitting on the tray. He took a big bite, and spoke around it, "But hungry...too."

"That's completely disgusting," Guyon said calmly, and as Peter stared at him in disbelief, having seen him mix alternate bites of pickled fish and marzipan before now, he grinned and added, "You're supposed to do that with *cheese.*"

He poured wine for himself, unsure whether Peter had been serious about the tea or not.

"No...the blackberry jam is for the cheese," Peter asserted and held out his empty cup, waggling it at Guyon. "Really at this point, I'm not that particular. You kept me in bed for two days on starvation rations...and not even doing anything interesting to make up for it."

"I know. I'm cruel beyond," Guyon said cheerfully, pouring wine into the proffered cup. "Unforgivable, appalling - oh, *cagar*, two days!" He was supposed to have signed de Tourvel's papers a day before. He was supposed to have Maurice dealt with for good. And instead -

He thumped his head onto the table with a groan.

"No, Gui...hitting your head is bad." Peter looked around and quickly slid the plate of bread under Guyon's head as a cushion. "Second only to having it hit for you."

"Thank you for that timely reminder," Guyon said rather crumbily, and raised his head, frowning. "Bread - Pèire - *what*?" He laughed, sudden and surprised. "Very effective. I wish you *would* hit me over the head, and please make it with an anvil..." *Damn Maurice, damn him, is it too much to ask for a few quiet moments where I don't have to be thinking of betrayal and this damned place and what it means?*

"Really, I honestly prefer your brains right where they are," Peter said, his voice turning serious. "What's wrong?"

"I had Maurice arrested, and I was supposed to sign the paperwork yesterday," Guyon said gloomily. He knew there was no way Peter was going to let him get out of that particular little oversight. Maurice was working against the Crown, and far more than anything he might have done to Peter, that was, essentially, the kind of thing they were in the Languedoc to find. He waited, dismally, for the explosion.

Peter closed his eyes, "Damn Robbie, why didn't he get the man to leave when Giraud did?" He opened his eyes and looked at Guyon, "Does he really hate me so much? Or was I just in the way of whatever the hell he was trying to accomplish with what seems to be just him and a few hired toughs?"

It was so entirely opposite to anything Guyon had been expecting him to say, that for a moment he was on the verge of launching into the reasoning he had already prepared - *I was tired, I'm sorry, I know I need to put what we do first, I swear this is the only mistake* - before what Peter had actually said caught up with him. "Peter...no. No, he just...he's *afraid* of you." He shrugged, helplessly. "You're so...untouched by all this, so - so incorruptible, and he - he just saw your death as a solution to his fear." *And I should have known what he would do.*

"God, I'm not incorruptible. No man is." Peter said, with complete conviction. "I just -" Peter stopped short, at that, letting

340

out a long breath of air, "Best go then...get it over and done. I...Christ's bones, Guyon, I'm sorry. I can't think of anyway to get around this, even if he is your uncle."

"*Great*-uncle," Guyon said with a small smile. "I don't need a way around it, *car-mi*. Maurice damned himself from the second he contemplated putting you in danger - and don't even *try* to tell me that's irrelevant, because it may be to de Retz and Corvay and even the English Queen, but it is *not* to me."

"I know." Peter said simply. "You always take care of me."

"I come and help, too late after the fact," Guyon said rather bitterly, "but so far we've been lucky. But I swear, I'm not - I'm not going to take revenge on Maurice. I'll do it by the law." He could not keep the anxiousness out of his voice, or, he suspected, his expression.

"I never had any doubt of that," Peter reached over and took Guyon's hand. "Finish eating and go see de Tourvel. I'm sure he knows that it's been worry over me that's kept you."

"Yes..." Guyon suddenly made one or two connections he would rather not have done, and winced, gripping Peter's hand and remembering the last time he had done that, so sure he had done something irredeemable, that Peter had closed himself off for good. *Don't. Don't.* Breathing a one-word prayer into another's palm..."I'll go now. Get it done. Maybe I'll *want* to eat, afterwards. And then, when I get back..." He looked straight at Peter, the look he had practiced for years on his students - "you can tell me just what everyone said to you that night."

Peter returned the gaze, his eyes clear and blue as summer skies, "But none of it's important now, you see? Because...because you said the words."

"*Ah*." It was a small sound that felt as though it had been twisted out of him. Peter, as always, had managed to disarm and wound him at once, all unintentionally. *You break my heart.* "As simple as that, then?"

"As simple as a piece of string."

Guyon laughed, and realized that he was still holding on to Peter's hand, and that he did not need to let go, did not need to hide. "How true," he agreed. "But is it as *long*?"

Peter's lips twitched, "Hurry back and we'll find out."

"Just for that," Guyon said in his blandest tones, "I'll find Jeannine before I go. To keep you company while I'm away..."

"I knew it was too good to last," Peter put a hand on his chest, melodramatically. "A few short days and you leave me to live in torment."

"The purest expression of love is suffering," Guyon said sanctimoniously, before sputtering into laughter. "Or something. I'm going. I love you. Don't kill Jeannine, I don't think there's room to hide the body..." He leant across the table, took advantage of Peter's stunned silence and slightly open mouth to kiss him, and left. *This, Maurice? This you can't kill in me. No matter what you say or do. This is my bell song.*

This drowns out knowledge.

*

Margarittes Hall, July 1646.

Our hearts are doubled by the loss,
Here mixture is addition grown ;
We both diffuse and both engross,
And we whose minds are so much one,
Never, yet ever, are alone.

The exploration of the kitchen, eating and cleaning up enough afterwards to keep them in Esmée's good graces, had almost managed to wear Peter out. His head was pounding by the time he was done and he was wearily making his way back up to his room to rest when Jeannine appeared, like some kind of dervish. She had her hair tied back in a very business-like manner and a studiously serious expression on her face.

I'll have to tell Vincennes about that look. Maybe he could practice it in the mirror.

Somehow, Peter managed to keep a straight face when he greeted her, "Good day, Jeannine."

"You know what time of day it is? You *must* be better. I mean - yes, good day to you, chevalier." She looked as though she would very much like to swear. Had he been Guyon, she probably would have.

"Much better but not whole quite yet. I fear I might have overdone a bit. My head is aching and I was just going to lie down and rest." Peter made a move toward his room. "Thank you very much for your concern."

"Then I'll come and read. Quietly. By the fire." She held up a book. "I came ready, you see?"

"It's really not necessary for you to sit with me," Peter told her. And it might be a bit awkward since his plan had been to climb into bed naked and hope his headache was gone by the time Guyon returned. He had strategies to implement.

"Oh, it really is," she said earnestly. "Because Guyon said lots and lots of things and talked about some kind of sleep that isn't sleep, and if you go to that kind of sleep while he's gone and I'm here, and I'm not there, he'll actually *kill* me."

"But..." Peter scrambled for some line of reasoning. He didn't even know if he would be *able* to sleep with Jeannine there, watching him. "It would not be proper for you to be in my bed chamber alone..."

It wouldn't, really, although he knew that de Tourvel trusted him, and God knew *nothing* would happen.

Her eyes slitted into very real amusement. "Do you know, I have the strangest feeling that I am completely safe?" she said, and suddenly laughed. "It's proper. My maid, Costanza, is downstairs, Guyon told me to stay, and my father knows. I don't think you can *get* more proper, do you?" She looked, suddenly, completely and frighteningly innocent. "Unless you think Costanza should be there with us, as well..."

A sudden flash of devilry went through his head, as he imagined doing something, anything, that would convince Jeannine that she was not quite as safe as she imagined. Robbie had done something of the sort to Sarah when she first began to tag after him, grabbed her and kissed her hard. Not the sweet kiss you'd give to an innocent girl to introduce her to what was to come, but the rough and demanding kiss of long time lovers. It had backfired on him - Sarah, innocent as she was, knew even then what she wanted and gave it back to him with just as much force. Left the man out of breath and half hard, looking for something to say. Of course, Peter had knocked him down for it, she was his sister after all.

Somehow, Peter had the feeling that such tactics would be just as big a mistake with Jeannine.

"Ah, very well, then..." He agreed with a sigh. "But you'll have to wait until I say it's clear before you come in."

She nodded contentedly, then scowled. "And if it's more than five minutes," she said, lifting a small jewelled timepiece on a fine gold chain that hung from her waist, "I'll come in anyway. And I bet you'll blush more than me!"

"I don't doubt," Peter growled and slipped past her into his room. For a moment he considered locking the door, but knowing Jeannine she'd either stand outside and yell at him for hours, something his headache would not be very amenable to, or try to go out and climb in through the window.

He sighed and cursed Guyon, and quickly removed his boots

and climbed into bed, fully dressed.

"Are you decent?" Jeannine poked her head around the door, and snorted with laughter even as she came in. "Don't answer, I don't want to know. Why are you dressed in bed?"

"Too much trouble," Peter lied. "Just need a nap and then I'll be up and around before Guyon returns."

He lifted one hand up to his head. Damn, his head was pounding even worse now, but sleep would probably take the worst of it away.

"Do you want some of the pain quencher?" Jeannine asked, sounding genuinely sympathetic. "I know how to mix it..."

"No!" Peter said sharply, then softened his tones. "No. No thank you, Jeannine. I don't often take drugs. Sleep is what I need more than anything."

She bit her lip, looking angry, then nodded, ducking her head to hide her expression. "Yes, chevalier," she said softly, and, true to her word, settled herself in the high-backed chair by the fire, opening her book.

Peter had not really meant to hurt her feelings, and searched for something that might make Jeannine feel better without making himself feel worse, "You could, perhaps, read to me until I am able to fall asleep, do you think?"

It would not be the same as listening to Guyon, but Jeannine's voice was not unpleasant.

The smile with which she looked up from her book was startling, not because of its secret, tucked-in corners, but because of the look that went with it, as though she were inviting him in to some small exclusive gathering. "Of course," she said softly. "I should have thought, when you saw what I had...I'm sorry. Of course I will. I'm halfway through," she added, as though he should know what she was talking about, and began, pitching her voice quiet and low - *Guyon must have been teaching her that, too* -"Common friendships may be divided; a man may love beauty in one, facility of behavior in another, liberality in one, and wisdom in another, paternity in this, fraternity in that man, and so forth: but this amity which possesses the soul, and sways it in all sovereignty, it is impossible it should be doubled.

"If two at one instant should require help, to which would you run? Should they crave contrary offices of you, what order would you follow? Should one commit a matter to your silence, which if the other knew would greatly profit him, what course would you take? Or how would you discharge your self? A singular and principal friendship dissolves all other duties, and frees a man from all other obligations."

Singular and principal. That, indeed, was what he felt for Guyon. That and so much more beside. Compelled, restrained, duty-bound and free - all these things that Guyon had given to him, seeming contradictions that all meant that they now belonged one to the other, above all others and all else.

No one else had ever explained those feelings to him as clearly as Montaigne had. Probably because few others had ever felt them the way that Montaigne had.

"The secret I have sworn not to reveal to another," Jeannine continued softly, "I may without perjury impart it unto him, who is no other but my self. It is a great and strange wonder for a man to double himself; and those that talk of tripling know not, nor can reach into the height of it. "Nothing is extreme that hath his like." I love the one as well as myself, no, more, and let those that would see what I have enter-love -" She broke off, and there was the sound of muffled laughter - "Oh, that's...really not subtle! Sorry. Um - 'enter-love one another, and love me as much as I love him: they will multiply in brotherhood, a thing most singular, and a lonely one, and that which is also the rarest to be found in the world'."

"Does it need subtlety?" Peter whispered softly, his eyes closed against the light from the windows. Peter had always felt, well, not always because at the first there was François and Peter would no more have hurt him than he would purposely hurt Guyon, but as the two of them had grown closer it was as if their thoughts were the same. Yes, they often had disagreements and arguments, but most of those were from equal stubbornness or too much truth, rather than the opposite. The willingness to protect, each for the other, beyond common sense at times.

"Well, I always assumed that when love involved *entering,* it was considered politic to disguise the fact," Jeannine said calmly. "In literature, anyway. It would be a bit difficult in bed sport."

"Oh, yes. Of course, you're right." Peter dragged his thoughts back, suddenly realizing that this was not necessarily a topic he should be discussing with Jeannine. He frowned, "Guyon does know you're reading this, yes?"

"Guyon," Jeannine said irritably and in her usual sharp tones, "*lent* it to me. *Honestly.* I think he's the only person in the whole of France who doesn't treat me like a babe in arms."

"It is hard to imagine that you are not when you pout," Peter pointed out, grimacing at her tones. "Would you care to continue?"

"Would you care to be soothed and sleep?" Jeannine snapped back, and it was the first time she had ever treated him as she did Guyon, and the first time he had really and truly understood just how much familial love, and how little romantic, was between the two of them.

"I would care," Peter gave her back the same pitch, "to be up and out and with Guyon. But instead I am here, in bed, with a pounding head and someone snapping at me."

"And that would be why I offered you the pain quencher!" Jeannine's voice was starting to rise to uncomfortable levels.

"And fantastic," said a dry, and very welcome voice from the doorway, "I just learned *why* I came back so fast. My horse will be delighted to learn his efforts were not in vain."

"He's treating me like a child-"

"She's whining and-"

"You started it because-"

"And my head aches and-"

"Jesus *Christ*," said Guyon blankly. "How *old* are the pair of you - *no*, that doesn't mean I want an answer, for the love of *God*. Jeannine, go home. Peter -" His mouth twitched downwards in a sudden inverted grin. "Shut up, hm?"

"Sorry," Peter said, sheepishly, and did.

Wonderful, Scudamore, and you were just saying that you wanted to be with him. With him to share what he had to be going through, and instead you get into an argument with Jeannine and just make it worse. How does he put up with you?

"I was only doing what you -" Jeannine started, and was taken in a firm and uncompromising grip beneath her arm.

"Quiet. Out. Home," Guyon said firmly. "Argue it tomorrow. *Home*, Jeannine, your father will want your company, do you understand?"

She drew in a sudden, startled breath, her annoyance forgotten. "Oh. Oh, *Guyon* - you-"

"*Home*," Guyon repeated, and Jeannine left the room without another word.

Peter didn't understand. He didn't understand at all. But still, it got Jeannine out and Guyon there with him so it rated on the good side as far as he was concerned. Still, he remained silent as requested, his many questions unasked.

"Maurice," said Guyon in an utterly inflectionless voice, "has been found guilty of treason without my participation. His fate is to be pronounced in due course. Of course, as a member of our family, he will be permitted to escape into exile, and I will not be permitted to know the date, in case I - prove myself a true de Chesnay and take justice upon myself, I suspect, given that I have just had to strip off my shirt in full view of a courtroom to demonstrate what happens when we are permitted to take justice into our own hands. After a very thorough inspection, I was kindly allowed to dress, and as an especial treat, taken to identify a rather ripe corpse as a man I killed. And what I really did not want or need after that, Peter, was to come back to a brawl more suited to infants!"

"Sorry," he said again. The only word he allowed himself.

Idiot! Complete idiot!

He had allowed Jeannine to set him off, just as he often did with Sarah. He should know better, one would think, learn as he got older. But no, he made the same mistakes and now, instead of moving to hold Guyon, soothe him after what he'd been through, all he could do was sit and allow him to yell.

Only he wasn't yelling, and somehow that made it all worse.

Guyon sighed, and rubbed his hands over his face. "No, don't - it's all right, I'd have thrown shoes at her by that point." He made a face. "I'm just angry, Pèire, it's not at you. I'm angry and I feel humiliated and that, as you know, *never* puts me at my best." He shuddered, sudden and frantic, like a wet dog. "*God.* I had to show them my - they were *there* when it was done, I still had to -

348

ah!" It was a yell of pure fury, and he whirled around, kicking over the chair Jeannine had been sitting in, and then picking it up and hurling it at the wall, the tendons in his neck standing out. "*Damn* them!"

Peter climbed down off of the bed and approached Guyon as warily as one would a strange dog. Not because he feared what Guyon might do to him, but because he wanted to comfort him and was still as unsure as ever, if Guyon would allow it.

"I should have been with you," Peter said quietly. "I had thought it was only papers you needed to sign, not -"

He was furious, mostly at de Tourvel for allowing this, but also at himself for not foreseeing it.

"Oc, so did I," Guyon said tiredly. He prodded at the broken chair with his foot. "Forgive me. I thought the ride might...mm. Restore my usual good humor." He turned around, and quirked a small smile at Peter. "It's done. What does it matter how?"

"But it does," Peter said with understanding, sliding one hand up to rest on Guyon's shoulder.

It did. And the thought that his beloved friend had gone through, had his privacy invaded in such a way, just infuriated him all over again. They needed to be away. To get out of this place and soon.

"Yes," Guyon agreed. He turned his head, and pressed his lips to Peter's hand. "My sanity. My soul. I am glad you weren't there, even though I did want you, rather." He sighed. "Well. *Afterwards.* At the time..." Peter could feel the grimace.

"Guyon...you know I've told you that I won't press you to tell me things that you do not wish to...or aren't ready to..." Peter lifted his other hand to Guyon's left shoulder, looking deep into his eyes. "But soon, please, I so want to understand you. I want..." Peter drew in a quick breath, "*'The secret I have sworn not to reveal to another, I may without perjury impart it unto him, who is no other but my self.'* I want to tell you everything as well. Anything you want to know. No more looking without seeing for us, Gui, please."

"I know. I will." Guyon did not even attempt to smile, as though he already knew it would seem a mockery. "I just...I can't right now. I feel scraped out, like a melon rind. But I will."

"Come to bed with me then?" Peter asked quietly. "I want you with me. Please."

"Are you giving me sanctuary, Pèire?" Guyon did smile, then, small and sad. "For there is nothing I need more."

"Always," Peter told him. "Today and tomorrow and for as long as you will have me, so long shall I be."

Guyon opened his mouth, as though to say something, and then closed it again, shaking his head. He leant in, and kissed Peter, brief and sweet and free of any bitterness that might have been expected. "Thank you, *car-mi*," he said softly. "Thank you."

*

Guyon wondered if he had sounded mocking or evasive when he had asked Peter about sanctuary. In truth, he had been nothing of the sort, rather giving in to one of his rare moments of utter honesty that left him feeling, as they always did, uncomfortably exposed and as though he were recovering from a fever, tired and brittle and not too coherent. Unsure as to whether he wanted to be touched or not, whether he could stand reassurance or not, whether he could even stand to be looked at any more, he concentrated on not shivering too obviously, and wondered if there was at least something for him to feign absorption with.

What good is my work anyway?

He caught his breath, realizing that he had sat down in the righted chair, and was staring into the fire, desperate for the comfort of light, desperate to lose himself, and shuddered.

"Cold?" Peter's voice came from somewhere behind him, very close behind him. "Would you like a blanket? Or -"

Guyon shook his head rapidly. "No. Yes? I don't - it's not cold enough for that, is it?" *Move back, for God's sake move back, I can't endure this and not tell you everything now, when neither of us will be able to withstand the truth.*

"It is if -" Peter hesitated, then moved around to kneel at the side of Guyon's chair. "Today had to have been...difficult. No matter that you knew it had to be done. No matter the justification. To have your...privacy invaded. To have to -" Peter looked down, his long hair falling like a drape over his face, "I

350

wish I had been there. I wish it hadn't been needed. I wish...God, I wish too damn much, don't I?"

"Yes," Guyon said with a faint flicker of bitter amusement. "So do I. It doesn't seem to be a very profitable pastime." He schooled himself to calmness, relieved when the hand he reached out to touch Peter's hair was steady. "The wishing can't be doing much for the headache you claimed when I came in, either."

"It's still there, though it seemed to have gotten a bit better when Jeannine left," Peter gave a contented sound at Guyon's touch and moved closer. "But that's going to be here for awhile. Nothing's to be done for it but to wait. I'm more concerned about you at the moment."

"I'm all right," Guyon answered automatically. *Quite all right, and perfectly insane, thank you.* He swallowed down a plea that tried very hard to escape him.

Don't ask questions about longing
look in my face
soul drunk, body ruined -

"I seem to be suffering from Persian poetry," he added, trying to make it a joke.

"Hmmm..." Peter looked up then, studying his face. "Perhaps then, allowing its escape might relieve the pressure?"

"Not the kind of poetry to be shared," Guyon said softly. *Unless I wished to be sent to the Bastille to join the other poor lunatics on the lower levels.* "It'll pass. Like a fever, or your headache, it'll pass." *The memories won't, and the scars won't, but the poetry will.*

Maurice's voice mocked him from the shadows of his mind. *You destroy everything you touch. You were born evil, do you think we didn't recognize that the moment you drew breath?*

As though mimicking the words, his breath stopped and caught, sharp and almost painful, as though there were some hard object lodged in his throat. "It's all right. Really. I'll tell you - later. Tomorrow, when it's eased." He managed a smile. "Enough for now, hm?"

He caught a flicker of something - Worry? Sadness? - as it passed over Peter's face. Those expressive eyes usually held little back from him, but perhaps it was Peter's own pain they were shielding. "As you say," Peter mumbled, then lay his head down in Guyon's lap, his arms stealing up to wrap around him.

Guyon had quite genuinely thought, until the warmth and trust and comfort of that familiar touch, that he had not wanted proximity, not even Peter's. As soon as it was given, though, he understood quite differently, understood that it was an aid to his faltering defenses, not another break in them. He bent over, curling into safety and consolation and *sanctuary, thank God,* brushing his lips gently against Peter's head.

"Mmmm...nice." Peter said softly, nuzzling in closer. "I - Do you want to go to bed? Or just sit here for awhile longer."

I would be quite happy to never move again, so long as you could keep the shadows silent like this, Guyon thought, closing his eyes. Aloud, he said only, "Oh, I'm not that cruel to your knees, I think bed is infinitely preferable, car-mi."

"My knees might ache, but my head feels much better here," Peter sighed again, less contentedly this time, and rose to his feet. "Bed..."

Guyon rose too, not banking the fire as he usually did. He was unsure whether he wanted more light or less, but a room blazing brighter than a comet would certainly not help Peter's headache, and leaping flames in a grate would demolish what was left of his self control. He did not even pretend to be able to do more than divest himself of shoes and stockings and his breeches, the thought of removing his shirt at all, even to change it, a step he could not quite contemplate. He arranged the bolsters against the headboard so that he was sitting upright on the bed, his back cushioned and protected, and smiled wryly at Peter's quizzical expression. "If you think I make such a good pillow," he explained, "I may as well be one in comfort."

Peter smiled then, slipping into bed and resuming his former position, his head in Guyon's lap and the rest of his length stretched out over the bed. "You're far too good to me, you know? Should tell me to take the damn drugs and make me sleep alone for being so idiotic...but I'm glad you didn't."

"You hate drugs," Guyon said, smoothing his fingers over Peter's temples. "More than even I do, I suspect. I don't know why, but it's you, you would never protest without reason. And

352

tonight, I can't tell you that it would be all right, to trust me, that it would be safe, because...I am not safe, not at the moment, and I won't betray you like that..." He trailed off, wishing he didn't find it so hard, now that he had admitted to his love, to conceal anything at all from Peter.

My lies of omission. My sins of the unspoken.

"Perhaps I should have stuck to Persian poetry after all..."

"No. No, Gui." Peter held him tighter. "You would never hurt me. Not on purpose. Not unless - " Peter's voice trailed off, then came back strongly reasserting itself, "You wouldn't."

"No, not on purpose," Guyon agreed, feeling exhausted both by what he was admitting to and what he was concealing. "I'm sorry. I have to sleep." The sudden appalling lassitude that had used to overcome him when he was a scholar had him well and truly in its grip. He snorted softly, unable not to find amusement in his next thought. "You know damn well that there's nothing either of us can do about it and I *will* sleep, anyway."

"Yes. You should." Peter smiled, loosening his grip and shifting to allow Guyon to lay down next to him if he wished. "Me too if I want this damnable headache to go away." He looked up then, straight at Guyon's face, his eyes searching, "I love you."

"Yes," Guyon said. He still found it impossible to repeat the words, worried that his voice might turn them, parrot-fashion, into an empty mockery, devoid of all feeling. A little of the Persian mystic's words escaped him despite himself. "They say there is a window from one heart to another - How can there be a window where no wall remains?"

"Mmmm..." Peter seemed to accept that as an answer, if the smile on his face were any clue. His eyes were already closing though, as if Guyon's words, his mere presence, were all that he needed to find his rest.

"Out beyond the worlds of wrongdoing and rightdoing, there is a field," Guyon said softly. "I'll meet you there. When the soul lies down in that grass, the world is too full to talk about. Ideas, language, even the phrase *each other* doesn't make any sense..."

He was lost in a haze of half-sleep, where he could hear the words and even see them, but knew himself to have fallen silent, before he could remember the rest of the poem well enough to translate it.

*

There were many things that Peter now looked forward to seeing when he awoke, unexpectedly, in the middle of the night. Guyon's sleeping form, or two clear eyes hovering above him in the dim light and the flash of a smile that meant he was going to get kissed senseless, and on more than one occasion, no more than a tuft of curly hair peeping out from under the edge of the blanket where his ever-cold lover had scrunched down into the warmth.

What he did not expect to see was a seemingly vast stretch of empty white sheet.

"Guyon?" Peter peered into the dim light, but there was no answer and no sight of the other man in the room.

He sat up, lighting a candle and looking for his breeches and stockings. Guyon's clothing was gone, but he was fairly sure that he had not gone far. He did wonder, however, what had lured him away from the warmth of their bed to wander through the chill of the house.

Dressing quickly, Peter headed downstairs towards the kitchen. If Gui could not sleep and didn't want to disturb Peter with his restlessness, that would be the next likely place for him to go - the kitchen with its night-banked fire and some warmth.

It took him a moment, when he entered the dimly firelit room, to realize that Guyon was actually there, sitting with his back to the heated stone of the fireplace, he was so still. Not the focused, attention-catching stillness that he tended to fall into when he was trying to work something out, or marshaling his thoughts ready to write, but something that was more like a deliberate withdrawal of self, a concealment of presence - ridiculous, since he was in plain sight, but still the only thing that came to mind.

"Guyon? Gui?" Peter spoke the other man's name softly, not wanting to startle him. What was he thinking? Were regrets flowing through his head? Or was he simply caught up in the plans he had been making earlier that week - plans for his land, and its stewardship?

Guyon slowly raised his head, and for a moment, Peter thought surely it was another man sitting there, so different did he look. His face was expressionless save for his wide frightened eyes, gazing out at something that had Peter looking back over his own shoulder unconsciously.

There was nothing there...or - Peter looked harder, his eyes flashing into shadows and every corner of the room. No...nothing...quite. Or something, and *not* quite. He saw nothing tangible, but somehow he knew...knew something was there. He felt it with his entire being, like a cool draft against his skin from a place where there was no gap or wind. His eyes shot back to Guyon and he called again, "Guyon?"

Guyon's eyes turned towards him, unseeing and dark, before they cleared a little. "You don't want," he said with a visible and audible effort, "to be here."

"Entreat me not to leave..." Peter whispered softly, moving slowly closer. He felt as if sudden movement would be wrong, but whether it was the fear of provoking a dangerous creature into action, or fear of having Guyon bolt like a frightened one, he wasn't sure.

He was not expecting the sharp laugh, biting as a whip, the only thing moving in the air between them. Guyon's eyes were still fixed and huge-pupilled, midnight caverns in his blank face. "I don't think you want my God, Peter. Go away." He drew a breath, audible and harsh, and a little expression came into his face, though it was impossible to identify in the dim light. "Please."

"No." Peter's answer was as simple as it was quick. "There's something..." He turned then more sharply than he had dared before, and looked into the shadows. "Something..." There it was again, that...something. He still couldn't see anything but, suddenly, the hair on his arms was standing on end and it felt as if something icy were touching him - cold fingers brushing over face, neck, shoulders. Real or imagined? Peter couldn't tell, but either way, if it held Guyon locked in its grip it was wrong and needed to be stopped.

"*Don't you dare.*" It was a hiss of real terror. "Don't. It's not real. *None* of it is real, do you understand? It's in my head and that's where it should stay. Now go away."

Peter wondered for a moment if Guyon were actually still asleep. If he was in that half-conscious state where some people could still function, but were not completely there. But no, Guyon's face held none of that dreamy distance that such people had, his was rather as if he were facing something nightmarish in his wakeful state and knew there was nothing that he could do to save himself. Save himself from whatever it was that Peter had felt. He moved closer, kneeling down on the hearth and putting one hand over Guyon's where they rested on his knees, "No...I don't know what's here...what's happening...but no."

"Oh God, can't you just for once -" Life was coming back into Guyon's voice and eyes. "Peter, you have no idea what - *it's not real*, and we are not having this conversation, now or ever. Now leave me alone." He sounded utterly sure, fixed and confident, but his eyes flickered to the corners of the room when he looked up, and whatever he found there deepened the small tight lines of fear around his eyes and mouth.

"No, I can't *just for once*," Peter said stubbornly. "Conversation or not...something is frightening you, and that's wrong...*unacceptable*. So, I am not leaving you here alone." Peter tightened his grip on Guyon's hand, "If you want me to leave...you're coming with me."

"It makes no difference," Guyon said dully. "It's in my mind, so - " He broke off and sighed. "It makes no difference," he repeated. "I'm damned anyway." He choked out a half-laugh. "Or insane. I wonder which is worse, hell or the asylum..."

"It's not in your mind," Peter whispered. "I feel it too, even if I can't see it." His grip tightened again as he continued, "So...no matter where you go, I will be there too." ...*for whither thou goest, I will go; and where thou lodgest, I will lodge: thy people shall be my people, and thy God my God...*And this, whatever it was, would be his as well, apparently.

"Jesus Christ," Guyon said, a more familiar wildness starting to replace the despairing black mirth in his eyes. "Peter, don't you understand? They burn people for this, they don't just put them in prison and send them into exile under a claim they escaped! For God's sake -" He stopped, and sighed. "For God's sake," he repeated more quietly, "have some sense, if you think there's something here, get away and stay away. Because this association is not one you want. I love you, but don't make me -" And then he was silent, utterly still, his eyes wide and horrified and giving no clue as to what he had been about to say.

"That's it..." Peter was taking Guyon out of here. This place, this horrid dark hall with all its memories and...demons. Peter froze. Demons? Suddenly the remembrance of a very strange conversation flooded through his mind...one where Guyon had asked him about his beliefs. It had seemed a very odd thing at the time...but now?

"Christ." Peter dragged Guyon to his feet, pulling him toward the door leading to the garden.

"What the hell do you think you're - Peter, don't you ever listen? You can't take someone away from their own mind, you can't be *with* that mind from the outside, what -" Guyon, stumbling behind him, was protesting with unfeigned anger.

"No...I'm listening. You are not." Peter dragged him outside. "It doesn't matter if they're real or not."

"Don't be so ridiculous! Obviously it matters, since I've never heard of entering a delusion being a desirable state, and oh, Christ, I am not having this conversation, I *refuse*!"

"Then don't!" Peter was at the end of his patience, becoming frightened and worried on top of it. He was in no mood to cut his punches. "Ever, if you don't want. I'll fight in the dark. These...whatever they are, or aren't...real or in your mind...they're frightening you and that's enough for me, damn it. I will keep them from you? Don't *you* understand?" Peter had switched to English mid-way through his angry words. French was just too soft for what he wanted to say, "Just come with me now!"

"I understand *you*, but - listen, it's not - it's only me - you shouldn't have to -" Guyon stopped then, unexpectedly, seeming to have completely run out of words. "Right," he said then, all inflection leaving his voice and the dead blankness of before returning. It was as though Peter had defeated the last of whatever fight had been left in him, that whatever reserves he had been using to combat his fears, he had used up to try and fight the help being offered him, instead. "Where to?"

Peter hadn't really thought that far ahead, something had just told him that they needed to be out. Out under the sky. No walls. No more unnatural dark, shut up in the tomb-like interior of Margarittes. "Here..." He led Guyon away from the Hall, running into the stables, briefly, to grab blankets to keep them warm. They smelled slightly, of hay and horse, but it wasn't unpleasant, or not half as unpleasant as the nearly palpable miasma of the Hall.

"You can't actually outrun what's wrong with me," Guyon said after a while, his voice still even and calm and almost casual-sounding. Had it not been for the utter lack of the faint, wry humor that Peter took for granted lay beneath even the more bizarre of Guyon's remarks, there would have been no connection at all to the quiet horror of what he was saying. "I tried. I went all the way to Paris. I came back, and held my hands out willingly to be shackled at the pelourinho, and still. Still." He didn't even sound as though he was trying to make sense, which was somehow more telling than anything else.

"Nothing is wrong with you." Peter's denial was vehement. "If being haunted by...by...No, it's not something anyone would choose. How could it be?" And they punished him for this? Peter would attest that the crime was obviously punishment enough.

"Peter, I was guilty of the crime they accused me of." Guyon looked at him with bleak, uncompromising eyes that were regaining their usual translucency. "I still am. The only difference is that then - I thought I was innocent. That's why I didn't want to come back here, that's what I didn't want you to know."

"I already knew..." Peter said softly. He had led them a good half mile away from Margarittes by now, behind a small ridge that hid the Hall from sight. "But it doesn't matter. It won't matter."

"It matters!" Guyon stopped walking, his voice clear of everything but pure horror. Even in the dim light, whatever fear had been riding him was being obliterated by a slowly growing frustration. "Peter, it matters. It matters more if you know - and I think I have the right to ask *how* you know, and *what*, by the way. Because if you know, if you truly do know, then why the *hell* aren't you afraid? Why aren't you afraid of *me*?"

"How could I be?" Peter felt frustrated, confused. He

understood what Guyon was saying...but he didn't understand what Guyon was saying. The words but not the meaning. "I went to the church. There are some things that even de Retz can not expunge, it seems. Your uncle's accusations are still in the record. But they're wrong, Gui. This is not something you asked for, so how could any of that be true? Do you have any control over this? Use it to hurt people?"

Guyon blinked at him in utter confusion. "What? No, of course not, but it's part of me. I thought it wasn't, I swore it wasn't, and he was wrong in *how* he accused me, but not in what I am, not in -" He swallowed, audibly. "I still have the words," he added then, his voice a whisper. "I always did have them, I just didn't realise...and then, after Giraud...*after*," he said more firmly, as though it were his conclusion, "I chose not. But I have them. I could write them, I could turn around and use them faster than your sword could ever move, I could let every second of black despair possess me enough to cut someone to the heart, flay them alive in front of me, and all of it would be words...*and I would glory in that use*."

"Words hurt people..." Peter said in soft agreement.

"Yes," Guyon agreed quietly. "Words hurt people. Do and have. Mine can - mine *will*. Words damn and torment and give no peace, and my father gave me that for a well-taught legacy."

"Lots of people use words to hurt." Peter had the scars from quite a few, so he knew that to be true. Scars from Robbie, from his sister, Hell, even a few from Brian, though those had healed to silvery traces by now.

"Yes," Guyon agreed tiredly, but the note of defeat was back in his voice. Whatever it was he had been attempting to explain, apparently Peter had failed in some way to understand him - or if he had understood, he had not managed to convey the fact to any degree. "Yes, they do." He was shaking, not from his always-present chill, the strange inward frost that Peter had long since grown used to, but from some tension that refused to leave him.

Well, if Peter couldn't remove the interior source yet, then he'd worry about the more immediate and external one. He spread one of the blankets on the ground, and wrapped the other around Guyon. "Yes, I know, it smells like horses, but I didn't have time for anything better. Sit and I'll build a fire."

"Ah, yes, why not. Then you can demonstrate that source of continual amazement to me - how you can light them outside and only ever put them out inside," Guyon retorted, but the familiar complaint lacked heat or even much inflection. He sat down on the blanket obediently, withdrawn once more.

"Ah, my skills can not be confined to the tiny space of a grate." Peter shrugged, trying to keep his tone light, as he gathered wood and built the fire. "No...I've just had more practice with this. I don't have to be neat or tidy. Don't have to worry about smoke. Just...Fire." Peter finished and walked back over to flop down on the blanket next to Guyon. He hesitated for a long moment then plunged ahead, "Guyon...I need to ask…When I was back from Toulouse...feverish...or any other time...did you ever say to me, 'Shall I tell you the moment I knew that you lived'?"

The sparks from the fire seemed to be reflecting straight into Guyon's eyes, absorbed and quenched by their odd translucency as he looked straight at Peter with all the old uncompromising clarity of thought and will, his blank resignation swallowed up in something that was not anger and was certainly not tolerance, and yet was a very long way from hope or joy or anything that any man might see outside of the hidden dark corners of the soul. "Now why," he said softly and dangerously, "would you ask me such a thing?"

"I heard them." Peter picked at a corner of the blanket, looking anywhere but at Guyon. "In that horrid little shack of a barn. As I sewed myself up and lay there...drifting, barely conscious...I heard you. Those words..."

"That's not possible," Guyon said too quickly. "You cannot have heard it, for I never said it. I *wrote* that and I burned the letter. I never - I didn't once - it's not possible. I swear, I never said that to you. I wrote it. I thought it. When you were away, when I thought you were in Poitiers, I wrote - oh, God, I wrote a great many things - but that? To you? No. I never said it." He didn't sound certain, though, despite his definite, emphatic phrasing. He sounded terrified.

Peter looked up at Guyon, no trace of fear in his own eyes, *never* any fear of Guyon, "I heard them. In your voice. It - I often think that's the only thing that kept me going."

"No." Guyon shook his head, vehemently. "That's *not possible*! *I burnt what I wrote*! I thought it and never said it! You cannot have heard that voice, Peter, you cannot have heard those words - not from me, because I *never said them*! And if you did...if you did, then -" He stopped, swallowed. "Oh, God. If you did, then either it was not me and this is all some delusion my madness has created, or - that night was real and I have truly damned you after all."

"Then perhaps I am the one who should be feared? Maybe I drew the words from your head...heard the unspoken? " Peter's voice had dropped down again, as if saying the words louder might make it true. "Don't fear this, Gui? Don't fear me or yourself. How can it be bad when it has given us nothing but good? I might have died there, in that shack, but your voice gave me hope...kept me going on towards home and you."

Guyon put his face in his hands. After a while, he said quietly, "It was a letter. One I thought I would never send, one I burned. I asked you - 'Shall I tell you the hour I knew that you lived? Do my thoughts ever brush against yours? They fly from my body and must go somewhere - where are you? I would follow and reclaim them, if I could.' I had no thought of you ever knowing I had even put such a thing down in ink, let alone that I had once, truly and honestly and openly, asked that question of God - and myself - and you. It was really you I was asking, I suppose, though I assumed you would never know." He took a quick, deep breath, dry-washing his face with his hands, and looked up. "I tried so hard to follow, all that wanting, I didn't even dare think your name to myself, because it would have been unendurable. And it still, somehow, reached you, and - I'm glad. I *am* glad, Peter, but oh, God, why the hell did you think I was sent to the pelourinho? What did you think this was all for?"

"Jealousy." Peter's jaw was tight. "Because you are so much better than...this place, these people...your brother...your Uncle...So much of it is obvious, Gui. It's there in the way Maurice treats you."

All true, all so very true, whether Guyon believed it or not. Nothing but earthly concerns had fueled his condemnation.

Nothing but earthly pettiness, envy, and Peter suspected, lies.

Guyon shook his head slowly, and there was a look on his face of such terrible sadness, and such love mixed in with it, that Peter thought it another phantasm, like the sense of *something* that had made his skin crawl in the kitchen. "No," he said at last. "Because they thought me guilty of practicing mysticism. Because they found me *guilty* of practicing it. You only read Maurice's accusation and statement, not the final decision. Not what de Retz removed - how could you, after all, since it was no longer there to read? Heresy and witchcraft, Peter, I told you - God, I even told you that Twelfth Night, do you remember? All the things that make the Languedoc famous, all the things I am - and yes, they burn people for this. But not me. Not me, because - I agreed to the subjugation of the flesh. Because I had never - *have* never seen an angel, I have never...never anything. I had always denied it, fought against even the feeling of my own soul, and never believed that what I was could ever be more than what I seemed. Never. I took de Retz's concealment and forgiveness and tried to live the innocence I protested and proclaimed. Until you. Until a night when I lit every candle I possessed, and I tried so hard, so very hard...I was afraid for you. That is my only excuse. I was afraid. Unreasoning, unthinking, utterly terrified. When I went to the pelourinho, I thought I was innocent, I thought that I simply *felt my soul*, a little too much, but - that was all. But you...I knew you were alive, and all I had tried not to be...it stopped mattering."

"Then I thank God that it didn't. And I thank you," Peter said softly, "for without that, I would have given up. I...I was quite ready to. To just lay in that barn and never move again. To just bleed out on the hay like some injured animal. You saved me."

Guyon shook his head. "No. *You* saved you. I...I just..." He made a small, helpless gesture. "I don't know."

"Gave me hope. Made me want to live." His lips twitched for only a moment, "Brought me home to torment you for weeks..."

"Don't - you're *joking* about this?" Guyon was shaking violently. "You don't know! You don't know!" There was raw anguish in his voice. "Everything they thought me...that I tried not to be...that I *bled* not to be, all gone, because my love is *corrupt*, and Maurice was right! I tried. I tried." Guyon kept saying that, and finally, Peter started to understand what he meant. He had tried not to love, and when that had failed, tried not to admit to it. *Not because he's been told love is wrong. Because he's been told his love is wrong.* "I'm either mad or evil, and no-one could want that..."

Peter leaned in, his lips pressing against Guyon's neck for several long moments, as if he needed to imprint them there. "I love you. Nothing will change that. Nothing you can do. Nothing you can say. I would die for you and call it satisfaction. I would live for and with you, and call it peace."

*

All your love has ever done for this family is to warp, and taint, and corrupt. You call it love and cost us everything. You were born evil, Guyon, did you think a few half-meant good deeds could change that?

Maurice's savage, scathing words, devoid of all understanding or acceptance, still echoed in his mind, jumbling together with all the words of years before, his brother's calm acknowledgement, Maurice's damning testimony.

His own screams.

I am not this thing! I cannot repent!

He could not. No more than he could deny any longer that he *was* what they had called him, what he had agreed to say he was for the sake of being accepted once more. But not in God's name. If that had ever been possible, the pelourinho had certainly stripped that away from him.

But Peter...

I would live for and with you, and call it peace.

Peter had bravery beyond all reckoning. The man who had lain down with a monster, not knowing what he did, had held on to that same monster willingly, all its hideousness revealed to him, and not faltered for a second.

He owed him honesty, owed him an end to his lies of omission. Owed him the last of his defenses, the final wall between himself and this love that he could no longer prevent.

"The night before they came for me, I told François. *I only feel my soul within me.* I swore I was no mystic. I swore it during and after the whipping, I swore it in my insanity and delirium after that. I vowed it to the Church, and de Retz did not believe me and pardoned me despite it. But *I* believed it. I believed everything I had said, the more so because - because afterwards, after the whipping, I *couldn't* feel it. And I was...surviving. Content, almost. Until I saw you - and I felt my soul within me once more."

He turned his head to glance at Peter, not trusting himself with more. How could he be loved, allow himself to be loved? He couldn't allow Peter to be brought down with him if he were again accused.

On that most dangerous of topics, then, no more. But the rest...*I have loved you for so long I think I forgot the words* - the rest he could say. "It was as though all my life, I had been searching for something. You read the letters. To Giraud. That I could...I could learn, and write, and still there was more, that I would never be - filled, I suppose. But even when you were wary of us, even when - when you were uncertain, it was...I love your mind. Did you know that? Your mind, your - your soul, I - everything. It is as though this was my purpose in life, as if my own gifts were half-given, half-used, before I met you."

"You overwhelm me. If you only used them in half, what will they become?" Peter gave a small sharp laugh. It held little amusement though in truth, his eyes downcast. "I know what my life was and what it is now. I know what you have given me, driven me to become for my own sake. I'm not naive, Guyon. I know you have faults...dark places that for some reason you don't think you can share with me. But, let me say again, I love you. And that will not change."

Guyon caught his breath. *Don't you see? I may not have a choice as to whether I share those places with you or not, any more!* His hands were wrapped around Peter's arm, his body betraying him before his thoughts had even reached a point of formulating coherent strings of words. *Don't let go. If you love me, don't ever let go. Even if I ask, even if I try and make you. Please.* "I don't think there's anything left," he said, and his voice shook. "I think - you said you wanted to know, I think, I think that's all, I don't - I think that's all. I'm so sorry," he added, more cogently. "If I'd known...even suspected, that you would feel this, that Toulouse had been for both of us..." *You would have still taken him to your bed, and broken the laws of man and God, and with joy in your heart, so don't lie to him now, when you found enough courage to stop hiding.* "I would have confessed and loved a great deal sooner," he finished, surprising himself.

"Oh, Gui..." Peter's laugh was half relief and half sob, as he pulled Guyon tighter into his embrace. "It doesn't matter. None of it. We're together now and God damn anyone who tries to change that."

Guyon choked on something that started out as a laugh, and ended up as something completely different, and sounded perfectly appalling. That Peter could mention God, that he had not killed off the last of this beloved, astounding man's faith in the divine and the infinite, was almost too much to bear. "Or at least a certain amount of smiting," he said shakily, trying to ignore the way his eyes were burning. He pressed his mouth to the small warm hollow between Peter's shoulder and collarbone, and simply breathed.

"Yes...smiting." Peter growled but his arms tightened around Guyon. "And I think they should begin with Uncle Maurice...and then Corvay. Or perhaps the other way around, hmmm?

"Oh - no, let them get some practice in first..." Guyon realized that he had longed for the safety of this, the ability to hide and yet be seen, since he first took off his shirt in front of all the curious, prurient men who had agreed with Maurice years before as to what he should undergo. He wasn't even sure Peter could *hear* what he was saying, since it was being muffled against his neck. "Then Corvay can take longer." He swallowed, his throat feeling oddly thick, and sniffed, realizing that the burning behind his eyes had eased because he was crying, as though something had broken inside him, and he could not find the place to mend it and stop. "How annoying. I've become a watering-can."

"Gui." Peter's voice was full of concern. "I didn't mean...I never meant - just -"

Peter's hand brushed over his cheek, smoothing away the

tears. No more words came from him now, as if he'd said them all and only waited for Guyon to accept.

"You damn well *better* have meant it," Guyon said, and half-laughed, the inexplicable grief beginning to subside to a manageable level, and bringing with it an understanding of what had hurt so. "You know...all the people I tried to change for, to give them what they wanted, to be...better, worth loving in their eyes, and it didn't matter, I never could be. And with you...I tried the opposite, I tried to defend myself from you with every weapon in my arsenal, and yet you'd fight the legions of hell for me and by Christ, I think you'd win. It sometimes feels...too much. Too much loss on the one hand, and too much unearned joy on the other, and I can't - can't seem to shut it all away, any more."

"Good," Peter whispered softly, pulling the blankets tighter around them and looking into the fire as he spoke. "Because earned and love have little to do with each other. But if it comes to that, you have, you know, earned more than I'll ever be able to give back. Do you know that you have taken all my loneliness and banished it? That the pain I felt when I first arrived in France has gone? That I can't call myself Sansfoy any longer, because you've returned my faith? That's something I never thought would be true."

Guyon half-smiled, thinking of his own arrogant statement, only days before. *I've got enough faith for both of us.* He had not only been wrong about that, he had been wrong about the possessor of that faith. "You gave yourself the worst name possible," he said quietly. "You never lacked faith. You were, and are, fidelity incarnate." *Even when it is undeserved.* He let go of Peter's arm with one hand, and wiped it awkwardly over his face. "My head may be pounding as much as yours," he admitted.

"Sleep then, it's the best cure." Peter shifted around until he was leaning against a largish rock that lay nearby. "The fire's good for awhile and I'll keep watch to make sure no vicious sheep try to nibble on you in the dark." He patted the ground between his legs offering a warm and fairly comfortable place for Guyon to rest.

"You're obsessed with sheep. I keep telling you, they're ambulatory clouds, we don't *have* sheep..." He didn't particularly

366

want to examine why even that feeble joke made him feel like crying all over again, but he had a suspicion it was an effect rather akin to lancing a boil - the best you could hope for was that all the infection was removed the first time. He moved into the place indicated, wondering when it had become the sum of his contentment, to relinquish his sense of self into the silence only Peter seemed able to give his frenetic mind.

"If it looks like a sheep and smells like a sheep and baaas like a sheep...it's probably damn well a sheep," Peter's lip twitched. "Is that a thesis?"

"Er." Guyon blinked at him. "Well, it's a stunning misuse of logic, so I regret that I am forced to say, *yes*." He chuckled, starting to feel more like a member of the human race again. "Of course, it could be an especially woolly variety of goat, and *then* where's your thesis, hm?" He shifted until Peter's heartbeat was against his ear, a constant, familiar rhythm that was part of the wonderful, blessed mental silence he was starting to luxuriate in.

*

The Languedoc, July 1646

Coming and staying show'd thee, thee,
But rising makes me doubt, that now
Thou art not thou.
That love is weak where fear's as strong as he ;
'Tis not all spirit, pure and brave,
If mixture it of fear, shame, honour have ;
Perchance as torches, which must ready be,
Men light and put out, so thou deal'st with me ;
Thou camest to kindle, go'st to come ; then I
Will dream that hope again, but else would die.

After weeks of people ignoring him and conversations stopping when he entered a room, never mind the fact that he still struggled badly with the Occitan slur, Peter was suddenly finding himself approached by complete strangers. Everyone, it seemed, wanted to divorce themselves from the scandal that was Maurice and protect their homes.

Peter credited the miraculous change of heart to Guyon's actions. *Amazing what having one man strip himself bare, literally and figuratively, can do to loosen people's tongues...*It was almost as if his very existence shamed them into doing what they should have all along.

He was hard put to it not to let his surprise - and his resentment - at the change show though, but the fact that Guyon behaved as though nothing had changed, as though only the information was relevant and nothing more, was enough to keep him from showing anything more than polite, surface gratitude.

"It wouldn't exactly help if I were to start screaming at them about hypocrisy, would it?" Guyon said wearily one night, sorting through yet another bundle of entirely useless documents, designed to prove that the sale of two cows had in fact been to another inhabitant of the area, and not to Spain. "After all, if I'd known scars had more effect than streaming blood, I'd have come back and walked around dressed in my breeches and no more years since...*honestly*, I am so *sick* of livestock!"

"Even the sheep?" Peter attempted to joke, but it fell flat with the weight of the mass of mundanity they were buried under. "Christ, and I thought estate paperwork was boring. But still, we're getting what we need, more or less."

"Mm," said Guyon. He appeared to be making a replica of Leonardo's flying machine out of three of the bills of sale. "Yes, they're all terribly, terribly innocent." He yawned. "I think someone should tell de Retz that innocence is boring. Vice, squalor and sin for me, please." The paper flying machine rather spectacularly failed to fly, traveling just as high as Guyon threw it and then plummeting straight back down. "Huh."

"I think your windage is off," Peter observed, picking up the contraption and handing it back. "Do we go through Maurice's papers next? Do you think he's stupid enough to leave anything useful for us?"

"That would be nice," Guyon said wistfully. "And yes. We can disprove our commission simply by boring everyone to death with it, I think. Any more proof of guiltlessness, and a conspiracy might be suspected - and we'd probably have to come back and try to disprove *that*, then. And...I suppose it wouldn't hurt to be thorough with Maurice." He laughed, not entirely in amusement. "I'm wearing gloves."

"You do that." Peter nodded. "I'm taking my sword."

"To stab papers?" Guyon brightened a bit. "What a marvelous idea. Can I do that to my students, when we get back?"

"No and no." Peter rolled his eyes. "But everything I've had to do with your uncle since I have arrived has been far too threatening. I just thought I'd threaten back...even if it is only estate books and old love letters."

"Love letters?" Guyon said in mostly unfeigned, if exaggerated horror. "Peter, that's a disgusting thought. I'm *definitely* wearing gloves."

Peter began attempting to make some order out of the chaos on the desk, "I didn't say it was requited love." He paused for a moment, "Actually, just the opposite might explain quite a lot."

Guyon's eyebrows raised. "Disappointment makes you insanely obsessed with your own version of right and wrong, and think you alone know God's true word?" He snorted. "That's a fairly appalling excuse, even for you trying to see the best in everyone."

"I wasn't trying to see the best. I'm actually doubtful that there is a best in your uncle's case." Peter picked up one scrap of paper and looked at it thoughtfully, "I was actually thinking about the poor object of his affections." Peter handed Guyon the paper in his hand, "What is this?"

"A piece of paper," Guyon said gloomily, looking at it cursorily, and then started to smile. "It's one of Corvay's strips. It's one of Corvay's missives! Where did you get that from? Whose pile?"

"This one..." Peter picked up a bill of lading. "Monsieur Philippe...doesn't that figure...Philippe Favoy. You know him?"

Guyon frowned. "I think so...he's one of the merchants in Carcassonne, a - *of course*. Bulk supplies. Corvay wants supplies stopped from going to the army!" He stared at the little paper in his hand. "Jesus God, we have him. Whether Favoy followed these instructions or not is irrelevant, we *have our proof*! You *genius*!"

Peter snorted, "No.. I merely spotted something that looked familiar. You are the one who deciphered it. But still, this scrap is very little as far as proof, don't you think? I want no chance that he can talk his way out."

"He sent it. It's signed in code, but it's signed. And if there's this? There *will* be more. Somewhere in all this mess, there are going to be five or six more of these. You know he never deals with only one person, and he might have known about Giraud, but he didn't deal with him directly - or if he tried, he was refused, and found a more...let's call it *subtle* - way." He made a face. "I'm not so sure about Maurice..."

"These..." Peter pointed at the slip in Guyon's hand. "They are so small...inconsequential nearly. It's possible your uncle could have overlooked one or two. Now that we know what we're looking for, we really need to search through his things."

"We do," Guyon agreed, his animation fading. "But I'm...afraid of what we might find. Not that it might condemn him, I - the more personal stuff." He sighed. "God, I'm a coward. How do you *stand* it?"

"I *stand it*, because it is utterly untrue." Peter frowned,

"Everyone has things they would prefer not to do. The proof of bravery is how you deal with those things."

"Right," Guyon agreed. "I'm strongly tempted to deal with it by means of a bottle of aguardente and unconsciousness." He made a small, wry face. "I won't. I'm just *tempted.*"

"Honestly, Gui, I'd do it alone, but I'm afraid I'd miss something important."

"As if I'd let you, anyway," Guyon said, and rubbed his hands over his face. "I tell you something, if there's anything in there that causes a repeat of the other night, I'm going down to that nice little cell of his, and slitting him open with a letter-opener, exile be damned." It was the first time he had admitted, however obliquely, to what Peter had suspected for a while, that while Guyon's demon-ridden night had been both frightening and unnerving, it had not been a unique incident since their arrival in the Languedoc. He wondered how often it happened in Paris, on the nights Guyon claimed work and left early, or sent him back to the Hôtel d'Orsay.

"It won't repeat." Peter told him. "I'm with you now. Together the two of us will hold them at bay and they will not touch you. You do know that, don't you?"

"No," Guyon said with weary, transparent honesty. "I don't. But I believe you when you say it." He sighed, and got to his feet. "All right. Let's get it over with. I'm not spending perfectly good time that I feel is designed for infinitely more pleasurable pursuits, worrying over what *might* be."

Peter stepped closer, slipping behind Guyon to whisper in his ear, "I promise you, we'll get this done, and then I will make sure that you won't have a single thought to trouble you. I will drive you into mindlessness, pleasure you so well that you will have no room left to think, only to feel."

It was a promise that Peter would enjoy keeping. He needed that escape, that release, as much as Guyon, and the thought of making Guyon incoherent, was a trial he was more than prepared to attempt.

"Oh, *bribery*," said Guyon, sounding both amused and far more content. "I like this. I *anticipate* this." His voice warmed into slightly tentative teasing. "Mindlessness, Peter? Good God,

371

how you value your skills!"

Peter chuckled, "I give my all for success.. And if I fail? I try again."

Guyon choked with unmistakably delighted laughter, and turned to kiss him. "A reminder of what you've promised," he said quietly. "Come on. Let's go and see whether Maurice ever washed his socks."

*

Maurice's room was not anything like Peter had ever imagined. In spite of the overall scruffiness of the rest of the house, and Maurice's own air of general neglect, his rooms were almost opulent. It was as if he had gone through the entire house and gathered anything of worth to keep in his rooms. The overall effect was that of an elegant rats' nest. Silk hangings on the bed, highly embroidered cushions on the chairs, the dresser and étagère covered with small pieces of art - carvings, statues, expensively framed miniatures.

"God. It's going to take forever to search through this." Peter almost groaned. Well, at least it was also much cleaner than they had expected, which had to be counted a plus.

"Only if you're expecting the curios to be *all* hollow and full of pa - oh, I remember this." Guyon's voice had changed completely as he picked up a small jade elephant, so pale as to seem almost transparent. "There's a whole set of them, there should be some with howdahs...God, that was an inspired toy, you almost can't break jade, you know -" He stopped, and looked over at Peter, going slightly pink. "I mean, the drawers first?"

"Yes...Drawers..." Peter smiled softly at Guyon. It was nice to see him relaxed after going through so much in the last few days. But relaxed he was and Peter would do his best to keep him that way. "You want desk or bureau?"

Guyon looked at both cluttered objects, and grimaced. "Oh Lord. Bureau, it looks more...er...papery." He rolled his eyes. "And my vocabulary improves by the day, have you noticed?"

"Anything that spares me the possibility of sorting through your uncle's underdrawers is fine with me, " Peter chuckled and moved to the desk. "Have fun."

Guyon blinked at him. "*Thank* you," he said, in tones that implied just the opposite. He began sifting through the top layer of clutter, breaking off only to wonder if Maurice had thrown anything out in his entire life.

"Hmmm...Dearest Maurice, I can't wait to see you again...My heart yards? No...yearns...." Peter held up a piece of paper to the light and read, "for the sight of you."

"Oh, please tell me you're making that up," Guyon said, sounding thoroughly nauseated.

"I am," Peter chuckled. "It's actually a tailor's bill...although what he might have had tailored I'm not sure, considering the look of his clothes."

"Linen, I would have thought," Guyon said absently. "He was reasonably clean, as a general thing. Hmm. Oh *lovely*, he kept a record of our activities, I *knew* the old bastard was -" He broke off with an exclamation of distaste. "Oh, now *I* need a bath," he said with feeling.

"What?" Peter moved to Guyon's side, a frown on his face. "What does it say?"

"It's a very *detailed* record," Guyon said, his face screwing up into a knot of unhappy revulsion. "Oh, including every moment of *attempted* 'intimacy', *aren't* you glad I kept refusing you?"

"In light of this...yes? But otherwise, no." Peter shook his head. "I just want to know how he got so...detailed. Was he watching us in our rooms? How?"

"Spyholes, I think - well, obviously, sorry, but - there must have been some added. Probably as soon as we chose the room." Guyon was evidently struggling against a fit of depression, nicely mixed with guilt. "And sound *does* carry, it's why my normal voice is always so low. I'd got into the habit well before I left here for Paris..." He flipped through the pages. "God, I treat you badly. I'm keeping this, to remind me."

"Don't." Peter reached out to touch his hand. "None of that's important. What is important is finding out who was helping him. No one man could have watched us that closely."

"Oh, just when I thought I couldn't feel sicker about it, you found a way," Guyon said. "Everyone who works outside, it seems, and your favorite kitchen boy - " He shook his head. "It wouldn't have occurred to any of them to do other than what he told them to."

Peter looked at the pages and sighed, "So...do we have to turn in the lot of them? Were they in on this little...scheme or just doing what Maurice told them to do? Yes, all right, I *know* they were doing what Maurice told them to do, but was it just because he's in charge or because they were part of the dissidents?"

Guyon looked at him for a long, blank moment, and then laughed, not the odd, choked noise that meant the amusement came from his own black pool of humor, or the sharp sound that always echoed with defeat, but the genuine sputter of delight that had been so rare since they left Paris. "Bèl-mi...most people here don't understand about dissidents. They're loyal to the families, to their lords, to the Seigneurie. They assume that's enough. I suppose it *is* dissension, but -" His hands went out, as though releasing a bird. "They don't even know what they are dissenting with."

Yes, Peter supposed that would be true of most of the people in the village at Hawthornden as well, loyal to the *Laird* and not much else. To each other, as well, but mostly to him and his family.

"Good. Even with this..." Peter waved a hand at the pages in Guyon's hand, "I'm just as glad that we don't have to turn them in. Of course, that does beg one other question."

"I shudder and tremble at the very thought," Guyon said, "but please, continue..." His eyebrows were starting to rise.

"Are they loyal enough that this," Peter waved his hand at the pages again, "will go no farther? Or at least not far enough to hurt you?"

"Or you," Guyon said quietly. "I don't much care what is said about me. But yes, to answer the question. They are."

Peter wasn't worried about himself. He was, after all, the Marshal of her Majesty's troops in France, and he doubted that much weight would be given to the scribblings of a few servants. Guyon however...

"Good. Good." He huffed out a breath and turned back to his inspection of the desk.

He heard Guyon let out an angry little breath behind him, but assumed it was to do with the cluttered layers of Maurice's bureau, rather than anything more personal, since he had, after all, accepted Guyon's word for the trustworthiness of the men in the area.

"Hmmmm...bill, bill, bill, document for transfer of ownership of perambulating clouds...bill," Peter frowned.

"Are any of the bills *paid*?" Guyon didn't sound very hopeful.

"Not that I can see, but they are all recent," Peter checked the dates again. "Looks like dear Uncle Maurice, decided to break the bank about the time he received your letter. Damn him. And...is he authorized to sell things from the estate?"

"Probably not," Guyon said wearily. "What's he been selling? And what, incidentally, has he been doing with the money if not paying bills?" He ran a hand over his head. "Oh hell, creditors. All we need."

"Looks like mostly livestock...but also some bits and pieces of furnishings and..." Peter held one paper closer to the light. "apparently quite a few acres of land to a Monsieur de Valette."

"Which acres?" Guyon asked, sounding worried. "I don't mind if he's selling off the grazing areas, especially if he's decided to go into cloud barter. But the vineyards are *not* to be touched, and I'll have to pay this de Valette their worth..." He sighed. "It would be so nice if de Tourvel had done what was asked and just kept an eye on things. I am *not* giving everything up to do what Giraud could not and manage this place. If necessary, I'll sell the lot and send Giraud the proceeds, but I'm not taking over as some unpaid and ungrateful bailiff."

"I'm not sure...it says land and gives acreage but I'm not familiar enough..." Peter walked over to where Guyon was standing and handed him the paper. "You look."

Guyon scowled at the paper for a moment. "Well, that's nonsense, the land doesn't exist," he said, chewing at his thumbnail. "I doubt de Valette will be pleased when he tries to use a fiction for functional purposes..." He made a small, impatient sound. "Why would anyone buy land unseen?"

"Stupidity...or because someone vouched for it...or..." Peter paused, his brain racing as he considered other possibilities.

"What if it wasn't really *land* that was bought?"

"Well, it wasn't," Guyon pointed out practically. "Since it doesn't exist. So what, then? De Valette doesn't exist either, and this is all money for -" He stopped, and groaned. "*Services rendered*," he said grimly.

"That would be my guess as well," Peter agreed. Of course this bit of paper, obviously, would not withstand close scrutiny, so that meant - "Guyon? I don't think your uncle was planning on remaining here much longer."

"Are you suggesting there is a God?" Guyon asked dryly, and then - "Oh. No, I suppose not, he must have known he'd be found out if he was accepting payments...they can always be tracked." He came over to the desk, peering at the papers there. "Let me see the bills, then..."

Peter gathered them up and carried them over to Guyon. "And here is a letter from a someone in Paris, about purchasing some...*objet d'art.* That explains this room a little. He'd gathered up anything that had value into one place, makes it a damn site easier to know what you've got. Also keeps people from noticing what's missing."

"Or *not* missing, even when supposedly sold." Guyon, as always, had gone straight from unhappy surprise into logical conclusions. "And not here, when bought. I think he was a money conduit, selling land that didn't exist to buy art that would never arrive. It's not a bad cover, really, no-one would check..." He waved a hand. "Except you, but then I don't think he expected anyone like you to arrive..." He frowned at the bills. "Oh," he said then, in a different tone of voice. "Oh, do you know, it would be so nice sometimes if I knew why Corvay hated me so much as to forget caution simply in order to twist the knife..."

"He hates you because you're more intelligent than he is," For Peter the answer was that obvious. "I don't mean that you know more, *although you do,* but you have a capacity for growth that he does not and never has had, It infuriates him."

"Enough," Guyon said with quiet venom, "to use the codes I devised for him with which to contact my uncle. He must have been laughing himself sick."

"Sick enough to die, one hopes." Peter grimaced and

continued with his sorting. "You have anything over there?"

"Yes," Guyon said, cold and angry. "Yes, I have something. We know where Martelle got the instructions as to *Carcassonne's brother*. Not Giraud, after all, Pèire-mi, you can stop hating him so." He sighed, and laid the papers to one side, a small, neatly accusing pile. "Maurice. All the time. Working for Corvay before he found either of us." He was white with temper. "So you can stop blaming yourself for my involvement, my friend. It seems you can lay all accusations firmly at my family's hearth."

Emotions flew through Peter like demented pigeons - anger, regret, guilt, anger again. Most of that directed at Corvay, but some for Maurice and yes, himself. "So Corvay knew all along that Giraud had nothing to do with this...and blackmailed you with it just the same?"

"Oh, Giraud would have been involved in something." Guyon gave him a small, apologetic smile. "Anything to do with Spain, and I've got no doubt he'd have been the first in line to offer assistance. But he had nothing to do with Corvay. *Knowingly*, at any rate. The blackmail was entirely appropriate."

"Hmpff," Peter snorted out a breath, not adding anything. Peter had reasons for hating Giraud that, of course, had nothing at all to do with his involvement with Spain, but Guyon already knew them and considering the events of the last few days, he did not wish to bring them up. "But does any of that link back to Corvay directly? The papers, I mean. They're written in your code?"

"Yes," Guyon said. "The last four, anyway, the earlier ones are in the autokey you first gave me." He laughed. "All so Corvay could run a war and prove his power. *Christ*. Not a single thing we've done has been for our countries. It's all been for Corvay and his own ends. *All* of it, right down to the warning we tried to send about the attack in May, which I'll wager never got - oh Christ, Peter, I'm *sorry*."

Peter had stiffened at Guyon's words. All that work, his and Guyon's. Trying so hard to get it done so that the King could be warned of Cromwell's plans - warned and prepared. And all of it in vain, because Corvay was trying to incorporate his power. Men had died. Some of them Peter had known. It was unacceptable.

377

"Guyon," Peter slipped into English as he often did when upset. "I don't care if any of this convicts the bastard or not. It's not going ta continue. I'll see him in Hell first, by my own hands."

Guyon closed his eyes, and nodded. "You should 'ave let me create proof," was all he said, referring back to their conversation in Douai. "I am so very sorry."

"Don't be sorry, Gui. You've done nothing. Just tell me that this is enough ta convict him. Or tell me what else we'll be needin'."

"It's enough. It's more than enough. It's straight treason, Peter, no matter what else he's done or what else he knows or what else we know. It will convict him."

Peter gave a tense nod, "Then lets get this all settled. Finish what needs finishin' and get back to Paris so we can put the bastard away."

"Yes." For some reason, Guyon was looking at him with sorrowful but unmistakable apology. "I will be as fast as I can." He smiled, then, crooked and unhappy and sincere. "I shall need a lot of ink."

Peter froze again, but for an entirely different reason this time, his French coming back to him just as quickly as it left. "Sorry, Gui. Sorry. I know this has all been - Just tell me what you need and what I can do to help."

"Just ink," Guyon said gently. "I have everything else I need. It's just...tidying, now. And then we can go."

Peter stepped forward and wrapped his arms around Guyon. "Ink...I can manage that. And a few other things."

"You manage a great many things," Guyon agreed, and brought a hand up, holding the back of Peter's neck. "Just - don't start managing guilt, please?"

"I'll try not to," Peter told him, and then gave a small grimace. "Lets take this all someplace else...back to our room. Then you can work on that...And I'll do my own work."

Guyon nodded. "There's not much of this to do, it stands as is. I just want to make copies. And *then* deal with the estate." He made a face. "And pass it to de Tourvel."

Peter nodded, "Of course, you know what I'll be doing..."

Guyon looked at him with the odd blankness that meant his

mind had already moved on to what *needed* to be done, rather than what was happening. "Er. No?" He blinked. "No, no idea."

"I, my most beloved, will be finding and covering every single damn spy hole in our room."

*

Climbing out of the magpie hodge-podge that was Maurice's room was a great relief to Peter. Even though it meant more time inside searching through the library, the work rooms and where ever else Guyon thought they might find anything of significance, at least he could do it without the fear of breaking either an ankle in the mess or breaking something else that might actually have some monetary or sentimental value. If he'd had to duck under Maurice's low hung chandelier one more time, he'd have developed a permanent hunch in his shoulders...and if he had forgotten to duck one more time, he was going to have a permanent lump on his still healing head.

The library, at least, had windows that opened easily to allow in light and air, and he could stand in his normal posture without fear of his life. All in all, he thought it was an improvement, even if all the books were badly in need of dusting.

"Aaaaachoooo! Damn..."

"Are you reacting to the number of words here, or the dust?" Guyon asked from his ridiculously comfortable-looking position on top of the book-ladder. Considering he was, in fact, balancing on a thin wooden platform that would have daunted a cat, he had no right to look even a quarter as relaxed as he did. He certainly should not have been swinging one booted foot as though he were in his preferred window seat.

"Yes!" Peter grumbled and scrubbed his kerchief over his nose. "Both, actually. Are you finding anything at all? Or have you simply become enthralled with what you're looking at?"

It would not surprise Peter in the least if Guyon had given over searching to read through a familiar text, he'd seen it often enough at home.

"No, and no," Guyon said dryly. "Or rather, yes and no. Or perhaps yes and yes." He chuckled. "I thought it might be something Maurice had annotated and used as code, the way we started doing before Douai, but it's just my father's inherent inability to leave anything alone without inserting notes about - hm. Drains, apparently. Good Lord."

Peter replied carefully. This was the first time he'd ever heard Guyon speak of his father so easily and he did not want to spoil the mood. "Yes, Uncle William used to do the same. I have books on the Peloponnesian wars that are so scribbled over that the original text is almost a mystery."

"If it's Thucydides, it's a mystery *anyway*," Guyon pointed out. "Good God, I will never be a householder while I have the choice left to me, if it does this to your mind. A whole script's worth of commentary on the effects of jackdaw nests, and the man wasn't even writing some coded message or metaphor. He had, in fact, carefully examined the kind of twigs that had the most deleterious effects on guttering." There was a faint snort from the top of the ladder. "Fascinating though the workings of his mind are, I do *not* think this is helpful. Especially since Maurice and Corvay are more akin to the workings of sewers than gutters, and less helpful than both."

Peter carefully stepped up on the bottom step of the ladder, peering over the top of the page, "Your father, however, seems to have enjoyed it a great deal. He must have, to have spent so much time on such a trivial subject."

"I think he was just easily sidetracked by a new concept and needed to investigate it thoroughly before putting it in the stacks that passed for his mental storage," Guyon said with a faint, wry smile, obviously fully aware of how familiar that would sound to Peter. "It was certainly a private enjoyment, if it went any further than that..."

"But still, I'm thinking most of the disrepair here can be laid at Maurice's feet, not your father's." Peter ventured cautiously. "And even if neither you nor I enjoy the mundane trials of being a householder, we both know how to accomplish it, how to keep things running. You don't just learn that on your own." Peter paused there, "Unless you're going to tell me you 'read it in a book'?"

"Well, some of it, obviously," Guyon said lightly, "but no, by observation. I used to -" He shrugged. "It was a way of being with him. I pretended to help at first, and later I got real tasks to do, and then at the end -" He stopped. "At the end it didn't matter to anyone but Giraud, so I suppose I should be grateful to him," he finished flatly, his comfortable slouch turning into something more resembling a coiled spring as he realised how close had come to talking of the things he never mentioned to anyone. Peter, as was becoming horribly common, found himself quite unexpectedly resenting François, both for knowing so much of this before he had even met Guyon, and for being dead and so unable to pass on either help or information.

But since none of that would be the least bit helpful, he simply leaned in, and rubbed his cheek, catlike, against Guyon's now tense shoulder, "I...I wish you'd tell me about him Gui...He seems like he was rather amazing in spite...or maybe because...of what he was. I want you to meet all of my family, and I'd like to know a bit more of yours than just Maurice."

"Oh, Maurice is a fair enough representation, as far as such things go," Guyon said with a small shrug. "I don't know, really. He was...fascinated by the unknown, I suppose. Brave." He breathed out a half-laugh. "He should have been a Templar or born five hundred years ago and gone on a Crusade. They might have found something to occupy him there."

It would have suited Astor de Chesnay, Peter was certain - probably because it would have suited him as well. "Sarah claims that's what Rupert dragged me off to. She wasn't best pleased when I became a soldier, even if it meant that she and Robbie got Hawthornden to themselves."

Peter was trying to relax Guyon, give information as well as receive it, trying to make it all as easy as possible. He wanted to know Guyon's father, through Guyon - partly because he knew Astor's death still affected him so strongly, and partly from a very real curiosity.

"Peter, believe me, you are very far from being like my father." Guyon's voice was hard. "I said he *was* brave. He stopped being that when he decided that rather than survive in pain, he would leave the rest of us to endure it for him and take his own life. I'm like him, I have that same cowardice, that same weakness, but you? Never in this world."

It seemed that relaxed conversation and Astor did not, in fact, go together.

"Everyone has their weaknesses." Peter argued softly. "Everyone."

This was a fact that Peter firmly believed in and more so, he knew exactly where his own lay - not five inches away, wearing a face like a thundercloud, lightning flashing in his eyes.

"And I have more than most, yes, granted," Guyon said snappishly. Apparently perfect honesty between them did nothing whatsoever to improve his temper or soften his approach - then again, very little other than unconsciousness had ever achieved either of those things, so it shouldn't have been a surprise. "I come from a glorious heritage of belief, truly! To think that it is acceptable when mourning to either summon the spirits of the dead or to follow them - what would you call that, a family likeness?"

"I call it love." Peter said quietly. "Sad and heartbreaking, but still love. Love like you had for me. Love that got me home from Toulouse. Love that brought you after me in the Grotte. I'm sad that loneliness brought your father to his end...but I *can* understand it."

"Oh, I understand it," Guyon said, and sighed, the tension going from him along with his annoyance. "I also feel it. The one thing I don't have to do is like either fact. And it wasn't loneliness - or not just loneliness - it was obsession. I am - that worries me. That I already am. That it's too late, all I've ever wanted to avoid becoming, I've always been." He hunched up one shoulder, protective and apologetic and a little defiant all at once. "I just managed to ignore the possibilities for a long time."

Peter dropped his head, unsure of just what Guyon was saying. Did he meant that he was having second thoughts about what was between them? That he felt their love had made him weak? "I think we're stronger together. The two of us. We complement and strengthen each other. *I* could never regret it."

"I don't regret it," Guyon said, sounding surprised. "Is that what you thought I meant? No, I regret who and what I am, but not - I don't regret that I love you." He said it with perfect ease, as though he were still talking about books and papers and drains - not the stilted casual words that he used to describe his father, but the quick unthinking calm that meant he had not even needed to consider which words he used. "I don't know about stronger, though - although yes, perhaps in some ways...hmm..." He trailed off, lost in thought, following his own mind into the strange tangents that Peter could still not quite anticipate.

"But Gui..." Peter hesitated, "...all that you are - who and what - that is what I love. Vaguely infuriating or dryly amusing...confusing as Hell or crystal clear...all of you. And I never think you weak...I've had too much proof of the opposite."

Guyon looked at him, his eyebrows raised to an almost ludicrous height. "Good God, you're deluded," he said, and grinned, suddenly and surprisingly. "By all means, remain so, it's an enchanting view of the world!"

Peter smiled sweetly in return and pushed Guyon off the ladder.

"Unlike this," Guyon said in a mildly pained voice, having saved himself from worse than a bruised side by virtue of catching one of the rungs with his right hand as he fell. "Ow."

"Yes...Vaguely infuriating..." Peter nodded, and crossed his arms, lounging back against the ladder, "but never weak. Although, we do need to work on your balance."

"My balance," Guyon said in the prim tones of an outraged maiden aunt, "is indisputably magnificent." His mouth twitched, a tiny betrayal of his desire to laugh. "Unlike that of the ladder," he added kindly, just as the runners yielded to pressure and moved the whole thing sideways.

Peter let out an undignified yip as he jumped away from it, landing safely, if somewhat inelegantly next to Guyon. "Yes, yes...I'll bet you think that's justice, don't you?"

"And considering where we are, of the poetic variety," Guyon agreed serenely. His eyes gleamed with what Peter had no doubt was utterly unholy amusement.

"God, I love you like this..." Peter laughed, "My own demented academic. Are you going to let me kiss you or are you going to shove me away and say we're still being watched?"

He leaned in closer, not *quite* touching Guyon.

"Oh, if we're being watched?" Guyon didn't even seem to need to breathe before he responded, it was so quick. "Let's give them a purpose to it. And no, I won't *let* you do anything. But I might, on the other hand, actively encourage you..." He *was* breathing. Peter was close enough to feel the faint warmth on his skin, somehow more of a physical presence than the light hand on his arm.

It felt even warmer against his lips. Warmer still as he drank it in with his kiss, his arms pulling Guyon closer. Then inferno hot as his entire body awakened to this - this joy that was his love. His love and his lover, his friend, his demented academic, all that he wanted, whether Guyon was his father's son or not.

*

Guyon, who found copying dull, and estate management worse, spent a great deal of time allowing small splatters of ink to drop from his quill onto the strips of trimmed paper he was using to check originals against his own work, as he watched Peter turn their room upside down looking for spyholes.

"I don't think," he said in slow amusement, "that there will be one in the outside wall."

"I'm not taking any chances," Peter muttered as he stared at the window frame. "And besides, I'm fixing this as well. I'm tired of feeling that icy draft when I get out of bed."

"It's summer, the draft is warmer than the inside," Guyon couldn't resist pointing out. "Peter, when I said tidying, I didn't mean I wanted you to fix the whole house, you know? Not that you're not more interesting than the precise cocktail of soil and gravel needed for vines, but..."

"Estate work is always boring to me. Yours. Mine. Anyone's. That's why Robbie runs Hawthornden and not me." Peter explained. "You acted like you knew nothing of sheep, Gui. Nothing at all. And you probably spent just as much time around them as I did." Peter was grinning and amused and utterly relaxed. Apparently being with someone who was poring over arable plans was a morning entirely to his taste.

"Yes," Guyon said vaguely. "I was a seven year old expert,

384

and the knowledge has remained with me to this day, I found it all so intriguing." He rolled his eyes. "Don't be an idiot."

Peter bumped his shoulder, jogging his arm just as he tried to make a notation on one of de Tourvel's careful plans. The nib skittered across the page in a series of small splodges, and Guyon sighed in exasperation. "*Peter* -"

"You just liked giving me a hard time."

"I *also* liked giving you a hard time, yes," Guyon said in cheerful agreement.

"I do sort of love you, you know?"

Guyon flicked ink at him, undeterred by the sentiment. "Oh good, that means you can stop babbling on about useless woolly quadrupeds and read up on how to drain marshland."

"Hey...wool soaks up a lot of water." Peter's lip twitched, and Guyon snorted.

"You know," he said, feeling rather aggravated, "obsession isn't actually an attractive look on you..."

"Even when it's you I'm obsessed with?" Peter moved impossibly closer. "Does that make a difference?" He dropped his chin onto Guyon's shoulder, and kissed his ear.

Guyon groaned. "I'm never going to get this done, am I?" he enquired rhetorically of the ceiling, then pushed his papers to the side. "Obviously, but then I have my priorities in the right order..."

Peter chuckled into Guyon's neck. "Do you want me to behave? I can, you know. I did for a very long time."

Guyon shook his head, half-laughing. "You were a complete distraction, whether you behaved or not, and no, I don't want you to."

"I was a distraction?" If the morning sun wanted competition, it had it now, the smile Peter wore was just that bright. "How?"

"Because to my great chagrin, I found I was more interested in paying attention to you than my books." Guyon's smile was rueful, as he turned round in his chair. "Not so much a distraction as a change in world order, I'm afraid."

From sunshine bright to a carp impersonation in only a few moments, it was an amazing sight. "I...I distracted you when you were still at the school?"

385

Guyon's eyebrows shot up. "Well, yes," he said patiently, "of course you did. I suspect I was alarmingly close to writing terrible troubadour allegories, in fact. Fortunately, self-respect took over."

Peter closed his eyes and shook his head, laughing at himself. "I had absolutely no idea. I thought you were only tolerating me because you felt sorry for me."

"Yes, my toleration levels have always been renowned," Guyon said with a snort, "and as to my ability to feel sorry for people, well, I hear it's unparalleled." He shook his head, and got up from his chair, before putting his hand on the side of Peter's face. "I thought you were too kind to admit you saw through me. Does that make us equal in ignorance, then?"

"At the very least," Peter nuzzled into the hand. "Thank goodness we seem to have grown up a bit."

Guyon laughed quietly. "That wasn't hard to achieve, you must admit."

"No other way to go, I'd imagine." Peter leaned in, resting his forehead against Guyon's.

"Mm, no." The main difference was that Guyon was willing to be distracted these days, and perfectly content to remain so. "And you need to either make sure that damn door is bolted, or leave me to paperwork."

Without a word, Peter crossed over and bolted the door, leaning back against it.

"That wasn't very industrious of you," Guyon said amusedly, before walking over and kissing him thoroughly.

Peter gave a contented sigh when he was finally released, "I do not feel in want of industry at the moment, thank you..."

"Really?" Guyon looked even more amused. "Is laziness the order of the day, then?"

"No...I believe this is the order of the day." Peter pulled him in for another kiss, long and languid.

The noise Guyon made was close to a hum, but quieter, contented-sounding. He leant in, slightly off-balance, gripping Peter's shoulders.

Sliding his hands down Guyon's back, Peter pulled him closer yet, tight against him, "I do believe you have discovered my favorite field of study."

"The duty of all licensed tutors," Guyon agreed solemnly, but his voice slurred slightly over the consonants. Peter's hands slid up under his loose shirt, and Guyon leant forward slightly, pressing his open mouth to Peter's throat, feeling the long-fingered hands move over his body with the surety of ownership.

"I will be sure to apply myself to this," Peter gasped slightly at the feel of lips and teeth moving over his throat, and ground his hips against Guyon's, his growing erection bumping against a matching one, in a firm greeting.

Guyon couldn't keep his hands still, fingers twining in Peter's hair, slipping under his shirt collar to caress his skin. He was dizzy from want, nothing but his own weight, pressing forward, kept him upright. "Christ." The exclamation was almost amused. "Let me get on the bed. Or at least on the floor..." He laughed, then, the humor inward-turning as ever.

"Yes...now..." Peter's words were a demanding growl. "Where?"

Guyon's eyes glittered. "Well, I was thinking here, but if you have a preference for another room, I'm sure I can try to accommodate that..."

"Guyon..." Another growl, and Peter bent down, picking him up over his shoulder and carrying him to the bed.

"Bastard," Guyon said laconically, and bit his shoulderblade.

"God..." Peter paused for a moment as a shudder of reaction shook through him. He panted for three breaths then settled them both on the bed.

Guyon reached for him, his hands a little unsteady, not as unmoved as his voice would have suggested. He kissed Peter quickly, aimlessly, with none of the precise erotic focus he had shown before, his mouth twisted in a little quizzical smile. "What?"

"That was..." Peter looked down at him. "You bit me..." The tone of voice was strange, breathy, not like his usual self.

Guyon drew back slightly, a faint smile of puzzled agreement quirking at one corner of his mouth. "Mm, and so?"

For the first time since Guyon had known him, Peter blushed with something more than embarrassment, "It...felt good."

Guyon's gaze turned speculative. "*Did* it?" The faint smile turned into a grin, and he brushed a hand over the open neck of Peter's shirt, drawing the collar to one side and over his shoulder. He watched in fascination as Peter's skin shivered, and pressed a kiss above the collarbone, then repeated the action, letting his teeth be felt through his tight lips.

A loud moan escaped Peter's lips and his skin turned an even rosier shade, "Gui...please..."

Guyon stopped and looked at Peter, his eyes warm and wicked at once. "That's new to you. How interesting." He leaned in again and breathed delicately on the target, cold after the warmth of his mouth, and pressed his hard lips to the same spot again, blunt teeth not-quite breaking skin, ruthless pleasure.

"Oh, God," Peter moaned, eyes drifting shut. "You are delighting in tormenting me, aren't you?" One eye opened. "Don't stop."

"Wasn't planning to, no," Guyon agreed. He punctuated the statement with a catlike flicker of his tongue, warmth amidst the cool air he was breathing onto the reddened skin, interspersed kisses and small bites with gentler caresses, his hands soothing over Peter's sides and chest under the shirt.

"Oh, Gui, you...that's just..." Whatever it was became lost in an insistent rattling of the door handle, and a series of thuds that were probably kicks.

"God *damn* it!" Guyon snapped.

"Guyon? I thought you wanted these books." It was Jeannine. "Why is the door bolted?"

Guyon slammed his hand over Peter's mouth. "Do *not* answer that," he said urgently, and scrambled off the bed, before tipping half the covers over Peter. "Stay." He went to the door, and unbolted it, before opening it wide enough to slip out of. "Books," he said flatly, mouth quirking in skeptical query. "Oh yes, so I see. Two whole books. My, my. I must truly have impressed you with my urgent need of them." His expression was scathing.

"Well, you said you wanted them...you didn't say when." Jeannine peeked around him. "Did I wake you...you look..." She took in Guyon's disheveled clothing, her eyes traveling down him with not one bit of embarrassment, "Well, sort of sleepy..."

"The word you're looking for is interrupted," Guyon said bluntly, "the word for you is unwanted, and the next phrase I will teach you is go away. Are we clear?"

"I interrupted?" She peeked past him again. "What did I interrupt? I thought you said you were working on how to drain that piece of land over by the lake."

Guyon looked at her with narrowed eyes. "I am." He stepped sideways, blocking any chance she had at looking through the doorway. One thin eyebrow arched in challenge. "And?"

Jeannine looked at him with a frustrated frown, "I thought maybe Peter was here...helping you."

"Yes, and so?" Guyon's voice began to sharpen with real temper. He was not going to have even a variation on this discussion where Peter might hear.

"My, you are grouchy." Jeannine looked at him. "Perhaps you should take a nap. It might make you less so."

"What a superb idea," Guyon said with emphasis. "In that case, you'll excuse me." He took the books from Jeannine's hand, and inclined his head with as much politeness as he could muster.

"Do you know where Peter is?" Jeannine asked before he could shut the door. "Father wanted me to ask him to stop by later..."

Guyon leant his head on the door frame, and gave himself over to slightly hysterical laughter, muffling it with one arm. "Of course he does," he said eventually. "Tell him Peter will be by later. Now go away."

"Well, there's no need to be so grumpy..." Jeanine turned and flounced off down the hall.

Guyon looked up at the gallery ceiling, and wondered for what felt like the thousandth time why he had ever thought coming back would be even possible. "Christ," he growled under his breath, and went back into the room, rebolting the door with force, and banging the books down hard on the desk.

From the look of the bed, there was either an ongoing, very localized earthquake, or Peter was having convulsions. He had bit down on the corner of one of the pillows, trying to muffle the laughter that was rolling through him uncontrollably.

"Oh, keep laughing," Guyon said sourly. "Really." He was thoroughly bad-tempered.

"But you...And she ...'did I wake you?' " Peter went off in another roll of laughter.

"And when you've quite finished," Guyon said acidly, "perhaps you would like to consider just how funny it would have been had the door not been locked? Or if you had answered it? Truly, cause for mirth, but forgive me if I don't quite find it in me to share it!"

Peter suddenly sobered, "First off, the door was locked. We made sure of it, just as always. Second, do you think I would be ashamed to be found in your rooms? That I'm ashamed that I love you? I know we can't go out and shout it from the roof tops but Christ!"

"No," Guyon said, holding onto his temper by virtue of clenching his hands around the edge of the desk, "I don't think either. I think Jeannine is a God-damned menace, is what I think!"

"She's just a little girl, Gui...Silly and curious and trying hard to learn to be a grown up. And she's afraid." Peter climbed off the bed, his clothing still undone and hanging on his lean frame. "And she's lonely."

Guyon nodded sharply. "I know. I do know, and I'm going to at least get her out of here, but I cannot stand this being - being watched all the time! All she has to do is say one wrong thing -" He broke off. "I'm sorry. Of course, you're right, she wouldn't. I'm being absurd."

"She'd never do anything to hurt you, Gui. She really does like you." Peter lifted one hand and placed it against Guyon's cheek. "But you're right...being watched is getting to me too."

"Not for much longer," Guyon said. "The price may be Jeannine's company, but I was done with this place six years ago. It hasn't changed."

*

Guyon had given his word to Jeannine that he would get her to Paris, but he had not envisaged quite how disappointed her

390

father was at the agreement they had come to. Not that he did not understand that his ferociously brilliant child deserved better than the home that had once been designed for the large family he had dreamed of, and a father whose main ties now were to the past, but he had imagined her as settled, going off to something stable of her own, a new family and a new life that would be something he could understand as well as something she needed.

But Guyon had no intention of tying either himself or Jeannine to the things they so desperately wanted to leave, not by some mockery of a sacrament or some dispassionate agreement of a loveless legality that would keep them both safe, and, as kindly as he could, he was repeatedly making that clear to de Tourvel, thanking God for the fact that simple courtesy prevented the Captain from trying the same suggestions on Peter.

"Really, Monsieur, Madame de Neuillant has received many such commissions," Peter tried to reassure the Captain. "She guides her charges in proper behavior for both town and Court, if they are so blessed as to have an entrance there. And I promise you, she will have any help that I can offer."

Guyon had several rapid and nightmarish images cross his mind in quick succession, mostly involving the list of ingredients that Madame de Neuillant had given him when Peter had dyed his hair and skin with walnut and oak-leaf juice. "Rose petals," he muttered involuntarily, and Peter kicked him.

De Tourvel gave the two of them an odd look, "She's respectable? And more importantly, will she love my girl and take good care of her? I know she's smart and witty but she's bound to be at least a bit homesick. She's never been away before."

"She is highly thought of by the Court and by the Church," Guyon said smoothly. "And I don't know whether she will *love* Jeannine, but she will certainly protect her and keep her busy." He didn't dare meet Peter's eyes, in case one or the other of them thanked God for the fact of Jeannine's potential occupation audibly.

"Well, not too busy to write home, I hope..." de Tourvel gave a small sigh of acceptance and then a laugh as the doors flew open admitting Jeannine.

"I knew you'd say yes! I knew!" She threw herself into her

father's surprised arms and kissed his face. "Thank you! Thank you!"

"Paris," Guyon muttered under the sound of her delighted exclamations, "will be paying for assassins." He jerked his head towards de Tourvel. "For *him*, when they find out he said yes."

"Guyon -" Peter began, but was interrupted when Jeannine, obviously far more excited than even he had suspected, bounced out of her father's arms and planted a damp teary-eyed kiss on Guyon's cheek.

"Thank you too, Guyon."

"And perhaps you could never say that in public," Guyon said with acid kindliness, stepping back and kissing her hand politely. "I won't be misconstrued by your gratitude, thank you all the same."

Jeannine withdrew her hand, laughing, and turned toward Peter, who took a step back and held up his hands.

"No thanks necessary...really," but he winked at de Tourvel who grinned and slapped him on the back.

"You're too tall to kiss anyway," Jeannine giggled and went back to her father's side.

Guyon ran a hand over his face, concealing a very real urge to laugh. "Yes, I shall talk to Madame about getting you shoes that will stop that from being a problem, in future," he agreed. "One day you may wish to kiss someone even taller than Peter, and then where would you be if you can't reach?"

"Pssh..." Jeannine waved her hand. "I shall just carry my Latin crib with me where ever I go. I will look intellectual and have something to stand on in case of such an occurrence."

"Jeannine," de Tourvel spoke up then. "Please, leave your poor Papa at least some nerves. I'm worried enough about you as it is."

"Yes, you surely don't think that a crib book would make you look intelligent, do you?" Guyon asked, feigning worry. "Good thing you're sending her away, Cap, that's almost embarrassing..."

"And besides that," Peter added in. "carrying something that heavy could lead to embarrassing muscles. Something a lady would never admit to having."

Jeannine looked at Peter and nodded, obviously taking his

word as truth. Guyon on the other hand, who knew he was merely passing on something he'd heard his sister say, had to hold back a snort. Peter and women were never an easy mix, and he wouldn't notice if she were built like the slenderest willow or had muscles like Atlas.

"Cap, I want you to take control of the estates," Guyon said abruptly. "I don't want to ever have to come back here. If something goes wrong, I trust you to deal with it."

"Um," said Jeannine. "I think...this is where I go and pack." She dropped them all a neat little curtsey, and turned to go. "*I'll* come back, you know," she said suddenly. "One day."

"Damn right you will," de Tourvel called after her. "I'm not going to Paris just to get a glimpse of you."

He sighed as the door shut with a click, then turned back to Guyon, "Yes...I had a feeling you'd want something like that."

"But you hoped otherwise?" Guyon still found it hard to feel real kindness towards de Tourvel, these days. If the voices in the night had all but gone, the dream-hazed memories had not, leaving him constantly aware of the ways de Tourvel had seen him exposed, humiliated - and how he had watched and never once moved to try and intervene or save. "I never gave anyone reason to hope that."

"No...no you didn't," de Tourvel was quick to agree. "But I some how I still hoped. Ah, well, what is it that you wish me to do? Hire a bailiff? Oversee him? I'm not sure I can manage it all alone."

"No." Guyon shook his head. "I want more than that. A bailiff, yes, but I need someone who knows about the vineyards. And wine. Giraud will need money, and I - am finding I might not object as much as I thought to a little. Oversee them both, by all means, but I want this place as nothing more than lands and produce. No more enshrined religion, no more of my family save the name. Turn Margarittes into whatever will pay. Maybe in time...we'll be forgotten. I think I would like that."

De Tourvel nodded slowly, "I was rather expecting that as well."

Bright blue eyes were watching him, Guyon knew, but Peter kept his counsel to himself for the moment.

"You once said I had the ability to go where no-one would find me," Guyon said quietly. "I'm - thinking of going somewhere where no-one will *want* to find me. I'll write, from there, but - I would like it...I would *prefer* it -" This was harder than he had thought. "I would prefer it if you forgot you knew anything of me but my name."

Once again he felt Peter's eyes on him, heavy with questions this time, questions that he did not want to answer here. He kept his eyes glued on de Tourvel instead.

"Yes...I..." the Captain was almost speechless. "I see. I suppose I understand that. I'm sorry that you feel that way, but I understand it."

"Thank you," Guyon said quietly. "Tell Jeannine to be ready to leave the day after tomorrow. I won't make life harder for you by giving her less than a day in which to pack." He brought out a folded paper. "This is a list of the inns I propose to break our journey at." He knew that he sounded like the stiffest and most uncaring being alive, but as ever, he could put no emotion that he truly felt into his voice.

"I'll be sure she's ready. She can take our carriage, never use it much anyway," de Tourvel nodded. "Just...treat her well, Gui. She's all I have...and..."

"She'll be safe," Peter stepped in to reassure the older man. "I'll make sure of that."

Thank God for Peter, Guyon thought for the hundredth time in his life. *I can't offer anything any more, not even my word. All I want is Corvay's destruction, and I can't think beyond that, I can't care for more than that. He's played countries like chess, and men for his pawns, and all I can truly think of is stopping him in any way I can.* "I promise," he said in his most prosaic tones, "only to beat her for five minutes on the hour every other Wednesday."

"What -?" de Tourvel looked at him for a moment, then continued dryly, "That will be a treat for her. I usually do that on Thursdays."

Peter snorted, and the atmosphere once again returned to a more relaxed state and remained so until they took their leave five minutes later.

*

Peter felt some relief that their travel plans were finalized, that Guyon had arranged all, and that they were leaving so soon. He did, however feel a bit of uneasiness over some of what Guyon had said to de Tourvel.

You once said I had the ability to go where no-one would find me

*I'm - thinking of going somewhere where no-one will **want** to find me.*

Surely those words were directed to de Tourvel alone. Guyon was going no where without Peter if it could be prevented. Or so Peter hoped.

"Gui?" Peter spoke up on their ride back to Margarittes. "I have a question."

"Mm?" Guyon didn't sound forbidding, just mildly interested. "Ask away."

"Are you truly going away?" Peter tried to make his voice as steady and nonchalant as possible. "Aside from back to Paris, I mean."

Guyon gave him a look of utter puzzlement. "We're going to Scotland, aren't we?" he asked. "Or has that changed? Oh well, no matter."

"I had thought we were, but from what you said to de Tourvel..." Peter gave an eloquent shrug. "...It sounded like you were going somewhere alone. And not very pleasant if no one would ever want to find you there. But if that's what you want..."

Guyon's mouth twitched, and his eyes lit up with a familiar unholy glee. "Peter, you do *remember* what everyone thinks of Scotland, don't you? *No-one* would want to come and find me. Absolutely no-one. As to alone..." He shook his head. "Not if it's my choice, no."

"Oh." Peter was silent for a long moment, before he spoke up again, "It *is* my home you know."

"And you *did* invite me," Guyon agreed serenely, before pulling his horse to a stop. "Alright, I confess. I wanted to worry him, and I wanted to hurt him, and I wanted to do it in style while all he can think is that I might let Jeannine down. Because God knows, *I* never needed anyone not to let me down, did I? So I indulged in overstatement and melodrama, and I expect he'll be vaguely relieved when he finds out where I've really gone." He shrugged. "It was childish. I know."

"No. It's understandable. Very understandable." Peter let out a long slow breath. "But I don't really ever think of Hawthornden as someplace people would avoid. I thought you'd changed your mind." Peter looked out over the vineyards. "I'm sorry."

"I'm getting very good at shooting my arrow over the house, aren't I?" Guyon said ruefully. "I think a definite moratorium on apologies is called for. I may love you, but I do not love the rest of the world. And I don't want to hurt you, but sometimes I do, because there are times when I *do* want to hurt everyone else, and you ...ah, you're there, and it's inadvertent. If I'd thought, I'd have said something else, because I certainly don't think of Hawthornden as a place to avoid." He paused, and when Peter turned back to look at him, he saw that Guyon's neck and face were patched with embarrassed red. He shrugged, and half-smiled. "It's your home. How could I?"

Peter gave a snort of amusement, "Because it's cold and on a rock and surrounded by sheep? Actually sheep, not ambulatory clouds. And because my sister is there and although she loves me you're not sure how she's going to take the fact that *I* love *you?*"

"But that's just fear." Guyon really smiled then, the sudden brilliant look of joy that Peter would never get used to in fifty years. "They say it keeps you healthy, you know. It's your *home*, Peter. You think I care about anything except that it matters to you? I'll wear socks and learn about sheep and I'll send for every fashionable frippery from Paris for your sister, and none of it will matter, because it is you and yours."

"Then you'd better put spur to that decrepit beast," Peter told him. "Because I have the sudden urge to kiss you senseless and I really can not do it here."

Guyon's eyebrows flickered upwards. Then his smile turned into a look of pure devilry, as he suddenly and surprisingly did just what Peter had suggested, not letting up until they were actually in the courtyard, and it was impossible to tell if he was more breathless from laughter or the ride.

*

Thank God they were leaving. It was a litany that pounded through Peter's head as he helped Guyon make their few preparations for their own departure. A few new servants were hired, neither of them really trusting anyone who served Maurice, but the rest Guyon left in de Tourvel's more than capable hands.

Peter's latest batch of dispatches had shown him no good news. The war raged on. King Charles had made Oxford his capital, but eventually the city had surrendered to Parliament. There had been word that the King was safe, at least, although held by the Scots. First near Oxford, then Nottingham, now actually in Scotland, if the reports were to be believed. Word of Rupert was even sketchier, although they had heard reports of him harrying ships throughout the Irish sea, stopping supplies from reach Parliamentarian troops.

And then there was Charleon, the damnable boy. He should be with his mother, giving her support, but instead he was off in the channel Isles, isolated even from Rupert, as if this whole thing was just some grand romp activated merely for his pleasure.

The whole thing frustrated Peter to no end. He wasn't sure where he should be or what he should be doing, other than having the forcible conviction that it was *not* here or doing this.

Guyon, unsurprisingly, was at once more resigned and more unhappy about the situation. He was under no illusions that he could do anything to change events, and laboring under a great deal of guilt that he had been oblivious to the time when he could have at least prevented Corvay's interference. His only attempt at alleviating Peter's frustration had ended up very close to reigniting all their old arguments - for Guyon's idea of consolation, inevitably, was to point out that the war was over, that Parliament had won, that there was nothing more for anyone to do.

He appeared to have blithely forgotten the fact that Peter was both Royalist and Scot, that the monarch he was sworn to was being held prisoner by his own countrymen, and his loyalties were, for once, forcibly divided. Guyon, who had forsworn his country for his boy-king years before, was wholly incapable of sympathy on the subject, though he was as patient as he could be with Peter's frustration and longing to do anything other than continue the last measures of Corvay's Languedoc dance.

So, mostly they both just did what they could do, the mechanics of their leave taking filling up enough hours to keep arguments at bay, at least with each other. By this point, Guyon had new servants to direct, and Peter, somehow, had been corralled by an overly excited Jeannine, who was demanding he tell her about Madame de Neuillant, her lodgings, her habits, and who her friends were. That was where the more obvious storm was brewing, as Peter's affection for that bastion of society barely extended beyond polite formality on most occasions, in spite of his recommending her to de Tourvel.

"Will she teach me about politics?" Jeannine demanded, and without waiting for a response, swung on Guyon. "Or will *you*? Not that you know any." She sniffed. "All *book*-learning." It was perfectly evident that she was spoiling for a fight to rid her of some of her tension, and equally obvious that Guyon had no intention whatsoever of gratifying her, as evidenced by the studious calm with which he looked up at her from his work.

"I am, indeed, a political babe-in-arms," he said over Peter's badly stifled snorting fit. "Ask anyone in Paris. Should you wish to take an interest in politics, I have no doubt that one of Madame's lovers will be well-versed in all such dealings."

"Lovers? She has lovers.. Like more than one?" Jeannine rounded back on Peter. "Is she delightfully wicked? Do dashing strangers vie to share one night in her arms?"

"Why do you ask me?" Peter snorted. "All I can say in truth is that *I* will never be one of them."

"She has power and influence," Guyon said in the same calm voice, "and believe it or not, one may possess both those things and be entirely without wickedness. Guile, deceit, and outright falsehood, however, are her stock-in-trade." He grinned. "They'd *have* to be, really, she's bound to have to exaggerate now and again."

"Oooh." Jeannine smiled smugly, as though she had discovered a marvelous secret. "You *like* her."

"Yes, I do," Guyon agreed serenely, and went back to his papers. "She's well-read, intelligent, amusing, and impossible to bully. She also has a marvelous line in skin remedies and an appalling sense of humor as to how one should pay for them." His smile was as closed and secretive as Jeannine's when he looked up a second time, and all of it private and for Peter. "I like her very much indeed."

And that, Peter thought, was probably why he, himself, did not. Although, he was not jealous of Guyon's liking for the Madame, he felt all at sea in her company - big and stupid in a way that the scholars had never made him feel. When she was present Court just felt more like *Court*. More puzzling than ever and a place he could never hope to actually fit.

"What're you doing, anyway?" Jeannine peered over Guyon's shoulder. "Oh, *codes*. Dull. You just love making everything more difficult than it needs to be."

"Well, so do you," Guyon retorted, "and at least I have the courtesy to keep my complications on paper."

"*Nice*," Jeannine said scathingly. "You could at least tell me what they are..." She had her best coaxing look on.

"No, I couldn't," Guyon said cheerfully, "because *I* will only turn traitor when something a damn sight more worthwhile is offered to me than the faint hope of your silence. Speaking of those who don't turn traitor, I'm going to need Peter's help in a few minutes, so go and find something else to do, please."

"But I'm packed, I think, and ready and....." Jeannine sighed at the irritated and resolved look on Guyon's face. "I suppose I should spend as much time with father as I can before I leave. He will miss me so."

"It's so sad that he's lost his mind," Guyon agreed inflectionlessly, and Jeannine kicked his chairleg as she passed him, setting him rocking. "And be *ready* in the morning, I am *not* waiting for you!"

"I will..." The words floated back to them as the door closed with a snap.

Peter moved closer to where Guyon was sitting and working. "Did you really need me for something? Or was that merely a ploy to allow me to escape?"

"I need to tell you what the autokeys are for these codes," Guyon said, rubbing a thumb between his eyebrows. "Unless you want all Corvay's poor little pawns cut off and isolated when he goes to the Bastille, someone's going to have to take over the message service. And since I *devised* the codes for the message service, it would be a bit idiotic if I kept the ones I made for Corvay, wouldn't it? You're the only one who can authorize these particular ones, so I need you to have them memorized, *Maréchal.*"

"Oh...yes. Sorry, Guyon. I have allowed other things to distract me from what we are trying to accomplish. It was extremely remiss of me." Peter was quite sincere in his apology, although it wasn't merely for being distracted. He knew they had been bordering on an argument all day and that was not how he wanted to begin their journey.

"Bah," said Guyon pithily. "You're not distracted and you're not remiss, you're angry and the truth tasted sour. I should have said the war is over *for now.* You and I know that Scotland has its own agenda, but he's still their King. There will be another army, there will be more battles. I'm sorry, though, that France will not help. It seems wrong. And if it were not for the fact that one idiot and one traitor are quite enough for a single family, I would pledge all I could of the Languedoc to you. But I cannot. This coding, this endless fussing with numbers and letters - it's all I can give." He made an odd little gesture with his hands, as though he were letting the papers fall. "I'm sorry it's so little. I'm sorry I'm not from your country. I'm sorry I can't change either fact."

Peter slumped and looked down at his feet. "No...I was allowing my frustration to rule my head and taking it out on you. I do that far too often, really, and I don't know why you put up with it." And, as always, even with Guyon's protestations of love, there was always the doubt in Peter's mind that he would *continue* to put up with it. "It really is a great deal, Guyon...and I would have trusted no one else to do it."

"That," said Guyon with horrible sweetness "is because no-one else *could.*" The false saccharin of his tones dissolved into a sort of choke. "Stop looking like that, *bèl-mi,* I've never asked you not to be human, I hope! I won't abandon you because you're

400

venting perfectly understandable annoyance in my general direction, I am *more* than capable of giving it back to you - accompanied by a good thump, if necessary!" His eyes glittered wickedly. "Or something more entertaining, for preference..."

"Oh? And just what did you have in mind? Puzzles? Word games perhaps? A nice afternoon walk?" Peter tried to brush his earlier mood away. He could rarely resist teasing Guyon, if given even the slightest chance.

"Chess, naturally," Guyon said in the same tones. "Although I am never sure whether I should centralize my knight, or merely *castle long*." The innocence in his voice somehow managed to make him sound utterly profane and wholly debauched with it.

"Ah...well, I suppose that is all dependant on your opponent's game...whether he plays tight or loose..." Peter replied leaning in just that much closer. "Although, even watching you play alone is...quite...stimulating."

"But I prefer more coffeehouse play," Guyon said, and then laughed. "As long as it's you setting the traps..."

"I only set traps for you, Gui." Peter chuckled as well, "No one else would ever be as challenging."

"Are you flattering my vanity, my pride, or my self-belief?" Guyon enquired wryly, but he was still half-laughing. "Whichever it is, you caught all three."

"Is it flattery to tell the truth?" Peter leaned in to place a nibbling kiss on Guyon's shoulder.

"In no variation," Guyon said evasively. While he was happy to boast, he was always uncomfortable with praise. "You know, this chair isn't very -" There was a small splintering noise, and Guyon leapt up, narrowly avoiding sending Peter's teeth through his lip. "Er. Stable," he concluded on a guilty-sounding chuckle.

"Then hooray for tomorrow and to going home," Peter laughed, pulling Guyon against him now that he was standing. "Home, where the furniture might not be much better, but we at least know its foibles."

"I like my desk," Guyon agreed. "And my bed, and my room, and my door, which has a *lock*..." He kissed Peter almost in punctuation of the concept.

"Ah..." Peter nodded and crossed to the door. "But this one

does as well. See?" He shot the bolt with an almost feral grin. "No one coming in...and no one leaving."

"Either way," Guyon murmured, "my pity all lies with the idiot who would try..."

"There are no such fools here," Peter moved back to his side, gathering him in for a kiss. He made it wet and rough and demanding, but asking for nothing more than he'd have given himself.

Even after more than a year, Guyon still startled beneath his touch, as though this were something wholly new, utterly unexpected and overwhelming at once, his response always, at first, one of quiet, delighted amazement. It was more convincing as a declaration than any of his sudden announcements or poetic paraphrases, his body unable to dissemble each and every time.

Peter cherished every small sound, drawing them in like the sweetest of nectars, his mouth covering Guyon's as a benediction, a blessing, an offering that thrilled him each time it was accepted. *This,* Peter thought, *this is what makes us whole.* Not the act itself but rather the sharing, the giving and receiving. That was the perfect explanation, and somehow, no explanation at all.

*

Corvay was not, in any way, as petty as he sometimes seemed. Each of his actions was calculated, thought-out, in some ways - though he despised the knowledge of this particular truth - profound. He was not insightful as to the nature of the men he owned, nor did he wish to be, but having the power of simple facts at his fingertips granted him a great deal more than that, enabled him to see beyond motive and desire and the strange inner beliefs that could drive a man, and to the simple absolute of what must, and would, be.

Sending the two men who had no idea how aware he was that his grasp over them was quite as tenuous as he knew it to be, into the morass of intrigue that was the Languedoc, had been for nothing so simple as revenge for their actions in Douai. While there was a part of him that applauded that, knew that it was an act of sense and intelligence that he had taught them, however painfully, there was part of him that resented their success. But he had not sought revenge for it, nor even for Peter Scudamore's later rebellion in saving Guyon's brother. His decision, in the end, had not even been to reinforce his control, nor to remind them of the fragility of their positions, though of course it would achieve each and every one of these purposes.

Corvay cared little for power over individuals. He held Maurice de Chesnay in his hand, and had for years, had known years before the final severing of Giraud and Guyon's brotherly ties that he would one day have them to use, as well. He owned Peter Scudamore as surely as God and the King, and for every twisted reason that came with those ideals. It gave him satisfaction, to know these things, but it was not the power he craved, nor even a particular pleasure.

But to hold the Languedoc! That, he would give up lives for, to know that the quiet, stubbornly independent, curiously loyal demesne belonged to him, not to State or Crown or Church, but to him - that was worth the hazard of the die, worth the destruction of his own name. He wanted the power of the devil himself, to stretch out his hand and claim dominion over the earth, or at least part of it, and that this could only be achieved by controlling the small human souls that inhabited it was less a pleasure than a necessity.

To send in the one man who both loved and hated that strange place and prove its calumny to the world was not something he had taken lightly, nor had it been some thoughtless quirk, born of blind hatred, to send the English Queen's Marshal, the one man of any status in France whom France could not claim as its own, with him. Corvay knew that whatever transpired in the lands near Carcassonne, whatever happened to Guyon and Peter, whether it broke their partnership entirely or simply caused the rift of incomprehension that already lay between them to grow deeper, it was irrelevant.

Guyon would try to save the Languedoc, because it was his home. And Peter would enforce that, would commit himself entirely to whatever quixotic idea came from the unreachable intelligence which was almost a separate entity from Guyon, and make it a fact. No other of Corvay's agents could be trusted to follow their hearts so stubbornly, no others be so blind to the very real division between possible and ideal as to set themselves aside as unnecessary.

Their loyalty to each other and to their nebulous concept of right and justice would achieve exactly what he wanted, and give him control. Not in the way he had led them to believe he wanted, by proving the Languedoc rebellious, but by proving it loyal, and thinking they were defying his wishes.

They would, believing they did all for the best and out of a sense of right and justice as innate to them as their hatred of his motives, think it a triumph to prove his spoken desires impossible. They would falsify records and claim no Spanish alliance existed. They would destroy all that was overtly set in place and call it evidence that none of what he had commanded them to prove existed. They would think themselves the saviors of that small state divided against itself, and in doing so, unite it against all they believed in, because they could not bring themselves to hide their manipulations, could not force dishonesty upon the world, could not lie and say it was for any other reason than to save the inhabitants that they did these things. And behind them, the unity would be against the very thing that might have saved the Languedoc entire, would be against the pretence of a belief that had never belonged there.

And when it was done, and they returned to lay his lack of proof at his feet, they would have no idea of what they had driven underground and made more dangerous, because they would have fostered a resentment that belonged only to those who believed themselves to be doing good - the hatred of the saved for the rescuer, a malleable and bitter thing that fit his purpose far better than the differing convictions he would never be able to pull together.

He knew that showing them this, in the years to come, would be a personal delight. That in doing so, he was making their loyalty to one another questionable was another private joy.

But it was not his reasoning, and it was not his only motive, and if he could gain a little hidden delight as well as the greater one, that was his own compensation for having to seem, in the public eye, to lose his power and his dignity, his own personal salve for what he would have to, however briefly, endure from the world.

Maurice de Chesnay, who kept a close watch on them, even in the privacy of their room, even in the times when they assumed themselves away from all those who could hear or see their actions, wrote with no little confusion, but utter trust. At first, the letters gladdened Corvay, for it was all as he had imagined it to be, and then, slowly, the first doubts began to creep in.

Guyon showed no signs of breaking - not within this strange friendship of which Corvay was never certain, not within himself, not with the Languedoc. He turned cartographer, spoke to de Tourvel, began to put the house in order, and made no move. Peter Scudamore bent his abilities to discovering Guyon's past - and to nothing else, no enforcing of whatever they had devised, no show of his abilities to make men believe in him and his ideals. They had turned inwards, not realizing perhaps what they did, healing what had gone before rather than thinking of what was to come. Maurice was frustrated, and Corvay bewildered.

There were no signs of the intimacies he knew existed and had convinced Maurice of, nothing save one evening at de Tourvel's, when the watcher outside the great windows of de Tourvel's cabinet had seen Guyon kneel before Peter, shaking his head, and heard him speak of Tolon.

Tolon, Toulouse, Corvay's greatest error, for the results had brought the two together in a way that nothing else perhaps could ever have done, had exposed their souls one to another by force, and left all Corvay's ruses worthless. Corvay was quite sure now that Guyon not only suspected what he had done to Peter on that mission, but knew it as a certainty, knew of what had been done from start to finish. Guyon knew how Corvay had used Giraud's name, of, perhaps, exactly what he had always planned for the Languedoc.

Guyon knew all these things and hated him for it, the actions of Douai had been revenge, pure and simple, not some devious plan to rob him of authority, but straightforward rage and determination to give him back in doubled form what he had brought about. He had almost succeeded, stripping Corvay of de Retz's support, at least, and possibly that of Douai, though that could never be certain.

Guyon de Chesnay was learning the art, not of a spy, but of a spymaster, teaching himself to know the art of corruption and yet hold himself apart from it, as he had once bent his mind towards casuistry and debate. Just as he had conquered each deficit in his learning while at the Sorbonne, he was overcoming his qualms and fears as to his own nature, embracing it without mockery or grim acceptance, but with slow care. And he was confiding this learning, not in words, or gestures, but by the very changing essence of his understanding and being and soul, to the one man in France who might just command the loyalty Corvay needed.

They were not tools. They were a storm that could tear apart all that Corvay had built, and he, believing them blind to themselves, had not foreseen it. Guyon would have forgiven no other man for invading the privacy that he still thought was his - Peter had read those long-ago, damning letters, and been discovered in doing so, yet de Chesnay had forgiven him, accepted that this must be, seemingly held the gradual erosion of his walls to be inevitable - because of who was doing so.

De Tourvel spoke to Scudamore of Astor, his daughter to de Chesnay of forgiveness, the records of Guyon's trial and conviction were found, such as they were, and yet the final rift did not take place, and nothing, nothing, was as Corvay had planned.

Peter Scudamore could command hearts and armies. Guyon de Chesnay could give him the power to do so, unfettered.

And God help him, he had unleashed the two of them on the one place that might just bring itself to accept the inevitability of their strength.

Corvay began to set in place the only resource left to him. If he could not have the Languedoc, he would have an end to the two who had lost it for him. He might not care for motive, he might not believe that a man's inner soul was what mattered most, but he knew just what could make a man like Guyon destroy all he loved.

He had to believe he was saving it.

*

The road to Paris: July-August, 1646

Love, nature's plot, this great creation's soul,
The being and the harmony of things,
Doth still preserve and propagate the whole,
From whence man's happiness and safety springs:
The earliest, whitest, blessed'st times did draw
From her alone their universal law.
Friendship's an abstract of this noble flame,
'Tis love refined and purged from all its dross,
The next to angels' love, if not the same,
As strong in passion is, though not so gross:
It antedates a glad eternity,
And is an heaven in epitome.

It amazed Peter at times, the amount of *things* that people thought they simply could not do without. He realized that few people lived as simply as he and Guyon tended to do, but really, how many dresses did one girl need? Especially since she'd probably order all new ones when she got to town and saw the differences between what she had been wearing and what the ladies of the court wore.

"Six, seven...and eight. Are you sure that's it, Jeannine? Sure you don't want to pack your bed curtains and the chamber pot too so you'll feel more at home?" Peter had taken to speaking to the girl just as he did to his sister, Sarah. It just seemed more comfortable and less likely to give her any romantic ideas regarding him.

"And a winding-sheet," said Guyon from the mounting-block. He had elected not to participate in any of the loading of boxes - though it had not prevented him from giving them all a running commentary on just how it was being done wrong. "For when she's murdered."

"I am not arriving in Paris looking like a pauper." Jeannine stuck her tongue out at Guyon. "Nor am I going to get half-way there and realize that I've left something important behind."

"Oh, just casually mention your dowry...four or five times a day. No-one will care what you wear. Well." Guyon suddenly looked worried. "As long as it isn't *too* transparent. Can we *go*?"

"Yes...yes. I'm quite ready, although I still don't understand why I can't ride with you, at least part of the time." Jeannine looked longingly at the horses.

"First off, goose, you're not used to spending such long hours in the saddle, and the type of swagger that a saddle sore rump would give you would not be at all fetching." Peter held out his hand to help Costanza into the carriage. "And second of all, I do not want Guyon to be charged with murder after the first five miles."

"I ride as well as Guyon!" It was an automatic protest.

"Yes, barelegged and over a blanket. The perfect way to arrive in Paris, my little hoyden," Guyon agreed. "I take it back, Peter. You ride in the carriage with Costanza, and I shall race Jeannine to Paris cross-country."

"I'd win!" Jeannine huffed, but turned and allowed Peter to hand her into the carriage as well.

"Thank God." Peter sighed as he closed and latched the door behind her. "Are you ready, Gui?"

"No," Guyon said dryly. "I need to pack some curtains." He grinned. "*More* than. Do you want me to fit a bolt on the *outside* to that carriage door, before we go?"

"No," Peter swung up into the saddle and settled himself comfortably. "But I may want something to stop my ears if we don't ride out ahead...quickly."

Normally Jeannine's fuss and prattle would have amused him, but not now. Now he only wanted Guyon's company and to get home as soon as possible, and the thought of how much slower their travel was to be due to the laden carriage was not a happy one.

Guyon simply slid onto his horse from the mounting block, completely without false pride at physical abilities he had never pretended to possess to any great extent. "If we go *fast*," he said enticingly, "we can get to the first hostelry at least two hours before they do..."

A slow smile spread across Peter's face as he considered exactly what could be accomplished in two hours of complete privacy. Then he sighed for just a moment. "But is that safe, do you think? You know this area far better than I do..."

Guyon made a face. "As safe as anything is. Oh, all right, *reasonably* fast. An hour." He sighed. "This is going to be *hell.*"

"This was your idea. Well, more or less..." Peter gave the coachman a nod and he and Guyon set off down the road.

"How?" Guyon demanded, with not altogether unreasonable outrage. "I thought sending her to Paris would be a good idea. I *never* said 'And I'll be happy to escort her'. I *certainly* never said *you* would be happy to escort her. And I promise on my life, I never gave anyone the idea that you had any sort of *entree* into the kind of society she wants!"

Peter shrugged, "We must have said something between the two of us. Ah, well, it's only a few days and then we can leave her with Madame de Neuillant. I'll squire her around to a few places and give her what little cachet I have, and we can wash our hands of the whole thing, yes?"

"Oh, you optimist," Guyon muttered. "But yes. I hope so. She'll be too busy bathing in rose petals and milk to bother us." There was a distinctly evil tinge to his smile. "Or was it *vinegar* and rose petals, I can never remember..."

"The former," Peter rolled his eyes. "Unless you think *she* would be idiotic enough try to darken her skin with walnut juice? No...that would not be the thing, would it?" He flipped back his hair and did an impression of Jeannine, "I can't go out in the sun. My skin must be as pale as cream if I don't want to look like a bumpkin."

Guyon snorted. "More likely freckles," he said amusedly. "And lemon juice does *not* work on those. Despite all claims to the contrary. And *stop* doing that, it's disturbing..."

"Yes, Guyon." Peter batted his eyes with a laugh and then looked back over his shoulder. "How long before they're settled enough to actually leave the drive, do you think?"

"Oh, God." The sound Guyon made was very close to a whimper. "Now I know *why* Lot's wife turned into a pillar of salt. I am not looking back. I am not, I am not...*move*!" he yelled back at the unfortunate coachman.

There was the sudden sound of the coachman's whip, followed by a very unladylike squeal and a thump. Peter was amused to see a mischievous smile on the coachman's face

"Floor, you think?" Guyon said speculatively. The expression on his face was almost identical to that of the coachman.

"Yes," Peter's lip twitched. "It sounded rather too hollow to be the squabs."

"Excellent," Guyon said in his most languid tones, grinned, and set his heels to his horse.

Barking out a laugh, Peter was quick to follow.

How fast is fast? he wondered. *And exactly how much faster than that can we manage without feeling too guilty that we left Jeannine on her own?*

It seemed that fast was *as possible*, and, as promised, involved a fair amount of cross country. Despite being nowhere near as skilled at riding as Peter, Guyon knew the area well, and, if not as skilled as a cavalry rider, was more than competent, so that Peter did not have to restrain himself as much as he had thought. He still slowed too soon for Peter's liking, but his reasoning was clear when he pointed behind them and to the left. "They're the cloud of dust," he said in explanation. "And that's our hour. You know, we *could* make for the Spanish coast..."

"No." Peter shook his head. "There is one major thing wrong with the Spanish coast."

Guyon raised a slightly dusty eyebrow. "There is?" He looked alarmingly wistful.

Leaning closer, Peter whispered intensely, "Too many Spaniards."

Guyon snorted, and his horse mimicked him, skittering sideways a little, startled by the sudden noise and movement.

"*Oh-*!" he said in exasperation. "Idiot beast. We'll have enough interruptions, *thank* you!" He got it back under control, and leant over, close enough to tease, not quite kissing. "And what's wrong with Spaniards?" he asked, his tones more suited to someone promising the delights of the Orient. His breath smelled faintly of the rosemary from the de Tourvel garden.

The remembrance of the delights of that warm sweet mouth held Peter's attention for several long moments, before he realized that he had, in fact, been asked a question.

"Oh...aren't we at war with them...or something?" He shook

his head to clear it.

"But the Scots aren't," Guyon said coaxingly. "And we're going to Scotland, so...we *could* stretch the point..." His eyes seemed impossibly large at his odd sideways and upward-looking angle, his smile a shadowy slant against the sun. "You have dust on your eyelashes," he said irrelevantly.

"And possibly several other places," Peter reached out with one hand, his thumb tracing the edge of Guyon's mouth. "But you are not a Scot, beloved, which although I thank God for it, could be a problem."

"They *like* the Languedociens..." Guyon sighed. "You're right. Back to Paris." He made a face. "I feel almost tempted to stay..."

"My home is where you dwell," Peter smiled, as he recited, "in golden sunshine or salt sea, in ice or sand or meadow green, where you are so shall I be." He gave a small chuckle, "But we'd have to replace all your books."

"They're just *things.* Like the globe. Not the funny vase-thing, though. I need that. But everything else...I wouldn't care about. I would just leave it..." Guyon looked disturbed, frowning into the bright light. "*This is a stolen season,*" he said in Occitan, and then laughed, and shook his head. "No, you're right. Out of this damn country, before I see some ghost even you can't banish."

Peter leaned in then, just the slightest bit further, brushing a kiss over Guyon's lips, "Do you think we could still manage that two hours?"

Guyon grinned, sudden and brilliant, his eyes green slits in a sun-bleached face. "I think *I* can," he said, and the teasing note was back in his voice. "Can you keep up?"

"Just watch me," Peter grinned and signaled for his beloved to take the lead.

The passage from one day to the next, in whose doorway we find ourselves snared, awaiting eternity.

And as he had on their first Twelfth Night, Peter followed Guyon, the snares just as tight, but ever more welcome.

*

It was oddly nice, not to have to worry about keeping who they were at least reasonably quiet, a rare oasis of unpretending calm in what seemed like an endless haze of miserable concealment. Guyon happily left Peter to deal with accommodation and suitable rooms for Jeannine, and went to wait in the courtyard, settling himself in the shade by the well with some of the river-chilled wine, rolling up his shirtsleeves and deciding that he didn't much care if he were taken for a degenerate ostler, as long as he could cool off slightly.

They had pushed themselves and their horses rather hard on the ride, each of them prodding the other to do just a bit better - a bit more speed, a better path. It had, Guyon had to admit, been a rather enjoyable trip and as a bonus, they might actually be as much as two and a half hours ahead of Jeannine and the lumbering carriage.

He rolled his jacket up and put it behind his head, leaning back on the impromptu pillow with a small sigh of contentment, and closing his eyes. He did not open them at the sound of footsteps.

"Have some wine," he said genially. He was fairly sure he had recognized Peter's step, but he was imbued enough with a drowsy well-being that he didn't really mind if it was a complete stranger.

He felt a puff of breath against his cheek, then lips closing over his own just briefly,

"Hmmm...that's a good vintage." Peter chuckled and sat down next to him.

"Let him kiss me with the kisses of his mouth: for thy love is better than wine," Guyon said, opening his eyes. He still could not prevent the faint mockery from entering his voice, but at least he was learning to use the words. "It seems nothing is free from sentiment. Sunlight is a terrible thing."

"Aye, and so it is," Peter agreed, pressing the cool wine bottle against his slightly pink cheeks.

"Oh." Guyon, who had never burned in his life, was suddenly and inexplicably embarrassed. It seemed somehow peculiarly intimate, to know someone so well that every infinitesimal change in hue and texture of skin was noticeable. He felt as though he had been caught staring at someone in the baths, breaking an unspoken but no less strict taboo. "Well, at least there's shade here."

Peter suddenly chuckled, lowering the bottle from his face, "I never thought in my life to hear you complain about being too warm."

"I - *oh*." Guyon went red. "I'm not," he mumbled. "I'm being...concerned, or something, and obviously the sun has softened my brains, because this is *wonderful*." He retrieved the bottle, and drank deeply, willing the blood to recede from his face.

"Thank you," Peter said, his hand coming up to gently trace over the warmth of blush on Guyon's cheeks. He was oddly quiet, as if trying to solve some puzzle set before him.

"I can hear the mice," Guyon said, trying to make a joke of it. "They're pedaling your cogs again." He frowned a little, still smiling, and reached up to wind a strand of Peter's hair around his finger. "Now you see *this* is spun light. Sunlight and spun light, *God* I love words!"

"And yet so seldom say the ones you mean," Peter chuckled quietly, seemingly content for the moment, to just sit in the shade with Guyon's fingers twisted in his hair.

"A hazard of love," Guyon agreed, wondering if Peter would understand what he was saying. "It can never be expressed in the way desired except by others. They stole the words long since and made better use of them, and we are poor little parrot-shadows, mouthing brilliance to sooth inadequacy."

"I don't require brilliance, Gui. I'm far too simple to really appreciate it." Peter smiled softly, leaning over against him. "I don't ask for much more than this."

But you are *brilliance*, Guyon thought, *and I, as they once foretold, am made shadow by it.* "I told you once, you ask too little," he said, and smiled. "But I still won't find you a phoenix, Peter, you'd forget to feed it."

"Ah, then it will just have to remain Marceau the mouse and I," Peter nodded. "He's followed me from the Louvre, I think. The pickings there were too slim once we left. And mice are much simpler pets anyway - they find their own food."

Guyon chuckled. "Scavengers born," he said softly. "Hm. Speaking of crumbs, are there any?" He shook himself out of his odd mood.

"Oh, yes, that's why I came out here in the first place." Peter stood up, reaching his hand down to Guyon. "There is food...and a nice cool room to eat it in."

"And that's supposed to please me?" Guyon grinned up at him. "*Cool.* Oh, how I suffer to please *you*!" He took Peter's hand, and let himself be pulled upright, enjoying the sudden feeling of floating in a green dazzle of shadow as the light shifted over his eyes. "How much freedom is left?"

"Shhh..." Peter placed one finger over Guyon's lips. "You'll spoil the mood. I, personally, am hoping for a broken axle, at least, that will keep them until sundown."

"I am dutifully praying," Guyon said solemnly, feeling the slightly calloused skin of Peter's finger move against his lips as he spoke. He felt as though love and sunlight had mingled to send his blood spinning through him in glowing delight. "Dear Lord. We humbly beseech thee to break their axles." The laughter bubbled out of him like champagne, an uncontainable and incandescent overflow of too much feeling.

"Amen." Peter concluded, and then pulled Guyon toward the inn.

*

The *Oiled Fish* was just as unprepossessing as its name, at least from the outside. Inside at least, it was warm and dry and very clean. He and Guyon were used to less savory accommodations, but Jeannine, he was thinking, was not. He arranged for two rooms, not shared, *thank God*, and meals for later, before retreating into privacy with Guyon.

"I think," Guyon said dreamily from the window, where he had opened the catch and was sitting with one leg balanced against the frame, and the other dangling outside against the sun-baked wall, "that this is the epitome of peace. Short-lived, valuable, and full of sun."

"Indeed," Peter agreed. "All three and most especially, I'm

thinking, the first."

Jeannine's imminent arrival, broken axles notwithstanding, made any thoughts of peace rather fleeting.

"Ah, she'll be too busy sulking to trouble us much today," Guyon said cheerfully. "It will take time before she's a true disruption." He smiled. "She thinks depriving us of her company is a hardship. So long let her sulks last."

"Sorry." Peter moved to join Guyon at the window, soaking up what of the sun that he could with all the enjoyment of a well-fed cat. "Jeannine is the very last thing I want to think of just now."

"She's like mosquitoes." Guyon rubbed his arm consolingly. "No matter what, they find a way in and leave irritating itchy marks behind them." He leant out of the window at a slightly perilous angle, craning to see around the corner. "Not even a cloud of dust yet, be Epicurean, car-mi, and stop fretting."

"Epicurean?" Peter leaned in and wrapped his arms around Guyon. "Yes, I think that will be my new title. I'll give up Marshal and take that up instead."

"Mm - *no*." Guyon tilted his head back, his eyebrows raised. "I've only just got used to loving the Marshal, I prefer not to confuse my emotions overly. But add it, by all means," he said generously. "What's one more name to your many?"

Peter snorted. Titles...Titles...what were they, anyway, but ways to define more duties, more work. "The only one I really want is...*'Yours'*."

Yes, he was quickly working his way toward the more juvenile protestations of love, but that this moment, he was more than serious.

"The revenue is atrocious," Guyon said mildly, "but it's one I'll gladly bestow." He scowled a little. "Inadequate, though, since every man and his cousin use the possessive towards you as though you were a parcel. So it will have to be a title self-conferred and no other way, since everyone can claim you, and I, alas, may not protest."

"Please protest," Peter told him, resting a suddenly tired head on Guyon's shoulder. "Protest a lot. I don't begrudge them all, really, but sometimes it's just so....so..."

Peter's hand fluttered around, no more eloquent than his words had been, he was sure.

"Ah." Guyon, who Peter knew thought titles both a mockery and a nuisance, sounded nothing but sympathetic. "Shall I protest with vigor and with eloquent venom, or simply by glaring every time some unfortunate uses the prefix 'my' in your direction?" He shifted, swinging his leg back in and turning so that his back blocked the sun from the window and anyone's curious gaze from the room. "After all, I am a skilled and practiced Cerberus, though I only have one head..." He put his arms around Peter, his perch making him for once slightly greater in height. He smelled of sun and the herbs he always packed his linen in, and faintly, sharply, of sweat and horse.

"Perhaps, I should have Morel write something out in your favor," Peter chuckled, pressing his face against Guyon's chest. "A claim or deed...something. Of course, that would give *you* a greater responsibility."

"I'll tell you a secret." Guyon's voice was a soft rumble against Peter's mouth, humming tangibly through his chest and throat. "I *like* responsibility. At least for you. Didn't you know? And I'd no more relinquish it than fly out of this window."

"I love you," Peter let the words come out, still startling in their newness. "In spite of your lack of wings."

"Which is a very good thing, because if they were a prerequisite, you'd be having a streak of dreadful luck," Guyon said, sounding amused. "You *really* hate being the Marshal, don't you?" he added seriously. "I'm sorry. I promise, after we deal with Corvay, we'll find a way to release you, we'll go somewhere, wherever you want, do *whatever* you want. I know we all spend our lives in shackles, but *you* should choose them, this time."

"It's not so much that I hate it, it's just -" Peter paused. Not so much what? He had never put it all into words, but now he wanted to. "It's just that I hate having people look up to me because of a title in front of my name. Especially since so much of it is a lie. They speak more respectfully to me at Court now...but all the time I know they have knives ready to shove into me at the first sign of weakness."

"Is that better or worse than when they used the knives

without hesitation?" Guyon asked gently. "It's not a lie, Peter. It's part of who you are, just as Hawthornden is even though you leave it to Robbie's care. It's not the title your cadets look up to, or that my students admire. It's - a hook, a tag, makes them able to put their respect for you into a word. And you know what Court is, nothing will ever change that."

Peter suddenly snorted, "And we'll be turning Jeannine loose in that. Which shall we feel sorry for, do you think?"

"Neither," Guyon said. "I think they're perfectly well-matched and that thanks to her affection for you, your own Court will have a beautiful, intelligent, and terrifying ally." He chuckled. "I can play Machiavelli, too, when I choose."

Peter chuckled again, softly against Guyon's chest. "And now we've come full circle. Can we talk about something, *anything,* else? Philosophy...economy...ancient Gaulish chemistry..."

"Ancient -" Guyon choked on a combination of the next word and a delighted little shout of laughter. "I always knew there was more to them than mistletoe and human sacrifice," he said then, and the odd note Peter had heard in his voice in the courtyard was back, as though something that amazed him had taken up residence in his every awareness, and he was on the verge of understanding it enough to share, "but *chemistry*? You think they sought the Philosopher's Stone and the green swan?"

"All right...so it was probably more like...'Heat and wood make fire...fire good.'" Peter gave a deep and throaty grunt. "But I was really only looking for a change of subject."

"Ah. Well, we could try a practical application of your fire principle?" Guyon asked, and when Peter looked up, amused but wondering what exactly he was talking about, his mouth was curling into a wholly unambiguous little grin. "Or heat, at least."

"See? That's another reason I love you. You have the best ideas." Peter moved back to allow Guyon to step down from the window.

It was more a little swung jump, Guyon using his arms to make sure he landed on his feet without stumbling, and the half-triumphant, half-embarrassed little smile he gave Peter showed that he knew exactly how he had shown off the strength so few people were aware of. The smile faded into something a great deal more speculative as Peter started to laugh, the rare look of total outward focus that nothing but books had ever seemed to visibly inspire in Guyon until the Languedoc, an oddly intent expression that was closer to tangibility than even sunlight or snow.

It was almost overpowering at times to have all of that directed towards him. Overpowering and magnificent and so amazing that it made his heart ache with the feeling of that gaze concentrated on him.

"What did you have in mind, exactly?" Peter caught himself running his tongue slowly over his bottom lip.

"Oh, experimentation, isn't that the source of all alchemy?" said Guyon with attempted lightness. His voice caught a little in his throat, sounding almost as rasping as it had after his thesis defense. He tilted his head in assumed consideration, his eyes starting to glitter with amusement as well as arousal. "Let me try - hm." He stepped closer, leaning in, and almost as gently as a brush of silk from a passing sleeve, his tongue mimicked the path along Peter's lower lip that his own had just traced.

So gentle, but so intimate that Peter could not hold back his groan of appreciation, "Once more? Please? You need to....establish a firm baseline."

"Ah, trust you to know the right words," Guyon said against his mouth, and there were so many layers to the meaning in that soft voice that Peter's own breath almost stopped, only to leave him in a little gasp as the brushstroke of Guyon's tongue was repeated, this time mimicking the process, mirror-like, almost before he had quite stopped.

He pulled Guyon closer, his own tongue searching, invading Guyon's mouth as if he could draw out every secret the man ever had, all the words he ever spoke.

"Perfect..." he breathed softly, sometime later, finally breaking the kiss.

"Oh, so *that's* what perfection is," Guyon began, mocking even while he fought for composure, and then cut himself off, laughing, and tugged Peter towards the bed. "While coherency and sense remain," he said rather dryly, before pulling Peter onto the thin mattress.

He landed rather ungracefully, but with the feeling of Guyon now pressed against him, grace was one of the last things on his mind. "You have your perfection and I'll have mine"

"Oh, I will," Guyon agreed with complete sincerity. He ran his hands under Peter's shirt. "Now how am I to generate heat with obstacles such as this?" he demanded, his eyebrows quirking together.

"Friction?" Peter said, his voice cracking as Guyon's questing hands grazed over him. "Or we could remove them. Or both."

"Oh, both, I hate choosing," Guyon said fervently, and kissed him again. "The experiment was to be based on *touch*, you know," he pointed out after a moment.

"Right. " Peter agreed quickly, then narrowed his eyes with a teasing look. "But you'll have to remove yours as well, if you're expecting much in the way of friction."

Guyon didn't look as amused any more, but he didn't flinch or withdraw, either. "Ah, *real* empiricism," he murmured, before sitting up and pulling the linen over his head, emerging with the air of a cat who was determined to convince the world that falling off an edge was precisely its intent. His eyebrows raised. "Well?" he said expectantly.

"Yes, very...." Peter looked at him for several long moments. Guyon hated this. Hated to be looked at. But sometimes Peter could not resist. The compact frame, lean muscles, all of it drew him in.

Guyon was frowning at him now and he gave himself a visible shake. "Oh...yes...sorry."

He drew his own shirt over his head, and tossed it, haphazardly toward the foot of the bed.

"I'm *so* sorry," said Guyon in dangerously sweet tones, "did I interrupt your thinking process?" He used his weight to push Peter backwards, his hands resting on either side of Peter's shoulders as he knelt over him. "I *hate* interrupting, of course...

"Oh, no...feel free...really." Peter's breath caught in his throat. *Beautiful. Perfect and* - "I never mind your interruptions."

"You," Guyon said almost dreamily, "are infinitely too tolerant." Then he kissed Peter with a great deal less calculation and a lot more force, and more than a hint of teeth. "I *expect*," he

419

said at one point, drawing back to inspect the results of his 'experimentation', and lifting one hand to start tracing patterns over Peter's throat and chest, "to be *minded*."

"Yes, sir..." Peter said breathlessly, pulling Guyon back for another kiss.

He had never realized before that Guyon's entire body could convey a grimace, even when his mouth was both hidden and occupied - which was something Peter definitely intended to consider at some later point, when the occupation didn't involve *him*.

"Alright...what?" Peter drew back, his expression, he was sure, oddly stuck someplace between frustration, lust and worry.

"Titles," Guyon explained irritably, and somehow managed to say all he was feeling with that one word, even if the explanation as to *why* was sorely lacking. As Peter continued to look at him with what he suspected was a blank expression worthy of a village idiot, he scowled, and added briefly, "Hate 'em."

"Agreed," Peter chuckled. He had them, and neglected them as much as he could reasonably manage. Hawthornden he had, more or less, given to Robbie, his deed to the estates in Briton still lay in a drawer, untouched.

"So don't," Guyon said, and touched his thumb to the corner of Peter's mouth, his expression suddenly tender. "You astound me," he murmured, and then shook his head, laughing, before returning to his self-appointed process of attempted discovery.

That was his beloved, mercurial as winter seas, quick to temper, quick to joy and -

Whatever else Peter had been thinking was suddenly driven from his head as sharp teeth bit down on his shoulder. "Yes...."

This time, Guyon's smile curled *into* his skin, hard and warm and triumphant. His tongue flickered out, soothing and arousing at once, and his mouth moved, promising and threatening at once, over Peter's collarbone and the small triangle of sunburned skin at his throat, resting there for a moment in a sort of apology to the already too-hot skin, before he bent his head further, curving his neck down without moving his body. Peter could feel the small, fine tremors all the way through him, from the balanced check Guyon's arms and shoulders were holding on his weight.

"Anything...." Peter cleared his throat, "Anything empirical?"

It was getting more and more difficult to be understandable. Guyon's touch always seemed to rob him of any innate sense he owned. And the fact that he was fairly well pinned down, kept him from concentrating on anything outside of the brush of skin on skin...lips and teeth and...

Guyon lifted his head and grinned at him. His weight shifted so that he was pressing down on Peter, and he moved quite deliberately from side to side, the motion small and insistent and relentless. "What's *your* conclusion?" he asked rather raggedly.

Peter was busily gulping in air like a marathon runner and had to find a moment to answer. "Conclusion...already tol' you.... 's all perfect..."

He shifted his legs, spreading them wider, then wrapping them around Guyon, pressing him closer.

"Stupid...damn..." One of Guyon's deft blunt hands was moving between them, and that really *was* friction, almost unbearable as the fabric of his breeches moved with what felt like astounding roughness over too-sensitized skin, but Guyon's intent was to alleviate, not cause discomfort, and he distracted Peter with the sharp, ice-and-burning sensation of breath and teeth and surprisingly hard, hot lips moving from his sunburned skin to his nipples, his tongue flickering back and forth and his other hand somehow soothing everywhere his mouth could not be, until he stopped, the cessation as much of a sensation as all that had preceded it, and he realized that what had felt like an incredible, tortuous eternity had been seconds, while Guyon undid lacings one-handed. For once, the triumph in his eyes seemed completely justifiable.

"Talent..." Peter laughed out, almost manically between gasping breaths. He wanted more. Wanted it now. He shifted again, up into that pressure of hands and hips that was too much and still not quite enough.

He could see the same almost feverish need in Guyon's eyes, narrowed in greenish slits of concentration, feel it in his taut body, and knew that while sometimes Guyon might draw things out deliberately, loving to give new meanings to torment, to take them both over the edge they were often not even aware of in a combination of frustration and laughter together, it was not true now. Then Guyon's hand slipped slightly backwards under his weight, his braced arm giving a little, and he *did* laugh, and suddenly all the desperation was gone with that one small shift, to be replaced by pleasure.

"Yesss," Peter hissed, his freed hand sliding up and around to the small of Guyon's back pressing him in tighter, hip thrusts slow and delicious. "Love you.... "

He still half-expected the response of shuttered eyes and silence to that, not the real, open delight that seemed to burn through Guyon's whole body, the way his head bent down until his lips were almost touching Peter's, so that when they formed the words in silent response, he could see nothing but the strange translucency of Guyon's wide eyes, a new horizon.

I love you.

It seemed that alchemy was empirical after all.

*

There were some things in life that were a constant. The rising and setting of the sun. Cold winters, warm summers. The late night sound of Guyon's pen scratching over paper. And now, apparently, the late evening threatening of the young girl that they had volunteered to deliver to Paris.

"That's done then." Peter entered their room at that evening's inn and collapsed back on the bed. "I've given her the nightly lecture. Explained, again, very thoroughly I might add, exactly why she must stay in her room - my brain will want washing later, by the way - and locked her in good and tight. If we don't reach Paris soon...I may resort to chains."

Guyon made a face at him. "I think she'd enjoy that a little too much. She could moan and bewail her fate. Loudly." He yawned, and stretched. "Or just make the manacles clank, and emit hollow groans..."

"Oh, she'd love that. She'd probably try to frighten someone enough that they'd make her a legend - The Ghost of the Chained Virgin." Peter rolled his eyes hugely, then sat up to pull his boots off.

"I think we started a legend all the way from Carcassonne to Paris," Guyon said, automatically kneeling to tug the boots free. "Most Unvirginal of Virgins. Weeping at six pm daily."

"Christ yes..." Peter's tones were emphatic. "And thank you." He wiggled his freed toes. "You're far too good to me, you know?"

Guyon looked at him with almost ludicrously-raised eyebrows. "Um, and that would be because? How? What?" He screwed up his face, and said thoughtfully - "I could *bite* your feet. Would that make you feel less burdened by my goodness?"

"Those feet have been trapped in those boot for a good eight hours, Gui. More likely it would make you feel less burdened by your dinner."

Guyon blinked at him. "Uh...in fact, the thought alone might be sufficient in that regard," he admitted. Then he frowned. "Wait, we had dinner?" He flopped full-length and face down onto the bed beside Peter. "I'm losing my mind. I can't remember dinner. Not at all..."

"Yes, yes. I starve you. I put you on a forced march across the vast wasteland of France with no food and little water." Peter chuckled and aimed a teasing swat at Guyon's backside. "Don't worry...food should be brought up at any moment. You won't waste away.

"Hm. Didn't think I would," Guyon said cheerfully. "'M just relieved to hear I'm not eating fantasy suppers *and* forgetting their consistency." He wriggled into the counterpane, ruffling it up so that it supported his chin. "Nice bed, for once."

Peter chuckled and leaned in to drop a light kiss against Guyon's temple, "Nicer bed partner. Do you suppose we'll make Paris tomorrow? Will we be able to drop her off immediately or will we have play nanny another night?"

"I already wrote to Madame de Neuillant," Guyon said smugly. "She'll be removed from Paris to the Comtesse's chateau the moment she sets foot on our cobbled streets." He grimaced. "She'll also come *back*, at some point, but hopefully we'll be gone by then..."

"If God is good, " Peter chuckled. "If he's better, perhaps she'll be wed by the time we see her next...and we'll not have to worry about her ever again." Peter's words sounded harsher than they were meant. He actually liked Jeannine, loved her like he loved his sister if the truth be known, but neither one of them had been prepared for the mischief that one very headstrong fifteen year old girl could get into.

"I think," Guyon said wryly, "that I am more worried about the idea of her marriage than anything else." He did not elaborate, but Peter, after Maurice's little revelation, was curious.

"Why is that?" Peter asked quietly, reaching out to twist one of Guyon's curls around his finger.

"Because she intends her marriage to be one of convenience and strategy and *title*," Guyon said dryly, "while she becomes the mistress of someone *interesting*. And I truly don't know which unknown victim I feel sorriest for." He sighed. "I think she may be contemplating Charleon for the latter, by the way."

"God save us..." Peter shook his head. "Can she not just fall in love like a normal girl since her father is obviously not forcing her to marry someone of his choosing?"

Guyon's mouth twitched. "She *did*," he said unhelpfully.

'Then why are we going through all this?" Peter frowned...then chuckled. "Let me guess, she fancied herself in love with someone already married? Your brother?"

"Um." Guyon laughed a bit. "No. Not Giri, she had more sense than *that*, thank God!" His smile turned a little sour. "The seigneur of Brocéliande and Hawthornden, the Maréchal of their most English Majesties in France, Peter Scudamore himself."

Peter's laugh was explosive, "What?! Christ, Gui, your sense of humor can be so odd at times. She saw me as an escape, I'm sure, but no more than that."

"No," Guyon said quietly. "Well. Yes. But she thought herself in love with you, too." He sighed. "She probably was. Add to my sins that I destroyed a young girl's dreams."

"But...I wouldn't. I couldn't." Peter's tone was almost shocked. "I mean, really. Not that it's not flattering, I suppose, but...Christ! Are you sure, Gui?"

"Oh, yes," Guyon said with absolute calmness. "Your charms are all-conquering, it seems. And I was - less than apparent, it would seem, about my - ah - *prior claim* - to commanding such affection. However." He smiled. "I finally found the courage to tell her, and no she seeks other prey."

"Thank God for that at least," Peter shook his head. "Sad. Although I'd find it much easier to feel sympathy for her if it had been your brother. Or you, for that matter."

"Oh, thank you very much," said Guyon acidly. "Charming. Really. Good thing you've got such a high opinion of yourself - shall I call her in and make it formal?" He was not quite joking.

"I merely meant," Peter gave a tug to the curl still wrapped around his finger, "that I could understand her being in love with you. That's so very easy. But in love with me? I don't even know how *you* can be."

"But -" Guyon turned onto his side, his eyes serious. "Pèire, that is your saving grace. You inspire love. In all of us. Of varying kinds, but...love, nonetheless. I heard what the Palatine said of you. *You can command armies.* Through loyalty. Through love." He wrinkled his nose. "Pfft. Sentiment. And yet true."

"If I can, it is only because I had a good teacher," Peter asserted, a slight blush tinting his face. "Rupert has always been very giving of his ideas and ideals. I merely put them into practice and had the luck that it seemed to work."

"Hm-mmm. Luck, of course," Guyon said wryly. He tugged at Peter's collar, bringing him closer, and kissed him, a soft, sweet touch of affirmation. "But still love."

"But yours is the only love I covet...ever."

"Well, you *have* that," Guyon said seriously. "Is there nothing else you think you may want?"

"Dinner." Peter gave a definite nod, his eyes twinkling. "And you."

"Well, one of us is here, one is most decidedly not." Guyon grinned at him, stretching out. "Go and be...authoritative." He rested the side of his face on the rucked-up folds of counterpane.

"Yes, Guyon." Peter gave a melodramatic sigh, "Your wish is for your humble servant to obey." He slipped off the bed and began looking for his boots.

"Could just shout," Guyon said helpfully, in the tones of a man who had no intention of moving at all. "You know - *where is my dinner*?"

"Um. Here, messieurs?" cam an anxious voice from outside the door. Guyon rolled onto his back, put a pillow over his face, and shook with laughter.

Peter gave it a playful shove, as if suffocating him, then went to open the door, "Come in, my girl. Please ignore the lunatic. We only let him out on alternate Wednesdays."

"Of which this is one," Guyon said amusedly. The girl laughed, putting out the covered trays and wine on the table.

"If you want anything else..."

"We'll call for it," Guyon agreed smoothly.

The girl bobbed a curtsey and moved toward the door, and if her glance lingered on Peter for more than a moment, he certainly didn't notice. "This smells promising," Peter made a show of lifting the covers.

"Bread and cheese?" Guyon said hopefully. "Apple?"

"At the very least," Peter said, tossing one in Guyon's direction. "But I believe this is beef stew...and actually made from beef."

"Oh God, don't, I feel like Tantalus..." Guyon bit into the apple. "Well, at least it's an apple," he added, rather indistinctly. He watched Peter suspiciously as the stew was tasted. "And?"

"Could use a bit of spice, but not bad," Peter shrugged and dished some up. "And the bread looks fresh as well."

Guyon took a piece of bread and a bowl, and began eating stew by the simple means of folding it up in the bread and stuffing it into his mouth. "'S easier than knives and spoons," he said, a little shamefacedly.

"And faster, apparently." Peter just chuckled and sat down with a spoon and his bowl.

"Well, *yes*," Guyon agreed. "Too much time doing - soldier things. I'm always thinking of my stomach. More than Thucydides or Aristotle, I think of food..."

Peter's eyes were twinkling as he looked at Guyon, "Only food then, and naught else?"

Guyon's whole face seemed to become a smile, at times like this, being asked the most ludicrous of questions and not having to disguise his answer. "Food, love, desire, you...all essentials, I can't separate them..."

"Please, God, you never shall," Peter's words were soft and heart felt. He was still in that odd stage where he expected to awaken at any moment to find that all Guyon's words of love were still unsaid and his own heart aching at being denied what it most wanted.

"Oh, no, never, I don't have the patience for *that* untangling!" Guyon laughed, and then said, "Besides, it's more like breathing. I mean, I *could* do without food, if I had to. But not breathing. Nor you."

Peter sat down his bowl and moved to sit next to Guyon, "You'll never have to, because I'm here as long as you wish it. I promised, I'll never try to leave you again. You'll have to send me away. Just -" There was a long pause, as if Peter wasn't sure how to say what he wanted, " - if you ever do send me away. Make it quick. Just say it at once. A clean cut."

Guyon, with faint horror, thought of just how much he was going to have to control his temper and his tongue, in order to make sure Peter *didn't* think that was what he was doing. It didn't really bear contemplating. "I'll...keep that in mind," he said unenthusiastically.

The words seemed to comfort Peter though, as if they were what he wanted to hear. "Thank you."

Guyon wondered what *exactly* he was being thanked for, and decided he was probably better off not knowing. "Mm." He put his own bowl aside and kissed Peter instead of trying to give any sort of concrete response, thinking that this was one instance in which he simply didn't trust words themselves, let alone his ability to use them to effect.

There was a soft chuckle from Peter, "I'm sorry. I've completely put you off, haven't I? Finish your dinner." He picked up the apple he'd tossed to Guyon earlier and began to slice and core it. "Sometimes I just need to have things out and said. It's better than worrying about them."

Guyon thought about pointing out that having things out and said only added to *his* worry, but just shrugged instead. He was starting to wonder if he was ever going to trust himself to speak again. He got to his feet, taking the bowl back over to the tray and looking at the other things on it with no particular sense of interest. He settled for a cup of wine, and went to steal slices of apple from Peter. "You know," he said conversationally, "Three eggs cost more than a chicken?"

Peter looked at him oddly, "Are you thinking of setting up a henhouse?"

"Hm? No...I was thinking of Jeannine's concepts of frugality. I hope *someone* teaches her how to run a household."

"Is that not part of Madame de Neuillant's job?" Peter popped a piece of the apple into Guyon's mouth.

"More teaching her how to *luxuriate*, I think," Guyon said wryly. "Remove all traces of country from her."

"Ah." Peter cut of a bit of apple and munched on it thoughtfully. "I'm not sure which one I pity more. Madame de Neuillant for making the attempt...or Jeannine for having that done to her. I rather like her country rashness, you know?"

Guyon nodded. "It keeps her bearable," he agreed. "But I'd rather see her change and be able to survive, than stay the same and go under. Or be forced back to the Languedoc and some horrendous marriage no-one sane would want. I cannot *believe* de Tourvel thought of me as a suitable concept."

"I can." Peter said, then continued when he saw the perplexed look on Guyon's face. "I mean think about it. He could see at least some affection there. Friendship, if nothing else. He knew you'd not beat her or try to break her spirit. Plus, you've a head on your shoulders and could take over his lands for her one day. She could do far worse and he knew that."

"I'm also insane, probably a heretic, and definitely degenerate, who would break her heart and spirit and ruin her life before vanishing into either academia or the Bastille," Guyon added more prosaically. "I'm sure she *could* have done worse, but I do rather worry as to *how*."

"De Tourvel never believed any of that of you, Gui." Peter shook his head. "But if you plan on doing any of that to me...I suppose I should pick a date and get in on the betting back in Paris. That way I'll at least have the money to sustain me." The comment was casual, Peter's attempt apparently, to get past his earlier comments.

Guyon raised an eyebrow at him. "I couldn't really make your life any worse," he pointed out, "so that doesn't bother me. And it would take more than a scruffy Occitan with a sharp tongue to break *you*, my dear. Not that I plan on trying."

"I'm rather attracted to scruffy, as it happens." Peter leaned in, dropping a kiss on his beloved's unshaven cheek.

Guyon laughed. "Good thing, that, since you'll never get anything else from me..." He grinned, imagining the effort it would take to ensure even vague respectability each day. "I think you have a secret desire for tree-bark."

Peter snorted out a laugh, "Trust me, my dear, even as a soldier I was never quite that desperate."

"Oh? Not *quite*? Just *how*, then?" Guyon put on his best salacious look.

"Let's just say that a strong wrist is useful for more than one type of sword play and leave it at that, shall we?"

Guyon snorted into his wine cup. "Oh, I think I'll definitely leave it there...until I want to embarrass you horribly, of course," he added, unable to resist.

"As if you need more ammunition to be able to manage that," Peter crunched down on another piece of apple, then took Guyon's wine to wash it down.

"But it's more *implication*," Guyon said with horrible, fervent sincerity, taking the remains of the apple and eating the core. "I can make people think true horrors, all with one word..."

"I know." Peter had been on the sharp end of that tongue too many times to deny any of its powers. "I've seen the aftermath.... And carry the scars."

"Can I see?" Guyon demanded, like an eager schoolboy. He stuck out his tongue at Peter, demonstrating his ability to have eaten an apple core without breaking the skin of any of the pips. "I've never caused scars before. Are they distinctive and elegant?"

"Very, but internal alas." Peter wrinkled his nose at the sight of the pips. "I don't know how you can do that."

"I stick them at the front of my mouth," Guyon said, choosing to take the question literally, and spitting them out into his hand. "So I don't risk biting them. And internal? That's no fun. Aren't you supposed to have that soldierly ability to *strip your sleeve and show your scars*?"

"That's only for impressing the ladies," Peter explained, "and since there are no ladies that I wish to impress, I have no need of such abilities."

"Oh." Guyon looked, briefly, disappointed. "You impress them anyway," he said then, and then smiled, the rare, genuine expression that so few people got to see. "And me. You impress me. Even without scars."

"I do?" Peter seemed genuinely surprised by that idea, but struck a preening pose. "It's my swordsman's physique, isn't it? You have a long-standing attraction to long legs and wiry muscles."

"The long legs especially," Guyon agreed urbanely. "Oh, no, wait - that's *envy*, which is a little different...the muscles are very impressive, though, yes," he added with an air of a man humoring a lunatic.

Peter leaned closer, his eyes sparkling, "I *could* show you my scars. If you were interested."

"I thought you said they were internal?" Guyon's smile ruined the suspicious note in his voice.

"Only the ones that you put there," Peter chuckled. "I've lots of others you know? I can even tell you the circumstances where I gained them, if you like. Of course, I *will* have to get undressed...."

"Oh, obviously," Guyon agreed. "Empirical proof, and all that..."

"And you'll have to get undressed as well."

"To compare and contrast?" Guyon asked wryly. "But I only have one story..."

"No..." Peter placed a hand over Guyon's lips, silencing him. "Because I'll be damned if I stand around stark naked, while you keep your clothes on. That's all I meant."

"Oh." Guyon reddened slightly, looking down his nose to give Peter's hand a cross-eyed, meditative look that meant he was planning something reasonably evil to save his equilibrium. "I suppose that's reasonable," he added around Peter's fingers. He was very carefully *not* biting.

Peter gingerly removed his hand from Guyon's mouth, "Where shall I begin?"

"With your sleeve, of course," Guyon said in reasonable tones. He was still giving Peter's hand nastily speculative looks.

"As you say." Peter slipped his left arm out of his sleeve, and pointed at three inch long silvery mark, just at the inside of his elbow. "Robbie's to blame for this one."

"Robbie is?" Guyon peered at the pale mark. "How?" Revenge for being silenced forgotten, he ran a finger lightly over the faintly raised skin.

"I was ten. He and Brian were eleven and very superior about their advanced age." Peter shook his head. "They wanted to go...oh, someplace, I don't remember where now...and didn't want me tagging after. They shut me up in the pantry. I got this climbing out the window."

"Unique to the end," Guyon said. "Most boys of ten would have got this breaking *in* to a pantry."

"It wasn't kept locked," Peter chuckled. "My mother understood the fact that young boys were always hungry. But we were expected to let the cook know what we were taking."

Guyon snorted. "I'm sure you were terribly dutiful about it," he agreed in patent disbelief. "What else?"

"Hmmm..." Peter slipped his shirt off the rest of the way. "I'll go over the ones from Poitou, since you know about those...but here..." He pointed at a crescent shaped scar on his right bicep. "Sarah."

"*Sarah*?" Guyon's eyebrows shot up. "How on earth -" He blinked. "Well, I'm impressed, I admit. What *did* you say to her to provoke this?"

"Oh...I was being a brother," Peter shook his head. "I said something offhand and probably very mean about her looks. I should have been more careful in my choice of moments though, and not said it when she had a hot curling iron in her hands."

"Possibly not, no," Guyon agreed. "It's...an interesting shape?" His mouth twitched. "Very unheroic. I can see why you tend not to explain this."

"If anyone asks, I just look mysterious and say a woman did it. Most of them don't press further." Peter laughed then crossed his arms. "Shirt."

Guyon stared at him for a moment, his mind completely

blank. "Shirt," he agreed amiably, and then - "*Oh*. Um, right." He took it off quickly, rubbing at the back of his neck and feeling decidedly awkward. "Shirt." He snorted at his own ridiculous behavior. Peter hated to be looked at far more than he did, and if this was his somewhat odd condition for Guyon finally being allowed to do more than try to observe without being caught staring, he was perfectly resigned to it.

"Oh...hmmm..." Peter sat on the edge of the bed and tugged his stockings off, pointing to the outside of his left calf. "That was a musket ball...a skirmish in some little place. Nothing important or brave. A few shots exchanged and we all went our separate ways. It just creased the skin and wasn't serious but hurt every step I took for a week or two."

"Mm. Wouldn't have been Powick Bridge, that little unimportant place, would it?" Guyon asked mildly. Off Peter's surprised look, he chuckled, and sat beside him, tracing the small grains of powder still visible in the scar, startling little flecks of blue. "I got into Corvay's reports. And you know I love reading." He grinned.

"Um, well..." Peter scratched at the scar, not looking at Guyon. "It wasn't major for me...I was terrified that I'd been hurt and would be sent home."

Guyon laughed in surprise. "You're hurt so we don't want you? You truly thought that was what would happen?" He shook his head. "I am trying very hard to imagine you letting anyone send you *anywhere*, if you were fighting for this cause you hold so very dear. And failing abysmally."

Peter chuckled, "Well, in my defense it did bleed quite a lot for such a small thing and, well, I had no home to go back to, so that was a valid concern. The Palatine just laughed at me."

Guyon thought that Rupert's laughter had probably been the kindest thing anyone could have done for Peter at that point in time. "I don't blame him," he said lightly. "Very young, very foolish."

Very brave, and utterly admirable. What was I doing then? Tutoring my first students, wholly ignorant of it all. I had never held anything more lethal than my clasp-knife, never known intent to harm, let alone kill. "I would have laughed at you too."

432

"It was what I needed," Peter nodded, "and rather reassuring, actually." He reached down and tugged Guyon's stockings off, rubbing his hands over the each instep in a firm caress. "I like your feet."

"My *feet*?" A small, surprised bubble of amusement distorted Guyon's voice. "Why, for God's sake? You love ice so much?" Then he smiled. "But I do have one good scar there, so perhaps you're right." He turned his right foot to the side, displaying an oddly perfect circle of flattened, silvery skin just on the side of his heel.

"They're good and sturdy. Strong. Not huge like mine. They suit you." Peter shrugged. "What's that from?" Long fingers reached out to stroke over the scar, feather light.

"Oh, Henri, François and I decided to learn cupping," Guyon said shamefacedly. "And we practiced on each others' *feet*, because I wouldn't take off my shirt, and arms are too visible, and - " he gestured at the scar. "I'm not sure what it does about humors, but it makes *lovely* blisters."

"I can imagine." Peter nodded, his fingers rubbing more purposefully, as if they would take away the small hurt. "Never let anyone take your blood," his voice was a bit absent sounding when he continued, "you might have need of it later."

"I'll bear that in mind," Guyon agreed. "You should take your own advice on that score, *bèl-mi*."

"Indeed," Peter agreed, coming back from where ever his mind had wandered. He stood then, unfastening his trousers and slipping them off, leaving only his drawers.

Guyon reached out a hand to touch the visible edge of the scar on Peter's hip. "Ah, this one I know," he said softly. The pen calluses on his fingers rasped slightly as he touched the raised skin. "Your *graz-dieu*." He knew that Peter did not understand why he called it a grace, knew that Peter did not see it as Guyon had always done, the line between the death that could have been and the life that was. The line between the brilliant, beloved Falkland's choice to ride into death and Peter's determination to survive and make others do so with him. *Your graz-dieu and mine.*

His horror of suicide would never fade, and his reading of

Falkland's decision in the midst of battle had only reinforced it. *Those I love will hold their lives cheap.* The earliest, most painful lesson.

Peter, unaware of his thoughts, nodded. "Newbury, of course. I should have been a bit faster."

"Hm." Guyon lowered his eyelids, concealing his changeable irises and his thoughts. "You were fast *enough*."

"I didn't suffer half as badly with that as from that stupid cut at Poitiers." Peter absently ran his hand over the more recent scar, still pink against his tan skin. He did not mention the still-lurid scar that showed in his hairline, neither of them as yet confident enough to make a jest of what Guyon's family had almost caused.

"Well, you didn't have an inept casuist repeatedly failing to stitch it up properly," Guyon pointed out dryly. His feelings about the entire episode were ones he kept very carefully buried beneath as many layers of sarcasm as he could find.

"And if I hadn't actually fought with you to keep you from doing it..." Peter gave a wry grin. "Anything you did had to have been an improvement over the first attempt."

"*Yes,*" Guyon said with feeling, and then, passionately, "I hate that scar. I hate what it stands for. I wish -" *I could have stopped it, could take it away, could erase that betrayal -* "that the sea were ink," he finished, disgusted with himself.

"I can't hate it in spite of all that," Peter took Guyon's hand and raised it to his lips. "That was when I first realized that you cared for me, at least as a friend, you worked so hard to make me well. You were so patient with my horrid moods and boredom. I'm sure I could have tried a saint."

Guyon laughed. "You probably could, and there were none to hand, alas..." He shook his head. "I took it out on everyone but the most deserving," he admitted. "I could have happily *murdered* you. Or tried. I would have enjoyed trying." He got to his feet as well. "I think I would have been very ineffectual, what with wanting you alive, but - I think I would have enjoyed the brief moment of conviction that I *was* trying, at least..." He shook his head, and leant in to kiss Peter.

"I'm very glad you didn't murder me," Peter chuckled and reached out toward Guyon's breeches, starting to unfasten them.

"Mm," Guyon agreed. "It would have made later developments...difficult." It was bliss to be able to touch and be touched, to fall easily into the first movements of the dance that was older than the first dawn and as new. He closed his eyes, still learning the feel of skin by heart, still not quite remembering either with mind or fingertips, still trying to commit his discoveries of what elicited a quick breath, a small shift, to memory.

There was a knock at the door, and his entire body jumped in involuntary reaction to the sound, his heart hammering. "*Jesus*," he gasped, and then, furiously, "*What*?"

"I'm here for the tray, Monsieur, if you have finished your meal." the girl's voice carried through the door a bit timidly after Guyon's growl.

"Oh *God*," said Guyon, rapidly using up his mental allowance for blasphemy before his next confession. He looked at Peter, then down at himself, and sighed. "And I suppose I'm nominated due to more clothing?" he asked wearily, and stacked the dishes on the tray before opening the door and handing it over with more force than grace. "*Thank* you," he said irritably.

"You're welcome, Monsieur," The little maid stared at Guyon's bare chest speculatively, nibbling at her bottom lip. "Are you sure you need nothing else?"

I am not going to answer that, Guyon thought, *no matter how much I'm longing to.* A snort of laughter, very badly disguised as a cough, from behind him made him grit his teeth. "No," he said in his nicest tones. "Only sleep. But thank you, again."

The maid gave him a brilliant smile, all gap-toothed and winsome, which made him suddenly wonder exactly how old she was. *Or how young.* And her walk as she went down the hallway, contained far more swish and swing than he was sure was absolutely necessary.

He shook his head, half-amused and half-bewildered, and wondering why he never seemed to be able to successfully convey his complete lack of any sort of interest. "Next room," he said dryly, "we get a lock on the *inside.*"

Peter was stretched out on the bed grinning like a lunatic when he returned, "Is Monsieur sure he wants nothing else?"

"*Monsieur,*" said Guyon with irritable emphasis, "is quite sure that he *does* want something else, starting with peace and quiet and time to *concentrate*, because he was in the middle of something very important."

The manic grin softened at the irritated words, "Important?"

"Obviously," Guyon said with all the hauteur at his command, which he recognized he was rendering fairly ineffectual by smiling - *like the lovesick fool I quite undoubtedly am,* he thought resignedly. "It's you, after all."

He quickly felt better about his own foolishness, because a blush suddenly began stretching over Peter's skin. "I -" Peter began, then simply reached out one hand. "Come here then."

Guyon crossed over to the bed, taking Peter's hand in his, and letting the strong grip pull him onto the worn and clean-smelling counterpane, reveling in the gift of touch. "Nothing is as important to me as you are. Not in this world or the next, not in my mind or heart. Nothing, ever, comes before you." *Romantic, sentimental, trite*, he thought. *I am reduced to the maunderings of a wine-sodden adolescent lout.* He half-laughed, half winced at himself. "It's unfortunate how ludicrous truth can sound," he said then.

"If it's truth, then it's never ludicrous," Peter kissed him gently. "Never."

"Hm. I like the way you hear words," Guyon said with a smile. "I will have to learn all the languages I can find, and make it sound new each time I say such things." He kissed Peter back, the small thrill of amazement that still raced through him at being able to do this catching him, as always, unawares; startling him into saying, "I love you."

"And *that* will always sound new, no matter the language. I love you too, Gui."

"Well, you have no sense," Guyon said in his most prosaic and dampening tones. He pressed his mouth to Peter's throat, to the hollow where the strong pulse beat, running his tongue lightly over the faintly-lined skin above his collarbones, where the line of sunburn was shading slowly to a less painful hue. "No sense, no taste, no discernment..." He punctuated each word with a kiss.

"I beg to differ..." Peter's voice had gone rough and breathy.

436

"My taste as never been in doubt. After all...the wager in town is when you will tire of me...not the reverse."

Guyon doubted that such speculation existed anywhere but Peter's unfounded worries. For the thousandth time, he managed not to express his feelings at whoever and whatever had made Peter think such things were to be taken for granted and spoken of as facts, and said in a commendably even voice, trying to conceal the sudden angry protectiveness that had swung through him - "Well, I hope you laid money down against it, then."

"Well, since I was eavesdropping I couldn't really say much of anything, I'm afraid," Peter smiled softly. "But I would have, because I'm going to do everything I can to make sure you never do."

"Oh, it's a safe bet," Guyon said in the same light voice, careful not to betray his sudden, furious longing for names and revenge. "Besides, you know eavesdroppers have rights to embarrass those they listen to. It's an odd thing, but always works..." He kissed Peter's shoulder, silent apology for the words that had obviously hurt.

"I'm afraid I would have embarrassed myself even more," Peter answered, once again twisting a finger around one of Guyon's curls. "But thank you."

"Hm. Nothing to thank me for. If I'd been *there*, to say what I thought, *then* you could have thanked me." He wondered what it would take, to make Peter sure of him - wondered, too, how much his own fears had contributed to this uncertainty, how much he should be damning himself, rather than the unknown participants of the wager. "Love doesn't stop. That's why it frightens people. It's so very all-consuming..."

"I know, " Peter stopped his restless fidgeting with Guyon's hair and kissed him. "I believe I told you once, that it didn't matter if you returned it, or if you never said it, that I would keep right on loving you. That hasn't changed. It can't. I was terrified though, to say it and to feel it."

"You?" Somehow that had never occurred to Guyon. That Peter *should* have been afraid, and of him, was not something he had ever questioned. But that he had been afraid of the emotion itself surprised him. "You kept that hidden." *I would have been kinder, perhaps, if I'd known. Not much, I'm incapable of much, still, but a little.*

"No one says something like that, without an idea about the response, without being afraid, beloved. No one."

"Well, I learned something new," Guyon said, unable to keep the surprise out of his voice. "But - not now? You're not afraid now?" *Of me? Please?* He touched his hands to the sides of Peter's face, gave him his best look of quizzical innocence. "Truly, I'm very nice. Not at all frightening or ogreish." He felt himself going red at the rather blatant untruth. "Really."

"You've given me everything I dreamed of, Gui, how could I be?" Peter's lip twitched in a small smile and he wrapped his arms around Guyon, pulling him closer. "Give me one kiss, and no more: If so be, this makes you poor, To enrich you, I'll restore for that one, two-thousand score."

"A thousand times a thousand, and a thousand more?" Guyon said teasingly, but he gave the requested kiss, letting himself feel the quiet satisfaction that it was no longer mimicry, but his own means, even if they were probably still clumsy compared to others Peter had known. "Now I want my payment." He smiled, putting his mouth back to where the pulse beat in the hollow of Peter's throat. "But I want it in installments, please. So that it takes forever." He kept his eyes closed against his own dissolution into endearments.

"Gladly." Peter shifted and claimed Guyon's lips in a demanding kiss, long and hard. "One," he breathed softly when he pulled away.

"Mm, you pay with *interest*." Guyon would never be able to tease like this fluently, but he knew, too, that he would never have to learn, since Peter was the only one at any of the earth's imagined corners who could laugh at him with impunity. He saw the brief struggle *not* to find his bad pun amusing in the blue eyes, and did not even try to hide his victorious smile when Peter gave in. "Should I make it compound, like the Paris bankers?"

Whatever Peter was going to respond was lost in another knock on the door. "Guyon? Are you awake? I can't sleep, and I'm bored. Can we go for a walk, or something?"

"Guyon is *busy* at the moment." Peter called out loudly.

"Then I'll go for a walk by *myself*," came the retort. Guyon thumped his head onto Peter's shoulder.

"She would, too," he said gloomily. "*Hell.*" He sat up, and began pulling on his clothes. "I don't *believe* this."

"I'm going to kill her. Slowly and painfully." Peter thumped his head back against the pillows with a groan. "Or...Or I'll wait until her wedding night...and come knocking at *her* door."

"With friends," Guyon agreed, shoving his feet into his boots. "*Drunk* friends. And mandolins. Possibly small drums." He leaned back, and kissed Peter with a great deal more regret than desire. "I'm sorry, bèl-mi."

"It's not your fault." Peter sighed, sadly. "Go on...I'll just lay here and dream of chains...and ropes...and really big locks."

"And methods of application," Guyon said. "Be inventive. Really." He took a deep breath, and went to the door. "I should put you on a leash for this walk," he said to Jeannine, as he left the room. "Put you on a leash and *drag* you."

He wondered just how many times he could be interrupted before he actually lost his mind.

As he closed the door, he heard Peter say, with frustrated amusement in his voice, "I knew there was a reason I've kept my wrists strong."

*

If Peter had begun the trip back to Paris with some odd idea in his head that Jeannine was some odd conglomeration of a child and a simulacrum of his sister, he was quickly being dispelled of that notion. Jeannine was at moments childlike, but that was more because it suited her purposes rather than any childlike qualities still infesting her attitude. She was also conniving, manipulative and stubborn beyond belief when she was thwarted. When she was bored, she was even worse. Right now, she was bored...immeasurably.

"But Peter, the garden is sure to be deserted. I've been cooped up in that stuffy old carriage all day and I need the fresh air. A walk would be just the thing to help me settle down for a good nights sleep." Her voice was pleasant and coercive, but Peter had heard it before.

"Ah, yes," Peter answered her back, "then you try to convince me to admire the shrubbery and you sneak off to God knows where, and I spend the rest of the evening searching for you."

"But that's not my fault," Jeannine replied sweetly. "You're just inattentive. I hadn't *gone* anywhere."

"In terms of 'you hadn't gone to Avignon', perhaps," Guyon said acidly. "In terms of 'not doing what you weren't supposed to', on the other hand, it was a total failure." Peter was slowly coming to terms with the fact that not only were all Jeannine's wiles transparent as glass to Guyon, but they always had been. It made his readiness to believe Maurice's claims of an imminent marriage all the more ridiculous, since the only thing Guyon wanted to do with Jeannine was to get her safely into the hands of Madame de Neuillant as fast as humanly possible. He had about as much patience with her as a striking snake disturbed from a summer sleep.

For her part, Jeannine merely disregarded what Guyon said. In that regard at least, she was like Sarah, who had never listened to him when he tried to forbid her something.

"But Peter, it really was a very uncomfortable day and I just know I'll never sleep." Jeannine had obviously fixed her sights on convincing the less stiff-necked of their little party to humor her - him. He knew she'd probably chosen well, he certainly was little proof against a pout and a sigh. He just hated that it was so obvious.

"Alas, resign yourself to insomnia," Guyon said without a trace of sympathy, and then, rather more grimly, "*Behave*, damn it." Whatever had transpired between them during Jeannine's abortive attempt to attend a village dance had left them completely out of charity with one another.

"I'm not doing anything." Jeannine blinked at him, guilelessly. "I'm not. Am I, Peter?"

"Um..." Peter squirmed in his seat. "Not yet?" *Damn.* This was exactly why he was no good with women. They confused him, *utterly.* Of course, so did Guyon at times, but somehow that never bothered him.

Guyon, unhelpfully, shook with brief and completely silent

laughter. "How very true," he murmured. "You know, if you'd shown the slightest signs of trustworthy behavior, Jeannine, this wouldn't be an issue. We could have safely left you in Costanza's company, retreated to a safe distance, and allowed you as many walks as you liked. You have no one to blame but yourself for this. And *stop* bullying Peter, or I'll take the key to your room from you, and lock you in from the *outside*."

"I'd never bully Peter," Jeannine's protest was as quick as it was insincere. "I don't, do I?" She leaned into him, her eyes large and doe-like, soft lips parted little more than a breath away. "I'd never *want* to do that."

"Um..." Peter blushed. *Damn it*. It was ridiculous. He could see exactly what she was doing, but somehow that omniscience was not helping him. "Guyon?"

Guyon made an odd sound that was incredibly close to a sneeze. "Jeannine?" His voice was as soft and coaxing as hers, and she drew back and blinked at him, a little confused. His return smile held all the reassurance of a razor blade's edge. "Key," he said with a dangerous lack of emphasis

"Humpf." Jeannine slouched back to her previous position, crossing her arms over her chest. *Thank God.* Peter sent a grateful expression toward Guyon. He hadn't been sure just how far Jeannine would have gone to coerce him and really did not want to know.

"Can I at least choose dinner, since I'm being held prisoner?" She quickly sat up and unfolded her arms. *She's a smart girl.* Peter suddenly thought. *No sense in covering up one of your major assets.* His eyes went wide. Where the hell had that thought come from? Jeannine was too young and sisterly...and yes, his own sister had found her children under a cabbage leaf and she and Robbie had never had sex. Peter was enjoying his foray into denial far too much.

Guyon's head tilted a little, his eyes narrowing in assessment. Then he shrugged. "Why not?" he asked lightly. "As long as you remember you have to eat it as well." He looked over at Peter, and his mouth pulled down at one corner before twitching up again uncontrollably. He raised a hand and rubbed at it with his thumb, and stifled a small laugh.

"Of course." That quickly her pout was dispelled and she stood up, smoothing down her dress and strolling, almost elegantly over to where the innkeeper stood.

"That was...odd." Peter gave a sigh of relief as she moved out of earshot. "I feel like I'm some part of a strange school exercise on flirtation and manipulation."

"You are," Guyon said amusedly. "So am I, on those alternate Wednesdays so spoken of. She just doesn't like my return approach as much as yours, so I get free time." He patted Peter's shoulder sympathetically. "At least she likes you?" It would have helped if he hadn't sounded quite so uncertain about the fact.

"I hope so...because I find her completely terrifying." Peter let out a long slow exhalation of breath. "Let me fight battles and wage wars...but God keep me from women."

Guyon stared at him for one incredulous moment, before dropping his head into his hands and finally giving in to the laughing fit that had been threatening all evening. "Um. Yes..." he managed in a stifled voice, before succumbing once more.

"It's not funny!" Peter whispered fervently, but Guyon's laughter was contagious and he found himself joining in.

"You and Saint Augustine," Guyon said eventually, raising his head. "Only you're the reverse. 'Give me women, Lord, but not yet!'"

Jeannine, coming back over, actually looked thrown. "Oh. Er, should I go away and come back?" she asked hesitantly.

Yes! Peter wanted to exclaim. Although, at that moment he wanted nothing more than for her to go away and not come back. Guyon in a teasing mood? Guyon laughing brightly as if everything in life was a glorious joke, just for his amusement? It happened far too seldom.

"Yes," Guyon said, with barely credible seriousness. "We are going to debate on the nature of women, and you should not be listening. It might corrupt you irretrievably." He looked up at her with utterly translucent eyes.

"Oh, poo." Jeannine chuckled. "Then I surely will want to stay in that case."

"*Lemora*," Guyon said unlovingly. "I should have guessed. What are you going to make us eat, anyway?"

"Blood and raw flesh," Jeannine answered coolly, returning to her seat. "What else would a leech wish to eat?" Peter dropped his head into his hands and shook his head, conceding defeat. Defeat in what, he wasn't sure, but the feeling was the same.

"Just blood, I always thought, my dearest parasite," Guyon said cheerfully. "Oh, well, that takes care of the wine, I suppose, I always wanted to commit living blasphemy."

And leave it to Guyon to be not only horrifying, but dangerous with it.

"All the time you spend drawing blood and you've never tasted it?" Jeannine's expression was as sweet as her words were sharp. Peter suddenly wondered if he should take notes. The wicked banter that the two dealt between them was very like what Guyon had often traded with François. Was this something he should learn? He wondered at that. Could he learn it, even if he wanted to?

"Only when I'm quite, quite sure of its purity," Guyon replied with perfect innocence. He smiled, and Jeannine went suddenly red. "Ah, the wine," he added smoothly, as a servant came over. "No, just leave it, that's fine..." He arched an eyebrow. "Thirsty, Jeannine?"

"I - Yes..." Jeannine simply nodded, the blush still on her cheeks. *Fault to Guyon.* Peter managed to keep from laughing, mostly. No, he did not think he would attempt to learn that trick of speech. He wasn't quick enough he knew, to keep up with Guyon's verbal sparring. Best to keep *his* to a blade of cold steel rather than trust his tongue.

Guyon, seemingly absorbed in pouring the wine, looked up at him suddenly and grinned, fully aware of the point he had won, and utterly unselfconscious about his means of doing it. He handed Jeannine her wine cup, and brushed his finger over her nose, a quick, rare gesture of consolation from a man who despised such things. "You know the rules, pica," he said kindly. "Don't play that game -"

"Until you're ready to play to the end," they chorused together. Jeannine's blush was fading. "I forgot," she admitted.

It was oddly familiar, this feeling of being left on the outside. It was once again watching Guyon and François, joke and tease and touch, and knowing that he'd never be part of it, never keep up. He took the cup that Guyon poured out for him, "So what are we to have for dinner?"

"Leeks," said Jeannine cheerfully, and then - "Ow! Guyon, that *hurt*!"

"You want to know what else I can come up with as well as taking your key?" Guyon asked, his eyebrows both raised in a way that promised doom. Jeannine sighed, the sound of the thoroughly put upon.

"We *are*. Well. *Also* leeks. They have a vegetable garden, and they cook things with that stuff that grows in water...oh, you know. Rice. And goose. And that funny bread." She pointed across the room, and Guyon rolled his eyes, pushing her arm down.

"Yes, very polite, sweeting - *well, well.*" His voice had taken on the more familiar resonance of real interest. "Peter, their cook is Eastern."

Peter's lip suddenly twitched, "How Eastern?"

"That *funny bread* is barbari," Guyon said, making a face at him. "So...all the way to Persia Eastern."

"If he's a decent cook, we're in for a treat then." Peter smiled. This is something he actually knew - good food was good food, no matter the language, and he had spent months with Rupert. Rupert who was always more than willing to try new things...then inflict them on his captains.

"You know about Persia?" Now that he had finally allowed himself to admit her charms, Jeannine looked about forty times more seductive when she was genuinely interested rather than feigning it, Peter noticed worriedly, and he realized why Guyon was so determined to get her into the comparatively safe hands of Madame de Neuillant as soon as he could. They were both responsible for far to many extremely impressionable and very young men for her presence in their company to be a good thing.

"Some," Peter admitted, then wondered if he should have denied it when Jeannine's excited gaze turned on him more fully. "Tell me." She wheedled. "I've never been anywhere."

Guyon rolled his eyes to the ceiling. "Poor deprived child," he said dryly, but the look in his eyes, when he lowered them again, was as pleading as hers, and Peter remembered that while he would never have admitted to anything so obvious, Guyon's sole experiences of 'going anywhere' had been primarily within France and usually on Corvay's business.

"Very well," Peter began to weave them a tale, telling of his travels with the Palatine. He told of the air that was so hot and warm that it felt like soup, of the winds that blew everyday and the beauty of the people. Of nights scented with incense and jasmine, and days at the bazaars that outdid even the fairs and markets of Paris. He told how oranges tasted first thing in the morning after a long night's watch, and of strong coffee, served in tiny cups, that could jolt you into wakefulness.

"And the muezzin calls, O Allah Akbar, Ash-hadu al-la, ilaha illallah, Ash-hadu anna Muhammadan, rasulullah..." Guyon said in his deep voice, a chant and a paean.

"You have to give them the honor of their Faith." Peter nodded. "Even if you don't agree with it. They adhere to it strictly, most of them by choice."

"It's our faith too," Guyon said to a wide-eyed Jeannine. "His Palatine prays for it. God is the Greatest, and I bear witness that there is no lord except God. Make haste towards prayer. Make haste towards welfare. Make haste towards the best thing, for God is the Greatest, and there is no Lord except God."

"Aşkin Cemal Olsun," Jeannine whispered, and Guyon went red, and then very white as the sudden heat faded from his face.

"*No!*" He swallowed wine and added - "That's different. That's - I'm sorry. I'm - not well. No, Peter, stay. I - I simply need to sleep." He crossed the room, stumbling a little, and Jeannine was very red again when she said quietly.

"I'm sorry. Really."

Peter watched Guyon's departure with a sad smile, "No, it's alright, Jeannie...It's new for him. He can't tease yet. And I don't think..." He shifted, stopping that train of thought. "But that leaves more dinner for us. Rice and goose...you'll like it."

"Given that I ordered it," she said sharply, "I hope so." Her beautiful golden eyebrows raised in expectation of a response.

"Yes...indeed." Peter's answer, he knew, left much to be desired. He really wanted nothing more than to go after Guyon, hold him and love him until he felt no more strangeness.

"Oh -!" For a moment, she sounded like Guyon at his most exasperated. "*Learn*, Pèire. *Peter*." She went redder still. "You say that it will be wonderful because *I* have ordered it, and I say - do my tastes suit yours? - and you say?" She smiled hopefully.

"I hope so...because I'm hungry?" Peter tried to bring his mind back to the conversation at hand, knowing that Jeannine would be much more manageable if given a bit of attention.

She blew out an exasperated little huff. "*No*. Play."

"Play?" Peter was totally confused. Not that this was uncommon for him when women were concerned, but usually he at least recognized *what* it was that they wanted, if not why. "Play what?"

Her eyes went wide. "Oh *Dio*. Guyon will kill me, that's why he said not to - you say that you are only hungry for beauty." She looked nervous.

"Beauty is not very filling to the belly, Jeannie...trust me on that one." Peter sighed. "And *please,* just tell me what it is you're trying to get me to do. It will be much quicker than all of this...whatever it is we're doing now."

"Teaching you." For once, she was straightforward, her eyes as greenly uncompromising as Guyon at his most implacable. *God, the eyes of the Languedoc, the very devil!* "I say one thing, and you respond. We amuse. We catch and pass and *amuse.*"

"Of course," Peter let out a tired sigh. "There are reasons that I avoid such conversations, you know? Because I am *very* bad at them."

"But Guyon teaches us." Her eyes were kind, now, and understanding. "You survive by words."

"No...Guyon survives by words. I am merely the muscle that enforces them." Peter shook his head. "But I will try...if it pleases you."

"It pleases *him*." She grinned, and her bottom teeth had a little, endearing crossover in the front. "Tell me - oh, Peter!" She leant forward, infused with something he had no name for. "Tell me of the Palatine!"

"That is much easier than what you were asking before," Peter chuckled. "The man is everything you could want in a commander - strong, brave, forthright...a bit of a bastard at times, *if you'll excuse my language*, but that's alright. It makes him approachable, human. I'd trust him with my life. I...I trust him as much as I trust Guyon." Peter suddenly realized that his words were true. He did trust Guyon that much. Maybe this was his first step to learning to not do things *for* his beloved and, rather, trust him to do them for himself.

"He sounds..." Jeannine stopped, and laughed. "I think I *will* take my dinner to my room. Costanza will love to chastise me. I shall see you in the morning, Scudamore." She dropped a little, formal curtsey, laughed, flicked her fingers, and was gone, followed by three eager serving men. They had, Peter noticed, taken the wine with them.

"Wonderful..." Peter climbed to his feet, muttering softly. "Now I get to make sure that she arrives and that they do not linger..."

Having disposed of the serving men - or rather watched Jeannine dismiss them - Peter went back to their room, and, with some alarm, noted that the plates being brought out were untouched, and the brandy being taken in replaced an empty wine bottle.

He intercepted the brandy and carried it in himself. "The food was not to your taste? I could order you something else."

"Oh, good Christ. Do I look in need of a nursemaid?" Guyon, who had been lying flat on the bed with his eyes closed, sat up, disconcertingly awake. "*No,* Peter. I am suffering from the pangs of love, so leave me be."

Peter raised his eyebrows at the rather unequivocal and certainly unexpected statement, "Ah...I had no idea the feeling would strike you so unpleasant. Shall I leave?"

"Given that it's you who strike me, it would be only courteous to remain and give the *coup de grace*, don't you think?" Guyon's voice was calm and almost dismissive, but his whole body leant outwards, silent yearning. "*Dear God.* I want you."

"And you have me," Peter said, half-amazed at this new openness. He had always been afraid of Guyon's hidden fire, but it seemed it was no more than an ordinary desire, even if it frightened the possessor of it. But not him. Unconcealed, it was

447

too close to truth to worry him, being its object.

Guyon, seeing neither his astonishment nor his acceptance, laughed, tired and harsh. "Yes, *that* I know. But can I *have* you, love and my light and my dear, will you *take* me?" He curled away from the window and from Peter, silent negation. "It's not - it's foolish, I know that. Only sometimes..." He rolled onto his back. "I *yearn*, I *long*, I *desire*."

For the first time in a very long while, Peter was almost as confused by Guyon as he had been by Jeannine earlier. Why should he feel the need to state it so plainly, when it was clear in every line of his body? Unless he was wrong in his assumptions - but no, Guyon's words had cast all that aside before he even began to think. To Guyon's plainness came a little imp of his own evasion, an irresistible desire to tease and prolong this unusual openness. He opened his eyes wide. "But Gui - I *do* have you. You're as embedded in me as my soul."

Guyon thumped his head back into the bolster with a force that would have rendered him unconscious had it been a wooden frame. "Oh, Christ! Pèire! Don't you realize even now why I left the room? I cannot, will not, will *never* show to the world that desire. Because it is not for *them* to remark upon. Only for you."

Peter stared at him for a moment, and then nodded. "When we get back, then?" They would never have that kind of privacy while they travelled, even if it was only the constant awareness that they were responsible for Jeannine, that there were people they did not know surrounding them, that to lose sight of the reason they were returning to Paris, and thereby fall into the trap of believing that this time of comparative freedom truly could mean anything of the kind, was their very own edge to a fearful precipice. "Gui, I don't think it's wise -"

To give in, to let you or myself be seduced by the honesty we've wanted for so long - because if we do, we'll forget everything else, and we can't afford to.

Guyon nodded, his expression almost grim in its determination, understanding of all that Peter wasn't saying clear in his washed-glass eyes. "When we get back," he agreed. He smiled a little at that, the amusement inward-turning as ever, but not, for once, with any underlying bitterness. "That is, if I remember what to do when interruption is not imminent."

*

Paris, August 1646

Like to the Indians scorched with the Sunne,
The Sunne which they doe as their God adore:
So am I us'd by Love, for evermore
I worship him, lesse favors have I wonne.
Better are they who thus to blacknesse run,
And so can onely whitenesse want deplore:
Then I who pale and white am with griefes store,
Nor can have hope, but to see hopes undone.

Riding into Paris after all their weeks in the countryside had been a bit of a shock, so many people and horses and carts and business. The noise was horrendous and much more jarring than that of cock crow and lamb bleat. And Jeannine was determined to see it all, her head hanging out the window of the carriage like hound catching a scent. After the third admonition to pull it back inside, Peter had given up and dropped back beside Guyon to ride the last mile in more peaceful company. Not even Jeannine had lost her decorum enough to holler out to them across the intervening distance.

Guyon gave him a sympathetic look, his eyes narrowed as though by doing so he could block out the noise and the glare of sun on high polished stone walls. He had made no attempt to force Jeannine to desist, perhaps because he had recognized the futility of it before she had even started to show her frightening degree of interest.

"Just a few hours more," he murmured quietly, "and then we can...reacclimatize in peace."

"Please, God, yes." Peter mumbled fervently. There were times when he actually liked Jeannine and enjoyed her company, but he was too tired, too anxious to be home and settled, for this to be one of them. "We'll send the carriage ahead to Madame's, shall we? Make her walk? That might settle her down enough to be reasonably demure."

"Better she sees exactly what she has to deal with, I think." Peter always forgot that Guyon liked most people, as long as they didn't actually impinge on his life to any degree that he considered to be inconvenient. Madame de Neuillant had been once and casually kind to Guyon, and as far as he was concerned, that was all he needed to know about her. "Besides, I'm quite sure Madame will be far more inventive in ways of wearing her out than a mere *walk*."

"I'm not sure I really want to know that." Peter chuckled. He could only imagine what Madame's methods included, but they seemed to be successful, whatever they were, turning out young women of apparent breeding, no matter what their actual backgrounds held.

Guyon grinned at him. "But now you do, and you will be imagining the very worst for *days*." He cast a glance up the road to where Jeannine's head was attempting to revolve like an owl's as she made a valiant effort to take in everything at once. "You may actually find it surprisingly soothing to contemplate..." They were turning down towards the Rue des Esclangons, and he made a face. "Perhaps we could just leave her here to wait and disappear to your hôtel..."

"As much as I wish we could...." Peter let his voice drift off. Guyon knew he wouldn't do it. Peter knew he wouldn't do it. Sometimes Peter's sense of honor and duty could be annoying and frustrating, even to himself.

"I know, I know," Guyon's sigh was small, and somehow managed to combine amusement and resignation together in one brief exhalation. "We're going to do it all as properly, just as her father would want. Although *why* he wants it like this is one of the world's greatest mysteries."

"Do you think de Tourvel entirely naïve as to what his daughter has planned for herself?" Peter wondered. They had never discussed this but Peter was sure that marriage alone was not in Jeannine's plan.

"Deliberately, yes. Actually? No. I think he knows just what she has in mind - *and* that for someone like her, it's her best chance of being content, if not happy in the way he might prefer. Cap might love Jeannine with all his heart, but he's well-versed in the reasons he'll never get anywhere at court and never could. But - his money counts for her when it couldn't count for him, and -" He shrugged. "He knows."

Peter nodded. He'd felt sure that Jeannine's father at least suspected, but suspecting and knowing could be two very different things.

The carriage finally drew to a stop in front of Guyon's home and Peter dismounted to hand Jeannine out and down to the street.

"Is this Madame's home?" Jeannine looked rather disillusioned with the appearance of the place.

"No," Guyon said with rather obviously strained patience, "it's my school. And my home. And Gottfried and Ännchen van Hesselink's home. And you *will* be polite about it, brat, or I will make you wait in the carriage and tell every sausage vendor and fruit seller in the area to come and offer their wares."

"I would never be impolite to your friends, Guyon..." Jeannine answered him back, then paused, "...well, except for Peter, but he doesn't count."

"Ah, it's nice to know where I stand in the grand scale of things," Peter said wryly as he directed the coachman back to the stables.

"I don't *want* to know where I stand," Guyon muttered for Peter's benefit, his eyes gleaming with a peculiar inner mirth. "Come on, let's face the hordes. And Gottfried."

Peter nodded and moved forward to open the door, but before he could it flew open of its own accord.

"Peter! Guyon!" Ännchen, her curls pinned back and an apron covering her skirts, practically bounced out the door. "Welcome home. Oh, we've missed you both so much. The students are about to drive Gottfried out of his mind and I do believe that Lt. Wycombe has developed an unhealthy attachment to my cook's lemon tarts, he has stopped by so frequently to see if we've heard from you."

"Such a joy to know our sparkling personalities left a void," Guyon said amusedly. "Anna, this is Jeannine de Tourvel, who is going to be a pupil of Madame de Neuillant's. Soon, in fact," he added with only slightly exaggerated relief.

"Ah, I see." Ännchen nodded and held her hand out to Jeannine. "Welcome to Paris, Mademoiselle. Now...all of you come in and sit. I will ply you with wine and tea and lovely food and you will tell me of your journey and -"

"Anna, who are you -?" Gottfried appeared in the journey. "Ah, the bad pennies have turned up."

"Oh, we're not bad at all, we're beautifully new-minted," Guyon retorted with a quick smile, before adding brightly, "Have you killed anyone yet?"

"Not yet, but it's been close," Gottfried slapped him on the back with a large grin. "Ännchen, lets get our friends inside and...Oh, hello?"

Apparently, he had just noticed Jeannine, something she would find rather lowering, Peter thought.

"Gottfried, Jeannine," Guyon said wearily, having apparently run out of patience with lengthy introductions. "She's going away in a few hours, so you don't have to be nice."

"Ah, but I always leave being ill-tempered to you, my dear. You know that." Gottfried chuckled and took Jeannine's hand for a moment. "Now, let's get in off the street before we stop traffic completely."

As they entered the cool hallway, still smelling mysteriously of new paint and old socks together, there was the sound of concentrated thumping from the main teaching room, and Herr Kirschner's exasperated voice bellowing for someone or other to sit down. The thumping intensified, and then a very angry Kees, his sketchbook under one arm, stamped into the hallway, past them all without a glance, and slammed out into the street.

"That," Guyon said wryly, "was our painter-in-residence. What's the matter with him?"

Peter, who had been watching Jeannine take this all in with no small amount of amusement, looked up too, "He's not been annoying you has he? I know his Royal commission may have been put on hold while we were gone but -"

"No, I suspect it was Andre," Ännchen huffed. "Monsieur Morel would try a the patience of a saint."

"Now, Anna, y -"

"No, Gottfried, it's true. And if he doesn't stop making calf eyes at David, Henri is going to knock him down."

Guyon groaned at that little piece of unwanted intelligence. "Let him," he said pithily. "Maybe some sense will be knocked into his head at the same time."

Jeannine turned wide eyes on him. "And you said you liked things uncomplicated!"

"I do." Guyon shrugged a little. "Events tend to conspire against me..."

There was another crash from inside and Ännchen smiled distractedly, "I hope that wasn't the new map holder."

"Here...let's go," Peter encouraged them all towards the door,

"Do you want me to -" Guyon began at the same time, gesturing towards the noise, and there was a Germanic roar of fury from Herr Kirschner's unmistakable voice that drowned out his last word and silenced all the continuing noise. "Oh. Never mind. Er, yes, let's go..." He took the opportunity, as Gottfried politely escorted Jeannine through, to brush a kiss over Ännchen's cheek. "Thank you," he said quietly, and Peter remembered that the last time they had seen each other, things had been infinitely unsettled and probably very worrying for Ännchen, who made no secret of her affection for them both.

Ännchen blushed merrily, reaching out to give Guyon's arm a small squeeze, "You're welcome. I'm glad you took the best advantage of your trip."

"We both did," Peter assured her with a smile. "We both did."

"Yes," Guyon agreed with the old, evasive wryness that Peter had not missed in the slightest, "we went away and changed the world. Astounding what a little southern air can do."

Peter held back the sudden urge he felt to grab Guyon and kiss him until he was either insensible, or admitted in front of Ännchen at least, that he loved Peter. A dangerous thought here in the middle of Paris and he squelched it immediately, but it was still a delicious idea for the short time he held it.

"So, what has our very dear Monsieur Morel been doing to irritate everyone?" Peter asked instead as they moved inside. "Apart from being too much himself?"

"Oh, you name it, he annoyed it," Gottfried said wearily. "He even managed to get up de Barrion's nose, and the man's got a surprising tolerance for idiots these days. He just *will not learn* the basic survival skills around here, including when to shut up."

Ännchen settled them all in her sitting room and went off to give orders to the cook and call her father up to join them. The place had not changed in the few weeks they had been gone, unsurprisingly, although somehow Peter had expected it to. He looked over to where Guyon was chatting with Gottfried and smiled. So much was the same and so much had changed. Changed for him at least.

He drew his thoughts back and turned toward Jeannine, who was fidgeting like the youngster she was, "Madame is not expecting us until later in the day, and will most likely not be at home. It would do us no good to go there directly, so relax."

"She'll send for you, anyway," Guyon added, before turning his attention back to Gottfried and a pile of badly-scrawled papers. "Ännchen can give you a tour of our own little labyrinth, if you've got that much energy." He laughed. "A brief glimpse of how you will *not* be living."

"It's very nice here, I'm sure," Jeannine answered him back quickly. "Well, except for your rooms, I'd expect. Piled to the ceiling with papers and books and odd bits that you've left laying when you got distracted."

"You do know him," Ännchen had reentered the room and laughed delightedly. "I'm always afraid that I'll mistakenly clean away something important."

"*Everything's* important," Gottfried and Guyon said together, and then both choked. "Not that your housekeeping isn't a thing of joy and perpetual wonder, darling," Gottfried added quickly.

"Just a little disconcerting," Guyon said serenely, mischief in his eyes. "*Did* you ever find the astrolabe treatise, Gottfried?"

Gottfried nodded sorrowfully. "It was in with the Plautus comedies."

"Good organizing," Guyon said, his mouth twitching.

"Oh you." Ännchen swatted at his arm. "Come, Jeannine, I will show you around our little bit of Paris...starting with Guyon's rooms. They'll need to be aired anyway."

Jeannine rose obediently, "I'll help you." Her eyes twinkled suddenly, "And make sure everything gets in the proper order."

"You touch, you die," Guyon said cheerfully. "I doubt anyone will miss you for at least a week. We'll just pretend to have been delayed on the road."

"Grouchy bear," Jeannine mumbled just loud enough for

Peter's ears as she followed Ännchen out the door, laughing.

"God, let that message arrive *soon*," said Guyon pathetically. "I can't stand much more of being nice - and yes, as you both very well know, this *is* me being nice. Incredibly nice. In a most praiseworthy manner."

Peter stepped over to Guyon's side and gave him a soothing pat on the back, "Your patience has been a thing of legend the entire trip. Shall I ask Ännchen for a bit of cake as a reward?"

Guyon's eyes narrowed. "You're bribing me with *cake*?" he demanded incredulously. "That's just not good enough!"

Peter leaned in closer, dropping his voice down to a sultry growl, "What would you prefer that I bribe you with?"

"That's enough." Gottfried laughed, covering his ears. "I'm not sure I want to hear the answer."

But Guyon's expression had changed, hardened into the odd determination that he usually showed in a debate or with the scholars, when he was about to say something that mattered to him and that he was terrified of, knowing it would reveal far too much of his inner self. His voice was light, however, belying the uncompromising clarity of his eyes. "Oh, just love. Why would I ask for anything else?"

The words caught Peter's heart, twisting it and slamming it back into his chest with an almost painful beat of happiness, "What else indeed? But you have that already, as much as I have to give. Do you not wish for more?"

"Mm." Guyon frowned, pretending to consider, before shaking his head. "No, I think not." Then he laughed. "Apples, maybe?"

"I'll have some shipped from Brocéliande immediately," Peter chuckled. "I think -"

What he thought was interrupted by another crash and a peal of laughter from the direction of the stairs and the schoolroom.

"Do I want to know?" Gottfried asked rather tiredly, getting to his feet.

"Almost certainly not," Guyon said in the same tone.

"I'll go." Peter shook his head and went toward the stairs. He'd recognized the laugh as Jeannine's and if she was causing trouble, he would definitely be dealing with it.

"Oh noble martyr," Guyon said mockingly as he left the room, and Peter resisted the impulse to turn around and stick his tongue out. He really *had* spent too much time with Jeannine.

There was another peal of laughter as Peter reached the schoolroom door and he paused there. Jeannine with a bemused Ännchen standing behind her, was surrounded by a veritable court of young men. Most of them students, of course, but Peter could see that some of his Cadets were there as well, Thomas being foremost among them. His hand was stretched out toward Jeannine as if he were offering her something, although from where Peter stood he could not say quite what.

"It's the Marshal." A sudden urgent whisper called out and all the Cadets suddenly snapped to attention. Well, at least they hadn't totally gone lax while he was away.

Ännchen gave Peter a look that he had become intimately familiar with in the last few days, the look of the total innocent watching their life somehow start to turn on its head and evade their control completely. The calculated sweetness in Jeannine's smile was far more horrifying.

I'd rather relive Newbury than deal with whatever she's come up with this time, he thought gloomily.

"Really, Jeannine," Peter put his best irritated older brother look on his face. "Is it necessary for you to disrupt things even here?"

"But sir, Mademoiselle de Tourvel was just -" Thomas began.

"Yes, I know what Mademoiselle was just." Peter snapped, "And I was not addressing you, Cadet."

Thomas fell silent, standing even stiffer than his *at attention* pose warranted.

Jeannine gave him a startled look, as though realizing she had finally crossed some line she had not even understood existed until that moment. She opened her mouth to say something, and Ännchen forestalled her.

"We'd better go and see whether my father has actually locked himself *in* the cellar," she said cheerfully. "Come on." Despite her tone, she gave the room full of young men an extremely unsympathetic look as she ushered Jeannine out.

Peter turned back to the room as they left, eyeing all the

young men. "Hmmm...gone a few weeks and what do I find? My cadets lounging about in the middle of the day. Are there no duties to be preformed? No drills? Has Cromwell surrendered at last and made my job redundant? Explain this to me, Cadet!"

The question was directed to Thomas, who was slightly senior to the rest, "We're off-duty, sir. And...we do have friends here, sir."

Now that was an amazing idea. One Peter had nurtured, of course, but he'd no idea it had taken root to this extent. "Understood. But, the students are not quite as *off-duty* at this time of day."

"Not at all, in fact," Guyon's voice was pure unadulterated acid from behind him. "You." He jerked his thumb at his students. "Out. I want to have a few words in private, if it's not *too* inconvenient - *ah, Monsieur Morel.*" If it were possible, his voice sharpened. "Haven't we already had this conversation about where you should be and where you are allowed to be and *why*, please, have you not paid attention?" His eyes swept scathingly over the room. "*Move*, gentlemen!"

Exchanging decidedly worried glances, the students trooped past him. Guyon stayed for another moment, his expression grim. "Count yourselves fortunate you've only let down the Marshal," he said coolly. "*I* would be less understanding." He closed the door behind him, and the beginnings of a crisp explanation as to why he was so annoyed could be heard starting in the hallway, fading away as he herded them down into the secondary teaching room.

Peter snapped his attention back to his cadets, "Now...who would like to explain to me, how you all came to be here, disrupting the work of this establishment, off-duty or not?"

There were several starts all jumbling out at once before Peter pointed at one Cadet. Roger Deighton, Peter realized, another of those involved in the bet that he had overheard being made. "You.. Deighton. You tell me."

"They said we could, sir?" Deighton apparently thought this was the perfect answer, because having got the five words out, he relaxed considerably. There was a lot of nodding in agreement.

"They said you could?" Peter frowned. "Who, exactly, said

you could?"

He could not, for the life of him, imagine Gottfried offering an invitation to what would surely be chaos.

"Kees and Philippe?" It somehow came out as more of a question than an answer.

Peter managed to restrict himself to a mental groan. *Of course it was. The only two whose official purpose is so varied they could be used for a fresco.* "You decided that because a part-time painter and a *secretary* told you it was perfectly all right to come and disrupt a house full of students, that's just what you'd do?" he demanded incredulously.

"He's your secretary? Sir?"

"Not for much longer if he keeps this up," Peter muttered under his breath. "And what, exactly, did you think you'd be doing once you arrived?"

There was a certain amount of shuffling, and not all of it was from the increasingly red-faced Deighton. "Morel," came the muttered answer at last, and then, belatedly, "Sir."

A puzzled and rather disturbing image flashed through Peter's brain at the thought of anyone 'doing' Morel, and he had to clear his throat before he continued, "Ah, yes, the ever-trustworthy Monsieur Morel...What had he to do with all this, precisely?"

"*What in the blind **hell** did you think you were doing involving Vincennes in your infantile game of one-upmanship?*" Guyon's temper was usually controlled well enough for sarcasm, but that had been a real yell of pure fury, coming through two closed doors, three stone walls, and along most of a hallway. "*My God, you childish, irresponsible little liability! Get out of my school! Get out of my sight!*"

"Um, that," said Deighton.

Surely Morel had not admitted to Guyon about his little...bet. He'd told Guyon it was ongoing, warned him more or less, but still having it put in your face was altogether different. Rather like having overheard it in the first place.

"Out with it." Peter growled. "Now."

"We...sort of...Kees said...and I said...and Philippe was pretty annoyed, and then there was a wager, and Vincennes tried stopping it and then Morel asked de Retz for a loan because he couldn't pay and he blamed Vincennes and everyone was really angry and we didn't get the money anyway."

They all have rocks in their heads, Peter thought numbly.

"And Morel was smug and Kees said we could get him back and he had a plan and he actually didn't but it's really easy to make Morel angry so we did." There was a pause. "So we're here, sir."

"And just what was the basis for this...wager, Cadet?" Peter's voice was as hard as steel and just as cold. He wondered if they would tell him or if they'd make up something. Of course, it could be a completely different bet, but that was not something he would be laying odds on.

Deighton scratched at the back of his neck. "It's..."

"A debate about the merits of scholars and soldiers that got out of hand, sir," said Thomas. "And unforgivably, we used yourself and de Chesnay as living examples on which to put our money. Doctor Vincennes took...extreme exception."

Hmmm...perhaps he should talk to her Majesty about training Thomas for the diplomatic corps, he was obviously too good at prevarication to remain a mere valet.

"I can imagine that the good doctor would, indeed." Peter said almost to himself, then turned back to his Cadets. "Your bets have little to do with me, but disrupting a civilian establishment does. Go back to the Hôtel and inform Lt. Wycombe that I'm back and that you are all to have 2 days remedial duty. Perhaps, the extra drill will put some sense into your heads. Dismissed."

The sound of Guyon expressing the last of his bad temper forcibly and succinctly to Gottfried filtered through as they all escaped.

"*I did not invest in this place to have it turn into a sink of depravity that Corvay can prey on at will, damn you...*"

The rest was inaudible, but Peter felt that he might be having a similar conversation with Lt. Wycombe before the week was out.

*

With Jeannine sent off to Madame de Neuillant's capable

hands, carriage, boxes and all; Gottfried placated and somewhat enlightened as to the reasons for Guyon's annoyance, and his own somewhat quieter wrath provoked enough for a few restrictive ideas to be put in motion at the school; enough somewhat startling dishes tasted and approved of to satisfy Ännchen; and Herr Kirschner's cellar having been chosen from and sent on ahead, Guyon and Peter were free to make their somewhat embarrassed escape.

"I would have offered you a bed for the night," Guyon said with an unusual lack of double meanings, "but it seems that your presence is more required at the hôtel than mine is at the school."

"Apparently so," Peter frowned. "It would seem that Lt. Wycombe needs a few reminders of how discipline should be upheld. No, I can't believe he knowingly allowed this to happen, but he needs to keep his eyes open. I just won't have this."

"They're young, they have pay, they get undercharged for everything, and they're all bored," Guyon pointed out. "Of course, the cadets have no excuse at all." His little sideways grin was an invitation to amusement. "Oh, Peter, haven't you realized? They are as angry as you about how little this country will help. Morel is simply an easy focus. I don't blame the cadets. I *don't*, no matter how annoyed I may be with the whole idiotic group, and no matter how much I may want to lock the students into their rooms or send them to the Sorbonne *now,* I understand. Yours are homesick and they loathe Cromwell, and they don't understand how you can be so calm, and they'll try and shake you until you show them it's impossible. And mine simply want to get their places and be feted for their superior intelligence, and neither is going to happen. We just need a little patience - and perhaps chains."

Peter chuckled a bit at that, "I like that image, but they'd only rattle them at me until they drove me mad with the noise. Ah, Gui, I don't think I was ever quite that young...not in the way they are, at least. I began running Hawthornden before I was their age, that was something that Uncle William just couldn't do. He had the skills, he just wasn't sure how to apply them in a sensible way."

"But I ran away to Paris, and was protected from ever being

responsible for anything but learning," Guyon said as kindly as he could. "I think you were older than me in years from the time we could both speak, all birthdates aside. But I..." He could feel the blood rushing hotly under his skin. "I know the frustration when one sees and cannot remedy. You have always *been* the remedy, *chérâme*. I know what it is only to resent and struggle and wish. You have always had...oh! The power to *be*, to *do,* to *assist.* You fight, while the rest of us long." He shrugged. "You command armies. The rest of us - we simply fight *in* them."

"No..." Peter put one finger over Guyon's lips. "I command armies, but *you* command me. Heart and soul, beloved, always."

"But not mind," Guyon said anxiously. "Never let me command that, for it must be yours entire. It is too...astounding, too strong, it should never be possible that anything should force it upon another path."

Peter glanced around, then leaned in and placed a quick kiss on Guyon's lips, "I do believe you just said I was headstrong...stubborn. And you are absolutely correct."

Guyon resisted, with difficulty, the temptation to either bite or snarl in response. "Mm," he allowed himself as his only reply. "Oh, come on! Let's terrify the children and get some damned privacy!"

Lt. Wycombe was waiting for them, knowing, after arrival of the Cadets that Peter had sent to him that he would be wanted. He waited in Peter's office, seated, not behind the desk but to the side at the small secretary's table that Philippe normally used. He came to attention quick enough though, when Peter stepped in.

"At ease, Lieutenant." Peter said, taking a seat behind the desk. "Do you mind telling me why you have allowed my cadets to think they have the run of the town in my absence?"

Wycombe's eyes widened with anger for a brief moment, before lowering to the table. "I was unaware that I had, my Lord Marshal," he said stiffly.

"No, I didn't think you had," Peter gave the other man a frustrated frown. "But, you know the political air at the moment and young men, especially soldiers, need more guidance at those times. They need a strong hand, even if it means they hate you as much as they follow you through loyalty. You can be stern without being cruel and they'll appreciate the fact that you don't let them get away with much."

"And *do* encourage them to only meet my students outside the school," Guyon interjected softly. "They are not good influences upon one another, you know this?"

"Yes, Seigneur."

"And I'm not the damned Seigneur!"

"But you *are*." Wycombe blinked. "It was announced in the Court annals."

Guyon swore, profoundly and feelingly.

Peter chuckled softly, "You can run away, but you can never hide completely from Court gossip."

"Oh, stuff an old sock in it," Guyon said, feeling his nose wrinkle quite involuntarily. "Ludicrous!"

"Look, Wycombe," Peter tried to retrain his face in a more businesslike expression, "I think we just need to keep them busier. That way they have less time to get into trouble. This place could use a good coat of paint, inside and out. Get those damnable merchants to provide something sturdy and neutral and put them to work."

"Yes, my lord Marshal. Will they be given expenses for cleaning their uniforms?"

Guyon, with difficulty, stopped himself from laughing.

Peter snorted, "You don't paint in uniform. They do have other clothes...I've seen them. I don't care what they look like, I just want them busy."

"Yes, my lord Marshal. Now?"

"No, Wycombe," Peter shook his head. "It will be dark soon enough. Just do the punishment drills, send them off so tired that they'll be glad for something as mundane as painting tomorrow."

"Yes, my - yes, sir." Wycombe offered a tired grin. "They know them by rote from your absence."

"Hmmm...well, yes, I'm sure they do." Peter sighed. "Well, I'm not planning on leaving again any time soon so we'll have that sorted out."

Guyon stopped himself from interjecting - *but we are, we are, I thought* - and kept his face expressionless, simply offering Wycombe a nod as he left the room. Once the door was close, he could not stop himself from beginning - "Pèire, I thought we -" and then silencing himself. "I misunderstood, forgive me."

"We...Yes, we are, Gui. I mean, of course we are. To Scotland." Peter smiled. "But we can take a month or two before we're off. Get them all settled. Get someone brought up to give Wycombe a hand...or...I'm considering taking on a pensioner or two. Just because they've been injured too much to fight doesn't mean the lads can't learn from them."

He paused there, to stand and step closer to Guyon, "We can't leave immediately anyway. We have to be sure that Corvay is settled, one way or the other."

"I know." Guyon swallowed. *I thought we were starting anew, but it's all the same sad roundelay, and I will sell my soul for you, but oh God! I long for escape!* "I'm sorry, I'm jaundiced with traveling, I think, and I am selfish enough simply to want to run, I admit."

"So am I," Peter slipped his arms around Guyon's waist. "And homesick, I must admit. I want to go and be surrounded by the comfort of familiar things, and see them all in new ways, because you're there to share them."

"I will give you an entirely new perspective," Guyon agreed with the wryness that still took him over, at times. "I told you. I am *not* good at responsibility, even when I see it's mine." He thumped his head into the hollow of Peter's shoulder. "Damned soldier."

"Damned indeed," Peter chuckled. "For having to wait before spiriting you away to my rock full of sheep."

Guyon snorted. "Clouds, bèl-mi, clouds, I don't believe in sheep..." He tilted his face up, and kissed Peter, still reveling in the joy of being able to do so and have it mean more than simple desire or want. "Believe in you," he muttered roughly, drawing back.

"As you should, for I am feeling quite substantial, thank you very much." Peter pulled Guyon back and closer, pressing his body against him. "Quite, quite substantial."

"And you brought your sense of humor with you, how kind," Guyon said amusedly. "Not too flattering-swift, then?" He put his hands at the sides of Peter's neck, letting each small change in skin brush against his palms and fingertips. "*God.* The touch of you."

"*Say* the name. Moisten your tongue with praise, and be the spring ground, waking." Peter whispered softly, moving closer to kiss Guyon again, "Let your mouth be given its gold-yellow stamen like the wild rose's. As you fill with wisdom, and your heart with love, there's no more thirst."

"I have begun," Guyon said in his most austere tones, "to slake my thirst." *Ah, God, the beauty and delight of you!* "And in you I have found a banquet under the heavens." He let his mouth curl up into a small, private smile, giving the only person who had ever understood his need for words, his own borrowed deliberations in return. "*Kush Geldi,* Pèire."

Peter's eyes were pure azure brilliance when he answered - "You, too, are welcome here."

*

They moved then, out of the office and down the hall toward Peter's private rooms, pushing the door open together and stepping inside.

The flame which they had fed on the road home, became something cauterizing, the last fire that removed lust forever and made it something transmuted. Caught fast in both friendship and desire, like stars in the depths of a reflecting sea, they were drowned and helpless but there, there and held and with one another, and found grace and care and courtesy enough to laugh even amidst obliteration.

And they seemed in each others' eyes to be reborn in their love, knowing each other like they never had before; gone were both the desperation and the uneasiness, to be replaced with the comfort and familiarity of friends who were now lovers. *Like Guyon's old boots,* Peter suddenly thought. *Well worn, and just right.*

Guyon was fierce and strong and somehow pliant in his arms, always on the verge of laughter, contented even when Peter removed his shirt, even when he ran his hands over the thickly scarred back. Instead of the small, familiar inhalation of tense demurral, Guyon breathed out amusement and desire, unfettered and blended inextricably, when, greatly daring, Peter licked at the thin white curl of a scar that lay between shoulder and throat.

This was what he had waited for, Peter acknowledged to himself, this surrender of all. He had waited for Guyon to know, at last, that nothing about him could drive Peter away, or make him less loved. No matter what Guyon had done in the past, no matter what might happen in the future, Peter would never stop loving him. There was no part of Guyon that troubled him now, nothing hidden from him, no demons lurking in shadows of his soul, - just this man, mystic, scholar, *beloved*, sharing all that he was with Peter.

The ultimate surrender, and the most ordinary, no pillar of fire and water, no annihilating conquest of one soul or body by another, simply two friends, two lovers, two beloveds, equal and unequal as all humanity eventually must be, smoothing out the ragged edges of too long a division, a slow and constant tide of love and private comprehension, running like cool spring water and melding the whole.

They slept in the aftermath, motionless, their bodies wrapped around each other in an intricate pattern of limbs, and awoke during the night to smile, and grumble good naturedly at each other about dampness and chill and the brightness of the moon shining in through the uncovered window.

"It makes sleep impossible," Guyon pointed out, and then laughed, softened with the gentleness that Peter now knew had always been there, and was somehow a part of the banked fires he had always withheld. *He's not exactly...like other people.* That long-ago warning. *François, he is precisely like, what in God's name were you playing at, to make him so closed?* "I like you in silver, though." The teasing was still tentative in origin, but even in moonlight, Guyon's eyes betrayed confidence as to its reception. *Another new thing. Will I ever tire of learning your variety?*

"My color, do you think?" Peter sat up, allowing the light to flow over him as he spread his arms.

"Mm, I must debate, gold or silver, sun or moon..." Guyon's strange eyes looked like coins in the bright reflective light. "This is more dramatic, I think." He sat up, leaning in to kiss the hollow of Peter's throat. "A more striking armor."

"But sunshine for you, for all you hide yourself away from it," Peter chuckled. "It turns your skin to burnished bronze and tips your hair with light. I've tried to catch it, you know, twisting my fingers into it. But it moves when disturbed, like reflections on the water."

Guyon tilted his head, like a curious cat. "A Bronze Age lake, then?" He held up his hands, the difference in color between them and his arms startling in the bleaching light, so that he looked gloved. "Or dipped in the river Styx?"

"In mud," Peter said then, taking them one at a time and pressing his lips to the palms. "That was your trial by fire, I know, caring for me when I was so...fractious. You deserve far more than you received for staying through that."

Peter reached down to the foot of the bed and found a quilt to pull over them, smiling when his fingers encountered the small neat hold in the corner, "I bought this for you."

"Hmm?" Guyon was half-smiling in puzzlement. "And I'd rather not be dipped in mud - you know, that was easy, not a trial. All I had to do was panic."

"You panic? Never." Peter chuckled at the mere idea. "But this...the quilt. I bought it for you and you and François blithely hung it over the window in my old Louvre rooms. Put holes in it before I could ever even offer it to you. Not that I had any idea how I'd manage it."

Guyon laughed, looking genuinely surprised. "Oh, not blithely! We thought it was some heirloom you'd curse us for using!" He ran his fingers over the torn edge. "You gave it to me anyway, it was a great consolation."

"I did...and you offered to have it patched. To stitch it yourself or have Ännchen do it." Peter chuckled at the memory. "And I had to say no, and I'm sure I sounded very ungrateful for the offer."

"You didn't, in fact, sound any different from usual," Guyon said wryly. "I didn't notice except to know I'd got it all wrong again." He shrugged restlessly. "You keep apologizing for that time, but I feel *I* should, I did nothing but irritate you enormously."

"I was irritated at myself, Guyon." Peter admitted. "I felt that I had failed her Majesty and myself. I let someone under my guard and paid the consequences. All I wanted to do was get home...and then when I managed it, I barely knew I was there. It was very lowering. And then there you were, helping me and all I wanted was to feel well enough to enjoy your company and not burden you with my weakness."

That was all true, he had felt a worthlessness during those days that he had allowed to color everything he did. He was lucky that he hadn't completely alienated everyone he knew.

Guyon snorted, suddenly and unexpectedly, before putting his head in his hands and laughing. "Very - very - *lowering*?" he managed at last. "And - hah! - we were basking in your survival - *oh God*..." he trailed off into incoherent sniggering. "Stitches," he managed at last. "And *Vincennes*, and the goddamned *linen,* and mice, dear *God, mice*! And all the time you were -" His words dissolved once more.

"It's not funny." Peter scowled, but it was all for show. "Really, Gui, I felt horrible. I hurt and everything had gone wrong...and then I had to burden you with it. I was glad to be alive, yes, but...I didn't know if I'd heal right and then what would I do? The Queen would have no use for a crippled Cavalier. And...Stop laughing, you brat." Peter pulled the blanket up over his head.

The only thing it served to do was make Guyon's next snorting fit rather wet in its effect. "How *old* are you?" he howled incredulously, and even muffled, there was a sort of glee in his voice. "You *hurt*? No, I'm sorry, I missed that - oh God oh God oh *God,* you *lunatic,* you utter chevalier!" He sobered then, all intense and precise, pushing the quilt back and Peter against the bedpost with it. "You would have been taken over by a gaggle of well-meaning Sorbonne scholars. You would have been trained to study until Benichou accepted you. And you would, quite incidentally, have been *mine*." Any amusement visible on his face was decidedly inward-turning. "Crippled my *foot*," he added.

"Yes, well, I didn't know any of that then, did I?" Peter excused himself. *And you are forgetting that François was still there...or would I have been to you what all of François's women were to him?* "And what would you have taught me? I'm no artist, nor doctor. I would have no patience to teach others...I barely manage with the Cadets. I can not see myself as a philosopher or astronomer, and certainly not a clergyman."

"Perhaps I would have made you into a master of debate," Guyon said teasingly. "A logician, a lawyer, a scientist...the list is endless!"

"Words are your area of expertise." Peter leaned closer, "I am more a man of action."

Guyon, instantly diverted, laughed. "Prove it," he said challengingly, opening his eyes wide and sitting back against the headboard with his arms folded. "Make me a thesis."

"Hmmm..." Peter considered. *A thesis?* "I would contend that certain actions invariably lead to certain reactions...at least as far as you are part of the equation."

"Synthesis. The definition of invariable is that it does not alter. Do my reactions never alter? Do they never, in fact, *vary*?"

"Ah, poor choice of words, I see..." Peter reached forward, and ran one finger deliberately over Guyon's chest, pausing to tease a nipple. "Perhaps, I should have said that they, within an acceptable degree of variation, lead to certain reactions."

Guyon's sharp little breath was utterly undisguised in its interest, wholly unconnected to Peter's argument. "And this acceptable degree - stretches how far?"

"Oh, it's wholly dependant on immeasurable outside factors, so therefore not as predictable," Peter frowned, then leaned in to place his lips where his fingers had just traveled. "Have I lost my case already?"

"I think you may be winning," Guyon said in his most expressionless voice, which Peter was beginning to learn meant he felt too many things to begin and try to convey them, and then laughed, and pulled Peter towards him, tangling his blunt fingers in Peter's long hair, and kissing pure joy against his mouth. "And as we all know, to the victor go the spoils..."

This.

This was love.

This was joy.

This was everything he had wanted for so very long
Because it is me, because it is you.
"A proven synthesis..."

*

Guyon woke all of a piece, his mind already half-way through the day to come before he had quite finished dreaming, meaning that he was out of bed and putting water to boil and finding clean clothes in the chest he had somewhat unofficially annexed before he was really aware of what he was doing. Peter was looking at him from the bed with an expression of sleepy amusement.

Guyon scratched at his forehead. "Oh, don't *even*," he said, trying not to laugh.

"What?" Peter said, with blue-eyed innocence covering his face. "I was merely thinking that, as you are so industrious, you could make coffee?"

"I *could*," Guyon agreed. "But that would be taking for granted that you had coffee *here*, rather than having your poisonous swamp-leaves brought with your hot water of a morning." He matched Peter's innocence as well as he could, though in his case he rather thought his repressed smile might be ruining the effect.

"Ah, well, if you can't be troubled, I suppose I'll just have to call for Thomas to take pity on my sad coffeeless state." Peter looked forlornly down at his scattered clothes. "And to clean up and.... I also need a bath...."

"Yes," Guyon said agreeably, looking through Peter's rather frightening cupboards for something that wasn't a product of Herr Kirschner's cellar. "I also need a bath. Shall I horrify the bathhouse with my unkempt state, or can I prevail on the Lord Marshal's courtesy for hot water myself?"

"By all means, please do." Peter sat up on the edge of the bed, yawning and scratching absently at his stomach. "As a matter of fact, I insist. Because Thomas's smiling, helpful morning face is something that should only be experienced with company...or a large glass of whisky."

"Do I want to know how often you've chosen the latter?"

470

Guyon asked, his eyebrows rising. "Because the former, you know, leads to thoughts of homicide." He slanted a teasing little smile over his shoulder.

"Most frequently I just keep my eyes closed...stubbornly...rather like a mole," Peter chuckled, stood, and padded over to where Guyon was rustling through cabinets. "Good morning, by the way."

"Ah. You noticed." Guyon shook his head at himself, laughing a little. "That it's morning. And I was right, by the way, you look more striking in silver than in gold. Sunlight makes you...accessible, and I prefer mysteries..." He straightened up, and kissed Peter briefly, before making a small face. "And also hazel twigs and perhaps some mint leaves, my mouth is vile."

"Doesn't matter," Peter said, and drew him back for a deeper kiss. "Now it's a better morning."

"It's a hot morning," Guyon said with a faint grimace, but he returned the kiss with interest, if little passion. For once that seemed to have faded into a mere hum of pleasure at touch rather than a sudden burgeoning of need simply at the feel of Peter's lips on his. *Am I growing accustomed to this joy?* he wondered, sudden and startled at himself, and was about to say something to that effect, to share this new discovery with its inspiration, when there was a knock at the door, and he sighed, pulling a shirt on. Peter might find nothing strange about greeting any and all of his men in whatever state of dress he happened to be in at the time, but Guyon still felt the need for caution, even if it was mere formality.

"Who's there?" Peter grumbled out at the door.

"Thomas, sir. I wondered if you were ready for breakfast and if you'd like tea or coffee?" If the young man's expression matched his voice, then Guyon pitied Peter for having to deal with such outright good humor every morning.

"Coffee please...and Mr. de Chesnay has arrived as well, so do bring enough for two, Thomas, please."

"Yes, sir." There was a pause and then, "Welcome home, sir. I'll have it for you shortly."

Welcome home? Guyon mouthed at Peter, getting a little grin that was pure mirth in return. As Thomas's footsteps were heard

471

receding, Guyon said quietly, "Have I converted you to good taste at last, *chérâme*?"

"I thought my good taste was proven in the company I keep," Peter answered, and went to tug on his trousers. "Or at least, the company I awaken in."

"No, that proves you have no sense, nothing about your *taste*," Guyon pointed out. Peter's invitations to word games were few and rare and something he held utterly, privately dear. "Although it perhaps says a great deal about what you *wish* to taste..."

"I do find *your* taste to be completely to *my* taste," Peter grinned. "Hearty and flavorful, I'd describe it...with a strong hint of spice."

"You make me sound like a joint of beef - or purloined venison!" Guyon laughed. "Or perhaps an unfortunate soup..." His amusement turned to speculation. "Soup requires more than one ingredient, I think...and isn't it often *barley* that thickens it?"

"Beef is not the joint that I crave," Peter quipped, his eyes now twinkling. "And anyone who's seen you in the bath would know that, barley or not, you don't need any thickening."

"The only man alive *displayed* to his best under water," Guyon agreed solemnly, "which is rather fitting since you are the commander of tides...*oh God damn it*." The last was a savage hiss as Thomas knocked perfunctorily on the door before coming in with breakfast.

"Thank you, Thomas," Peter was barely able to restrain the laughter in his voice. "Just set it down."

"I'm sure you'll like this," Thomas was seemingly oblivious to having interrupted anything. "That new cadet - Riviere, I think his name is - his father was some kind of horribly fancy chef in some Lord's house. I don't know all the details but his cooking is a treat."

Thomas swept the covers off the dishes, setting two chairs at the table, laying out silver, as he chatted away.

Guyon moved hurriedly to the window, his shoulders shaking with badly-controlled laughter, and opened it to step out onto the balcony into the early sun. He startled a small flock of pigeons from the ledge, the purring sound of their wings as they took flight hiding the small hiccup of amusement that escaped him. He stared out over the city, breathing slowly and carefully so as not to let any more laughter loose, and felt the heat of the day already pressing down on him, baking off the stones that seemed to have stored it overnight.

"At least it's high enough here for the worst of the smells not to affect the air," he murmured, thinking that in this one respect, at least, he would miss the Languedoc.

"That's fine, Thomas," He could hear Peter's voice from inside. "We haven't been starving ourselves, you know? Just...Well, it doesn't matter what we were 'just'...we're back and ...No, just leave that for now. You can empty it later on and ...."

The 'and' was lost to him, as Peter apparently and quite firmly, ushered the redoubtable Thomas out the door.

Guyon poked his head back around the balcony door. "What on *earth*?" he asked, looking at what was apparently breakfast rather than a banquet for several starving giants.

"Amazing, isn't it?" Peter shook his head. "Either Thomas thinks that we need to keep our strength up...or...No, there is no *or*. I refuse to even speculate on what that boy has in his head. He keeps me organized and my rooms neat and for that I'm more than grateful."

Guyon laughed. "Well, at least he can make coffee," he pointed out cheerfully, pouring himself a cup and taking a roll. "Agh, I forgot, I can't," he remembered a second later, putting the roll back. "De Retz."

"De Retz can surely wait an extra ten minutes for you to have a roll, Gui." Peter chuckled. "You do not think he will be quite *that* anxious?"

"No, my beloved heathen, I do not. And even if he were, he can wait an hour if I feel so inclined, and be damned to his schedule and his clock both, but I *must* go to shrift first, since I refuse to give Corvay the death-knell while I stand outside grace - and for *that* I should have fasted. But I still want my coffee, even so."

"I understand," Peter nodded. Guyon knew that Peter's own faith was as strong as his own, although he followed it a way that many would consider lackadaisical. His was the soldier's way, with little time for ceremony. He prayed on his feet, giving thanks to God for life and all its wonders, as if he spoke to a beloved Father rather than a deity. Not for Peter were kneeling and priests giving a benediction or a punishment. Although he believed in all the sacraments, he spared them little time.

"I'll...I'll feed you when you get back then, yes?" There was, however, room for trepidation in his voice...small worries about what was to come.

Guyon smiled. "You feed me body and soul," he said honestly, draining his coffee, and offered what reassurance he could that it was nothing to do with the small measure of peace they had found together which was sending him to the confessional. "But you cannot absolve me of how I feel about Maurice, *car-mi*." He grinned. "Your approval is soothing, but distinctly un-Christian, I'm afraid." He put his cup down. "Damn, no bath," he added, and stripped off his shirt to make do with decidedly-lukewarm water, some elderly toweling, and some very hard soap.

It was, if nothing else, an exercise guaranteed to banish the last of any residual sleep, as was the re-arrival of Thomas, with a message from the English Queen that Peter was to attend her *immediately*.

"No breakfast for either of us, then," Guyon said with mock-sympathy, and got a scoop of cold water in his face for his troubles.

*

If Peter disliked the time he spent at Court, he absolutely *hated* the hours wasted while he waited in her Majesty's antechamber. Long hours of inactivity were always difficult, but long hours of inactivity, where he had to seem interested in who else was being kept waiting, and where he had to sit on a stiff chair and wear his nicest clothes had to be even worse.

When he was the Queen's cavalier he did a lot less of it because it would have been difficult to insure her Majesty's safety from so far away, but as the Marshal it seemed to be a regular occurrence. He much preferred it when they simply corresponded or met casually rather than these summonses. And this one, in particular, was one he had been dreading, for Charleon had returned to his family, as full of himself as only a teenage boy could be and even moreso since he was a teenage boy who also happened to be a Prince.

Rupert, not so long ago, had written a rather scathing letter filled with suggestions about just how the Royal arse could be got away from its impromptu tour of the islands and got back to sit its Royal self in the St-Germain, and rather painfully at that. Suffering from his own troubles, however, he had been unable to follow and put his suggestions into practice, and Charles had forgotten, with the serenity of absence, just how likely it was that these would turn from suggestions to certainties as soon as Rupert caught up with him.

And catch up he had, eventually, and so they were blessed with the Prince's own self, and his mother's plans for him. Plans that, it would appear, included Peter somehow. Although, how her Majesty thought he could contribute with his new duties was yet to be seen.

Peter gave a little huff of breath. It was too bad really that he could not put the Prince through his paces like he'd do a new recruit. It might do him good.

But there was something else to the Prince these days, something that Peter was unwilling to unleash and his mother seemed to have no idea even existed, something born of the misery that his father's treatment by his country had engendered in him and his father's treatment of Rupert had confirmed, a jaded, snarling, carefully-hidden violence that was far beyond his years. Perhaps it might serve the young lion better to be sent to the Sorbonne, and put through his paces in the frustrated hothouse environment of the debating chambers, until he could rely on more than simply the fingernail-clenched control he seemed to have acquired for himself in the years since Peter had last seen him. What Peter was very, very sure of was that whatever Charles was trying to hide, he wanted absolutely nothing to do with it.

Fortunately, judging from Charles's expression as the Queen explained her ideas for Peter's new duties, it was as unpalatable to him as it was to Peter himself, and not only because he had never been one to be ruled by petticoat government in any but the most blatant of ways.

And that was something that Peter, fortunately, was quite willing to take advantage of, if only in the loosest of terms.

"Of course, your Majesty," Peter agreed amiably, "if that is your wish...and the wish of his Highness.. I am ever at your service."

"It is not his Highness's wish," Charles said acidly, "because his Highness has long since gone beyond the need for observation or babying. What his Highness needs is the autonomy to at least judge what will benefit him in his incomparably impossible situation, and forgive me, sir, but that does not include the wardenship of your invented post and title."

"Newly invented, it may be, your Highness, but like you I am also doing what I can in this...impossible situation." Peter stiffened. "I'm working with what I have at hand in hopes that it can, in some way, be of benefit."

"And I'm sure it will be, but not to me," Charles said simply, and Peter was reminded of something Guyon had said, that there were some men no-one could follow, not because they were superior, not because they were placed above others by some divine touch, but because there were places within them that had been made too distant, too private, to closed away to be touched. Perhaps Rupert could have found some nerve to play upon, spoken in the right tones of need and duty and obedience and forced some six-month, unwilling agreement from the uncrowned Prince, but no-one else, now, could find that impetus, could go far enough to reach him on his lonely pinnacle of painfully-maintained belief in his destiny.

"Which is quite acceptable," Peter continued, "because I'm not doing this for *your* benefit, but that of their Majesties."

There, that was said, now he waited for the Prince to have his final words and hopefully her Majesty would see how abhorrent this was to both of them and have done.

"It will not, though," Charles said, and shrugged his shoulders, not in dismissal, but restlessly, as though the lace and silks and heavy rich doublet weighed as heavily on him as they always did on Peter. "It will benefit no-one if I am seen to be in need of - warding. I must be seen to have at least some power of my own, so I might have the right to explain. And I don't doubt that you are skilled, but - I *must* show whose son I am. I must apply to the Hague, to Spain if I must, to the Scots for certain, to Mazarin while I remain here, and forgive me, ma mere, but no-one can teach me the art of being supplicant and heir at once. I cannot be seen to rely on advisors until that is what they are perceived to be, and not nursemaids chosen by a loving parent."

Henrietta Maria's face went cold then, as cold as any parent whose teenaged son had just implied that she, although she loved him, did not know what was best, "I only want you to have people around you that can be trusted. Trusted to advise you and trusted to help keep you safe for me. You are my son, Charles. How can I do less?"

The sentiment was good, but the timing was not. Peter knew this. Charles knew this. They simply had to convince her Majesty.

"Your concern is understandable, your Majesty," Peter agreed. "But in this instance, I think his Highness is correct. Perception is important and right now anything that is *perceived* as a weakness is, in fact, a weakness."

Charles's dark eyes flashed over to him, surprise and gratitude in their hard depths, and he picked up on Peter's lines as quickly as any scholar. "I will be thought Catholic simply for being here. I will be seen as within the sphere of your influence. Everything I do must be seen to contradict that, that I am - all that my father is, but more." He flinched even at saying it, and Peter knew what it must have cost him to say that. For a subject to hint that his King was easily led might be forgiven - in time. For a son and heir - never. But Charles was right, and all three of them knew it. His only chance now was to seem above those he loved, and Peter thought that might be the closed dark place within him, the place where he would never believe that to be true, and knew it was essential to pretend it was so.

The expression on the Queen's face told all, flashing from mother, to wife, to Monarch and back, all within a few seconds. "Very well. I'm sure you will do as *you* think best no matter what my opinion in the matter. Thank you for your time, Marshal. You may go."

Peter bowed to them both and moved to make his retreat.

The sound of an exasperated, steeped in misunderstanding row began behind him, and Peter, much though he adored his Queen, had a fleeting sympathy for his Prince, who was learning both the price and the necessity of intransigence at once.

"I am not antagonizing him, ma mere," was the last thing he heard, "I am ensuring he understands that I cannot afford to need him." And then, very softly, "Yet."

*

Guyon, absolved of all save the sin of pride, left an extremely amused priest behind him after a half-hour talk which had left a good deal unspoken and a great deal more tacitly understood. The pride, the priest had pointed out with what Guyon had to admit was complete justice, could never be absolved, since Guyon was never going to repent of it. That the pride was in the fact he did not see the absolution of other, rather more venial sins as being necessary to his state of grace, they had decided not to touch upon.

He made his way to de Retz's chambers, in which he was holding official audiences, still wearing his nightshirt under an open robe and looking less like an Archbishop that a somewhat debauched courtier, his round, pleasant face unshaven and his eyes deep-circled. He might have donned his night-clothes, but any use he had got out of them other than increased comfort for sitting at his desk was obviously very minimal indeed.

"My Lord," Guyon said quietly, as Andre Morel hovered in the background, looking, for once, less concerned with himself and with eavesdropping than worried about his employer. "I came to see you at the earliest possible opportunity."

"No," de Retz contradicted him, but not without a bit of amusement in his tired voice, "you came to see me as soon as it was convenient. No problem though, de Chesnay, I fully approve of rest after a trip such as yours must have been."

"If you approve of it so, why not take your own approval as a benison and to your doubtless extremely comfortable bed?"

Guyon asked gently. He liked de Retz, mostly as an inherited feeling from François, who had loved and protected him to the full extent of his not inconsiderable abilities, and partly in remembrance of a long-ago bishop who had saved a seventeen year old of no account from the Church's condemnation, for no other reason than that he had liked the boy's mind and held it as being worth more than the rules.

De Retz flicked a hand at Morel, who bowed and backed out of the room, closing the door behind him. "Because I do not approve of the things I must do, at times," he said obliquely. "And I will not trap you in *this* web, de Chesnay, you have endured enough spider-silk, I think."

"More than," Guyon agreed. "But I have our proof." He laid the little sheaf of papers in front of the Archbishop's ringed hands. "I give you Corvay's treason, in open writing."

De Retz did not touch them immediately, as if almost afraid of their possibly contagious state, "In his own hand? You're sure? You know that Corvay's power is such that it will take that, nothing third hand or less sure."

"In his own hand," Guyon said softly. "In the code I designed for you and François, before ever he thought of me, or I had heard of him. I have left copies in the Languedoc and with my brother in Portugal."

"God be praised," de Retz breathed vehemently, and opened up the papers to read. "This will work, I'm certain. Well done."

"You know," Guyon said in a sudden access of spite, thinking of what those papers had almost cost him - and what they *had* cost him - to obtain, "sometimes *I* don't like you very much, either. For the record, since we seem to be having one taken, what with you commemorating others' work in God's name. And *speaking* of names, my lord Archbishop, I was greeted with the highly unwelcome news of my elevation to the *Seigneurie*. I'm rather hoping it's inaccurate."

"I have only arranged for you to have what was already yours in all but name," de Retz did not look up from his study of the papers. "And rightfully so with your brother's departure."

"And the minor consideration that I did not want these things never actually crossed your mind, did it?" Guyon asked wearily.

"God rot the lot of you, I was *content* in the Sorbonne until you and Corvay used me for a cat's paw. You never wanted my true skills and you never wanted Peter's. You wanted the Languedoc. You and Corvay both, you wanted the Languedoc, and the place has nothing to give you and never did. All this treachery and double-dealing and people's *lives - do me the courtesy of looking me in the eye!* - and you used loyalty and honor and Peter's good name as a disguise. *How dare you?*" He was shaking with rage. "You think taking what belongs to my brother and giving it to me like John the Baptist's head on a plate of lies is *compensation?* That a marshal's baton that will never stand service and lands he may never see can *ever* make reparation for what you have done to Peter?" He drew a deep breath, fighting to control his voice. "These papers free us from Corvay. But *by God*, they free us from you as well. *It ends.*"

De Retz looked up at him tired and nonplussed, "Some one should stand for the Languedoc, de Chesnay. Should it not be you as soon as someone else? You, at least, will consider more than your own gains." He drew a deep breath, shaking his head, "I have done many things of which I am not proud, and those I will settle with God. This...this at least, I have some hope of leading to good, in spite of your arguments. And this..." He waved a hand over the papers, "...will do more."

Guyon closed his eyes, shaking his head. "You will never understand," he said wearily. "*Giraud* stood for the Languedoc. He put it above France, which is what it takes, what it *means* to stand for something. You *stand* for it. And I - I cannot give it that, because I will always stand for France before everything. For God, for my country, for my King, but that is...a matter of conscience. Private." *And Peter above all and any of it, but I am never going to tell you that.* "I am not *equipped* for this, I never was. I want no more to do with the Languedoc, or Corvay, or the court. Let me go back to my ideas and my teaching and my writing, *please.*"

"Your brother stood for it in a way that was not acceptable, Guyon," de Retz's voice was rough but not unkind. "He kept it separate in a way that would *never* be accepted. You must see that. We must all be together in this...political climate. Otherwise we will be found weaker and wanting."

"You create the climate, and then wonder how it is the rest of us cannot bear to live in it," Guyon said, his energy leaving him. *I cannot fight this. Not even for Peter - because Peter would agree with him, would call it honor and right and see only another way of keeping his oath. It would be better at times had I been born blind and deaf, shut away from all the outside world for eternity, rather than see and hear and still be trapped by my mind's clarity.* "I see. But I do not have to agree, even if I have to obey."

"The climate was created by Cromwell and Corvay and those like them...but that does not mean that I will allow it to wash me away in its storm." De Retz spoke commandingly, but no longer spoke to convince. "As long as you do not move against me, I will still hope we can remain...friends."

And there de Retz slumped in his seat, "I'm so very tired, Guyon. So very, very tired. Let me dress and we'll get this thing done, shall we?"

Oh, don't make me pity you, don't make me worry for you or want to help you or care, Guyon thought in useless, already futile prayer. "As you wish, my lord," he said tonelessly, knowing that he was as bound as ever before, and though the ties were silken this time, they were stronger even than Corvay's irons of grief and guilt and fear.

De Retz stood, but before he could leave the room, a knock sounded at the door. It was Andre Morel.

"Excuse me, your Grace, but I have a message for Monsieur de Chesnay." Andre stepped in and delivered it to Guyon with no further prologue. The missive was plain, no address, and sealed only with an unshaped blob of wax. "A boy just brought it."

"Pursued by creditors?" de Retz laughed. "You can pay them all now, I think."

"Witty, my lord, very witty," Guyon said, rolling his eyes. "What have you put the students up to *now*, Andre?" he teased, sliding his finger under the fold and breaking the wax.

De Retz snorted, and went into his dressing room. Andre glowered. "Oh, go away," Guyon said irritably. "I'll shout if I need to reply."

"Sir," Andre muttered, and went out again without even the

courtesy of a bow. Guyon shook his head, and opened the paper.

And the glass sphere of his world shattered around him.

He should have expected it, really. Something from Corvay - no pleas for silence, of course, but threats. He would have been fully prepared to take action against anything the man threw his way. But this he could not fight against.

Whatever happens to me, I can promise you this. You will see Peter Scudamore at the whipping post, if not dead.

He remembered. He had always sworn that it was lost to him, but he remembered every lacerating blow, every second of torment that had driven the breath from him so that he could not even scream for mercy. He remembered it as he fought to breathe, as the cold cloth of despair clogged his airway and all succor was driven from him.

I cannot recant!

But for Peter -

And Peter above all and any of it, he had thought, scant moments before.

Including love. Including life and breath and sanity and hope. *Above all.*

He would have condemned himself, he would have gone happily to a noose, to the block, would have embraced the executioner even if the man suffered from leprosy; kissed him full on the lips and taken him gladly and willingly to a suppurating bed, and still come onto the platform afterward to put his neck out for the axe, to prevent this.

All that I am...

It will not be your hands shackled there.

"Oh God! God!"

Fourteen youths and fourteen monks...

His limbs were water, the air suffocated him, the feeling both long-forgotten and suddenly familiar - and he choked on it along with the regained and new-felt presence of the invisible, intangible, foul wet cloth that was suddenly pushed down into his throat to stifle his prayers.

"No, no, no..."

I am not this thing! I cannot recant!

He remembered. He remembered everything, cold and clear,

and yet remembered the warmth of the sunlit morning, too. He remembered the slow rise of the bloody mist into the August air.

My heresy for my faith, will that suffice?

Pèire-mi, car-mi, my heart...

The cold hand at his throat relinquished him, the stifling cloth was withdrawn from his mouth. And he knew what he must do.

My heresy for my faith.

My faith for my heresy.

It will not be your hands shackled there...

"It will be," he murmured. "Though it cost me my soul, it will be."

Even when it costs me my life, it will. It will be. I will repay.

Guyon, blind and sick with grief and knowledge, crumpled the paper in his hand, and flung it in the direction of the hearth. "My lord, it seems I must return to the Hôtel d'Orsay for a while. I'll attend on you to see Corvay within the hour," he called, amazed at the clear steadiness of his voice. There was a muffled grunt in response.

But for one moment, he could not move, could not force himself into the first step that would mean the beginning of his damnation.

I love you, he thought, as he had over a year before, kneeling by Peter's bed in the stifling Louvre room. *With all I am. With my life.*

He forced iron into his joints, tasted it like blood on his tongue.

It will not be your hands...

"Yes," he whispered. "It will."

He walked past Andre Morel, and out through the corridors of the Louvre, into the burning sun of mid-morning.

With all of my divided soul.

With my heresy for my faith.

Aşkin Cemal Olsun.

Peter, I love you.

*

In spite of the relief Peter felt in returning to Paris, in

realizing that the Prince of Wales was more than capable of looking after his own interests, and in spite of having the information they needed to begin to finally rid themselves of Corvay, Peter still felt unsettled. It had been a long trip with many highs and lows, pains and joys, but surely that would all now be ended. They were back in Paris, Guyon was with him now, finally, in the way he wanted. His in fact and in love.

Then why did he feel as if he were missing something very important?

Peter gave a tired sigh and tried to concentrate on the reports that the very meticulous Lt. Wycombe had prepared for him. The man was, indeed, quite comprehensive, listing out improvements, punishments and where he felt advancement was due. All Peter really needed to do was review it all and place his signature at the bottom of the page.

Mark it done.

Mark it finished.

He squirmed in his chair, trying to find a more comfortable position. This wasn't an unusual task for him, really, he'd done much the same thing dozens of times before. *Just read the damn thing, Peter, and have done.* But he couldn't help feeling that something was wrong. That somewhere in these reports, or the information they had brought back from Carcassonne, there was something that was not connecting in the way he had expected.

Drawing a deep breath, he finally reached out for his pen and scrawled his name at the bottom of the report: *Peter Scudamore, Marshal of their Majesty's forces in France.*

Done.

"I keep telling you - you need a secretary." Guyon, choosing as always to announce himself by talking as opposed to any more conventional way, came into his room. "Too many papers, I think. You'll need to burn them before you go back home - a final glorious and satisfying conflagration of the useless."

"Indeed, you may be right," Peter smiled at Guyon, feeling less unsettled just by having him there and safe. "But Wycombe puts so much work into the damnable things that I feel guilty if I don't read them."

"All I can assume is that you actually enjoy guilt," Guyon

said dryly. "Well. No more of that, at least. You will be free and back in Scotland in days."

Back in Scot - What was that supposed to mean? Suddenly Peter felt a dizzying wave of foreboding sweep over him.

"Oh, I don't expect that will happen anytime soon." Peter tried to maintain his equilibrium. Surely, Guyon was just speaking from insecurity, wondering if Peter was now going to leave him. "And you were to return with me, I thought. That's what I hoped, in any case."

"No." Guyon wandered over to the mantelpiece, and ran his finger over the top of it. "Good God, they dusted. No, I'll be staying here. De Retz will need help, and I'm ideally placed to give it. And there's no need for you to stay, now."

Peter felt the words like a punch in the stomach, but bit it all down. He couldn't let his own past insecurities color what they had gained, "Well, if you don't think you can be spared, I'll just stay until you can. I do still have duties, you know? None of that has changed."

"But the Queen has already agreed to release you," Guyon said lightly. "Isn't that what all this paperwork is for? And you've always said you wouldn't stay where you were unwanted."

"No, this paperwork is just the normal business of maintaining a command." Peter's eyes, moved over Guyon's face, looking for a clue as to where all of this was coming from. Guyon had walked out this morning and all was fine...but now it was not? What had happened between then and now? "And her Majesty agreed reluctantly, and certainly does not expect me to be gone tomorrow."

"Well, even you couldn't pack in a day, I agree," Guyon said. "Maybe Friday?" He should have been laughing, by now, his eyes alight with his own brand of maverick humor, but his face was stern and set, at odds with his light voice. "I don't know when there's a ship leaving port, but doubtless you could command one in any case."

"Guyon, what are you talking about? I can't leave now. We need to present the information that we've gathered and - " Peter looked at him with a puzzled expression. "That's not it, is it? This is something else."

"Not - else, no. This is it. What there is." Guyon didn't even try to smile. "You're going back to Scotland, and I'm going with de Retz to Corvay, and then - well. And then he will be on trial." He grimaced. "I'll write and tell you about it."

"No." Peter's denial was short and sharp. "This was not what we had decided. Whatever happens we're facing it together...we stay together. What -"

He didn't understand what was going on, but he was going to get to the bottom of it. Either Guyon was leaving with him or he was staying here, those were the two acceptable options in all of this insanity.

"No, *you* decided, and rode roughshod over me again," Guyon said, completely calmly. "I didn't. I thought I could leave, but - even I can't lie that well. Together has become a farce, Peter, and I can't continue it."

"No...no.. You said you'd teach me. All the codes...all your auto keys. You'd be there and take the time." Peter suddenly felt like a deserted child or as though he was trying to scoop up the ocean in a sieve, lost and out of control. "I don't understand."

"Well, that was before I was stupid enough to say I loved you." Guyon sighed. "I wrecked it. Peter, there's no way I can stay with you - not and lie like this. And you would need that lie, you'd wait every day for me to give in and repeat it, and I can't, I won't." He looked pained. "You said it yourself - you have nothing to offer me. You *certainly* do not have what my mind craves. What my intellect craves. I am becoming - bored. I fight it, but -" he shrugged. "Friendship and the undoubted physical pleasures you bring are not sufficient."

For several long moments there was silence, the words hanging there like they were written in fire on the sudden darkness of Peter's heart, burning him from the inside out.

"It was all a lie? All of it?" Peter felt hurt and angry and hopeless. Was this some kind of horrible justice that Guyon was trying to visit on him? He had lied. Told Peter he loved him, only to tear it way now - perhaps in some horrid recompense for Peter's trying to do the honorable thing in the Languedoc and let Guyon go his own way. All of his feelings tangled, crossing each other and battling to be foremost, leaving him simply bleak and confused.

"No." Guyon looked suddenly, impossibly, sad. "Not all. Not when I said I was incapable of love." His hands spread outwards, empty. *I'm unarmed.* The old gesture of absolute truth. "This is what I am. What I always was. I won't lie any more. And I won't ask you to forgive me."

"No," Peter's negation was soft and utterly calm this time. "There is nothing to forgive. It is my own fault, really. I should have known that faith can not be regained once it is lost and that love never comes to the faithless. I'm the same fool I have been from the beginning and shall always be. Go then...I - I won't trouble you any more. I have things to settle and then I'll be gone." He turned hollow eyes to Guyon, "I'm sorry you felt...coerced into something you didn't want...that was never my intention."

"No. I know that. Your intentions are always of the best. But they're like all good intentions, Peter - they pave the road to hell. And I've seen too much of that place to walk down that path any longer." Guyon drew a quick breath. "I'm sorry for any pain I've caused," he said with awkward formality. "Go with God, Scudamore."

Peter didn't reply to Guyon, just picked up one of the reports from his desk and held it up in front of unseeing eyes.

God only walks with the faithful.

There was a long silence, and then a shift of air as Guyon left the room.

For the first time ever in all his times of leaving, he closed the door behind him, and not even his footsteps could be heard through the thick wood - but Peter knew each time they fell, knew as they crossed the gallery and went down the stairs, knew as they paused, briefly, in the hallway, and knew that Guyon had turned, that his hand was on the newel-post, the beds of his nails white with the grip he would be exerting on it.

Then the faint sound of the main door closing drifted up, and he might have imagined it all, save for the one, absolute, irrevocable truth, the final fact that even the master of debate could not have overcome, even if he had not laid it out himself for the world's acknowledgement. Guyon was gone.

487

*

Whatever happens to me, I can promise you this. You will see Peter Scudamore at the whipping post, if not dead. And I shall still be alive to watch your understanding that you are the cause of his destruction. The English Marshal, lost to the world's condemnation, and you, Guyon de Chesnay, left to the awareness that you took from the man whom you have upheld as the source of all that is excellent and bright, his one shining virtue - his honor. And yet you know that, I tell you nothing you are not cognizant of. Destroy me, and I swear I shall take him with me.

But he had avoided that. He had lied for the first time in his life with something more than omission, used words in the way he knew best to annihilate the truth.

The truth is...

He clenched his teeth over the cry that threatened to escape him, bit the inside of his lip until he tasted blood, and walked alongside de Retz as though nothing concerned him but the Archbishop's demands.

"This is it, de Chesnay. We've got him as surely as if we had witnessed his own hand signing the command." De Retz gave a sure nod. "Nothing he can do will stop this."

"No," Guyon agreed. "Nothing." *I hope. He will kill me for this, and Peter is safe, believing me recusant. Dear God, let nothing stop him!* "You chose your hounds well." He managed to say that without any bitterness, managed to make it into a mere statement of fact.

"Yes," de Retz looked at him oddly for a moment before continuing. "And reward them when I can. Don't think I will forget this."

No, Guyon thought, *but it will not matter.* For he would be gone and Peter would accept nothing, he knew.

"My lord...whatever else comes of this, whatever else you may be forced to do..." He stopped, and then drew upon his sad remnants of belief. *I won't let him take my home from me. Whatever else, Peter. I cannot and will not allow that.*

We *won't. You and I, Guyon.*

"The Languedoc...the Languedoc must remain inviolate. It has suffered enough."

"Indeed," de Retz nodded his agreement. "A few men amongst thousands...we have far more traitors here in Paris it seems, than ever were there."

And I am among them, Guyon thought wearily. His mouth tasted like metal, like a plum stone sucked upon too long. He wanted to spit it out. He wanted to spit out his soul, his betrayal.

The bell was silent, still, and he would not reach out to Peter to set it swinging.

I am forfeit. I forfeit.

The truth is...

He did not knock at Corvay's door. He merely opened it and walked in, brushing past the man acting as secretary for the day unannounced, de Retz a pace behind him. *The truth is...*

The sputtering secretary was dismissed wordlessly by Corvay. He didn't look surprised to see them, nor resigned, he looked as he always did, as if he were in complete control of the situation.

"Ah, Monsieur de Chesnay..." He rose from his seat, "And your Grace. To what do I own the honor of *your* visit today?"

"The reading of some items," de Retz said calmly. "De Chesnay, if you would?"

"Item one," Guyon said flatly. "That you have treated with the Spanish. Item two. That you have promised to the English crown in exile that which you cannot deliver. Item three. That you have conspired with the enemies of France against his Majesty the King. Item four. That you have promised the destruction of his Majesty's demesnes, specifically that of the Languedoc, in exchange for monies already paid. For this the crown of France and the church of Paris demand that you be tried and proved a traitor."

"Ah, serious charges then indeed." Corvay nodded, almost solemnly. "And I assume you have proof to back them up. No, of course you do, or you would not be confronting me with them." He picked up a knife from his desk, a small dagger used for the opening of sealed correspondence. "But then, you also know that I will not fall alone?"

"I know," Guyon said quietly. He ignored de Retz's small, startled movement by his side, and walked over to lean across the desk. "I always knew. You were right. But you forgot, Corvay, you forgot. I have also always known what was said of me, that while to François was given Michael's tongue of justice, and to de la Roche all of Raphael and Gabriel's song and beauty, to me were given the words of the Angel of Death, that I was the Islamic Azrael made flesh. I always knew. *Aşkin Cemal Olsun*, Luc. I set Peter Scudamore free of all you would accuse him of. And no man will convict another of error if he wishes to keep his own name pure."

"I do not believe that," Corvay gave a brief sardonic chuckle. "Scudamore would allow no such thing. People may not speak a word, de Chesnay, but your cavalier wears his heart on his sleeve for all the world to read. They could not see him look at you and not believe."

"They will now." Guyon allowed himself a small, sour smile. "Everything he has ever feared of me, I confirmed. Every secret belief he ever concealed, I brought into light and acknowledged. He does not *believe* that I was false. He *knows* it for a certainty."

"Ah, so you have kept him safe by tearing his heart out," Corvay nodded slowly. "The whipping post might have been kinder."

He straightened slowly, "But that would take him out of my reach, wouldn't it? I owe you something for that, I believe..."

"Payment owed," Guyon said, and smiled, extending his hand. "We owe God a death, Corvay."

"I have never made deals with God, my little scholar." Corvay snorted. "He has too much leeway."

There was a sudden movement and the letter knife that Corvay had been playing with flashed forward, pinning Guyon's hand to the table. Right through bone and sinew, *"Payment received."*

*

There was pain. There had to be pain. Guyon knew it and yet could not feel it, the air leaving him in a soundless gasp as he

490

stared at his pinned hand, a bleeding, shattered butterfly against the dark wood of the polished desk. He could see, with abnormal clarity, a few white splinters of bone against the dark blue-grey of the protruding metal, the gleam of red torn tendon rivaling the jeweled hilt of Corvay's dagger. His fingers twitched, slow and blurred in his vision, utterly beyond his command, like a shot bird.

"Holy Christ!" De Retz, moving fast to stop Corvay as he lunged for the door, and failing, a sword point at his throat.

"*Fall back, little priest.*"

Guyon felt, rather than saw de Retz step back, his vision beginning to go grey at the edges, his breath clawing at his throat. He wanted to scream and laugh. He had given up all, and he still lived. That was not how it was supposed to play out.

There was a furious yell from the corridor, and a spate of Russian - *Boronskaya, they should have named* him *shadow and ghost* - but Guyon's world view was narrowing, crystalline and faded at once, a series of faceted impressions. He moved his hand, fast and sharp and upwards, feeling the hilt slam against the bones as he tore himself free from the wood.

"Get me David Somers," he said to de Retz, and at the other man's open-mouthed, silent protestation, yelled with all the strength of his despair - "Do you want Corvay or not? *Get him for me!*"

He could hear them scurrying off, yells in the corridor, doors opening and closing, but none of it mattered. All that his mind could process at the moment was that he was still alive and that, somehow, that was the sharpest cut of all.

Payment deferred, said an all-too familiar voice, and there was the nasty, unkind laugh following it, the one that he had first heard in his student rooms, when he was battling for Peter's life. He gasped, coming back to reality.

"Oh God," he whispered. "Pèire..."

*

His desk was finally cleared of work. Cleared because he had knocked everything onto the floor with agitated sweep of one long-fingered hand. Reports, maps, letters, all of it scattered as if by the wind, and laying on the floor, detritus to his unsettled mind.

How could this be true? How could Guyon have said those words? Those dark and evil words...

"I wrecked it. Peter, there's no way I can stay with you - not and lie like this. And you would need that lie, you'd wait every day for me to give in and repeat it, and I can't, I won't."

And how could he have not? Perhaps that was more to the heart of the matter. He had forced Guyon's hand again, somehow. Coerced him, by his actions, into speaking words he had not meant. He knew that Guyon had feared for him - as a friend only, it seemed now - and had not wanted him to leave...Perhaps Guyon felt the lie kinder while he convalesced.

Oh, God. It would have been kinder still to let him leave. Better than the dark pit that Guyon had left behind. Better than this future, not only of bleak sadness, but now unending pain that he had done something so truly dishonorable.

How could he endure?

Guyon was stronger than he was, despite all his claims of weakness, made of goddamned adamant through and through. He cried out in agony for François when he dreamed, and not a word of that escaped him awake, he smiled and had somehow come to find true pleasure in his existence once again. But then, François was dead. You could live with the dead, you could live with grief. However hard, however painful, it was possible. But with the living -

He could not do this. He could not see Guyon on the street, in de Retz's antechamber, dear *God,* Corvay would come to court, they would be each and every day trapped in the same room, accusing the same man of the same things and recalling, always recalling, the words that Guyon had so carefully turned to choking dust.

I have loved you for so long that I forgot the words.

How could he ever hear that low, clear voice speak again, and not remember that?

And he had thought them to be true. He lifted the bottle of whiskey to his lips. That and a small broken coil of string, twisted and frayed, were the only things remaining on his desk since the beginning of his outburst. Only those...oh...and one thing more.

His pistol.

It was primed and ready. His shirt open, chest laid bare to take the shot where it would do the most good - his heart. He would no longer need that frozen organ, so best he stop its workings entire.

And yet. And yet. The one thing unfeigned, the one thing that could *not* be a lie, because it had not been from Guyon's lips that he had learned it, but from those of de Tourvel, calm and unaccusing and reciting the facts of his friend's death, of Guyon's last-held secret.

Yes, of course he knows what his father did for them. If Guyon's overcome his horror of cold steel for your sake, you must have influence beyond imagining.

Guyon's terror, his pure, unadulterated dread, of the despair that led to suicide. *I may as well send him a note and give him the blame with clarity. He'll take it.*

He deserves *it*, Peter thought with unaccustomed bitterness. *He must have known what he would cause. Is this what he wanted?*

Peter didn't know. He wasn't sure and could do nothing more than mark himself as a damnable coward.

But for which crime would he be marked? Living or dying? Both were almost equally terrifying at this moment - Living without Guyon or dying a death that would condemn him directly to hell?

Will you pray for me, Guyon? he thought wildly. *'All the souls in hell' - I've heard you say that as you light the evening candle - will you pray? Even as one of the many? Will you remember?*

He was almost unaware of the gun in his hand, and yet utterly, terribly conscious of the small circle of cool metal against his skin.

"Iff you are pozink," said a worried voice from his doorway, "iss not one I haff requested."

Kees.

Peter had forgotten the time. Hell, he had forgotten anything

493

at all existed outside the four walls of his office. And perhaps, that was true...for him. His life all condensed down to this one moment...then shattered by an interruption.

Somehow he wasn't surprised.

"Iss off courze not my place to be sayink," Kees continued, "bud unlessen you are soddenly mat, iss unforkivable sin whass you is goink to do, yes?"

It took Peter a moment to work out what, exactly, the rather scatterbrained painter was saying. Not, given the amount of whisky he had consumed, that a sodden mat wasn't an apt description, but it seemed rather unlike Kees to so bluntly state such a thing.

Suddenly mad, he realized, and a fittingly insane laugh strove to get past his constricted throat.

"I am indeed *mat*, as you say," Peter answered, and a noise escaped him that was somewhere between a laugh and a sob. *Even that is undecided.* As undecided as he felt himself.

"Den ze court it will forkive," Kees said. "Continue. I zhall skitch. Will need mush red, bud iz goot for de anadomy pratize."

Now Peter did laugh, harsh and cold, broken, "Do you think I would care in death what the court would forgive?"

"Nod ad all. Bud I zhall be needink de excuses for to give dem, vor I will not be zo happyful." Kees poised his pencil over the paper. "Forkive interruption, iss all most interrestink. Iss also, I t'ink, why I am almost knocked over by blint Occitan leavink hôtel, yess?"

"Yes." Peter's hand trembled and he lowered the pistol, laying it on the desk to take up the bottle once again. "He is the one to whom forgiveness is owed. I - I have done the unthinkable..."

He tossed back his drink, then threw the empty bottle and listened to it shatter against the cold stones of the hearth, "It seems our...friendship is at an end... An end of all -"

Well, that was before I was stupid enough to say I loved you.

He had made Guyon stupid enough to lie. He had brought that sparkling intellect low enough to match his own and it was unforgivable.

"Ah." Kees sat down in the chair opposite him. "Ya, zo, he conffezionaled to de luff. Iz nod vor to be killink zelf. Iz to be

494

tellink him you do nod share. Iz zo bat, vor soltier to be luffed?"

"No -" Peter's voice cracked on a true sob this time, quickly reigned in. "Nor for a scholar I would have thought. But I would be wrong. He does not love me, ya see? It was all pretense. A pretense that I forced him to for friendship's sake...and...and now even that is done."

Peter reached down and absently picked up the bit of string, winding it tight around his thumb.

Kees was silent, for a time. Then he said quietly, "I am alzo de scholar. I wadtch de peoples, vor to put in deir facess de li'l bid off soul. Perhapz you are off de right. Iz all done. Bud nod, I zink, in de way you imagine. A *scolare*...he hass - de reasonink, alwayz, ya?"

"Yes, he does." Peter nodded, dropping the thread on the desk and running his now empty hands over the grip of the pistol. "He does and he told each and every one of them to me quite clearly."

- you have nothing to offer me.

You certainly do not have what my mind craves.

I am becoming - bored.

Friendship and the undoubted physical pleasures you bring are not sufficient.

"Quite...quite clearly."

"Den you are havink one choisse only," Kees said, and leant forward over the desk, taking the pistol out of Peter's lax grip. "Iss to *argue*. And dis?" He waved the pistol around in demonstration. "Iss not argue. Iss *loozink*!" He thumped the gun down on the desk in emphasis, and his clenching hand forced the trigger downwards. There was a noise as of splintering ice - or glass.

Peter turned his head quickly, and saw that one of the great windows to the balcony had been shot out.

"Oh dear," said Kees innocently. "Iss goot dat vass not you, ya?"

One part of him quickly agreed, but another part wanted to call back the bullet, re-aim the shot.

"You don't understand, Kees. I have fought. I have argued. That is what caused this." Peter shook his head at the irony. "I coerced him into something he apparently did not want...and now...he's told me..." Peter crossed his arms on the desk and leaned to rest his head against them, his voice becoming muffled as he continued, "He's right though, in everything he said. Every word."

"Ant zo? Zo he iss right. Iss nothink. *Nothink.* Iss mistake, you fix." Kees's small dark face was more monkey-like than ever in its intensity. "Or maybe...Pieter, maybe you are to be asskink de *why*. Not...not vor de *why me,* but de *why*."

"Or may-be," said the drawling, halting voice of Boronskaya, "you are to sim-ply to be kill-ing the creat-ure *Corvay*."

Peter turned so quickly that in his drunken state he almost toppled from his chair, "Yes. Yes, Alexei...that will be done. If not by me then by the courts. He -"

A frown crossed Peter's brow. Why was Boronskaya even there? He didn't often come by the Hôtel, and then only on some errand. "What's wrong?"

"Your spymaster is destroyed by de Chesnay," Boronskaya said in quick Russian. "But it is a Pyrrhic victory. The cost was our mystic's hand."

*

The Hôtel d'Orsay, Paris, August 1646

Flye hence, O Joy, no longer heere abide
Too great thy pleasures are for my despaire
To looke on, losses now must prove my fare;
Who not long since on better foode relied.
But foole, how oft had I Heav'ns changing spi'd
Before of mine owne fate I could have care:
Yet now past time I can too late beware,
When nothings left but sorrowes faster ty'de.

It was amazing, Peter was to think later, how small words joined together in a particular way could change one's life.

I was stupid enough to say I loved you.

If those words had torn Peter's world to shreds then the ones that Boronskaya had just uttered meant the end of Guyon's. Peter found himself hoping against hope that it, at least, had been Guyon's left hand - that Corvay's traitorous actions had not taken away Guyon's second voice. For if words were the tools that Guyon used, the written form was surely as important as the spoken.

Boronskaya was still looking at him, waiting for a response, his eyes beginning to narrow with anger beyond that at whatever had happened in Corvay's rooms. "You think I'm lying?" He was still speaking in Russian.

"No...No." Peter said, shaking his head. "It's just...Will he be alright? No...I'm sure de Retz...Sorry, I'm just a little..." Peter paused and took a deep breath, trying to circle his mind back to what *was* important. It wasn't his feelings, his heartbreak at Guyon's earlier words, that were important. It was going after Corvay. Now. Before he could make a run for it. "Corvay will go to his home first. He will have money there..."

"How very pragmatic," Boronskaya said, leaving it unclear as to who he meant. "So where is this home of his?" He was obviously ready to set out immediately.

"It's in the Rue Ferou," Peter answered, finally coming back to himself. He moved to strap on his saber, lacing his shirt and looking for his cloak. "It's not far, thank God. "

"Zhall I call ze guard?" This from Kees. Peter had forgotten he was even there.

"Yes...Tell them to form a cordon but not to approach the house." He did not want to take the chance that Corvay would slip past them.

"No," Boronskaya said, putting out a hand. "The Cardinal's guards will already have been sent. De Retz was being very - *forceful* - when I left. He has -" He broke off, looking narrowly at Peter. "Sent for Ibn Ibrahim, as well," he added, in a slightly altered voice. "You have been drinking."

"Yes," Peter admitted. "Quite a lot, actually. And when I have dealt with Corvay...I'll probably drink some more. But, if you think that's going to matter...that I will not be able to do this...then go to Guyon. He could probably use a friendly face."

Because drunk or sober, he was going to go after Corvay. Drunk or sober he was going to kill the man...but not because he was a traitor. Peter truly believed that his traitorous actions were for the Court to address, and he would have done all in his power to make that so. No, Peter's reasons for killing Corvay would be personal.

The dark-velvet eyes widened in amusement. "You think *I* care if you drink? So long as you keep your feet under you, it's no concern of mine!" Then Boronskaya grinned. "And also, if you *cannot* do this, all the more reason for my being there, and *make sure*."

"I won't need you." Peter said, sharply then moved for the door. "But I appreciate the thought."

"You might," Boronskaya pointed out with an unexpected little flash of annoyance, "be even more glad of my sworn word as observer, than my thoughts."

Peter paused in the doorway, taking a deep breath, "Yes...I'm sorry. You are, indeed, right. I've just.... I've just had a very bad day."

Apparently, whisky improved his powers of understatement. He'd have to remember that in future.

Boronskaya gave him a slightly incredulous look, then shrugged, gesturing towards the stairs. "After you," he said politely.

Peter would never clearly remember that trip to the Rue Ferou. His worry over Guyon, combined with drink and the numbness of despair, all joined together to wrap him in a cloud. He felt as if he were alone in the depths of the Grotte once again, with only the light of one small candle to lead him. Unfortunately, this time the light was merely the fire of hatred he felt for Corvay, rather than that of Guyon coming to save him.

His next clear thought was not until he was outside the house, remembering the last time he had stood there, and Guyon's clear little appraisal of the man who waited within.

He's completely lacking in personal perception, had you noticed? Information and manipulation, yes, but understanding? No.

Corvay would have no idea of his true purpose in coming here.

One cannot walk the line of the diameter without peril.

The forbidden path, the straight line that must never be more than an outline drawn in invisible sand. *The line that is the center.* The line Guyon, with his clear uncompromising vision of future and present, chose each time, the line Corvay enticed others onto with promises that he could make all different. And Peter, for this one moment of time, this one situation of his own making, who moved within the circle and not through it, knew himself to be better than both.

He had honed his craft through long hours of Marcelli's interminable 'again'. Honed it to where his body moved of its own accord with little direction from his mind - it ran, it fought and it mastered, with all the emotion of a clock, its mechanism running perfectly with no direction.

"Well," said Boronskaya from behind him, "I think it will be easier on the same side of a door, don't you?"

"Impatient?" Peter said, as he went to the door. He didn't bother knocking, simply opened the door and stepped inside. "His office is through there."

"Impatient, me? Never," Boronskaya said. "But you might want to get to the Louvre, so I was thinking perhaps a little...briskness." He laughed aloud, the sound rich and rolling and bringing Corvay to the door of his office. "Ah, the devil himself," he said lightly.

"Will you come with us?" Peter was sure of Corvay's answer even as he asked, but form was form, and he was sworn to uphold it. "Surrender yourself to the crown?"

"The Crown Imperial or the battered fiction of England?" Corvay retorted. "Not a choice I would make either way, Scudamore, so I fear your answer is *no*."

"Then I fear -" Peter paused, giving Corvay a cold speculative look. "No. There is nothing here to be feared. I will take you back, or you will die. Those are your options."

If Peter had thought he was a cold blooded killer after his duel with Lesueur, he had been wrong. This, *this,* was true cold bloodedness. He knew that he meant every word he spoke and intended to carry them out.

"You're always so...simplistic," Corvay said on a sigh. "Die? Yes, I might. Or you might die, or perhaps I shall leave you alive and wishing otherwise...no, I think you may find the options are endless."

"And you always make things more difficult than they need to be," Peter moved forward, blade drawn, forcing Corvay to take some action.

"I never thought you averse to complications before now," Corvay said, stepping back and reaching out to the side to where his sword leant against the wall. "As long as they came from others - have they taken the hand off yet, by the way? Or didn't you wait to see?" The thin rapier flicked upwards. *Diestro.*

"Of course, they haven't." Peter stepped forward again. "Your aim was too true, surprisingly enough. You did very little damage."

Amazing what he could do when he knew how unscrupulous his opponent was - the lie fell from his lips with the soft sound of conviction. "Guyon will be transcribing your trial for the Court's amusement."

"Ah, but not for yours," Corvay said silkily, his blade moving across, this time, almost catching under Peter's wrist. "You have no idea how he is, do you?"

Peter didn't answer, all seriousness now. He blocked it all from his mind - the slight shift of Boronskaya at his back, his thoughts of Guyon, the small niggling worry that, just possibly, he might not be good enough.

He slipped into position, blade and eyes directed at Corvay's face, his own body in profile to present a lesser target, his feet apart and settled into the light and shifting movements of *La Destreza.*

He had seen Corvay in the training rooms, too, fast and brutal and rarely holding to any code of honor. He was expecting the hard, almost painful replies to each tiny hint of a movement that he made, but he had forgotten the difference between Marcelli, who demanded pure skill, and a man who would use his other hand not for balance, but to behave as though he were pugilist and swordsman both.

Still, he barely flinched when, in the middle of his riposte, Corvay picked up a large letter seal and threw it at him. He simply raised his off-hand and blocked it, completing his movement with a slash to Corvay's face. It landed, cutting the man's nose, cheek and lip in a long impossible severing of skin and muscles and binding tissue. Blood poured from the gash, covering the lower half of his face in a gory mask.

The lit candelabrum that followed a few moments later, was more difficult to ignore than the seal had been. It struck, catching fire to the edge of his cloak.

"Christ!" Peter was shaken out of his numb state, snatching at the cloak to remove it.

The candles spilled from their holders and rolled across the floor, catching papers in a trail of flames and wax as they went. Dimly, Peter was aware of Boronskaya cursing somewhere to his right, and there was a sudden ripping noise as the Russian tore at the tapestry on the wall. Corvay, his left hand pressed to his face, his sleeve and shirt front already sodden with blood, came at Peter once more. The cloak on the floor continued to burn, and there was a sudden incredible blaze of light from Boronskaya's direction, along with a shout of "*Kerosin!*"

"Burning the evidence, Corvay?" Peter held his gaze steady, shifting away from the flames. "It will do you no good. What we have is duplicated and safe."

Corvay's mouth, what Peter could see of it, curled into a

501

parody of a grin, teeth and gums showing through the divided upper lip. "A bonus to light your way..." was all he replied, and spat red.

"There is only one person in all the world that does that," Peter asserted, "And you are not he."

Peter took another step, then had to pause as a burning curtain gusted out between the two of them, flames and sparks obscuring his opponent for several long moments.

It was like the duel with Lesueur, the sudden cloud hiding Corvay from him, the involuntary covering of his eyes, but it was no clear voice of iron that floated out across to him this time, no instruction to *Block!* but Boronskaya's accented soldier's roar.

"Pyotr! *Strike now!*"

He did. Moving with blind faith that Boronskaya would not steer him wrong. And thank God he did, or Corvay's blade would have slipped up and under his ribs in the next instance, almost surely piercing his heart.

Even so, Peter did not come away unscathed, Corvay's blade skittering up the length of his own, slashing open his arm.

Corvay was somewhere behind the burning curtain, should have been moving, should have been coming forward, and was not. It had not been just Corvay's sword that had made contact as Boronskaya shouted. Peter took a step forward, towards the pile of burning cloth and paper and *dear God he's somewhere in there*, and was caught back.

"*Kerosin!*" Boronskaya shouted again, and then, right in his ear and far too loud, "*Oil!* In the tapestry, it was soaked -"

It was then that Peter finally noticed the damage, noticed everything he had tuned out in his concentration on Corvay. The fire that was burning not just the curtains and the tapestry, but the entire room...probably the entire building. The crackling of it was loud as it ignited cloth and paper and wood, loud enough that Boronskaya's shout was necessary. And there before him, where Corvay should have been standing, or lying fallen...was instead a vision of God's own Hell. The timbers of the floor had collapsed, taking Corvay to the lower level, and one more step would have sent Peter to join him. The room below was pure flame, leaving Peter to wonder if Corvay had set light there before they arrived, thinking to be gone long before any meeting could take place.

Of course. He had thought Peter would go first to Guyon, giving him much more time.

"*Move!*" Boronskaya yelled into his ear again, and Peter resisted the impulse to smack him away. "Stop staring and *move!*" He pulled *hard* at Peter's arm this time, turning him around towards the door, and then shoved at his back with a curse that Peter had never heard before. "Out! Out of here!"

No! Peter wanted to wail. He felt cheated, painfully cheated...and then horrified that he could feel that way about the death of another being, no matter how evil. He stumbled down the now-too-long hallway that lead towards the front door, coughing horribly and trusting, somehow, that Alexei was following him.

The final shove that sent him stumbling out of the door was proof positive that the boyar had, indeed, kept possession of all his wits and his life. "End of the street," Boronskaya rasped, hauling him along. "Come *on*, damn you, I'll not roast for your foibles!"

Peter nodded, not sparing breath for talk as he moved down the street. He searched vainly for a bit of his shirt that was not covered in sweat and soot, on which to wipe his burning eyes.

"Water...." He managed to croak out, pointing towards a rough trough used for horses.

"Pump," said Boronskaya even more briefly, and of course there was one beside it, it probably supplied the street. He took first hand at working it, gesturing to Peter to put his injured arm under it first, and seeming to regain his breath by the second, despite the added effort.

Peter hissed as the water hit the cut, cursing Corvay and himself before moving to sluice the soot off his face and out of his eyes. To be honest, he was also worried that some stray spark was, even now, nesting in his clothes or hair, so he wasn't tidy, splashing himself with enthusiasm, before trading places with Boronskaya.

He hoped his efforts hadn't been as wholly unsuccessful as the Russian's, of whom it could only be said that his skin was a faint grey rather than a smudged black by the time he finished. His silvery hair stayed a resolute shade of charcoal, only wet, and when he rinsed out his mouth with water, spitting with vigor, it was apparent that his interior was a close parallel in appearance.

The house behind them lit the whole scene. Fortunately for its neighbors, it had a rather large garden area around it, one more plus for someone with Corvay's needs, setting it apart from its fellows. A loud crash signaled the collapse of more timbers, and the frame of the house collapsed in upon itself.

"He's dead...surely." Peter wheezed and coughed as the sparks flew up.

"I hate the man too," Boronskaya said rather sputteringly, spitting out black-specked water once again, "But dear God, I hope so! No-one deserves to be alive in *that*!"

Peter realized that while he had spoken nothing to Boronskaya but French, the young Russian's only contribution in that language had been the frantic word *oil* as he tried to get Peter to see the devastation around him. Other than that, he had spoken nothing but his mother tongue. Without the halting little drawl, he seemed a different man, scarcely a trace of the courtier remaining. "Alexei -" he began, but Boronskaya was not listening, using the pump himself as he scrubbed at his head.

He owed the man a lot, he knew. If not for his quick action, Peter might now be resting at the bottom of that fiery mass of timbers with Corvay's sword through his heart.

The thought made him shudder and brought him back to himself. "You should get back to the Louvre, Alexei. Guyon...Guyon will need a friend."

And *God*...it couldn't be him, no matter how he wanted it. It couldn't be him.

*

Guyon had never experienced pain like this before. His back had been agony, but this was something new, a sickening, frightening grind that seemed to reverberate through his whole being. His thoughts tried, and failed, to connect, to grasp at what he needed to do, the mocking voice that Peter had promised him was gone forever and which was the only thing he feared kept speaking with terrible clarity in his ears, setting them to ringing, telling him what he knew to be true.

Boronskaya has gone to the Hôtel d'Orsay.

Peter will go to the Rue Ferou.

He could not think, he could not move, could do nothing but struggle not to cry out and clutch at his wrist, feeling things somehow loose and wrong even there. The dagger still remained in his hand, glittering with beautiful malevolence. *I am become a weapon.*

"In here...In here." Peter heard de Retz speaking to someone. Heard it as if from a distance, remote and outside his island of pain.

"Guyon, Ibn Ibrahim will be here soon," the voice that spoke to him now was calm, familiar. "I'm going to give you something to knock you out so he can work on your hand right away.

It was David. At least, he *though*t it was David. Gone were his usual drifting tones, to be replaced with a strength the other man rarely showed to any but Henri.

"No," he managed. "No. Not that. Something other." He drew in a breath, fought for sanity and words. "You've got to - I've got to get to -" Another peak of agony, and this time he almost *did* scream. "Corvay. At the Rue Ferou. And Boron - *Christ*! - Boronskaya went to Peter...he *knows.*"

"Yes...yes...I'm sure Peter knows and will be here as soon as he can," David assured him. He didn't understand. "He wouldn't let you be alone, Guyon. Just calm down and I'll give you something to make you sleep."

"*I don't want you to put me to sleep I want you to wake me up,*" Guyon snarled out on one long breath, and strove to focus on David's face, knotting his good hand in the man's shirt. "Peter. Is with. Corvay. Now *get this damned knife out of my hand and DO something*!" The last was more a shriek than the roar he had intended it to be, but he was rapidly getting past the stage where he cared or was even capable of judging what anyone sounded like, let alone controlling his own voice.

"Christ!" David gripped Guyon's good hand where it clutched at him. "I can't do that. You know I can't...not if you ever want to use that hand again. You need to wait for Ibn Ibrahim to get here and let him remove it. You said that Boronskaya went to talk to

505

Peter, surely he wouldn't let Peter go...well, there...alone?"

"Doesn't matter." Guyon was losing all ability to explain, and knew it. He let go of David's shirt, dropping his hand back to hold onto his wrist again. *I've done something unforgivable and I have to tell him, even if it never is forgiven, I have to tell him...*"And if you won't -" He deliberately gripped the jewelled hilt in his good hand, feeling strengthless and sick and wondering if he even had the ability to keep his eyes open much longer, let alone do as he threatened - "*I will.*"

"Christ, God..." David believed him, knew how stubborn he could be if he set his mind to something. "Fine. Right. Just...oh, hell...It's going to hurt, Guyon. Really a lot. And I might be damaging it even more...and...and there'll be blood."

"There's some *left*?" Guyon said in dark amusement, and met David's eyes in a moment of clear, grim understanding. "It's all right, David. The blame..." *I will survive this for now and get to Peter. I can. I will.* The pain tore at him savagely. "The blame is mine."

And then so was something that felt remarkably as though forked lightning had made its way into his hand, as David's hand replaced his on the dagger's hilt, and he started to draw it upwards.

"Peter's going to kill me...Peter's going to kill me..." David mumbled under his breath. "There now...it's out and...You still with me, Guyon?"

David was wrapping his hand in a heavy padding of cotton and gauze in some, he was sure, vain attempt to keep the blood on the inside.

"Alas, yes," Guyon agreed. "But not, I think, for long. *Drugs*, David."

"I have something I can give you, but I don't advise you to take it." David's face was a mask of unhappiness. "Really, can't you wait? I'm sure Peter is fine."

"No," said Guyon, covering all questions. "Just get it."

"What do you think you are doing?" demanded a sharp, angry voice, and Guyon winced. Ibn Ibrahim.

"He's got it in his head that he's leaving. Can't tell him otherwise." David defended himself. "Had to take out the knife,

506

he was going to yank it out himself."

"Not you, *him*," snapped Ibn Ibrahim, and Guyon mustered what was left of his energy.

"I want drugs that clear the mind."

"A nap and a surgeon is what you want."

"No. It isn't." Guyon took a deep breath, hoping he was not about to succumb to nausea and disprove his point himself. "I have to get to the Rue Ferou, and I won't like this."

"Well, I'm glad that's decided. You won't." Ibn Ibrahim nodded. "Give him something to knock him out, David. I want to see what damage you've done. Vincennes! Get my bag in here."

Vincennes came in, went a peculiar shade of grey, and stared at Guyon's hand. Guyon hissed in a breath. "You come near me, Vincennes, and you'll live to regret it."

"Er, seriously, do whatever he wants," Vincennes said fervently to Ibn Ibrahim.

"*What*?"

"Really," Vincennes said, nodding. "Because otherwise we're dead."

"A man of sense," said Guyon wearily. "David -"

"Besides," said the man of sense. "I'm almost betting he'll not get farther than the street before he passes out...so it's all moot."

"You know better than to bet," said Guyon with a faint flicker of returning wit. "Or so I was told."

Vincennes's pallor was replaced by a scalding wash of red embarrassment. "Uh..."

"There's these powdered leaves, they -"

"Then put them in water and *give them to me*," Guyon said with all the ruthlessness he possessed. *And Peter above all.* It beat in his mind like a trapped moth, fighting to incinerate itself.

"You won't be able to have anything else for five hours, Guyon...Five hours." David's face was pale. "Are you sure? I'll go...I'll get Peter."

"You won't." It wasn't sickness that washed through him now, but bitter, terrible grief. *I am losing all my walls and my control, dear God have mercy on me, show me some kindness and let me win this fight.* "He won't come. I - made sure. It has to be me. I have to do this."

507

David sighed sadly, and handed Guyon the potion.

"Has anyone noticed I'm still here?" demanded Ibn Ibrahim. "De Chesnay, listen to me. If you leave that hand now, you risk amputation."

Guyon laughed, and swallowed the horrible, bitter little drink. "Too late," he said. "You think I'd put my body above my soul?"

"I think you're insane," Ibn Ibrahim shook his head. "But you will do what you will do. Keep it as immobile as possible and get back here as soon as you can.?

"I'll go with you," David said. "I'm going to thump Peter, what did he think he was doing putting a game with Corvay over you?"

"Because," Guyon said, starting to feel blissfully detached and quite calm, "I told him I didn't love him and he bored me."

There was total, horrified silence.

"He believed you?" Vincennes managed to squeak out. "Really, Guyon, I know we tease Peter about being a muddle-headed soldier, but it's just that - teasing. How could the man believe you?"

But it was David, looking into Guyon's eyes, who said to them all very quietly, "How could he not?" and Guyon smiled, the expression almost as hard to endure as the receding pain.

"How indeed?" he asked with equal softness.

"You really are -"

"I know what I am," Guyon agreed, and wavered to his feet. "But I'll not have Peter's death added to my sins." He took a deep breath, and stepped forward, feeling strange and numb and utterly clear-headed, and as though he were entirely separated from his body, a mere collection of thoughts and perception and the terrible, clawing pain that seemed so remote and yet felt so appalling. "If you're coming with me, David, move."

*

The walk to the Rue Ferou was probably worse for David, Guyon reflected, since he was more preoccupied with keeping a reasonably straight line and his thoughts from wandering off with amazing thoroughness into a labyrinth of Cicero and Plotinus and, for some reason, Euclid. Since all those things were preferable to wondering how he could be in so much pain and still upright, he was quite willing to let David dictate both pace and direction, and retreat into his strangely crystalline thoughts until he was needed.

Since from myself, my other self I turn.

"Who said that?" he wondered aloud.

"Who said what?" David looked puzzled as he guided Guyon around the last corner and into the Rue Ferou. "Oh, my...."

The devastation facing them was horrible...black smoke and soaring flames, both upper floors caved into the basement.

All Guyon could think of was the look on Peter's face as he loosed his words like Apollo's plague arrows, of his final empty little phrase -

Go with God, Scudamore.

"No," he protested in dull fear, telling himself *I would know, I would know, I would have known*, and all the time hearing the voice cry *You will be the author of it*! as though from some dimly-remembered nightmare.

"Surely no one is inside there." David's fervent voice broke the sudden silence. "They couldn't be...I mean, I'm sure that...Peter isn't in there."

Guyon started to walk towards the house. *If I am closer, I will know, I will be certain. If I am closer...*

It was the rolling, sonorous curses that stopped him half-way, the familiar sound of Russian expletives carving through the smoke-filled air.

"Alexei," he whispered, his knees almost unhinging with relief.

"It's not my fault that it took this long to burn through. Stay under the pump, damn you, until I can be sure that's the last one."

"And Peter, thank God," David whispered, as two grayish sodden figures came into view, the light from the fire making them seem eerily ghostlike.

"*This is the most inefficient fucking water I've ever encountered*!" Alexei yelled in Russian. Peter's voice had been hoarse and a bit ragged, but Alexei sounded entirely unaffected.

"Huh?" said David.

"Apparently," Guyon said, leaning against the nearest wall

and wondering how his mind could remain this clear when everything else was shutting down almost completely, "our French water is inadequate.".

"It's not the water, you idiot, it's the damn padding in that coat." Peter was obviously stressed, switching from French to English to Russian as he spoke. "It's so thick that it took that long to burn through. You weren't even wet there the first time. Inefficient water my arse!" The last few words broke into a magnificent coughing fit.

"Are you -" Alexei suddenly choked, but on laughter, his words dissolving into a sort of squeaking set of wheezes as he went into a fit of almost-giggles that rivaled Peter's coughing. "Are you i-insulting my c-oat?" He was back in French, along with his sputtering mirth.

"I think," Guyon said from his strange new pinnacle of pain and detachment, "they're all right."

Peter's coughing fit diminished slowly, "Ya sound like an ass, yersel'. Come on, Alexei, we need to get back to the Louvre. Guyon might not want to see me but...I can't *not go*. I have to know for my own sake that he's alright."

The words caught sharply against Guyon's heart, and twisted painfully. *Even now,* he thought. *Even now, he has grace.*

He could not find the energy to move. David was cursing him, for some reason, pushing him back against the wall, and none of it mattered. *It was worth everything to see you safe,* he thought suddenly, and smiled.

"We go." Alexi agreed. "Our lit-tle mystic, will want you there, Pyotr, this I know."

Peter coughed some more before he answered, his voice as bleak as the grey ash that covered his face, "No, I refuse to delude myself. It hurts too damn much. He doesn't want me there. He said that I made him lie and forced him into something that he didn't want. He may not hate me...but that is as far as I can go."

"I ought to cut your heart out slowly and feed it to you," David growled, and Guyon sighed, turning his head to look into blue eyes that were just the wrong shade, and English fairness that was somehow wrong.

"I wish you would," he said, before turning his attention back to Peter. "Hello," he called, and smiled, raising his bandaged hand before he could think.

The world became decidedly grey and wool-filled for a while, the only thing anchoring him to it David's renewed cursing.

*

By the time Peter was halfway toward the rather ill-assorted couple by the wall, he could hear David cursing himself and Guyon more thoroughly than the most inventive of Boronskaya's epithets after he got Peter out of the house. Guyon, white-faced and expressionless, was ignoring him, his translucent eyes fixed on Peter. "Never again," David growled. "*Never* again. I hope he *does* chop your damn hand off. I'll *help*. I'll volunteer with the saw!"

Peter approached Guyon, cautiously as any nervous cat, looking worriedly at the mass of bandages concealing whatever damage Corvay had done to his right hand. "You shouldn't be here. That - You need to get to the surgeon, Guyon. Now. Please."

"'S all right. I can wait all day to have my hand amputated." Guyon sounded completely detached, and Peter, terrified, realized that it was from reality.

"No. Dammit! You're not having the bloody thing amputated. We're going to Ibn Ibrahim now...I don't care if I have to wake the whole Sorbonne." Peter looked at him, his jaw tight. "Please, Guyon. I beg you."

"I think he's the one who wants it amputated," Guyon said dreamily. "He's waiting for me in de Retz's rooms. But I made David bandage it up and give me American powdered leaves, and came here. Instead. They've done something *incredible* to my mind."

"Yes," Peter agreed. "They have. But please...now..." He gently took Guyon's uninjured hand and tried to lead him away.

"You killed Corvay," Guyon said, stopping still. He laughed bitterly. "Of course you did. Of *course* you did. It was all for nothing."

"No...it was for you. And for me. And now we're free." Peter looked at him, his eyes searching his face, looking for something that would convince Guyon to go.. now..."You're...you're finally free, to do whatever you wish. Be whatever you want to be."

Guyon laughed. He laughed until he shook with it, and the movement jarred his hand, stopping his amusement instantly. "Yes. So are you. And now that Corvay won't be going to the courts, I find I am *extremely* unwilling to persist in lying to you. Which I was." He frowned. "David, my mind's working too fast for my mouth. What *are* those leaves?"

David looked up, "Coca leaves...work fast, yes?"

"Definitely work fast, yes," Guyon said wryly. "So lying to you, Corvay, coca leaves - can you blame me for not feeling like scampering off to have my hand removed?"

"It doesn't matter. Nothing matters but getting you to the surgeon. Once...once that's taken care of, we'll talk. When I'm sure it's you talking and not the pain, or David's damn leaves, I'll stand and listen to whatever you want to tell me." Peter promised. "But please, Gui...you're bleeding."

"Oh." Guyon peered at his hand. "I thought it stopped doing that. Sorry, I'm probably frightening dogs and small children." He sighed, sounding infinitely sad. "I'm not a stoic. I thought I would be. But I'm not."

"I don't want you to be stoic. I want you to move your damn feet." Peter demanded. "If you don't, I swear I'm going to bloody well pick you up and carry you all the way there."

Guyon looked at him assessingly. "You would, too," he said with a faint smile, and started walking. "Your wish, as you can see, is my command -" He caught his breath, his free hand automatically coming up and covering the bloodstained bandages, but even that small instinctive touch caused him visible pain. "Give me a moment, just -" There were beads of sweat at his temples and along his lip, and for a moment he just stood still, breathing shallowly.

Peter turned to David, then, "What else can you safely do? Please, David."

"I can't." David looked uncharacteristically furious. "I can't, and I told him I can't, not for another five hours. *Nothing.*"

"God..." Peter's eyes squeezed shut for just a moment. "Alexei...Please, go ahead of us and make sure they're ready. I'll

512

get him there as quickly as I can. David...just...move..." He slid one arm around Guyon...and got him moving again.

"Told you I wasn't a stoic," Guyon said apologetically. "I'm sorry. I'm sorry I lied. I promised I never would, and I did, and I'm so sorry, and I'd like this damn drug to stop *now*, it's removing all my walls and filters, worse than you do..."

"I forgive you." Peter told him, not knowing what the apology was for, and not caring as long as Guyon moved. "I'd forgive you anything, don't you know that by now?"

"No," Guyon said, looking down at his feet as thought they belonged to someone else. He quite possibly thought they did. "I deliberately made it unforgivable. You were supposed to hit me. Never want to speak to me again. Might have been something about darkening doors in there...but you didn't." He sounded as desolate as Peter felt. "It's unforgivable. And it was a *lie*."

"No..." Peter answered him back but would not allow him to stop moving. "I'm sure you only said what you felt, Guyon. I don't hold it against you. Truly. I - I always pushed you. I kept telling you what you didn't want to hear because I loved...do love you...so desperately. That was what was unforgivable, I can see that."

"It was a lie," Guyon repeated dully. "Start to finish. I was lying from the second I started. I was lying because I wanted Corvay in court and he would have taken you down with him. And I wouldn't allow it to happen, not when this time *I* could save *you*. So I thought of all the things you've always said you were afraid of - and I made them into my words and sharpened their points and loosed them at you. I love you. Of course I love you. And I made you doubt it." He sighed. "How dead is Corvay?"

"You don't have to say that, Guyon. Just wait, alright? When this is done, when David's drugs are out of your system, if you still want to tell me any of that, I'll listen. But not now, please..." *Because if you change your mind it really will break me.* "Just keep moving."

Guyon smiled at him with a sort of resigned sorrow. "Yes, Peter," he said softly, and tried - and failed - to cling to his renewed silence as they went the rest of the way to de Retz's rooms and the irate Ibn Ibrahim.

*

The trip back to the Louvre was just as horrific as Peter had feared. Guyon, almost in shock with pain, saying whatever came into his brain - some of it babbling and some of it all too clear to Peter. He claimed to have lied to Peter, that he did, in fact, love him. Peter knew better than to trust that though. Men said lots of things, he knew, when they were in pain, or frightened, or under the influence of drugs. Things that weren't true once they lost their pain and fright and sobered up.

But none of that really mattered to Peter at the moment. All that mattered was that Guyon be healed as best as was possible. Healed and comforted, if not by him. He'd do whatever it took to make that happen. Then, when it was all over with, he'd see how Guyon felt about him.

Right now, Ibn Ibrahim had pulled Guyon from his grasp and he and Vincennes were examining Guyon's wound to see how best to proceed. Peter waited, impatiently, for them to tell him what they needed, or wanted from him.

"I won't need to take it off," Ibn Ibrahim said curtly. He was glaring down at the injury as though it were some sort of personal insult, but his touch must have been at odds with however he sounded, because Guyon, who had flinched from his *own* quick brush of fingers over the layers of bandages, was perfectly still under his examination. "The veins at your wrists are collapsed, which means the blood flows slowly. So less bruising, less impediment, less fear of gangrene. An old injury to them?"

"Very," Guyon said dryly. His eyes were closed. "I'm not looking at it. I'm not going to look at it, I have no intention of knowing what it -" He bit down on his lip, stopping the flow of words, and took a slow breath. "So you'll have to be without visual aids." His eyes flickered open, and found Vincennes. "New form of tutorial, chér. How your tutor's hand works, from the inside out - *Christ*, can I have a gag, please?"

"What will you need to do?" Peter spoke softly from the shadows where he stood. "No...just tell me what you need from me? More light? More candles, surely? Blankets."

514

He shifted nervously. He had never felt quite so useless in his whole life. Even his time on the battle field had not prepared him for this. He'd seen friends hit with musket balls, cannon balls and chain shot, bones broken, limbs severed and insides spilling out from saber cuts, but this - This was the person he loved more than his own life, and there was nothing he could do.

Ibn Ibrahim did not answer. It was Vincennes who spoke, instead, as he got out three sheets of beaten copper and a silvered-glass lantern from the battered leather bag that must have been Ibn Ibrahim's. "You can cut his shirt sleeve off," he said briskly. Peter wondered how he could sound so calm, and then saw the fine white line around his mouth, clearly visible among the bright freckles.

"Just cut the damn *shirt* off," Guyon rasped irritably. "I'm not going to want it without a sleeve, am I?"

"Instruments case," Ibn Ibrahim said to Vincennes, ignoring them all. He snapped his fingers at Peter. "Writing desk." He pointed across the room at the little folded object.

Peter jumped to the command as if it were Prince Rupert himself giving it, rather than the small, intense man before him. He handed him the writing desk and then moved to cut away, Guyon's shirt, giving Vincennes a quick short nod of gratitude. The younger man obviously had some idea of how useless he felt and was trying to make him feel less so.

Vincennes had lit a candle, placing it in the little silvered-glass lantern, and the sudden reflected light was almost dazzling, sharp and spluttering as a firework for one instant before the wick was trimmed and the little box closed, an almost white beam of light shining out steadily.

"Here," said Ibn Ibrahim. He had placed one of the sheets of copper on the writing desk, and gestured to the right side with one hand. His other was still holding Guyon's wrist. "You know that you can have nothing to ease the pain, now?" he said suddenly, addressing Guyon.

"I knew that after the first seven times you yelled it at me," Guyon agreed. "*My* decision. I told you."

"Very well." A long look passed between them that Peter could not read. "Your decision," Ibn Ibrahim agreed at last, and his thin mouth flickered in an almost-smile. "I repeat what I said before. To save your hand, I am going to peel back your skin. I am going to extract bone splinters. I am going to repair what I can of muscle and tendon. Can you keep still?"

Guyon snorted out painful-sounding laughter. "*No*," he retorted.

Swallowing hard, Peter stepped closer, his eyes locking onto Guyon's, "I'll help. I'll hold him still so you can work."

He could do this. He would ignore Guyon's pain in order to hold him steady and still, with the hope that it will make things better in the end. *He could do this.*

"Self-sacrifice is unattractive," Guyon said harshly. "Vincennes -"

"Is going to be holding copper sheets and pouring a lot of water," said his erstwhile pupil. "I can wreck de Retz's floor, that'll be interesting..."

Guyon closed his eyes for a brief moment, shuttering everything away. "Right," he said. It wasn't agreement so much as an unwilling kind of yielding. "You don't have to," he said to Peter, quietly. "Truly."

"Guyon, for once in your life, shut up and let someone help you," Peter's voice was rough and raw, but he smoothed a gentle hand over Guyon's forehead, brushing the curls back from his sweaty brow. "It will be alright."

"I told you. You really need to work on your definitions." The pulse in Guyon's throat beat visibly and fast, and for a moment, he looked completely terrified. Then he grinned, sudden and savage and utterly unlike himself. "All right. Let's start, if we have to."

Peter looked up at Ibn Ibrahim and Vincennes and gave them a quick nod to say he was ready as well. Then he moved into a position where he could hold Guyon steady and still without being in the surgeon's way.

"Guyon, I want you to listen to my voice," Peter told him softly, as the surgeon and Vincennes moved to begin their work. "There is nothing, nothing, more important than that. You don't have to answer after this. You don't have to do anything but listen. Do you understand?"

Guyon's eyes were almost completely transparent, the pupils contracted to pinpricks and the irises colorless in the glaring light, but they were still clear and focused as he looked straight at Peter. "Yes," he said quietly. "Yes, I understand." He swallowed. "*Aşkin Cemal Olsun*, Pèire. *Ou hibouka.*"

"I'm touched," said Ibn Ibrahim dryly. "Shut up."

Peter was oddly prepared for this. He'd tell Guyon all the things that he had wanted to say, the things his heart had stored up over the time since Guyon had come to his office and ripped his heart out. It would be so very easy to tell him of his hurt and pain and try to hurt him back, now, when he couldn't retaliate. But somehow, Peter couldn't find it within himself, even as hurt as he had been.

"I love you, Guyon. Whether you ever want to hear that again or not, it's true. I'll stay away if you want, but it won't change anything. I'll just be loving you from where ever I am." The words were simple and earnest.

"I know," Guyon said with quiet sorrow. "It's you who don't."

"I thought there was going to be only one person here talking," Ibn Ibrahim snapped.

"Long as it's not me," Vincennes said helpfully, and was the recipient of three incredulous stares. He shrugged. "Needed saying. I do *speak* Arabic, Guyon." He added honestly, "Now."

"*Inshallah*," said Ibn Ibrahim, looking more as though he wished he could put them all in a sack and drown them, than as though he believed his word of prayer, and his horrendous little knife made the first cut.

Peter braced Guyon, held him as still as he could, "Guyon...Guyon...listen to me, beloved. There is nothing more important than that. We're here together after all the things we've been through and this is just one more thing. We'll get through this, together, I promise."

Guyon made no reply, biting down on his lower lip. His eyes were still fixed on Peter, in a silent plea for belief.

Ibn Ibrahim stopped cutting, and began to use a small pair of pincers on the exposed flesh. A steady stream of water ran onto de Retz's expensive carpet from the pitcher Vincennes was holding, the faint rose tint of it slowly deepening.

517

"Whatever you honestly and truly want from me is yours. You know that." Peter said softly, fighting back the painful lump forming in his stomach, and the one in his throat. God this hurt, hurt like the words that Guyon had said to him.

Together has become a farce, Peter, and I can't continue it.

I am becoming - bored.

Friendship and the undoubted physical pleasures you bring are not sufficient.

Every one of those words was engraved on his soul like a firebrand. But this hurt even worse, because he was sure that when this was over, and the pain and the drugs wore off, Guyon would simply walk away again, leaving him even more broken

"That's because - God loves irony," Guyon managed on a sort of broken gasp. Pain was driving the lucidity from his eyes, blood welling in a bright set of indentations on his lip as he spoke. "This hurts. This hurts."

Ibn Ibrahim's face was carved from illuminated marble in the light and black shadows of the lantern, fixed and immobile as he used a tiny file on the jagged edges of bone. The water poured again, a thin, constant sound overlaying the faint rasp of roughened metal. "Move the copper," he said quietly, and the light suddenly intensified and warmed at once.

Peter reached over and snatched a small roll of gauze off of the instrument tray, and held it up in front of Guyon's mouth, "Open your mouth so I can put this in. Then you can bite on it and not hurt yourself. Please, Gui. I know it hurts. I know so very well. And scream if you need to. Sometimes it helps."

His voice was still calm and soothing, his body only betraying the tension and pain he was feeling. *If there were any way, I would take this pain myself. I've had it before.* Guyon was strong, he had no doubt of that, but he was a scholar, not a soldier, and shouldn't have to suffer this kind of pain.

Guyon nodded, his face seeming to draw in and contract as he made an effort towards control, to doing as he was told. He unclenched his jaw, biting down on the gauze, and for a fleeting moment, his wide eyes showed genuine amusement, showing as clearly as though he had spoken aloud just how little he appreciated the taste of the material. He turned his head away restlessly, his hair soaked with sweat and dragging against the chair back, a pulse beating as fast as a bird's heart in his temples.

Ibn Ibrahim took up a second knife, trimming torn muscle away, now, a malign and demon-born cook in the fiery light of the balanced copper sheet. Guyon's hand was an anatomy sketch, a corpse's remnants with one skinned and pulsing vein overlaying it all, the neatly flayed skin folded back over the planed and shattered bones.

Vincennes kept pouring water, his right hand steady as it held the copper sheets, catching reflected light and the shimmer of the liquid.

Leaning in, Peter could not, somehow, resist placing a kiss against that rapidly beating pulse in the fragile hollow of Guyon's temple. *This is madness,* he thought suddenly, *Cruel madness.* But still Vincennes and the surgeon worked, each movement sending a shock of pain through Guyon.

There had to be something more he could do.

"A North Country lad up to London had strayed,
Although with his nature it did not agree.
He wept and he sighed, and so bitterly he cried,
How I wish once again in the North I could be!
Oh the oak and the ash, and the bonny ivy tree,
They flourish at home in my own country."

Peter crooned the lyrics into Guyon's ear, as soft and as gentle as a mother comforting her babe.

Guyon muttered something through teeth and gauze, a slur of Occitan and pain. Tears escaped his closed eyes, slow and somehow heavy, as though overladen with salt.

"Catgut," said Ibn Ibrahim curtly, and for the first time, the light trembled.

"*Thanks be to God.*" There was no doubting the sincerity of Vincennes's prayer.

The quick, spare hands moved quickly now, repairing and binding where before they had cut and rendered useless, patches for the now-silent tailor of words.

"Bandage it," Ibn Ibrahim instructed Vincennes at last, and straightened, bending over Guyon and looking into his face. "Good boy," he said, rubbing a thumb over Guyon's white cheek.

He took the mangled gauze out from between the clenched teeth. "Good boy."

"You're done." Peter looked up, wondering if his eyes looked as haunted as he felt.

"I'm done," Ibn Ibrahim agreed. His hawk's eyes were almost as bright as the light that Vincennes was finally extinguishing, piercing the sudden sense of dimness. "You should believe him." There were lines on his face that Peter had never noticed before, reminding him that no-one really knew how old the Arabic physician was, that Vincennes and Guyon had always joked that he knew the secrets of the world's creation. "This was for you."

"Shut - up," Guyon growled faintly. "Thank you...but shut up..."

"Sssh, sssh, sssh," Peter whispered softly to Guyon, soothing one hand through his hair. "You need to rest. No more worries. Let me take care of this, please Gui?"

He didn't wait for an answer, all of his thoughts too painful to think of much beyond the practicalities. "What do we do now?"

He looked at Vincennes and the surgeon, asking about medications and changing the dressing and everything he'd need to do to help Guyon during the next several days. After that some decision would be made, Peter was sure, about Guyon's future and whether he was to be any part of it.

"I *can't* sssh," Guyon said pathetically, cutting across the explanations of when things needed to be changed and just what painkillers and opiates and sleeping draughts were in which prepared vials and twists of paper that Vincennes was laying out. "I want a drink. And can someone go and burn David's collection of leaves now? My mind won't *stop*..."

"It will soon enough," Vincennes told him. "And when it does, you're going to collapse like an empty wine skin."

Peter listened to the last of the instructions then asked, "Where -? I hate to beg the Archbishop's indulgence, but Guyon can scarce stand, I'm sure, let alone get back to his rooms. Is there someplace...?"

"Have the official bedroom," de Retz said, emerging from it. "Oh thank God, you've stopped. My *carpet*!" It was a sort of howl, before he collected himself, shaking his head. "Sorry. The bedroom is - a showcase, I have morning audiences in it. But the bed really is a bed." He looked nearly as bad as Guyon. "Christ, de Chesnay. You've got a constitution like iron."

Peter left polite replies to everyone else for the moment. All he could think of was getting Guyon someplace to rest. He gently moved his injured arm so that his hand rested against his chest, then slid his hands under him and lifted him gently into his arms.

"Did he leave my fingers?" Guyon asked anxiously. He still hadn't looked at his hand - not that he would be able to tell at the moment in any case, since it looked more like a misshapen mitten than anything belonging to the human body. "Did he?" He was shivering as though he had been dipped in ice, his limbs refusing to obey him even as he tried desperately to gain control over his own balance.

"Yes, beloved, it's all still there, every finger. I promise you." Peter carried Guyon towards the bedroom, moving as smoothly and gently as he could. He relished the chance to use the loving words again, uncaring of who might hear them, for he feared that it would be all too soon that they would again be forbidden.

Guyon curled onto his good side as soon as he was laid on the bed, burying his head in the pillows. "Is this all it takes to get luxury?" he asked through chattering teeth. "Or would be, if it were warmer." He shuddered. "Oh God. When can I have the opiates? Screaming's so undignified." His voice was jumping and slurring as though he were drunk - *worse,* Peter thought, remembering the deadly smooth tones that had accompanied the flask of aquavit, at François's funeral. *Which reminds me...*

He covered Guyon as warmly as he could, then went back out into the other room to collect all the vials and papers and things that he'd need to care for the injured man. "How long, Vincennes? How long before I can give him this?"

He wasn't certain when Guyon and David had made their damnable agreement.

"Can give it to him in an hour or so," said David in a very subdued voice from the doorway. "I put a *lot* in that drink."

"And still not enough," Peter said, tight lipped. "Damn it, David. How could - No, I can't be any angrier about this than I was about the aquavit you shared with him on the day of François' funeral. The man is impossible to say no to, as I very well know. But you shouldn't have let him put himself in more danger for me, David. He's worth ten of me any day and he could have..." Peter took a deep breath. "An hour, yes, fine."

"Right," said de Retz, having finally got either control of himself or his perceptions, or, least probably, the situation - and quite honestly, Peter couldn't have given a damn which it was. "Somers, I need a secretary. We're going to the Cardinal. Practice coherency on the way by telling me what you two did. Scudamore, I want to talk to you later. *At length*." He didn't look sick any more. He looked angrier than Peter. "Everyone who isn't the English Marshal, out of my rooms. *Now*."

There was a flurry of activity and the room was quickly cleared of everyone but Peter. Then even he was gone, seeking instead the warmth and comfort of Guyon's living presence, if not his touch.

"New definition of unbearable," Guyon said from the depths of an incredibly small curled-up ball at the top of the Archbishop's State bed. "This. I can't get *warm*." Even the edges of the pillows under his head were trembling visibly.

It was probably shock, Peter was sure, and the letdown after so much stress. "It won't be much longer, then I can give you something for the pain. You won't feel so cold when you sleep."

But still as much as he didn't want to do it, he tugged off his boots and crawled up on the bed next to Guyon, doing his best not to disturb the thickly wrapped hand. "Here, maybe this will help." He wrapped himself tightly around Guyon.

"It helps," Guyon whispered, in defiance of all the evidence, since he did not seem to be feeling any warmer at all, judging by the shivering. The icy fingers of his good hand wrapped slowly and fumblingly around Peter's arm. "Don't go."

Peter felt that lump again, rising up in his throat, large and slick. Still, somehow, he managed to choke words out around it, "I'll stay as long as you need me to."

"Self-sacrifice -" Guyon said, and stopped. He didn't say anything else until the clock in the other room told them the hour had passed, and even then he was silent until he had somehow swallowed the horrible-smelling liquid that Vincennes had left.

"Thank you," he said then, and his eyes were dark, and still so sad, as though some spring of life in him had failed. He had not moved his hand from his chest. "Stay?"

"I will," Peter whispered to him fervently. *God help me.* "I will."

*

It was a toss-up, Peter thought, as to which one of them was worse company. Guyon, drugged out of his pain, incoherent or depressed in between times or he, worried and numb, feeling the pain of his own injury and trying not to show any of it to Guyon. The strain was stretching him thin, like catapult line, one more turn of the crank and he'd break, whipping out to damage anyone close.

Anyone, please God, but Guyon.

Peter was struggling. Drowning. Mired twelve inches deep in a morass of worry and his own pain. No, it wasn't purely physical, but it effected him just the same. And Guyon's continual swings between seemingly abject apology and numb acceptance of his situation, drove new spikes into him daily.

Whatever had been said to everyone by Guyon between Corvay's leaving the Louvre and Peter finding the spy master at the Rue Ferou had obviously been both revealing and deliberately, personally devastating - and absolutely inward-turning in both. David, despite all his competence towards Guyon, was equally obviously furious with him; Vincennes was frightened by him; Ibn Ibrahim, who came to make sure that no-one had missed any signs of infection, was gentle and almost tender. De Retz left everyone to it, and made no complaint about his rooms. And Guyon, the unwitting centre of it all, was too drugged and agonized by alternate hours and minutes to do or say anything that might alleviate the situation. It all felt far too much like a powder keg to Peter, and one with a very short fuse.

"I have food for you, Gui," Peter tried to sound enthusiastic as he gently shifted Guyon, propping pillows around him until he was almost sitting up but cushion from all most any movement. "I'd tell you Ännchen made it but I don't want to put you completely off food. No, I had Cadet Riviere send it over from the Hôtel. Good beef broth and.. Hmmm baked apples of some kind...mashed up so it shouldn't be too difficult."

"I don't remember anyone extracting my teeth," Guyon said. It would have been an enormous relief had he snarled, or snapped, or even used the sharp twist of mockery that always stung, but instead his voice was completely flat, lifeless and emotionless. And that meant the end of the cycle of powders and draughts, and the slow spin into the clear-headed, terrible agony that marked down time until the next dosages and the painful, unhappy ravings that were not always even comprehensible. Peter had no idea whether Guyon was even aware enough to have started dreading it, but after less than forty-eight hours, each of which had seemed interminable, he certainly had.

"I meant on your stomach. Food and drugs don't always agree...I seem to remember that." Peter frowned. A lot of the hours he passed after his return from Toulouse were still a mystery to him, so he might have this all completely wrong. "That's right, isn't it?"

"Oh." Guyon's bleak, translucent gaze refocused from whatever inner vista was currently occupying him, and he nodded in an agreement that might have been connected to Peter's question and might simply have been a return to the anxious, persistent need to acquiesce with everything he thought Peter could possibly want from him.

"Well then...food..." Peter put the tray on the bedside table and drew up his chair. "Do you feel a bit like a bird in his nest? Only I hope this is a bit more appetizing than whatever they get."

Peter was babbling and he knew it, but if he didn't keep up this constant barrage of banalities, one of them would start talking about something more important, and as long as Guyon was under the influence of drugs, Peter just couldn't hear it.

"Argos," Guyon said wearily, and then - "You're right. I don't think food would be a good idea. I'll just - I'll wait." His mouth shook a little when he tried to smile, as though covering some great emotion - but it wasn't emotion he was covering, Peter knew, it was the start of the dizzying slide downwards into pain once again.

"You should try to get some down while you can. I...I know it's not pleasant but...could you try?" The in between times were the best chance to get food into him, even if it came back up once the pain got bad.

Guyon's stony face softened into a sort of wry acceptance. "I can try," he agreed, and there was the faintest sound of humor in his voice. *The question being whether you'll be glad I did, later,* remained unspoken and yet very audible indeed.

"Good," Peter gave him a half smile and spooned up some of the broth, testing it, then raising it to Guyon's lips. "A little bland, but not too bad."

The look Guyon gave him was a rather hysterical combination of *please shut up* and *how the hell would you know* and, approximately half a second later, *oh God, this is horrible, and I'm embarrassed.*

"It could be worse, Gui...it could be quail eggs."

"Or herb broth." The amusement was a little more definite, that time, if rusty-sounding. "Although if you're lucky, you don't remember."

"I remember the quail eggs." He did, sadly. François had, somehow, liberated dozens of the undersized treats, and brought them to his Louvre rooms while he was recovering. "They stared at me...two of them, like tiny blind eyeballs...I dreamed about those damned things."

"I hid them in a kettle and François boiled them," Guyon said then, and while it sounded a little disconnected, it was almost certainly true. He put up his good hand. "No more. Really." True to depressing form, he had managed five more spoonfuls before the sadly familiar refusal. "Sorry," he added miserably.

"I understand," Peter sighed and sat down the bowl. "Not even a bite of apples? I know you love them."

"Not cooked I don't," Guyon said, and curled up into the pillows like an unhappy snail retreating into its shell.

"Oh, sorry," Peter felt disappointed and hurt. He had asked Riviere to cook the apples, thinking they'd be softer and easier for Guyon to digest. He tried to send the disappointment away, there was no way that Guyon could have known everything he was doing to tempt him to eat.

There was a knock at the door and Peter went to answer it.

"Supplies," David said, far too cheerfully, and waving a parcel at Peter. "I talked to some of the botanists at the gardens and there's a really nice apothecary, he's a bit old but he knows his stuff, and Ibn Ibrahim came up with a few ideas after he took a look at Vincennes's hangover cure. So *something* should work."

"Yes...yes, David. That's good." It would be good if it *did* work, because watching this cycle of unconsciousness and pain was going to make him ill before it made Guyon better.

"'S fairly strong, but we just won't tell him, right?"

"Yes, I can imagine just how well he'll take *that* piece of brilliance in a few days," Henri, less cheerfully loud than David, but equally contrasting in voice and appearance to the grey lassitude Peter had just been faced with, chipped in from the corridor. "Are we allowed in, Peter, or are you playing the dragon?"

Peter glanced back over his shoulder, and spoke quietly, "No...You can come in. Maybe seeing something besides my face will help."

God knows nothing else seemed to. No matter how Guyon felt about him, Peter hurt when Guyon did, and right now he felt like he'd been run over by a sixteen horse coach.

"I've got new drugs," David said brightly and loudly, and Guyon lifted his head enough to give him a hazy but still remarkably potent glare.

"I heard," he said sharply, "just like the rest of Paris. And I'm not deaf."

Henri thumped David painfully and audibly in the side, and moved over to the bed. "You want us here?" he asked more quietly.

"Do I get a *choice*?" Guyon snarled. "You *are* here."

"With new drugs," David chimed in, unstoppably, and Guyon just closed his eyes.

"So measure them out and *go away*."

"You need to get yourself settled, my dear." Henri carefully refluffed pillows and straightened blankets. He sniffed at the broth on the tray and then looked up at Peter, eyebrows raised at the barely diminished contents. Peter just shrugged.

"And I'm settled, and now you can go," Guyon said, proving incontrovertibly that ungrateful was currently as nice as he got.

"After the nice new -"

"Oh, David, put an old sock in it and chew," said Henri wearily. "We all know he's going to take the damn stuff, so just - please, try and have a little restraint."

David pursed his lips. "Well, if you want to take control, you can see if the hand needs draining again," he said sweetly, and Guyon looked at him as though he were contemplating mass murder.

"I'll help," Peter offered. "Just show me what to do."

Peter had not seen Guyon's hand since Ibn Ibrahim had wrapped it up. Oddly, that worried him more than Guyon's attitude. Somehow, not seeing it was worse, like a big horrible secret that Guyon was keeping from him.

But maybe that was the point. No trust. No intimacy of any kind.

"*No,*" Guyon said, and his face, impossibly, went whiter and more expressionless.

"I'll make a deal, then," David said. "Drugs and no Peter, or we do the stoicism routine and Peter can have a nice long look."

"And that would be our cue to leave for a nice long *walk*," Henri said firmly, taking Peter by the arm. "Ah! Not an argument you want to have, my dear sweet Marshal, believe you me."

"No, it's - No, I understand," Peter said softly. But he didn't. Not really. Still he followed Henri, taking deep breath of air once they were out in the corridor. Air not scented with blood and drugs and Guyon's misery.

"I feel," Henri said to the vaulted ceiling, "as though I keep having this conversation in a sort of repeating bad dream. Or overhearing it." He shrugged. "*Walk,* my lord Marshal, or I'll drag you."

"What?" Peter scowled for a moment. "You needn't growl at me, Henri. I know I'm not wanted here...so walk. No argument."

"As I said, it repeats," Henri said. "And gets no better with repetition. I don't give advice, I'm not made for it, and you know that. But I'll tell you something David won't. Those drugs will be far worse than aquavit could ever be. And incidentally, *that* is what they're going to be mixed in." He stopped, and grinned mirthlessly at Peter. "So learn to take hardship lightly, Peter, because that's all you'll be getting for a long, long time."

Peter nodded. This was something he understood. Guyon at his worst, as he had been the day of François' funeral. It would be rough. That was something else he understood. And that he would deserve every damnable thing that Guyon through his way, he accepted

...that was before I was stupid enough to say I loved you.

...there's no way I can stay with you - not and lie like this. And you would need that lie, you'd wait every day for me to give in and repeat it, and I can't, I won't.

He had forced Guyon to tell lies. No punishment...no vile words would be enough.

Not even Henri's warning, however, could have possibly prepared him for what was to come, for Guyon's bitter, uncontrolled jumble of myth and fact and desperate longing for François, the final admission of why he could not longer sustain the lie. Guyon was still bound to a dead man, and his every word proved his desire to follow him.

And the one thing that Peter, loving Guyon even in his vilification, refused to grant. He just sank deeper and deeper into himself, enduring the curses, the harsh words, sometimes even the blows that Guyon dealt him, with a quiet pain-filled stoicism. He tended Guyon as best he could, only leaving his side when David came to change the dressing, something he still was not allowed to witness.

"Patient-hearted Odysseus," Guyon said at one point. He sounded as though his heart was breaking, even though he laughed while he said it. His eyes stared out through the window like black glass, the pupils huge and unchanging.

"Hmmm?" Peter looked up, tiredly. It was beginning to get to the point that it was difficult to tell which of them was the one in recuperation.

Odysseus, patient hearted? But he hadn't been, not really. Or at least not patient-hearted enough that he remained celibate, keeping himself only for Penelope. If any were to claim that title, it should be she, putting off suitor after suitor, in spite of overwhelming pressures.

Peter gave himself a little shake, realizing how his mind had wandered, "Gui, I don't understand.."

The bleak, unchanging eyes stared past him. "There wasn't one, so it couldn't have been home." Guyon was looking at something that might have been there once, or never at all. "He died."

I know, Peter thought desolately. *I know.*

He stood and spoke the words out loud this time, "I know. I miss him too."

It was true, now as ever, Peter did miss François. Missed his teasing, his wisdom and his love for Guyon, even as he ached with his jealousy of it. François always seemed to make things easier between them. Settling Guyon in ways that only he seemed to understand. Helping Peter with brief and sensible commentaries on life. Peter could not say that he ever completely understood François Villon, but he would never deny that he loved him.

"It's the drugs," David said when he came back that evening, and there was no possible response to that, except for Guyon's expressionless voice saying into the quiet -

"Giant-slayer."

David's hand involuntarily went to his throat, and Peter remembered Guyon, outside the Richelieu chapel, drunk and blind with grief and his hand closing around David's throat.

"That is the only thing you may not say to me...David, my cherubic giant-slayer David, I will not be condescended to!"

And through all of it Peter only wanted to ask, *How much longer?*

How much longer will Guyon need to be drugged nearly insensible? How much longer before he healed enough to decrease the dosage? How much longer - How much longer until he was coherent enough to tell Peter to leave.

For that was Peter's razor-edge. Wanting Guyon to heal, but dreading it with the same breath - for Guyon's return to clarity could mean his own banishment.

"My love is an arquebus," Guyon said incomprehensibly, walking the line of his own diameter without fear or true understanding of what he did, and it all began again.

*

Does it hurt?
Does it hurt?
Yes, in the wrong place, in the wrong time.
I have cut out my heart, and thrown it to the dogs.
"This, it is too true, is the dog of a man who perished far away..."
"Sssh, don't..."
"Patient-hearted Odysseus," Guyon muttered, and laughed.
He could see it.
There the dog Argos lay in the dung, all covered with dog ticks. As he perceived that Odysseus had come close to him, he wagged his tail, and laid both ears back; only he now no longer had the strength to move any closer to his master...
"There wasn't one, so it couldn't have been home."
There wasn't one, because I am Argos.
"He died."
"Gui, I don't understand..."
"It's the drugs."
"Giant-slayer." Guyon laughed again. *That is the one thing you may not ask me. David, my cherubic giant-slayer David...*
Forget not yet, forget not this...
"The mind that never meant amiss..."
But he had, oh, God forgive him, he had...he had meant all of it, meant each word to find its bleeding home and stick there to rot.
"All that hath been and is..."
I did not think I would have to live with it!
The pain seared into him, and he could not tell where it came from.
"My love is an arquebus." He wept.
My beloved is unto me as a cluster of camphire in the vineyards of Engedi...Kush Geldi, thou art welcome. Thou art not welcome. Not well come. Aşkin Cemal Olsun. "Ah God!" It

seared through him. "François!" *Forgive me, forgive me, my darling friend forgive me...*

I have seen no signs of love in him.

Stay with me, stay with me, Guyon, little scholar...

"No, no, no! I promised! *I promised*!"

"No I damn well can't!" An English howl of frustration, David, David who carried leaves instead of a sling, who had treasures in his mind as great as those of the father of Solomon - "Peter, listen to me, it *will* kill him!"

Aşkin Cemal Olsun.

"I can't hear the bell." It mattered. Dear God, he had to hear it. It was still, so still, it had been still for hours. No reverberation, no swing of joy nor of despair. "I can't hear the bell. I can't *feel the bell*!"

"Sssh..."

Why could no-one understand?

"Please, please, please..."

Cool air, and the sound of the Angelus. He laughed, and drew in a breath of sunset, tasting it on his tongue like cold water, swallowing it like glowing wine. The deep tones sounded within him -

Not so deep as a well, not as wide as a church door..

"It is enough, it will serve..."

Warm arms around him. "It's all right." Did Peter cry gall or salt? Which had he cried, in the days after Toulouse, after Poitiers?

Little scholar, stay with me...

"No. A cluster of cypress, a bouquet of henna. My beloved is to me..."

My beloved has turned his face away; and I will never see the light shine upon it again.

Aşkin Cemal Olsun.

"Nothing."

Nothing.

The truth is I love you.

"There rust, and let me die."

Silence. Silence, and warmth, and the faint shudders that could have been tears or exasperation or hatred or all three of them.

But not love. I killed it.

How would you know?

What do you usually do when you want to know the answer?

Not love, not love, not love. He had killed it.

What do you usually do -

He laughed, and smashed the muffled pain of his hand outwards, knowing the impact to be stone, and ignoring the horrified cry that wrapped him around as closely as the arms he lay in.

"*Gui*! Guyon!"

I know where it hurts, now. He laughed again, and his heart throbbed. *Rust and ashes, torn paper for his amusement. Not rust, no, dust, rust and dust and my mind is filled with sand...*

In front of him, lying on de Retz's balcony in the setting sun, Achilles lay in the ashes and wept, poured dust on his golden head and howled for grief, tore at his own wrists and dyed his face with blood and dirt.

My beloved is dead. My love is dead. Love is dead, love...

The cypresses are stripped bare, the leaves are burning. My heart is inditing. Can a heart indite with grief?

...and darkest clouds of grief o'erspread
Achilles' brow; with both his hands he seiz'd
And pour'd upon his head the grimy dust,
Marring his graceful visage; and defil'd
With black'ning ashes all his costly robes.
Stretch'd in the dust his lofty stature lay,
As with his hands his flowing locks he tore...

"Whom I honoured most of all my comrades, loved him as my soul. Loved him as my soul. More than my soul. Loved and loved, and my soul is gone, all immortality is gone, him have I lost..."

The great bells stopped.

"Beloved, don't, hush..."

What do you usually do?

He drew in a breath, felt Peter's arms relax, and spat out venomously, "My God, don't you know? I read a book."

And in soft cypress let me be laid.

When the flames took him this time, he did not even scream. Wavering in the fire, Patroclus's shade wept with François's hazel eyes, and reached out with cool fingers to soothe the burning pain.

Come away, death.

"So sorrow still, on sorrow heaped, I bear the husband of my youth..."

Little scholar, stay with me.

"No."

So loved, beloved, so loved, my love, forgive me.

He sobbed, and did not know whose grief it was, *what* grief it was -

I have cut out my heart and thrown it to the dogs.

Argos, Argos, covered in ticks and lying on a dung heap.

"Odysseus..."

Achilles, golden amidst his invulnerable bruises of all-encompassing sorrow, mourned, and held up steel, cutting away his hair, the blood still streaming over his hands. The hero of Greece held out flayed muscle, torn and tattered, exposed shattered bone and dark marrow to the world, and wept.

Guyon screamed.

"*No!*"

*

So this was Hell. Not a fiery pit of condemnation as many believed, but rather a cold fear, wrapping itself around your soul until you could scarce breathe let alone contemplate your sins. And at times like this, Peter felt all of his sins so strongly that he wondered if he'd ever breathe again.

"My love is an arquebus." Guyon looked at Peter and wept. "No, no, no! I promised! *I promised!*"

"David, please." Peter looked at David, his expression desperate. "It's not helping. It's making him crazed but it's not helping. Can't you do something?"

"No I damn well can't!" David's face was a mask of frustration. "Peter, listen to me, anything else now *will* kill him!"

"But this..." Peter slipped into English, hoping somehow that

Guyon would be less likely to understand him, "...this is killing him too. He's so cut off and he still hurts."

"And if he can't find a way of surviving his own mind, he's better off dead anyway," David said in the same language, as though he understood and agreed with Peter's reasoning. "It won't kill him to see a few shades. But it bloody well will if he has to keep feeling the amount of pain he's in!"

"How do I do this, David? Just tell me that? He seems so frightened sometimes that it just makes me ill and I don't know what to do." Peter closed his eyes for a moment. "He'd hate this so much. Hate showing this to anyone...especially me, right now."

"To you? No, I don't think *especially* to you. Just generally. Mostly generally. He'd *really* hate knowing I could see, you know he never made a sound when I - anyway, the dosage'll go down soon and he'll be sleepy and incoherent 'stead of scared and loud and incoherent." David's explanations were comprehensive, but they always seemed to lack something essential, such as the point whoever he was talking to had been trying to make.

"I can't hear the bell." Guyon's voice was full of aching despair. "I can't hear the bell. I can't *feel the bell!*"

"What bell?" David asked.

"It doesn't matter," Peter felt bleak and worn out, emotionally and physically. He moved to sit on the edge of the bed, one hand reaching out to brush Guyon's curls away from his face. "Sssh..."

"Please," Guyon said, Guyon who so rarely asked for anything for himself without mockery or a thousand layers of obliquity. For a moment, Peter wondered if he was actually *seeing* him, asking for something, and was instantly plunged into a renewed fear that, whatever it was, he wouldn't be able to give it. But the clouded eyes were still unfocused, and it was still his inner, hellish world that Guyon was speaking to. "Please, please..."

Outside de Retz's room, the cathedral bells could be heard faintly

"Open the window, David." Peter said softly, and when David protested, "Just open it. Please. It might not help, but...."

He climbed into bed with Guyon, somehow remembering that the only times after Toulouse that he felt any true comfort were when either Guyon or François held him - drew him close and made his aching body relax with soft words and warmth.

"Sssh," He whispered softly to Guyon as David opened the window, letting in cool evening air and the sound of the bells. "Sssh...It's alright."

For a few, astounding minutes, it seemed to make a difference, the unhappy overstrung tension in Guyon's body relaxing slightly as he drew in a deep breath of the cooler air, sighing it out with a small laugh free from all the jagged, wild bitterness of before.

"No." But it was not a denial, so much as a continuance, Guyon sounding almost fond as he went on, "A cluster of cypress, a bouquet of henna. My beloved is to me..." His voice trailed off, and all the tension was back, the beautiful voice cracked and hoarse. "Nothing."

Yes, nothing...

Nothing was what he was to Guyon. No matter how much he tried to deny it. No matter what Guyon's hasty words had been after his fight with Corvay, he knew it was true.

Together has become a farce, Peter, and I can't continue it.

He fought back bitter tears, remembering David's presence all too well. He, as much as Guyon, wanted no one to see this pain.

Guyon, fighting something that might have been Peter, or his past, or the knowledge of what the drugs were doing to him, or perhaps the demons Peter had once sworn would never return, moved with sudden, horrendous deliberation and smashed his bound hand onto the stone wall of de Retz's chamber as hard as he could. He was laughing, the savagery of earlier back full force.

"*Gui!* Guyon!" Peter grabbed him, body, arm and all, pulling him into the cocoon of arms and pillows. "David! David! Oh, *Christ...*Come look."

He could see it already, blood seeping through the cotton and gauze. But still, somehow, he managed to hold Guyon still as David began to unwrapped Guyon's injured hand, then hid his face against Guyon's neck while he worked.

He doesn't want me to see. Doesn't want to share himself with me. All Peter could do was honor Guyon's request.

"This is getting ridiculous," David muttered, working fast.

Obviously there hadn't been very much more damage done, despite Guyon's best efforts, since he didn't sound even mildly concerned. "Can't you just curl up and sleep like anyone normal?"

The responding laugh had absolutely nothing to do with David. It didn't sound as though it had very much to do with sanity, either.

"It's time for more of your favorite drink anyway," David said, the bed shifting as he got back to his feet. Peter wondered just whose mind he thought would be irretrievably lost first.

Peter remained where he was, half-wrapped around Guyon's somewhat more docile frame. He'd probably fight taking the drugs. He always did. If Peter remained where he was, however, he'd have better leverage for the fight to come.

"It's going to be alright, Gui. I'll do whatever I can to keep you safe. Anything...but you need to help too. Don't fight this, please. And then...then when you're more recovered, I...I'll still leave if you want me too. I just can't leave you like this." His voice cracked, although he had been trying to keep it short and quiet. As much as he liked David, some things just *were* private.

Guyon was talking again, quiet and indistinct now, and somehow sorrowful. "More than my soul," he said with sudden clarity, and then became indistinct once more. The bells stopped, and so did he.

Perhaps they really are working. Perhaps it's going to get better now. Perhaps -

"My God, don't you know?" Guyon said with a venom Peter had never heard turned on anyone but Corvay before now. "I read a book!"

And it was David, returning with the cup, who flinched at that.

"Sssh, Beloved...please...don't." Peter whispered insistently, cherishing that one word, the word that meant they belonged together, even knowing it for the lie it was.

For once, either what he was saying got through to Guyon, or whatever hell Guyon was inhabiting decided that even souls in the Styx needed the occasional respite, because he was quiet, drinking David's mixture without complaint, though his eyes still looked past everything tangible, out to the balcony and the sunset.

He said something about sorrow, quietly mournful, but nothing more than that, and David's worried expression began to lighten a little.

Peter relaxed just slightly, listening as the last few notes of the bell chiming from the cathedral at last fell silent, leaving the room in a quiet, almost haunting, stillness.

"No," Guyon said into it, calm and clear, and then, returning for some reason to whatever had been obsessing him before, "Odysseus." He was crying quietly, inconsolable, but hazy with it, as though the drugs were detaching him even from the hell-broth of raw emotions his life had become.

"Shhh..." Peter soothed him with hand and voice, as one might soothe a small child with night terrors. *"Thou sail'st with others in this Argus here; Nor wreck or bulging thou hast cause to fear; But trust to this, my noble passenger; Who swims with virtue, he shall still he sure (Ulysses-like) all tempests to endure, And 'midst a thousand gulfs to be secure."*

But the security he had hoped to represent was not to be. Whether Guyon had even heard him was debatable, as he cried out, the sound thin and breathy with some unnamed terror, a desperate refutation of all the things that were visible only to his clouded, altered vision.

It was like the night in the Languedoc, Guyon seeing things only he could see. Then, at least, he had let Peter in. Had let him calm and soothe him with actions and words. But now all Peter had was this. Desperation and an uneasy feeling of truce - more like two sides of a long-fought feud than anything else. Peter was counting the days, the minutes almost, until it ended. Until he wasn't needed and was sent off alone. He wondered how he'd face it, how he would survive.

He looked down at Guyon, but his blankly staring eyes held no answers.

"Achilles," Guyon whispered again, his voice a flat ache of misery. "Achilles."

*

Peter stood at one end of the large state chambers, not *quite* at attention, but not *quite* at his ease, either. He had not had a lot of contact with Cardinal Mazarin since his arrival in France and, *please God*, he had hoped to continue that trend. But now, here he was, awaiting that same gentleman's arrival without the reassurance of her Majesty's presence.

That Mazarin would be aware of his duel with Corvay, had not surprised Peter in the least. That he would want to see Peter afterwards was even less surprising. Peter had killed the Spy Master of France with forethought and extreme malice and although the reasons were clear and the legalities of the situation witnessed by Alexei Boronskaya, it would not be something that was easily overlooked. He had purposefully set the entire French intelligence gathering force back by months at the very least, because not only had he killed the man himself, but their battle and the subsequent fire had destroyed whatever records might have been used in his place.

None of this would be overlooked, English Marshal in France or not.

Alexei, understanding this with far more clarity than Peter had been capable of in his worry over Guyon, had been invaluable over the past couple of days, acting as unofficial messenger between Mazarin and de Retz, who still found civility towards one another a trial, smoothing over the fact that Peter was unavailable on the first two times of asking - at first because he had absolutely refused to leave Guyon, and the second time because the miracle David had promised had occurred, and Guyon was well and truly asleep, and was likely to remain so for some time. Alexei had promptly pointed out, not terribly nicely, that it would probably benefit everyone's chances of survival if Peter followed his example, and that he was perfectly capable of sitting in a chair and watching someone breathe, if Peter was worried about whether Guyon would continue to do so unsupervised.

His pithy common sense had come as a wonderful change from Guyon's confusion and David's evasions, and it had been surprisingly easy to manage an uninterrupted six hours, completely unmoving, in the vastness of de Retz's state bed, Guyon an oddly comforting if equally immobile presence beside him.

While Peter slept, Alexei had arranged for clothes suitable for attending the Cardinal to be brought and laid out for him, had ordered a bath, and had somehow made everything in the room both tidier and more bearable in atmosphere. The thought of leaving Guyon, unbearable before sleep, suddenly seemed both possible and less a betrayal than a necessity.

I am going to owe Boronskaya more than my life, at this rate, Peter thought wryly, and straightened as he heard the sound of voices and footsteps heralding Mazarin's arrival.

It came as a shock to see de Retz with him, in full official regalia. He had grown used to the man wearing only the minimal trappings of office, in the privacy of his home or rooms. He was used to the slightly soft, youthful features, the kind and comprehending eyes that always seemed to perceive the layers of Guyon's mind and soften them with a grace that Peter was forced to acknowledge was the man's own touch of the Divine spark.

The *grace of God*, the blessing that he so calmly bestowed on others, had always been integral to the Machiavellian little man, making his very real sins of the world easily forgivable.

He gave me absolution, Guyon had said, a long year before. But he did not look, today, as though that was something that he was either empowered or wishful to grant Peter. He was cold, and remote, and hard amidst the beauty of his robes, a brocaded foil to the red unsheathed power that was the Cardinal.

For the first time, Peter realized this was not to be some question-and-answer, the graceful antiphony he had become used to in churchmen. This was to be the ecclesiastical judgment of Paris, already decided upon without desire or need for his explanations.

He greeted Mazarin with the utmost ceremony, waiting for him to seat himself before kneeling and kissing his ring of office. De Retz waved away a similar courtesy, moving to stand behind the Cardinal's chair.

Mazarin gave his permission for Peter to stand and then looked him over from head to toe with an assessing eye. Peter for his part, merely waited.

"You have caused us inconvenience of the most extreme,

Marshal." Mazarin's Italian accent overlaid his English with a strong, almost dancing lilt. It lent a peculiar sort of humorous note to the words, though there was no amusement at all in the dark face. "The spymaster was a bitter necessity to us. We desired for his trial, and would not have had him executed until his secrets had been given to France. Now we are as much in the dark as before, and there can be no illumination, for you have destroyed it. There is no replacement for knowledge. The library at Alexandria's burning cost the world greatly, but cost Paris not at all. You have provided us with an inferno equal in destruction, equal in effect to politics, to our security. No one man's life is equal to this, not can be. The Archbishop has stated your case most eloquently. But you fail to have comprehended the essential difference between the public and the private, and so now I must judge your sins and not his. This does not please me, and in displeasing me, you have displeased France, to whom you are beholden, if not as a subject, then at least by gratitude for her gifts."

"I understand, Monsignor." Peter spoke calmly and with the utmost respect, but his calm did not quite reach his eyes, and surely not his mind. He did understand that his actions had cost France in general, and Mazarin in particular, quite a bit, however he still did not consider that he had any other choice but to do exactly as he did. He had confronted Corvay with every intention of bringing him to the justice of the courts, in spite of what he had done to Guyon. Things had not quite turned out that way, and the fault was not his, but he did not expect that Mazarin wanted to hear that.

"I would have been a great deal happier," Mazarin said with an extremely personal bitterness that he must have decided he wanted Peter to know to its fullest extent, dropping the plurality of his position with a calculated force, "if you had *understood* before you issued your challenge. As it is, you have displayed what can only be called in the kindest of interpretations a *complete lack of perception.*"

Peter straightened even more at that. *What the hell had de Retz been telling the man?* "With all due respect, your Eminence, you weren't there, and neither was the Archbishop."

"No. And *that* we shall treat upon in a moment." Mazarin leant forward, and Peter saw that he was not simply sitting in official condemnation, but very, very angry indeed. "Would you perhaps care to enlighten me as to what peculiar power a man under official arrest *had*, that two loyal subjects of their respective Crowns saw death as their only means of escape? Because, Marshal, I am prepared to believe many things. But that you should both hold the power of Church and Crown so lightly as to believe you were placed beyond all protection but your own is nothing less than an *insult*!"

Behind him, de Retz stirred, drawing Peter's eye. *Tell him of the Marqués*, he mouthed

"Aside from his crimes against the state, his assault on private citizens, his conspiracy to murder? He was also a blackmailer of the foulest kind, sir. He threatened Monsieur de Chesnay with the murder of his brother if he did not do his bidding." Peter stated the facts baldly, with little embellishment. "For those crimes alone he deserved to die, but still I would have brought him to justice, if I had any choice in the matter."

Very, very delicately, de Retz brought a finger up and scratched at his nose. It had the fortunate side-effect that when Mazarin turned his head to look at him, his mouth was completely hidden. "You support this? You believe this?" he demanded.

De Retz lowered his hand. "I would not have asserted as much if I did not," he said rather dryly. Peter remembered that de Retz did not, in fact, *like* Mazarin. Their unspoken yet well-known enmity had been the force behind one of Corvay's less intelligent moves, and the cause of two murders.

"Your Eminence, your Grace, I know what my actions have cost you, but you should not, must not, think that I gave no thought to their outcome or the consequences of them." Peter looked a bit grim. "Personal matters aside, Corvay was playing both ends against the middle and taking France into the line of fire with his every step."

"Are you so completely arrogant as to think I do not know that?" Mazarin was on his feet, and as small a man as he was, he filled the room. "Why do you think his papers were so *essential*?" He took a breath, and said in a very quiet voice - "I do not care if you tied him up by his heels, eviscerated him with a heated poker and extracted his brains with a spoon. I *do* care that you burned up his house!" He sat down again, seething. "Oh, get out," he said at last, in French. "Go to Brocéliande - *I am not suggesting!* *Forget all thoughts of Scotland, Marshal!* - and take that God-damned little Sorbonne reject with you." He swung his glare on de Retz. "And you. *Out!*"

"Does his Eminence wish *me* to go to Brocéliande?" de Retz asked, just the wrong side of sarcastic.

"His Eminence wishes you to go to the devil! *In Paris*, my Lord Archbishop, where I can keep what remains of my eyes on you!"

"Yes, your Eminence," said de Retz, and scratched at his nose again, before bowing. "You heard, my Lord Marshal."

"I did," Peter answered stiffly. "And I say again, you weren't there, your Eminence."

But apparently, it did not matter, he was dismissed like so much waste and sent off to rusticate until either the Cardinal's good humor returned or he was sent for. Well, he'd damn well go, and happily. He'd take Guyon and...well, hopefully Guyon would wish to go with him. Cardinal or no Cardinal, he'd not take him unwillingly. His beloved, *yes, still that returned or not*, would need to make that decision himself.

As the doors closed behind them, de Retz snorted, choked, and burst into obviously long-withheld laughter. "Ah, Lord, God, that was *worth* it," he said at last, wiping at his eyes with an embroidered sleeve. "I'm sorry you had to endure that, Scudamore. But if he doesn't get to lose his temper and make us all feel like ants, he's quite capable of simmering away until we all end up at the Place de la Greve. But oh!" He trailed off into renewed laughter. "*You weren't there, your Eminence.* No, he damn well wasn't, you couldn't have paid him!" He sniffed, and shook his head, sobering. "Come, walk with me, my lord Marshal."

"I'm glad that I added to your amusement, your Grace," Peter said dryly, but fell into step alongside de Retz.

"Yes, your joy's overwhelming. Almost tangible." De Retz sighed. "Well, I'm glad you're going. It will give us all space to

542

clear the debris away. And for God's sake, take that lunatic English herbalist with you before I decide he would make an ideal snack for the lions at the menagerie."

"I will offer, but I fear you may have to appeal to de la Roche, for a guarantee," Peter gave a weak smile. "After some of the words I had with Monsieur Somers, he may not think I am the best company."

"It's not an offer," de Retz said dryly. "It's an instruction. He can't shut up and he nearly had *me* in the Bastille when he acted as my secretary. Take whoever else you want, just get him out of my immediate vicinity. Besides -" he gave Peter an oddly sharp look - "he may be useful to you once the bandages come off de Chesnay's hand."

"As you say," Peter shrugged. This appeared to be his day for receiving ultimatums. He'd do as he was asked or -

If Guyon didn't want to go with him, then perhaps he'd go with David and Henri and Peter could.... What? Remaining was not an option. But he'd give the run of the estate to Guyon and find someplace nearby to stay.

Peter's stomach ached with the pain of those thoughts. He and Guyon had not been able to have any serious talk, the latter being in too much pain and frequently drugged insensible to combat it.

"Corvay," de Retz said, apparently to a nearby plant, "left a letter for de Chesnay with me, which I gave to him on the day of what I believe was several ultimatums. My fire burns somewhat erratically, and I confess to curiosity. I retrieved it from the grate." He stopped walking, inspecting the plant carefully. "Do you think this is greenfly?"

"That would be the 'lunatic herbalist's' area of expertise," Peter answered distractedly. "Was the letter important, do you think? Or just more of his threats?"

"The letter was important, in as much as it was personal to de Chesnay. To you, to me? No. It was not important. To a man who has only ever been given cause to fear for one other living soul, and touching upon a matter which he knows to be achievable? It was enough to make him take a personal vow of crossing the Styx. Did you not hear the Cardinal, Scudamore? *Two* men who knew what was to befall saw their lives as cheap that day. And they did not include Corvay, David Somers, Alexei Boronskaya, or myself." He reached into his heavy sleeve, and extracted a singed piece of folded paper, that had once been very tightly crumpled and badly smoothed out. "A piece of the puzzle, Marshal," he said, and handed it over.

Peter looked over the missive, recognizing at once Corvay's crabbed script. "He was grasping at straws here. He knew we had him."

In spite of his calm words, Peter's heart was pounding furiously. Corvay had threatened him. Tried to use whatever small amount of affection that Guyon had felt for him as a weapon. Was this what Guyon had been trying to tell him the night of the fire? That this threat had caused him to say things that weren't completely true? Be that as it may, Guyon had been much too cold and calculating in his speech, for it to all be a sham.

Together has become a farce, Peter, and I can't continue it.

You certainly do not have what my mind craves. What my intellect craves.

Every word had been pounded into his heart like a spike.

"Yes, he did," de Retz agreed. "To an extent, I am to blame for this. I was the one who had the official condemnation of de Chesnay revoked, six years ago. I knew that his one remaining weakness was what he calls his *duality*. The division of his soul. Mutated and made heresy by his brother's actions - and kept private and hidden until your arrival. He would never have known, if you had remained in England. And Corvay would never have known the full extent of the fear he has for the whipping-post if *I* had not revealed it to him." He smiled wryly at Peter. "Oh, yes. I was the one who gave him that particular piece of information. So that Guyon would never again have cause to feel threatened by it. I wanted Corvay to *protect* him." He sighed. "God forgive me, I trusted blindly on the one occasion I should not have done. And Corvay, knowing where the seeds of true insanity lay in a man I was sworn to protect in all matters of the spirit, set out to destroy him using a dagger sharper and more deadly than any steel he held in his hand that day in his rooms. It wasn't *you* he was threatening, Marshal. He was telling Guyon de Chesnay that the only redemption possible to him was death. And de Chesnay sought to save you from something he believed would be done - his deepest and most abiding fear, of seeing *you* at the pelourinho, of his own particular *estrega* made flesh - by forcing you to believe there was nothing left for you in France."

"It was not a thing that would be so easily accomplished, your Grace." Peter frowned. "Or I would not imagine it would." He shook his head, "I can understand that fear. Guyon and I - Our friendship has been strong, if nothing else. I have seen those scars. He would not wish that on anyone.

De Retz took a deep breath. "Scudamore -" he began, and then sighed, shaking his head. "No. Never mind. It is not *my* task to impart learning, or to force it upon an unwilling mind." His mouth twitched into a smile that seemed oddly shallow. "Go and tell de Chesnay of your destination. I will be glad to have the occupancy of my rooms returned to me."

"As you say, your Grace." Peter gave him a bow and went off through well, remembered hallways towards de Retz's rooms. Maybe this was actually what they needed - to get out of Paris. A place for Guyon to heal without worrying thoughts of students and the possibility of letting people down. A place for him to prepare for whatever his future life might hold, even if it were to be all alone.

My lies are sins of omission, Guyon had told him once. And in Peter's rooms, he had omitted *nothing*.

The seeds of true insanity, de Retz had called it.

Peter wondered if it would be better, *more honorable*, of him to give Guyon that solitude, since it truly seemed to be what he really craved. But he could not completely let go of hope.

I have loved you for so long that I think I forgot the words.

I am the owner of so many words, and the master of none of them.

Friendship and the undoubted physical pleasures you bring are not sufficient.

What was the lie?

*

The *Quai*, Paris, late August 1646

Lost, shipwrackt, spoyld, debar'd of smallest hope,
Nothing of pleasure left, save thoughts have scope,
Which wander may; goe then my thoughts and cry:
Hope's perish'd, Love tempest-beaten, Joy lost,
Killing Despaire hath all these blessings crost;
Yet Faith still cries, Love will not falsifie.

The *Quai* had been conceded as neutral territory by both the students of de Chesnay's school and the Cadets of the English Guard. The fact that both Guyon and Peter frequented the place, often together, might have had something to do with the peace being kept, or it might have been the large, very scarred individual that worked behind the bar and his equally large musket.

It was a gloomy little group who assembled there. Reduced to gleaning what information they could from rumor and hearsay, the cadets had learned quite soon that the students at de Chesnay's school, usually an impeccable source of fact, were as confused and as lacking in useful information as everyone else.

"I've tried to sweet-talk Madame, but she will tell me nothing," Leon Tarbes muttered quietly. Leon was a student of music and cousin, through his French mother, to Thomas Williamson, Peter's valet. He was also Madame de Neuillant's current lover.

"A'cos of her seeing right through you," Philippe said somewhat less than sweetly. As the only one officially in both worlds, he was taking the lack of knowledge extremely personally.

"She a'ways sees trou hem." Kees van Rijn asserted. "But she tells hem."

"Not this time," Leon said, his head on his hand, a perfect pose of depression that Kees was almost unconsciously sketching as they talked. "Hasn't the Marshal come back at all, Tom?"

"Only twice in the past week." Thomas gave a perplexed frown. "He met with Wycombe, cleaned up, changed and left again. He looks awful...worse than - But I've heard nothing about his arrest either, so that has to be good, doesn't it?"

"Christ protect us all, for we were once as young as you sorry lot," said the cheerful voice of Charles de Barrion. Now a licensed tutor at the Sorbonne, he inspired tentative dread in Guyon's students, and bewildered wariness in the cadets, who were never sure quite where he stood in the tangled but somehow simplistic friendships of their Marshal. He took his robe off as he spoke, calling over his shoulder, "You still hoping for cold wine, Pierre?"

All eyes, student and cadet, flashed in the direction of the bar, half way hoping to see the Marshal standing there.

"I always hope, Charles. What is the world without a little hope?" Pierre Vincennes answered his friend back, as those same eyes dropped just as quickly in disappointment.

"A dull and empty place, like the eyes of these poor fish here," de Barrion responded. "And how is the terrible task of sorrow-drowning and unrequited studently and cadetly love going, my dears?" He flung his robe over the back of the settle and sat down with a faint grunt. He looked unusually tired, in the harsh light, the summer exams having been a trying time for all concerned, and his first year as both a sponsoring tutor and official debater having proved, he had said loudly and publicly on several occasions, to remind him of just why people were in awe of Guyon de Chesnay.

That he only received grunted replies and half-hearted ones at that, was not particularly auspicious for further conversation; the younger men, as one, suddenly finding their drinks horribly interesting.

"Ah, really? How fascinating." De Barrion's entire voice was an eyeroll. Vincennes, collecting wine and cups from the tavern owner, snorted, not even bothering to disguise his amusement.

"We're worried about the Marshal," Roger Deighton suddenly blurted, then sighed and attempted that again in his limited and broken French. "Nous - nous inquiétons...pour le maréchal...et Monsieur de Chesnay."

"Yes, well, you can join the rest of us," Vincennes said rather snappishly. His normal levels of tolerance had decreased rapidly in the days since the bet, and the red-headed doctor that everyone

547

had come to see as an ally had become more of an irritable instructor on behavior and good manners. He sighed, and relented. "The Cardinal's probably going to banish them for a while, I heard."

"Banish?"

"Where?"

"Can he do that?"

"Corvay was a bad piece of work. Got what he deserved from what I can tell." That was Roger Deighton again, blunt to the point of painfulness.

"No-one's disagreeing, except for where a few people might have liked it slower," de Barrion said wryly. "But really, children, you can't go around burning down official houses full of official documents and not expect someone to get a little bit annoyed with you. And no, he can't *do* that, Philippe, but he can strongly suggest it, and wise men tend to do as the Cardinal suggests."

"And whut ov M'sieur?" Kees ventured, finishing off his sketch of Leon and moving lower on the page to absently begin one of de Barrion. "Is he to leave?"

"We heard he was hurt. Was he with the Marshal?" Thomas' voice was a bit anxious. If nothing else, he knew how any harm to Guyon would effect Peter.

Vincennes and de Barrion exchanged glances. "Sort of," Vincennes said vaguely. "And yes, he's hurt. Badly. Corvay put a knife through his hand." Kees shot him a startled glance, and showed him a quick sketch in the corner of the paper. "No, actually *through* the bones, Kees, not between them."

"Christ." Roger took a deep drink of his ale.

"De Chesnay will go with the Marshal then. He won't trust anyone else to nurse him." Thomas murmured softly.

"Vill he go?" Kees asked, giving Vincennes a long look.

"He'll go," Vincennes agreed quietly, and ruined the solemnity of the atmosphere by adding "Even if we have to truss him up like a Christmas goose first."

Philippe snorted, "You're a brave man if you attempt it."

"You know," Vincennes said in tones that lowered the temperature quite considerably, "I consider that man to be one of my dearest friends. I owe him my career. And I had to stand and pour water into his hand while Ibn Ibrahim turned him into a living anatomy lesson. And he didn't make a sound. So you'll forgive me if I don't really feel like making the usual jokes at his expense."

There was a horrified silence.

"You're being sententious again, Pierre, that's my job," de Barrion said lightly into it, and the tension eased.

"The Marshal leaves...and de Chesnay, he leaves too?" Kees sounded as if the idea confused him. "Where do they go?"

"Doesn't Peter have estates in Brittany or something? They'll probably go there," de Barrion said casually, as though the whole thing bored him.

"Bot' ov dem?" Kees asked again, clearly puzzled by something.

"Of course," Thomas elbowed him, causing his pencil to scutter across the page.

"Of course," Vincennes echoed, fixing Kees with a hard look.

"Of course, naturally, and obviously. Yes, we're really not improving our vocabularies here, gentlemen, shall we move on from this fascinating point of debate as to the various meanings of *both* and *together*?" De Barrion sounded both impatient and exasperated.

Kees just shrugged and looked back down at his page.

"How soon will they go, do you know?" Philippe asked. This would affect him the most. For his employer to be away from town was one thing, but to be banished for an undisclosed period of time was quite another.

"No," Vincennes said unhelpfully. "As soon as they can, I think."

"Will...will Monsieur heal? I mean...Christ." Leon looked a bit ill as he glanced down at the sketch that Kees had made.

There was a long, uncomfortable silence, while everyone tried, and failed, not to follow the direction of Leon's gaze. "We don't know," de Barrion said at last, quietly. "It's a case of being grateful for what there is." At the blank looks he received, he added, more gently than his usual acerbic style, "He's alive and he still has his hand."

*

Peter was far more than willing to quit Paris for the moment. There were too many memories here for him to retain any reluctance. His times of dreadful loneliness, François' death, and always, Guyon's painful words pounding themselves into his head. There were times that he could still hear them echoing off the walls of his office at the Hôtel d'Orsay, bringing with them the stench of remorse and regret.

No, leaving Paris would be no hardship for him, and in spite of their current ill feelings, Peter would not, could not ever regret that Guyon was to go with him. The logistics of the move, however, were straining him mightily. Guyon was undoubtedly still in a great deal of pain - how was he to transport him to Brocéliande without making it worse? He would have to arrange for a carriage, that was for certain, to make the three day trip. A good one, well sprung, and padded. And...Yes, it was just as well that de Retz said he should take David and Henri along with him, he would need the help.

And all of this without Guyon's direct permission. He was too pained and drugged to make any sensible decisions at the moment, but still Peter felt rather like he was packing him up like an extra piece of luggage - luggage that might possibly be angry when it regained its sensibilities. Still, as Guyon had taken charge of his care after Poitou, he must take charge now. He entered de Retz's state apartments with a sigh, removing his hat and unbuckling his sword as he entered the room.

"The weight of the world?" asked Alexei Boronskaya, "or just the weight of the Cardinal's displeasure?" He waved an elegant hand at the room. "I bribed. They cleaned. I contemplate wizardry, but Guyon said I should be burned if I did. Then I helped him take not very hot bath, and he said I should burn anyway." He snorted. "So I give him more drugs. He was not grateful, but he sleeps."

"Possibly only half, and yes..." Peter answered the actual questions first, then continued absently. "You shouldn't have to bribe them to do their job, Alexei." He quietly approached the bed, reaching out with one gentle hand to smooth the hair away from Guyon's sleeping face.

"I am not the Archbishop." Boronskaya shrugged. "I have gold. Not influence. Is expected." He gestured at the great jewel-studded chain of office that he wore. "This tells people what I am, no?" He sighed a little. "*He* knows different. Take him to Russia, Marshal. There we give those like him honor, not to call them heretics."

"He's not a heretic!" Peter snapped suddenly, then looked at Boronskaya, with wide tormented eyes, "He's...Guyon. Damn it all to hell, Alexei. They want us to leave. Now. How can I do that? How can I take him when I'm not even positive he'd want to go with me if he were in his right mind?"

Boronskaya blinked at him, the large dark eyes shuttering up slowly like drenched night-time flowers. "But he does not have a right mind, except for wanting to be with you," he said quietly. "Not for now, and now is all that matters. Later perhaps he will shout. Then he will say all is as he would have made it be, and he will let it go. They say you leave, so you leave."

Peter felt himself let out a long slow breath, as if all his tension were releasing at the same time, flowing out and scattering on the floor like leaves in the path of the wind. It was a lightening feeling. "I hope you're right, Alexei. But even if you're not, I don't supposed I can make anything worse, eh?"

He settled himself down behind de Retz's desk and pulled out parchment and paper. "I need to send word ahead to Brocéliande and arrange for a coach and, God, talk to Ibn Ibrahim and let Jeannine know what's happened...and..." His voice trailed off. What he really wanted to do right now, at this very minute, was crawl in bed with Guyon and hold him. Hold him until he had the feeling of the other man's living body firmly fixed in his mind.

"I will go to Ibn Ibrahim." Boronskaya patted his shoulder. "I will get coach. I like the ambassador's coach. Very comfortable." He grinned. "You write to your estates. They can get iron cage ready."

"To keep my bird from flying?" Peter grimaced, torn between amusement and pain. "Thank you, Alexei. I appreciate everything you've done for us...not just this but..." Peter had lost all his words. Boronskaya had been more than helpful to both of them since his duel with Lesueur, in fact, and Peter was uncertain of the reason. That Alexei liked both of them, he was sure, but - *no,* he was seeing suspicious behavior where there was none. Boronskaya was their friend, had been from the beginning and that was his motivation. That and only that.

"In Russia," Boronskaya said, "our priests marry." He looked as though he expected that statement to be of some enormous help and import, and when Peter did not respond, he sighed heavily. "Is no matter. Carriage." He nodded, and left the room.

"His second job is as Delphic Oracle," Guyon said drowsily.

Peter forced himself to stand slowly and walk over to the bedside, rather than throw himself across the room and into Guyon's arms. It wasn't prudent, either because of their estrangement or the pain that Guyon was still dealing with. "Hello. How do you -? I mean, can I get you anything?"

Guyon frowned. "Less clouds. Or wool. Fog." There was a very long pause. "In my head," he added with a painful attempt at clarity.

"No," Peter told him gently. "You really don't want that, Gui. I know the lack of clarity is probably a bit...frightening. It's a normal reaction to the drugs you've been given. But we haven't any choice at the moment, it's the only way to keep the pain under control."

"Ah. Control." Guyon swallowed. "All that glitters..." He sighed, and shifted restlessly under the layers of blankets. "We're leaving?"

"Yes, at the Cardinal's insistence," Peter said simply. "I believe that Brocéliande is probably our best choice at the moment. I...I hope you don't mind that I'm arranging every thing to take us there." Peter straightened, "It's the only place I could think of, but I daresay that it's big enough that you won't even know I'm there."

"So why are we going?" Guyon asked. He looked thoroughly confused.

"Because Mazarin is...annoyed with me." Peter shrugged.

"Oh." Guyon scowled into the middle distance. "And we can't go somewhere and I'll know you're there?" He made a face. "I

think I lost word order."

"It's alright," Peter reassured him. "I just meant that if you didn't want to see me...you wouldn't have to." It would break his heart into even smaller pieces, but he'd keep away.

"Oh. I see." The slightly clouded look of incomprehension was leaving Guyon's eyes, to be replaced by the dragging, weary sadness that Peter associated with returning pain. "The things I'm not allowed to say because you don't believe me. I forgot." He closed his eyes. "You're right. Drug me."

Peter tensed, "No, you may say anything you wish. Silence has never been a stricture that *I* have put on *you*."

"Oh, *very* good," Guyon said, his eyes still closed. "And I can add to my sins that I taught you cruelty. *Magister* indeed!" He laughed, the sound sharp and harsh. "*Lay on thy whips, o love.* Do I sleep in a lax bed?"

"I'm sorry." Peter dropped his head. "You do not deserve such words from me. I - We are going to Brocéliande, if you've no objection to the plan. I'm not sure for how long. Until Mazarin cools off, or I am no longer in disgrace, it would appear." He tried to move to a safer topic, to hide within the mundane.

"I don't object." The harshness left Guyon's voice, leaving it completely emotionless, flat and dead and utterly without tone. "I deserve everything given."

Peter stood still for several long moments, blinking back his pain before he trusted his voice to speak, "Then I should get my letters written so that every thing can be made ready."

"Yes," Guyon said tiredly. He opened his eyes, and the old look of opaque glass lay across them, concealing his thoughts as much as the haze of drugs and pain overlaid his words. "You should." The brackets of pain at the corners of his mouth twitched into a small attempt at a smile. "Do you mind if I watch?"

"No, of course not." Peter answered, softly, still unable to deny Guyon anything. "But you should try to get as much rest as you can, the trip is going to be quite rough on you, I'd imagine." It would. Peter only remembered his trip from Toulouse to Paris in vague snips of coherency, a cloud of pain and dizziness overwhelming everything else. This would be easier, certainly, but he doubted it would be much more pleasant.

"I expect it will," Guyon said with a faint return to his usual dryness. "But worse for you. *I* just have to ramble and complain. *You* have to listen. Ah, coherency. It must be time to return me to my wool and fog."

Peter looked up, "Yes, I'm afraid it is. " He moved to mix the potion that he had been given - one for pain, one for preventing fever, one for God knows what other than Vincennes and David had assured him that it would help. It was just the pain medication on this hour though, and he brought it carefully to Guyon's bedside. He sat down on the side of the bed, helping Guyon to raise up with a touch that was as gentle as any mother guiding her newborn to the breast. "Drink it all, please."

Guyon snorted. "You mean I can't drink half and - I know. No jokes." He grimaced, raising his good hand to the cup to tilt it, and swallowed with an expression that suggested boiled slugs had been a prime ingredient. "And now I feel the need to sandpaper my tongue," he said revoltedly. "I never want to know what goes in that."

"And you wondered that I fought you," Peter could not hold back a small smile as he lowered Guyon back down on the bed. "But it works."

"I know it works." Guyon sighed, looking cross. "I don't want it to."

"Yes, you do." Peter said it by rote. No one wanted to be in pain, Guyon was simply chaffing at the loss of clarity the drug brought. That was understandable. It had been wearing enough to Peter, let alone someone like Guyon, whose mind was his proudest possession.

Guyon's mouth twitched. "*No*," he said with a fair amount of exasperated amusement, "I *don't*. There may not be much of my mind remaining, but..." He looked suddenly appalled. "It's not important," he finished in a whisper.

"Guyon," Peter said suddenly, his hand moving unerringly to wrap around the wrist of Guyon's uninjured hand. "This is only temporary. Your hand will heal. The pain will go and there will be no more need for drugs. Please, believe that."

"Oh, I believe that," Guyon said, but the horrified look was still on his face. "That's not. It's not. I don't -" He gritted his teeth.

"I believe you," he said at last. He slid his hand down so that he could return Peter's grip. "Don't worry."

"You might as soon tell the sun not to shine," Peter said softly. "I always have and always will."

"I'm doing that next," Guyon retorted obliquely, his words beginning to slur. "Call me Canute. Only with sun..."

"Rest," Peter told him, tucking the blankets around him. "I'll be here when you wake." *As I shall always be, beloved, if you allow it.*

Guyon's mouth twisted slightly, the worryingly familiar look of sorrow returning to his eyes as they clouded over with sleep and opiates. "I won't ask you to promise," he said, and in his voice was the finality of someone utterly defeated. He curled onto his side, cradling his hand against his chest, and the next words were a whisper that Peter was quite certain he wasn't meant to hear. "I lost the right."

*

Peter watched as Henri and Boronskaya helped Guyon into the carriage. Henri clambered in after him, awkwardly, and as Guyon fumbled a hand out of the open window, Boronskaya took it and pulled him forward. Even in the warm sun of early September, there were deep lines around Guyon's eyes, but as Alexei reached around his neck in some strange embrace, they lightened, and he was suddenly smiling, a gleam of real joy in his tired face. "*Saint-Segùr.* Alexei -!"

"*Saint-Christoph.* For my travel-tutor." Alexei had left gold around Guyon's neck, Peter realized, and remembered, as if from a time spent in another world, the little cross Guyon had tucked into François's sleeve, before the Watch removed his body.

I gave him the Saint-Segùr...

And now Alexei had replaced it, something Peter had never thought to do, an added failure to his long list of inadequacies.

Guyon's mouth pulled inwards, and his good arm was suddenly crushing Boronskaya to the window, his lips pressing against the man's ear and cheek.

Somehow the sight sent a wrench of pain straight to Peter's

heart. He wanted to wrench Alexei away and take his place. He wanted to stay well back and allow Guyon to enjoy his first moments of true animation in days. He wanted to do both and neither - mostly wanting to just stop feeling the way he did - hurt, confused and sad. None of that was conducive to what he knew he needed to be. He needed to be more lighthearted, to distance himself from all his sorrows so that he could care for Guyon as he should.

He straightened his shoulders and stepped forward, "Are we...are we all settled then? Where's David?"

"Hiding from you." Henri grinned from the other horse. "He's in the carriage. All prepared and loaded with, er, *sweetmeats.*"

"With swee - Oh, yes." Peter nodded and turned. "Alexei, thank you again, my friend. We'll send you word of our safe arrival."

He didn't wait for an answer, afraid of what he'd see in the other man's eyes, but instead moved to mount his horse. He had opted to ride, not sure he could watch the pain in Guyon's eyes for hour after hour and not want to do something. Something violent, like striking David until he drugged Guyon unconscious.

Alexei tapped the roof of the carriage, and Guyon's white face became a blur of pallor as it moved, a sudden glimmer of blond betraying David's presence beside him. Henri laughed, and spurred after them, but Alexei caught Peter's bridle before he could move.

"*Dismount.*" The voice of the boyar, cold and uncompromising.

Peter looked after the carriage, but did as he was asked, swinging down off the horse with only slightly less than his usual grace.

"Yes, Alexei?" Somehow Peter had known it would come to this. In spite of all his help, something had been brewing between them.

"*Yes, Alexei.*" The voice was still gentle, and yet so mocking. "Do you think me a child? I am called like you. *Peter, Pyotr, Pèire, Pierre,* little *Pierrot.* I am *Alexandrovitch,* Pyotr *Alexandrovitch,* no Alexei, I. I am son of the Tsar. Son of the Tsar and I told you. I told you. Take him to Russia. I told you.

But you told me." He caught Peter in his arms, held him tight and kissed him, on forehead and cheeks. "For your *escholiante,* my tutor. For the love you bear, for your country, for the wife he knows I must take!" He laughed, and took off his great fur robe, and his heavy gold and ruby-pearl collar, placing them around Peter's shoulders. "He is to be cherished, your little mystic. Your spirit, yours, we cannot have him." And then he crushed Peter to him again, and kissed his lips. "Go with God, my darling dear."

Peter sagged inwardly, resting against Boronskaya for just a moment before he spoke, "I do cherish him. I do. Nothing has changed in how I feel for him. It's...It just hurts to know he may never feel the same. And now? How can I burden him with my love or my hurts, when he is so broken himself? How?"

He straightened then, pulled himself together as if it were an actual physical putting together of pieces. When he spoke again, it was in slow but clear Russian, "Thank you, Alexandrovitch. I will try. Truly."

"Ah, now." The deep flower-eyes were velvet, absorbing light with kindness. "Be a little kind, *Pierrot*. Just a little. He hurts too, more than in body." Boronskaya held onto the horse's bridle as Peter remounted. "Truly." The smile was a quiet caress, and then he made a sudden gesture, sending Peter's horse caracoling on its way.

*

They had sketched out a travel plan. They would alternate in the carriage, with Henri and David, who had ridden from Rome to Paris, taking over the horses each time they stopped at an inn or way post. But by the time they were twenty miles outside Paris, Henri, who had been letting Peter ride outpost while he took a kind of vanguard, was dropping back and tying his horse's reins to the pillion, calling a halt.

Before the carriage had even slowed, he was swinging inside, and David hoisting himself out. By the time Peter dropped back and came in, he could hear the litany.

Yes, for sure. Yes, in truth.

David had pulled the leashed horses to a stop as the carriage halted. "He won't," he said incomprehensibly, as Peter rode up.

"He won't, what?" Peter frowned, glancing at the carriage. Guyon? Henri? Which he and what won't he do?

"Tell me, David." He demanded an answer, although he was almost certain that he did not really want to hear it.

David quirked a smile at him. "Well, you told him." Equal incomprehensibility. "Henri, get out, we're on course..."

"What?" Peter looked wildly at the carriage, then growled, "David...I can't."

Get in there? No. That was too terrifying a thought. Besides, Guyon would not want him, would he?

"Oh, bugger you," David snarled, and a surprisingly strong arm shoved at him, hard enough to make him lose his seat and grab at the door edge. "*There*," he said with satisfaction, as Henri clambered out without even a backward glance. *Someone* tapped on the carriage roof.

"Walk on," said Henri's voice, and Peter was left facing Guyon, a white-faced harlequin with diamond-edged shadows around his eyes and mouth.

*God...*The word did not leave Peter's mouth, but he quickly fought to school his expression, so fearful was he of his shock showing on his face. "Guyon? Are you -? No, of course you're not alright. When did David last give you your medicine?"

He slid down on the bench and began digging through the supplies that David had left behind. This he could do, at least, keep himself busy, too busy to allow his own pain to intrude upon Guyon.

"I am pain-killed." Guyon's voice was flat and absolute. "Not very much. But enough. *Sit still.*"

Peter froze, then forced himself to sit back in the seat, his eyes lowered towards his own hands. Hands that were whole.

Another crashing wave of guilt struck him full on. *He was whole and Guyon was not. It was his fault this happened.*

"You said. You said. *When David's drugs are out of your system, if you still want to tell me any of that, I'll listen.*" Guyon swallowed. "There's nothing in my system. Ask them."

"Guyon...." Peter's voice was a disbelieving croak. "You didn't? You never -? You shouldn't. I'm not worth your pain.

558

Ever. I would have waited." *Forever.* His mind filled in the last word.

And this was his fault as well, Guyon in pain while he waited for Peter to talk. Damn David, how could he have allowed anyone to suffer like this, let alone someone he professed to hold as a friend.

"Oh. Oh, I forgot. It *doesn't count if there's pain.*" Guyon grimaced. "This isn't about waiting. Oh, God, I don't know. Perhaps it is." He tried to smile, and shrugged. "I lied, Peter. I am the master of debate, I know how to use each word to strike home. You gave me each and every syllable. That you wondered why I stayed with you. That you were not clever enough." He looked sick. "That you were not *enough.* So I used those words to make lies. I made lies. *I lied.* I lied. I lied. I lied. I lied by omission and lied with words. *Nothing* can be enough without love. *Nothing.* Nothing. I love you." The shadows deepened beneath his eyes as he drew back. "I love you so very much. I love you. My all in all. And I lied."

Peter felt his face flush and then go pale. His nerve failing him so badly that he still could not look up, "You must have felt some of it...or you could not have been so convincing." And God that hurt...even if he accepted it as being a lie, there must have been some truth there, however small.

"No. *You believed it.* So it was easy." Guyon sighed. "I confirmed. I did not state - *dear God, Pèire!* - *Listen*! **Listen**! I make the world believe what I say is true. I *make that happen.* And...I made it happen. I made you believe. Please. Listen. I used every skill I have to *make you believe.*"

"You succeeded." Peter blinked back his pain. He could still hear the words as if they had just been spoken. He was boring, stupid. He gave physical pleasure but, of course, that wasn't enough. Nothing was enough. *He* was not enough.

And worse, it had only confirmed what he had always suspected that people felt - that Guyon felt. All of it true.

He released a ragged breath, "Why would you lie?"

"To save you." Guyon choked on something that was not a laugh. "To save you from the *pelourinho.* Better you hate me. Better you hate me because I would die. And then it would not matter, so it would not matter, so - it would not matter. You would hate me and I would be dead, and ah, it is bearable."

"Then you failed." Peter told him quietly. "I was hurt, aching. I felt like my heart had been ripped from me." He turned his head, finally able to look at Guyon. "But I never hated you." There was the sound of a choked laugh that Peter realized was coming from him, "How could I when you only spoke the truth that I feared."

"Oh *Christ*." Guyon, impossibly, was laughing. "By my God and Savior, oh, *Peter. Peter*. I wanted that. God help me, I wanted that, I wanted you to feel that, I wanted you to *know* that - *it was a lie*. All of it. Oh, God, all of it, all of it. You are more brilliant than every heaven I have ever seen. My sun, better than stars, better than the brilliance of water, more than glitter, more than gold, all and my all of all in all - *Pèire*. How could you doubt this knowledge. How could you doubt the truth of my soul?"

"Because I have no faith." Peter's words were bitter but heartfelt. "I wanted to believe but...No one but you, Guyon. No one has ever -"

He lost what few words he had then, closing his eyes and biting his lip to try to calm himself.

I make the world believe what I say is true. I used every skill I have to make you believe.

And he had succeeded, for Peter still believed, in spite of Guyon's protestations. And how could he trust what Guyon said now? For by his own words he could use his skills to convince Peter that lies were truth.

His own pain was not important. Not nearly as important as the poor suffering soul in front of him. Pale and fevered looking, Guyon was almost like a specter sent to haunt him with recrimination for his hasty words.

"That was why I could cause that belief. Because no-one save I has ever seen past it." Guyon's good hand came out. "*You* gave me the words. *You*. I never thought them. I never thought *of* them. *The truth is I love you.*"

"I love you. I never stopped. I never could."

"*Thou very idiot.*" Guyon's eyes were full of tears. "Oh, Pèire. Then I failed in every way. *That was what you were supposed to do.*"

"And since when," Peter choked out, "have I ever done what I am supposed to?"

"Well, I'm counting, and so far? You tally never," Guyon said with a faint flicker of bitter resignation, and, to Peter's relief, leaned back and closed his eyes.

*

Brittany, August 1646

Love's a thing, as I do hear
Ever full of pensive fear
Rather than to which I'll fall
Trust me, I'll not like at all
If to love I should intend,
Let my hair then stand an end :
And that terror likewise prove,
Fatal to me in my love.
But if horror cannot slake
Flames which would an entrance make,
Then the next thing I desire
Is, to love and live i' th' fire.

The journey to Brittany seemed endless. It did not matter what drugs David gave Guyon, nor which he refused to take, nor which he acquiesced to. The pain of his hand slowly became a fact of life, intolerable and yet of course to be borne, because it was there, as much part of him as his heartbeat, as constant and imperative as his breathing, and it was almost a relief to vanish into the strange numb haze of the sleeping powders, once the disorientating factor of the incredibly heavy opiates was removed. It was a relief, because no drugs in the world could change the bitter truth of his realization - that no matter what he said, no matter what he did, no matter what truth he painfully and unflinchingly revealed, Peter did not believe him.

Or rather, and worse, he *did*. But he believed the lie, the one moment of untruth Guyon had ever given in his life. Guyon could have crossed the Baring Straits in an open fishing boat to prove his sincerity, and would not have done a thing to erase the words he had spoken in Paris.

You would always be waiting for me to say something I cannot give.

And now that all he wanted to do was give it, was to say it, now that it was utterly all-consuming, he was flinging it all into a void.

And worse, a void that he had created with his own words. It

562

was ironic that the thing that had always given him himself, had now taken the one thing outside of himself that he truly wanted. For no matter how often Peter said he loved him, it was obvious he still did not believe it returned in more than words. Words with no feeling behind them. He wanted to shake Peter, press Love into his skin until he had to believe. But that option was lost to him for the moment. Lost with the drive of Corvay's dagger.

I'm a child, he thought in weary self-disgust. *A child who thinks that to say 'I love you' keeps away the monsters and banishes demons, who think that very fact of love itself is enough to grant forgiveness for the unforgivable. But Peter is not God or de Retz, to grant absolution, and prayer has never been efficacious when it is selfish.*

The only company he wanted was Peter's, the only company he could not bear was Peter's. His mind, still half-fogged, was trapped as well, in the unending circle of despairing acknowledgment that had become his only recognizable emotion.

And Peter...Peter was kindness itself. Bestowing touch and comfort in all the ways that Guyon knew he was capable of. Gentling him with his voice when he could and holding him against the raise of pain when nothing else worked. And what could he say? Do not love me when you don't believe it returned? Don't comfort me when you won't let it be returned? Don't love me?

He was aware enough, even at his worst, to know that if this lack of belief was almost intolerable, it was still *almost*, that if he did say those things, there was a strong chance, these days, that he might be obeyed - and that - that would destroy him, finally and utterly. Let the world think it was fear that he would never use his hand again that kept him silent, that it was pain and drugs that made him remote.

Never give your word.

His father had been right. It was he who had been the fool, he who had lacked the wit to understand why that promise had been forced from him.

There should have been more to that bleak statement, the other side of that coin's truth. *For you cannot take it back, and when it is not wanted, you will have lost your soul.*

563

The bell swung within him still, but the prayer's calling was no greeting of his joy's internal sun. It was the tolling of a midnight funeral, the hollow echo of loss. It rang, unceasing and cold, giving him no peace.

And as it rang, he managed gratitude, managed acceptance, managed even to smile, at times.

By the time they had been at Brocéliande for a week, the haunted look had begun to leave Peter's eyes. For that, at least, he could be truly thankful. And the place seemed pleasant enough, from what sights trickled in between his drugged fogginess and pained awareness. Perhaps this would be better than them trapped in Paris, with Peter's duties and his students, and too many friends to be comfortable with, but who would want to know 'how he was'. Here there was only Henri and David, thank God, and they were enough.

Henri, who had his own strange forms of kindness that Guyon had almost forgotten about, was willing to spend hours reading to him, simply telling David and Peter that if they wanted to mangle the French language, he was at their disposal between the hours of noon and two, and was quite willing to give lessons over luncheon. However, since Guyon was *reliant* on interpretation, he said, it seemed deeply unfair that they inflict their attempts on such a wholly captive audience.

And David, all rough concern that was so unlike his usual drifting pleasantness that it almost frightened Guyon at first, wondering if this change meant something horrible was happening and his hand would have to come off. But no, David had shown him the work that Ibn Ibrahim had done, and how it was healing, at least on the outside. And it was David who changed the dressings when Guyon wanted it done, but dreaded allowing Peter to see it. And it was David who listened and gave him hope and spoke to Peter in their barbaric Anglais, which somehow seemed to make him feel more at ease. And Peter's ease was something that Guyon could not attend to at the moment...not without wanting to fall at his feet and beg him, *Please let me love you. Please believe me.*

Helpless to prevent himself, he drifted further into the half-dead world of drugs and the words of others. *Mine are dead*, he thought once, as Henri cheerfully misinterpreted a new thesis from Paris that should have roused him at least to some kind of scathing dismissal, but instead seemed as far from him as the Hesperides, both virtual and real. *And I am the author of their death.*

All his skill and all his careful study in precision of meaning, wasted and gone, useless as his hand. It began to seem a symbol of all that was wrong with him - an unmoving appendage that had been peeled to the bones and found wanting, reduced to its bare elements and left a mangled, repulsive mockery of something that had seemed so strong.

"Good morning." It was Peter, stepping into study where Guyon sat, a book held unseen on his lap. Peter, who smelled of outdoors and sun and just a bit of horses, who gave him a tentative smile.

That was another thing that he loathed. Time passed and left him unaware of its movement. He could complete one thought in a second, and half of one in an entire afternoon, and without the people who came to light the candles, or greet him with the time of day, he would remain locked within his own internal timescale, oblivious to all else.

"Apparently so," he said dryly, from somewhere behind the thickening ice that seemed to separate him from everything, and then, reduced to the obvious - "You've been out?"

"Yes," Peter moved to open the heavy draperies, letting light into the room. "I was making arrangements for the Ambassador's carriage to be returned...and for the use of one here, should we need it."

"Oh." Guyon contemplated that thought with a sort of vague horror. He didn't have any intention of getting back in a carriage, and if that was how he was to be reduced to traveling in future, he didn't think he would be going anywhere at all.

At least not from choice. Besides, I won't know how they move a coffin.

It was a bleak, surprisingly clear thought, as though all his contemplation had led to that little moment of finally understanding where every road his thoughts took him down ended up. "You all ride," he pointed out. "Or were you planning on a state visit to your tenants?"

"What?" Peter looked back from whatever had caught his eye outside the window. "Oh, no...but you never know. Best to be prepared in any case. And what *is* David doing out there?"

"I have no idea," Guyon said with absolute truth, since he had not looked out of the window since he unwillingly left his bed, nor seen David since the early morning hell of cleaning his hand and dressing it. He got to his feet, still suffering from the strange unbalanced feeling that keeping his hand still engendered in him, and went to stand beside Peter.

He was left none the wiser when he looked. "No," he said, "I really have *no* idea."

"Do you...Do you want to go find out?" Peter ventured. David was either doing some odd sort of exercise which involved bending in half as far as he could, then reaching out with his left hand and describing a strange circle with his finger, or he was painting imaginary pictures on the bottom of the hedge.

Guyon shrugged. "I suppose so," he said, wishing he could make himself sound even vaguely interested, since it would obviously please Peter if he demonstrated some signs of not being a slightly warm automaton. He didn't particularly care what David was doing or why he was doing it, and the most feeling he could muster about it was a small sense of relief that he wasn't doing it inside or making anyone else participate. On the other hand, to find out meant going outside, and he was starved for air that hadn't been trapped in the great house for what sometimes tasted like centuries. "Yes, actually." He managed one of his smiles, and wondered why they always made Peter flinch a bit. He didn't think they looked any different to when they were genuine. "If only because then I'll know what you're about to ask him to stop doing."

Peter's smile was still tentative, like he expected Guyon to ask him to stop, but he opened the outside door and lead the way out into the morning sunshine. "David, what are you doing?" Peter asked as they approached.

"Hedgehog."

"Hedgehog?"

"Yes."

"All is explained," Guyon said sarcastically to a nearby bush. The sun didn't seem to be touching him at all, but at least the air was clean. "Or rather, isn't at all. *What*?"

"We have one." David said, with an emphasized attitude of patience. "Appropriately in the hedge."

"Correct me if I'm wrong," Guyon said exasperatedly, "but aren't they, in fact, *nocturnal*? Perhaps its idea of hedgehog bliss is *not* to be woken up by a demented herbalist at its equivalent of three in the morning."

David scowled at him, "Yes, yes...but I think it's hurt. So cheese and apples."

"Ah," Peter nodded slowly. "You're trying to lure it out?"

"It's afraid, you see. Although, Cook says it's usually quite tame."

"It *also*," Guyon said irritably, "eats meat. Not cheese, and not apples. Although I believe they like milk. If you put out a bowl of last night's stew, you'd probably have more - *what*?" They were both staring at him as though he had just announced the Ark of the Covenant was in the attic. "What, what, *what*?"

"Just amazed, as always," Peter smiled softly, "by the vast range of your knowledge."

"Stew." David said, unbending himself from his undignified pose and moving toward the back of the house and the kitchen doors.

"Yes," Guyon said dryly. "Just call me the patron saint of all things prickly and flea-ridden." He snorted. The hedgehog, hurt or not, had probably decided to leave the *area*, let alone the hedge. He knew exactly how it felt.

Peter's look was odd and somehow painful when he turned it back on Guyon, "Let's walk."

Guyon sighed, the faint traces of irritably amused life leaving him. The thought of spending time carefully not saying all the things he wanted to, Peter's silent endurance hanging over them both like a damp shroud, was almost more than he could stand. But he had caused it all, and so knew he *had* to bear it, that it was his penance and his damnation at once. "Of course," he said quietly.

"Damn it, Guyon." Peter froze before they had even taken a

step. "That wasn't a command it was a suggestion. It's not a bloody forced march, it's a stroll in the sunshine. If you don't want to go, say so...just don't...don't be so...damned....calm..."

Peter's voice, which had started out angry and rough, ended up soft and rather lost-sounding as it trailed off.

"I'm afraid I'm not quite capable of the wailing and breast-beating you all seem to think appropriate," Guyon snapped back, his sudden anger escaping him before he had time to realize it and control it. "I'll pour my ash on my head *mentally*, I think." He closed his mouth, pressing his lips together, and took three shallow breaths through his nose, swallowing all the other words that were crowding his throat. "And for all our sakes, *alone*."

He turned and made his way back to the house, knowing that he had only made things worse, knowing that if he did not learn to keep silent, he was going to immolate even their sad remaining rags of friendship, and somehow unable to stop himself from lashing out, from wanting to hurt someone else and make them feel the pain that he was forced to suffer.

For the first time, when he entered his room, he turned the key in the door.

I'm not locking you out, Peter, he thought. *I'm locking myself away. It's the only thing left I can give you...*

*

Peter watched Guyon walk away. He seemed to be doing more and more of that lately. *How long*, he wondered, *until it would be the last time? Until Guyon gave up on him and left?* And how long after that until he put an end to his own pain? Only this time it would not be due to anything Guyon had done or said, but rather his own fault for not believing. Faith took so long to regain, fear so long to over come.

He was starting to understand that Guyon's way of feeling fear was nothing he could relate to, but rather it was as strange and detached as his other peculiarities. More and more, these days, Peter was thinking of François's warning, kindly meant and, at the time, utterly incomprehensible.

You must have noticed, he's not - exactly like other people.

It had been a wonderful truth for a long time, but this withdrawal and isolation was the other side of it, the part that Peter imagined Guyon would never show to anyone if he could help it.

But knowing that did nothing to stop how much pain it caused.

And watching Guyon's withdrawal pained him even more, because Peter knew that he was the root cause of it. That his lack of faith and refusal to believe Guyon's simple words were driving his friend, his beloved, into this icy cavern that even he could not breach. Peter felt guilt, so much guilt, for hadn't Guyon done the same to him? Told him that he didn't really feel the love that he knew was there? Had even forbidden him to say the words. God, how much that had hurt. But here he was, doing that very same thing to Guyon.

It was not surprising that Guyon chose, more often than not, to shut himself away literally as well as figuratively, but it just made everything that little bit harder - *one* fortress of guarded silence would have been bad enough, but when it was reinforced with actual walls and doors, it truly was impenetrable.

He should go and apologize, try to coax Guyon back outside for the day. It was the sad state of his heart that even a day spent with a sullen and angry Guyon was better than one spent with out him completely.

All his good intentions about expressing regret for something he wasn't sure he had actually *done*, however, vanished as soon as he realized that Guyon's door was not just closed in silent forbiddance, it was, in fact, *locked.*

Locked. Locked. Was Guyon behind it, frantically packing his things to leave? Had this been the final straw?

"Guyon?" Peter's panicked voice rang in the hallway, "Please don't. Please. I'm sorry...please."

There was a muffled sound of real annoyance, and then that of the key turning in the lock. Guyon flung the door open with a force that suggested he had somehow found a way of putting all the strength of his right hand in to his usable left, and glared at him without a trace of wryness, or exasperated fondness, or anything that Peter realized he had begun to take for granted. The look on Guyon's face now was usually reserved for Andre at his worst

"Don't what?" he asked. "Sleep? I thought that was everyone's sworn intent, me and sleep."

Peter just stared for a few moments, looking into those suddenly sharp eyes. "No.. never mind...I just..." He turned sharply and stalked off down the hall. He couldn't do this. Couldn't be on pins and needles all the time with not knowing which way to jump. He stopped before he reached the end of the hall. But how could he not? He loved Guyon and no attempts at indifference could block that out of his mind. He was stuck. There was a time when he would have appended 'and happily so' to the end of that statement, but now all he could do was wait and pray and hope that things would improve.

He turned again, knowing just how foolish he must seem, and yet without any idea of what else to do other than keep trying, but it was not two steps back towards Guyon's room when he heard the small, distinct sound again.

Guyon had re-locked the door.

*

He locked the door. He locked the door. He locked the god-damned bloody door. Peter didn't know what to do. He didn't know if he was angry or hurt or...merely resigned. If this was his punishment for loss of faith or Guyon's way of chiding him for his disbelief. No, that was unfair. Guyon was normally outspoken to a fault. Telling people even what they did not wish to hear. Except when it came to him, for some reason. Christ!

For some reason, all he could think of was raised black eyebrows and a sharp voice saying - *well, why don't you have a think about it?*

But that time, Guyon had been the one in perfect physical health, and Guyon had been the one to walk away, and Guyon -

- had left his boots behind in an access of real temper.

And never struck back, save for that one, sharp, uncontrollable little demand. And God knew, he could have. He truly could have. He could have said -

What if I want to weigh down my cloak with stones and walk into the Seine, chevalier, what then?

Could have said -

I will always ask you for the one thing your integrity cannot give.

Could have said -

I grow bored.

Could have said -

I have loved you for so long that I forgot the words.

Could have said -

"I need you to help me mend a harpsichord."

"Could have - Um, what?" Peter blinked, his mind coming out of its whirlwind of regret and anger. "Henri? You said - What did you say?"

"I need you," Henri repeated patiently, "to help me mend a harpsichord. You have one. It needs restringing. Help."

"I do?" Peter frowned, he might have seen something of the sort when the steward was showing them through the Hall, but he couldn't remember having been far more concerned with how Guyon was feeling. "But really, Henri, I don't know anything about them."

"I don't really care, as long as you can pull very hard on something and not forget about what you're doing and wander off," Henri pointed out. "And you have the unmistakable virtue of two hands."

It was a real oddity. Henri would find ways of making Guyon tolerate him, would devote hours to finding something to occupy that frenetic, unhappy mind, and then turn around and dismiss the whole thing as an inconvenience.

"Certainly...I don't appear to have other plans." Peter looked fleetingly back up the stairs then turned to follow Henri.

"Do you know what's absolutely sodding amazing?" Henri continued in perfectly spoken, horribly precise English. "I've known him for nearly ten years, and it's the most forthcoming he's ever been. Right. Pliers. String. Pull. Excellent, thank you." He began to hum nastily through his teeth and tweak metallic strands in what seemed an unnecessarily painful way.

Peter held on tight, in spite of the numbing vibrations,

"Forthcoming? About what?"

Henri snorted around the pliers. "Oquow. Ow. Owowowowow. Yaip. Uh, anything? Can you pullsh ti'er?" And who knew that giggles went right the way up metal strings and into your elbow and hurt?

He could take the pain though. Truthfully he needed the distraction, or he'd be back up the stairs pounding on that locked door and saying things that did not need to be said. Things he would regret the moment they were out of his mouth. Peter pulled the wire tighter, "Is that enough?"

Henri grinned around the pliers, and then let them out of his jaws to grasp them in his strong musician's hands and wrench. "Dunno, Peter, izzit?" He twanged the string, and nodded. "That's good." He wasn't grinning, and he wasn't smiling, and his lean dark face was creased with fury as he leant across the fragile instrument and said - "You have David for your guerdon. Well, fair is fair, I shall fly Guyon's banner. He lost his hand, you stupid bastard, don't you understand? He lost his other voice, and all you can do is tell him he's a liar - and I am going insane with being fed up enough to spit!" And then it was as though all that intensity were a mirage, as he bent into the harpsichord and said - "The one to your left, please."

Peter obediently shifted his grip to the next strand. "I deserve that, I know." Peter said quietly. "I'm trying, Henri, really. Christ. I've fought in battles, seen men ripped apart, blown up and bleeding. Had it happen to me more than once. But none of that frightens me as much as this does. To have that faith again."

"Fai'zzzz eazzzzzy," Henri pointed out. "Lovezzzzzz no'." He started tweaking the string with his hands again. "Did you know I was in love with him once? Thought I was, anyway. Ran away all the way to Rome - let go a bit, thanks - to get away from what he said that night. Next one, three down." The next words were almost incomprehensible, and would have been entirely so were it not for the fact that Peter could place them in context. "Love' tha' l'il idio' like ma'. O' tho'ht I di', 'nyw'y."

Loved that little idiot like mad. Or thought I did, anyway.

He laughed at Peter's grunt of effort, and started playing chords. "Met David. Learned what love really was. Came back to

Paris. Saw Guyon love this mad bastard dead in Poitiers. Saw the mad bastard come back." Chord, melody, chord, dischord, plange, cadence. "Keep trying, Peter."

By now, even Peter's teeth hurt from the vibrations, "I intend to, Henri. I have no other choice. Even if...if everything he's said is a lie...I still love him. That has never stopped."

"Well, it's a funny kind of love to drive a man to his - "

"Dinner?" David asked sweetly. "Given that our little half-handed cretin's locked his door, I take it we're on our own. And yes, I know we think it's lunch, but they seem to think we desperately want our main meal right now, and I simply won't disillusion..." he trailed off. "'S a hawk moth caterpillar. On the door frame. Hehe. I'll give it to M'sieur Prickles, he can hatch a hawk."

Peter slumped, "Are we done here, Henri?" He wanted out. Out of this house and into the fresh air. Air with no recriminations or accusation. He wanted to get on his horse and tear across the meadows like the Angel of Death riding towards a battleground. But no...he had promised Guyon he would not do that. So a walk it was to be...if Henri were done with him.

Henri closed his eyes, and sighed. "We're done," he said, sounding as tired as Peter felt. "We're done."

"Then...enjoy your meal, Messieurs, and your day," Peter turned sharply, going towards the door. Was he really being selfish, as Henri had implied? Guyon had lost so very much because of this...because of him. Was he, in part, allowing guilt to keep them apart? He didn't know, but he hoped that whatever part of him that was holding the restraints grew tired and released them soon.

Maybe I can make him *rewire a harpsichord.*

*

It had not occurred to Guyon that his behavior came across as both unnecessarily distant and as cruel. Had he been only physically in pain, he would have attempted to deal with it with more grace, had he been perfectly healthy when the inevitable results of his appalling lie came back to torment him, he would have turned the full abilities of his mind and spirit onto a solution. But with both forms of private, agonized, insoluble agony rendering him physically and mentally incapable at once, all he could do was retreat to manufactured safety and try to insulate the rags of himself against any further pain.

"Open up..." David's voice came through the thick muffling of his chamber door. "'S time and I brought you things..." David, precise as always.

Guyon opened his eyes - when had it become easier to keep them closed, even when he was awake? He supposed since it had become so painful to look and not see Peter, or look and see him, always with that expression of quiet, disbelieving pain -

And I put that there -

"Guyon, that means you open the door."

Guyon nodded, and got to his feet, the odd feeling of imbalance assailing him again as he stumbled across the floor and turned the key. He opened the door and immediately turned his back on David. It might hurt to look at Peter, but he didn't want to see anyone else, either, not and sense the silent accusation, the revulsion, the outrage. The unspoken, and worse, the spoken questions.

David waved in a servant who sat a tray down on the table and then scurried out, "Lunch, so they tell me, but enough food for ten." He held up his wash basin, "Before or after?"

"Before," Guyon said quickly. It wouldn't actually make any difference to his appetite - everything tasted like ash and smelled worse and seemed to enhance the pain - but at least it provided him with an excuse. "That way I get rid of you sooner." His voice lacked the necessary humor to make it anything less than a deliberate insult.

"Making that your life's work then, are you?" David frowned, setting out the things necessary for cleaning and rewrapping Guyon's hand. "Getting plenty of practice at least."

"And yet here you are," Guyon said acidly, "so the practise is obviously needed, wouldn't you say?" It seemed bitterly unfair that he was stranded in Brittany with three of the four men in the world who were definitely unafraid of him, and equally unafraid of giving him everything he handed out straight back - to differing degrees.

"Yes...If you actually want to succeed. Hand." David looked at him expectantly.

Guyon sighed, and extended it towards David obediently. He would have paid money to imbue his muscles with the same steely calm he could wrap around his voice, but his body had always been the one thing that betrayed him, and this horrendous little ritual was never going to be the exception. His whole arm shook, the hand making involuntary, savage little flinches as skin memory informed it of what came next. "Trust me," he said with a coldness he was a long way from feeling, "if I didn't want to succeed, I wouldn't be trying." Except for the fact that he didn't, except for the fact that he would have paid all the money had had for Peter's support - except for the fact he had forfeited it, could never expect it again, and would rather endure this alone in limbo forever than be made to feel its lack.

David slowly and gently began unwrapping the bandages from Guyon's hand, "He'd be here you know, if you'd ask. He wants to be. Turn."

"If I ask?" Guyon's voice, too, escaped his control, shooting upwards in a mixture of incredulity and pain, as even David's gentleness sent precise agony screaming through his bones and muscles. "Because begging works so well! If he can't - if he doesn't - it's not up to me any more. It's not. He has to make that leap, and he - he won't."

David was silent for a long moment, continuing his work as if afraid to allow one to conflict with the other. Finally, he handed Guyon a bit of linen, "There. Dry that and we'll rewrap it."

As Guyon slowly and painfully obeyed, trying not to cry out at every touch of the cloth, David continued, "You're making his choice easy then, aren't you?" His voice had little of its usual haziness as he added sharply, "And easy on yourself."

Guyon had no idea what expression was on his face when he looked at David, but whatever it was, it had enough force to it to make David raise one hand and concede - "All right, not that easy."

"Not easy at all," Guyon said tiredly, trying to dry his fingers without moving them. "And I'm not doing it to be easy on myself." *I'd have walked into the lake with stones in my pockets long since, if I were.*

"But begging is not what Peter wants, I expect, " David gave a shrug. "He just wants what he had." David cut gauze and linen, preparing the new bandage. "Smaller this time. Not as bulky."

"Enough to cover it with a glove?" Guyon asked hopefully. The pain he could bear, was bearing, but the looks he got, the constant reminder that he was reminding people - that Peter had seen -

He stopped himself from crying out with an effort. *You've seen me flayed down to bones and nerves and sinew. All of me. I wouldn't want it, either.*

"Should be," David considered. "Wouldn't though. 'll heal better with air."

"No," said Guyon, his throat closing over with panic as he watched the bruised, bleeding, mutilated skin disappear under David's careful wrapping. He couldn't say anything else for a moment, his heart pounding so fiercely in his head and chest that he thought if he even breathed, he would be sick. "No," he repeated in a whisper. His hand twitched, as though agreeing.

"Will." David assured him. "I can understand the glove, but Peter won't care. He just - But you're not listening are you?"

Guyon stared at the table, watching the grain of the wood blur and focus with each beat of his heart, rhythmic swirls of pain and disorientation mixing with clarity, a kaleidoscope of unwanted sensation. "No, I'm listening," he managed. "What does he just?"

"He just needs to know that you're still you," David tilted his head. "The you he loves an' not the other one."

Guyon's laugh tore something at the back of his throat, it was so hard and sharp, a noise that surprised him as much as it seemed to startle David. "But I *am* the other one," he said. His vision was starting to blur completely, fraying at the edges. "I always have been. And you're right. It's not who he loves. Who could?" He drew a deep breath, trying to retain even a little of his once-vaunted control. "Please go away now, David," he said quietly. "Please."

David gathered up his things, shaking his head, "You're wrong, Guyon. If that was who you'd always been, Peter wouldn't have to begin with. And I'm certain he did."

"Exactly," Guyon said as the door closed. "Did."

There is no greater misery than a joy recalled in sorrow.

When I am from him, I am dead till I be with him...

He would always be dead, now. In every way that mattered, he would be dead. Unending, unendurable, unchanging -

Am I already in hell?

He closed his eyes again, and the pain took him over, shaking him from head to foot, out of his control completely.

Yes. God help me, yes. This is hell.

*

No-one had come near him for the length of the September afternoon, leaving him to thoughts of autumn and dying leaves and the beginning of a preparation for renewal, months hence - a renewal that for him would never come.

The night he had spent as Peter lay in the barn near Toulouse was nothing compared to this. Then, he had been reaching out to something infinite, intangible, his whole being a prayer. Now, his whole being was turned towards another, towards someone who refused to be reached, refused to allow him entry, refused him and all he helplessly, unstoppably, gave.

I think by some secret ordinance of the heavens, we embraced one another by our names.

Are you ever going to finish reading Montaigne?

I am what they have called me. But not to God. Only to you.

Guyon's good hand pressed against his mouth in a fist, trying to contain things even he was not quite sure of, trying to stifle the scream that seemed to be always there, so that words had to be pushed past it.

Payment owed, Corvay had said, as the searing, unimaginable pain drove into his hand. *Payment **deferred***, had been Guyon's response then, as he fought not to let that same scream escape, the sound that had never left him, but stayed echoing in the endless cavern of his mind, never voiced and never absent.

He dropped his hand to the table, and picked up the dagger, thinking of when he had wrenched it and his hand free from the table, of David's hand on his, later, pulling it free from bone and tissue.

It wouldn't hurt as badly, this time, or at least not for long, and even if it did, it would hurt less then being reminded of what he had said.

Undoubted physical pleasure is not enough -
Payment deferred.
Not enough. I grow bored.
Payment deferred.
Not enough.
Deferred.
Not enough.

"Enough!" Guyon shouted to the empty room. He held the dagger in his hand, studying the way the light glinted off the steel It was a small thing, really, the blade only six inches long. Beautiful in its own way.

"Guyon?" Henri's voice drawled out from the now opened doorway. "What do you think you're doing?"

"Contemplating the beauty of all things deadly. This blade...it could be a scorpion or a viper, but would people fear it more or less." Guyon sighed. "Get out, Henri."

"I will beg your pardon, and refuse," Henri said with gentle implacability. "Not all deadliness *is* beautiful, incidentally. Aconite is a revolting shade of yellow."

"So is your tongue in the mornings, but fortunately I am not the one who deals with it," Guyon responded automatically. "*Please*, Henri, leave me *alone*." God. He had once been possessed of strength in his voice and the power to enforce it. Now he sounded like a whining child.

"Don't be a bigger fool that you already are, Guyon." Henri hissed.

"That would be what I am trying not to be." He could be contained. He could restrain himself from lashing out. "There must be a way to remedy this. If only Corvay's aim had been more true..."

"And you think that would do it?" Henri huffed out a breath. "That would have fixed everything? Made it so much simpler...if you'd have died?"

"Yes," Guyon said, amazed as ever at his contemporaries' inability to see the obvious. "That was what I had originally intended, you know. For Peter to be able to mourn - and relinquish."

"And you think he'd do that? God, you really are an idiot."

"Well, I know that," Guyon said dryly. "But of course he would. I *know* he would. I've given him my love, and he -" He choked on emptiness, on desperation, on tears that were not Henri's to dry. "Payment deferred, Henri."

"You gave him your love and then you yanked it back...because you thought that would allow him to find peace?" Henri's look of amazed incredulity was almost palpable. "Christ can't you see it almost killed him? Is killing him? Every day, by long slow steps, he's dying inside...and you're spooning in the poison."

"*Damn you!*" Guyon was on his feet before he knew it, snarling into his long-term friend's face, forgetting the pain in his hand. "Why do you think that I wish it had been different? There would have been peace."

"Yes, peace. But only for you." Henri's voice dropped down to almost a whisper. "Peter would have followed you within the hour."

"Peter," Guyon said coldly, "would find his own cock to crow his denial, as he does each day we stay here. Don't you dare play me, Henri, or I swear to God I'll unstring tendons to make David my lute instead of Peter's banner!"

"Peter would have had a pistol to his head before you bled out," Henri snapped. "And *this time* he'd succeed in his attempt."

The world, for a strange, dizzy moment, paused in a spiderweb of panic. "This time?" Guyon asked quietly. His voice floated out of him in thin, frightened tones.

"Yes, this time." Henri said, his tones cold. "That beautiful mahogany desk in his office might have had a rather gruesome decoration added to it, if not for the Queen's baby artist."

"You lie," Guyon said, his voice still not quite his own, trying to find some strands of certainty with which to tether himself to the world. "Peter would *not*."

"There are some things that no man should be made to live

through, Guyon," Henri said harshly. "Especially, some one who feels as much as Peter."

"*You lie!*" Guyon's arm was across Henri's throat before the next breath could escape either of them. "You lie as you lie in that goosefeather bed, *you lie! Aşkin Cemal Olsun,* Henri, I would -" He stopped. "*No.*" It came out of his mouth past constricted horrors of lungs and throat. "*No.* No. *You lie!*"

"I do not!" Henri's fingers were scrabbling at Guyon's arm, trying to pull him away. "Guyon!"

"Oh *God*!" Guyon spun away, caught at his own breath as though he were the one half-choked. "I should have - I *did* - I - *where is he?*"

Henri gasped, taking in air and coughing, "You can't...go after him...like that. Christ, Guyon, are you going to...try to kill us all...one at a time?" He rubbed at his neck.

"You *wish,*" Guyon snarled, and ran out of the small room.

*

Peter was supposed to be looking at the account books. He was also supposed to be looking at plans for breeding of stock, storing of seed for the following years planting and the ideas his vintner had for improving his wines. He was, however, doing none of it. Instead he was staring blankly out the window at the overcast skies and wondering if it was a reflection of how he felt.

Overcast, cloudy, and pained muddle. It was a feeling he was, unfortunately becoming intimately familiar with. So familiar in fact that David had begun offering him some of his drugs in the hopes they could find something that might artificially lift his spirits. As if any of that would help.

He lay down the paper he had been studying, or failing to study, and propped his chin up on the palm of his long fingered hand. What more could he do? He hurt, dammit, but he didn't mean to hurt Guyon. But he also wasn't sure if he could find enough faith within himself to allow Guyon in again.

Guyon had given him his faith back.

Guyon had smashed his faith like a cheap mirror.

He wasn't sure what he needed to do to put himself and his

faith back together.

Peter wondered, as he stretched his aching body out on the study's sofa, if it was his destiny for people to try to beat sense into him when it came to his affections. First Robbie, long years back, and now Henri. Both of them so sure they knew what he should do. Both of them caring about the outcome. Both of them so positive that he wasn't capable of working his way through it on his own. And both of them so utterly wrong.

Oh, not about what the final satisfactory outcome should be, but the fact that he wasn't capable of the task. He was, if left to his own devices and his own slow and meticulous process of evaluating his own fears and emotions, more than capable, he was sure, of deciding what was best for his own life.

When Robbie had first recognized that Peter was attracted to Brian, he said nothing. He didn't encourage or discourage. Robbie had known for some time of his attraction to men and although he didn't understand it, he accepted it as part of what Peter was. It didn't keep him from steering likely females in Peter's direction, but he didn't get upset when Peter turned them down, either.

But Brian gave no real clue that he thought of Peter as anything more than one of his best friends, so if he seemed to touch Peter frequently, why it was no more frequently than he touched Robbie. It simply meant more to Peter, lost in the throes of youthful lust and the loneliness of his position as Lord of the Manor at such a young age.

Things would probably have gone on just as they were if Peter's eighteenth birthday had not rolled around. It had worried him at first, Robbie and Brian inviting him to go out with them to celebrate. The last time they'd done that he'd found himself shoved into the arms of a pretty girl named Sally, who was more than happy to help him lose his virginity. This time, however, they wound up in a tavern, drinking to the wee small hours. Sarah had come to fetch Robbie and had left a slightly less drunken Peter to see to it that Brian didn't fall off a cliff or break his neck on the way home.

"Do dee dee round the hill...with...hmmmm..hmmm...." Brian sang drunkenly as they neared his cottage. *"Round*

the hill and down ta the...lalala.. What's the words there, Peter?"

"Valley...?" Peter suggested, really having no clue what Brian was singing.

"Round the hill and down to the valley...and...Look! My house." Brian pointed and giggled. "Come on then. I think I have some whiskey inside."

"I think we've had 'nough. Heads gonna ache tomorrow as it is..." Peter shifted, trying to encourage Brian towards the door. They managed the last few steps and Peter leaned his friend against the wall while he got the door open.

"Peter...Peter...Peter... There's niver enief...uh...never enough whiskey, lad..." Brian leaned towards him, swaying unsteadily.

"You're about to fall over...I think that's prolly enough." Peter moved forward to prop up the other man.

That was his first mistake, he suddenly found himself wrapped in the affectionate embrace of his friend, noses mere inches apart.

"You're probably right, Peter," Brian said softly. "You're a smart one I've always thought. And so, so beautiful..."

Brian's lips descended on his and Peter didn't have the energy, or the will to push him away.

They stumbled inside, still kissing, shedding clothes as they both hurried towards the bed, touching, kissing...hands on each other, stroking until they both came with loud groans of satisfaction. They were both asleep almost immediately after, the sex and the drink making it a necessity.

Peter was awakened the next morning by the expedient of a large hand, Brian's, swatting his bare backside.

"Roll yer sel' out, Perry-lad. We've got a bit of work ta be done today." Brian's voice, sounding disgustingly not hungover, echoed in Peter's head. "Coffee's on the stove and there's a bit of bread on the sideboard. Didn't

582

think ye'd be able ta stomach much more'n that."

Peter slowly sat up, willing the meager contents of his stomach, what ever had not been whiskey, to stay just where it was. "Uh...thanks. Why're you in such a hurry though..."

Brian was standing at the basin, splashing what had to be icy water over himself, then scrubbing. Peter absently scratched at his own belly, and grimaced. He needed to wash as well.

"Lots ta do, I told ye. I don't want ta be too late doin' it either." Brian dried himself off hurriedly and tugged on his trousers. "I'm supposed ta meet Ellie later on."

Peter froze, and choked out, "Ellie?"

"Oh, yeah...she's a fine girl, that Ellie. I'll have her in the bed and on her back after two whiskeys."

"Oh..." Peter felt his heart begin to pound painfully. "I thought maybe we could...."

Brian gave a chuckle, as he pulled on his shirt, "I'll ask her if she has a friend, if ya like?"

"No." Peter managed keep his voice from squeaking, but only just.

Brian came back over to the bed and putting one hand on Peter's cheek, leaned in to kiss him. "You're one of my best friends, ya know? We'll hafta do this again sometime."

Then he straightened, tugging on his stockings and shoes, "Stay if ya like, Perry-lad. Just close up when ya leave."

And with that he was gone, leaving Peter alone.

Alone. Like he was leaving Guyon alone...

He'd eventually confessed all to Robert, in explanation of why he'd not been spending the usual amount of time with Brian. He already knew that he and Brian had felt differently about what had happened and he just needed to give himself time to work through it. He'd hoped for a bit of sympathy from the man he thought of as his older brother, but what he got instead was Robert telling him that Brian never took sex seriously and that Peter was daft and should just get past it as quick as possible.

Even though he knew it was true and that he was already trying to do just that, the words stung.

And now, here was Henri, telling him to get over his pain and move forward as quickly as possible.

Peter sighed and shook his head. He didn't like what he was doing. Didn't like himself much for doing it. *God, when had he become so cowardly?*

He was treating Guyon like Brian had treated him, like his own feelings were the only ones that mattered. He knew, inside where it truly mattered, that Guyon loved him. Why could he not admit it? Would he be any worse off if he was wrong? And if it were the right decision...he'd have Guyon back.

He closed his eyes and took a deep breath. Sometimes you just had to step off the edge of the cliff and hope the water below was deep enough to buoy you up over the rocks.

He'd do it. Today. He'd not let another sun set on this painful travesty that their lives had become.

He'd take that step off the cliff of his fear...to accept Guyon's word and the chance that he'd be hurt again...and hope that his faith would buoy him up, over the rocks that Guyon's lie had been. He'd do it.

There would be no more looking back.

The door opened, and was closed again with a soft precision that somehow jangled every nerve Peter possessed. He turned in his chair to see the object of his Fortune's Wheel contemplation standing with his back to the painted wood, unmistakably furious and yet contained with it, the air around him almost shimmering with the heat of pure rage.

"It seems I'm not the only liar, then," Guyon said, and the words were small and hard and crystal-clear, falling into the room like something terrible and molten.

Peter straightened up, tiredly, "What are you saying, Guyon? What is it that you imagine I've done?"

This had become the pattern of their interactions lately, all sharp and recriminating.

"I just had a conversation with Henri," Guyon said, still in the same voice, still not moving. "He said something about you and success with a pistol. Of course, he might have meant *lack* of success with a pistol. Since you're alive."

"Yes." Peter said, blandly. "I was either too brave or too cowardly to pull the trigger. Who knows which? In any case, Kees interrupted me and...I'm here."

Guyon nodded, slowly. "Mm." Peter had never heard that particular tone in that familiar syllable before. He was used to amusement, contemplation, embarrassment, sometimes all in layers and sometimes concealing a great deal of something else that Guyon either did not want to or could not say. But this time, it wasn't concealing anything. It was flat, cold absorption of a fact. "Yes, I see. I suppose I owe Kees a debt." Usually, that sort of statement would have been said with sincerity, with wry humor, with *something*. But not this time. It was said with the same red-hot, utterly contained anger as he had first spoken with. "What do you think?"

"I don't think that's up to me." *God,* he was tired of this. Tired of hurting and being afraid and not knowing which way to turn or how high to jump. In spite of his earlier decision, the next words just came out, "Perhaps, you'd have been more grateful if he hadn't."

They were sharp and unfair, and Guyon was undeserving of them, but Peter could not wish them unsaid. He had been balancing on the edge of this cliff for long enough. This needed to be settled one way or another, so he could tell Guyon his decision and move forward with no more doubts.

"No, I don't think so," Guyon said quietly, contemplatively. "But then, I suppose it doesn't matter. I was supposed to be dead, and I would have been happy, thinking you free of me. So - no, I'm grateful to Kees. Since I'm alive without having to withstand anything save the lack of your love. I'm fortunate, hm? I can count myself blessed. See you alive. *Know what I've done.*" The last words were raw and torn-sounding, despite the constant quiet level of Guyon's voice, the rasping sound of someone who had been screaming for hours.

Peter hung his head. He did love Guyon still. Loved him with such intensity that he was often afraid that it would burn him out and leave only a rotting husk behind. In that moment he again knew himself for a coward, because as much as he loved Guyon, he was terrified of being hurt so badly again.

God! What had happened to him? What happened to the man who had loved so much that he was willing to settle for whatever pieces he could have? Friendship, if nothing else, had meant as much to him as a touch. Could he find that again?

"Guyon? I -"

He stopped, and looked up in time to see something that had replaced the anger in Guyon's strange eyes - what? Hope? Love? Despair, that had clogged his last words? - flicker and die.

"Mm. You. So you are. Yourself." Guyon's face was set in hard lines. "And prepared to commit the only unforgivable sin. What would you think, Peter, if I did the same?"

Peter shook his head, "Do not taunt me, Gui. I know I should not have. I was just - Christ, I was frightened and cowardly and...I just couldn't face it."

"Ah. And if *I* cannot? You gave me the desire to live and the will to do so, and now you withdraw it and leave me a shell, because everything you told me was a lie. And I, damn my soul to hell, cannot live with the knowledge that it was I who made it so. You don't want what I've become. You don't want who I am. Love isn't supposed to be a death sentence, but I don't want to live seeing what I made your life!"

"I never lied to you. Never. I loved you...I still love you..." Peter said it with a tired sounding voice. "Don't you see, Guyon? I didn't try it because you did not love me, but because I still loved you. It wouldn't stop. Even if you'd sent me away, I would have still loved you. And...and I don't know if I could have kept myself away."

"It wasn't supposed to be an option." Guyon's voice was utterly inflectionless. "I intended for Corvay to take my life, not my usefulness. I don't think - I don't think anyone's in question that death is a kindness more than I deserve, but - I can't live with this. I'm sorry. I can't." He swallowed audibly. "I love you, and I lied, and you're never going to forgive me - you took the string off. I can't look every day and know that whatever you say - whatever you try and make me think is real - it isn't. What's real is what's gone, what I destroyed. And I'm a coward, far more than you are, I know it, but - *I can't*."

"*Christ....*" The words fell from Peter's lips, clattering to the floor between them. He'd driven Guyon to this with his distrust...with his faithlessness. He'd sworn never to lie to him, and yet, what else had he been doing with his refusals to listen and believe? Was that any better than what Brian had done to him so long ago? Professing love with one breath then removing it, come sober daylight? None of that mattered. None of it. He loved Guyon and -

"It truly doesn't matter." Peter said out loud. "You could drive Corvay's blade into my own heart, and as it stopped beating your name would still be on my lips. I love you, Guyon. I have, I do, and I will. God help me."

Peter crossed the room, pulling Guyon against him, before either of them could step away from this. "I'm the coward, Gui. I've admitted it to myself and now I admit it to you. I'm a craven idiot who lost faith and then refused to see when it was somehow, miraculously handed back to him." His voice cracked then, full of emotions that he could no longer hold inside. "I...I still have it, ya know? The string. I cut it off because...I thought you'd not want it there anymore. But I couldn't...I couldn't just throw it away."

There was a long silence, while Guyon remained utterly still in his arms, the compliant lifelessness of his limbs almost familiar, and then he took a small, shaking breath, and that too was something Peter knew, and couldn't place. It was the second, deeper breath, sharp and very audible, the movement of Guyon's arms to come around him with a tentative grip, that reminded him.

Guyon, outside the Richelieu Chapel, grieving and agonized and willing himself towards death over François's loss.

"I love you," Guyon said then, frightened and quiet and utterly uncertain, and that, thank God, was new.

"And I you." Peter whispered the words. "With all I have and all I am."

"Can I apologize for doubting that later?" Guyon sounded a bit more like himself, a faint wry shiver to his words now, rather than the metallic, flat despair of before.

"You can," Peter chuckled softly, "but you don't need to. That could begin a circle of apologies that could keep us to the end of time."

"I don't mind that," Guyon admitted, and then snorted. "Oh God. I haven't improved in my expression of sentiment at all. I meant the end of time part."

"It doesn't matter." Peter whispered. "None of it matters."

And somewhere outside the hall the chapel bell rang. *Calling the hour, of course*, Peter thought, but somehow he knew it was also ringing for them - for love, for joy, for life.

*

Guyon did not know the parallels that Peter had drawn between his behavior earlier on in the study and his aquavit-induced reaction after François's funeral, but he would have applauded the perspicacity of that theory, if he had. After François's death, he had willed himself quietly towards his own end, not seeing any hope for a future without the one thing that had ever kept the endless length of days before him bright.

Peter had changed that, given him hope, and *more* than hope, a reason and a purpose that went beyond duty or attempts to avenge the senselessness of François's brutal death. He had given him friendship, freely offered, given him a sanctuary that even in the depths of despair, it had been impossible for Guyon not to recognize.

But he had not admitted the degree to which he had given his heart, then, nor had he allowed himself to surrender the last citadel of his body and mind together. Despite all that had begun during Peter's absence in Toulouse and Poitiers, Guyon had been himself entire, and knew it.

Now, though -

It was as though he had been drowning for days, had forced his head up time and again above murky waters of something unnamed and horrendous, and now that Henri had forced him to put a name to it, made him see the unforgivable for what it was, the waters had at last closed over him, and yet the bottom to these depths was nowhere in reach.

Forgiveness, ironically, had come at the one second he needed it the most - and that one second had made it too late to change a single thing.

So he stood, unsure if it was himself that Peter loved, or some idea of 'Guyon'. If Peter could love who he was now as much as he had professed to love who he had been. It wasn't something he could even ask, could even explain really, and not only because he was afraid of what the answer might be.

Instead, he just tried to be what he thought Peter wanted. Did all he could to please and let time draw them back into comfort with one another. Or so he hoped.

"He just needs to know that you're still you. The you he loves an' not the other one."

"But I am *the other one."*

He was both. He was the man who had stared into the blazing lights of candles until his eyes and mind were seared, all for the sake of a love he had believed to be impossible. He was the man who had rejected that love, refuted it coldly and calmly and with all the ruthlessness befitting the monster he had once proclaimed himself.

He was half himself and twice himself, and none of it was bearable any more.

"I'm sorry, I was - what did you say?" He was aware that Peter had spoken, but it was just sound, the water seeming almost tangible, muffling and distorting everything into unintelligibility.

"I asked what you were thinking about," Peter spoke so softly to him these days, like he was trying to gentle some half-wild creature. *Appropriate,* Guyon thought. *Because I feel half-wild, torn and exhausted with all this...trying.*

For a moment, his mind went blank, before he dredged up a smile, wondering, as he always did now, why it made Peter look away. "Swimming," he said. *Oh God, the lies of omission never stop.* "I'm not really sure why."

"Do you like to?" Peter sat down next to him. "We did all the time when we were young. There's a lake not too far from Hawthornden. The water is like ice at times, but it never seemed to discourage us."

"Yes, I like to." The smile felt a little more natural, this time. "It was...rivers, for us. Well, you've seen them." *I think that was the closest I have ever come to being allowed to be happy with you.* "I like to," he repeated, feeling as if even this much conversation was an effort he was incapable of.

"I wonder where there is around here..." Peter's voice trailed off, but then he continued, as if a swimming spot were one of the most important things he could consider at the moment. "It's too cold for you now, of course, but come next summer... I'll ask some of the children, they'll be the one's who'll know. They always do."

"And probably don't find it too cold until it freezes over," Guyon agreed. He wished he felt capable of suggesting something to do, some topic of conversation, something to keep the ebb and flow between them smooth, but he felt distanced, still, and isolated, his mind aching with every carefully chosen word. His hand throbbed incessantly, the effort of concealing the very real pain draining him of all ability to think or act as he knew he should.

It was like being silenced, like being gagged, knowing that his instinctive movements, to touch, to reassure himself of reality, all the small necessities that he had come to take so for granted, were blocked to him now.

Peter was saying something else, a question in his tone, and Guyon gave up trying to participate. "Yes," he agreed, hoping that the answer was not expected to be the opposite. "Of course."

*

Brocéliande, Brittany, September 1646

Tis true our life is but a long disease,
Made up of reàl pain and seeming ease.
You stars, who these entangled fortunes give,
 O tell me why
 It is so hard to die,
Yet such a task to live!
If with some pleasure we our griefs betray,
It costs us dearer than it can repay,
For time or fortune all things so devours,
Our hopes are crossed,
Or els the object lost,
 Ere we can call it ours.

It was Peter's considered opinion that the sooner things could be brought back to normal for the two of them, the better. If Guyon were to be comfortable and relaxed in the knowledge of Peter's love and Peter's acceptance of his own affections, it would make dealing with the changes in their lives just that much simpler. Fewer distractions meant they could concentrate on bringing Guyon back to his full health, rather than conflicts and recriminations.

Of course, with Guyon, nothing was ever simple.

Or, if it was, Peter always had the edgy feeling that somehow, he was getting everything wrong.

In this case, it would have been easier if he had been *told* he was getting things wrong, instead of being forced into a series of deductions that were all probably more inaccurate than his original set of premises, and all compounded by the fact that Guyon, in direct contrast to what *was* normal for him, seemed to be prepared to agree to anything Peter wanted.

Would Guyon like to go for a walk? Yes, of course. Would Guyon care for some lunch? He could eat something, if Peter was hungry. Would Guyon like to go over the books with him? Yes, he'd be delighted to have a look.

It was worrisome...and almost a little frightening.

The other aspect of it, which Peter took just that little bit too long to realize, by which time Guyon had obviously managed to convince himself of some God-knew-what insane idea about *concealment*, was that it seemed as though everything in the damn world required two fully functioning hands.

Such as going over books.

Or getting up from an armchair.

Or, in Guyon's usual way of over-emphatic, gesture-punctuated conversation, talking. Which probably explained why he wasn't doing very much of that, either, at the moment.

"I'm tired of this," Peter finally announced, closing the leather bound ledger and looking at Guyon with a sigh. "I can think of at least two dozen things I'd much rather be doing. How about you?"

And that look, at least, was easily definable. Total panic usually was, and Peter was trying to remember the last time he had seen that expression on Guyon's face, because it was actually *familiar*, and Guyon didn't panic. He shouted, he lost his temper to one degree or another, he flayed unfortunate souls who had got too close to him alive, just with words, and he definitely worried, even if he hid it with furious sarcasm. But panic? Until then, Peter would have sworn it was an alien emotion to him.

Apart from when he's trying to tell you something about demons in the middle of the night.

Oh hell.

"Guyon," Peter slipped closer, moving slowly and deliberately. He slipped gentle arms around his beloved, relieved on his own part that he could call him that again. "You know that I'm not expecting anything from you right now, don't you? Things won't get better over night, I know that. You know that. But they will *get* better...eventually."

"Mm." It wasn't - *quite* - an agreement, but at least it was very much Guyon, and not an anxious, obliging facsimile of him. "Yes. Sorry." He made a wry face, as though he had bitten into a disguised lemon. "I'll learn to use other words, eventually."

They both pretended not to notice the small flinch back from the idea of *using words*.

"I'm sure you will," Peter tried for a tease. "If you were so constrained I'm sure, eventually, the top of your head would fly loose from the resultant pressure."

It earned him a brief, flickering smile, at least. "So what were these two dozen things?" Guyon asked, straightening. "I'm hoping, by the way, that one of them *isn't* riding, because *no*."

"Not horses, at least," Peter's lip twitched but he did not pursue that train of thought any further. "A glass of cool cider and a long nap seem to top my list at the moment. Care to join me?"

"It's Ragnarok," Guyon said. "You're *advocating* inactivity? And that was *not* a criticism. Just surprise, because yes. I would."

"Mmmmm..." Peter smiled happily, nuzzling down into Guyon's neck. "You go on up...I'll get the cider and meet you there." His voice was a almost a purr.

Guyon relaxed, briefly - too briefly, damnit - before the faint, edgy anxiousness was back, and he nodded, moving away. "I - right. Yes." He made a vague, awkward gesture with his good hand, and then left the room, walking slightly carefully, as though expecting to lose his balance, or something to attack him as he went.

Peter sighed softly as he watched him go. This was going to be more difficult than he had expected.

*

When Peter arrived upstairs a few minutes later, cider in one hand, cups in the other, it was not, as he had hoped, to find Guyon relaxing. Rather than having kicked off his boots and flopping down in the middle of the bed with a book, which would have been his normal reaction to the suggestion of rest or a nap, Peter found him standing, somewhat stiffly, in the middle of the room.

He was staring at the bed, an odd expression of worry and fear on his face, his bottom lip red, Peter was sure, from being bitten. He held his injured hand against his chest, the rest of his body wrapped around it protectively. It was a stance so unlike him that Peter found himself paused in the doorway, half embarrassed at catching him in such a raw state. It seemed wrong somehow to see so much of his beloved stripped away.

Clearing his throat noisily, he put a smile on his face and

entered the rest of the way, "Here now. Cider good and cold. "

Guyon started slightly, his expression of worry smoothing out into a small smile at Peter's voice, but his stance did not change. Either he was completely unaware of it, or it had already become second nature to him - a kind of self-containment that he had somehow arrived at as a last bastion against the world. "Do we actually have things here that *don't* involve apples?" he asked, his voice a little raspy.

"Apparently, not much," Peter said softly. "I mean...as far as local drink is concerned. Would you rather have wine? I could go -"

He waved vaguely back at the door, but didn't really want to go. Not that he minded the errand, but Guyon standing like that was almost frightening in an odd and disquieting way.

Guyon shook his head. "No. Don't -" He stopped, shaking his head, and looked down at his hands, moving them away to his sides almost angrily. "I just wondered. I wasn't complaining."

"And I was just offering," Peter said softly and moved to fill the cups, offering one to Guyon. "In another few weeks they'll have the harvest and the pressing. If you're tired of apples now, you'll hate them by the time that's done with."

"No." Guyon shook his head, his smile a little less like a shield this time. "I *like* apples, remember? It's - hm. A bit like luxury." His eyes gleamed with faint amusement as he took the cup." Better than olives, I think."

"Depends on what you want, I 'spect." Peter sat down, stretching his booted feet out in front of him. "Can't make oil from apples, after all."

"There's - probably a way," Guyon said, moving over to the window seat. It was familiar, it was *right*, Guyon preferred window-seats and always had, he always took the ridiculous and behaved as though it were possible, and yet his eyes kept asking *Am I getting this right yet*? and it was completely unnerving Peter. It was as though Guyon was trying to remember ways of behavior, to prove that he was himself - as though he were on trial, in some strange way.

Peter quirked his lips into the semblance of a smile , "Much easier to let apples be apples and olives be olives, don't you think?"

And you be yourself, Gui, please....

He would have paid money for Guyon to yell at him just then. To call him an idiot for some silly thing he'd said...or to touch him in that offhanded way he had, casual and yet so tender.

"Mm, but that would assume I *wanted* easy." Guyon put his cup down on the windowsill, looking out. "To be the inventor of apple oil - think there's money in it?"

"I suppose it would depend on its applications," Peter mused, attempting to relax into a somewhat more normal state himself. "Would you use it for cooking? Lubrication? Medicines?"

Guyon turned to look at him, his eyebrows starting to raise. "I'm almost afraid to ask what you'd be trying to medicate," he pointed out, and then - "Damn. I'm sorry, can you - no, never mind." He slid awkwardly out of the window seat, and went over to the bed, unfolding one of the blankets from the end with an impatient shake of his good hand and putting it around himself with a sort of haphazard precision that was almost funny. "Still cold," he said in wry apology. "Some things really *don't* change."

"I consider this a good thing," Peter stood and moved to Guyon's side, straightening the blanket with gentle care. "You could just get in the bed, you know? I did suggest being lazy and having a nap. You'd be warmer."

"Mm." It really *wasn't* agreement, that time. "I mean. Yes. I would be. But I can't -" Guyon rubbed the back of his good hand down his nose, sighing. "I don't *use* a bed, I haven't since we got here, the windowseat's better." And about the only thing that could be said in favor of that nasty little statement was that at least he hadn't moved away while making it.

"I don't...I mean I'll stay over there." Peter pointed back to the chair. "I didn't mean -"

Words, Scudamore, they really can help sometimes.

"Not that I don't want...when you feel better.. But not.... *Christ!* Telling me to shut up would probably be a kindness..."

Guyon looked at him in complete bewilderment. "It probably would," he said. "I was referring to the fact I can't get *out* of the damn bed without either screaming in pain or rolling onto the floor and trying to get up that way, which is really very undignified. What are *you* talking about?"

Peter could feel the flush of red as it traveled up his neck, "Well, I know how badly *I've* been sleeping and...." He cleared his throat, "I guess I just couldn't face the bed without you there and...The couch in the study isn't too bad really, just a bit short..."

And really, could he sound like anymore like an idiot?

"Um." Guyon's thumb had traveled to the corner of his mouth, and was pressing at a distinct twitch there. "Er, Peter, I thought you arranged these separate rooms so that you didn't *have* to share a bed. I've been rather looking at this damn thing as a living example of just how much you don't -" the humor died out of his voice and eyes. "Of what I'd lost," he added, more quietly. "At least I *fit* on a windowseat."

"I didn't claim there was logic in it. I'd just come in here at night...ready to sleep...and see that vast space and - " Peter shook his head. "I've missed you, Gui. Talking to you...being with you."

"I'm not much company at the moment," Guyon pointed out rather unnecessarily. "I - it hasn't been all that bearable on this side, either. Browne started to seem like - the ninth hell, actually, most uncomforting."

"You're all the company I could want, Gui." Peter said softly. "I'm a lunatic. I just want to sit here and look at you...have you close with no -"

Peter bit back the words, unsure of how they'd be taken.

"No what?" Guyon asked quietly. He didn't look mocking, or apprehensive, more as though he were unsure he were actually hearing what Peter was saying. His good hand stopped pressing at his mouth, and reached out to touch Peter's arm, instead. "No what, *chérâme?*"

"No fears." Peter said, "No locks." He drew a shaking breath, needing to get this out, get it said and get past it, "That almost killed me. My own damn fault, I know. I'm sorry."

"No. No, it's not - it *wasn't* your fault." Guyon, for once, seemed to be having no better luck with words than he was. "I - I'm used to being able to *retreat*. Into myself. Get away behind the walls in...in my mind. And I can't. I can't, they're gone. It was inexcusable, it's not an excuse, but - I was hurt, and I wanted to hide." He shrugged, lopsided and miserable. "It just seemed the only way. I know - I know it was cowardly. I know. I just - I just didn't think I could *survive* any more hurt. Any. So I -" He looked thoroughly miserable. "I'm *not* a good person," he finished apologetically.

"You did what you needed to do, Gui." Peter said softly. He understood that need, God, now more than he ever had before. He had been ready to lock a few doors himself, hide and not come out until everything stopped hurting. "It's done now though, I hope...but if you still feel like you need that...."

God, please say no.

He'd give Guyon his privacy. Give him whatever he damn well needed, but it would kill him just a little, every time he heard that lock click.

"It's done," Guyon agreed. "Done, and no, I don't need it, I certainly never wanted it, but - the walls - I can't seem to rebuild them. I'm sorry." He sighed. "I saw how you look at me now. I just - I can't be who I was. I *can't*."

"Then be who you are." Peter's voice broke. "That's all I want for you. But...do you think that whoever you wind up being...can still want me?"

It sounded pathetic and miserable, Peter knew, but he couldn't keep the words back. And there it was, as quick as the words, that fear, black and ominous as a storm.

"*That*," said Guyon, with the first faint return of the tones of bedrock certainty that were so much more familiar, "is the one thing everything else is changing *around*. Pèire - everything else that I have loved, and thought lost - Giri, my home, the Sorbonne, François - I could let go, or shut away. But with you - I couldn't. I couldn't stop loving, even when everything else crashed down and ended, I couldn't stop. *Want* you?" There was a sharp, incredulous break in the clear voice. "*Christ*. You *possess* me."

"*Thank, God.*" Peter almost gasped. He moved closer, gently wrapping his arms around Guyon. "I love you so much that -"

He had to stop there, the words catching in his throat. All he could do was shake his head and hold on.

Guyon, for once, made no half-embarrassed attempts to neutralize what had been said - *Christ! Sentiment!* - or to move

597

away. His only response was to hold on in return as well as he could, and the only sound that escaped him was a small sigh of pure, unmistakable relief.

*

It was sometime later that Peter managed to force himself to loosen his tight but careful grip from around Guyon. There were more things they needed to settle between them, but now he felt they had time. Time for decisions made with the sure knowledge that they would make them together. Less desperation, he hoped. Less sullen silences on both parts. More laughter. Hell, even more arguing would be a relief, a return to normalcy. But it would be the arguing of two people exercising their skills at debate and not that of two trying to wound the other before they could be hit themselves.

"Gui?" Peter questioned softly. "Will you move in here with me? Into my rooms, I mean?"

And there was the panic-stricken look again, but *thank God* it was at the bed itself and not at Peter. "Pèire..." *That's real, that's him, that's unfeigned, that's hope* - "I would, but -" His good hand came up again, to cradle around the wrist of the hurting one - *hurting, not damaged.* **Hurting.** "You'll have to help me up."

"You say that like you think I won't." Peter looked at him. "I will help you however I can. Whatever you need. Always."

Peter had been aching to do this. Every twitch of pain, every uneven step, every sad look that Guyon had given his bandaged hand had cut Peter to the quick. Damn pride and restraint, all of it had hurt him too. Not physically, of course, unless you counted the inability to sleep and the resultant foul moods, but a pain just as real, cutting into his heart as sure as a blade.

"You -" It was as though he had suddenly realized that to breathe was to kill something small and defenseless, seeing that look in Guyon's eyes. "Oh. I'm sorry, I should have - you don't *mind*?" There was no false modesty in the translucent eyes, only dawning, tentative wonder.

"Do I -?" Peter closed his mouth and then his eyes, wanting to be sure of his control when he next spoke. "I have done as much for strangers on the battlefield. How much more would I do for you? "

"Strangers on the battlefield," Guyon said in his driest voice, "have a tendency not to say things such as 'please don't let go.' If they do, I believe that something is amputated. Which I would rather not occur."

Peter didn't know whether to snort out a laugh, or a sob. This was what he'd been missing most of all, that dry acerbic wit. "If given a choice the doctor might go for that sharp tongue first in any case, so I doubt it's a worry."

"Christ's *sake*!" Guyon looked, for a moment, as though he were contemplating whether or not to replicate the problem of what to do with a sharp tongue, but instead he put his good hand back up to his mouth, and rubbed over it. "*Pèire*. I'm *asking*, damn you. I'm *asking*."

"Ask," Peter said simply. "Tell me what you need from me and it's done."

Guyon shook his head, his left hand unconsciously cradling the right. "Achilles lay in the ashes," he said, incomprehensibly. "Why should I think I deserve better?"

Peter stopped for a moment, a worried look on his face. This was Guyon at his most enigmatic and he wanted to get this right.

Nervously, he spoke at last, his arms outstretched in supplication, "Thou art my life, my love, my heart, The very eyes of me, And hast command of every part, To live and die for thee."

"B-bid me to live," Guyon said, and his good arm and his bad together knocked Peter's back to his sides, even as he hissed in pain at the awkward movement. "I - I give. I give. *Damn it*!" And then he was shaking, really shaking, not just from cold, but something beyond that, and Guyon, self-contained, utterly self-possessed Guyon, wrapped his good arm around himself, and lifted a face all furrowed and contorted with embarrassed grief when he said "Oh Pèire. I cannot turn Protestant. Forgive me?"

"Nor will I, Gui...but I will bid thee love, if you will allow me the same." Peter said softly. "Now come and rest. Our last few days have been...difficult. Let me warm you."

He waited for the inevitable squawk that always followed him trying to care for Guyon in any but the most superficial manner.

"If you could bear it, I would allow it," Guyon said quietly, and for the first time, Peter realized that the bright green of the eyes, the spark amidst the transparency, the little, personal, confident flame that he had once noticed, was not bright and burning for him *because he could see it*, but bright because the green was red-rimmed, and red-laced, and raw with tiredness. "I'm tired, Peter. I'm cold, and I'm so tired..."

Peter drew him over to the bed and sat him down on the edge so he could pull off the shabby boots. He also smoothed off the trousers and then gently helped Guyon to lay back on the bed before covering him with blankets. It only took a few more moments for Peter to remove his own clothes and slip in on the other side, taking care not to jostle Guyon too much. "Warm enough?'

He felt so awkward. He wanted to hold Guyon, touch him, reassure himself that they were there together at last, but he wasn't sure how to do it in a way that wouldn't hurt him or if Guyon were even ready for even that much intimacy between them.

Well, Scudamore, if you can tell him to ask, shouldn't you do the same?

Guyon nodded, curling up into a bundle of cloth and shivers, and then - "No. *No.* I don't mind idiocy, but - I'll be damned if I endure it without you! You never hated it before, what did I - oh. Well. I see." He pulled the blankets in tighter, and bit down on a corner.

Peter moved closer, "Let me...can I? *Damn.* I want to warm you, just...Tell me how to move, where I can put my hands and arms that won't hurt too much."

"I don't *care*," Guyon said rather desperately. "Agony is preferable to -" He turned, awkward and all limbs and joints, huddling into Peter and pushing his face, like a tired cat, into the crook of his neck. "I'm *cold*," he repeated exhaustedly.

This, at last, was something Peter knew how to do. He pulled Guyon's uninjured hand closer, lifting his shirt higher to it could rest against his warm bare skin. The injured hand he left in the space between them, it would be warm soon enough. He moved his legs tangling them with Guyon's chilled ones and his arms wrapped gently around him. "Better?"

Guyon simply made a small, cross, tired noise; and Peter, who was used to comparing him to anyone who was not a soldier, was suddenly and forcibly reminded of his long-ago lieutenant, lacking a leg and trying to convince *him* that all would be well.

But Guyon was not, never would be, and felt for him none of a lieutenant's responsibility. He said nothing of who to take care of, who to watch over, named no names. He simply stammered out - *Guyon. Stammering. Impossible.* - "Tell me you'll always love me, n-no matter what h-happens."

"I never stopped loving you, Gui. I never could." Peter took a deep shuddering breath. "I will always love you, no matter what."

And then he gave what Guyon *never* asked him for, "I promise."

I can give you this.

*

Guyon had not exaggerated how difficult it was for him to get up from the bed, and that he was leaving Peter's silent, sleeping comfort made it infinitely harder. But the pain...

His hand ached, his mind beat unceasingly. *Let me go. Let me go. Please.*

He looked at Peter's face, serene now with the smoothed-out placidity of deep sleep. *Have I told you? You are beautiful. Bèl-mi. The light and beauty of my eyes.*

Behold, thou art fair.

He did not want to leave. But he could not bear any of it - not the pain, not the regret, not the despair.

God. God.

He wants you to be what you were, can't you see that?

Too well.

I grow bored -

Oh Christ, Peter, even if you forgive me the seventy-times seven, I will never forgive myself that!

"I'm sorry," he whispered into the silence of the room, and held the door open, looking for one last time at all he had ever known of earthly joy. "I'm sorry."

He moved down the hallway in a strange form of trance, holding himself as still as he could, even as his feet placed themselves with precision.

The sleeping draught was already on his table, outlined in Breton moonlight.

Merlin's lake. Was that what he drank, did Viviane give him rest eternal with mandrake and hemlock?

Five measures to each vial.

Five measures more than I need.

He poured the contents into the pitcher of watered wine, and poured out a careful cup. *Henbane and mandragora, God bless all herbalists for their love of centuries-past efficacy.* The room was dark except for the moonlight streaming in, and he would not commit the final blasphemy of lighting candles, would not risk reaching out for all that had become his faith and his belief.

I am dead till I be -

"No," he said quietly. "No, no, no more. No more."

Light them for me later, Pèire. And forgive me.

The first cup was hardest, faintly bitter, drying his mouth - and after that, it was easy to swallow, and swallow, and long for something to quench his growing thirst.

Thirst for what? Love? That he had refuted, long before, from his brother first - *It is done. And so am I -* and then from Peter. *Not enough -* he had not lied the one time, but a thousand, with every breath he took from that moment on, he had lied, every time he laughed away some declaration of love, he had lied.

My only sins are lies of omission. He had lied with every word he had spoken, lied by living, lied by existing, by breathing, by writing, by teaching.

And if he had any sort of courage, he would have taken a knife, dear *God* he would have taken Corvay's dagger, and ended it.

But he was not, and never would be, that brave.

Forgive me.

*"But I do not seem as wretched
as I am, wherefore a great ill comes to me;
but God can't harm me more by death;*

and of that too I shall be glad..."

Peter had sent troubadours to sing that to him. Peter. Peter, who would mourn his death, even knowing what he was. Peter, who had contemplated the greatest sin because he thought his love was not returned. Peter, who had faced down and defeated the unforgivable, who always would, no matter what. "Of that too I shall be glad," he whispered. "I love you. Until death."

Something - demon or deity - should have responded. But there was nothing but silence.

"When I take a full view and circle of myself without this reasonable moderator, and equal piece of justice, death, I do conceive myself the miserablest person extant."

Montaigne knew nothing. He only had to survive loss.

I must....I cannot - live without all that others saw as being good in me removed. Better I lie dead at their feet than this. Death they could mourn. This living mockery of all they held dear is a travesty of a life, a travesty even of exile.

Were there not another life that I hope for, all the vanities of this world should not entreat a moment's breath from me.

He could not remember who had written that, nor why it mattered, nor why it had once been of such importance. It had, it had, but now all he could feel was the pure and desperate relief as he felt that his own breath was slowing, slowing. Soon it would stop. He drained the cup again.

"I love you."

Silence. He had spoken complete, finished, perfectly judged words into silence, and watched them held to be not enough

He wanted to say how much, how very much, for once, he wanted not to count, but -

That's not how it works, that's not how it is.

"I love you." The words were out of his mouth once more, held on dry lips before he could practice them, realizing that they were the last ones he would ever speak, and finding nothing more fitting to end it with. He tried to put the cup neatly on the table, wondered if he should try and reach the bed, but already his fingers were too heavy, his legs beyond his use, and he was wrapped up, wrapped up and possessed, possessed by memory and longing, possessed by no living man who could understand the meaning of his words, caught and bound on the dying sounds of the last syllable into all he longed for.

"You."

The cup fell to the ground.

*

The room was a soft diffused blur, lit only by the light of the fire. It seemed almost foggy...so foggy that Peter wasn't sure exactly where he was - the Hôtel, Brocéliande, or maybe his old rooms at the Louvre. The window was open, so maybe the night mists had simply drifted in, the fire not enough to hold them at bay. Guyon was standing before the fire, one arm draped along the mantelpiece as he stared into the flames. Peter was for some reason sitting in a chair rather than in bed where he last remembered being.

"You'll always see me like this, you know?" Guyon spoke softly, half turning toward Peter. "Just like this."

The breath caught in Peter's throat as he realized that, instead of being covered in leather and clutched against his chest, Guyon's right hand was whole, bare and stretched out towards him.

"It's impossible, you know?"

Impossible, but true. That was how Peter saw him. Perfect in body as well as in mind, no matter what damage he had been dealt. "That's because I love you."

"I know." Guyon said simply. "You love *this* me."

"I love all of you. Any of you." Peter said it again. "You just have to let me."

"But it's gone, Peter." Guyon's voice was calm, "Nothing you feel or believe can bring it back because the bell is gone."

"The bell? What bell?" Peter was completely confused now. "What do you mean?"

"None of it matters. I no longer matter." And with that, somehow, Guyon walked into the flames. Peter tried to go after him, drag him out of the consuming blaze, but found that he was tied to the chair. Heavy coils of rope held him fast, and chains locked him in place.

"No, Guyon! You can't do this! You won't do this! I refuse to allow it!" There was a sudden flash of darkness, the flames were replaced with another view; Guyon's bed chamber.

Guyon stood at the side of his bed, cup in his hand. He was taking long draughts of the liquid and refilling it from a pitcher he held in his other hand.

"Of that too I shall be glad," Guyon whispered. "I love you. Until death."

"Guyon, what are you saying?" Peter hissed, still struggling against his chains. "I can't be without you. Remember Montaigne - 'All things being by effect common between them.' All things, Guyon. Our thoughts, our judgments, our honor and our lives...as if we had only one soul between us. That's how it's been for us. How it will be. I can't deny it, no matter what has been said."

"Montaigne knew nothing. He only had to survive loss. I must....I cannot - live without all that others saw as being good in me removed. Better I lie dead at their feet than this. Death they could mourn." Guyon's voice was flat and dull, despite the harsh words.

"What are you doing?" Peter continued his struggles. "What – what are you -?"

"It was easier when only a string held you, wasn't it?" A familiar voice came from the shadows, as Peter struggled against his bonds. "Easier to escape and lighter to be held. *This* binding is far more difficult than physical bonds. Will you tell me the moment you knew that *he* lived?"

"François?" Peter looked around frantically. "François... you've got to help him. You must. Help me. Please."

"Gladly," the tone was half-way mocking, and oh so familiar. "Just bind him to you, leather and string, heart *and soul.* You're a smart fellow, Scudamore...you'll see the way."

"François! Please..." But the presence was fading, and with it the room - all going dark and cold, covered in mists.

*

Peter rolled over, mostly asleep, and cold. It wasn't unusual, he often kicked off the blankets during the night and had to look for them as he cooled off. He reached out one hand, feeling blindly for the edge so he could snuggle back into the warmth, but he found nothing

Nothing?

No blankets, no warmth, and no Guyon.

He sat up immediately, gazing around the dim room, "Gui?"

This was a puzzle, especially since Guyon had told him how difficult it was for him to get in and out of bed. Perhaps he had awakened in pain and had gone off quietly to find his medication, rather than waking Peter up.

"Idiot."

Given the way Guyon had veered between a desperate need for comfort and an unhappy adherence to what little independence he had remaining to him - *what kind of fool sleeps in a windowseat when they're ill and hurt anyway?* - it made a strange kind of sense that Guyon would choose to exercise one of the more difficult sides to his nature in the middle of the night. Sense, that was, if one had dealt with prolonged exposure to Guyon's foibles in the past. With a sigh, Peter got up himself, and went to see exactly what point his errant lover had got to before his body had let him down *this* time.

This was his payback, he knew, for those miserable weeks after Toulouse. He had tormented both François and Guyon horribly with his refusal to take Vincennes' potions and drugs. Fought them even. So this? No surprise that Guyon was just as stubborn as he had been, it was only his due.

He wandered down the hall, watching the shadows in case they held Guyon's form. He found nothing though and was now approaching the door to Guyon's room.

The door was open a small crack, clear sign that Guyon had got that far, at least. *And probably taken whatever David's dosing him with, and gone to sleep. Goats have more sense. Tree-climbing Moroccan goats have more sense.* He sighed, and pushed the door open.

"Guyon? Are you in -" His eyes took in the cup, laying on the floor. Then, just past it, a bare foot. "Gui?"

He moved forward and knelt down beside the too still body. "Guyon?" He reached out one hand, and gently shook him.

There was no response, and Guyon's body rocked bonelessly under his ministrations. "Guyon!!"

There was no response. No irritable, confused mutter, or slurred complaint of cold, or startled, slitted eyes squinting in perplexity at him, in silent demand that he explain what, exactly, was wrong with him. Nothing. Even the gloved hand was left unprotected, lying by Guyon's side instead of against his chest as it always was, now.

Peter shook him again, harder this time, but there was still no response. It was only the fact that he could see the very slow but steady rise and fall of Guyon's chest that kept him from panicking completely.

He looked around the room then, saw the empty vial and the empty wine bottle on the table, near the bed.

There was no way that this was an accident. Guyon had tried - No, he wouldn't do that. He'd told Guyon that he accepted his love. Told him that they needed to be together. Surely Guyon wouldn't have tried to - His mind recoiled at the thought.

No. No. He couldn't have driven Guyon to this by his delaying.

"David..." He'd go get David.

He didn't stop to think that David would be about as pleased to have someone crash into his room in the middle of the night as any other normal man - which was to say, not at all, and justifiably not. But when he yelled David's name, the responding howl of fury and startled pain was Henri's. The all-too naked body he could see, however, was definitely David's.

Peter grabbed his arm, tugging unceremoniously toward the edge of the bed, "Come on. It's Guyon. He...he won't wake up, David. He..." Even in his urgency, it was more than he could bear. Fear, pain and guilt caught him all at once, in a breath that felt as though it were being dragged over shards of broken glass. "Hurry, please..."

"Ah, *what*?" David looked utterly befuddled, and it was Henri who moved, still rubbing the inside of his thigh and pulling on a shirt as he did so.

"*Move*," he said, shoving David towards the door.

"Clothes!"

"David!"

"Jesus, you're all mad..."

"Hurry..." Peter pleaded. He rushed ahead, wanting to get back to Guyon as soon as possible, just in case...just in case...No. Nothing was going to happen. It couldn't. He wouldn't even think of it.

He dashed back into Guyon's room and gathered him up into his arms.

"Peace, tranquility, bloody poppies, what do I get? Apples and you three..." David was into a full-on grumbling session when he arrived seconds later, still naked. He grabbed Guyon's hooded cloak from the hook by the door, and wrapped himself in it, his long bony legs sticking out at the bottom and looking decidedly ridiculous. He moved quickly, however, checking the vial on the table and the pitcher, and sniffing at the dregs, before pouring them onto his fingers and tasting the drops. "I don't know what he meant to do," he said more quietly, "but all he's done is guaranteed himself a long nap and a headache."

"Thank, God." Peter's exhortation was a pained gasp as he rocked Guyon in his arms. "He was so still...I thought -"

He couldn't say anymore, just sat silently, waiting for the accusations he knew he deserved. This was his fault. He'd not convinced Guyon. He'd waited too damn long. He didn't know what to do now. Surely, this would be it. His stupidity had done this to the strongest, most intelligent man he knew, and there was to be no forgiveness.

But the accusation that did come was not aimed at him, and was utterly unexpected. "*Did you know*?" Henri spat out. He should have looked as ridiculous as David, dressed only in a shirt, but somehow he didn't. Anger came off him in waves. "David! Is that why you gave him so little each time?"

"I knew it was possible." David's chin came up sharply, but no scholar of Magister Benichou's could be outfaced, and while it was easy to forget where Henri, the organist of the Richelieu Chapel, had studied years before, he had nonetheless once been a member of the most unholy Trinity the halls had ever produced, the boon companion of François Villon and Guyon de Chesnay. François, who was dead and lost to them all, and Guyon, who had been trying to lose himself, and the only one left capable of communication in this hideous moment was a blazingly angry Henri, realizing that he could have been left behind.

"Possible," Henri repeated flatly then, and the scintillating, astounding rage was swallowed up in soft disbelief. "*Right*." He turned around, and knelt down beside Peter. "*Christ*, Peter. Are you all right?"

"Am I -?" The kindness broke down the last of Peter's reserve. Was *he* alright? Was *he* alright? No...and he'd not be alright until Guyon awoke and settled his life for him. Told him to go. Told him he'd hate him. Told him to stay. "Henri...."

Peter could say no more than that, his face buried against Guyon's curls as he choked on fear and misery.

Henri made a small, pained sound beside him, and put a hand on his shoulder, offering up his silent presence in a peculiar kind of comfort. He stayed there, saying nothing, neither waiting for some kind of response nor demanding anything, and did not take his hand away.

*

Guyon had thought to wake in a torment beyond anything he had experienced, something surpassing human understanding, and yet, God willing, an agony removed from life even if perpetual.

Instead, he felt as though he had drunk heavy wine all night and slept for two hours, his head thick and painful and sluggish, his limbs weighted and aching.

I'm alive, he thought in horror. *Dear God. I failed. I'm alive.*

His second thought was, *I can't move.* And a sudden fear crossed his mind that his failed attempt had, somehow, left him paralyzed and more damaged than he had begun. But no, he was just covered, weighted down by the heaviness of Peter's body draped over his own.

Christ. Oh Christ. All that he had been unable to bear any longer, magnified and enhanced and terribly *there*. And he was still the same mutilated, fragmented mockery who should not have existed.

The thought was intolerable, drawing a small tight gasp from his throat that he stifled as quickly as he could.

Peter's grip tightened around him, but his eyes didn't open. He looked, Guyon thought suddenly, strangely diminished, as if he had shrunk somehow, or caved in on himself.

"Pèire?" He wondered just how bad this was going to be. Not only a failure, but a breathing reminder of inadequacy, of all that he had wanted to escape, of all that he had forced on Peter and now would be unable to evade.

There was no reply but a soft whimper and a shaky intake of breath. Peter's face was blotchy and creased from laying against his shirt.

So the failure had been that costly. He supposed failure was hard for a man like Peter to accept, even if he could have never been in doubt of what he had attached himself to. *I'm sorry. I couldn't even give you this. I couldn't even die.*

Peter's eyes suddenly flew open and he lifted his head, "Guyon? You're awake? Thank God. I... I almost lost you. I never want... *Christ.* I'm never leaving you alone again. What did I do? What? I tried, but it was wrong. So wrong obviously. And God...don't leave me."

Guyon heard the words, and made no sense of them. Recriminations and accusations he had been half-ready for - but aimed at him, blame placed where it should be, not this nebulous self-accusation. "You?" he managed. "You *didn't.*"

"I know I didn't. I'm sorry.... So sorry." Peter closed his eyes as if struggling for words. "But I tried. I'm just... I didn't do it right. Didn't use the right words. Didn't give you what you needed. Waited too damn long."

Guyon didn't understand. "Waited?" His mind was still fogged, thoughts swimming through it with unpleasant, syrupy slowness. "For what?"

"To tell you. None of it matters. None of it. Change. Stay the same. None of it. " Peter's voice cracked.

Guyon's heart beat more quickly, real physical pain attacking him before he was ready to withstand it. "But you - you were going - you kept giving up - *what?*"

"No! Never leave unless you sent me... But you tried and... not even friendship remained. But not now. You told me. Don't

610

take it again. Please." Peter blinked -*were those tears* - as he finished his rambling, disjointed plea.

"Peter. Peter. Take what? My life? You didn't want it, what else should I do?" Guyon wished he had used the dagger, used a gun, used *anything* but his craving for sleep, and been safe from this. "What *else* should I do?"

"I want it. I thought I told you. Christ... I know I'm not good with words but -" Peter closed his eyes for another long moment. "I love you. It's not worth much, but I do. And if you want me to go, I'll go. And if you want me to stay, I'll stay. But you said – you said -"

It was odd, how a full grown man could suddenly sound like a small lost boy.

"You said you wanted me..."

"I *do*!" The words left Guyon before he could think about how contradictory they must seem beside his recent actions. "That's why I can't go on. I *do*. Your love - it's worth everything, and I can't keep...*wasting* it on someone I'll never be again!"

"I don't understand." Peter looked desperate. "I don't know what you mean.   I don't know how to show you what - Tell me. Just don't - God, tell me what to do."

"I can't. I don't - I can't." *I can't.* "I don't even know what to do for myself. I *failed* at the one thing that had some purpose. I love you so much, *too* much. You keep giving everything up for me, and it's all - it's more than I can bear."

"What do you think I've given up?" The desperation gave way to confusion. "Nothing I could possibly have given up could mean more to me than you do."

"But it's *not me*!" Guyon had caught Peter's desperation, it seemed, giving his own muddled thoughts over in exchange. "Peter, please. Understand this. I *can't* mean anything any more, I'm *dead.*"

"No! I don't know why you're doing this...why you're saying this." Peter was moving back toward frightened.

"Because it's true! You want things to go back, the way it all was - and it's *not possible*, because I killed it. When I said those things - Jesu, didn't you listen to me in the Languedoc? - I planned them, I chose them carefully, I *knew what I was doing.*

And I can't forgive *myself.*"

"*I* forgave you."

"I know." He was never going to make Peter see that this was the unkindest cut of all. That he had forced Peter into having no choice but to forgive the truly unforgivable.

"But you have no idea why, do you?" Peter said, soft and uneven.

"No." It was never going to stop, this pain of incomprehension. *I am dead after all. I am in the hell I imagined.*

"And I suppose saying, 'Because I love you' is not going to be enough?"

Guyon, mute, shook his head. He wanted to agree, wanted this to be explicable, wanted to tell Peter that of course, yes, it was. And to the man of the journey from the Languedoc to Paris, who had not stood in front of the English Marshal and lied to him, the man who had never turned his scathing fury outward onto the only thing he cared for, it would have been.

Peter sighed and stood up, "Guyon, do you trust me?"

"You know I do." Guyon felt numb, his mind empty of everything but defeat.

"Do you think I would lie about this?"

Guyon shook his head again. *The problem is you never lie.*

"Then look at me now, and know I am not lying." Peter commanded him, standing next to the bed and looking down. "I love you. I *know* you love *me.* You are my very heart and if you take that...if you go...you will take it with you. I will never love anyone but you...my most beloved and irritating friend. The you that was. The you that you think you are now. The you that you will become tomorrow. That's how it is and will *always* be."

Guyon opened his mouth to protest, and closed it again on the simple, choking fact that it was true. It was true because how could he feel that and deny that Peter did? Or, conscienceless, decide only he was capable of those emotions, those beliefs? *It's always been true. It's you who's refusing to see. Not him. It never was.*

I'm damaged. Irreparably.

And it makes no difference to how he feels.

He took in a small breath, feeling it ache in his throat and trickle, painfully, into his lungs. "Yes," he said at last. It was all he could manage, a single croaked syllable.

"And you'll stay here with me? And no more...." Peter stopped as if he couldn't pass the words from his lips. "You'll stay?"

"Yes." That time was easier, though without the stranglehold on his vocal chords, he was beginning to feel just how bad an idea drinking the entire vial of sleeping draught in a pitcher of wine had been. There would actually have been advantages to death, in comparison.

"Good." Peter gave a relieved looking nod. "Now...drink this."

This was water, sweet and pure, a balm to his throat. "David says that will help wash everything away."

"Oh *God*," Guyon said with feeling. "David *knows*?" He was starting to reconsider the idea of hell - and would have said something to that effect, except for the way Peter looked, his determination a very thin veneer over the still-remaining desperation.

"'M sorry..." Peter muttered. "I found you. Probably scared him, and Henri, out of several years growth, bursting into their room like that. And...um...David's a lot thinner than I would ever have thought."

The joke might have been inappropriately timed, but it was an attempt at normalcy, that Guyon appreciated.

"*How* much thinner?" Guyon asked with morbid speculation. His head was pounding with a precisely vicious ache over his left eye. "You don't need to apologize, though I think I do."

"Only if you feel you must," Peter muttered. "And as for David...you *do* remember the horse I brought back from Toulouse?"

"Vividly and rather unpleasantly, yes," Guyon said. "Do you think you could sit down? Only tilting my head up is harder than it really should be."

Peter eased back down on the bed. "David is almost that bone thin...and Henri...he's not very happy with me either."

"Because you...interrupted them?" It was unlike Henri to be annoyed about that sort of thing, but given the atmosphere recently, Guyon could well imagine that the last thing Henri had wanted to deal with was the results of another of his failures.

"Um, no. Because I startled David and he bit Henri in a rather sensitive spot. Look, Gui, I know I'm babbling like a lunatic and none of this is important and the only reason I'm doing it is because you scared the shit out of me and I'm still so keyed up that my mouth is running away with me. " Peter took a sighing breath. "I know we have a lot of hard work between us. Just tell me that you think we can do it. That you're willing to try."

Was that it? As simple as that, to try, even to agree to try, and have it be preferable to the long peace and the blankness he had craved? Guyon did not think for a moment that he had increased in worth, that he was any less of a failure, that what he had said and done was in any way ameliorated - but *Peter did*. And in the end, that mattered more than his despair. "Yes," he said. "I do. I am. I *will*."

"Then that is enough," Peter carefully stretched out on the bed next to him, one hand twisting in the tail of Guyon's shirt. "I've got no string, y'see...until you put it back on me."

String. The little piece of knotted string that had started all this and damn near finished it as well. "You'll. Have to get some." Guyon whispered, and was intensely proud of the fact he had managed words. He certainly couldn't manage a smile, or a joke. "I love you." Which managed to be both true and sublimely irrelevant all at once. He was almost impressed with himself.

"I know," the simple words rang with truth as the two of them relaxed into sleep.

*

"Mmmgh, cold." Peter grumbled several hours later. The late afternoon sun shone in the windows but gave no warmth to the room. Some how, as usual, all the blankets had been dragged away from him and were now wrapped firmly around Guyon in an odd sort of cloth cocoon. He found it somehow endearing, although a bit inconvenient since he couldn't, just now, jerk them away as he usually would, pulling blankets and Guyon back to his side of the bed in a tangled but comforting heap.

The cocoon twitched. It didn't seem very likely to hatch any time soon, given Guyon's loathing of being disturbed out of warmth and comfort, but then there was an indistinct mumble from inside the layers, and a far more distinct curse. "'M stuck," Guyon said irritably and clearly.

"Oh..." Peter moved at once to gently disentangle him, peeling the layers back as if removing the skin from a delicate, easily bruised piece of fruit. "Alright?"

"Mm." There was still some of that frozen distance in Guyon's eyes, mingled with sleepy, slightly pained annoyance. Then his expression cleared, warming into familiar, wry amusement. "Did I leave you to freeze again, bèl-mi?"

"As always," Peter chuckled, then straightened the blankets and settled himself against Guyon's warmth. "But that's alright. It's the only time I get to wield my vengeance by sticking *my* cold bits against *you*, with no guilt."

"Guiltless vengeance, I'll have to try it some day." Guyon shifted, accommodating Peter as best he could without jarring his hand

"Gui?" Peter spoke his name questioningly, then hesitated. The walking on egg shells feeling was still there, even with their renewed understanding. He still felt the pressure of *getting this bloody well right, damn it.*

"Yes?" There was the same faint worry under the light question, proof that Guyon was not as unmoved as he so often seemed.

"I'm glad you're here." Peter felt almost pathetic in his raw honesty, but he had to say it. Had to be sure that Guyon knew it.

"I - good?" Guyon's voice was unexpectedly tentative, closing over a world of unspoken fear that Peter knew he would never be allowed even to guess at, let alone enter, if Guyon had his way. Considering where that had almost led them, it wasn't a practice he felt even vague tolerance towards.

"But -" Peter took a deep breath, moving to hold Guyon as tight and as close as he could. " -you need to stop doing that. You need to stop being afraid of telling me things. You need to know - *to know, Gui* - that nothing about you is frightening to me.

Nothing about you will drive me away. You said you trusted me." He didn't say it, but he begged it just the same; *prove it.*

"I do." Every time, it was a surprise at how quickly Guyon said that - and a relief. "I'm...working it through. I - I'm glad to be with *you*. But here? I'm still not...I don't know. I *meant* that damn stuff to be final. I know I shouldn't have - but I did, and I can't...I can't make it so I never felt that." He was shivering a little, by the time he finished.

"I'm not asking that." Peter smoothed comforting circles over Guyon's hip. "Just don't shut me out. Let me help. Tell me what I can do and let me do it."

"I don't know what you can do," Guyon said helplessly. "Resurrect Corvay so I can kill him *myself*?"

"Not even for you, *chér*," Peter grumbled softly, trying to joke off the feeling he had at even the mention of the man's name.

"No, I know." Guyon's voice softened into apology. "Do you remember what I once said about how it felt - to have choices taken from me? I feel as though every time I claw back a little belief that I *can* choose, and every time I try, something - something appalling happens. Or I *do* something appalling. I thought - after the Languedoc, I really thought -" His voice shook, and steadied. "I thought I would be allowed just that small joy. And I took it away and did what I've always accused you of doing - I took away the choice for both of us because I was afraid. I did *everything* I hate others doing. It's so hard to live with that." It might have sounded self-pitying, but for the faint trace of disgusted wonder to the words.

"No..." Peter hushed him softly. "You did what you thought was best, Gui. I...I might have done the same."

But he couldn't have. He didn't have it in him to tell such a lie, he knew. He would just have left Guyon without a word, probably, and gone to his supposed death. The same in the end though, leaving Guyon behind to pick up the pieces.

"No, you wouldn't." There was a sudden shift in Guyon's tones, into deep affection. "You aren't capable of causing that kind of pain. But then - no *sane* man is." There was no horror in his voice as he said what they both knew, only a kind of disconsolate resignation.

"I would have done it differently, yes.... But it would still have been done." Peter told him. "You remember Argenteuil, I'm sure."

He had taken Guyon's place on a dangerous mission. Well, a mission that was supposed to be dangerous, but turned out to be just another one of Corvay's machinations. He had told the messenger that Guyon was not to be found, and went off in his place. He had not really expected to return.

"Yes. Which gives me even less of an excuse, considering my reaction." Guyon sighed, before a quirk of humor came into his voice. "Er, my *initial* reaction, that is."

"I think I far preferred the latter one," Peter relaxed slightly. "It was most...pleasurable."

That had been the first time they were together, kissing and touching. When Peter knew that his lust was not only that, but more.

"I wish..." Guyon started, and then stopped. "No, maybe I don't." He kissed Peter's shoulder. "Browne was right about love."

"Browne was right about a lot of things," Peter smiled, still remembering that first time together. "What specifically do you mean?"

"I love my friend before my self, and yet methinks I do not love him enough: some few months hence my multiplied affection will make me believe I have not loved him at all..." The words were still accented and slurred, but Peter suspected it was an enhanced version of Guyon's natural accent, rather than an inability to pronounce them, these days.

"That's all true, Gui. True for him, I'm guessing, and true for me." Peter raised one hand to Guyon's cheek, a small smile on his lips, "Does Browne comment on the stupid things we do to prove our love? Or to protect it?"

He knew the answer, but was trying to make a point that Guyon would understand.

"He doesn't get especially detailed about it," Guyon began, and then sighed and admitted, "Yes."

"And what does he say?" Peter caressed the cheek under his hand, feeling the scruff of beard against his palm.

"That we make our faith into a buckler and don't feel the edge of the sword when we turn it on ourselves in trying to protect the ones we love." Guyon pressed his face into the touch.

"We've both felt that blade. We just need to know how to recover from it. To not let the self-sacrifice become more important than the love."

"He doesn't say anything about how to do *that*." But there were traces of hope in Guyon's voice now, as well as the fear.

"Then we'll figure it out together." Peter's voice caressed as gently as his hand. "We always work best as a team."

Guyon nodded. His eyelids looked bruised when they lowered - David's solution had been too weak to kill anything but a sick cat, even taken in full, but it had been enough to put most people down into a heavy sleep for over a full day and night. Guyon had managed less than a third of that time in total. "Yes. I keep forgetting that, but yes. *Infinitely* better."

"You should try for some more sleep. We've an hour or two until dinner, I think." Or if not they could just hold the damn meal for them. "Your stomach should be able to handle food by then. I'll wake you when it's time."

"But you'll stay?" The question was almost inaudible, but it was something to pin another patch of his slowly rebuilding hope to, because Guyon had *asked*.

"Of course," he replied at once, "*if* you promise to leave me at least one blanket?"

"But I don't make promises," Guyon said mockingly, and while it might have been inward-turning, it was free from bitterness. "Though I can *intend* to leave you two. Being generous like that."

"Hmm." Peter gave a considering sound. "We'll compromise. I'll stay here, with my arms around you, and we'll share the blankets. Deal?"

"Perfect," Guyon said, and there was no trace of irony in his voice.

*

Feeling as trapped by his own desire to stop causing others pain as he ever had by Corvay's machinations, Guyon forced himself to experience to the full the physical and mental agony that he had tried with such determination to evade completely. He could have allowed himself simply to continue to drift back into sleep over the following days, let the last of David's mixture leave his system, and knew it would have been easier that way, that he could have created a little period of grace in which he did not have to consider what he wanted and what he had done. It would have been yet another act of cowardice, though, and he was not prepared to give in to that small seductive voice again, for that way led the oblivion he had longed for - and promised not to grant himself.

He had hated the drugs David had given to him in Paris, hated and feared the things they had done to him, both the lassitude and the terrifying, vivid sights of some Greek Hell that he was completely unable to bear. But the pain in his hand had lessened scarcely at all, and even the sleep David's potions had forced on him was not enough to quite kill it, the very real physical agony filtering through no matter what he did.

It was not only the unbearable knowledge of what he had done to Peter that had led him to attempt his own personal draught of Lethe, but the fear that the pain would never stop, that this was, now, to be his life, a succession of small and futile attempts to render even breathing bearable, a new set of evasions to undertake whereby he concealed from everyone how bad things were - hour by hour and throughout dragging, interminable minutes.

Despite his promise, it was becoming something he was unsure it was possible to continue.

"You're feeling it. You look...grayish." David Somers looked up from where he had just finished rewrapping Guyon's hand. "Really, you should do as I say."

"Mm. Your expertise, I hear, is woefully lacking in all things save a knowledge of my intent." Guyon, who had been told by a still livid Henri just what David had worked out before he had even decided it for himself, was in no mood to be kind or forgiving. It had been small consolation to him that Henri, who truly believed suicide to be the one unforgivable sin, was as angry with David as he was with him, and had not scrupled to express his feelings to either of them.

"So I have been told," David shrugged off the insult as easily as Guyon had given it. "But that does not make it correct.

"My intent? No, I've been told *that*, myself." Guyon glared at David until the guileless pale-blue eyes looked up at him. "You weren't even giving me enough to block me into sleep. So why should I listen to you, again?"

"Because I'm right." David snipped off the end of the gauze and tied it. "Because pain is a bad thing. And because you in pain is hurting Peter."

"I'll manage. It'll pass." He left unspoken *no-one has noticed until now, when Henri made you reassess your work,* and *I have to keep hiding this, I have to retain something that is a part of who I was.*

"No," David said simply, "it won't. You'll push and push and the pain will get worse until you can't hide it any longer." David turned, packing things into his bag. "Then Peter will want to force you to take the drugs...then he'll feel guilty that he did."

"I can't do anything about how Peter feels," Guyon said with perfect honesty. He couldn't. Every decision Peter had made, every change of heart and mind he had subjected them both to, had been entirely outside Guyon's influence. "And if you think he would force me to take whatever those hellish little concoctions of yours are, you are *very* wrong." He did not drop his gaze as David looked at him with a mixture of hurt and betrayal and real anger that hurt almost as much as though it came from Peter or Henri. "I don't trust you any more, David," he said then, spacing each word evenly. "I don't actually dare. You have *no idea* what those damn things did to me."

"You are wrong." David looked suddenly unlike himself. No more easy-going drowsy friend, but rather a stone-faced man with anger in his eyes. "I know exactly what they did. That's my job. I know you hated them, how you reacted, but I still know what they did."

"Did you," Guyon asked with his own cold rage, the one that had been building since he learned he could not touch Corvay, "design them specifically with me in mind?"

He had the satisfaction of seeing David blanch, and shook his

620

head wearily, schooling his expression into blandness. "Revenge, David?" he asked then, keeping his voice perfectly smooth and pleasant, utterly non-threatening. "I see. I do hope you found it sweet?"

"No, damn you." David dropped his eyes. "Because it only hurt him more. Hurt them both, really."

"I could have told you that it would do, if you'd asked," Guyon said. "You should have talked to Henri, at least, if not to Peter or to me. I still walk sanity on a thread, while overall you gained nothing and I lost very little, and the only ones to truly suffer were those you wanted to pay me back for."

David had little to say to that, "Will you tell them?"

"I never tell anyone anything unless I have to, do I?" Guyon pointed out, and then rolled his eyes impatiently. "*Obviously not*, since even if I don't much care whether you live or die, I do count Henri as a friend, and *he does*. And to be honest, David, I have not got the energy, these days, to deal with talking Peter out of what he will undoubtedly want to do to you in return."

A breathy grunt was the only reply to that, and the sound of David closing the latch on his bag with an audible click.

"I never wanted you to be hurt," David said quietly. "I just wanted you to feel some of the pain that you had given out. What I've given you since we arrived here has been correct. If you'd taken what I first tried to give you, it would have helped."

"*David*," Guyon said, and to his shame, his voice cracked. "Oh God, you idiot. Did I teach you nothing when you came to the debate classes? You cannot make someone feel pain without hurting them, that's the premise of every logical nightmare since debate began. You did nothing to me that wasn't already there. I saw nothing I did not already know, felt nothing I had not felt a thousand times over. You should have spoken to François, long before, and you should have *damn well put a thesis together before you started this*!" He rubbed his good hand over his face. "Come here," he said then, leaning forward in the chair.

David stepped closer warily, "I know that. I meant no *lasting* hurt. And yes, I was stupid and it was wrong. I.... I was very angry."

"Mm." Guyon gestured towards his shirt. "Pull it up," he said, hunching forward over his knees, making it clear what he expected David to look at, his back already exposed before the material was moved. *I am tired of causing this in others. I am tired.*

David's hands, usually swift and sure with things, hesitated before they drew the shirt up. He managed to hold everything in but a small hiss, before he released it the cloth, letting it flutter back down to cover Guyon once again. "What -?"

"That was what I came back from the Languedoc carrying." There was no way of making it kinder for either of them. "That was why I said what I did to Henri before he went to Rome. That was the *last* price I paid for my insanity. I was seventeen when that was done - and my brother did it. And that was what Corvay threatened Peter with, and why I lied. I *never* do anything without just cause or good reason, even if I keep those motives hidden from others. *Now* do you understand?"

"Christ...." David's face was covered with thoughts of horror. "No...I can see...*Christ!* "

"Make me walk the line of the diameter again," Guyon said coldly, sitting up, "and I'll kill you myself. Henri loves you and Peter likes you, but right now, I am *very* close to hatred." He smiled tightly. "The last man I hated rotted in the Carcassonne jail through the summer months. So don't expect me to trust you, David, and while I understand what you did? I won't forgive you for a long time. Because I saw Achilles flay himself alive in front of me, and Peter, as you know, is that and more to me. *You have no comprehension of what pain is to me.* Start praying that I never decide to teach you."

*

David Somers was not normally a cruel man, his actions toward Guyon notwithstanding, nor was he stupid. If he gave off an air of one who was in a drugged haze most of the time, it was more because if kept him from having to deal with a lot of unpleasantness. It also helped him control his temper, because if people did not take you seriously, neither did they attempt to confide in you about many things.

The only complete exception to this rule had been Henri de la Roche. From the first Henri had seen through David's little subterfuge, somehow knowing, without David giving him the least bit of encouragement, that there was more there than most people saw. It had made David hold him in highest regard before he ever knew he loved him.

Peter, although he didn't seem to be able to tell when David was drugged or sober, treated him with an indulgent friendship, almost as if it didn't really matter. As if he saw David's value even if he chose to escape reality on a fairly regular basis. That was more than David could resist, and put Peter second in his affections, only after Henri.

David could not stand the thought of either one of them being hurt. That had prompted his actions toward Guyon in the first place. But David now found himself shortsighted. His actions had actually been the ones to hurt both Peter and Henri.

Doubly unforgivable, then, and the more so because if Guyon had no love or indulgence for him, he had always granted him the kind clear eyes of reality, willing to grant him the harsh tolerance he did to so few, simply by virtue of the fact those he cared for wanted him to.

It had seemed like a Judas-gift, until now.

Will you tell them?

Obviously not.

Uncompromising did not mean unkind, but God, he would have given a great deal not to learn that fact by virtue of Guyon's moment of revelation.

There was nothing for that except for him to tell Henri. Not because he was afraid that Guyon would renege and do it, but because he should. And because if he did not, now, it would eat at him until Henri noticed and asked him. Then, he'd have to tell and watch those wonderful dark eyes turn hurt and scornful. He hated that, hated when he disappointed Henri. It didn't happen often, because Henri, thank God, did not expect too much from him, but when he did....

He hated it.

And hated himself worse.

"Brooding's catching, is it?" Henri asked, breaking off

623

playing as soon as David entered the room. "You brought a cloud with you, you'll warp my strings." He held out his hand, shifting over on the music stool. "Never mind, my dear, you're doing your best."

"No, I'm not!" David snapped out. "Or I wasn't. God, Henri, I've done the stupidest thing. Completely and horridly stupid."

"Uh-huh," Henri agreed. One hand rippled out a little stretched chord. His other took David's in his, and pulled him down onto the stool beside him. "That would be why I've been so annoyed with you."

"You're going to be more annoyed with me now," David managed. God, he didn't want to do this. "You...you might even hate me. I know I hate myself so it wouldn't be surprising, really."

Henri blinked. "All right," he said. "I can't really imagine anything that bad, but go on..."

"First...I...I never meant to hurt Guyon, not really....and I never wanted him to do what he did. Please tell me that you believe that." David's voice was desperate, only a few steps from begging.

"Yes, I *know* that," Henri said patiently, "I don't have to believe it. You wouldn't have done that to Peter, apart from anything else, so obviously." He turned sideways, taking both David's hands in his. "And if that's first, what's second?"

"In Paris..." David looked down at their joined hands, wondering how fast Henri would pull away when he told the truth. "...I purposely gave Guyon drugs mixed with aquavit, knowing how he reacted to it. And..." He looked up at Henri's face, expecting to see anger, at the very least, but instead found a sort of kind sad understanding, and Henri was neither letting go nor turning away.

"I know that," Henri said gently. "You might play the scatterbrain, but I didn't think you'd forgotten the funeral."

"No...but that's not all, Henri." David took a deep breath. "What I gave him was wrong. It drugged him but he still hurt. God, I wanted him to hurt. He'd hurt Peter so badly."

It sounded like a lame excuse now so long after the fact, but at the time it had seemed so utterly unfair that Guyon did such a thing to Peter. It had made him angry, so very angry.

"You gave him the wrong drugs," Henri repeated flatly. "In aquavit. Because he'd hurt Peter. David, I love you. I've sworn to God and man to love you until the day I die and beyond, but sometimes, you make my head want to explode, did you know that?" He didn't look angry, even now, simply bewildered and a little hurt, and trying very obviously to understand. "Why would you do such a thing to *anyone*?"

"I was angry. He'd...he'd just ripped Peter's heart out...like...like he'd done to you." And that was the crux of it, wasn't it? It wasn't really for Peter, but for revenge. Revenge and jealousy. Peter was just an excuse.

Henri opened his mouth, blinked, and closed it again. "I take you've learned it was nothing like at all?" was all he said, suspiciously mildly. "I *have* spoken to him since then, you know. He had his reasons - *aha*." All bewilderment vanished from his expression. "He *told* you. Well, well, well."

"He showed me." David said, closing his eyes again, momentarily. "How could we allow that to happen, Henri? How can the Church? I...I know I let him feel the pain...but I never would have actually damaged him."

"Because he's -" Henri sighed, and unexpectedly leaned in and kissed David. "I'm not angry," he said surprisingly. "He used to be this odd mixture of arrogant and vulnerable, and he was a walking prayer to be kicked. You just saw him reverting to that, that's all. I know you wouldn't have actually damaged him, if you'd known, but you're not here telling me because you let him feel pain, you're telling me because you're scared you *did* damage him." The dark, intelligent eyes were full of compassion. "You didn't, David. You couldn't. You didn't know him before he'd met Peter. He was broken a long, long time before you even met him - believe me, he's *better*, these days."

"Peter could do that. Could heal him." David looked at Henri, his eyes large and dark. "Make him whole...like you did me."

"*Is* doing," Henri said firmly. "So do us all a favor, please, if and as you love me, *and stay out of it*." He kissed David again. "Until you're asked," he added with a grin.

"I'll try," David said, his lip giving a small twitch of amusement. "Even though it will be hard. You do know what an interfering busy-body I am." Yes, between bouts of wanting the entire world to simply go away and leave him the Hell alone, of course. "And Henri?"

"The harpsichord lid will crack if we try," Henri said, his mouth twitching. "Oh, not that? What, then?"

David giggled delightedly at the thought of them on top of the harpsichord, "I love you."

Henri laughed. "Yes, and I love you, was there something you came here to tell me?" His eyes crinkled up into little slits of amusement. "Or were you just interrupting me because you and you alone can?"

"I've always felt it was in my best interest to exercise that prerogative whenever I could." David nodded solemnly. "It's always led to such delightful amusements."

"I'm so glad you enjoy it," Henri said agreeably. "Now kindly lock the door so we can go back to normal, would you?"

David Somers, in spite of the fact that he often gave the impression of one who was in a drugged haze most of the time, was no fool. He locked the door.

*

Usually, dinner was devoted to the sheer enjoyment of Peter's cook employing all his skills to tempt Parisian tastes. That said tastes were confined to a musician who never knew what he was eating, a herbalist who knew every detail, a soldier who simply did not care as long as it filled his belly, and a man who seemed to prefer fruit to real sustenance, did not seem to deter him for a second.

"You know, Guyon," Henri said one evening, "It would be *so* nice if you ate food and not sit here and pick at grapes. It makes me feel like a glutton."

Peter looked up from his contemplation of his wine glass with a gentle smile, "He's right, Gui. You've lost some weight as well. You should try to eat a bit more. Here...try some of this salmon."

Guyon made a face. "You actually *want* me to feed my brain?"

"Brain food and fodder." David suddenly chuckled, as he

stole a piece of chicken off of Henri's plate.

"Feed your brain, your body...hell, even your toes." Peter smiled at him. He really was concerned, Guyon had lost quite a bit of weight since they left Paris. Weight he could not well afford. "But eat."

"It feels like oil," Guyon said rather sharply.

"The food?" Peter looked at Guyon's plate and then his own. Not that he paid very much attention to what he ate, but it had all seemed fine - tasty and well prepared. "Would you like something else instead?"

"No, my hand," Guyon said. He sounded a bit surprised. "It goes in...waves. Like oil. And the grapes help."

Now Peter inspected the grapes. They looked perfectly normal from where he was. "The grapes help with what?"

"They cut through the...oil." Guyon made a small face at him. "Don't fuss, Peter. We knew it would hurt. But it *does sicken!*"

"I can't help but fuss if you hurt, Gui," Peter frowned and then turned to David with a questioning look.

David shrugged. "He wants to sleep, not be pain-free, and I'm no doctor."

"He's here, too," Guyon said acidly.

"Maybe we should have asked Vincennes to come along." As a thought, it was a good one, but as a practical plan it left something to be desired. Guyon barely allowed David to help him, he would have roasted Vincennes alive.

"Oh, *what* a lovely plan," Guyon said. "What did he ever do to you?" Even in the candlelight, he was horribly white. "Hm. Hate to ask, David mine, but is there something not of the opium-like character that stops the...oil?"

"Are you alright?" Peter stood up, moving closer to Guyon. "Maybe you should let me take you upstairs."

"I don't think upstairs will stop it," Guyon said with an evident effort at being kind.

"No.. but I think it might be better for you to lay down than fall down." Peter told him. "David, is there anything that will work better?"

David widened his eyes. "Why yes, little knight, many things!"

"Then why are you not giving it to him?" Peter frowned and looked at Henri for support.

"Because *he*," Guyon said with emphasis, "refuses it."

David made a face at him.

"That's ridiculous, Guyon. I won't have you in pain." The words were out before Peter even thought about them. "I mean...*Christ*. You know what I mean, Gui. There's just no sense in hurting when you don't have to."

"It makes me stupid," Guyon said. He looked utterly woebegone, white and tired and thin, and the only thing Peter wanted to do was hold him close and make idiotic promises about 'no harm to you, ever again'. He would, of course have been slapped, both hard and deservedly, but it was very hard to remember that this was the man who had defeated Corvay in every intellectual way possible, especially when he sat there all exhausted and leaning back in his chair as though movement was beyond him. "Please no?"

Peter understood the refusal, even if he hated it. In the days after Toulouse they had dumped innumerable drugs down his throat. They had taken the pain away, but left him groggy and unaware of almost everything. How could he send Guyon, for whom intellectual awareness had always been a matter of pride, into that dreary twilight world. "No one will force you, Gui. But you need to eat and... I won't let you waste away. I can't."

"It rolls up my wrist," Guyon said, as though no-one else were in the room. "It rolls up in waves, like some slick of nausea and slow pain, and I can feel the bones, and *nothing stops it.* And food makes it so much worse..." He looked up at Peter like a pleading child, his clear eyes begging *make it stop, make it stop.*

The sight made Peter want to cry, or tear his heart out so he would not feel his deficiencies. He wasn't a doctor and he wasn't sure what he could do. If there were any way, he'd take the pain for his own. But he couldn't. "I'm sorry...."

"Thou very idiot," Guyon said, amused and suddenly altogether himself. "What for? Because I hurt and am tired - *oh.*" He stopped and laughed. "Go and eat walnuts, gentlemen. *Now.*"

"But we want to see you capitulate," Henri said with enormous sincerity.

"I have, I do," Guyon responded. "Now go."

"Yes, maitre." Henri was laughing as he took David by the wrist and a bowl of fruit and cheese in the other hand, tucked two open bottles of wine under his arm, and towed his lover and his gains out of the room. "*Told* you he'd be all right..."

Peter watched them go with no little relief. As close as he was beginning to feel to the two after the last few weeks of Guyon's convalescence, this was a conversation they needed to have alone. And *Christ*, it was one he really did not want to have at all.

Guyon looked about as eager to have the conversation as Peter felt, his expression nakedly apprehensive. "I don't want opiates," he said abruptly. "I'm not losing my words again."

"Gui," Peter shook his head. "I don't blame you. I never *want* to have to take anything like that again, myself. But - if I need to, I will. Never casually. Not that. But in need." He moved closer to Guyon, brushing a thumb over the pale, pained, cheek. "I think for you. *Just now*. There may be a need."

Guyon shook his head. "I can bear it. It's only bad in waves, there are times it hurts less..." Even if Peter hadn't known a damn sight better than that from his earlier unguarded comments, the fact that Guyon was so unlike himself as to be pleading and looking close to tears with it was the equivalent of a placard around his neck that read 'I am no longer capable of making decisions for myself.'

But, *dear God*, how could he take that away? His riding rough-shod over Guyon's wishes had been one of the major stumbling blocks between them.

"Guyon, you need to do this. Just until you've healed somewhat...then it will be over." Peter drew a long shaking breath. "Please let me take care of you in this. Trust me."

He didn't even feel guilty for that blatant little piece of manipulation. Guyon's insecurities about showing Peter that he meant what he had said in the Languedoc and here in Brittany, and *not* what he had said in Paris, were simultaneously more convincing than anything he could have said, and a very, *very* useful weapon to hand when he was too tired to conceal them. Peter was prepared to use the final argument of 'if you really do love me,' if he had to, just so that Guyon would be forced into agreeing to take the drugs, and believing it was from a sort of choice. Resentment, Peter could and would deal with, if he had to. Guyon looking like a days-old corpse with the ague, he would *not*.

"Of course I trust you," Guyon said quickly. "If you think - I know you hate drugs. So yes. If you say it's necessary."

Thank God. And he'd worry about retribution and revenge - that Guyon would surely visit upon him when he was strong and well - at some later date.

"I think it is, beloved. As much as I hate it, I think it is."

Guyon made a small, wry face, that didn't do very much to conceal the way his mouth shook. "It frightens me, a little," he said in far-too-light tones. "I - I worry. What I might say. And I won't mean it, and they won't be my words, and -" he broke off, his face twisting. "Sorry. I - I just -" He shrugged, helplessly. "I'm afraid. Ridiculous, hm?"

"No," Peter tried to reassure him. Words were Guyon's strength, to lose them would make him feel like Samson shorn. It was a very real fear. "I know when I came back from Toulouse I must have said horrible things to you. There were things in my head that still haunt my dreams and I know they got tangled up and twisted with what was reality. Whatever you say will be taken as such by me, Guyon. I will understand."

"You just thought I was a murderous old woman," Guyon said with a flicker of amusement. "Oh, and Corvay. I must tell you, I wouldn't blame you for being insulted if I return that particular favor." He swallowed. "You...things seemed to be at least based in reality. In events." He cradled his hand to his chest, unconsciously protecting it. "When Vincennes let me have the drugs, after Ibn Ibrahim had -" He broke off. Even if Guyon had remembered that from a time when he was well and sane, there were still no words for what Ibn Ibrahim had done. For what David had exacerbated. "I know I raved, but - I saw Achilles. Mourning. I - I don't want to know what I said."

"It doesn't matter." Peter cracked out the words. "None of it matters. The only thing that does is that you heal and, please God, not hurt so much while you do. I'll keep you from everyone

630

else if you wish. In our rooms and no one else allowed in."

Somehow, miraculously, he had said exactly the right thing. He wasn't sure which part of it had finally got through past Guyon's stubborn terror, but whatever it was, the fearful, unhappy tension suddenly left him, and he nodded, slowly. "Promise?" he said, and it didn't even sound half-way to a joke, despite the small attempt at a smile that went with the shaken little word.

"I do." The words were promise and bond.

"All right," Guyon said, taking a deep breath. "All right." His smile looked almost genuine. "It's going to taste disgusting, isn't it?"

Peter's lips quirked up in a half smile, "If there is any justice in the world."

"For once," Guyon said wryly, "I find myself rather hoping there is not." He flung his good arm out dramatically. "Alas, my fate is sealed. Do your worst, tyrant..."

Peter stepped into the space, wrapped his arms around Guyon, and as he gentled his face down into the junction of neck and shoulder he whispered softly, "No, my worst I shall save for when you are well. It's all so much better when you fight back."

The small shiver that passed through Guyon's body told him that he had made his point.

*

If Peter on drugs was an angry wet cat, then Guyon on drugs was a fly with one wing. He spun about helplessly, unable to settle on direction or task. His normally razor sharp wit was dull and disjointed and his speech even more slurred than when speaking his native tongue. It was rather, Peter thought worriedly, as if Guyon were not there at all, but rather a mere shell with everything that was Guyon drained out of it. It was frightening, although David reassured him again and again that once he healed and they weaned him off the drugs he would be just as he was.

Henri, with his strange, startling kindness, understood faster than any of them what was needed, and set Guyon the task of writing down each troubadour verse as he remembered it - in English, and with his left hand. Dulled and bemused, Guyon did not question the strange command, but painstakingly and painfully put his left hand to work, forming letters that looked like a child's attempts at script. The results, however, were anything but.

Then, has man any right in love? No,
but fools could think so
just as, if one'd like to, he could accuse
the Occitan of not being French
or the ship of sinking before reaching port -
alas! for such a crime I'm taken by death
because otherwise, by Christ, I don't know what I did wrong.

It was correct, Peter knew, but that he chose that verse was probably rather telling. Telling in what way though, was something Peter wasn't sure he was up to deciphering just then. He felt as if his own intellect had been driven away with Guyon's, leaving only the worry behind. He was constantly tired from sitting up to watch over Guyon in his sleep. His appetite had fled as well, leaving him looking almost translucent, only that showing that his soul was still in residence and not off walking the mental hells that Guyon seemed to reside in. But he kept all of this to himself, instead simply doing what he could to distract the other man. Reading the verses as Guyon wrote them out, rubbing tense shoulders until they relaxed in sleep and just...being there.

And then one morning, after he had painfully and unpleasantly fallen into a deep sleep, Guyon, still silent, put a paper into his hand, his eyes wide and anxious. "Please," he said, halting and unsure. "*Je vous en prie.* My mind...on paper. It works. I tried..."

From long sighing and grievous wailing
only the one I try to exalt myself for can deliver me
since now, for only appearance's sake
I have stirred a wholly new song.
I walk up the slope and don't complain
since the paths of truth move me to think gently
Go up, heart! you do well if you suffer
go on, as long as you don't fail the one you love.
Gold shall be viler than iron
before I renounce loving the one I am devoted to.

632

The words hit Peter's chest rather like a cannon ball, knocking the wind from him and leaving him aching with emotion. That Guyon could do this...give these words to him when all he should really be doing was trying to get well...it was all too much. Peter blinked back tears and pulled Guyon close. He had so many words to say, but none of them came out beyond a choked, "I love you." This then, was how he was repaid by God, given relief and guilt in one lump, first sweet then sour, all commingled in a broth of love. He was more than prepared to drink it all down, take it into himself until it became a permanent part...Guyon was his, undeniably and irrevocably. And he was Guyon's in that same complete way. He yearned for Guyon to heal so that he could tell him how truly it was so.

"Words," Guyon said, painfully, and then, for the first time, chose Occitan, not while concealing, but while desperately trying to explain. "I killed them, Pèire, but not in translation! Not in translation!"

"No...no you didn't," Peter buried his face against Guyon's shoulder. "They were perfect. Utterly perfect."

"Does that mean you will sleep?" Guyon, robbed of pretence, was as anxious and as tired as Peter.

Peter chuckled, brokenly, "I'll try." Leave it to Guyon to worry for him at such a time. "For you, I'll try."

"Mm. How if...I don't want...try." Guyon slammed his good hand into the wall. "I *don't* want you to *try*. I won't break! I won't...I promised not to try to cross the Styx, and no, I won't. So *sleep*, Peter, because Christ, if you kill yourself, tell me how my promise holds?" He was ashen and shaking by the time he finished, the effort of sentences visible.

"I know...I know..." Peter took the good hand, quickly checking it for damage as he raised it to his lips. "I'll try...it's just, I worry for you so much. And some of this is my fault." He took a deep breath. "I'm not strong like you, Guyon. You need these drugs and I understand that. You need them and I want you to have them while you heal. But...I'm afraid they'll take you from me too. It's irrational, I know, but that's it just the same."

"Because they do." Guyon's eyes were translucent and clouded all at once, an exhausted reflection of comprehension.

"They do. I warned. You. I warned you. I say - I will say -" He clamped his lips together, his eyes darkening with impossible pleas.

"No.. no..." Peter put a gentle hand on Guyon's face. "It's not forever...it's just - I'll look at it as if I'm watching you through a window while you work. I can see you...and almost hear you...and you can do the same to me. We just have to wait until the weather clears and we can open the window. Then we'll be able to touch and hear and all will be well."

"I can - think the window is badly-made. Curse the maker. A lot?" Guyon had Peter's hand in his, between the good one and the gloved, immobile facsimile, and pressed his lips to it. "Don't...be angry. When I do. Curse. You're not...not the maker."

"I won't." Peter assured him softly. "I'm just the one standing there, worrying that instead of the window opening, it will somehow, all of its own, shatter and cut us both to shreds. God, I'm useless. You know how I worry, Gui. But so...no sleep." Peter sighed and gave him a crooked smile. "Save me from the glass?" It was silly to say and silly to ask, but he wanted Guyon to know that even in this state, in pain, confused by drugs, Peter relied on him for so much.

Guyon smiled, small and sweet and tired. "Come," he said with quiet assurance, and took Peter's hands between his, leading him awkwardly to the bed. "You lie there." He had not let go, and did not, even when Peter, obediently and embarrassedly, lay down. He curled in on top of Peter, his back to the window. "I am...glass. It hits me first, I survive. You sleep. If I am glass, I can fight glass, yes?" His good hand smoothed over Peter's face, and his eyes were mocking and kind all at once, pure Guyon despite their odd haziness. "Sleep."

*

Brocéliande, October 1646

I did not live until this time
Crowned my felicity,
When I could say without a crime,
I am not thine, but thee.
  This carcase breathed and walked and slept,
So that the world believed
There was a soul the motions kept,
But they were all deceived.
  No bridegroom's nor crown-conqueror's mirth
To mine compared can be;
They have but pieces of this earth,
I've all the world in thee.

Peter hated to see Guyon like this, no matter the small improvements he could see were being made now that Guyon was able to admit the full extent of his physical discomfort. In pain, listless, giddy and ridiculous from the drugs, half-lost in a dreamworld of Occitan poetry, half struggling to combine the small pockets remaining to him of mental clarity with his muddled and confused day-to-day life, it was a such a far cry from his usual stoic behavior that it made Peter's heart ache. But they both endured, somehow biding their time while Guyon healed and slowly reduced the vast doses of the drugs that threatened to take over that fine mind with amazing ease.

"Aphasia," Guyon said grimly and coherently, a few days into David's course of treatment, cradling his wrist in his good hand. He had the unbandaged but still-inflamed thumb pressed against his cheek in an attempt to cool it. "Next I shall be asking for a *hay* drink, instead of *water.*"

"Then I shall send you out to drink with the cattle," Peter told him simply. He'd learned that lightness was the way to answer such comments from Guyon. At least if he didn't want to be snapped at.

"It would probably be more beneficial than whatever it is David keeps putting in every drink you give me," Guyon retorted. "There are ways I foresaw my life after Corvay's death. An opium addict, no matter *how* docile, was *not* among them."

"It shouldn't be for too much longer," Peter said hopefully. "But you may not thank us when comes to the end." As bad as Peter knew the pain was now, the drugs, including valerian and God knew what else David had mixed in his odd cocktail, were keeping Guyon's pain down to a dull ache. Just because his hand had healed enough for the amount of drugs he was taking to have been changed and slightly reduced, did not, unfortunately, mean the underlying pain would have diminished enough for them to be completely unnecessary. Add to that the inevitable craving that his body was bound to feel after such prolonged use and Peter knew they had a completely new nightmare waiting to happen.

"I don't feel all that thankful now," Guyon said with masterly understatement. His sole means of entertainment, during his increasing periods of coherent thought, seemed to be in expressing just how much he hated all the changes each drug made to his mental processes.

"I know, beloved, I know." Peter drew him closer. "But you may once your hand heals enough to begin your exercises. It's going to hurt. Very much." This was something Peter knew first hand, although none of his hurts had ever included the type of damage that Corvay's blade had done to Guyon's hand.

"You mean very much *more*." Guyon leant into him tiredly, rubbing a too-prominently bony face against Peter's shoulder. The last couple of weeks had stripped what was left of youth from his features, and the man who had called himself Death's Dancer no longer wore the disguising mask of softening innocence. The lines around his eyes and mouth were carved as deeply now as though he had been ten years older, the last year under Corvay's harsh tutelage written plain for all to see.

It was a writing that Peter longed to erase, for all that it was impossible. Oh, he could help put some weight back on the too-lean frame, maybe even coax a more content and relaxed expression onto the face that was now all planes and angles instead of softness, but he could not give back innocence, no matter how hard he tried.

He wondered, once again, if it were right for him to put Guyon through this. Through life with him and all the intrigue and pain he seemed to gather like flies to honey. He knew, of course, what Guyon's reaction to any attempt on his part to keep him away from it would be. "I won't lie and say it will be easy, but you have the heart for it." Peter placed a kiss on the top of the curly head. "And the stubbornness."

"Oh, *that*!" Guyon laughed, and tired facsimile of the usual delighted howl that it was, it was no less genuine. "Well, yes, stubborn I am more than capable of." He grimaced up at Peter. "Anyone who can get your long-legged and ridiculous self out of the *Grotte* is evidently more than stubborn enough."

"Stubbornness on your part," Peter agreed. "I, however, can only plead insanity for my own bit in that." Insanity and jealousy and stupidity for allowing the words of Guyon's uncle to influence what he was already feeling.

"Hm." Peter had not realized how much Guyon emphasized his odd little quirks of speech with touch until it had been forcibly stopped, and the mobile features did double duty. "Insanity, twisted sentiment..."

"Yes...but all done with the best of intentions," Peter smiled softly at him. "And relief that none of it was necessary in the end."

"Ffft." Guyon bit his shoulder, replacement for the usual strong-fingered grasp around his neck. "String. *String*, Pèire, yards and yards of *string*. I made tea on the end of a length of *string*. Not necessary?" His good hand came up and flicked Peter, rather painfully, on the end of his nose. "Let me beg, plead, and *insist* to differ."

"Ouch," Peter gave a momentary scowl. "I am not your teether nor your sparring dummy and I'll thank you to cease in your attempts to make me either. I meant unnecessary on my part, beloved brat."

But Peter could not resist the way his hand strayed to his bare wrist. No string adorned it now, of course, that he had removed the night of his aborted meeting with whiskey and a pistol. He had a vision of Guyon replacing it, tying the knots and putting it in place with a kiss. An overt sentiment, he knew, but one that he could not help. It suddenly came to Peter that Guyon might never be able to repeat the little ritual, never tie the knots again and replace it. It was like a dagger through his heart and it was all he could do to restrain a pained gasp.

Guyon narrowed his eyes at him, drawing back. "And the scent of burning martyr drowns out even our smoking chimneys," he said, but his voice was gentle. "What bit you?"

"You did, obviously," Peter tried to turn it into a joke. "I might have been a bit...premature in asking you to stop."

"Such a lack of wisdom..." Guyon agreed, and reached up to kiss him instead. "*Bèl-mi.*" It was always different, now, hearing those slurred syllables, knowing that it was not some casual, flung-away endearment, but Guyon's own, peculiar expression of *sentiment.*

You are the light and beauty of mine eyes.

Peter drank it all in, the touch and the sentiment, like a man dying of thirst. It was always like this, no matter how often it happened. He wondered if there would ever come a time when this affection, this love, would become commonplace between them. Somehow he doubted it, his lover being far too volatile for any long-term comfort. And that thought, as much as anything else, banished his earlier worries. Guyon was a fighter. He would heal.

*

In the normal course of things weaning, like so many other first separations, was designed by nature to be a step forward in life. But when the weaning must be from something acquired, something learned, or forced upon the body, something which under normal circumstances would be rejected and has been made into a crutch for survival, it is no such matter. The body, left to crave something for which there are no adequate substitutes, no further nourishment to suit the absence of what has been made unavailable, becomes reduced to lack, and need, and desperation, and, in Guyon's case, adding to the hell-brew of uncontrollable miseries, the return of a slow and debilitating pain that never truly eased.

So rather than enjoying the returning clarity of his mind, Peter could only see the pinched furrows in the other man's brow, the darkly shadowed eyes and the hiss of agony that incautious movement caused.

Peter had railed at David, "Is there nothing else that can be done? He hurts, damn it! How can we expect him to work at recovering movement and feeling when every tiny thing makes him feel like the knife is being driven through his hand again?"

But David had just stared at him, sympathetic but unhelpful, and unusually unforthcoming about just why he was so acquiescent to Guyon's wishes, when he had never shown any signs of being so before, and in the end Peter did understand the necessity, even if he hated it. David gave Guyon other drugs - an odd cocktail that helped somewhat, but not in any major way, due to Guyon's refusal to allow it to be mixed with aquavit. Peter was sympathetic to his reasoning if not the result, but had hounded David to 'find something else' so often that Henri had barred the door to the stillroom, to give the blond apothecary a bit of peace.

Disturbingly, Guyon took no part in any of the 'discussions', bar his point-blank refusal to let David use an aquavit base for any of his mixtures. He obligingly drank vast amounts of willowbark tea, and said nothing at all of its complete inefficacy until Henri pointed out that since it didn't even cure mild headaches, it couldn't possibly be doing any good. He seemed to think that he had earned the nightmares that the valerian subjected him to - either that, or he had lived with bad dreams for so long that he could not tell the difference between those caused by drugs and those he tended to suffer from in any case.

He was in a continual state of bad temper, without ever getting angry - perhaps more because he simply lacked the energy to do so than because he was not. He seemed to have simply accepted that things would not improve, that the pain would be constant, and he seemed utterly prepared to have completely lost the use of his hand. It was getting to the point where his reaction to aquavit would, if nothing else, have made a welcome change from the sheer monotony of low-grade, perpetual snarling, and withdrawn and inward-turning sullenness that seemed to presage an explosion that somehow never came.

"Come on, Gui. You have to do this, please." Peter sat across from him, the first two fingers of his right hand held up and extended between them. "Just squeeze as much as you can."

The look he received in return was wearily assessing. "Is this for my benefit, or yours?" Guyon enquired with faintly scathing and evidently feigned curiosity. "Because since I really don't see what good it's doing *me,* it must be another salve for your singed conscience, and I keep telling you - there's no need."

Peter's jaw tensed, "Of course you don't see what good it's doing, because you aren't bloody well doing it."

There were more days like this than not, Guyon questioning and hopeless, Peter frustrated and pained. And more than that, he felt lost and frustrated and bitterly angry at Corvay for doing this, and at himself because he couldn't kill the man a second time.

Guyon's mouth twitched with sudden, unexpected humor. "Well. No. I suppose that is one aspect of negativity I should take into account..." He sighed. "Oh, all *right*." He wore a glove over his hand now, only David - and that on very, very rare occasions - allowed to see beneath it. Peter had no idea whether it was still bandaged, or stitched, or what state it was really in. What seemed quite definite was that Guyon found it next to useless. He raised it now, tilting his head as though to assess some way of trying this without causing pain, and then, with a small sigh of resignation, tried what Peter had requested.

His thumb curled in perfectly, was obviously capable of exerting whatever pressure Guyon wanted, but since that would have meant putting pressure on the damaged palm as well, that was obviously not going to be something Guyon tried. Mockingly, he curved his little finger inwards towards the pad of his thumb, a crab's pincer.

"Fine," Peter let out a huff of air and scooted back. "Don't take this seriously. Don't take me seriously. I'm just a big dumb Scot anyway and don't know anything about wounds or treatment or how to regain strength after an injury." He turned away, walking to the window and feeling only more anger at himself for his loss of patience.

"Sarcasm doesn't suit you," Guyon said. "I *know* you know all that, but you don't seem to have *listened.* I am never going to be able to use this thing properly again. *I've* accepted that, for God's sake, why can't you?" In the past, it would have been a demand -

now it was more a faintly irritable query to which he did not seem to really expect an answer.

"Because it's not true." Peter's answer was hot but quiet. He didn't want to hear this. Didn't want to hear Guyon's acceptance of his injury like it was already a foregone conclusion. It wasn't. If he could just get Guyon to understand that, it would be the first step for getting decent usage back into his hand. "I wish *you* would accept *that*."

"Oh, Lord," said Guyon wearily. "Peter, there comes a point where hope ceases to be a virtue and optimism becomes simply -" He stopped abruptly, not even the start of the next word escaping him, and there was silence. "All right," he said at last. "All right. I'm sorry. Whatever you want."

"It's not just what I want." Peter's temper was hovering near the edge and he knew it. He knew that if he didn't calm down he'd be ruining his own hand by smashing it through the glass of the window. "You have to want it. Want it badly enough to work through the pain, because yes, I damn well know it hurts. It's going to. Probably for quite some time yet. I want you to do this. I want you whole again and I don't care if the first thing you to when you are is strike me right in the face. Christ, I'll laugh and be glad you were able to make the fist you hit me with."

"But I can do that *now*, with my other hand," Guyon said, and then sighed. "Look, I meant it. I'll do whatever you say. But I'm not stupid, and I do know the difference between the fact it's hurting to use and the fact I can't *stand* anything touching the palm or the back of my hand. I really, really can't. Isn't there another way I could try what you want?"

Peter still could not bring himself to turn around, "Why don't you trust me, Guyon?"

The pain in his voice had very little to do with their current discussion. Guyon might as well be hiding from him in fear as it all amounted to the same thing. He didn't want Peter to help him, not really, and that hurt him all the way through. He wore that damn glove all the time, even in their bed, and that hurt him more.

"Why *what*?" The pure shock in Guyon's voice rendered it harsh. "But I - *of course* I trust you! I don't - what on earth makes you think I don't?"

"You won't let me help you. You don't...." Peter closed his eyes and shook his head, working for some kind of control. "You hide from me like you think seeing your hand will make me love you less."

"I *don't* think that," Guyon said quickly. "And it's not about letting you help me. It's not. It's about *letting myself be helped.*" There was a short silence, and then he added, slowly and painfully, "The only thing I could ever lay claim to was a certain amount of dexterity. That I could rely on my hands to be quick, and sure, and *steady*. Reliable. I know - I know I'm not good at fighting, but that wasn't really what I used them for in any case. And now I've lost that. I can't write for hours. I can barely manage legibility with my left hand. My mind has been locked up, and the only thing I have left is a certain amount of pride. And I *need* that. If I want to keep enduring this, I need to have that pride. And every time I give in, accept help rather than my own resources, however meager, I relinquish it."

"And when I was hurt, after Poitou...after the Grotte...Did it make me less that I let you help me?" Peter had hated it, because he knew it was necessary and he hated burdening Guyon with his care, but he never felt lessened by it.

"No," Guyon said. He sounded tired. "But that was different. You hadn't been lessened in the first place."

"Guyon, I am a trained soldier. I was struck down *twice* by people who should not have been able to get near me, let alone take me by surprise. That was quite...lessening."

"You are never, *never* going to understand me, are you?" Guyon asked in a somewhat muffled voice. "Peter...as bluntly as I can, then, you were not lessened because nothing had been taken from you that you could not regain, or set right. I cannot replace bone, or tendon, or erase *what this damned thing looks like*!" The veneer of resignation was stripped away, finally, not by rage but by pure, blistering frustration.

"So what does that mean?" Peter's voice was soft and far more calm sounding than he felt, "I leave you alone? You suffer but don't do anything that might help, even a little? And you never again touch me without that glove on?"

"You make it sound ridiculous," Guyon snapped, "and it

really is not! And I *said.* I'll do whatever you want. I'll even make an effort to believe it's going to help, what more do you want from me?"

"I don't know." Peter shook his head and sighed. "Maybe it's not you I want something from. Maybe I need it from myself. More patience...something."

More of something, because this, this just wasn't working. He hurt and Guyon hurt and he felt guilt overwhelming him daily. Guilt and heartache that he hadn't, somehow, prevented this. Guilt that he hadn't killed Corvay before he managed to hurt even the smallest hair on Guyon's head.

"Maybe you need to forgive yourself," Guyon said. "For not being God. You're the best man I know, but - you expect some sort of indefinable perfection of yourself. I don't know what it is, but - the Divine isn't actually attainable before death. Or possibly complete hermitage. I'd rather, incidentally, you avoided those options."

"Forgiving oneself is often the most difficult trial of all." Peter looked up then slowly moved back to the chair he had vacated earlier. He held up his two fingers again. "Don't squeeze. Just try wrapping your fingers around mine. Just the fingers."

Guyon smiled crookedly, and nodded. "Right," he said, and his eyes crinkled up a little with inward-turning amusement. "I'll try not to hurt you, shall I?"

"Please." Peter smiled but didn't feel any joy in it. He remembered how Guyon's hands felt on him, testing him, bringing him pleasure, holding him up. Another surge of guilt swept over him, but he squashed it back down.

Guyon's gloved fingers brushed his, the little finger curling easily around, the index finger managing to crook slightly. The other two stayed still. "You might not believe this," Guyon said rather tightly, "but I am, in fact, trying to move them."

"I believe you." Peter nodded. "Try again."

Guyon breathed out a half-laugh. "I should have been expecting that," he said dryly. There was no perceptible difference on his next attempt. "Don't tell me," he said, holding his other hand up. "*Again.* Just tell me when it's *stop*, hm?"

"Of course." And this time, Peter did smile.

*

"Let's live in haste; use pleasures while we may
Could life return, 'twould never lose a day."

David dropped the book he was looking at negligently down on the table, not caring that it almost upset the inkpot or that the spine now sported a definite dent. "Well, that was bloody depressing? Where are all the tales of "halcyon summers drifting into winded days of fall"? Really, I think the person who stocked this library must only have been here in the depth of winter and was suffering from some horrid debilitating illness."

Henri looked at him with unfocused eyes. "Or you invented their existence?" he suggested, after linking himself back from whatever world it was that had little black notes instead of letters, and probably had an equal amount of depressing symbolism in it. "I don't remember anything about winded days of fall. Or windy days of fall, either," he added after a moment's reflection, for Henri could never sacrifice grammar to imagery, something that tended to have a deleterious effect on his secular music-writing.

"Well, someone must have lived here before we arrived. I doubt this bloody great house has sat vacant since it was built. So no...not made up, except for the depressing bit...that was only conjecture." David flopped down on padded bench near where Henri was working.

"I don't see what's depressing about using pleasures," Henri pointed out. "I mean, *losing* pleasures, yes. Very depressing, poor poet, my heart agonizes over his distress, but using them sounds rather pleasant." He scratched at his forehead. "Am I being dense again?

"It's about dying, Henri," David told him patiently. "It's all 'use up the good things because you're not going to be around long enough to savor them. Not that I don't believe in living a full life, but...I just want to be in it long enough to enjoy everything at least twice...sometimes more."

"Well, that seems like a good mission," Henri said, still looking confused. "You're not thinking of departing this world any time soon, are you? I mean, we're all dying, dust thou art and

644

to dust thou shalt return and all that, but you should have told me if you'd been given advance notice of the process being brought forward..." His eyebrows were drawing together in a not-quite frown, half-humorous and half-puzzled.

David gave a rude snort, "No. No such luck for me or for you. Although..." He leapt to his feet, padding across the intervening space to wrap his long thin arms around Henri, "...given a choice, I'd rather not stay if you went ahead of me. Was any of that in either Peter or Guyon do you think? *God, such despair*...but I'd rather the drugs than a bullet for myself."

"Yes, but you don't deal in that kind of death." Henri was patient. "If you did, you'd say you'd rather the bullet than the drugs. The one thing that surprises me is that Peter wouldn't choose steel, but then what do I know of that kind of misery? I don't even know why Guyon decided death was preferable to battling on, you know I don't. I'm the one who never gives up, remember? I don't know how, even when I'm unhappy." He soothed one hand slowly down David's back. "You saw too much of me in Peter, David, and we're not alike. And Guyon isn't you."

His deep-socketed eyes were calm and thoughtful, no accusation in them. Henri had been thinking while he withdrew into his music, sifting through what he knew to find the answers he needed. "Not that I'm thrilled to know your mind works quite like you assumed Guyon's would, but I suppose it may come in useful at some point. Even if I don't want to imagine how or when." His mouth curved into a small smile.

"I'm going to miss him, you know," David said quietly, one finger drawing meaningless runes on Henri's chest. "It's been rather nice to have someone besides you around that I can trust."

"Eh?" Henri blinked. "What? Who? Who're you going to miss? What have *I* missed?" The little smile had turned into full-blown perplexity. "I don't think anyone's going anywhere, you know..."

"Oh, he'll find out." David said simply. "Guyon will tell him, or I'll let something slip. Once he knows he won't want anything to do with me."

"Guyon won't tell him," Henri said simply. "He knows Peter views you as a friend, and he won't jeopardise that - not because of you, or me, but because of Peter. And if you let something slip, Peter won't understand it. So that's never going to happen." He looked a little sad. "I told you, Peter's not like me. He doesn't see the evil in men first, or the connotations of harm. He sees you as a good man, and so anything you say? That's how he'll construe it. You'll have to tell him outright before he even suspects - and why would you?" Henri's eyes narrowed. "Unless you're joining in this recent craze for self-sacrifice, in which case I shall be forced to bind and gag you until I'm convinced it's passed."

"No...never that, my dear. You know me far too well to think it." No, he'd never come flat out and tell Peter the truth about the drugs he'd been giving Guyon, he actually did value the man's friendship. And that was the problem really. He'd tormented Guyon, not only because of Henri, but for the pain Guyon had caused Peter as well. Pain that the man had never deserved. It was a strange feeling for David. He'd so rarely had friends, let alone ones he'd wanted to protect, even from each other.

"Do I?" Henri tilted his head a little, the dark, slightly sunken features sharpening as he examined David. "Oh, well, that's all right then. David -" He stopped, his face screwing up into a sort of wince. "You do actually know what you did was *wrong*, don't you?" It was a genuine question, and more than that, a genuinely worried question, not coming from Henri's strange liking for Guyon, but from a deeper fear, that David had lost his moral compass again. It was almost nice, knowing that Henri put that before his friend's well being, but David felt a little guilty that the question had to be asked, even so.

"Yes. Yes, I do and I hate that I do. And I'd probably do it again, right or wrong because..." *Because why?* Sincerely, through all of it he hadn't wished to physically hurt Guyon, but he felt so helpless to protect Peter from the hurts that he felt that it was simply the easiest thing to do. He shook his head, "Sometimes I don't understand myself, Henri. I wonder that *you* ever do."

"Well, I go for the obvious," Henri said absently. "I don't pretend to sieve through your layers, love, you're not a threshing floor or eight-part harmony. You've wanted to hurt Guyon since we got to Paris, and Peter gave you a reason. That's fine, I told you, he makes most people want to do that. But Peter doesn't need your protection from him any more than you need his from me - or I need yours from anyone, or you need Guyon's from Peter." He snorted a bit, at the last.

It was such a ludicrous concept, in reverse, that David had to think about what the words had actually been for some time before they made sense.

And when they finally did make sense, David had to agree with them. He thought back to a long ago conversation with Peter, the one time Peter had thought that he might need to be protected from Henri. It had surprised him, the other man's quick leap to offer his defense - although not in so many words, his expression told the tale. Never had anyone but Henri attempted to defend him from anything and even though in this case it was unneeded, the fact that Peter would offer, so quickly and without question was just...Well, the man amazed him and still did.

Henri was watching him, his bony face still almost expressionless as he waited for David to understand - and David's expression must have changed when he finally worked out just what Henri had said, because the small curled smile returned, warmth replacing patience. "You know when I said you aren't like Guyon? You're not." David frowned, and Henri continued, "You believe in the sanctity of life, David, still. Guyon doesn't. He'll forgive you, in the end, because you did that to him, and he gave up thinking he was worth more years ago. But you try that on anyone else, and a word to the wise man I know you are - *never* let him find out." Henri didn't look as if it was giving him any pleasure at all to say the next words, but there was still love in his eyes, along with the warning. "He'll do what friendship would always stop Peter from doing. He'll kill you."

"And I'd deserve it..." David nodded slowly. Yes, that was right, wasn't it? You don't kill people. You don't purposely hurt them. He did believe that...mostly...although, it seemed that the individuals that he considered to be 'people' was a much narrower list than that of others.

"Not necessarily," Henri said wryly. "But then you've made a habit of ignoring what people deserve, recently, so it shouldn't surprise you that you're not the only one good at that little piece of avoidance." He looked rueful. "I'd rather not lose you to Guyon's crooked sense of order in the universe, if you don't mind too much."

"Well, that would certainly be my plan," David chuckled. "In the general scheme of things, I much prefer being found. Especially by you."

"Do you?" Henri's dark eyes turned speculative. "Well, I do still owe you." That was as oblique as Henri ever got in his life, and he did it out of kindness. David had been the one to find Henri, when they first met in Rome, and Henri never forgot that fact, claiming he owed David a found life, and still hadn't been given the chance to repay it. "General schemes have their uses," he added vaguely, but his kiss was anything but absent-minded or distant, the one thing that never failed between them as strong as ever, even if David knew he had been given the clearest warning of his life, just before it.

He'll kill you.

You have no comprehension of what pain is to me, Guyon had said after his confession, and David, as Henri had tried to predict would happen, was very aware now that he never, ever wanted to.

You're not the only one good at that little piece of avoidance.

But he was, possibly, the most skilled at it, and in the spirit of cultivating his abilities, he pushed all other thoughts save desire from his mind, and honed his talent.

*

The pain sometimes made Guyon foggier than the drugs had, stretches of time vanished into some blank nothingness for which he had, unfortunately, been conscious. He knew that there had to be something he could do to break out of it, compared it mentally to how the sun burned away the mist on the lake each morning, the way things that had been a blur of light shaded into crisp clean edges. He tried everything he could think of to keep himself from slipping into the numb, strange deadness that had replaced the crystalline clarity of David's powdered leaves from the Americas, replaced it and never really left him. He tried - and he failed, succeeding only in snarling at everyone, in alienating David, in frustrating Henri, who at least had the patience born of older familiarity - and in doing something to Peter that, even in the worst and the blackest of times, he recognized was unspeakable.

For Peter was still suffering from the aftereffects of that night of true and determined madness Guyon had forced upon them - not even the agonizing pain of before, nor the drugs, nor even the removal of the wonderful muffling blanket of opium and mandragora had stopped Guyon from seeing that. Guyon had forced himself, painfully and slowly and with moments of real despair, to accept that he had lost the use of his hand - Peter could not, *would not*, as though it were some personal insult, a source of greater grief to him than it ever could be to Guyon. His conviction and his fear felt on some days like an intolerable insult, and on others another burden of incomprehension that he could not withstand, so that Guyon felt he must give way beneath it, give way and give in and acquiesce to whatever Peter wanted or asked, just to take the desolation from the air, from Peter's voice, from his eyes.

The lack of outward expression that their love had begun to close itself into had become another form of agony to him, fearing as he did that the one thing they had both sworn was becoming as lost and damaged as his hand. It was a fear he kept as private as he did what he had come to see as a mutilation - the thick scar tissue and twisted shape of the one part of him he had ever been proud of. It had come to symbolize all that he loathed about himself - all that he hated about what he was capable of. And the last thing he wanted was for Peter to have to touch it, let alone to see what it had been made into.

It had been a long time since he had allowed himself to appear at all without the concealing glove, but it was still not second nature to him to put it on, so that he was forced to jam his hand hastily and painfully into the soft leather when there was a knock on his door in the afternoon, disturbing him from watching leaves begin to drift in the courtyard.

"Guyon?" Peter's voice was a bit hesitant, a sound Guyon seldom associated with a man who was so alive and vibrant. This he blamed himself for too, but wasn't sure what he could do to tear that sound away, other than start another argument - and

649

hadn't they torn at each other enough?

"As ever, I haven't changed my name..." It should have been a joke, the old half-reference back to his invariable response in a time when Peter had been incapable of hearing a word he said, but in the circumstances, it just sounded bitter and slightly malicious. He bit his lip, and tried again. "Here for the daily torment? Or a little leaf-watching?" He spent more time doing that than anything else, the great tree that could be seen through the study window beginning to turn into its autumn colors. In the twilight of half-felt pain and thorough unhappiness that his days had become, he could almost see them taking place.

"Either and neither," Peter said cryptically, as he stepped up beside Guyon and looked out the window for a few moments. "Something arrived for you. A package. It has a frank from Mazarin, but I didn't recognize the seal."

Guyon made a face. "You think he's recalling us? No, what use could I be to him now..." he trailed off unhappily, and shook his head, starting again. "You devised a treasure hunt so that it would take me an afternoon to find it?"

"No." Peter's jaw tensed and tightened, as if he weren't quite certain what words to hold in or which to let out. "I left it for you in the hallway. I wasn't sure where you were but I - If I hadn't found you it would have been there for you when you came back inside."

"Oh." Watching Peter hold back words, Guyon found himself doing the same. He wanted to say *Tell me what you're not saying*, and *why wouldn't you have found me*? and a few choice insanities about *wouldn't you have kept looking*? and possibly *string*, and he thought they could both survive extremely well without that particular Pandora's box of misery being opened up. Mostly because he suspected he would howl like some chained lunatic from pure despair if he ever let the words start spilling out. "I'll...go and open it, then." He tried out a smile. "You curious?"

"Yes. A bit." Peter, too, looked as if he were trying out his smile rather than using it naturally. They were both trying. They both wanted to get themselves back to normal, but it was hard...so terribly hard. "It's one of those oddish sized things. Not big enough for an elephant nor quite so small as a whisper."

650

"I wish it *were* whisper-size," Guyon said wryly. "I've never seen a package one could describe like that...come on." He slid out of the windowseat, standing awkwardly. He still found his balance needed adjusting in the first few seconds of becoming completely vertical, as though he had used his fingers for balance against the air. "You can tell me I'm opening it wrong."

Peter frowned, but didn't reply, falling into step just behind him as he headed toward the door. It was a strange reversal, wherein the *Scottish sheepherder* now followed his *shadow* where ever they went. It was not a comfortable feeling somehow, that they had fallen into this leader and follower mode, rather than walking side by side as they should.

But then, it had never really been comfortable when he had been the one doing the following, either - and he had, whether Peter knew it, or wanted to admit it - or not. Guyon sighed, and pushed the study door open, wondering whether to feel irritated or grateful for the fact that all doors were left unlatched now, unless he expressly chose otherwise. It saved his left-handed awkwardness, but he wanted to scream that he had not lost the use of *both* hands, only one, that he was only part cripple...

He swallowed the always-threatening vitriol down, and went towards the hall table, picking up the little box. "I don't know the seal either," he admitted with a shrug, turning it over. He recognized, with a grimace of real annoyance, that he couldn't hold onto it and break the seal - he couldn't even open it one-handed, because he wouldn't be able to get purchase on it. "Damn. Sorry, would you -" he held it out to Peter.

Peter, looked up from the patch of wooden floor that he somehow seemed to find far too interesting, "What? Oh. Yes...sorry, I should have thought -"

He picked up the box, but didn't open it, merely holding it steady for Guyon to do the honors.

"Oh, very helpful, very kind," said Guyon acidly, sliding his thumbnail under the seal and pulling the box free from the paper wrapping. The lid, lacking a catch, opened as he took it in his good hand, and he lost his grip, the box falling to the floor.

Peter, if I had both my hands, I would throttle you, he thought, bending to retrieve the box's contents. *If I were even a man any more, I would have the courage to tell you what I think of this so-called method of encouragement you are pursuing.*

He was to think, later, how ironic it was that he had thought that at the moment he held in his hand the first glimmer of hope he had been given in weeks, from the man whose opening phrase was always *Start again.* Maestro Marcelli, writing to him from Paris, and sending him a folded paper and something wrapped in cloth, which he ignored in favor of opening the paper. He gasped out a laugh as he read the few words.

You will drop this. Pick it up. Unwrap it. Put it on. And start again. As we all must.

Marcelli.

Guyon let the paper drift to the floor, and picked up the little cloth wrapping, shaking it loose with his left hand. He stared at the leather patches, the intricate straps connecting them, and his mind went completely blank.

Put it on.

"What...?" he whispered in bewilderment. "I don't - Peter, what *is* this?"

Peter stepped closer, and looked down at the bits of leather that Guyon held in his good hand. "It's - It's a sort of fencing brace. It's meant to help strengthen your grip and brace it at the same time. They're often used for beginners and after...injuries. He wants to help you, Guyon. This has Marcelli's mark on it, here." Peter turned the brace over to show the intertwined CW mark stamped into the leather. "He constructed it himself."

Guyon looked down at the little initials, and felt his mouth twist with something that was like grief, and like sadness, and yet was neither. Marcelli, who had never said a word during those long, miserable days while he watched Peter from the shadows, who had once told him that he would never learn the *Destreza* to any great degree because he feared not the line of the diameter, as most men did, but its centre. Marcelli, who did not know him, and who was still the first one to even hint at a knowledge of how deep this loss had gone, how intrinsically bound his hand was to his sense of self. "The patches will cover the scars," he said softly, "and the straps go round the base of the dead fingers. Not *quite* a fencing brace." He bit his lip, almost unbearably moved.

652

"But - bracing." He half-laughed at his own feeble joke.

"I did say he wanted to help you." Peter repeated, a small hopeful smile playing over his lips. "Can I -? I mean, would you like to put it on? I could go call David or..."

The look on Peter's face said that he was forcing himself to volunteer to do this, and that the last thing he wanted was an outside intrusion.

Guyon looked at him for a long moment, trying to gather what was left of his courage, knowing that whatever he did now was going to be irrevocable. *Call David,* he wanted to say, *call anyone, but not you. I don't want you to see this, ever.*

Payment deferred, said another voice, mockingly, and he flinched. He would not hide from that, not now that he had given his word. *What next, lock your door and mix the draught yourself?*

No. No. Unthinkable. But to take that step...

Don't worry, said François's laughing voice in his memory, *it's easy once you step off a cliff. It's all up to the ground, after that.*

Start again. As we all must.

He raised his hand, with the leather patch in the palm, and slowly, carefully, hooked the index finger of his gloved left hand through the straps, lifting it until it hung in the air, offering it towards Peter. "What, with my teeth?" he asked lightly. "I think you'd better do it for me."

Peter's surprise was palpable, if brief, and he stepped forward to take the bits of leather from Guyon's hand. "It goes this way 'round, I think. If you take off your glove it should be easy enough to figure out."

Guyon didn't trust himself to say anything that wouldn't come out either as undiluted venom or a whimper, and so just nodded. He stripped the glove off quickly with his left hand, not bothering to conceal the wince as the leather dragged over the scarring. He turned his head away, not needing to see Peter's expression when he finally caught sight of the purplish, twisted flesh, the distorted dents beneath the scarring where bone had been removed by Ibn Ibrahim's ruthless little saw and file, the still-present red lines of inflammation and the fading, sick yellow bruising adding shadowy, lurid horror to the whole.

But somehow, Peter just worked without comment, ignoring the whole as he had once ignored the scars on Guyon's back, instead focusing on sliding the bits of leather into place and lacing it all snugly.

"Is that too tight?" he asked as he finished up. "You might want to have the laces trimmed if you find they get in your way."

Guyon shook his head. "No. No, it's - it's comfortable. Well." He chanced a glance at Peter. "As it can be." He looked down at his hand. With the back of it covered by the leather, it looked almost recognizable again, the useless and wasted fingers held firmly together, feeling almost snug within their wrapping, the thumb and index finger delineated by the dark strap, obviously still functional. "Thank you," he added, and meant it. He hoped it showed in his voice. "Thank you for - all of it." *For treating me as though I'm still whole, still sane, still worth something more than mockery.*

"You're welcome," Peter answered, but he looked a bit confused, "Master Marcelli is much more responsible than I am, though."

He looked as though he wanted to say something else, but instead he just smoothed his thumb over the small bits of bare skin on Guyon's hand, as if he had waited to be able to do just that for too long.

"Hm," Guyon said, and his voice shook even over that dry little syllable, something inside him starting to unravel and unknot at Peter's touch, making him realize how much he had been craving this, how much he had needed it, not only as reassurance, but as confirmation of everything Peter had been saying.

Since when did gestures start to mean more to me than words? Since when did I fear the things you don't say more than I relish those you do, when did I begin to mistrust everything including silence?

The ground was coming up towards him fast, and he could only hope he survived the impact.

He put his good hand on the side of Peter's face. "True. But I'm prejudiced. It's the not loving Marcelli element that has my perception warped." He let himself smile, even though it hurt a little. His eyes burned, then, because the emotion that drove it was real, and it wasn't something he was feeling through a fog and he was, in fact, a long way from dead.

"I do love you. So much." Peter closed his eyes then, leaning into Guyon's touch. "I've been afraid of hurting you more, somehow."

Guyon spread his fingers out, against the rough-soft rasp of Peter's cheek, running his fingertips into the long hair. "It wouldn't have mattered. It *wouldn't*. Because it would have been you."

"That would have made it worse, Gui." Peter looked down, both hands now gently holding Guyon's injured one. "I never want to be the cause of your pain."

"I know." Guyon swallowed, trying harder than he ever had in his life to find the right words, the right phrasing, some way of making Peter understand the utter, essential truth of what he felt. "I know. But you are, sometimes. As I am yours. It's - how it works, I think. What we *want* doesn't really come into it. What matters is...is how we deal with it. With being the cause of pain. With having it caused. I've torn you to shreds for day after day, and I'm still doing it, and I would give *anything* to stop, and anything not to have ever started. And...I just have to have faith in all the other things I know, and hope you can have enough faith in me to survive me at my worst." He shrugged. "There. That was my honesty for the *month*, I think."

Peter chuckled, a little dry and painful sound, "God, how can we love so much and still do these things to each other. It seems to be a theme with us." He looked up then, searching Guyon's eyes with his own. "But nothing will make me leave you...unless you ask me to go. Nothing."

"And I promised you that I would never ask you once before, and still you were going to leave." Guyon did not mean it as a rebuke, simply as a reminder that words did not - *could not* - always work for them. "And I still have faith."

"I was trying to do what was right for you. What was good. What was best. I -" Peter scowled, but it was not, apparently at Guyon. "I never want to be your stumbling block."

"You make yourself into one of your own free will, what would you like me to do about it?" Guyon snapped back, surprised at himself. It was as though the flickers of real emotion that Marcelli's gift had evoked in him had been the first catching of flames under a fire of exasperation. "Christ! What do I have, a plague cross on the study door? On my forehead? On my *body*? What? You avoid touching me as though I were marked for buboes and infection!"

"I didn't think you wanted me to. You've been hiding yourself from me behind that damned leather glove, as if you thought I'd take one look and run away." Peter's words snapped out. Then he stopped, his body wound as tight as strings on Henri's damnable harpsichord. "You could show David...let him help you. But not me?"

"I don't care *what* David sees of me, I don't care what he thinks of me, if he's revolted by me it's his own problem!" *God*, it was a relief to say these things, as though something had been festering close to the bone, driven in to a place Corvay's dagger had found but not shown outwardly. "I *do,* however, care a very great deal about how *you* perceive me, and given that you already saw me flayed open like a miniature Marsyas, you'll forgive me if I don't want to keep reminding you of just what I've become to look at! Importunate desire, Peter, is nothing *but* repulsive, and at least there's no danger of my demonstrating that on David's behalf!"

"Well, good!" Peter railed, "Because if you did I'd bloody well have to knock him down! Don't you know that none of this means anything to me? I love you. I want you with me. I've wanted to touch you so damned much that I ache with it...but I can't if I don't know you want me too."

"What the hell do I have to do to -" Guyon started, and then stopped, feeling as though someone had simply reached inside his mind and heart and *squeezed*, sudden and unkind and absolutely stopping all chance of breath or words, because he was about to answer his own question, and it was like diving into ice-cold water without even testing it first, no preparation for the shock. *What do I have to do to make you see?*

Something, he thought, breath returning in a sort of laughing hiccup, *that he **can** see*. "There's a saying about Mohammed and a mountain," he said in an odd little gasp. "There's nothing about two Mohammeds. Or two mountains, for that matter." He reached up his good hand, and gripped the back of Peter's neck. "It's the *importunate* part I was afraid of," he said calmly, and let all his want and love and frustration show through in a small, savage kiss.

That Peter returned it, practically melted into it, was the final relaxation of control on both sides.

"Thank, God..." Peter whispered against his lips. "I couldn't have stood it much longer."

"Well, you should have *said,*" Guyon began, and a completely different sort of laugh caught in his throat, because he had been the one not wanting to hear words, so what good would it have done either of them even if Peter *had* said something? "Triple-dyed idiot," he grumbled, and then, with a quickness that seemed to belong to another life, added, "Me," before returning his attention to the sheer joy of feeling skin and breath and pulse that aroused his every sense, so close and yet so wonderfully separate, exquisitely distinct.

Peter pressed close against him, warmth and joy pouring out of him, as he nuzzled his face down into Guyon's neck. "I love you. Want you...always..." He chuckled softly, "Right now as a matter of fact."

"Then could we perhaps go upstairs?" Guyon asked, feeling more like shouting - for joy, for relief, for sheer exhilaration. "Only I think making a scandal and a hissing is a task well-filled by Henri and David..."

"More than," Peter agreed, vehemently, urging Guyon toward the stairs.

Guyon decided to tell Peter about the kitchen table, the imported brandy, and the cook *later*, and hurried.

*

Peter shivered as he poked at the fire, trying to coax it into something more resembling a blaze than a smolder. This was one apparent drawback to locking even the servants out of your rooms

657

at night, no one could come in early and do this for you. A small price to pay for privacy though, true enough, and for the luxury of not being awakened in the wee hours when it was done. He never had learned to sleep through someone coming into his room - ever.

He glanced back over at the bed, smiling at the picture his lover made...or would make if he could actually see anything of Guyon beyond the end of his nose and a bit of hair poking out from between pillow and blankets. Really, sometimes it was like sleeping with a hibernating bear the way he buried himself, and almost as dangerous to awaken.

The fire finally decided to cheer up and Peter added a few more pieces of wood before moving back to stand at the end of the bed and wondering - strategically speaking of course - where he could safely crawl back in.

"Did you kill it?" Guyon mumbled from somewhere amidst the blankets. "Only 'm not getting up." He emerged enough to show Peter a curtained slant of dark tangled hair and slitted, sleepy eyes. "Y're up?"

"Only just." Peter assured him. "Trying to get the room warmed. Go on back to sleep." He found an opening and crawled into the bed, being careful to keep his chilled hands and feet away from Guyon's warmth.

Guyon curled around him, determinedly sharing warmth, his bad hand tucked awkwardly between them. "Mm. You know, I miss François and our Sundays, sometimes." He yawned into Peter's shoulder. "Only I keep thinking it should rain, so it's perfect."

Peter tensed slightly but somehow, managed to keep his tone light, "I never thought I'd hear you say that you actually *wanted* rain, Gui."

François Villon still stood between them. And he probably always would. Peter fought hard not to resent that. He'd liked François, really he had. Loved him almost, as a brother, but somehow even now, nearly a year after his death he could still feel his jealousy of the time François had spent with Guyon.

"Only if it's *outside*," Guyon said amusedly. "That way it's nicer to be in." He shifted back a little, tilting his head on the pillows. "You always do that. Why?"

"If it begins to rain *inside*, then I'm definitely in for a bit of work having the roof redone," Peter leaned in and kissed Guyon's forehead. "Something that I certainly do not want to contemplate."

"No, although definitely to be avoided, I agree. François. You always...flinch. Does it still hurt so badly?" Guyon looked at him worriedly.

Peter sighed. He should have known that Guyon would not let this rest. The same attitude that made him good at deciphering codes and languages carried over into the rest of his dealings with the world. It could be a very good trait, unless you were on the unwelcome receiving end.

"Just some lingering guilt, I suppose." Peter said softly. "I'll get over it."

"Guilt?" Guyon frowned at him. "Pèire, Lesueur is dead, and at your hand. There is nothing to be guilty about, chérâme. Not even I cling to that, and I was there!"

Yes, Peter had fought and killed Christien Lesueur. Had given justice to François and to Guyon. So, true enough, he felt no guilt due to *that*. He'd done all he could.

"As I said, I'll get over it." Peter reaffirmed. "Do you want me to send for some breakfast? Or do you want to sleep more?"

"I want," Guyon said with enormous patience, "you to tell me *why* you still need to get over guilt. I keep telling *you* things. It seems only fair for you to return the favor, hm?" His eyebrows met in a quizzical little frown. "What's so bad, Pèire-mi, that you don't want to discuss it? God knows, I mourn him every day, but I don't turn to wood and iron when I hear his name -" He broke off. "Except I never *do*, do I. All right, mon bèl, what is this worm in your bud? That's not guilt, it's pain, I'm not stupid."

"You won't let this go, will you? Can't we just say...that I'm having feelings that I'm not very damn proud of and move on?" Peter looked vacantly up at the canopy over the bed, its pattern intricate but a bit faded. Faded like his jealousy towards François should have been.

Guyon's whole face was a scrunched question mark, as he shifted so that he was leaning over Peter and blocking the canopy

659

from sight. "Not really, no, because *what*?"

"Damn it, Gui, I'm still jealous. It's stupid - ridiculous in fact - but there it is." Peter turned his head, honestly ashamed of his feelings. "So it *is* guilt. Guilt that I could feel that way about someone I cared about...that you loved. It's François, damn it, and I should be past it."

"Jealous?" Guyon sounded thoroughly confused. "But *why*? There's nothing to be jealous *of*, it's not as though I loved him as I love you, and you cannot truly think I feel less because I gave friendship to him?" There was a brief pause, and then he asked, tentatively, "Can you?"

Peter tensed again, climbing out of the bed to draw on his trousers, "Really, Guyon, I'm not a child, even if my jealousy renders my maturity in question. You don't have to pretend. I've accepted that you loved François...and I'll deal with it. I know you love me. I do. Truly. You don't have to deny him out of some...fear that I'll let my jealousy overtake me."

Guyon sat bolt upright in the bed. "Wait, wait, *what*? *Deny* him? Deny him *what*, for God's sake?" The laugh that followed was breathy and short with embarrassment. "Peter, you think - you don't think - you *can't* think - good God. You *do*." Peter turned his head to see Guyon sitting amidst a puddle of blankets, for once unself-conscious about his nakedness, and staring at him. "You think François and I were *lovers*?"

"I was so jealous of him," Peter continued, unhearing, dragging his shirt up over his shoulders. "The time you spent together. When I saw all that affection that I couldn't share... You touching him. His kiss on your lips. Seeing you wrapped around him in sleep.... And then when he died. Christ, Guyon. I never wished him dead. No matter how jealous I felt. You know that, don't you?"

He stopped then, his eyes seeking out Guyon's, "I wanted to show him up, somehow. I had dreams of it. No credit to my friendship, I know but - I never wished him dead."

"I never thought you did," Guyon said, rather absently. He was still looking at Peter with a sort of bemused expression of burgeoning enlightenment. "Peter, you're not listening. Which is annoying me. François. Was not. My lover. Nor, by the way, was

I his, in case you think I am delving into Greek semantics. He was my friend, and dear to me beyond all my family, dearer to me than all save you, but he was *not my lover*. He *could not* have been. Do you understand me?"

Peter wasn't certain that he did. "What do you mean he *could not be*? He kissed me, for God's sake. He certainly didn't seem averse to being with another man."

Guyon snorted, the noise sudden and surprising. "I am very sure he was not. François loved love for its own sake, and was, he assured the world, skilled at displaying so. But I *was* averse. To all. And he knew that."

"But you -" Peter frowned, now completely at a loss. "I mean...well, you never...and when we -"

Yes, Peter, that was brilliant.

He shook his head and tried again for coherency. "You and François were *not* lovers?"

Guyon's mouth twitched, and Peter suspected it was not entirely with amusement. "No," he said with commendable calmness. "I told you that Twelfth Night. I had never given the answer answerless, nor asked for it. In plain language, Peter, the first time I was ever even kissed was by a drunken Scot who wished I was his dead friend. Which is *not*, incidentally, a mistake I have ever made."

"No. You wouldn't." Peter could say that with conviction at least. "I'm obviously fourteen kinds of a fool. I - Christ. I just - And François - And -"

Peter suddenly began to laugh. "I seem to have lost all facility for completing a sentence."

"So it would seem," Guyon said mildly. "Peter, surely to *God* you didn't think I - that I had -" He went red, the color covering his whole body in a wash of heat. "I hate to think of what impression you had of my former bed play," he said in a rather strangled voice.

"Well, Hell, it's not like I'd know. My own experience wasn't what you'd call vast." Peter suddenly paused in his laughter, as a thought suddenly sprang into his mind, "Wait. You didn't think I was involved with James, did you? "

Wide, utterly translucent eyes looked back at him. "No, Peter,

I thought you *loved* him. Which I suppose is its own involvement. And then, of course, Robert told me about Brian, so I knew that you *were* vaguely cognizant of what we were about."

"*Vaguely* is a most comprehensive word." Peter nodded. "And I *did* love James, but more than that, I was as grateful for his friendship as I was for that of François...and you. My beginnings at Court were just as awkward in England as they were here. But I can tell you beyond a doubt that if I kissed you, drunk or sober, it was *not* James Whitley I would have been thinking about."

"And since you have no idea what I'm referring to," Guyon said dryly, "that makes me all the more thankful I gave you my refusal." He laughed. "Come here, you fool. Unless you prefer me at a disadvantage." He gestured to his unclothed state.

"Now that is something I'll don't have to give thought to. This is one of the few ways I *ever* get you at a disadvantage." Peter said as he stood, slowly letting his shirt drop off his shoulders. God there were so many questions he'd like to have answered. So many thoughts, past and present that he wanted to bring up. But they could wait. There was time now, so much time. And all of it theirs.

"But you do so utilize it," Guyon said sweetly and poisonously, and then hit Peter with sharp accuracy across the shoulder with his good hand. "God *damn* it, Peter. I tell you the whole truth of my soul, and your response is 'but you were François's lover, and I'm jealous'? You have rocks, I tell you, rocks in your head!" But he was laughing, and when he kissed Peter it was like someone soothing a hurt, small and soft and gentle

Then, being Guyon, he bit Peter's lip hard, and any further discussion was lost in proving just how much they had found out about each other since that first, disastrous kiss.

*

Peter, it appeared, had a list for everything. Things to do to get the estates ready for winter. Things to do to keep his affairs in order back in Paris. Things to do to 'fix Guyon'. Not that Peter would ever have said that to him, or even, if Guyon was truthful to himself, think it. But still there were times it felt that way - upper arm exercises, lower arm exercises, wrist exercises and those interminable 'finger plays' all trying to coax his unwilling hand into some kind of movement or to compensate for it all if that continued to be impossible.

He'd kneaded more bread in the last month than they'd need to feed the town all winter long. Or at least it felt like it.

Still, there was some sense in what he said, although Guyon was certain it would make no difference to his hand's use, he had been far more sedentary than he normally would have and his whole body showed the lack. Where once there had been nervous wiry muscle, now there was only a kind of sallow thinness, with no tone or definition. He had his own theories as to the reasoning behind Marcelli's little leather gift - not only did the patches conceal the appearance of his hand, but they gave it a kind of brace, holding together the two fingers that he was slowly coming to accept would never work again.

But Peter saw his acceptance, painful as it was for him, as being part of his earlier despair, rather than realism, tried everything to convince him otherwise, to find ways of showing him that recovery was possible, that everything would 'return to normal'. Guyon, living with it, watching the tiny, infinitesimal changes in his whole hand and wrist, knew otherwise. He was beginning to compensate, the muscles in his thumb and index finger becoming slowly more defined than those in the opposite hand, the deep groove in his wrist hardening with every day that passed. As the pain slowly became a thing of intermittent attack, caused by unwary movement or touch, he became aware of *how* he could use what was left to him, and longed to explain that to Peter, so that he could work on what he knew existed, and not what Peter was trying, in all love, to force into being.

Telling himself that it was from a need for exercise, and not to avoid Peter's worried eyes and David's still guilt-stricken ones, he took to walking the grounds. Not yet confident enough to ride, he had still not come to any of the boundaries, and had begun to trace a route for himself. Not by nature shy, solitude had made him so, and he was both surprised and at a loss when the men working on the land began to recognize him, calling a greeting or

663

waving if the distance was too far to be heard, and not seeming to mind when he only responded with the awkward nod that had come to pass for his own greeting.

Since Peter seemed prepared to love this land, he looked at it with kinder and more assessing eyes than he had turned on any estates since he had left the Languedoc and mentally consigned it in its entirety to Giraud's care, years before. Wrapped in his silence, he noticed where things grew and had grown, the texture of the soil where it was turned up by boots or horses' hooves, the way the undergrowth was denser in some places than others. He saw where the berries were beginning to turn, and where the leaves had fallen early, where they had begun to pile into little drifts. He saw which way the trees bent, noticed from which direction the wind always blew, where grass was sparse and tough and interspersed with moss, and where it was lush and the last remnants of clover grew among it.

He learned Breton, on his walks, learned it by listening and calling it back to himself in his own mental habit of Occitan, blending and merging the familiar and the new until he was conscious of both only as speech. His mind fed upon it as though starving, his self-imposed isolation having left him greedy for something both new and not painful to the touch of memory. Henri's idea of poetry had been almost what was needed, but had still touched too closely upon all the old wounds, both self-inflicted and caused by others, to be entirely of comfort; and Peter was only completely confident of his treatment and of his behavior when they were alone and safely in the warm, increasingly cluttered chamber.

It was as though before that heavy door closed, they were all on trial, all attempting in their own ways to prove something, to be perfect, to make ruins whole instead of creating something new. Guyon knew it had to be him who took that step, who opened up the possibility of a new and different world, but he was not sure if he had either the ability or the strength to do so, as much as he craved for the point when he had both and could use them.

In a sudden strange blaze of afternoon-summer, there came a week when the mornings were cool enough almost to presage winter, and the afternoons burned like August heat from midday to dusk. Like cats, David and Henri disappeared into the mellow light after the noontime meal, and no-one wanted to enquire too closely as to why or where to. Peter *did* have to attend to things, different harvests claiming his attention and different managers vying for his opinion and his sole regard. Guyon, walking amid new spider-webs and the scents of harvest and hot damp earth, both understood and was glad of it, for the Peter who came to their bed in the cool night was a different man, and one he was glad to welcome into their strange rare privacy.

But still, he wanted the last barrier removed, the last caution and fear gone, and though he could not wipe out the memories of that one terrible night for either of them, he knew there had to be a way of making things new, as the days began again and again in cool fresh dew, all washed and glittering with the slow sun.

One of the men he met most frequently on his walks was Peter's coppicer and woodsman, who tended towards the same paths as Guyon and respected both his desire for silence and his need to learn at once. He had been shown paths and where things would change and where they were already changing, and all with few words passing, so that his senses were indulged without a need for contribution. It was this, as much as anything, that was restoring his equilibrium, he knew, and it was a pleasure, too, to be in the company of someone who seemed to enjoy the heat as much as he did.

"You should go to the lake, lord," was the greeting one day, and Guyon looked over in surprise, quirking a little grin.

"I'm no lord," he said automatically, as he always did, and then - "and why should I be doing that, hm?"

"Because you're well enough to see yourself clear, now," was the response, and Guyon did not even pretend to misunderstand as to what kind of clarity was meant.

"It would take the magic of your Vivien's own pool to do that for me, I think," he said softly.

"And that being in the forests, you'll not find that here. No, this is ours, we say it was Merlin's."

"And here I thought Merlin was in a crystal cave!" Guyon started to laugh.

"He is, lord. But *before* that, before he enchanted himself away from the world, we tell our children this was his." The woodsman laughed, too. "Merlin's magic in a little pool of mud and reeds. You should see for yourself."

"I -" Guyon was about to say something quick, and easy, and dismissive, but swallowed the facile words down, and nodded instead. "I will," he agreed. "Thank you."

"Today, then."

"And why today?" Guyon teased, though he had intended to anyhow.

"Weather's ending tonight, so if you're wanting a swim, best have it over with before then," said the man, touched his hat, and turned off down one of his own well-worn little paths.

"Weather's - how can weather -?" Guyon rolled his eyes in exasperation. "Well, let's hope the pool doesn't give me *that* sort of clarity, or we're all doomed," he said to a nearby blackberry bush.

He followed the path down over the sloping hillside, towards the thicker part of the woods that he had not so much as skirted yet, knowing that if he had needed to take a different path to the one he was already on, he would have been told. The undergrowth was thicker, though the trees were fewer, and though the path was worn, it was still covered in ivy and lined with brambles and goose-grass, catching his clothes and leaving little green marks that looked like children's fingertips had brushed against him as he passed by.

He was beginning to wonder of the pool's existence by the time he came to it, and when he did, he almost stepped straight in, it was so heavily fringed with grasses and reeds, as though it had simply come out of the path.

He had half-expected some strange change in the air, but the heat was still low and burning, the clouds passing by overhead in great white piles, the birds still called in the trees, and the faint wind had given way to no preternatural stillness of myth or legend.

"Merlin's lake," Guyon said quietly, and his voice was as it always sounded, quiet and a little resonant in his throat, no mystery there either. He began to skirt around it, stepping over thick roots that came up from the earth and went down into the water, avoiding the low-hanging branches of the weeping willows.

"Go for a swim," he muttered. "Go for a - oh, why the hell not, who's going to know. Well. Who's going to know in time to *stop* me, anyway?" He grinned, tugging off his jacket and shirt with the awkward quickness that was now second-nature to him, and kicking his way out of his battered boots with his usual gratitude for their well-worn ease in removal. He contemplated removing his breeches for a moment, before he decided that he would rather deal with wet clothing than with the effort required with laces and hooks, and one hand still not quite accustomed to its reversed task and the other aching and with clamped, pincered fingers.

He peeled off his stockings, laid them neatly on top of his shirt, and then paused. With a faint shrug, he unstrapped the leather guard, using his good hand and teeth as he had learned, put it with his clothes, and then waded in to the water, past the reeds.

It was, indeed, muddy, the softness of it almost a shock, clouds of it making his passage murky until the water was up past his waist and he could strike out a little, taking his feet from the sinking bottom.

The water was warm with the sun on the surface, the layer of chill beneath it a shock, after the double caress of sun-heat and mud. He gasped a little, feeling the pull and burn as he moved his right hand in the familiar curl of swimming, unthinking. He pushed his fingers together, imagining that they were held in place by the guard, and turned onto his back, moving his arms and feet just enough to float.

He looked up into clouds, infinite layers of white and grey in the moving masses overhead, reflecting sunlight from their soft depths into brilliant autumnal blue.

"Infinity," he said in wonder, and turned his head to the side, only to see the same thing reflected around him as the clouds of silt subsided, only this time broken and glittering with the movement of his body, into the sun and the deep green of the trees.

Let it go, he thought. *Let it go and be glad. Go home and stop trying to tell them. Just show them. Go home and show them.*

Surprising even himself, then, he kicked water upwards, in a kind of flung-out challenge to the air, and laughed into the sudden dazzle.

"*Yes!*" he shouted, not knowing why, or caring who heard him. "*Clarity!*"

*

It appeared that what Peter had been told earlier in the day had been true, although he had been tempted to laugh when his vintner had said the sunny days were drawing to an end and that, in spite of the nearly cloudless sky, they would have a storm before morning. He should have known better, Claude had lived here all his life, Peter barely one season. But in his defense the sky had been clear blue and bright, with merely the wisp of a few clouds, sheep of the sky, grazing across its surface.

Still and all, they needed the rain as they had needed the sun, the people and the land; respite one from the other. But Guyon would probably not be best pleased by this harbinger of the cold days to come.

Guyon had arrived back as the first drops of rain began to fall, and as sodden as though he had been caught in a downpour. To all queries, from the concerned to the irritated, he had simply responded that he had washed off in the stream, that he did not need a bath, and shouldn't someone make sure there were enough candles for the evening, since it appeared that light from any window was not going to be an option?

The imperturbability of his good mood had been almost familiar - and indeed should have been, save for the fact that Peter had not known it for a long, long time. Corvay had destroyed that adamantine armor of wry amusement months before.

What is this? Peter wondered as he directed the servants to do Guyon's bidding. And just in time too, for the clouds drew closer in the time it took for them to accomplish their task and the sky began to empty itself of every drop of laden moisture.

668

Peter moved to the window of their chamber, looking out at the courtyard where water was already running in rivulets, its stones brought into eerie illumination by the flashes of lightning. It could have been a oppressive sight, but somehow the coolness the rain brought lifted the heaviness away.

"Your coppicer," Guyon said from behind him, "told me the weather was ending. Isn't it an amazing phrase? It's..." There was a silence into which Peter was sure Guyon's good hand was waving in description - "perfect. *God.* Words." His laugh was rather muffled, and Peter turned around to see that he had got rather hastily and haphazardly changed, his feet still bare, and was toweling his hair off with his discarded shirt. "Have I mentioned that I love words?"

To say that Peter felt suddenly quite taken aback, would have been an understatement. In fact he felt quite sure that if he could see himself in a mirror at that moment, he would have looked rather like a beached cod, mouth gaping silently. "Not...not recently."

As a matter of fact, quite the opposite.

"I never said I liked *my* using them, you know," Guyon pointed out. "I just like them as they stand. And when they're new. Or - right." He flicked at Peter's jaw with his braced index finger, snorting a little with laughter. "Close your mouth, my porpoise."

Peter gave a little huff and closed his mouth, reaching up to twine one finger through a still damp curl. "So you've been off rediscovering the joys of words while I slaved away to get the cellars filled for winter. An equitable division, I'm sure."

He had to chuckle though, he did not begrudge Guyon his wandering time and he had enjoyed the work, rough and physical, stacking crates and hauling boxes. The Court would be appalled at some of the things he did.

"It seems...suitable," Guyon agreed, his eyes dancing with the private mirth that Peter had come to think was gone for good. "And I like *equitable*, too. Hm. I was wrong. I *like* words. I *like* this place. On the other hand, I *love* you, even though you refuse to accept things I tell you as fact."

"Such as?" Peter ventured, a bit tentatively. He did not want to endanger this strangely light mood with recrimination and dissention of any kind, it felt too good and he wanted to enjoy it as much as Guyon seemed to be.

"That I *accept* what has been done," Guyon said, a little more seriously. "So stop trying to make things as they *were*, see them as they *are*, and help me make what *is* into something more...workable." He reached up, and cupped Peter's face in his leather-bound hand. "I can still do this. Everything else I can learn with the other, and what does that matter, in the end?"

It's hard. It makes me feel like I've failed you. That I've failed us. Peter thought but did not say the words out loud. Things were changing tonight it seemed. "I'll try. I will. I just wanted to help somehow. It's kind of all tied up in those words, you know? I love you."

Guyon was nodding, though, as if he had heard what Peter had not said as clearly as what he had. He was *listening* again, Peter realized, the one thing that had always been his saving grace very much to the fore. "But you'll *have* to help," he said, and he did not drop his hand, or try to curl it away and hide it. "How can I learn to fight with my left hand if you don't teach me?"

"I will. You know I will." Peter said sincerely, then his lip twitched into a grin. "Although, you never *really* learned with your right."

"Then I can only improve," Guyon said serenely, "true? Or at least drive you only half-way to distraction, since you will feel bound to be horrendously patient..."

"I am always horrendously patient," Peter asserted with a laugh. What was going on? How *had* Guyon spent the day that so much change had been wrought? Peter didn't know and could only thank God and all the Saints that it was happening.

"Mm." The little multi-layered sound that meant so many things, and usually that Peter was being laughed at being one of them. "Of course." Guyon laughed, then, sounding surprised at himself. "I spent the day swimming in Merlin's Pool."

"Mm." Peter hummed back, attempting the same inflection and he was sure, failing utterly. "And did you see the man himself?"

"Don't be ridiculous, he's locked in the forest several miles away in a crystal cave," Guyon said, only a faint flicker at one corner of his mouth betraying his amusement. "No, I simply...cleared my head? I think that suffices as a description."

"As long as you didn't clear it of everything," Peter said softly, "I'll accept that."

Guyon blinked at him. "I hope not," he said, a little dryly, "because that would make it hard to know *how*, exactly, I had remained capable of speech. Or emotion. I think both may be...somewhat essential."

"And knowing how to find your way home was also a necessity." Peter added to the list. "Which I'm very glad you managed, because again, there's that, I love you thing that we're exploring."

"Oh, we're exploring it? It's a *thing*?" Guyon looked simultaneously amused, vaguely horrified at Peter's mode of expression, and oddly delighted. Even in the very peculiar purplish-yellow light of the first autumn thunderstorm, delight appeared to be winning out.

Peter nodded solemnly, "A wonderful thing. And I would not dream of exploring it with anyone but you. My guide, my navigator and my lodestar."

"Which makes you either a captain, a ship, or some form of sextant, all of which are somewhat disturbing thoughts," Guyon pointed out, and laughed as his statement was punctuated with an increased deluge against their windows. "You know...here and in Wales, they say Lancelot was one-handed. Of course in Wales they also say he played the harp, so -" he shrugged. "But - since you have given us all Avalon, it must make you Arthur."

"I would claim no such greatness as that, my dear, as well you know," Peter smiled at the conceit. "But if it would put you by my side, I would be a contented king."

"Then don't send me off to look for the Grail, and you'll have no reason to be otherwise," Guyon said, kindly turning six variations of the myth on their heads simultaneously. "I can't be Lancelot," he added. "He wanted adventure. I just -" He shrugged, half-smiling. "I don't know about contentment. But I think - I *think* - I am beginning to know about love. Since I do, after all, know you."

"I know." Peter nodded, then moved to the dressing table and plucked something out of the jumble that always seemed to accumulate there. "Then as my knight and brother, my heart and life and all...you must have a token." Peter hesitated then. Was it too much? Too soon? It felt right but so much always seemed to ride on such small symbols in their lives. "If you will allow...."

Guyon gave him a vaguely bewildered look. "I thought that was ladies at jousts," he said, sounding rather confused. "And I don't have a - er, never mind, let's forget I started that sentence, shall we? I *meant* to say, yes."

Drawing a knife, Peter made a quick cut of the leather lacing he held in his hand, then moved to Guyon's side. "It's not exactly string...but it binds just as well and will last much longer. It will bind you to me as I was once bound...as...as I wish to be bound again."

...bind him to you, leather and string, heart and soul. You're a smart fellow, Scudamore...you'll see the way.

Guyon was very quiet, almost disturbingly so, his eyes fixed on Peter's face rather than on the lacing in his hand, searching for something Peter hoped was either there or not, depending on what this most mercurial of men wanted. Then he nodded, his mouth shaping silent agreement, and held out his left arm with a crooked little smile, swallowing visibly. "Yes," he said then, almost inaudibly.

"With this I bind you to me, make you mine as I am yours...one heart, one soul, one being." Peter's hands shook as he tied the knot in place. "Always together."

Before the Languedoc, before Corvay's death, he knew, Guyon would have tried to laugh off any trace of solemnity, and would almost certainly have tried to distract Peter from the fact that he would never say anything of the kind in return. But the flickering mask of deliberate omission had long since been destroyed, and Guyon made no attempt either to deflect or negate what had been said to him.

"Let me return the favor," was all he said, his low voice a little hoarse.

"Yes...Please. " Peter knew his voice was as unsteady as his hands had been, and he turned quickly, both to cut a second

672

length of cord, and to hide some of the naked yearning he was sure could be read on his face.

Guyon took the lacing in his hand with an odd little smile. "I had *craved* -" he said quietly, and then shook his head, bending it over his task, pressing the cord in place with the thumb of his bad hand and tying the knot with slow care with his other, hardly fumbling at all. "All I am," he said quietly. "All I have ever been or may become. It's yours."

"You give me more honor than I rightly deserve," Peter said quietly, then took Guyon's hand and placed a kiss on the pulse point of his wrist, lingering as he felt the beat of blood thrum against his lips. "I love you."

"I can't *give* you honor," Guyon said quietly. "You *are* my honor." He took a small, shaken-sounding breath. "And my love."

*

Brocéliande, October 1646

Love is the shining Star of blessings light,
The fervent fire of zeal, the root of peace,
The lasting lamp, fed with the oil of right,
Image of Faith, and womb for joy's increase.
Love is true Virtue, and his ends delight,
His flames are joys, his bands true Lovers' might.

It was well into October before they heard from anyone other than Marcelli, leaving them in no doubt that Alexei was dissuading anyone who had not the sense to realize how much their privacy was needed from interrupting this time. Guyon wondered why he had not succumbed to Gottfried and Ännchen's undoubted insistence that they be at least allowed to know how they were, before coming to the conclusion that he was probably lying through his back teeth in the name of reassurance.

Jeannine, however, was impervious to lies and reassurance and blandishments all, and her letter was a testament to Madame de Tourvel's teaching, blending her own assurance that she knew and understood - and was doing her own part to protect them from the world's censure and scrutiny - with a practiced vapidity that left them both stunned and fearing a little for Parisian society when she finally emerged from her training.

> *My dear cousins,*
> *There, isn't that discreet and proper? And a beautifully unexceptional title that no-one could object to in a correspondent, now that I have finally been given permission to write to you. My dearest friend, hurt and languishing away in Brocéliande and I was not even allowed to write to ascertain your health. Yes, that ridiculous Russian that you have set to keeping track of me refused to tell me how to reach you before this. He's quite infuriating, you know? He came to see me, just after you left and gave me the entire horror story of how you were injured, Guyon, and then ended it all with, "It is not yet time for you to write. They both need time to heal with*

no interference." All rolled up and pronounced with that stuttery accent of his and a stern but kindly look that said he would accept no argument.

Here I rant and rave and I really should thank you both for sending him my way. None of the other girls have any visitors half so interesting as my 'mysterious Russian' and it has quite improved my standing - something which has proved uplifting, as I was about to vanish into the depths of boredom before his arrival.

Madame, I am sure, is a lovely woman, and well able to teach us all but, my goodness, classes in deportment and posture? Hours of complete boredom when you know I would so much sooner spend time reading and learning, a fact that the other girls seem to find unusual in the extreme. The hours Madame insists we spend doing that, they find as much of a waste of time as I do all those lost minutes examining the turn of my ankle, which no-one is ever going to see anyway unless by accident. It seems they think that looking pretty and being soft-spoken are all they need to advance themselves. Half of them can barely hold up their end of a conversation, let alone engage in a debate. And so many things to remember - how to stand, how to sit, how to walk! As if I have not been doing all three since I was a year old.

I make it sound as if there are dozens of us here, but nothing could be further from the truth. As a matter of fact, Madame has told me that the five of us are the most she has ever had in her establishment before. I think, as I am the latest arrival, that was meant to show me how grateful I should be. And I am...but my gratitude is for the two of you, rather than Madame, who I find to be more than a little disapproving of me.

I also have classes in dancing, which is a relief, for you know that I do have an excess of energy at times, and those few hours each day allow me to rid myself of the 'enthusiasm' that Madame seems to find so objectionable. And, I have been drilled and grilled about rank and social standing. Who is higher than whom. Who must be paid attention to and whom one can easily ignore.

It was rather gratifying to find that my connection to the English Marshal has set me above at least two of the other girls, placing me right in the middle of the group. Really Peter, had you any idea that you are a person of such standing? You have the ear of both la reine Anglaise and our young King...that makes you a very important person, according to Madame. She frowned at me horribly when I laughed and said you were 'Just Peter' and my friend.

The other girls took our afternoon walk to ask me dozens of questions about the Marshal. What is he like? Where did we meet? What are his plans for marriage. Yes, you are considered quite a catch as well, did you know? I'm sure you must, not even you are that blind.

And yes, I can feel Guyon scowling at me from here. Do not worry, grumpy bear, I put them right off any ideas they might have had regarding Peter. I told them that I 'had heard' that Peter was promised to someone, and I made it very plain that whomever he married would, of course, be expected to go with him when he eventually returned to Scotland. That worked the best, naturally, because while a young woman might believe that she could turn Peter's head from his promised bride, none of them wanted to leave France for Scotland. Madame overheard me and gave me her very first nod of approval. She seems to like you, Guyon, and the fact that I deflected the rest of them so well impressed her. She...Madame seems to know much more than she tells.

I will have to close this now, as it is time for my bath. Can you imagine? I soak in milk. Milk! And then lemon for my hair and rose oil for my skin. Don't frown, it causes wrinkles. Look down modestly when praised. Do not be afraid to laugh when things are amusing but do not bray like a donkey - not that I ever did that, I hope, but really, there is so much to remember! But I am determined to learn it all, just as if it were a text by Plato or your beloved Browne and Montaigne. I haven't forgotten the classics, you see!

Take care of yourselves, please. Write back to me soon and know that you are both in my thoughts and affections.

Jeannine de Tourvel

*

As was often the case in the afternoon, when Peter entered the house, all was silence but for the somber creaking of settling stone and timber. If he stopped and listened very carefully though, he could hear other things. The soft sounds of voices from the kitchens as the servants began preparations for the evening meal, the clack of spoon in bowl or knife on board. He could hear behind him, the stables where the grooms worked at cleaning or repairing. And then, ever so faintly, the rustle of paper and the slow scratch of pen on paper.

The sound heartened him and made his soul leap with gladness no matter how often it occurred. The sound meant that Guyon was working, reading and making notes, his nimble brain occupied with something other than the difficulties he still had with simply moving the pen across the page.

He was getting better. And although he would deny it, Peter was sure; he was more pleased with his own progress than he'd thought he would be. True, his hand would probably never be what it was, but it was so much better than Guyon had at first expected that everyone had been cheered by his advances.

Peter stepped quietly to the door of the small study and leaned against its frame, drinking in the sight of his love, like a sailor drinks in the sight of the sea.

"And there my love did sit, pensive and engaged - a true tribute to that which is called knowledge," Peter spoke softly, smiling all the white. "Hello, Gui. Busy day?"

"Not unless you count translating some of Jaufre Rudel for you illiterate heathens," Guyon said, laying the pen down. "*Do you count Jaufre Rudel as busy?*" He turned his head towards the doorway, his mouth curving into the quiet smile that was far more often seen these days than the brilliant grin which had once haunted Peter's dreams. He got to his feet. "I hope not. Also, I think we have pigeons in the roof."

"Ah, that would explain the purring I have been hearing..." Peter moved over to give Guyon a quick soft kiss, "...and here I thought it was you...."

"Yes, like a well-fed cat. Place me in the sun and watch me bat at dust motes," Guyon agreed. "They're more...one-note conversationalists, it would seem. Poor Rudel is doomed to a mental rhythm of repetitive cooing - and *you* have been helping with the apple harvest." He sniffed, and laughed. "I hope you brought some product of it back for the gannets."

Peter snorted out a laugh, "Well, I had noticed that David's belt was let out another notch, but I wasn't going to mention it. Really though, if they did eat five times their weight, it would still be worth supplying them. As angry as I was with David there for awhile...I've rather enjoyed their company. They're certainly easy guests, requiring little attention to keep them happy."

"Anger and sweetness are equally as wasted on David," Guyon agreed vaguely. "I suppose, yes, as guests - or gannets - go, they seem easy enough. But then I'm not their host, you are, my absentee friend...are apples so enthralling, then, or was it the hat which enticed you?" He looked through the doorway at the battered straw object that Peter had left on the hallway table. "I think the local donkey is looking for that."

"He was, but I told him I was bringing it home to my beloved, and he gifted it to me with no complaint," Peter chuckled. "Actually, I wanted you to go back with me to taste the pressing. You've spent long enough in here and the day is bright and cool and...Please?"

"You or pigeons and Rudel, the indecision is crippling me," Guyon said amusedly. "You do *know* my only contribution is going to be 'yes, it tastes of apple', don't you?" He laughed a little, then, and waved his left hand in a sort of negation. "Would a simple *yes* have sufficed, chérâme?"

"Yes," Peter said. That was the answer he wanted after all. Just the pleasure of Guyon's company after a day spent in satisfyingly simple exertion. What could be sweeter? "They won't care what you actually think of the pressing, Gui. The important thing is that we are there. That's what will mean everything." Peter wondered if such things were done at Guyon's family estates in the Languedoc. He hadn't seen anything of the sort when they were there, but then, it hadn't been harvest.

"I don't actually think they're going to care whether I'm there or at the bottom of the ocean," Guyon said, his eyes starting to crease up into laughter, "but I'm always happy to watch people stutter and fall over themselves when you say something nice to them."

"Why do I think it more likely that you just want to be there to laugh when I get mixed up and use the wrong dialect?" Peter chuckled, remembering the perplexed look on the estate manager's face when he had absently spoken to him in Occitan.

"Mmm - because I am, as you rightly said, in a more *purring* mood today, and so I only want to laugh at everyone else?" Guyon picked up a sheaf of paper and swatted him with it. "And they're not dialects, my beloved heretic, they're *languages*!"

"As you say," Peter agreed, amiably. "Just as English is English is English...except when it's not. Come now...do you need to change shoes? Find something warmer to wear?"

Guyon stared at him. "Eng - English is Eng -" He opened and closed his mouth like a carp, then shook his head. "Good God. And no, thank you, I am not yet either senile or six, and I refuse to wear good shoes for an apple pressing."

"Not six? Well then, Oh Ancient One, are you ready to depart?" Peter gave an exaggerated bow, gesturing toward the door like a mummer.

Guyon narrowed his eyes at him as he passed. "Are you saying I'm - oh, Lord, I refuse to waste any more of the day on your orchard-addled attempts at wit." Then he paused in the doorway, and sighed. "At the risk of proving your point, I don't have ink on my nose, do I?" he asked rather plaintively.

Peter's lips twitched, "On your nose? No. No ink on your nose."

"Which means?" Guyon's eyebrows drew together, his expression faintly threatening.

"You've got a bit of a smudge, just there," Peter reached up, chuckling and rubbing away the trace of ink from his friend's cheek. "There. Completely presentable and very *not six.*"

"Oh good," said Guyon with suspicious mildness, and Peter saw the glint of pure devilry in his eyes far too late, before Guyon reached up and kissed him with an almost malicious thoroughness. "Nor are you, apparently," he said in the same vague tones, but his mouth twitched at one corner, a faint uncontrollable flicker of mirth.

"No...um..." Peter blinked, attempting to get back his breath. "You know...cider is very overrated..."

"No, no," Guyon said, "how can it be, when the day is *bright and cool*, and you said *please*?"

"Indeed," Peter sighed, and then shifted somewhat uncomfortably. *The man is the very devil when he gets in these moods. And I'm not enough Saint to keep my mind focused.* "I suppose we should go then?"

"Well, yes," Guyon said serenely. "It's part of it, after all." He smiled, oddly without mockery, at Peter's blank look, and brushed the index finger of his damaged hand over the back of Peter's arm. "*Stay me with flagons,*" he said, "*comfort me with apples, for I am sick with love.*"

"May you never be cured," Peter's words were as fervent as the most devout acolyte's prayer.

"No, it's fatal," Guyon said as though he were announcing that he had in fact found the elixir of life. "Or - terminal, at any rate." He laughed at his own solemnity. "I don't know. Something lasting. *Enduring*, since I test the Lord Marshal's endurance."

"Aye, you do...always," Peter's lip quirked again, but he stepped back. "And we'd best go or I'll scandalize the servants by putting it to the proof right here in the study."

"Good heavens, is that all it would take?" Guyon asked lightly. "We'd certainly better go, then, or I may feel the need to enlighten you as to what the stillroom has proved on many occasions..."

"And that is?" Peter retrieved Guyon's cloak and settled it over his shoulders. It wasn't horribly cold but there was a decided coolness in the air, as he'd said.

"Now since when do I repeat scandal?" Guyon asked, eyebrows quirking at either the gesture or his own comment, it was impossible to tell.

"Well, at least *that* door has a lock on it," Peter chuckled. Henri and David really did spend quite a lot of time behind that door...and no, he wasn't sure he really wanted to think much more about that. The pair had known far more about his own intimate behavior at one time, than he was still comfortable with - knowing about theirs was just- "And I'm guessing we should all be thankful for that or we'd have no servants left."

Guyon's expression turned decidedly speculative at that, but he made no further comment. "Apples," was all he said briefly, and went out into the bright autumn sun.

*

The festival for the apple harvest, which took place once it was certain that everything was put in storage or ready for use, was one of the local customs. Every year all the people from the nearby village gathered at the estate to help with the harvest. There was little pay, aside from their share of the harvest and a wonderful party in celebration of the task. A last little hurrah before the coming of winter and a retreat from the out-of-doors. It was nothing flamboyant or fancy, but rather a homely and comfortable celebration shared with no thought given to social standing, other than the 'Official Tasting' of the first cider press.

This was what Peter and Guyon found themselves in the middle of - townsfolk and estate servants milling through the orchards calling out greetings, jesting and jokes. There were a multitude of children tumbling through the leaves, playing hide and seek around the skirts of their mothers and legs of their fathers. There were children asleep on blankets here and there, some on their mother's shoulders, and everywhere giggling and laughter.

It was almost overwhelming to the two who had been so solitary of late.

"Go and...bless apples, or something," Guyon had said as soon as they arrived, and promptly made a concerted effort to blend in with some shadows under a nearby tree. But as it always did, his detached care made him into a sort of transported piper of

Hameln, and Peter, being urged to compliment and taste and approve, noticed that he was soon surrounded by children and some of the mothers, listening as he outlined some fantastical tale. The blunt fingers flashed through deep autumn light and dust motes, the damaged right hand scarcely noticeable amidst the quick explanatory movements.

He seemed to have an ever-eager stream of servants - mostly under four foot high - to replenish his cup, though his plate, as so often nowadays, remained untouched. Peter began to move over to remonstrate, and caught David's eye as he, too, was drifting forward, before they both broke into laughter at the thought of what the unwilling beneficiary of their concern would have to say about it.

Amidst their laughter, Henri, passing by, added something to the story, and as Guyon turned in overly-disgusted negation, shoved something that probably consisted mostly of apples, and was certainly, judging from Guyon's expression, extremely spicy, into his mouth. All protests were stifled by an anxious query from one young woman with a baby in her arms and a small son diligently smearing a pastry onto her skirt, and Guyon's snarl turned into equally anxious compliments. Henri grinned over at them, and made an invisible chalk mark in the air.

Peter lost sight of his friend then, being taken off first to this place and then that, offered more food than he could possibly consume in a week, but which he must, at least, taste for forms sake - and praise, of course. Most of it was good, some odd and some just...bad. But still, the bad was infrequent and always washed down with cider from the previous year's pressing.

He was, in fact, beginning to feel more than a bit unsteady on his feet as he made his way back to where Guyon had been seated. Unsteady, but happy and stuffed full of food, and now, wanted nothing more than to just curl up in the weak fall sun and have a nap, like one of the children.

"I think the apples may have blessed *you*," Guyon said amusedly as he sat down. It seemed that Henri had taken over the duties of storytelling. "With sleepiness."

"Mmm..." Peter smiled. "I have drunk at least ten gallons of cider, and eaten apple concoctions of every variety...plus, chicken, roast beef, and about eight kinds of cheese. I feel like the kitchen tabby."

He chuckled and leaned against Guyon, "And you, sirrah? Do you have any voice left?"

"Enough for some things, yes," Guyon said, and ran one finger over Peter's temple. "Mm. Brighter than the taste of evening air." It could have been a random comment, an embellishment to Henri's rather awkward tale of the music of the spheres, but the warmth in his eyes showed otherwise.

"I have a great wish at this moment," Peter spoke softly, "to share the taste of all of it with you."

"Poor deprived Scot." It was a soft mimicry of the brittle, desperate voice that Guyon had used the night before they left Paris, this one honey-laden and full of rich sun. "Did no-one tumble you among autumn leaves, then?"

"No," Peter admittedly dolefully. "Nor yet in the heather nor the great hall. I am horridly deprived."

"You are, you are..." Guyon was laughing down at him. "Shall I make you a bed of moss and a canopy of leaves, and keep you warm in crystal for all eternity, my Merlin?"

"Sounds rather a lonely place to be," Peter shrugged. "Unless you're sealing yourself in with me?"

"But of course," Guyon said casually. "Eh, *mes pichons*, my *picas*, my little thieves of hearts!" There was instant and rather disturbing attention, into which Guyon just laughed, soft and light as the afore mentioned leaves. "Your lord Brocéliande here, he does not know that Viviane is sealed in with Merlin!"

There was a babble of explanation about leaves and lakes and trees and reflections and magic mirrors, and among it all, Guyon just tilted his head back against the tree, and smiled, broad and open, his finger still running gently over Peter's temple, up over the thick scar that was covered by his hair.

Peter laughed at the different versions of Merlin's entrapment that the children were now vying to tell him. "A block of ice, is it? As large as a barn? And how does it stay frozen through the summer months?"

"Magic, of course," was the answer to that. And led to further comments on all the kinds of magics that Viviane and Merlin could wield. It appeared it began at simple illusion and made its way up to the possibility of raising the very dead.

"*Chut.*" Guyon's voice was serious if you did not know him, and an entire bubble of glee if you did. "But we do not try to raise the dead." His elbow dug painfully into Peter's side, clear indication that his drowsy state was officially at an end. "Terrible things happen." He chuckled. "*Worse* than my lord Brocéliande in a sheet."

"And worse than Monsieur de Chesnay, when he's awakened unexpectedly," Peter jibed back, and then turned to the children. "Just for your further education? If you wish to play a practical joke on a friend, be sure that you're wearing armor rather than a sheet, especially if he's the type to wake up swinging his fists."

A small lad, about four years old with sandy curls, plucked his thumb from his mouth long enough to ask, "He hitted you?"

"Yes, he quite did, but it was all my own fault for playing the trick in the first place, ya see?"

"*Magic* armor! Like Lancelot!" There was a general nod, and Peter turned a bewildered look on Guyon.

"I thought Lancelot was the false friend?" he mouthed.

"Ah, not here," Guyon said quietly. "He comes from this lake. *Lancelot du Lac,* the perfect knight." His voice deepened into the singing tones that had enthralled the Sorbonne, once upon a time. "And a stone floated across the lake, and in it was a sword, and a woman followed it, weeping. And she cried aloud 'Alas, alas, Lancelot, for you were once the greatest knight alive, and now you have lost God's grace!' And Lancelot answered: 'I always knew that I was never the best knight. And yet I am still the greatest, for I love my lord above all things." And he drew the sword from the stone, and the lady faded away, and she was as mist in the hills." He paused. "In every other version I have heard, he cannot draw the sword. It's only here that he's forgiven."

Here and in Wales, they say Lancelot was one-handed. Peter touched the still-bony wrist above Marcelli's leather patch, knowing now why Guyon was telling this story.

I cannot live with myself, he had said before his journey to Merlin's Lake, and had come back changed, and alive, and determined to make himself whole. In the guise of a story for children, he was telling Peter the *why* of it, and a little of his own peculiar *how.*

Unaware of his weaving skein of thought, Guyon registered his touch with a smile, continuing the story. His voice was soft and deep as a bell, ringing out as the shadows deepened. "And he knelt, and gave the sword to his liege lord, repeating, "I was never the best. But yet by thy love I may be the greatest."

The words drove straight to Peter's heart, but not with pain. It was more like a slow sweet ache that flowed outward from that strongly beating organ and suffused every inch of his body with its honeyed flow. He knew it then, for what it was - love. The same love he had felt for Guyon almost from their meeting. The same love that he had harbored through months of pain when he felt it not returned, then almost delirious happiness when, at last it seemed to be, and finally, through the dark time when it was denied and thrown back in his face. It was a constant. It didn't seem to matter what was said or done, for it or against it, the feeling remained. It was a comfort, somehow, that knowledge.

"And his liege?" Peter smiled. "Did he bid the knight rise and tell him that, 'as great as his love was, so would love be returned,' and that together they would forge a kingdom that would remain a legend?"

"No." Soft negation, and yet, oddly, confirmation too, gratitude in Guyon's eyes now as well as hope. "He said more than that. He said "You are greater than my right hand, you are the power of God for the rights that I proclaim, you stand for the fullness of love and the beauty of it, you are my sword and shield, you stand for my vows and my right hand to God." He stopped, and his eyes were a burning green, even in the dim light. "The fullness of love and the beauty of it..." he repeated.

"But they *did* maked an legend. They *did,* so!" It was the same sandy-haired boy who had asked Peter 'He hitted you?'

"Yes, they did. And we are granted the freedom to live in it." Guyon smiled at them. "And now that shadows cross the sky, you must bring *your* lord his *gratis.*"

At that the children jumped up and scurried off, followed back a moment later by the Master of the Press, filled cup in hand. The 'cup' in this instance was a large chalice made of cedar wood and full to the brim with cider, brandy and affelcello - the sharp, strong and sweet. The crowd gathered around as it was presented, with all due ceremony, to Peter.

He lifted it, having to actually use both hands as large as it was. "My first Festival as lord of Brocéliande...You have all made my friends and I welcome, more welcome than an exiled Scot would ever have believed possible. You have helped us all find a home here that we will always be glad to return to. So, for the first, this cup is dedicated to you, the good people of Brocéliande. For the second, I must dedicate this cup to your young king Louis and to their Majesties Charles and Henrietta, all of whom have brought me to this place. And for third, to my dearest friends, Guyon, Henri and David...and to other friends absent or no longer with us." He looked a moment at Guyon before he continued. "To François Villon."

With that Peter raised the cup and drank deeply, managing, just barely, to take in half.

Guyon spoke in rapid Breton, when the cup passed to him, and Peter knew that he was hoping none of those from Paris would hear what he said. "For François Villon. For our perfect knight, for our Galahad, may God give him peace. For the beauty of the earth, and those sovereigns who rule over it, those exiled and those yet to be crowned. *Aux Brocéliande, vivat la lengua.*" He passed the cup to Henri, and it was evident that he really had taken his third-left, for he was still swallowing as Henri spoke.

"Lord, this is our pleasure and our hope. *Aux Brocéliande,* may you have all the music of Gregory's great spheres." He gave the cup to David.

"For love, be granted joy, as I wish you peace." David's cherubic face was unusually solemn, and Peter remembered how seriously the Sorbonne scholars took oaths.

They're swearing themselves to me. He felt his blood sing as though he were truly Arthur, and looked away, embarrassed, only to meet Guyon's steady, translucent eyes.

Yes. Aux Brocéliande.

There was a cheer from the crowd as the cup was passed back to the Master, who carried it back to refill it and begin its rounds.

All present, from the eldest grandmother to the youngest child, would drink from it before his rounds were done, taking the oath to keep peace between them all.

After that, the only thing left was the bonfire and dancing. Peter wondered how many dances he would have to stand up for before he could, in all courtesy, sneak away.

"Little lord," said Henri, amused, and Peter was about to take loud affront until he remembered. *Little lawyer. Little scholar.* "Henri!" He knew how startled he must sound, and Guyon's bad hand fumbled at his wrist.

"There, now. Let it go." His voice was still slurring over consonants. "It's not so bad, hm? Your kingdom delights us, so be glad."

"My kingdom," Peter couldn't help giving a small snort of amusement. "But it is a wonderful place, isn't it? And I meant what I said, I never would have imagined that these people would have felt anything but animosity for their new foreign 'lord', but that's not been true at all."

"It's true magic," Guyon agreed. "It's Avalon, chérâme." He laughed. "Your Island of Apples."

"Which makes me *le seigneur des pommes*?" Peter chuckled, giving a bow to announce his new title. "And you, my knights, what is it to be next? A dance since the cup forbids us do battle?"

"No, the Sorbonne custom," David said in English, and turned quickly to kiss Guyon's lips. "There now, darling, give your sworn dear your answer answerless!" He laughed, and took Henri by the wrist to lead him into the eight-man dance.

"You never asked me," Guyon said in amused agreement.

Peter looked down at his feet, then back up at Guyon from under the veil of his hair, "I never thought - You always seemed to know the question."

"How could I?" Guyon's eyes were still as warm, in the dusk and torchlight, as they had been in the deepening sun. "I am answerless, my dear. And you have not asked."

"Will you stay with me?" Peter asked quietly, his voice as gentle as the trembling he could feel in his hands. "Will you love me?"

"And I will stay, and I will love you until time and time grow answerless." It was the first time Peter had heard the official answer, the deliberate and yet promising vagueness. "I give you my answer that has no answer, I give you the time that has never been given, I give you the stroke of midnight and the bell-tolls after and the time-steps between them, I give you my lips and my soul."

A wise decision, my dears, mocked François, laughing through stars and fire-sparks. *You cannot offend.*

Peter lifted his hand, placing them on either side of Guyon's neck, his thumbs resting gently against his jaw line, "I think then, that there is one more thing that I am owed."

"I do?" Guyon's eyes were clear and guileless, and there was a tiny frown between the thin dark eyebrows. His mouth contracted, and he bit his lower lip suddenly, and let it go. "Whatever it is, car-mi, it is yours."

"This and only this..." Peter leaned in and, as soft as a whisper, claimed Guyon's lips.

Guyon drew back, and his leather-bound hand cupped Peter's face awkwardly. "As always, you excel," he said softly, and the kiss that he gave Peter was no *answer answerless*, but a promise written upon marble and carved by water. "My most dear."

*

All Guyon's life, he had woken quickly and abruptly, with no hint of intervening drowsiness, simply a cessation of sleep that was as immediate in its surfacing as it was when he fell into it. He rarely remembered his dreams, and he rarely slept for long, and the fact that he always appeared to allow the oddly protective side to his nature surface when he slept in Peter's company was not something that he had ever really thought about. On the few occasions he had ever contemplated it, he had assumed that it was partly to do with all that had occurred during and after Peter's disastrous trip to Poitiers, and partly because it was also a wonderfully concealing way of ensuring he never had his back in contact with Peter.

Corvay's dagger had changed all of that, and he was still adjusting to the results. He no longer slept in short, intense bursts, but, thanks to David's new regime of mild sleeping draughts on a regular basis, slept for long, not-quite-under periods where he was half-aware and yet too fogged to do anything about what he might hear. He had hated it at first, before coming to find it quite pleasant - before, he admitted now in a rare awakening to a false dawn, accepting that he did not have to be the one alert, that it was not always his responsibility to take simply because it was night.

One of the more unpleasant aspects to recovery, Guyon had decided as the days passed and shortened, the last traces of summer finally disappearing into the chill of autumn that lasted longer with every morning and came earlier each night, was that he was more aware of the world around him. Without the rawness of pain or the craving for various drugs that had replaced it, he saw things without the prejudice of fear or the conviction that it was caused by or directed toward himself.

He was not worried by Henri or David, though he knew they were both finding ways of excusing their delay in Brittany - and finding the excuses harder to come by all the time. Contentment was a rarity for more men than just those who had been caught in Corvay's web, and an integral part of that prized emotion was the ability to let down at least some of the guard that was always a part of the oddly-assorted couple's Paris life.

Peter, on the other hand, was suffering *from* his contentment, and while the undeniable fact exasperated Guyon almost to the point of voicing his irritation aloud, he also understood it, and his understanding was silencing him. When they left Paris, Peter had needed the inaction, the peace, the soft tranquility of his estates, had needed above all to be given that knowledge that he belonged somewhere. But it was not a way that he could bear to live, nor a state of being that satisfied him, being too close to a life wholly of the mind to ever make him completely happy.

Guyon, recovering physically, was content to rest. But in his quiet ease, he was more aware than he had been for many years, and knew that what should have been further balm to the myriad of spiritual wounds that he, among others, had inflicted on Peter, was becoming a fresh irritant. Knowing that Peter would deny it if confronted, he struggled to find a means of leading him towards volunteering the knowledge freely.

He even used de Retz's communications in the end, desperate to provoke some reaction that was not the interminable consideration for his own well-being, and a total disregard for the fact that this new discontent was beginning to prove a barrier in its own right.

"The Archbishop tells me that your Queen's brood is nearly all returned to her," he said one morning, apropos of nothing and wondering if there was any better way of souring coffee than with unasked for Court news.

"Then I suppose we should be thankful that we're here and well out of it," Peter said, pausing with his cup half way to his lips. "For then it would all be feasting and 'Peter, you know that I depend on you for their safety' and let me tell you, as much as I adore her Majesty, her children are in need of a much firmer hand than I would be allowed to give them."

"Well, there's a grand precedent for spoiling royal infants at the Louvre," Guyon said dryly. "I wonder just how badly the Dieudonne's nose will be put out of joint at having the Duke of York's battle experience pushed in his face at every given opportunity." It was, he knew, one of his less clear invitations to a long exposition of Peter's feelings on the subject of the English King's sons' relationship with the army, but he was never sure as to how far he could push it.

"I'm sure his Majesty has much more on his mind than children at present," Peter said quietly, but his eyes took on a distant look, as if he could see the King he was speaking of, rather than his most Catholic Majesty of France, the frail and beleaguered Charles rather than the young determined Prince, see his sworn monarch through the stone walls of his confinement.

"Mm. Sheep?" Guyon suggested mildly. "Or rocks?"

Peter gave a small snort, "Possibly both. We've those aplenty that's for certain. More coffee?"

For one glorious moment of pure and blissful imagining, Guyon envisaged accepting and then pouring it over Peter's head. Not quite sure of whether he was as yet equal to dealing with the inevitable reprisal, however, he went for a blunter and less visible means of crab-coaxing. "I wonder if Thomas is inflicting his

morning cheer on Lieutenant Wycombe, these days," he said vaguely, taking the coffeepot.

"If there is any justice in the world," Peter's answer was as dry as sand. "That is one thing I do not miss. The lad's good, knows his duties, but there have been times when I wanted to throw my boots at his head in the morning...especially after a late night."

"How soothing it must be now that we keep such country hours," Guyon said with equal dryness. He gave Peter his best look of false innocence, for with Henri and David in residence, and his own liking for night-time conversation rather than daytime activities, it was extremely unusual for any of them to retire before midnight

"Indeed," Peter's lip twitched. "I think though, that Thomas is in bed by nine each night and up by five, unholy wretch. Not that I begrudge him regular hours, I just don't think he should try to inflict them on me."

"I think those should be hours banned by law," Guyon agreed, giving up. He had a horrible suspicion that Peter knew exactly what he was trying to do, and was using his own weapon of deflection against him. It was provoking in the extreme, but not enough for him to show it. He contented himself by emptying the coffeepot, taking the last of the bacon, and demonstrating his new ability to peel an apple one-handed with enormous slowness, guaranteed to frustrate anyone watching.

He knew he was winning when he saw Peter's hands twitch as if he wanted to reach out and take it away from him. Even more sure when Peter forced them down.

"So," Peter said by way of reopening the conversation. "What do you have planned for today? I'm pretty much at your service, if you wish."

Yes, Peter had brought all the estate books up-to-date, had inspected all the buildings and had sent out orders for repairs to be done to anything that would need it before the first snows, and was so far ahead that Guyon wondered why he was even bothering to pay his estate manager anything.

"I don't have any plans at all," Guyon said without raising his eyes from his task. "I thought I might design a bathhouse." He waited serenely for a response to this new piece of lunacy. In fact, he had already begun designs based on the ruins of the Roman hypocaust he had found nearby, and was waiting for word from a local stonemason as to the feasibility of his project. He had also begun to devise a system whereby some of the vines from his Languedoc estates might be imported, though he had not, as yet, informed Peter of that fact, since in that respect failure was almost inevitable on the first few tries, and he wished to keep that as much to himself as possible.

"A bath house?" Peter chuckled. "Then I shall have to stop calling you *beloved* and amend it to *beloved prune*. You'll get in the water and never come out."

But in spite of his teasing tone, Guyon saw Peter's hands twitch again, and the purposeful way he suddenly folded his arms.

"And I shall avoid having to actually inform the household of my bathing habits every time I want hot water, which is rather more to the point," Guyon said mildly, finishing his snail-like task and setting both apple and knife aside. He did not have to look to know that the twitch would have moved to Peter's face, and smiled with deliberate and impervious kindness. "Did you want the peel?" he asked sweetly. "You could throw it over your shoulder and see which initials it fails to make."

"No thank you. Sarah did that once when she was twelve and then locked herself in her room for two days when it failed to form an 'R'." Peter sighed. "I wonder how Robbie found them when he returned home. I've not heard a word from him, not that he's ever been much a one for letters."

"You would have heard soon enough if anything were wrong at home," Guyon said consolingly, and added, unable to resist the opening given him, "I would imagine his time has been consumed by *other* matters, hm?"

"So I'd imagine...the same things that I've been doing," Peter leaned forward, and picked up the apple peel, absently tearing it into smaller pieces that he then stacked on his own plate. "I wonder if he was able to get a good price for his rye?"

Guyon resisted, with incredible difficulty, the urge to either thump his head onto the breakfast-table or simply smack Peter across *his* head with his good hand. "Or he might be politicking," he said, giving up on any sort of subtlety in favor of a hammer and anvil of obviousness. "After all, the Laird's opinion would be wanted. And with the Laird absent, Robbie must be finding more duties still added to his role."

"I'm sure he has," Peter drew a heavy sigh and then with one finger reached out and knocked over his carefully constructed tower. "It's worrisome, Gui. Robbie is not the most subtle of men and...No, sorry, never mind. No sense in going over something I can't control."

"Mm." Guyon reached out and touched Peter's hand, a small, fleeting touch that was oddly like the one he had first used in the *Shoe*, over two years before, when he had skimmed his fingers awkwardly over broken skin and advised a new outlet for bad temper other than stone walls. "Is this a time to remind you that perhaps it is not *about* control?"

"I know. I know." Peter picked up a piece of the apple peel, shredding it into even smaller bits while he talked. "Robbie is fine. Sarah is fine. The children are fine. *I'm* bloody well fine...just going insane. Our wee bit of rock is not important enough for Cromwell to trouble himself with. I know that. I - Just - It's -" Peter slammed his hand down on the table in frustration. "I'm just too far away, Gui. You know what I mean?"

"Yes," Guyon said simply, wondering if Peter thought he was deaf, blind, or merely insensitive. One of the first conversations that had ever passed between them had involved just how far away Peter was, and Guyon, despite all his protestations to the contrary as to his interest, had been transcribing and developing codes for Corvay, de Retz, and even Mazarin for long enough to know just what Peter had avoided by arriving in France with his Queen. He loathed and detested politics with all his solitary, purist nature, but it did not, and had never, prevented him from seeing all the layers and half-truths that made up Government. "Yes, I know. Perhaps it is time you should start thinking about...alternatives?"

"Or maybe it's time I learn that final lesson in letting it go?" Peter shook his head. "Robbie, subtlety aside, is a big boy. I need to learn to trust that."

The words were said with surprising forcefulness, but Peter's expression contradicted them all, his worries still plain on his too expressive face.

But it's not trust you have to learn, Guyon thought. *It never was. It's forgiveness and understanding and acceptance, and you will not find any of those things here. And I am, I am finding them all, somewhere within me where I never even suspected their existence, and I am not ready to lose them yet. Not quite yet.*

Recognizing his own inadequacies in this matter, and wishing he had never started the line of conversation, Guyon sighed, and touched Peter's shoulder. "Perhaps," he agreed, and wished for the courage to say what was needed. *You don't need to learn anything. We'll leave whenever you like.*

But he said nothing more, leaving his hand where it was in silent and half-unwilling support, knowing that this once, his words would not help.

Whatever you decide, he thought then, relinquishing all thoughts of influence, and tried to convey that with his silence. *Whatever you need. Whenever you are ready and for whatever you may be ready for, I am yours to command.*

The bell swung inside him with solemn joy, deep and abiding acceptance, even as he sorrowed for Peter's loss.

Aşkin Cemal Olsun.
This is the glory of God.
Glory be to God.
To my God.
My God.
God.
Aşkin Cemal Olsun...

The glory of the world. The glory that was God and the swing of the bell and love, and love, and love, and the full circle that drew around to meet his heresy at the top of Fortune's Wheel once more.

Aşk Olsun.

*

www.ingramcontent.com/pod-product-compliance
Lightning Source LLC
Chambersburg PA
CBHW020240030726

47499CB00001B/8